LUCIAN

VIII

EUCLID

VIII

132

LUCIAN

WITH AN ENGLISH TRANSLATION BY

M. D. MACLEOD

LECTURER IN CLASSICS, UNIVERSITY OF
SOUTHAMPTON

IN EIGHT VOLUMES

VIII

CAMBRIDGE, MASSACHUSETTS
HARVARD UNIVERSITY PRESS

LONDON
WILLIAM HEINEMANN LTD

MCMLXVII

PATRIS MEMORIAE

Printed in Great Britain

CONTENTS

LIST OF LUCIAN'S WORKS

SHOWING THEIR DIVISION INTO VOLUMES
IN THIS EDITION

LIST OF LUCIAN'S WORKS

Volume VI

Volume VII

Volume VIII

PREFACE

The Solecist, The Ass, Affairs of the Heart, Halcyon, Demosthenes, Podagra, Ocypus and *The Cynic* were relegated to this volume because there are good reasons for doubting the Lucianic authorship of some if not all of these works, though they are found in *Γ* and other good manuscripts. *Philopatris, Charidemus* and *Nero* together with the epigram "*On His Own Book*" are certainly not by Lucian and are only found in a few inferior manuscripts.

In addition various letters have been ascribed to Lucian in inferior manuscripts; for details see M. Wittek's *Liste des Manuscrits de Lucien* in *Scriptorium* 1952. These are in the main *Phalaris Letters*, which were no doubt ascribed to Lucian because of confusion with his *Phalaris A* and *B*; but there are also ten *Scythian Letters* purporting to be from Anacharsis to (1) the Athenians, (2) Solon, (3-10) various other individuals. The style of these Scythian Letters has nothing to suggest that Lucian is the author, and the fact that they occur at the end of Lucian's *Anacharsis* shows how they found their way into Lucian's works. However, as one of the manuscripts containing the *Scythian Letters* is the respectable Laurentianus 57.51 (L), they have no doubt as good a claim to appear in this volume as such pseudo-Lucianea as *Charidemus, Philopatris* and *Nero*. Space however does not permit this; those who wish to read the *Scythian Letters* will find them on pp. 102-105 of Hercher's *Epistolographi Graeci*, or in F. H. Reuter's *Die Briefe des Anacharsis* (Berlin, 1963).

PREFACE

It should also be mentioned that the Lucianic manuscript Vaticanus Graecus 87 contains a dialogue entitled Τιμαρίων ἢ περὶ τῶν κατ' αὐτὸν παθημάτων, but this work is Byzantine and can be dated to the twelfth century A.D. It found its way into Vaticanus 87 because it is a satirical dialogue strongly influenced by Lucian in general and the *Necyomanteia* in particular. See H. F. Tozer's account in *Journal of Hellenic Studies*, 1881, pp. 241-270.

I have based my text for the *Solecist* on Nilén's Teubner, and for *Podagra* and *Ocypus* on Zimmermann's edition. Elsewhere I have prepared my own text by collation of the manuscripts; I have been considerably helped in this task by use of Nilén's accurate collations of Γ, B and E. I have also found Albers' critical edition of " *Demosthenis Encomium* " of great value. I also had the benefit of Harmon's translation of the *Solecist*, *Halcyon* and part of *Affairs of the Heart* (this title for the *Amores* is his), together with Rouse's version of part of *The Ass*.

I should like to thank the Rev. J. H. Davies for his help with *Philopatris* and Mr. W. J. F. Davies for correcting the proofs.

THE SHAM SOPHIST or THE SOLECIST

This dialogue has been rejected as non-Lucianic by many authorities on the ground that it is unworthy of Lucian's talents and seems to criticise a number of Lucian's own usages. Harmon agreed with this view and suggested that it may have been the work of an unknown schoolmaster who had lived in Egypt (cf. c. 5) and had read *Lexiphanes* (cf. c. 11). This view may well be correct. See, however, my article in *Classical Quarterly*, 1956, where I argue that this dialogue could indeed be by Lucian and is best taken as a spiteful and at times hypocritical attack on a personal enemy who has offended Lucian by criticising his Greek.

An attractive alternative interpretation is Reitz's suggestion that, if the *Solecist* is by Lucian, the contributions of Lucian and Socrates are intended to be ironical and constitute a " reductio ad absurdum " of the activities of the more extravagant Atticists of the day. This view has recently been supported by J. Bompaire (*Lucien Écrivain*) and B. Baldwin (*Classical Review*, 1962) who suggests that someone like Phrynichus of Bithynia, a contemporary of Lucian, or Moeris (of unknown date) may be satirised. This view has the advantage of making the dialogue reputable satire and also accounting for the condemnation of Lucianic usages, but is perhaps too subtle.

Lucian did have a great interest in linguistic minutiae and was capable of writing tediously on them, as in the *Slip of the Tongue* (vol. 6, pp. 171 ff.), which can hardly be a " reductio ad absurdum " as it was addressed to a patron rather than to critics. Lucian's pronouncements all seem seriously meant, and Socrates' views seem to be quoted with approval. Moreover, in general, they are just those views which one would expect of Lucian, as Socrates recommends Platonic usages (cf. *Lexiphanes* c. 22, F. W. House-holder, *Literary Quotation and Allusion in Lucian*, p. 44), but shows a sense of proportion by objecting to usages already obsolescent. If some Lucianic usages are criticised in this dialogue, we should bear in mind that Lucian was a prolific and at times careless writer who could be hypocritical in his personal feuds, and that the reference to Egypt in c. 5 perhaps suggests a late date when Lucian's powers were failing.

It is impossible to produce an adequate translation of this dialogue, as some of the deliberate mistakes are outrageously gross, while others could only have offended the hypercritical. I have contented myself with introducing an obvious blunder in the English, wherever there seems to be a deliberate mistake, however venial, in the Greek. It is hardly necessary to point out that any blunder in the English is not identical with the error in the Greek. The nature of any Greek blunder is explained in a relevant footnote.

ΨΕΥΔΟΣΟΦΙΣΤΗΣ Η ΣΟΛΟΙΚΙΣΤΗΣ

ΛΟΥΚΙΑΝΟΣ[1]

1. Ἆρά γε ὁ γνῶναι τὸν σολοικίζοντα δεινὸς οὗτος καὶ φυλάξασθαι μὴ σολοικίσαι δυνατός;

ΣΟΦΙΣΤΗΣ[1]

Ἐμοὶ μὲν δοκεῖ.

ΛΟΥΚΙΑΝΟΣ

Ὁ δέ γε μὴ φυλάξασθαι οὐδὲ γνῶναι τὸν οὕτως ἔχοντα;

ΣΟΦΙΣΤΗΣ

Ἀληθῆ λέγεις.

ΛΟΥΚΙΑΝΟΣ

Σὺ δὲ αὐτὸς φῂς οὐ σολοικίζειν, ἢ πῶς λέγωμεν[2] περὶ σοῦ;

Codices rettuli *ΓΩSUΨΝ. ΓΩS* = γ, *UΨ* = β.
[1] Personarum nomina *Λουκιανός* et *Σοφιστής* βγ: *Λυκῖνος* et *Σολοικιστής* edd.
[2] λέγωμεν Halm: λέγομεν βγ.

---

[1] The only other instance of Lucianus as opposed to Lycinus as a speaker's name in a dialogue is in *The Fisher*, where Lucian is defending his *Sale of the Lives*. This could mean that here too Lucian is replying in person to criticism. (Or it could mean that the dialogue is not by Lucian.)

THE SHAM SOPHIST or
THE SOLECIST

LUCIAN [1]

1. Is the man who is clever at detecting howlers in the speech of another able to guard against making them himself ?

SOPHIST

I for one think so.

LUCIAN

And the man who can't guard against howlers in his own speech can't recognise them in another ?

SOPHIST

True enough.

LUCIAN

And what about yourself ? Do you say that you don't make any [2] howlers, or how are we to describe you ?

---

[2] Lit. solecisms, ignorant mistakes in grammar and speech, of the type for which the people of Soli in Cilicia were proverbially notorious. Sometimes, though apparently not in this dialogue, a distinction was drawn between " barbarisms " (as meaning mistakes in the use of one word) and " solecisms " (as being errors in the syntax of a phrase).

φὴς οὐ for οὐ φὴς (cf. p. 26) is probably not a deliberate mistake; it cannot be one of the three mistakes admitted on p. 8 and φὴς μὴ is used seriously on p. 22.

LUCIAN

ΣΟΦΙΣΤΗΣ

Ἀπαίδευτος γὰρ ἂν εἴην, εἰ σολοικίζοιμι τηλικοῦτος ὤν.

ΛΟΥΚΙΑΝΟΣ

Οὐκοῦν καὶ ἕτερον φωρᾶσαι δυνήσῃ τοῦτο δρῶντα καὶ ἐλέγξαι τὸν ἀρνούμενον;

ΣΟΦΙΣΤΗΣ

Παντάπασί γε.

ΛΟΥΚΙΑΝΟΣ

Ἴθι νῦν ἐμοῦ λαβοῦ σολοικίζοντος, ἄρτι δὲ σολοικιῶ.

ΣΟΦΙΣΤΗΣ

Οὐκοῦν εἰπέ.

ΛΟΥΚΙΑΝΟΣ

Ἀλλ' ἔγωγε ἤδη τὸ δεινὸν εἴργασμαι, σὺ δὲ οὐκ ἐπέγνως.

ΣΟΦΙΣΤΗΣ

Παίζεις ἔχων;

ΛΟΥΚΙΑΝΟΣ

Μὰ τοὺς θεούς· ἐπεὶ σολοικίσας ἔλαθόν σε ὡς οὐκ ἐπιστάμενον. αὖθις δὲ σκόπει· οὐ γάρ σέ φημι δύνασθαι κατανοῆσαι, ἐπεὶ ἃ μὲν οἶσθ', ἃ δ' οὐκ οἶσθα.

---

[1] ἄρτι with the future is also condemned by Phrynichus and not used by the best writers.

THE SOLECIST

Well, I should be ignorant if I made them at my age.

Then you'll also be able to catch someone else out when he makes them and prove your point when he denies it ?

Certainly.

Come now and catch me in my howlers ; I'll start the [1] now.

Start then.

But I've already perpetrated the enormity, though you didn't recognise it.

Are you always joking ?

Good heavens no ! You let me get away with a howler because you didn't know any better. Pay attention once more. I say you can't catch me, because there are things what [2] you know and things what you don't.

---

[2] ἃ μὲν . . . ἃ δέ (for τὰ μὲν . . . τὰ δὲ) is fairly common in Hellenistic Greek; Lucian himself is guilty of this usage in *Timon* 57 and *A Professor of Public Speaking* 15. Cf. also *The Ass* 23.

LUCIAN

Εἰπὲ μόνον.

ΛΟΥΚΙΑΝΟΣ

Ἀλλὰ καὶ νῦν σεσολοίκισταί μοι, σὺ δ' οὐκ ἔγνως.

ΣΟΦΙΣΤΗΣ

Πῶς γάρ, σοῦ μηδὲν λέγοντος;

ΛΟΥΚΙΑΝΟΣ

Ἐγὼ μὲν λέγω καὶ σολοικίζω, σὺ δ' οὐχ ἔπῃ τούτῳ δρῶντι· ἐπεὶ ὄφελον καὶ νῦν ἀκολουθῆσαι δυνήσῃ.

ΣΟΦΙΣΤΗΣ

2. Θαυμαστὰ λέγεις, εἰ μὴ δυνήσομαι καταμαθεῖν σολοικισμόν.

ΛΟΥΚΙΑΝΟΣ

Καὶ πῶς ἂν δύναιο τὸν ἕνα μαθεῖν τοὺς τρεῖς ἀγνοήσας;

ΣΟΦΙΣΤΗΣ

Τίνας τρεῖς;

ΛΟΥΚΙΑΝΟΣ

Ὅλους ἀρτιγενείους.

ΣΟΦΙΣΤΗΣ

Ἐγὼ μέν σε παίζειν δοκῶ.

THE SOLECIST

SOPHIST

Just say something.

LUCIAN

But I've just made another howler, though you didn't notice it.

SOPHIST

How so, when you say nothing ?

LUCIAN

I am saying things and making howlers, but you don't keep up with me as I do it. I hopes [1] you can follow me this time.

SOPHIST

2. I'm surprised to hear you say I won't be able to recognise a howler.

LUCIAN

How could you recognise one when in your ignorance you've missed three ?

SOPHIST

What three ?

LUCIAN

Three whole bearded monsters I've just perjured [2] up.

SOPHIST

I think you're joking.

---

[1] A gross mistake involving (a) the late usage of ὄφελον for ὤφελες, and (b) its combination with a future indicative.

[2] ἀρτιγενείους is wrongly used for ἀρτιγενεῖς ("new-bearded" for "new-born").

LUCIAN

ΛΟΥΚΙΑΝΟΣ

Ἐγὼ δὲ ⟨σὲ⟩ [1] ἀγνοεῖν τὸν ἁμαρτάνοντα ἐν τοῖς λόγοις.

ΣΟΦΙΣΤΗΣ

Καὶ πῶς ἄν τις μάθοι μηδενὸς εἰρημένου;

ΛΟΥΚΙΑΝΟΣ

Λέλεκται καὶ σεσολοίκισται τετραπλῆ, [2] σὺ δ' οὐκ ἔγνως. μέγα οὖν ἆθλον κατέπραξας ἄν, εἴπερ ἔγνως.

ΣΟΦΙΣΤΗΣ

Οὐ μέγα μέν, ἀναγκαῖον δὲ τῷ ὁμολογήσαντι.

ΛΟΥΚΙΑΝΟΣ

Ἀλλ' οὐδὲ νῦν ἔγνως.

ΣΟΦΙΣΤΗΣ

Πότε [3] νῦν;

ΛΟΥΚΙΑΝΟΣ

Ὅτε τὸ ἆθλον ἔφην σε καταπρᾶξαι.

ΣΟΦΙΣΤΗΣ

Οὐκ οἶδα ὅ τι λέγεις.

---

[1] σὲ deest in codd.: add. edd..
[2] τετραπλῆ N: τριπλῆ βγ.
[3] πότε; *ΛΟΥΚ.* νῦν ὅτε . . . β.

THE SOLECIST

LUCIAN

And I that you don't know when a man makes howlers in his talk.

SOPHIST

How can anyone know when nothing has been said ?

LUCIAN

Things have been said and four howlers made, so that you would have achieved a great succession [1] if you had recognised them.

SOPHIST

Not a great one but the minimum requirement now that I've let myself in for this.

LUCIAN

But even now you didn't notice.

SOPHIST

When just now ?

LUCIAN

When I talked of your achieving a succession.

SOPHIST

I don't know what you mean.

---

[1] $\mathring{a}\theta\lambda o\nu$ (" prize ") is wrongly used for $\mathring{a}\theta\lambda o\varsigma$ (" task ").

LUCIAN

ΛΟΥΚΙΑΝΟΣ

Ὀρθῶς ἔφης· οὐ γὰρ οἶσθα. καὶ πρόιθί γε ἐς τὸ ἔμπροσθεν· οὐ γὰρ ἐθέλεις ἔπεσθαι, συνήσων ἄν, εἴπερ ἐθελήσειας.

ΣΟΦΙΣΤΗΣ

3. Ἀλλ' ἐγὼ βούλομαι· σὺ δ' οὐδὲν εἶπας ὧν ἄνθρωποι σολοικίζοντες λέγουσιν.

ΛΟΥΚΙΑΝΟΣ

Τὸ γὰρ νῦν ῥηθὲν μικρόν τί σοι φαίνεται κακὸν εἶναι; ὅμως δὲ ἀκολούθησον αὖθις, ἐπεὶ οὐκ ἔμαθες ἐκδραμόντα.

ΣΟΦΙΣΤΗΣ

Μὰ τοὺς θεοὺς οὐκ ἔγωγε.

ΛΟΥΚΙΑΝΟΣ

Ἀλλὰ μὴν μεθῆκα θεῖν λαγὼ ταχέως. ἆρα παρῆξεν[1]; ἀλλὰ καὶ νῦν ἔξεστιν ἰδεῖν τὸν λαγώ· εἰ δὲ μή, πολλοὶ γενόμενοι λαγὼ λήσουσί σε ἐν σολοικισμῷ πεσόντες.

[1] παρῆξεν S: παρῆξαι Ω: προῆξαι Γ: προσρῆξαι β: προῆξεν Mras.

---

[1] An intentional tautology.

[2] The intentional mistake may be ἄν with the future (cf. p. 26), though this is used occasionally in Attic and by Lucian (cf. *Fisherman* 29, *Anacharsis* 17, 25, 31, etc.); or the error may simply be the failure to use the more normal present (or aorist) participle with ἄν when with an optative protasis.

THE SOLECIST

LUCIAN

You're right there ; you don't. Advance forward into the lead [1] then, as you don't want to follow, though you shall [2] be able to understand if you should wish.

SOPHIST

3. But I do wish ; but you've said none of the things which men say in making howlers.

LUCIAN

Then you think what I said just now a trifling fault ? Nevertheless follow me once more, since you didn't notice what came rushing out.

SOPHIST

Good heavens, I certainly didn't.

LUCIAN

But look here's a hare who [3] I've just let rush out. Did it dash past you ? You can still see the hare to who I refer. If you can't, there will be hordes of the misbegotten hares whom [3] will dash past you unnoticed.

[3] The accusative singular λαγώ (though found in Xenophon) is a deliberate blunder as λαγώς is second declension. Lucian correctly has λαγών in *The Hall* 24.

The context perhaps suggests that nominative plural λαγώ is to be regarded as a mistake for λαγοί ; this, if seriously meant, is a piece of excessive pedantry based on the fact that λαγοί is Sophoclean, whereas λαγώ has no better authority than Eupolis. Generally speaking, however, λαγώς is Attic, λαγός Ionic and λαγωός epic, but cf. Athenaeus 9.400. Lucian has λαγώς three times and λαγωός four times but no nominative plural form.

LUCIAN

ΣΟΦΙΣΤΗΣ

Οὐ λήσουσιν.

ΛΟΥΚΙΑΝΟΣ

Καὶ μὴν ἔλαθόν γε.

ΣΟΦΙΣΤΗΣ

Θαυμαστὰ λέγεις.

ΛΟΥΚΙΑΝΟΣ

Σὺ δὲ ὑπὸ τῆς ἄγαν παιδείας διέφθορας, ὥστε μηδ᾽ αὐτὸ τοῦτο σολοικίζοντας κατανοῆσαι. [οὐ γὰρ πρόσεστιν αὐτῷ τὸ τίνα.] [1]

ΣΟΦΙΣΤΗΣ

4. Ταῦτα μὲν οὐκ οἶδα πῶς λέγεις · ἐγὼ δὲ πολλοὺς ἤδη σολοικίζοντας κατενόησα.

ΛΟΥΚΙΑΝΟΣ

Κἀμὲ τοίνυν εἴσῃ τότε, ὅταν τι τῶν παιδίων γένῃ τῶν τὰς τίτθας θηλαζόντων πιούσας.[2] εἰ [3] οὐ νῦν ἔγνως σολοικίζοντά με, οὐδὲ αὐξάνοντα παιδία σολοικισμὸν ποιήσει τῷ μηδὲν εἰδότι.

ΣΟΦΙΣΤΗΣ

Ἀληθῆ λέγεις.

---

[1] οὐ . . . τίνα del. edd..   [2] πιούσας om. N, edd..
[3] εἰ ex correctione Ω: ἢ Γ: ἢ εἰ U, N, Γ ex corr., Ω ante corr..

14

THE SOLECIST

SOPHIST

They won't get by me.

LUCIAN

But look they're already by you.

SOPHIST

I'm surprised to hear it.

LUCIAN

Too much learning has been your underdoing [1]; so you see there's another howler people make without your noticing.

SOPHIST

4. I don't know what you mean by that. I've noticed many people making howlers in my time.

LUCIAN

Then you'll know that I've done so too—on the day when you become one of the babies to whom their nurses give suckle. [2] If you hasn't [3] caught me making a howler this time, you'll be too ignorant to find any howlers no matter how big the childs [4] grow.

SOPHIST

True enough.

[1] The intransitive use of διέφθορα (common in late prose) is also censured by Phrynichus and others; διέφθορα is transitive in Attic.

[2] The mistake may be in applying θηλάζω in the sense of " suck " to humans; if πιούσας is retained, there is perhaps no deliberate mistake as θηλάζω in the sense of " suckle " has good authority, whether applied to humans or animals.

[3] εἰ οὐ may be criticised; it occurs occasionally in Attic, cf. *Zeus Catechised* 5, *Parasite* 12, *Praise of Demosthenes* 21.

[4] The intransitive use of αὐξάνω (not in the best Attic writers) is criticised.

LUCIAN

ΛΟΥΚΙΑΝΟΣ

Καὶ μὴν εἰ ταῦτα ἀγνοήσομεν, οὐδὲν γνωσόμεθα τῶν ἑαυτῶν,[1] ἐπεὶ καὶ τόδε σολοικισθὲν ἀπέφυγέ σε. μὴ τοίνυν ἔτι λέγειν,[2] ὡς ἱκανὸς εἶ κατιδεῖν τὸν σολοικίζοντα καὶ αὐτὸς μὴ σολοικίζειν.

5. Κἀγὼ μὲν οὕτως. Σωκράτης δὲ ὁ ἀπὸ Μόψου,[3] ᾧ συνεγενόμην ἐν Αἰγύπτῳ, τὰ τοιαῦτα ἔλεγεν ἀνεπαχθῶς καὶ οὐκ ἤλεγχε τὸν ἁμαρτάνοντα.

Πρὸς μέντοι τὸν ἐρωτήσαντα πηνίκα ἔξεισιν, Τίς γὰρ ἄν, ἔφη, ⟨φαίη⟩[1] σοι περὶ τῆς τήμερον ὡς ἐξιών; ἑτέρου δὲ φήσαντος, Ἱκανὰ ἔχω τὰ πατρῷα, Πῶς φῄς; εἶπε· τέθνηκεν γὰρ ὁ πατήρ σοι; ἄλλου δὲ αὖθις λέγοντος, Πατριώτης ἔστι μοι· Ἐλάνθανες ἄρα ἡμᾶς, ἔφη, βάρβαρος ὤν. ἄλλου δὲ εἰπόντος,

[1] φαίη (deest in βγ) add. Nilén: ἀποκριθῇ Ν.

---

[1] ἑαυτῶν for ἡμῶν αὐτῶν is the mistake, though found in Thucydides. Cf. *True Story* 1, 6, *The Ass* 8. For other Lucianic misuses of reflexive pronouns, see *Banquet* 45, *Hermotimus* 1, *Demonax* 17, *Dialogues of the Dead* 1, 3, etc.

[2] The infinitive for imperative may be meant as a mistake, though it occurs in Attic; cf. *The Ignorant Book Collector* 7, *Professor of Public Speaking* 10, *Mistaken Critic* 16, *Saturnalia* 21.

[3] Socrates of Mopsus is unknown. Mopsus is presumably a placename, and perhaps Mopsuestia in Cilicia. It is tempting, however, to identify Socrates with Demonax of Cyprus of whom Lucian says ἐπὶ μήκιστον συνεγενόμην (*Demonax* 1), that he was like Socrates (ibid. 5), that he criticised in a nice way (6), and had a healthy contempt for archaisms and barbarisms (26); but no Mopsus is known in Cyprus. The *Etymologicum Magnum* does quote once

THE SOLECIST

LUCIAN

However if we remain ignorant of these ones, we won't recognise any made by we [1] ourselves, for there's another one you missed. So never again to [2] claim you're competent to spot howlers made by others and to avoid them yourself.

5. Well that's my way of putting the matter; but Socrates of Mopsus,[3] whom I knew [4] in Egypt, used to put that sort of thing tactfully without showing up the offender.

To the man who asked him the hour [5] he was leaving home, he replied, " Who could answer such an untimely question? I've already left for to-day."

When another said, " I'm the possessor [6] of no mean hereditament," he asked, " How do you mean? Is your father dead then? "

When yet another said, " He's a townee [7] of mine," he said, " You didn't tell us you hailed from the wilds."

---

from " Socrates the grammarian " but the text seems doubtful.

[4] Or perhaps " under whom I studied "; cf. preceding note.

[5] Phrynichus censures the use of πηνίκα for πότε; but this passage seems to go farther and imply that πηνίκα should mean " at what o'clock to-day? " Perhaps ἔξεισιν is used loosely for ἀποδημήσει, but ἐξιών properly for " leave the house "; cf. Timon 4. Alternatively Socrates may be objecting to the use of ἔξεισιν as a present tense.

[6] In Attic prose πατρῷος should refer to patrimonial possessions and πάτριος to hereditary background. Cf. Timon 12, Scythian 4, Peregrinus 4.

[7] πατριώτης (as opposed to πολίτης) should only be used of non-Greeks as having no πόλις. Cf. Pollux, 3, 54.

Ὁ δεῖνά ἐστι μεθύσῃς, Μητρός, εἶπεν, ἢ πῶς
λέγεις; ἑτέρου δὲ ‹. . . λέγοντος› λέοντας,[1] Διπλα-
σιάζεις,[2] ἔφη, τοὺς λέοντας.[3] εἰπόντος δέ τινος,
Λῆμμα πάρεστιν αὐτῷ, διὰ τῶν δύο μ,[4] Οὐκοῦν,
ἔφη, λήψεται, εἰ λῆμμα αὐτῷ πάρεστιν. ἑτέρου
δὲ εἰπόντος, Πρόσεισιν ὁ μεῖραξ οὑμὸς φίλος,
Ἔπειτα, ἔφη, λοιδορεῖς φίλον ὄντα; πρὸς δὲ [5]
τὸν εἰπόντα, Δεδίττομαι τὸν ἄνδρα καὶ φεύγω,
Σύ, ἔφη, καὶ ὅταν τινὰ εὐλαβηθῇς, διώξῃ. ἄλλου
δὲ εἰπόντος, Τῶν φίλων ὁ κορυφαιότατος, Χάριέν
γε, ἔφη, τὸ τῆς κορυφῆς ποιεῖν τι ἐπάνω. καὶ
ἐξορμῶ δέ τινος εἰπόντος, Καὶ τίς ἐστιν, εἶπεν, ὃν
ἐξορμᾷς; Ἐξ ἐπιπολῆς δέ τινος εἰπόντος, Ἐκ τῆς
ἐπιπολῆς, εἶπεν, ὡς ἐκ τῆς πιθάκνης. λέγοντος δέ
τινος Συνετάξατό μοι, Καὶ λόχον δέ, ἔφη, Ξενοφῶ

[1] lacunam ante λέοντας (δέοντας β) statuit Nilén: . . . λέγοντος
λέοντας conieci: διαλέγοντας Rothstein.   [2] διπλασιάζει β.
[3] λέγοντας β.   [4] διὰ . . . μ del. E. H. Warmington.
[5] δὲ S: om. cett. codd..

---

[1] μεθύσῃς as a masculine nominative has poor authority;
Socrates rightly regards it as a genitive feminine.
[2] The mistake is now lost from the Greek; Socrates'
reply suggests he may be objecting to a poetic word for
two, or a dual form, or an incorrect reduplication.
[3] The mistake is in using λῆμμα (gain) for λῆμα (spirit).
[4] μεῖραξ should be used of girls.
[5] δεδίττομαι means " frighten " not " fear " in Attic.
[6] Phrynichus also condemns this tautological superlative
used in Alexander 30, Parasite 42, How To Write History 34.
[7] The intransitive use of ἐξορμῶ (not found in good Attic
prose) is censured but cf. Dialogues of the Dead 25, 2, True
Story 2, 4.
[8] The mistake is ἐξ ἐπιπολῆς (found in Nigrinus 35) for
ἐπιπολῆς. It should perhaps be written as one word,

When someone else said, " So-and-so is a drunken [1] mother's son," he said, " Does his mother drink ? Or what do you mean ? "

When someone else said " ⟨Twofold ?⟩ lions," [2] he said, " You're doubling your lions."

When another man said, " He's a man of talents " [3] (instead of using " talent " in the singular), he said, " Then he'll be in the money, if he's got talents."

When another said, " My friend, that filly [4] of a lad, will be coming," he said, " Why then insult your friend ? He's no girl."

To the man who said " I affright [5] the man and run away from him," he said, " Then you'll be the pursuer even when you're afraid of someone."

When another said, " My chiefest friend," [6] he said, " How clever of you to elevate him above your chief friend ! "

When someone said, " I speed [7] forth," he said, " Whom do you speed forth ? "

When a man said, " From [8] outside," he said, " From the outside, like from the bottom of the barrel."

When someone said, " He gave me my marching orders," [9] he said, " Xenophon also gave his troops their order of march."

---

as Phrynichus criticises it as wrongly formed on the analogy of ἐξαίφνης. Phrynichus rightly recommends the adverbial ἐπιπολῆς (found in Attic and *True Story* 2.2, *Dialogues of the Courtesans* 9.2); Socrates less correctly sanctions the late noun ἐπιπολή.

[9] Socrates objects to συντάττομαι with the dative (probably in the sense of " bid farewell to ", as ἀποτάσσομαι in this sense is condemned by Phrynichus).

συνετάξατο. ἄλλου δὲ εἰπόντος, Περιέστην αὐτον
ὥστε λαθεῖν, Θαυμαστόν, ἔφη, εἰ εἷς ὢν περιέστης
τὸν ἕνα. ἑτέρου δὲ λέγοντος, Συνεκρίνετο αὐτῷ,
Καὶ διεκρίνετο πάντως, εἶπεν.

6. Εἰώθει δὲ καὶ πρὸς τοὺς σολοικίζοντας Ἀττικῶς
παίζειν ἀνεπαχθῶς· πρὸς γοῦν τὸν εἰπόντα, Νῶι
τοῦτο δοκεῖ, Σύ, ἔφη, καὶ νῶιν ἐρεῖς ὡς ἁμαρτά-
νομεν. ἑτέρου δὲ σπουδῇ διηγουμένου τι τῶν
ἐπιχωρίων καὶ εἰπόντος, Ἡ δὲ τῷ Ἡρακλεῖ
μιχθεῖσα, Οὐκ ἄρα, ἔφη, ὁ Ἡρακλῆς ἐμίχθη αὐτῇ;
Καρῆναι δέ τινος εἰπόντος ὡς δέοιτο, Τί γάρ, ἔφη,
σοὶ δεινὸν εἴργασται καὶ ἄξιον ἀτιμίας; καὶ
ζυγομαχεῖν δέ τινος λέγοντος,[1] Πρὸς τὸν ἐχθρόν,
εἶπε,[2] ζυγομαχεῖς; ἑτέρου δὲ εἰπόντος βασανίζεσθαι τὸν παῖδα αὐτῷ νοσοῦντα, Ἐπὶ τῷ, ἔφη,
ἢ τί βουλομένου τοῦ βασανίζοντος; Προκόπτει
δέ τινος εἰπόντος ἐν τοῖς μαθήμασιν, Ὁ δὲ Πλάτων,
ἔφη, τοῦτο ἐπιδιδόναι καλεῖ. ἐρομένου δέ τινος εἰ

---

[1] λέγοντος γ: εἰπόντος β.   [2] εἶπε S: σου Ψ: μου cett. codd..

[1] Socrates objects to the late Greek use of περιίσταμαι for
" shun " (found in *Hermotimus* 86).

[2] Socrates objects to συγκρίνομαι with the dative
(perhaps found in *Parasite* 51) in the sense of " contend
with ".   Phrynichus similarly prefers διάκρισις to σύγκρισις
in the sense of " comparison ".

[3] I.e. " when using bookish language ", like Lexiphanes
(vol. v, pp. 291 seq.).   [4] νῶι is wrongly used for νῶιν.

[5] Socrates insists that μίγνυσθαι should only be used of
the man; the distinction is observed in tragedy, but not in
comedy or by Lucian; cf. *True Story* 1.8 (of women),
Dialogues of The Sea-Gods 3.2 (compound, of a man).

[6] The mistake is καρῆναι for κείρασθαι, criticised on the
ground that the passive should only be applied to animals
or ἄτιμοι.   Cf. Phrynichus 292.

When another said, " I got round [1] him and escaped without his noticing," he said, " It's surprising that one individual could get round another."

When someone else said, " He invited comparison to [2] him ", he said, " Yes, and he certainly invited criticism."

6. He was also in the habit of poking inoffensive fun at people making howlers when Atticising.[3] To the man who said, " This is the opinion of we [4] twain," he said, " You can also tell us twain we're wrong."

When another man was eagerly recounting a piece of local lore and said, " When that she had known [5] Heracles," he asked, " Didn't Heracles then know her ? "

When someone said, " I must needs be sheared," [6] he said, " Why, what beastly thing have you done that such an indignity should fall on your head ? "

When someone talked of being at war with his wife,[7] he asked whether she was a national enemy.

When another referred to his sick boy as suffering torture,[8] he said, " Why ? What is his torturer after ? "

When someone said, " He's advancing [9] in his studies," he said that Plato calls it " progressing."

---

[7] Perhaps Socrates insists that ζυγομαχεῖν should only be used of disputes with a σύζυγος, i.e. a wife, relative or associate; cf. Menander, *Dyscolus*, 17,250.

[8] Socrates objects to the figurative use of βασανίζεσθαι in the sense of " to be tortured " (not found in Attic).

[9] Socrates objects to προκόπτω, a word not used by Plato; it is used by Thucydides (though not of studies) and by Lucian (*Hermotimus* 63, *Parasite* 13) in just this way.

μελετήσει ὁ δεῖνα, Πῶς οὖν, ἔφη, ἐμὲ ἐρωτῶν
εἰ μελετήσομαι, λέγεις ὅτι ὁ δεῖνα;

7. Ἀττικίζοντος δέ τινος καὶ τεθνήξει εἰπόντος ἐπὶ
τοῦ τρίτου, Βέλτιον, ἔφη, καὶ ἐνταῦθα μὴ ἀττικίζειν
καταρώμενον. καὶ πρὸς τὸν εἰπόντα δὲ στοχάζομαι
αὐτοῦ ἐπὶ τοῦ φείδομαι αὐτοῦ, Μή τι, ἔφη, διή-
μαρτες βαλών; ἀφιστᾶν δέ τινος εἰπόντος καὶ
ἑτέρου ἀφιστάνειν, Ταῦτα μέν,¹ ἔφη, οὐκ οἶδα.
πρὸς δὲ τὸν λέγοντα πλὴν εἰ μή, Ταῦτα, ἔφη,
διπλᾶ χαρίζῃ. καὶ χρᾶσθαι δέ τινος εἰπόντος,
Ψευδαττικόν, ἔφη, τὸ ῥῆμα. τῷ δὲ λέγοντι
ἔκτοτε, Καλόν, ἔφη, τὸ εἰπεῖν ἐκπέρυσι, ὁ γὰρ
Πλάτων ἐς τότε λέγει. τῷ δὲ ἰδού ἐπὶ τοῦ ἰδέ
χρωμένου τινός, Ἕτερα ἀνθ᾽ ἑτέρων, ἔφη, σημαί-
νεις. ἀντιλαμβάνομαι δὲ ἐπὶ τοῦ συνίημι λέγοντός
τινος, θαυμάζειν ἔφη πῶς ἀντιποιούμενος τοῦ
λέγοντος φῂς μὴ ἀντιποιεῖσθαι. βράδιον δέ τινος

---

¹ ταῦτα μέν Mras: ταῦτά με Ψ: μέν cett. codd..

---

¹ Socrates (perversely or wrongly) takes μελετήσει, as
second person from μελετήσομαι (a rare late future) rather
than third person from μελετήσω (the normal Attic future).

² Socrates does exactly the same thing again, objecting
to τεθνήξω (an Attic alternative for θανοῦμαι) as opposed to
τεθνήξομαι (in current use, e.g. *Charon* 8, *Salaried Posts* 31).

³ στοχάζομαι is used quite wrongly for φείδομαι.

⁴ Socrates rightly objects to ἀφιστᾶν and ἀφιστάνειν as
non-Attic alternatives for ἀφιστάναι.

⁵ Socrates objects to the tautological πλὴν εἰ μή, though
it is probably Attic and occurs in *Dialogues of the Dead* 29.2
and *Salaried Posts* 9 and 23.

⁶ Socrates rightly objects to χρᾶσθαι for χρῆσθαι.

⁷ ἔκτοτε is a late usage (e.g. *The Ass* 45) also censured by
Phrynichus; Socrates retorts by inventing the preposterous
ἐκπέρυσι on the same analogy.

THE SOLECIST

When someone asked, " Wilt[1] so-and-so discourse ? " he said, " Why ask me if I'm going to discourse and then add so-and-so ? "

7. When an Atticiser said, " Shalt[2] shuffle off this mortal coil " (though he meant the third person), " It's better to refrain from Atticising in this world if you're going to curse me."

To the man who said, " I'm letting off[3] at that wight " (instead of " I'm letting him off "), he said, " Methinks you have missed your mark."

When someone said " to get putten[4] away " and another, " to get putted away," he said, " These terms are unfamiliar to me."

To the man who said, " save unless,"[5] he said, " It's kind of you to give us double measure."

When a man said " to enjoy usufract,"[6] he said, " That's a bad old word."

To the man who said, " hitherafter,"[7] he said that " Last year after " must be an excellent expression, seeing that Plato used " hitherto."

To the man who used the phrase " look here "[8] " instead of " look," he said, " You say one thing and mean another."

When a man said " I reprehend[9] you," instead of " I comprehend you," he said he wondered how the man could be a follower of the speaker and yet say he didn't follow him.

---

[8] Socrates seems to imply that ἰδού should only be used exclamatorily; in Attic the middle of ὁρῶ is confined to poetry and compounds; but cf. *Dialogues of the Courtesans* 2.1.

[9] Socrates objects to ἀντιλαμβάνομαι for " understand," as its normal meaning in Plato is " reprehend."

εἰπόντος, Οὐκ ἔστιν, ἔφη, ὅμοιον τῷ τάχιον.
βαρεῖν δέ τινος εἰπόντος, Οὐκ ἔστιν, ἔφη, τὸ
βαρύνειν ἢ νενόμικας. λέλογχα δὲ τὸ εἴληχα
λέγοντος, Ὀλίγων,¹ ἔφη, καὶ παρ' οἷς ἁμαρτάνεται.
ἵπτασθαι δὲ ἐπὶ τοῦ πέτεσθαι² πολλῶν λεγόντων,
"Ὅτι μὲν ἀπὸ τῆς πτήσεως τὸ ὄνομα, σαφῶς
ἴσμεν. περιστερὸν δέ τινος εἰπόντος ὡς δὴ
Ἀττικόν, Καὶ τὸν φάττον ἐροῦμεν, ἔφη. φακὸν
δέ τινος εἰπόντος ἐδηδοκέναι, Καὶ πῶς ἄν, ἔφη,
φακόν τις φάγοι³; ταῦτα μὲν τὰ Σωκράτεια.

8. Ἐπανίωμεν δέ, εἰ δοκεῖ, ἐπὶ τὴν ἅμιλλαν τῶν
προτέρων λόγων. κἀγὼ μὲν καλῶ τοὺς βελτί-
στους ἰέναι ὅλους,⁴ σὺ δὲ γνώρισον· οἶμαι γάρ

---

¹ ὀλίγων β: ὀλίγον γ.   ² πέτεσθαι rec.: πέτασθαι βγ.
³ φάγοι Fritzsche: φάγῃ codd..
⁴ ἰέναι ὅλους Herwerden: εἶναι ὅλους codd.: σολοικισμούς
Rothstein: ἰέναι ἐνόπλους Nilén: ἰέναι λόχους E. H. Warmington: εἶναι βόλους conieci.

---

¹ βράδιον should be βραδύτερον. Socrates condemns it as
even worse than τάχιον (for θᾶττον, the form used by Attic
and by Lucian, *Toxaris* 6 and 11), which at least was the
current form. Phrynichus condemns both βράδιον and τάχιον.
² Socrates wrongly insists that βαρεῖν should be intransitive; it is transitive in Plato *Symposium* 203 b, and in
Dialogues of the Dead 20.4 and *Aetion* 5.
³ Socrates objects to λέλογχα (εἴληχα is used in the best
Attic prose). Cf. ἐλελόγχει *Affairs of the Heart* 18, but
εἰλήχασι ibid. 24.
⁴ ἵπτασθαι is rightly condemned here, and is censured as a
barbarism in *Lexiphanes* 25, and by Phrynichus. It
occurs, however (in compounds), in *Judgement of the
Goddesses* 5 and 6, *Downward Journey* 2, *Dream* 16.

The form recommended by Socrates is probably πέτεσθαι,
as it is the best Attic form, is preferred to πέτασθαι by

THE SOLECIST

When a man said "more tardier,[1]" he said that was a different thing from "more quicker."

When a man said "to press,"[2] he said, "That's not the same thing as 'to depress' as you thought."

When someone said "gotten"[3] for "got," he said, "That's not used by many people, and they move in the wrong circles."

When a great number of people said, "flee[4] through the air" for "fly through the air," he remarked, "We can be quite sure that something flighty is involved."

When someone thought he was being scholarly by talking of a "woodhen,"[5] he said, "Let's call it a jill-snipe."

When a man said he'd eaten a potager of pulse,[6] he asked how anyone could eat so repulsive a dish.

8. So much for Socrates' views. But now let us return, if you will, to our contest of words as before. And I shall summon the best of them to come all and one,[7] and you must recognise them. For I think

Lucian (cf. *Lover of Lies* 13, *Dialogues of the Courtesans* 1.2, *Ass* 4, 12, 13) and is recommended by Phrynichus. πέτασθαι is expressly condemned in *Mistaken Critic* 29.

[5] Socrates objects to περιστερός (a rare masculine form found in Attic comedy) for the normal feminine form περιστερά (common pigeon); he retorts by inventing φάττος for φάττα (ringdove).

[6] Socrates objects to the usage of φακός for φακῆ. According to Herodian φακός should be used of raw, φακῆ of cooked lentils, but the rule is not observed in Attic comedy or late Greek. Socrates retorts by punning on φακός in its current sense of "bottle."

[7] Perhaps ὅλους in the sense of "omnes" rather than "totos" (cf. c. 2) is censured; or a mistake may be concealed in the (probably corrupt) infinitive.

σε κἂν νῦν δυνήσεσθαι τοσούτων γε ἐπακούσαντα
τῶν ἑξῆς λεγομένων.

ΣΟΦΙΣΤΗΣ

Ἴσως μὲν οὐδὲ νῦν δυνήσομαί σου λέγοντος· ὅμως
εἰπέ.

ΛΟΥΚΙΑΝΟΣ

Καὶ πῶς φῂς οὐ δυνήσεσθαι; ἡ γὰρ θύρα σχεδὸν
ἀνέῳγέ σοι τῆς γνωρίσεως [1] αὐτῶν.

ΣΟΦΙΣΤΗΣ

Εἰπὲ τοίνυν.

ΛΟΥΚΙΑΝΟΣ

Ἀλλὰ εἶπον.

ΣΟΦΙΣΤΗΣ

Οὐδέν γε, ὥστε ἐμὲ μαθεῖν.

ΛΟΥΚΙΑΝΟΣ

Οὐ γὰρ ἔμαθες τὸ ἀνέῳγεν;

ΣΟΦΙΣΤΗΣ

Οὐκ ἔμαθον.

---

[1] γνώσεως β.

---

[1] " Now also " is ironical. The mistake is κἂν for καί
(though not followed by an " εἰ " clause); this is common
in late Greek (cf. *Downward Journey* 13, 14, 20, *Nigrinus*
23). Alternatively ἄν with the future may again be

that now also [1] you shalt be able to do so, when you hear so many howlers one after the other.

SOPHIST

Perhaps not even now will I be able to do so with *you* doing the talking. However, speak away.

LUCIAN

How come you say [2] you won't be able ? For the door is pretty well ajarred [3] for you to recognise them.

SOPHIST

Well, say something.

LUCIAN

But I've already said it.

SOPHIST

You've said nothing for me to notice.

LUCIAN

Didn't you notice the word " ajarred " ?

SOPHIST

No, I didn't.

censured (cf. note on c. 2); for κἄν with the future, cf. *Zeus Rants* 32.

[2] Cf. note on c. 1.

[3] ἀνέῳγε for ἀνέῳκται is a mistake also censured by Phrynichus. ἀνέῳγα (not in good Attic) is used intransitively in late Greek; cf. *Cock* 6, 32, *Ship* 4, *Anacharsis* 29, *Dialogues of the Dead*, 14.1.

LUCIAN

ΛΟΥΚΙΑΝΟΣ

Τί οὖν πεισόμεθα, εἰ μηδὲ νῦν ἀκολουθήσεις
τοῖς λεγομένοις; καίτοι πρός γε τὰ κατ' ἀρχὰς
ῥηθέντα ὑπὸ σοῦ ἐγὼ μὲν ὤμην ἱππεῖς [1] ἐς πεδίον
καλεῖν. σὺ δὲ τοὺς ἱππεῖς κατενόησας; ἀλλὰ
ἔοικας οὐ φροντίζειν τῶν λόγων, μάλιστα οὓς
νῦν κατὰ σφᾶς αὐτοὺς διήλθομεν.

ΣΟΦΙΣΤΗΣ

Ἐγὼ μὲν φροντίζω, σὺ δὲ ἀδήλως αὐτοὺς
διεξέρχῃ.

ΛΟΥΚΙΑΝΟΣ

9. Πάνυ γοῦν ἄδηλόν ἐστι τὸ κατὰ σφᾶς αὐτοὺς
ἐφ' ἡμῶν λεγόμενον. ἀλλὰ τοῦτο μὲν δῆλον· σὲ
δὲ οὐδεὶς ἂν θεῶν ἀγνοοῦντα παύσειεν πλήν γε ὁ
Ἀπόλλων. μαντεύεται γοῦν ἐκεῖνος πᾶσι τοῖς
ἐρωτῶσι, σὺ δὲ οὐδὲ τὸν μαντευόμενον κατενόησας.

ΣΟΦΙΣΤΗΣ

Μὰ τοὺς θεούς, οὐ γὰρ ἔμαθον.

[1] ἱππεῖς SΨN: ἱππῆς ΓΩU.

---

[1] I.e. " fight in favourable conditions." See Plato,
Theaetetus 183 D, where Theaetetus is warned against
challenging Socrates to an argument. Cf. *The Fisher* 9.

The mistake is in not using the normal Attic —έας for
the accusative plural of a noun in —εύς. Lucian normally
has —έας (*Ship* 31, *Toxaris* 49, *True Story* 2.34, etc.) but
—εῖς occurs in *Ship* 46 and *Ass* 23.

[2] Perhaps ἔοικα οὐ for οὐκ ἔοικα is deliberate. But cf.
notes on φῂς οὐ pp. 5 and 27.

28

THE SOLECIST

What will become of us, if not even now do you
follow what I say ? However to oppose your initial
remarks I thought I'd call them [1] horsemen of mine
on to the open plain. Didn't you notice them
horsemen ? Why, you don't seem to be paying no [2]
attention to the discussion, particularly the one
there's just been between you and I.[3]

SOPHIST

I am paying attention, but you're not obvious
enough in what you say.

LUCIAN

9. I quite agree ; there's nothing obvious about
" between you and I " instead of " between you
and me." No that's obvious enough, but no god
would stop *you* from being an ignoramus except
Apollo. He at any rate learns [4] anyone who consults
him. But you didn't even notice him learning
them.

SOPHIST

Heavens no ! I didn't.

---

[3] σφᾶς αὐτοὺς for ἡμᾶς αὐτοὺς is a mistake unparalleled in
Attic and very rare elsewhere; but cf. note on ἑαυτῶν (c. 4)
and the late Greek use of σφέτερος for ὑμέτερος.

[4] μαντεύομαι in the sense of " give an oracle " is regarded
as a mistake, though found in Demosthenes and the normal
meaning in Lucian (*Alexander* 19, *Dialogues of the Dead* 10.1,
25.2, etc.); the usual Attic meaning (consult an oracle)
occurs once in Lucian (*Dialogues of the Dead* 23.1).

LUCIAN

ΛΟΥΚΙΑΝΟΣ

Ἦ [1] ἄρα καθ' εἶς λανθάνει σε περιιών; [2]

ΣΟΦΙΣΤΗΣ

Ἐοίκασί γε.

ΛΟΥΚΙΑΝΟΣ

Ὁ δὲ καθ' εἶς πῶς παρῆλθεν;

ΣΟΦΙΣΤΗΣ

Οὐδὲ τοῦτο ἔμαθον.

ΛΟΥΚΙΑΝΟΣ

Οἶσθα δέ τινα μνηστευόμενον αὐτῷ γάμον;

ΣΟΦΙΣΤΗΣ

Τί οὖν τοῦτο;

ΛΟΥΚΙΑΝΟΣ

Ὅτι σολοικίζειν ἀνάγκη τὸν μνηστευόμενον αὐτῷ.

ΣΟΦΙΣΤΗΣ

Τί οὖν πρὸς τοὐμὸν πρᾶγμα, εἰ σολοικίζει τις μνηστευόμενος;

---

[1] ἦ Baar: εἰ codd..   [2] περιιών γ.

---

[1] καθ' εἶς or καθεῖς is an illogical alternative for ἕκαστος and only found in late vulgar Greek.

30

THE SOLECIST

LUCIAN

Then do all them [1] mistakes each in turn escape
your notice ?

SOPHIST

It seems so.

LUCIAN

How did " all them " get past you ?

SOPHIST

I didn't notice that one either.

LUCIAN

Do you know of anyone who's setting his own [2]
cap at a girl with a view to matrimony ?

SOPHIST

Why do you ask me that ?

LUCIAN

Because there must be something wrong when a
man sets his own cap at a girl.

SOPHIST

What does it matter to me if a man who sets his [3]
cap at a girl is wrong ?

---

[2] The mistake is probably the tautological use of αὐτῷ
with the middle μνηστεύομαι ; Lucian does exactly this in
Salaried Posts 23.

[3] The sophist by omitting αὐτῷ misses the point.

LUCIAN

ΛΟΥΚΙΑΝΟΣ

῞Οτι ἀγνοεῖ ὁ φάσκων εἰδέναι. καὶ τὸ μὲν οὕτως ἔχει. εἰ δέ τις λέγοι [1] σοι παρελθὼν ὡς
ἀπολείποι [2] τὴν γυναῖκα, ἆρ’ ἂν ἐπιτρέποις αὐτῷ;

ΣΟΦΙΣΤΗΣ

Τί γὰρ οὐκ ἂν ἐπιτρέποιμι, εἰ φαίνοιτο ἀδι-
κούμενος;

ΛΟΥΚΙΑΝΟΣ

Εἰ δὲ σολοικίζων φαίνοιτο, ἐπιτρέποις ἂν αὐτῷ
τοῦτο;

ΣΟΦΙΣΤΗΣ

Οὐκ ἔγωγε.

ΛΟΥΚΙΑΝΟΣ

Ὀρθῶς γὰρ λέγεις· οὐ γὰρ ἐπιτρεπτέον σολοι-
κίζοντι τῷ φίλῳ, ἀλλὰ διδακτέον ὅπως τοῦτο μὴ
πείσεται. καὶ εἴ τίς γε νῦν ψοφοίη τὴν θύραν
ἐσιὼν ἢ ἐξιὼν κόπτοι, τί φήσομέν σε πεπονθέναι;

ΣΟΦΙΣΤΗΣ

Ἐμὲ μὲν οὐδέν, ἐκεῖνον δὲ ἐπεσελθεῖν βούλεσθαι ἢ ἐξιέναι.

[1] λέγοι N: λέγει cett. codd..   [2] ἀπολίποι recc..

---

[1] The mistake is ἀπολείπω, which is used of the wife leaving
the husband in Attic oratory, but of the husband by Lucian
(*Dialogues of the Gods* 8.2, *Double Indictment* 29).

THE SOLECIST

Only that the one who claims to know is ignorant. Well so much for that. But if a man were to come and tell you that he was divorcing [1] from his wife, would you allow him ?

SOPHIST

Of course I would, if he were obviously the injured party.

LUCIAN

But if he were obviously ungrammatical, would you let him do so ?

SOPHIST

I certainly wouldn't.

LUCIAN

You're quite right. For one shouldn't let a friend make a grammatical error, but instruct him how to avoid it. And if anyone were now to rattle at the door on his way in or knock it on his way out,[2] what effect shall we say it has on you ?

SOPHIST

None on me ; but we can say he wished to come in or go out.

[2] An intentional mistake as θύραν ψοφεῖν (cf. Latin " ostium crepat ") is regularly used of people going out and κόπτειν (" knock " " pulsare ") of people coming in. According to Plutarch *Publicola* 20, ancient doors opened outwards and when going out one rattled them as a warning to those outside, though this is disputed by some modern scholars (cf. W. Beare, *The Roman Stage*, pp. 287 ff.).

LUCIAN

ΛΟΥΚΙΑΝΟΣ

Σὲ δὲ ἀγνοοῦντα τὸν κόπτοντα ἢ ψοφοῦντα
οὐδὲν ὅλως πεπονθέναι δόξομεν ἀπαίδευτον ὄντα;

ΣΟΦΙΣΤΗΣ

Ὑβριστὴς εἶ.

ΛΟΥΚΙΑΝΟΣ

Τί λέγεις; ὑβριστὴς ἐγώ; νῦν δὴ γενήσομαί
σοι διαλεγόμενος. ἔοικα δὲ σολοικίσαι τὸ νῦν δὴ
γενήσομαι, σὺ δ' οὐκ ἔγνως.

ΣΟΦΙΣΤΗΣ

10. Παῦσαι πρὸς τῆς Ἀθηνᾶς· ἀλλ' εἰπέ τι τοιοῦτον ὥστε κἀμὲ μαθεῖν.

ΛΟΥΚΙΑΝΟΣ

Καὶ πῶς ἂν μάθοις;

ΣΟΦΙΣΤΗΣ

Εἴ μοι πάντα ἐπέλθοις, ὅσα φῂς σολοικίσας ἐμὲ
λαθεῖν καὶ παρ' ὅ τι ἕκαστον σεσολοίκισται.

ΛΟΥΚΙΑΝΟΣ

Μηδαμῶς, ὦ ἄριστε· μακρὸν γὰρ [1] ἂν ποιή-
σαιμεν τὸν διάλογον. ἀλλὰ περὶ μὲν τούτων
ἔξεστί σοι καθ' ἕκαστον αὐτῶν πυνθάνεσθαι· νῦν

[1] γὰρ om. β.

34

THE SOLECIST

LUCIAN

Shall we regard you as ignorant of the difference between a man knocking the door and rattling at it and completely unaffected by the matter, because you are an ignoramus?

SOPHIST

You're offensive.

LUCIAN

What's that you say? I offensive? Now in [1] this present time I shall be offensive in talking to you. I appear to have made a howler in saying "now in the present time I shall," but you didn't notice it.

SOPHIST

10. In Athena's name, stop! Say something that even I can understand.

LUCIAN

How could you?

SOPHIST

If you went through all the errors you say you made without my noticing and you explained where each error lay.

LUCIAN

Don't ask that, my good fellow, for that would make our discussion a lengthy one. No, as regards the errors I made, you may enquire about each of them separately. But at present let's tackle

---

[1] The solecism is νῦν δή with the future which is perhaps condemned as illogical; Plato uses it often enough with the future, though more frequently with the present (as recommended by Pollux) or to refer to the immediate past.

δὲ ἕτερ' ἄττα ἐπέλθωμεν, εἰ δοκεῖ, καὶ πρῶτόν γε
αὐτὸ τὸ ἄττα μὴ δασέως ἀλλὰ ψιλῶς ἐξενεγκεῖν
ὀρθῶς φαίνεται ῥηθὲν μετὰ τοῦ ἕτερα συντιθέμενον.[1]
μὴ γὰρ οὕτως ἄλογον ἦν ἄν. ἔπειτα τὸ τῆς
ὕβρεως, ἥν με φῂς ὑβρίσαι <σε>,[2] εἰ μὴ οὕτω
λέγοιμι, ἀλλ' εἰς σὲ φαίην,[3] ἴδιον.

ΣΟΦΙΣΤΗΣ

Ἐγὼ μὲν οὐκ ἔχω εἰπεῖν.

ΛΟΥΚΙΑΝΟΣ

Ὅτι τὸ μὲν σὲ [4] ὑβρίζειν τὸ σῶμά ἐστι τὸ σὸν
ἤτοι πληγαῖς ἢ δεσμοῖς ἢ καὶ ἄλλῳ τρόπῳ, τὸ
δὲ ἐς σέ, ὅταν εἴς τι τῶν σῶν γίγνηται ἡ ὕβρις·
καὶ γὰρ ὅστις γυναῖκα ὑβρίζει τὴν σήν, εἰς σὲ
ὑβρίζει, καὶ ὅστις παῖδα καὶ φίλον καὶ ὅστις γε
οἰκέτην. πλὴν γὰρ περὶ πραγμάτων οὕτως ἔχει
σοι· ἐπεὶ τὸ ἐς πρᾶγμα ὑβρίζειν λέλεκται, οἷον
ἐς τὴν παροιμίαν, ὡς ὁ Πλάτων φησὶν ἐν τῷ
Συμποσίῳ.

ΣΟΦΙΣΤΗΣ

Κατανοῶ τὸ διάφορον.

[1] ὀρθῶς . . . συντιθέμενον del. Gesner.
[2] σε deest in codd.: add. Gesner.
[3] σέ, φαίην ἂν ἴδιον Baar.
[4] σὲ L: σῶμα cett. codd.: σέ, ὦ μακάριε, Nilén.

---

[1] Lucian here gives elementary instruction on the
distinction between two obsolescent Attic words ἄττα with a
smooth breathing (= τινα) and ἄττα with a rough breathing
(= ἅτινα).

something othergates,[1] if you don't mind. In the first place to say " something " and not " some things " is clearly right when in conjunction with " othergates." To do otherwise would be illogical. Next there's the question of my having offended you, as you claim. If I were to put things differently and say I had offended against you, the phrase has a particular meaning.

SOPHIST

About that I can't say.

LUCIAN

Yes indeed, for to offend you is to offend your person [2] with blows or chains or in some other way, while to offend against you is when the offence is committed against anything that is yours ; for any man who offends your wife or your son or your friend or even your slave offends against you. You can take this to be true except in the case of inanimate objects ; for we talk of offending against inanimate things, as for example " against the proverb," to quote Plato's phrase in the *Banquet*.[3]

SOPHIST

I appreciate the difference.

---

[2] Lucian insists that ὑβρίζω τινά refers to physical affront to the individual's person and ὑβρίζω εἰς τινα is used of affront to his possessions ; the distinction is seldom observed in Attic or elsewhere or by Lucian himself.

[3] 174 B.

LUCIAN

ΛΟΥΚΙΑΝΟΣ

Ἆρ᾽ οὖν καὶ τοῦτο κατανοεῖς, ὅτι τὸ ταῦτα ὑπαλλάττειν σολοικίζειν καλοῦσιν;

ΣΟΦΙΣΤΗΣ

Ἀλλὰ νῦν εἴσομαι.

ΛΟΥΚΙΑΝΟΣ

Αὐτὸ δὲ τὸ [1] ἐναλλάττειν;

ΣΟΦΙΣΤΗΣ

Ἐμοὶ μὲν ταὐτὸν λέγειν δόξει.

ΛΟΥΚΙΑΝΟΣ

Καὶ πῶς ἂν εἴη ταὐτὸν τῷ ὑπαλλάττειν τὸ ἐναλλάττειν, εἴπερ τὸ μὲν ἑτέρου πρὸς ἕτερον γίγνεται, τοῦ μὴ ὀρθοῦ πρὸς τὸ ὀρθόν, τὸ δὲ τοῦ μὴ ὄντος πρὸς τὸ ὄν;

ΣΟΦΙΣΤΗΣ

Κατέμαθον ὅτι τὸ μὲν ὑπαλλάττειν τὸ μὴ κύριον ἀντὶ τοῦ κυρίου λέγειν ἐστίν, τὸ δ᾽ ἐναλλάττειν ποτὲ μὲν τῷ κυρίῳ, ποτὲ δὲ τῷ μὴ κυρίῳ χρῆσθαι.

---

[1] τῷ Ω, Γ?: τὸ cett. codd.: lacunam inter δὲ et τὸ coniciunt edd..

---

[1] The whole passage is obscure, perhaps deliberately so. Hypallage (here translated as " exchange ") is explained by Cicero, *Orator* 27.93, Quintilian 8.6.23 as equivalent to μετωνυμία (change of name); enallage (translated here as

THE SOLECIST

LUCIAN

Then do you appreciate also that it is called an error to exchange these expressions ?

SOPHIST

I shall from now.

LUCIAN

And do people call this " to change " ?

SOPHIST

That will mean the same thing in my opinion.

LUCIAN

How could " to change " be the same as " to exchange " ? One changes [1] one thing to another, for example the incorrect [2] to the correct, while one exchanges the true for the false.

SOPHIST

I have learnt [3] " to exchange " is to use figurative instead of plain language, while " to change " is sometimes to use plain and sometimes figurative language.

" change ") is a grammatical term for the substitution of one mood, tense, etc., for another. More logically Lucian would have said " the correct to the incorrect . . . the true for the false."

[2] τὸ ὀρθὸν 'correct' is also ambiguous, as it could also mean active as opposed to passive, or nominative as opposed to an oblique case.

[3] The sophist shows that he has indeed learnt the meaning of hypallage, but does not know the technical sense of enallage.

LUCIAN

ΛΟΥΚΙΑΝΟΣ

Ἔχει τινὰ καὶ ταῦτα κατανόησιν οὐκ ἄχαριν,[1] τὸ δὲ σπουδάζειν πρός τινα τὴν [2] οἰκείαν ὠφέλειαν τοῦ σπουδάζοντος ἐμφαίνει, τὸ δὲ περί τινα τὴν ἐκείνου περὶ ὃν σπουδάζει. καὶ ταῦτα ἴσως μὲν ὑποσυγκέχυται, ἴσως δὲ καὶ ἀκριβοῦται παρά τισι· βέλτιον δὲ τὸ ἀκριβοῦν ἑκάστῳ.

ΣΟΦΙΣΤΗΣ

Ὀρθῶς γὰρ λέγεις.

ΛΟΥΚΙΑΝΟΣ

11. Τό γε μὴν καθέζεσθαι [3] τοῦ καθίζειν καὶ τὸ κάθισον τοῦ κάθησο ἆρ' οἶσθ' ὅτι διενήνοχεν;

ΣΟΦΙΣΤΗΣ

Οὐκ οἶδα. τὸ καθέσθητι ἤκουόν σου λέγοντος ὡς ἔστιν ἔκφυλον.

ΛΟΥΚΙΑΝΟΣ

Καὶ ὀρθῶς γε ἤκουσας. ἀλλὰ τὸ κάθισον τοῦ κάθησο διαφέρειν φημί.

ΣΟΦΙΣΤΗΣ

Καὶ τῷ ποτ' ἂν εἴη διαφέρον;

---

[1] χρῆσθαι. ἔχει . . . ἄχαριν. ΛΟΥΚ. Τὸ . . . ΓΥ.
[2] τὴν γὰρ codd.: γὰρ del. correctores in ΓΩU: πρός τινα ⟨οὐ ταὐτόν ἐστι τῷ περί τινα⟩· τὴν γὰρ Rothstein.
[3] καθέζεσθαι Ν: καθίζεσθαι βγ.

40

THE SOLECIST

Once again you show a charming understanding of the matter. Again to show zeal to [1] another indicates that one is seeking one's private advantage, whereas to show zeal for someone means that one is seeking that person's advantage. Perhaps these expressions too are confused, but perhaps they are also used accurately by some. But it's better for everyone to be accurate.

SOPHIST

You're quite right.

LUCIAN

11. Do you know that there's a difference between " to sit " and " to settle " and between " to settle down " and " to be seated " ?

SOPHIST

No, I don't. But I've heard you say that " sit yourself down " [2] is a barbarism.

LUCIAN

What you heard was right. But I'm telling you that " settle down " is different from " be seated."

SOPHIST

How ever could it be different ?

---

[1] Lucian draws a correct if obvious distinction between σπουδάζω πρός τινα " court " (Lucian prefers σπουδάζω τινά in this meaning) and σπουδάζω περί τινα " be zealous for."

[2] Cf. *Lexiphanes* 25 and Phrynichus 236 where the non-Attic καθεσθείς is condemned as barbaric. Lucian has περικαθεσθέντες in *True Story* 1.23.

LUCIAN

ΛΟΥΚΙΑΝΟΣ

Τῷ τὸ μὲν πρὸς τὸν ἑστῶτα λέγεσθαι, τὸ κάθισον, τὸ δὲ πρὸς τὸν καθεζόμενον·
ἧσο,[1] ξεῖν᾽, ἡμεῖς δὲ καὶ ἄλλοθι δήομεν ἕδρην,
ἀντὶ τοῦ μένε καθεζόμενος. πάλιν οὖν εἰρήσθω
ὅτι τὸ ταῦτα παραλλάττειν ἁμαρτάνειν ἐστί.
τὸ δὲ καθίζω τοῦ καθέζομαι ἆρά σοι δοκεῖ μικρῷ
τινι διαφέρειν; εἴπερ τὸ μὲν καὶ ἕτερον δρῶμεν,
τὸ καθίζειν λέγω,[2] τὸ δὲ μόνους ἡμᾶς αὐτούς, τὸ
καθέζεσθαι.

ΣΟΦΙΣΤΗΣ

12. Καὶ ταῦτα ἱκανῶς διελήλυθας, καὶ δεῖ δέ γε[3]
οὕτω σε προδιδάσκειν.

ΛΟΥΚΙΑΝΟΣ

Ἑτέρως γὰρ λέγοντος οὐ κατανοεῖς; οὐκ οἶσθα
οἷόν ἐστι ξυγγραφεὺς ἀνήρ;
....[4]

---

[1] ἧσο βγΝ: ἧσ᾽ ὦ rec., Homer, *Odyssey* 16, 44.
[2] τὸ ... λέγω rec., edd.: τὸ ... λέγειν βΝ: τῷ ... λέγειν γ.
[3] δεῖ δέ γε Nilén: δὴ λέγε βγ: δὴ λέγω Ν.
[4] lacunam statuit Gesner.

---

[1] Homer, *Odyssey* XVI. 44. The distinction is between
κάθισον, " settle down " (aorist imperative of καθίζω used
instransitively) and κάθησο " be seated " (present imperative of κάθημαι).
[2] The distinction is primarily between καθέζομαι, " sit,"
and καθίζω " settle," used transitively.
[3] Lucian is perhaps complicating matters deliberately by
implying that καθίζω can be used both transitively and

THE SOLECIST

LUCIAN

Because the one thing, " settle down," is said to
omeone standing, and the other to someone sitting,
or instance " Be seated, friend ; and we shall
lsewhere find a seat," [1] instead of saying " remain
eated." Therefore let me repeat that to inter-
hange these is to make a mistake. Do you think
hat " I settle " is not very much different from " I
it " ? [2] We do the one to another person also,[3]
' settle " I mean, but the other " sit " only to
urselves.

SOPHIST

12. Once again you've given me an adequate explanation ; you ought always thus to instruct me in
advance.

LUCIAN

Can't you understand me, if I talk otherwise ?
Don't you know what is meant by a writer [4] ?

SOPHIST

— — — —

LUCIAN

— — — —

intransitively. Lucian himself uses καθίζω transitively
and intransitively, as well as καθίζομαι and καθέζομαι.
[4] Lucian may mean " Can't you read books on the
subject ? " The text makes poor sense unless we follow
Gesner in assuming a lacuna, perhaps involving the distinction between συγγραφεύς (historian of contemporary events
like Thucydides) and ἱστοριόγραφος (e.g. Herodotus).

LUCIAN

ΣΟΦΙΣΤΗΣ

Πάνυ οἶδα νῦν γέ σου ἀκούσας ταῦτα λέγοντος.

ΛΟΥΚΙΑΝΟΣ

Ἐπεὶ καὶ τὸ καταδουλοῦν σὺ μὲν ἴσως ταὐτὸν τῷ καταδουλοῦσθαι νενόμικας, ἐγὼ δὲ οἶδα διαφορὰν οὐκ ὀλίγην ἔχον.

ΣΟΦΙΣΤΗΣ

Τίνα ταύτην;

ΛΟΥΚΙΑΝΟΣ

Ὅτι τὸ μὲν ἑτέρῳ, τὸ καταδουλοῦν, ⟨τὸ⟩[1] δ' ἑαυτῷ γίγνεται.

ΣΟΦΙΣΤΗΣ

Καλῶς λέγεις.

ΛΟΥΚΙΑΝΟΣ

Καὶ ἄλλα δέ σοι πολλὰ ὑπάρχει μανθάνειν, εἴπερ μὴ αὐτὸς εἰδέναι οὐκ εἰδὼς δόξεις.

ΣΟΦΙΣΤΗΣ

Ἀλλ' οὐκ ἂν δόξαιμι.

ΛΟΥΚΙΑΝΟΣ

Οὐκοῦν τὰ λοιπὰ εἰσαῦθις ἀναβαλώμεθα, νῦν δὲ διαλύσωμεν τὸν διάλογον.

---

[1] τὸ Hemsterhuys: deest in codd..

THE SOLECIST

SOPHIST

I know very well, now that I've heard what you've said.

LUCIAN

Indeed you do, for you have perhaps thought that " to enslave " is the same as " to slave," [1] but I know there's a great difference.

SOPHIST

How do you mean ?

LUCIAN

Because you enslave another, but you slave yourself.

SOPHIST

Well said !

LUCIAN

You have many other things to learn, unless you will persist in thinking you know for yourself when you don't.

SOPHIST

No, I won't do that.

LUCIAN

Then let's postpone the rest to another time, and break off our discussion for the present.

---

[1] The distinction is between the active and passive of καταδουλοῦν (enslave).

LUCIUS or THE ASS

The most helpful accounts of the problem of the
authorship of *The Ass* and its relationship with the
Metamorphoses of Apuleius and the lost Μεταμορ-
φώσεις thought by Photius to have been written by
Lucius of Patras, are to be found in B. E. Perry's *The
Metamorphoses ascribed to Lucius of Patrae* and in
P. Vallette's introduction to the Budé edition of
Apuleius' *Metamorphoses*.

The evidence of Photius (*Bibl. Cod.* 129, Migne) is
as follows :

" I have read the *Metamorphoses* of Lucius of
Patras, a work in several books. His style is clear,
pure and attractive. Though he avoids innovations
of language, he is inordinately fond of marvellous
stories, and one might almost call him another
Lucian. At any rate Lucius' first two books have
more or less been copied by him from the work of
Lucian entitled *Lucius* or *The Ass* ; or Lucian has
copied his work from the books of Lucius. The
second alternative appears the more probable, if I
may indulge in conjecture ; for which was the
earlier we cannot as yet tell. For Lucian has, as it
were, filed down Lucius' books with their greater
bulk, has removed what he did not think suitable for
his own particular purpose and, using the original
phrases and constructions, has assembled what
remains in one book, calling what he has plundered
from that source *Lucius* or *The Ass*. The work of
both authors is full of fictitious stories and shameful

obscenities. Lucian, however, in composing this book as in his other works, mocked and ridiculed the superstitions of the Greeks ; Lucius on the other hand was serious and believed in the metamorphoses of men into other men and of beasts into men and back again, and in all the other ridiculous nonsense of the old fables, so that he wove all that into the fabric of his tale.''

It is generally agreed that both *The Ass* and Apuleius' *Metamorphoses* are derived from the lost work for the following reasons :

(1) The narratives of *The Ass* and of Apuleius not only are the same in outline, but have numerous verbal parallels. (Apuleius' version differs in being fuller, digressing to tell many other tales, and by introducing autobiographical elements and favourable references to Isis and Osiris into his final chapters.)

(2) Apuleius tells us (1.1) " Fabulam Graecanicam incipimus." (Attempts to show that this earlier Greek version was also by Apuleius have proved unconvincing.)

(3) Apuleius' version cannot be an enlargement of *The Ass* because comparison of *The Ass* 24, 36 and 38 (see notes) with the parallel passages in Apuleius show that *The Ass* must be an abridged version, and therefore taken from the same " fabula Graecanica " as Apuleius.

The question of the additional stories found in Apuleius is a difficult one. A few scholars allow him no originality at all except perhaps in the ending of his work, though a rather more popular view is that all the additional material came from Apuleius.

Perhaps the best solution is given by A. Lesky (*Hermes*, 1941, pp. 43 ff.) who suggests that some few of the extra tales were in the lost original.

So much of the Greek of *The Ass* seems unworthy of Lucian that most editors have rejected it as non-Lucianic. Knaut and Neukamm, however, have amassed a formidable list of peculiarly Lucianic usages in *The Ass*. Rohde explained the combination of Lucianic and non-Lucianic elements by suggesting that Lucius of Patras wrote seriously about the transformation of someone else into an ass, and that Lucian abridged and parodied this work, changing it only at the end by making the Ass-man announce that he is Lucian's adversary, Lucius of Patras. This ingenious theory is to be discounted because (despite what Photius says) the lost original was probably not serious (both copies show facetious touches throughout), and a Lucianic parody would surely have been full of malicious sabotage right from the beginning.

The most convincing explanation is that of Perry, who developed Pauly's suggestion that the original *Metamorphoses* was written by Lucian himself, while the epitome was made by another. If the *Metamorphoses* was a facetious satire on credulity and curiosity, what more probable author for it than Lucian, the writer of the *Lover of Lies*, *True Story* and the *Syrian Goddess*, particularly in view of what Photius says of the style of the *Metamorphoses*? This theory is chronologically possible, especially if the *Metamorphoses* of Apuleius is regarded as later than his *Apologia*. The main objection is that it conflicts with part of the evidence of Photius, but this can be discounted because the lost work was probably not credulous and serious, nor was its author Lucius of Patras, as no self-respecting author would confess that he had been an ass for a period ("ass" had much the same proverbial connotation to the Greeks as to us). Photius, indeed, could well have made a mistake in assuming that the Assman's name given in c. 55 was also the name of the author or that the title meant "Metamorphoses written by" (rather than "experienced by") Lucius of Patras.

Many modern authorities, however, believe that Photius chose the right alternative and that Lucius of Patras was a writer and earlier than Lucian, though they disagree as to his date. If they are correct, *The Ass* should probably be regarded as the work of a Pseudo-Lucian, not because its Greek is unworthy of Lucian himself (Lucian could conceivably be imitating the vulgar Greek of the original or of the genre), but because one can scarcely visualise Lucian as a mere epitomist, or as showing such restraint when parodying, or indeed as a plagiarist (though it could be argued that his disavowal of plagiarism in *Prometheus In Words* refers particularly to his dialogues). However, the writer of *The Ass* often shows an incredibly Lucianic turn of phrase. One could therefore regard him as an imitator of incomparable genius; but an altogether more probable alternative is that Lucian's own hand had some share in the composition of *The Ass*, and that the theory that Lucius of Patras was the writer should be dismissed.

The story of the Ass-Man and his lady lover, however, existed before Lucian's time. It was known to

Juvenal (*Satires*, 6.334), and Cataudella (*La Novella Greca*, pp. 152 ff.) speculates that it may have figured among the earliest Milesian Fables (cf. note on c. 51). We should therefore, while accepting Perry's theory, assume that Lucian's *Metamorphoses* was not completely original, but contained a certain amount of adaptation of earlier material to which he gave unity and greater literary form. His debt, however, to predecessors such as Aristides or Lucius of Patras (if he existed) was probably no greater than his debt to Menippus in the field of satirical dialogue.

ΛΟΥΚΙΟΣ[1] Η ΟΝΟΣ

1. Ἀπῄειν ποτὲ ἐς Θετταλίαν· ἦν δέ μοι πατρικόν
τι συμβόλαιον ἐκεῖ πρὸς ἄνθρωπον ἐπιχώριον· ἵππος
δέ με κατῆγε καὶ τὰ σκεύη καὶ θεράπων ἠκολούθει εἷς.
ἐπορευόμην οὖν τὴν προκειμένην ὁδόν· καί πως
ἔτυχον καὶ ἄλλοι ἀπιόντες ἐς Ὕπατα πόλιν τῆς
Θετταλίας, ἐκεῖθεν ὄντες· καὶ ἁλῶν ἐκοινωνοῦμεν,
καὶ οὕτως ἐκείνην τὴν ἀργαλέαν ὁδὸν ἀνύσαντες
πλησίον ἤδη τῆς πόλεως ἦμεν, κἀγὼ ἠρόμην τοὺς
Θετταλοὺς εἴπερ ἐπίστανται ἄνδρα οἰκοῦντα ἐς
τὰ Ὕπατα, Ἵππαρχον τοὔνομα. γράμματα δὲ
αὐτῷ ἐκόμιζον οἴκοθεν, ὥστε οἰκῆσαι παρ' αὐτῷ.
οἱ δὲ εἰδέναι τὸν Ἵππαρχον τοῦτον ἔλεγον καὶ ὅπῃ [2]
τῆς πόλεως οἰκεῖ καὶ ὅτι ἀργύριον ἱκανὸν ἔχει [3]
καὶ ὅτι μίαν θεράπαιναν τρέφει καὶ τὴν αὑτοῦ
γαμετὴν μόνας· ἔστι γὰρ φιλαργυρώτατος δεινῶς.
ἐπεὶ δὲ πλησίον τῆς πόλεως ἐγεγόνειμεν, κῆπός
τις ἦν καὶ ἔνδον [4] οἰκίδιον ἀνεκτόν, ἔνθα ὁ Ἵππαρχος
ᾤκει.

2. οἱ μὲν οὖν ἀσπασάμενοί με ᾤχοντο, ἐγὼ
δὲ κόπτω προσελθὼν τὴν θύραν, καὶ μόλις μὲν καὶ
βραδέως, ὑπήκουσε δ' οὖν γυνή,[5] εἶτα καὶ προῆλθεν.
ἐγὼ μὲν ἠρόμην εἰ ἔνδον εἴη Ἵππαρχος· Ἔνδον,

Traditio est simplex. Codices rettuli Γ et recentes
(N, Ψ, C, Vat. 87).

[1] Titulus Λοῦκις apud Photium et fortasse primitus Γ.

LUCIUS or THE ASS

1. Once upon a time I was on my way to Thessaly, having some business of my father's to transact there with a man of that country. I had a horse to carry me and my baggage, and I was accompanied by one servant. And so I was proceeding along my intended route ; now it happened that I had as fellow travellers men on their way back home to Hypata, a city of Thessaly. We shared salt[1] and thus we proceeded on that difficult journey until we were near the city, when I asked the Thessalians if they knew a man living in Hypata, called Hipparchus. I had a letter of introduction to him from home, so that I could stay at his house. They said they knew this Hipparchus and where he lived in the city ; they told me that he had plenty of money, but that the only women he kept were one servant and his wife, as he was a terrible miser. When we had come near to the city, we found a garden, and in it a tolerably comfortable cottage, where Hipparchus lived.

2. The others therefore said good-bye and left me, and I went up and knocked at the door. Though I had a long wait, eventually a woman did reluctantly answer my knock, and then even came out. I asked

[1] I.e. became friends and ate together.

[2] ὅποι ΓΝ. [3] ἔχοι ΓΝ.

[4] ἦν καὶ ἔνδον Courier: ἔνδον ἦν καὶ ΓΝC.: ἦν καὶ Ψ.

[5] ἡ γυνή rec., edd..

53

PSEUDO-LUCIAN

ἔφη· σὺ δὲ τίς ἢ τί βουλόμενος πυνθάνῃ;

Γράμματα ἥκω κομίζων αὐτῷ παρὰ Δεκριανοῦ τοῦ Πατρέως σοφιστοῦ.

Μεῖνόν με, ἔφη, αὐτοῦ, καὶ τὴν θύραν συγκλείσασα ᾤχετο εἴσω πάλιν· καί ποτε ἐξελθοῦσα κελεύει ἡμᾶς εἰσελθεῖν. κἀγὼ δὲ παρελθὼν εἴσω ἀσπάζομαι αὐτὸν καὶ τὰ γράμματα ἐπέδωκα. ἔτυχεν δὲ ἐν ἀρχῇ δείπνου ὢν καὶ κατέκειτο ἐπὶ κλινιδίου στενοῦ, γυνὴ δὲ αὐτοῦ καθῆστο πλησίον, καὶ τράπεζα μηδὲν ἔχουσα παρέκειτο. ὁ δὲ ἐπειδὴ τοῖς γράμμασιν ἐνέτυχεν, Ἀλλ' ὁ μὲν φίλτατος ἐμοί, ἔφη, καὶ τῶν Ἑλλήνων ἐξοχώτατος Δεκριανὸς εὖ ποιεῖ καὶ θαρρῶν πέμπει παρ' ἐμοὶ τοὺς ἑταίρους τοὺς ἑαυτοῦ· τὸ δὲ οἰκίδιον τὸ ἐμὸν ὁρᾷς, ὦ Λούκιε, ὡς ἔστι μικρὸν μέν, ἀλλὰ εὔγνωμον τὸν οἰκοῦντα ἐνεγκεῖν· ποιήσεις δὲ αὐτὸ σὺ μεγάλην οἰκίαν ἀνεξικάκως οἰκήσας. καὶ καλεῖ τὴν παιδίσκην, Ὦ Παλαίστρα, δὸς τὸν ἕτερον[1] κοιτῶνα καὶ θὲς[2] λαβοῦσα εἴ τι κομίζει σκεῦος, εἶτα πέμπε αὐτὸν εἰς βαλανεῖον· οὐχὶ μετρίαν γὰρ[3] ἐλήλυθεν ὁδόν. 3. ταῦτα εἰπόντος[4] τὸ παιδισκάριον ἡ Παλαίστρα ἄγει με καὶ δείκνυσί μοι κάλλιστον οἰκημάτιον· καί, Σὺ μέν, ἔφη, ἐπὶ ταύτης τῆς κλίνης κοιμήσῃ, τῷ δὲ παιδί σου σκιμπόδιον αὐτοῦ παραθήσω καὶ προσκεφάλαιον ἐπιθήσω. ταῦτα εἰπούσης ἡμεῖς ἀπῄειμεν λουσόμενοι δόντες αὐτῇ κριθιδίων τιμὴν εἰς τὸν ἵππον· ἡ δὲ πάντα ἔφερεν λαβοῦσα εἴσω καὶ κατέθηκεν. ἡμεῖς δὲ

[1] τὸν ἕτερον scripsi: τὸν ἑταῖρον ΓΝ: τῷ ἑταίρῳ recc., edd..
[2] θὲς codd.: κατάθες Courier.
[3] γὰρ om. ΓΝ.
[4] εἰπόντα Γ.

54

if Hipparchus was at home. " Yes," said she,
" but who are you that ask ? What do you want ? "
" I come with a letter for him from Decrianus, the
professor from Patras."

" Wait for me here," she said and, closing the
door, went in again.

Eventually she came out and invited us in. I
went in, greeted him and gave him the letter. He
was just beginning dinner and was lying on a narrow
couch, while his wife sat nearby, and by their side
was an empty table. After reading the letter he
said, " Indeed Decrianus is my dearest friend and the
best man in all Greece, and I'm glad that he sends
his own friends to my house with such confidence.[1]
But you can see, Lucius, how tiny my cottage is.
Nevertheless it is glad to offer its hospitality, and
you will make it into a mansion if you live in it in a
tolerant spirit." He then called the maid and said,
" Palaestra, give him the spare bedroom, and take
his baggage there, and then show him the way to the
baths, for he's come a long way." 3. When he had
said this, the darling little Palaestra took me and
showed me an excellent little room. " You will lie
on this bed," she said, " and I'll place a pallet over
there for your slave and put a pillow on it." After
she had said this, we gave her money to provide
barley for my horse and went off to have our bath,
while she took everything inside for us. After our

---

[1] Perhaps the miser is being sarcastic.

λουσάμενοι ἀναστρέψαντες εἴσω εὐθὺς παρήλθομεν,
καὶ ὁ Ἵππαρχός με δεξιωσάμενος ἐκέλευεν συνανα-
κλίνεσθαι μετ' αὐτοῦ. τὸ δὲ δεῖπνον οὐ σφόδρα
λιτόν· ὁ δὲ οἶνος ἡδὺς καὶ παλαιὸς ἦν. ἐπεὶ δὲ
ἐδεδειπνήκειμεν, πότος ἦν καὶ λόγος οἷος ἐπὶ
δείπνου ξένου, καὶ οὕτω τὴν ἑσπέραν ἐκείνην πότῳ
δόντες ἐκοιμήθημεν. τῇ δ' ὑστεραίᾳ ὁ Ἵππαρχος
ἤρετό με τίς μὲν ἔσται ἡ νῦν μοι ὁδὸς καὶ εἰ
πάσαις ταῖς ἡμέραις αὐτοῦ προσμενῶ. Ἄπειμι
μέν, ἔφην, εἰς Λάρισσαν, ἔοικα δὲ ἐνθάδε διατρίψειν
τριῶν ἢ πέντε ἡμερῶν.

4. ἀλλὰ τοῦτο μὲν ἦν σκῆψις. ἐπεθύμουν δὲ
σφόδρα μείνας ἐνταῦθα ἐξευρεῖν τινα τῶν μαγεύειν
ἐπισταμένων γυναικῶν καὶ θεάσασθαί τι παράδοξον,
ἢ πετόμενον ἄνθρωπον ἢ λιθούμενον. καὶ τῷ
ἔρωτι τῆς θέας ταύτης δοὺς ἐμαυτὸν περιῄειν τὴν
πόλιν, ἀπορῶν μὲν τῆς ἀρχῆς τοῦ ζητήματος,
ὅμως δὲ περιῄειν· κἀν τούτῳ γυναῖκα ὁρῶ
προσιοῦσαν ἔτι νέαν, εὐπορουμένην, ὅσον ἦν ἐκ τῆς
ὁδοῦ συμβαλεῖν· ἱμάτια γὰρ ἀνθινὰ καὶ παῖδες
συχνοὶ καὶ χρυσίον περιττόν. ὡς δὲ πλησιαίτερον
γίνομαι, προσαγορεύει με ἡ γυνή, καὶ ἀμείβομαι
αὐτῇ ὁμοίως, καὶ φησίν, Ἐγὼ Ἄβροιά εἰμι, εἴ
τινα τῆς σῆς μητρὸς φίλην ἀκούεις, καὶ ὑμᾶς δὲ
τοὺς ἐξ ἐκείνης γενομένους φιλῶ ὥσπερ οὓς ἔτεκον
αὐτή· τί οὖν οὐχὶ παρ' ἐμοὶ καταλύσεις,[1] ὦ τέκνον;

Ἀλλὰ σοὶ μέν, ἔφην, πολλὴ χάρις, αἰδοῦμαι δὲ
οὐδὲν ἀνδρὶ φίλῳ ἐγκαλῶν ἔπειτα φεύγων τὴν
ἐκείνου οἰκίαν· ἀλλὰ τῇ γνώμῃ, φιλτάτη, κατάγομαι
παρὰ σοί.

---

[1] καταλύεις recc.,

bath we returned and went straight into the dining-room where Hipparchus greeted me and invited me to recline beside him. The meal was by no means a frugal one,[1] and the wine was sweet and old. After we had eaten, we drank and talked as men do when a stranger comes to dinner ; and, after thus devoting the evening to drinking, we went to bed. On the next day Hipparchus asked me where I would now be going and if I would be spending all my time with him. " I shall be going on to Larissa," I answered, " but I think I shall stay here for three or four days."

4. But this was a pretence. In fact I wanted very much to stay there and find one of the women accomplished in sorcery [2] and see something strange, be it a man flying or turning into stone. Engrossed in my desire for such a sight, I walked round the city. I didn't know how to start my search, but walked around nevertheless. While doing so, I saw approaching me a woman who was still young and, to judge from seeing her in the street, was well off ; for she was gaily dressed, accompanied by many slaves and wearing too much gold. When I came closer, she greeted me and I answered her in like fashion.[3] She then said, " I am Abroea, if you know any friend of your mother of that name ; and I love you sons of hers like my own sons. Why then won't you stay with me, my child ? "

" I'm most grateful to you," I said, " but I'm ashamed to leave a friend's house when I have no fault to find with him. However, I stay with you in spirit, my charming friend."

---

[1] As might have been expected from a miser.
[2] Thessalian women were famous for their witchcraft.
[3] This phase may be due to unskilful epitomising; cf. notes on cc. 7, 24, 36, etc..

Ποῖ [1] δέ, ἔφη, καὶ κατάγῃ;

Παρὰ Ἱππάρχῳ.

Τῷ φιλαργύρῳ; ἔφη.

Μηδαμῶς, εἶπον, ὦ μῆτερ, τοῦτο εἴπῃς. λαμπρὸς γὰρ καὶ πολυτελὴς γέγονεν εἰς ἐμέ, ὥστε καὶ ἐγκαλέσαι ἄν τις τῇ τρυφῇ.

ἡ δὲ μειδιάσασα καί με τῆς χειρὸς λαβομένη ἄγει ἀπωτέρω καὶ λέγει πρὸς ἐμέ, Φυλάττου μοι, ἔφη, τὴν Ἱππάρχου γυναῖκα πάσῃ μηχανῇ· μάγος γάρ ἐστι δεινὴ καὶ μάχλος καὶ πᾶσι τοῖς νέοις ἐπιβάλλει τὸν ὀφθαλμόν· καὶ εἰ μή τις ὑπακούσει [2] αὐτῇ, τοῦτον τῇ τέχνῃ ἀμύνεται, καὶ πολλοὺς μετεμόρφωσεν εἰς ζῷα, τοὺς δὲ τέλεον ἀπώλεσε· σὺ δὲ καὶ νέος εἶ, τέκνον, καὶ καλός, ὥστε εὐθὺς ἀρέσαι γυναικί, καὶ ξένος, πρᾶγμα εὐκαταφρόνητον.

5. ἐγὼ δὲ πυθόμενος ὅτι τὸ πάλαι μοι ζητούμενον οἴκοι παρ' ἐμοὶ κάθηται, προσεῖχον αὐτῇ οὐδὲν ἔτι. ὡς δέ ποτε ἀφείθην, ἀπῄειν οἴκαδε λαλῶν πρὸς ἐμαυτὸν ἐν τῇ ὁδῷ, Ἄγε δὴ σὺ ὁ φάσκων ἐπιθυμεῖν ταύτης τῆς παραδόξου θέας, ἔγειρέ μοι σεαυτὸν καὶ τέχνην εὕρισκε σοφήν, ᾗ τεύξῃ τούτων ὧν ἐρᾷς, καὶ ἐπὶ τὴν θεράπαιναν τὴν Παλαίστραν ἤδη ἀποδύου—τῆς γὰρ γυναικὸς τοῦ ξένου καὶ φίλου πόρρω ἵστασο—κἀπὶ ταύτης κυλιόμενος καὶ γυμναζόμενος καὶ ταύτῃ συμπλεκόμενος εὖ ἴσθι ὡς ῥᾳδίως γνώσῃ· δοῦλοι γὰρ ἐπίστανται καὶ καλὰ καὶ αἰσχρά.

---

[1] Ποῖ codd.: Ποῦ Fritzsche.
[2] ὑπακούσει codd.: ὑπακούσῃ edd..

---

[1] Cf. Euripides, Syleus, Fr. 693.2.

" Where have you gone to stay ? "

" With Hipparchus."

" The miser ? "

" You mustn't say that, mother ; for he's been a splendidly generous host to me, so much so that he might even be accused of being too lavish."

She smiled, took my hand and led me aside, saying, " I would have you be on your guard against Hipparchus' wife in every way you can. For she's a clever witch and a fast woman who makes eyes at every young man. Any who won't listen to her she punishes with her magic ; she has transformed many into beasts, while others she has done away with altogether. You, my child, are young and handsome enough to please a woman at first sight, and, being a stranger, you are something of no account."

5. When I learned that what I had been looking for was in the house with me, I had no further interest in her. When eventually I got away from her, I made my way to the house, saying to myself as I went, " Come now, you who claim to be eager for these strange sights, bestir yourself,[1] I say, and devise a cunning scheme whereby to gain what you desire. Strip yourself at once to wrestle with the maid, Palaestra,[2] for you must keep your distance from the wife of your host and friend. If you try a roll with her, and test your strength and grapple with her, you can be sure that you'll easily discover what you want to know. For slaves know all that goes on, whether good or bad."

---

[2] The name " Palaestra " is derived from the Greek verb " to wrestle." Perhaps the pun could be retained by calling her " Ju-Jit-Su."

καὶ ταῦτα λέγων πρὸς ἐμαυτὸν εἰσῄειν οἴκαδε.
τὸν μὲν οὖν Ἵππαρχον οὐ κατέλαβον ἐν τῇ οἰκίᾳ
οὐδὲ τὴν ἐκείνου γυναῖκα, ἡ δὲ Παλαίστρα τῇ
ἑστίᾳ παρήδρευεν δεῖπνον ἡμῖν εὐτρεπίζουσα.
6. κἀγὼ εὐθὺς[1] ἔνθεν ἑλών, Ὡς εὐρύθμως, ἔφην,
ὦ καλὴ Παλαίστρα, τὴν πυγὴν τῇ χύτρᾳ ὁμοῦ
συμπεριφέρεις καὶ κλίνεις.[2] ἡ δὲ ὀσφὺς ἡμῖν[3]
ὑγρῶς ἐπικινεῖται. μακάριος ὅστις ἐνταῦθα ἐνε-
βάψατο.

ἡ δὲ—σφόδρα γὰρ ἦν ἰταμὸν καὶ χαρίτων μεστὸν
τὸ κοράσιον—Φεύγοις ἄν, εἶπεν, ὦ νεανίσκε, εἴ γε
νοῦν ἔχοις καὶ ζῆν ἐθέλοις, ὡς πολλοῦ πυρὸς καὶ
κνίσης μεστά· ἦν γὰρ αὐτοῦ μόνον ἅψῃ, τραῦμα
ἔχων πυρίκαυτον αὐτοῦ μοι παρεδρεύοις,[4] θεραπ-
εύσαι[5] δέ σε οὐδεὶς ἀλλ᾽[6] οὐδὲ θεὸς ἰατρός, ἀλλ᾽ ἡ[7]
κατακαύσασά σε μόνη ἐγώ, καὶ τὸ παραδοξότατον,
ἐγὼ μέν σε ποιήσω πλέον ποθεῖν,[8] καὶ τῆς ἀπὸ τῆς
θεραπείας ὀδύνης ἀρδόμενος ἀεὶ ἀνέξῃ[9] καὶ οὐδὲ
λίθοις βαλλόμενος τὴν γλυκεῖαν ὀδύνην φεύξῃ.
τί γελᾷς; ἀκριβῆ βλέπεις ἀνθρωπομάγειρον.[10] οὐ
γὰρ μόνα ταῦτα φαῦλα ἐδώδιμα σκευάζω, ἀλλ᾽
ἤδη τὸ μέγα τοῦτο καὶ καλόν, τὸν ἄνθρωπον, οἶδα
ἔγωγε καὶ σφάττειν καὶ δέρειν καὶ κατακόπτειν,
ἥδιστα δὲ τῶν σπλάγχνων αὐτῶν καὶ τῆς καρδίας
ἅπτομαι.

Τοῦτο μὲν ὀρθῶς, ἔφην, λέγεις· καὶ γὰρ ἐμὲ
πόρρωθεν καὶ μηδὲ ἐγγὺς ὄντα οὐ κατακαύματι μὰ

---

[1] εὐθὺς . . . ἀνακαγχάσασα (fin. cap.) paucis verbis minus
obscoenis suppletis om. N.   [2] κινεῖς Jacobs.   [3] ὑμῖν Jense.
[4] παρεδρεύοις corrector in rec.: παρεδρεύεις codd.: παρεδρεύσεις
edd..   [5] θεραπεύσει Jacobs.

Talking thus to myself, I entered the house. I found neither Hipparchus nor his wife at home, but Palaestra was busy at the fireplace preparing our dinner. 6. I immediately ' did make my start from thence [1] ' and said, " Palaestra, you lovely creature, how rhythmically you turn and tilt your buttocks in time with the saucepan ! And my word, how nimble too is the motion of your waist. Happy the man who dips his piece in such a dish ! "

She, being a most lively and attractive little wench, said, " You'd run away, young fellow, if you had any sense and any desire to go on living, for it's all full of fire and steam here. If you so much as touch it, you'll have a nasty burn, and won't be able to budge from here. No one will be able to cure you, no, not even the Healer God himself, but only I who gave you the burn. What's strangest of all is that I shall make you long for more, and you'll always submit to being treated with my painful cure and, even though you're pelted with stones, you'll never try to escape its sweet pain. Why do you laugh ? You see before you a veritable man-cooker. For its not merely these common foods that I prepare, but now I know about that great and glorious dish, man. I can kill a man, skin him, and cut him up, and I take particular pleasure in getting my hands right on his inside and his heart."

" What you say is quite true," I replied, " for even when I was still a long way off, you didn't just

[1] Cf. Homer, *Odyssey* VIII. 500, etc.

---

[6] ἀλλ' Courier: ἄλλος codd..   [7] ἀλλ' ἡ Jacobs: ἀλλὰ codd..
[8] ποθεῖν Peletier: πονεῖν codd..
[9] ἀνθέξῃ Courier.   [10] ἄνθρωπον μάγειρον Γ.

Δι' ἀλλὰ ὅλῳ ἐμπρησμῷ ἐπέθηκας, καὶ διὰ τῶν
ὀμμάτων τῶν ἐμῶν τὸ σὸν μὴ φαινόμενον πῦρ
κάτω ἐς τὰ σπλάγχνα τἀμὰ ῥίψασα φρύγεις καὶ
ταῦτα οὐδὲν ἀδικοῦντα· ὥστε πρὸς θεῶν ἴασαί με
ταύταις αἷς λέγεις αὐτὴ ταῖς πικραῖς καὶ ἡδείαις
θεραπείαις, καί με ἤδη ἀπεσφαγμένον λαβοῦσα
δεῖρε, ὅπως αὐτὴ θέλεις.

ἡ δὲ μέγα καὶ ἥδιστον ἐκ τούτου ἀνακαγχάσασα
ἐμὴ τὸ λοιπὸν ἦν, καὶ συνέκειτο ἡμῖν ὅπως,
ἐπειδὰν κατακοιμίσῃ τοὺς δεσπότας, ἔλθῃ εἴσω
παρ' ἐμὲ καὶ καθευδήσῃ. 7. κἀπειδὴ ἀφίκετό ποτε
ὁ Ἵππαρχος, λουσάμενοι ἐδειπνοῦμεν καὶ πότος
ἦν συχνὸς ἡμῶν ὁμιλούντων· εἶτα τοῦ ὕπνου
καταψευσάμενος ἀνίσταμαι καὶ ἔργῳ ἀπήειν ἔνθα
ᾤκουν. πάντα δὲ τὰ ἔνδον εὖ παρεσκεύαστο·
τῷ μὲν παιδὶ ἔξω ὑπέστρωτο, τράπεζα δὲ τῇ κλίνῃ
παρειστήκει ποτήριον ἔχουσα· καὶ οἶνος αὐτοῦ
παρέκειτο καὶ ὕδωρ ἕτοιμον καὶ ψυχρὸν καὶ
θερμόν. πᾶσα δὲ ἦν αὕτη τῆς Παλαίστρας παρασκευή. τῶν δὲ στρωμάτων ῥόδα πολλὰ κατε-
πέπαστο, τὰ μὲν οὕτω γυμνὰ καθ' αὑτά, τὰ δὲ
λελυμένα, τὰ δὲ στεφάνοις συμπεπλεγμένα. κἀγὼ
τὸ συμπόσιον εὑρὼν ἕτοιμον ἔμενον τὸν συμπότην.
8. ἡ δὲ ἐπειδὴ κατέκλινε τὴν δέσποιναν, σπουδῇ
παρ' ἐμὲ ἧκε, καὶ ἦν εὐφροσύνη τὸν οἶνον ἡμῶν
καὶ τὰ φιλήματα προπινόντων ἀλλήλοις. ὡς δέ τῷ
ποτῷ παρεσκευάσαμεν ἑαυτοὺς εὖ πρὸς τὴν
νύκτα, λέγει πρός με ἡ Παλαίστρα· Τοῦτο μὲν
πάντως δεῖ σε μνημονεύειν, ὦ νεανίσκε, ὅτι εἰς
Παλαίστραν ἐμπέπτωκας, καὶ [1] χρή σε νῦν ἐπιδεῖξαι

[1] Pro καὶ χρή . . . κοίμισον (p. 68) pauca minus obscoena
supplet N.

singe me but plunged me into a general conflagration ; you've been sending your invisible fire down through my eyes into my inward parts and roasting me, even though I've done nothing wrong. Therefore, in heaven's name, heal me yourself, with that bittersweet treatment of which you've been talking and, now that I'm already slaughtered, take me and skin me in any way you yourself please."

At this she gave a loud and delightful laugh, and thereafter she was mine. We agreed that, once she had seen her master and mistress to bed, she was to come to my room and spend the night there. 7. When Hipparchus eventually arrived, we washed [1] and had dinner, drinking a great deal as we talked. Then I pretended I was sleepy, got up and did in fact go off to my room. Everything inside the room had been beautifully prepared. Bedding had been made up for my servant outside, while beside my bed was a table with a cup. There was wine there, and hot and cold water had been left ready ; this was all the work of Palaestra. Over the bedclothes roses had been strewn in profusion, some of them in their natural state, some plucked apart, and others plaited into garlands. Finding the room prepared for the celebrations, I awaited my companion. 8. Once she had seen her mistress to bed, she hurried to my room, and we made merry as we offered each other toasts and kisses. When we had fortified ourselves with wine for the night ahead, Palaestra said to me, " Young fellow, you must remember that it's Palaestra [2] with whom you've come to grips, and

---

[1] There may be a trace of unskilful epitomising here; in Apuleius 2.11 Lucius spent the afternoon in taking a bath.
[2] See note on p. 59.

εἰ γέγονας ἐν τοῖς ἐφήβοις γοργὸς καὶ παλαίσματα πολλὰ ἔμαθές ποτε.

Ἀλλ' οὐκ ἂν ἴδοις φεύγοντά με τὸν ἔλεγχον τοῦτον· ὥστε ἀπόδυσαι, καὶ ἤδη παλαίωμεν.

ἡ δέ, Οὕτως, ἔφη, ὡς ἐγὼ θέλω, παράσχου μοι τὴν ἐπίδειξιν· ἐγὼ μὲν νόμῳ διδασκάλου καὶ ἐπιστάτου τὰ ὀνόματα τῶν παλαισμάτων ὧν ἐθέλω εὑροῦσα ἐρῶ, σὺ δὲ ἕτοιμος γίνου ἐς τὸ ὑπακούειν καὶ ποιεῖν πᾶν τὸ κελευόμενον.

Ἀλλ' ἐπίτατε, ἔφην, καὶ σκόπει ὅπως εὐχερῶς καὶ ὑγρῶς τὰ παλαίσματα καὶ εὐτόνως ἔσται.

9. ἡ δὲ ἀποδυσαμένη τὴν ἐσθῆτα καὶ στᾶσα ὅλη γυμνὴ ἔνθεν ἤρξατο ἐπιτάττειν, Ὦ μειράκιον, ἔκδυσαι καὶ ἀλειψάμενος ἔνθεν ἐκ τοῦ μύρου συμπλέκου τῷ ἀνταγωνιστῇ· δύο μηρῶν σπάσας κλῖνον ὑπτίαν, ἔπειτα ἀνώτερος ὑποβάλλων[1] διὰ μηρῶν καὶ διαστείλας αἰώρει καὶ τεῖνε ἄνω τὰ σκέλη, καὶ χαλάσας καὶ στήσας κολλῶ αὐτῷ καὶ παρεισελθὼν βάλε καὶ πρώσας[2] νύσσε ἤδη πανταχοῦ ἕως πονέσῃ, καὶ ἡ ὀσφῦς ἰσχυέτω, εἶτα ἐξελκύσας κατὰ πλάτος[3] διὰ βουβῶνος δῆξον, καὶ πάλιν συνώθει εἰς τὸν τοῖχον, εἶτα τύπτε· ἐπειδὰν δὲ χάλασμα ἴδῃς, τότ' ἤδη ἐπιβὰς ἄμμα κατ' ἰξύος δήσας σύνεχε, καὶ πειρῶ μὴ σπεύδειν, ἀλλ' ὀλίγον διακαρτερήσας σύντρεχε. ἤδη ἀπολέλυσαι.

---

[1] ὑποβαλὼν Ψ.
[2] τρώσας recc..
[3] πλάτος recc.: πλάτους Γ.

you must now show whether you've become a lad of mettle and have learnt many a wrestling hold."

" Indeed you won't see me shirking this trial of strength. Strip then, and let's start our wrestling now."

" You must follow my wishes as you demonstrate your prowess. I shall be like a trainer and supervisor, thinking up and calling out the names of the holds I wish, and you must be ready to obey and carry out all your orders."

" Well give your orders," said I, " and see how readily, how nimbly and how vigorously I shall display my holds."

9. She stripped off her clothing and, standing completely naked, began her instructions there and then. " Strip off, my lad ; rub on some of that ointment from over there, and grapple with your adversary. Grab me by both thighs and put me on my back. Next get on top of me, slip in through my thighs and open me up, keeping your legs poised above me and stretched out. Then drop them into position, keeping glued to your target. Go right into the assault, and push forward everywhere now with a sharp attack till your opponent is worn out,[1] and let your weapon show its strength. Then withdraw, attack on a broad front and stab your foe through the groin. Push forward again to the wall and then strike. When you notice that the resistance is weakening, that's the very time to lock yourself in close combat and grip your opponent by the waist. Try not to hurry, but be patient for a little and match your pace to mine. Now you can fall out from class."

[1] Or perhaps, taking the verb as middle, " till you are worn out."

PSEUDO-LUCIAN

10. κἀγὼ ἐπειδὴ ῥᾳδίως πάντα ὑπήκουσα καὶ εἰς τέλος ἡμῖν ἔληξε τὰ παλαίσματα, λέγω[1] πρὸς τὴν Παλαίστραν ἅμα ἐπιγελάσας, ᾿Ω διδάσκαλε, ὁρᾷς μὲν ὅπως εὐχερῶς καὶ εὐηκόως πεπάλαισταί μοι, σκόπει δέ, μὴ οὐκ ἐν κόσμῳ τὰ παλαίσματα ὑποβάλλεις·[2] ἀλλὰ γὰρ ἐξ ἄλλων ἐπιτάττεις.

ἡ δὲ ἐπὶ κόρρης πλήξασά με, Ὡς φλύαρον, ἔφη, παρέλαβον τὸν μαθητήν. σκόπει οὖν μὴ πληγὰς ἔτι πλείους[3] λάβῃς ἄλλα καὶ οὐ τὰ ἐπιταττόμενα παλαίων.

καὶ ταῦτα εἰποῦσα ἐπανίσταται καὶ θεραπεύσασα ἑαυτήν, Νῦν, ἔφη, δείξεις εἴπερ νέος εἶ καὶ εὔτονος παλαιστὴς καὶ εἰ ἐπίστασαι παλαίειν καὶ ποιεῖν τὰ ἀπὸ γονατίου.

καὶ πεσοῦσα ἐπὶ τοῦ λέχους ἐς γόνυ, Ἄγε δὴ σὺ ὁ παλαιστής, ἔχεις τὰ μέσα, ὥστε τινάξας ὀξεῖαν ἐπίπρωσον καὶ βάθυνον. ψιλὸν ὁρᾷς αὐτοῦ παρακείμενον, τούτῳ χρῆσαι· πρῶτον δὲ κατὰ λόγον, ὡς ἅμμα[4] σφίγγε, εἶτα ἀνακλάσας ἔμβαλε[5] καὶ σύνεχε καὶ μὴ δίδου διάστημα. ἐὰν δὲ χαλᾶται, θᾶττον ἐπάρας ἀνώτερον μετάθες καὶ κρούσας κύψον[6] καὶ σκόπει ὅπως μὴ ἀνασπάσῃς θᾶττον ἢ κελευσθῇς, ἀλλὰ δὴ κυρτώσας πολὺ αὐτὸν ὕφελε,[7] καὶ ὑποβαλὼν κάτω αὖθις τὴν παρεμβολὴν σύνεχε καὶ κινοῦ, εἶτα ἄφες αὐτόν· πέπτωκε[8] γὰρ καὶ λέλυται καὶ ὕδωρ ὅλος ἔστι σοι ὁ ἀνταγωνιστής.

---

[1] λέγω rec.: καὶ λέγω cett.   [2] ὑποβάλλῃς recc., edd..
[3] πλείους Jacobitz: πλείω codd..
[4] ὡς ἅμμα recc.: ὁ σαμμα Γ: ὅσα μίμα recc.: ὅσα νόμιμα Ψ: εἰς ἅμμα Courier.   [5] ἔμβαλλε recc..   [6] κύψον Guyet: κρύψον codd..
[7] ὕφελκε Courier.   [8] πέπωκε Γ.

10. When I for my part had obeyed every order with ease and our wrestling had come to an end, I said to Palaestra with a laugh, " You can see, teacher, how readily and obediently I have done my wrestling, but take care that you aren't getting out of order in suggesting holds. For you ask for one after another."

But she slapped my face and said, " What a chatterbox I have for my pupil ! Take care that you don't get some more slaps for using different holds from the ones I ask for."

So saying, she rose from the bed, and, after freshening up, said " Now you will show whether you're a youthful and vigorous wrestler, and can wrestle and go into action on your knees."

Then she dropped on to one knee on the bed and said " Come now, Sir Wrestler, here you have the centre of operations. Brandish your weapon, push forward for a sharp thrust and plunge it in deep. You see it lying unfolded there ; make the most of it. First, of course, you must go into a clinch with me, and then you must bend me back, attacking and gripping me tight, allowing no gap between us. If you start slacking off, you must be faster in mounting each offensive and must move to a higher point of vantage. You must put your head down and strike, and see that you don't retire quicker than you're told to ; you must arch your battleline into a wide curve, before making a gradual withdrawal. Then you must push down again in a controlled infiltration and keep on the move. Only then may you withdraw your spearhead from the field. For it's now limp and lifeless, and your opponent is drenched."

ἐγὼ δὲ ἤδη μέγα ἀναγελῶν, Ἐθέλω, ἔφην,
καὶ αὐτός, ὦ διδάσκαλε, παλαίσματα ὀλίγ' ἄττα
ἐπιτάξαι, σὺ δὲ ὑπάκουσον ἐπαναστᾶσα [1] καὶ
κάθισον, εἶτα δοῦσα κατὰ χειρὸς πάραψαι τὸ
λοιπὸν καὶ [2] καταμάττου, καί με πρὸς τοῦ Ἡρακλέους περιλαβοῦσα ἤδη κοίμισον.

11. Ἐν τοιαύταις ἡδοναῖς καὶ παιδιαῖς παλαισμάτων ἀγωνιζόμενοι νυκτερινοὺς ἀγῶνας ἐστεφα-
νούμεθα, καὶ ἦν πολλὴ μὲν ἐν τούτῳ τρυφή·
ὥστε τῆς εἰς τὴν Λάρισσαν ὁδοῦ παντάπασιν
ἐπιλελήσμην. καί ποτε ἐπὶ νοῦν μοι ἦλθε τὸ [3]
μαθεῖν ὧν ἕνεκα ἤθλουν, καὶ φημὶ πρὸς αὐτήν,
Ὦ φιλτάτη, δεῖξόν μοι μαγγανεύουσαν ἢ μεταμορφουμένην τὴν δέσποιναν· πάλαι γὰρ τῆς
παραδόξου ταύτης θέας ἐπιθυμῶ. μᾶλλον <δ'> [4]
εἴ τι σὺ οἶδας, αὐτὴ μαγγάνευσον, ὥστε φανῆναί μοι
ἄλλην ἐξ ἄλλης ὄψιν. οἶμαι δὲ καὶ σὲ οὐκ ἀπείρως
τῆσδε τῆς τέχνης ἔχειν· τοῦτο δὲ οὐ παρ' ἑτέρου
μαθών, ἀλλὰ παρὰ τῆς ἐμαυτοῦ ψυχῆς λαβὼν
οἶδα, ἐπεί με τὸν πάλαι ἀδαμάντινον, ὡς ἔλεγον αἱ
γυναῖκες, ἐς μηδεμίαν γυναῖκα τὰ ὄμματα ταῦτα
ἐρωτικῶς ποτε ἐκτείναντα συλλαβοῦσα τῇ τέχνῃ
ταύτῃ αἰχμάλωτον ἔχεις ἐρωτικῷ πολέμῳ ψυχαγω-
γοῦσα.

ἡ δὲ Παλαίστρα, Παῦσαι, φησί, προσπαίζων.
τίς γὰρ ᾠδὴ δύναται μαγεῦσαι τὸν ἔρωτα, ὄντα
τῆς τέχνης κύριον; ἐγὼ δέ, ὦ φίλτατε, τούτων
μὲν οἶδα οὐδὲν μὰ τὴν κεφαλὴν τὴν σὴν καὶ
τήνδε τὴν μακαρίαν εὐνήν· οὐδὲ γὰρ γράμματα
ἔμαθον, καὶ ἡ δέσποινα βάσκανος οὖσα τυγχάνει

I was now laughing heartily and said, " I wish to prescribe a few holds of my own, teacher, and *you* must get up and obey *me*. Now sit down. Next give me water to wash my hands, apply the rest of the ointment and wipe yourself clean. And now, by Heracles, hold me tight and lull me to sleep."

11. Such were our pleasant, frolicsome wrestling-bouts as we competed in nightly combat and covered ourselves with laurels. We found great enjoyment in this, so that I had completely forgotten about my journey to Larissa. Then at last I thought of gaining the information which had been the purpose of my athletic feats, and said to her, " Dearest, show me your mistress practising magic or changing her shape. For I've long had a craving for this strange sight. Or better still, if you can, work your own magic, so that you appear to me in one shape after another, for I imagine that you too are skilled in this art. This is no second-hand information but what I have learnt from my own soul, seeing that I who have long been called the adamant one by the women and have never cast these eyes of mine amorously on any woman, have been caught by you, and by your art you hold me prisoner, for you enchant my soul by the warfare of love."

But Palaestra said, " Stop joking. What magic incantations can conjure Love forth ? He is the master of the art. I, my darling, know nothing about these things, I swear it by your own dear self and by this bed that's brought such joy. For I cannot even read, and my mistress is very jealous

---

1 ἐπανάστα Γ.   2 καὶ om Γ.
3 τὸ recc.: ἐς τὸ Γ.   4 δ' supplet Courier.

εἰς τὴν αὑτῆς τέχνην· εἰ δέ μοι καιρὸς ἐπιτρέψει [1]
πειράσομαι παρασχεῖν σοι τὸ ἰδεῖν μεταμορφουμένην
τὴν κεκτημένην.

καὶ τότε μὲν ἐπὶ τούτοις ἐκοιμήθημεν. 12. ἡμέραις δὲ ὕστερον οὐ πολλαῖς ἀγγέλλει πρός με ἡ
Παλαίστρα ὡς ἡ δέσποινα αὐτῆς μέλλοι ὄρνις
γενομένη πέτεσθαι [2] πρὸς τὸν ἐρώμενον.

κἀγώ, Νῦν, ἔφην, ὁ καιρός, ὦ Παλαίστρα, τῆς
εἰς ἐμὲ χάριτος, ᾗ [3] νῦν ἔχεις τὸν σαυτῆς ἱκέτην
ἀναπαῦσαι πολυχρονίου ἐπιθυμίας.

Θάρρει, ἔφη.

κἀπειδὴ ἑσπέρα ἦν, ἄγει με λαβοῦσα πρὸς τὴν
θύραν τοῦ δωματίου, ἔνθα ἐκεῖνοι ἐκάθευδον, καὶ
κελεύει με προσάγειν ὀπῇ τινι τῆς θύρας λεπτῇ καὶ
σκοπεῖν τὰ γινόμενα ἔνδον. ὁρῶ οὖν τὴν μὲν γυναῖκα
ἀποδυομένην. εἶτα γυμνὴ τῷ λύχνῳ προσελθοῦσα
καὶ χόνδρους δύο λαβοῦσα τὸν μὲν λιβανωτὸν τῷ
πυρὶ τοῦ λύχνου ἐπέθηκε καὶ στᾶσα πολλὰ τοῦ
λύχνου κατελάλησεν· εἶτα κιβώτιον ἁδρὸν ἀνοίξασα,
πάνυ πολλὰς ἔχον πυξίδας ἐν αὐτῷ, ἔνθεν ἀναιρεῖται
καὶ προφέρει μίαν· ἡ δὲ εἶχεν ἐμβεβλημένον ὅ
τι μὲν οὐκ οἶδα, τῆς δὲ ὄψεως αὐτῆς ἕνεκα ἔλαιον
αὐτὸ ἐδόκουν εἶναι. ἐκ τούτου λαβοῦσα χρίεται
ὅλη, ἀπὸ τῶν ὀνύχων ἀρξαμένη τῶν κάτω, καὶ
ἄφνω πτερὰ ἐκφύεται αὐτῇ, καὶ ἡ ῥὶν κερατίνη καὶ
γρυπὴ ἐγένετο, καὶ τἆλλα δὲ ὅσα ὀρνίθων κτήματα
καὶ σύμβολα πάντα εἶχε· καὶ ἦν ἄλλο οὐδὲν ἢ
κόραξ νυκτερινός. ἐπεὶ δὲ εἶδεν ἑαυτὴν ἐπτερωμένην,
κρώξασα δεινὸν καὶ οἷον ἐκεῖνοι [4] οἱ κόρακες,

---

[1] ἐπιτρέψει rec.: ἐπιτρέψοι ΓΝ edd..

70

about her own art. But if the occasion permits, I
shall try to let you see my mistress changing her
shape."

Then, this being agreed, we went to sleep. 12. A
few days later Palaestra reported to me that her
mistress was going to turn into a bird and fly to her
beloved.

" Now's your chance, Palaestra," said I, " to do
me the favour by which you can, and I pray you will,
bring me relief from a craving that has persisted so
long."

" Don't worry," she said.

When it was evening, she took me and led me to
the door of the bedroom of her master and mistress,
bidding me put my eye to a tiny crack in the door
and see what was going on inside. I saw the lady of
the house undressing. Then she went up to the
lamp naked, took two grains of frankincense which
she put upon the flame of the lamp, and standing
there uttered a screed of words over the lamp. Then
she opened a large box containing a great number of
caskets, one of which she picked up and took out.
What it had in it I don't know, though from its
appearance I thought it was olive oil. She took
some of this and, starting with her toenails, anointed
herself all over. Suddenly she started sprouting
feathers, and her nose became horny and hooked ;
she had all the attributes and marks of a bird, and
was for all the world a night-raven.[1] When she
saw that she had grown feathers, she uttered a terrible

---

[1] I.e. a long-eared owl, the bird called νυκτικόραξ by
Aristotle.

[2] πέτασθαι Γ.   [3] ἦ N : ᾆ cett..
[4] ἐκεῖνοι man. rec. in Ψ : ἐκεῖνο codd..

71

ναστᾶσα ᾤχετο πετομένη διὰ τῆς θυρίδος.
13. ἐγὼ δὲ ὄναρ ἐκεῖνο οἰόμενος ὁρᾶν τοῖς δακτύλοις
τῶν ἑαυτοῦ βλεφάρων ἡπτόμην, οὐ πιστεύων τοῖς
ἐμαυτοῦ ὀφθαλμοῖς οὔθ' ὅτι βλέπουσιν οὔθ' ὅτι
ἐγρηγόρασιν. ὡς δὲ μόλις καὶ βραδέως ἐπείσθην
ὅτι μὴ καθεύδω, ἐδεόμην τότε τῆς Παλαίστρας
πτερῶσαι κἀμὲ καὶ χρίσασαν ἐξ ἐκείνου τοῦ
φαρμάκου ἐᾶσαι πέτεσθαί με· ἠβουλόμην γὰρ
πείρᾳ μαθεῖν εἰ μεταμορφωθεὶς ἐκ τοῦ ἀνθρώπου
καὶ τὴν ψυχὴν [1] ὄρνις ἔσομαι. ἡ δὲ τὸ δωμάτιον
ὑπανοίξασα [2] κομίζει τὴν πυξίδα. ἐγὼ δὲ σπεύδων
ἤδη ἀποδύσας χρίω ὅλον ἐμαυτόν, καὶ ὄρνις μὲν οὐ
γίνομαι ὁ δυστυχής, ἀλλά μοι οὐρὰ ὄπισθεν ἐξῆλθεν,
καὶ οἱ δάκτυλοι πάντες ᾤχοντο οὐκ οἶδ' ὅποι·[3]
ὄνυχας δὲ τοὺς πάντας τέσσαρας εἶχον, καὶ
τούτους οὐδὲν ἄλλο ἢ ὁπλάς, καί μοι αἱ χεῖρες καὶ
οἱ πόδες κτήνους πόδες ἐγένοντο, καὶ τὰ [4] ὦτα δὲ
μακρὰ καὶ τὸ πρόσωπον μέγα. ἐπεὶ δὲ κύκλῳ
περιεσκόπουν, αὑτὸν ἑώρων ὄνον, φωνὴν δὲ ἀνθρώπου
ἐς τὸ μέμψασθαι τὴν Παλαίστραν οὐκέτι εἶχον. τὸ
δὲ χεῖλος ἐκτείνας κάτω καὶ αὐτῷ δὴ τῷ σχήματι
ὡς ὄνος ὑποβλέπων ᾐτιώμην αὐτήν, ὅση δύναμις,
ὄνος ἀντὶ ὄρνιθος γενόμενος. 14. ἡ δὲ ἀμφοτέραις
ταῖς χερσὶν τυψαμένη τὸ πρόσωπον, Τάλαινα,
εἶπεν, ἐγώ, μέγα εἴργασμαι κακόν· σπεύσασα γὰρ
ἥμαρτον ἐν τῇ ὁμοιότητι τῶν πυξίδων καὶ ἄλλην
ἔλαβον οὐχὶ τὴν τὰ πτερὰ φύουσαν.[5] ἀλλὰ θάρρει
μοι, φίλτατε· ῥᾴων [6] γὰρ ἡ τούτου θεραπεία·

[1] τύχην Γ.
[2] ἐπανοίξασα Γ.

72

croak just as those birds do, rose up and flew away through the window. 13. I thought I was dreaming and felt my eyelids with my fingers, for I did not believe that my own eyes were seeing this or were awake. When eventually I had barely convinced myself that I was awake, I then asked Palaestra to give me feathers too, and to smear me with that concoction and allow me to fly ; for I wished to learn by experience whether, when my body was transformed from human shape, my soul would also become that of a bird. She stealthily opened the door of the room and brought me the casket. I now hastily stripped and smeared myself all over ; but alas I did not become a bird. Instead a tail sprang out from my behind, and all my fingers and toes vanished I know not where. I kept four nails in all and these were unmistakably hooves, while my hands and feet had become the feet of a beast, my ears had grown long and my face become enormous. When I looked myself over, I could see that I was an ass, but I no longer had a human voice with which to abuse Palaestra. But I did drop my lip and, confronting her with my appearance, looked up angrily at her as an ass does, trying as best I could to reproach her for my having become an ass instead of a bird. 14. She beat her face with both hands and said : " Unlucky one that I am, I have wrought great harm, for in my haste, misled by the similarity of the caskets, I took the wrong one, and not the one which produces feathers. But please do cheer up, my darling ; the

---

³ ὅποι Courier: ὅπου codd..
⁵ φύουσαν recc.: χρίουσαν ΓΝ.
⁴ τὰ recc.: om. ΓΝ.
⁶ ῥάστη recc., edd..

ῥόδα γὰρ μόνα εἰ φάγοις, ἀποδύσῃ μὲν αὐτίκα τὸ
κτῆνος, τὸν δὲ ἐραστήν μοι τὸν ἐμὸν αὖθις ἀποδώ-
σεις. ἀλλά μοι, φίλτατε, τὴν μίαν νύκτα ταύτην
ὑπόμεινον ἐν τῷ ὄνῳ, ὄρθρου δὲ δραμοῦσα οἴσω σοι
ῥόδα καὶ φαγὼν ἰαθήσῃ. ταῦτα εἶπεν καταψήσασα [1]
μου τὰ ὦτα καὶ τὸ λοιπὸν δέρμα.

15. ἐγὼ δὲ τὰ μὲν ἄλλα ὄνος ἤμην, τὰς δὲ φρένας
καὶ τὸν νοῦν ἄνθρωπος ἐκεῖνος ὁ Λούκιος, δίχα
τῆς φωνῆς. πολλὰ οὖν κατ' ἐμαυτὸν μεμψάμενος
τὴν Παλαίστραν ἐπὶ τῇ ἁμαρτίᾳ δακὼν τὸ χεῖλος
ἀπήειν ἔνθα ἠπιστάμην ἑστῶτα τὸν ἐμαυτοῦ ἵππον
καὶ ἄλλον ἀληθινὸν ὄνον τὸν Ἱππάρχου. οἱ δὲ
αἰσθόμενοί με εἴσω παριόντα, δείσαντες μὴ τοῦ
χόρτου κοινωνὸς αὐτοῖς ἐπεισέρχομαι, τὰ ὦτα
κατακλίναντες ἕτοιμοι ἦσαν τοῖς ποσὶν ἀμύνειν
τῇ γαστρί· κἀγὼ συνεὶς πορρωτέρω ποι τῆς φάτνης
ἀποχωρήσας ἑστὼς ἐγέλων, ὁ δέ μοι γέλως ὀγκηθ-
μὸς ἦν. ταῦτα δ' ἄρ' [2] ἐνενόουν πρὸς ἐμαυτόν·
Ὦ τῆς ἀκαίρου ταύτης περιεργίας. τί δέ, εἰ λύκος
παρεισέλθοι ἢ ἄλλο τι θηρίον; κινδυνεύεταί μοι
μηδὲν κακὸν πεποιηκότι. [3] ταῦτα ἐννοῶν ἠγνόουν
ὁ δυστυχὴς τὸ μέλλον κακόν.

16. ἐπεὶ γὰρ ἦν ἤδη νὺξ βαθεῖα καὶ σιωπὴ πολλὴ
καὶ ὕπνος ὁ γλυκύς, ψοφεῖ μὲν ἔξωθεν ὁ τοῖχος
ὡς διορυττόμενος, καὶ διωρύττετό γε, καὶ ὀπὴ
ἤδη ἐγεγόνει ἄνθρωπον δέξασθαι δυναμένη, καὶ
εὐθὺς ἄνθρωπος ταύτῃ παρῄει καὶ ἄλλος ὁμοίως,
καὶ πολλοὶ ἔνδον ἦσαν καὶ πάντες εἶχον ξίφη.
εἶτα καταδήσαντες ἔνδον ἐν τοῖς δωματίοις τὸν

[1] καταψηλαφήσασα recc., edd..   [2] δ' ἄρ' Jacobitz: γὰρ codd..
[3] πεποιηκότι διαφθαρῆναι recc., edd..

cure for this is quite simple. For all you have to do is eat roses and you'll immediately discard your bestial shape, and restore my own lover to me once more. But I beg you, dearest one, remain the ass for this single night, and at dawn I shall make all speed to bring you roses, which you will eat and be cured," and she stroked my ears and my skin as she spoke.

15. But though I was an ass in every other respect, in mind and intellect I remained a human, and was still the same Lucius except for my voice. And so I cursed Palaestra bitterly to myself for her mistake, and went away biting my lip to where I knew my own horse was standing along with a real ass belonging to Hipparchus. When they saw me coming in, they were afraid I was coming to share their fodder, and dropped their ears and were prepared to defend their bellies with their feet. When I understood what was happening I retired to some distance from the manger and stood laughing, though my laughter took the form of braying. " Oh, what untimely curiosity ! " I thought to myself. " What would happen if a wolf or any other wild beast were to get in ? I'm in danger, though I've done nothing wrong." Such were my thoughts, for I didn't know, poor creature, the evils in store for me.

16. When it was now dead of night and silence and sweet sleep reigned, a noise started on the outside of the wall as if of someone breaking in. This was indeed so, and presently there was a hole big enough to take a man. Immediately one man came through, and others followed in the same way, till many were inside, all of them armed with swords. Then they

Ἵππαρχον καὶ τὴν Παλαίστραν καὶ τὸν ἐμὸν
οἰκέτην ἀδεῶς ἤδη τὴν οἰκίαν ἐκένουν τά τε χρήματα
καὶ τὰ ἱμάτια καὶ τὰ σκεύη κομίζοντες ἔξω. ὡς
δὲ οὐδὲν ἄλλο ἔνδον κατελείπετο, λαβόντες[1] καὶ τὸν
ἄλλον ὄνον καὶ τὸν ἵππον ἐπέσαξαν, ἔπειτα ὅσα
ἐβάστασαν, ἐπικατέδησαν ἡμῖν. καὶ οὕτως μέγα
ἄχθος φέροντας ἡμᾶς ξύλοις παίοντες ἤλαυνον· ὡς
εἰς[2] τὸ ὄρος ἀτρίπτῳ ὁδῷ φεύγειν πειρώμενοι.
τὰ μὲν οὖν ἄλλα κτήνη οὐκ ἔχω εἰπεῖν ὅ τι ἔπασχεν,
ἐγὼ δὲ ἀνυπόδητος ἀσυνήθης ἀπιὼν πέτραις ὀξείαις
ἐπιβαίνων, τοσαῦτα σκεύη φέρων ἀπωλλύμην.
καὶ πολλάκις προσέπταιον, καὶ οὐκ ἦν ἐξὸν καταπεσεῖν, καὶ εὐθὺς ἄλλος ὄπισθεν κατὰ τῶν μηρῶν
ἔπαιεν ξύλῳ. ἐπεὶ δὲ πολλάκις Ὦ Καῖσαρ ἀναβοῆσαι ἐπεθύμουν, οὐδὲν ἄλλο ἢ ὠγκώμην, καὶ τὸ μὲν
ὦ μέγιστον καὶ εὐφωνότατον ἐβόων, τὸ δὲ Καῖσαρ
οὐκ ἐπηκολούθει. ἀλλὰ μὴν καὶ δι᾽ αὐτὸ τοῦτο
ἐτυπτόμην ὡς προδιδοὺς αὐτοὺς τῷ ὀγκηθμῷ.
μαθὼν οὖν ὅτι ἄλλως ἐβόων, ἔγνων σιγῇ προϊέναι
καὶ κερδαίνειν τὸ μὴ παίεσθαι.

17. ἐπὶ τούτῳ ἡμέρα τε ἤδη ἦν, καὶ ἡμεῖς ὄρη
πολλὰ ἀναβεβήκειμεν, καὶ στόματα δὲ ἡμῶν
δεσμῷ ἐπείχετο, ὡς μὴ περιβοσκόμενοι τὴν ὁδὸν
ἐς τὸ ἄριστον ἀναλίσκοιμεν· ὥστε ἐς τὴν τότε καὶ
ἔμεινα ὄνος. ἐπεὶ δὲ ἦν αὐτὸ τὸ[3] μέσον τῆς ἡμέρας, καταλύομεν εἴς τινα ἔπαυλιν συνήθων ἐκείνοις
ἀνθρώπων, ὅσον ἦν ἐκ τῶν γινομένων σκοπεῖν·
καὶ γὰρ φιλήμασιν ἠσπάζοντο ἀλλήλους καὶ
καταλύειν ἐκέλευον αὐτοὺς οἱ[4] ἐν τῇ ἐπαύλει

---

[1] λαβόντες ΓΝ: λαβόντες ἐμέ τε recc., edd..
[2] ὡς εἰς ΓΝ: εἰς recc., edd..   [3] τὸ recc.: om. ΓΝ.   [4] οἱ om. Γ.

went inside, bound Hipparchus, Palaestra and my
servant in their rooms, and proceeded nonchalantly
to empty the house, carrying out all the money,
clothes and furnishings. When nothing else was
left inside, taking the other ass and the horse, they
saddled us and fastened on our backs everything
they had brought out. We carried these heavy
loads and they beat us with sticks, driving us on in
their efforts to escape up the mountain by an unused
track. How the other two animals felt I can't say,
but for myself I was at death's door, for I was
unshod and unaccustomed to such travelling and to
walking over jagged stones with all that baggage to
carry. I often stumbled, but wasn't allowed to
drop down, as someone would immediately strike
my rump with a stick. I often wanted to shout
" Oh Lord ! " ; but only mustered a bray, and,
though I could shout the " Oh " loud and clear, the
" Lord " wouldn't follow. But I was beaten for
this too, as I was giving them away by my braying.
So I realised that my cries were useless and learned to
proceed in silence and earn myself immunity from
blows.

17. It was already day by now and we had climbed
up many mountains. Our mouths were kept
muzzled so that we couldn't graze and waste travelling time on breakfast. Thus for that day, too, I
remained an ass. It was actually midday before we
stopped at a farmhouse which, to judge from what
was going on, belonged to friends of theirs. For they
greeted each other with embraces and the occupants
of the farm invited them to break their journey,

καὶ παρέθηκαν ἄριστον καὶ τοῖς κτήνεσιν ἡμῖν
παρέβαλον κριθίδια.[1] καὶ οἱ μὲν ἠρίστων, ἐγὼ
δὲ ἐπείνων μὲν κακῶς· ἀλλ' ἐπειδὴ οὐπώποτε
κριθὰς ὠμὰς ἠριστήκειν, ἐσκοπούμην ὅ τι καὶ
καταφάγοιμι. ὁρῶ δὲ κῆπον αὐτοῦ ὀπίσω τῆς
αὐλῆς, καὶ εἶχε λάχανα πολλὰ καὶ καλὰ καὶ ῥόδα
ὑπὲρ αὐτῶν [2] ἐφαίνετο· κἀγὼ λαθὼν πάντας τοὺς
ἔνδον ἀσχολουμένους περὶ τὸ ἄριστον ἔρχομαι ἐπὶ
τὸν κῆπον, τοῦτο μὲν ὠμῶν λαχάνων ἐμπλησθησό-
μενος, τοῦτο δὲ τῶν ῥόδων ἕνεκα· ἐλογιζόμην γὰρ
ὅτι δῆθεν φαγὼν τῶν ἀνθῶν πάλιν ἄνθρωπος
ἔσομαι. εἶτα ἐμβὰς εἰς τὸν κῆπον θριδάκων μὲν
καὶ ῥαφανίδων καὶ σελίνων, ὅσα ὠμὰ ἐσθίει
ἄνθρωπος, ἐνεπλήσθην, τὰ δὲ ῥόδα ἐκεῖνα οὐκ ἦν
ῥόδα ἀληθινά, τὰ δ' ἦν ἐκ τῆς ἀγρίας δάφνης
φυόμενα· ῥοδοδάφνην [3] αὐτὰ καλοῦσιν ἄνθρωποι,
κακὸν ἄριστον ὄνῳ τοῦτο παντὶ καὶ ἵππῳ· φασὶ
γὰρ τὸν φαγόντα ἀποθνήσκειν αὐτίκα. 18. ἐν
τούτῳ ὁ κηπουρὸς αἰσθόμενος καὶ ξύλον ἁρπάσας,
εἰσελθὼν εἰς τὸν κῆπον καὶ τὸν πολέμιον ἰδὼν καὶ
τῶν λαχάνων τὸν ὄλεθρον, ὥσπερ τις δυνάστης
μισοπόνηρος κλέπτην λαβών, οὕτω με συνέκοψε τῷ[4]
ξύλῳ, μήτε πλευρῶν φεισάμενος μήτε μηρῶν,
καὶ μὴν καὶ τὰ ὦτά μου κατέκλασεν καὶ τὸ πρόσωπον
συνέτριψεν. ἐγὼ δὲ οὐκέτ' ἀνεχόμενος ἀπολακτίσας
ἀμφοτέροις καὶ καταβαλὼν ὕπτιον ἐπὶ τῶν λαχάνων
ἔφευγον ἄνω ἐς τὸ ὄρος. ὁ δὲ ἐπειδὴ εἶδε δρόμῳ

---

[1] κριθία recc., edd..   [2] αὐτῶν recc.: αὐτὸν ΓΝ.
[3] ῥόδα δάφνην codd.: corr. Gesner.
[4] τῷ om. ΓΝ.

serving them with breakfast and throwing down some
barley for us animals; my fellows settled to their
breakfast, but I, though miserably hungry, looked
round for something to eat, for I'd never yet had a
meal of raw barley. I noticed a garden over there
behind the yard. It was full of magnificient vegetables, and above them I could see roses. Unnoticed
by any in the house, for they were busy with breakfast, I went into the garden, partly to eat my fill of
raw vegetables, but also to get the roses in the
mistaken belief that, if I ate these flowers, I would
become a man again. Then I stepped into the garden
and ate my fill of lettuces, radishes and celery, the
vegetables that a man can eat raw, but these roses
were not proper roses, but grew on the wild laurel.
They are called rose-bays [1] and make a bad breakfast
for any ass or horse, for they say that to eat them is
instant death. 18. Meanwhile the gardener had
heard the noise and seized a stick. When he had
gone into the garden and seen his enemy and the
havoc wrought amongst his vegetables, he became
just like a severe nabob who's caught a thief, and
gave me a drubbing with his stick. He spared
neither my ribs nor my haunches, and what's more
hammered my ears and pounded my face. When I
could put up with no more, I kicked out at him with
both hind-legs, sending him on to his back among the
vegetables, while I ran off up the mountain. When
he saw me running away, he shouted for the dogs to

---

[1] Probably *Nerium oleander* rather than the modern
rhododendron; cf. Pliny, *Natural History* 16.79, 24.90, who
says that the Greeks used the names *rhododendron, nerion*
and *rhododaphne* for one and the same shrub and that it
was poisonous to cattle, but useful to men as an antidote
to snake venom. Cf. also ibid. 21. 77.

ἀπιόντα, ἀνέκραγε λῦσαι τοὺς κύνας ἐπ' ἐμοί· οἱ δὲ
κύνες πολλοί τε ἦσαν καὶ μεγάλοι καὶ ἄρκτοις
μάχεσθαι ἱκανοί. ἔγνων ὅτι δὴ διασπάσονταί με
οὗτοι λαβόντες, καὶ¹ ὀλίγον ἐκπεριελθὼν ἔκρινα
τοῦτο δὴ² τὸ τοῦ λόγου, "παλινδρομῆσαι μᾶλλον ἢ
κακῶς δραμεῖν." ὀπίσω οὖν³ ἀπῄειν καὶ εἴσειμι
αὖθις εἰς τὴν ἔπαυλιν. οἱ δὲ τοὺς μὲν κύνας
δρόμῳ ἐπιφερομένους ἐδέξαντο καὶ κατέδησαν,
ἐμὲ δὲ παίοντες οὐ πρότερον ἀφῆκαν πρὶν ἢ ὑπὸ
τῆς ὀδύνης πάντα τὰ λάχανα κάτωθεν ἐξεμέσαι.

19. καὶ μὴν ὅτε ὁδοιπορεῖν ὥρα ἦν, τὰ βαρύτατα
τῶν κλεμμάτων καὶ τὰ πλεῖστα ἐμοὶ ἐπέθηκαν·
κἀκεῖθεν τότε οὕτως ἐξελαύνομεν. ἐπεὶ δὲ ἀπηγό-
ρευον ἤδη παιόμενός τε καὶ τῷ φορτίῳ ἀχθόμενος
καὶ τὰς ὁπλὰς ἐκ τῆς ὁδοῦ ἐκτετριμμένος, ἔγνων
αὐτοῦ καταπεσεῖν καὶ μηδ' ἂν ἀποσφάττωσί με
ταῖς πληγαῖς ἀναστῆναί ποτε, τοῦτο ἐλπίσας μέγα
μοι ὄφελος ἔσεσθαι ἐκ τοῦ βουλεύματος· ᾠήθην
γὰρ ὅτι πάντως ἡττώμενοι τὰ μὲν ἐμὰ σκεύη
διανεμοῦσιν τῷ τε ἵππῳ καὶ τῷ ἡμιόνῳ, ἐμὲ δὲ
αὐτοῦ ἐάσουσιν κεῖσθαι τοῖς λύκοις. ἀλλά τις δαίμων βάσκανος συνεὶς τῶν ἐμῶν βουλευμάτων ἐς
τοὐναντίον περιήνεγκεν· ὁ γὰρ ἕτερος ὄνος ἴσως
ἐμοὶ τὰ αὐτὰ νοήσας πίπτει ἐν τῇ ὁδῷ. οἱ δὲ τὰ
μὲν πρῶτα ξύλῳ παίοντες ἀναστῆναι τὸν ἄθλιον
ἐκέλευον, ὡς δὲ οὐδὲν ὑπήκουεν ταῖς πληγαῖς,
λαβόντες αὐτὸν οἱ μὲν τῶν ὤτων, οἱ δὲ τῆς οὐρᾶς
ἀνεγείρειν ἐπειρῶντο· ὡς δὲ οὐδὲν ἤνυον, ἔκειτο δὲ
ὥσπερ λίθος ἐν τῇ ὁδῷ ἀπηγορευκώς, λογισάμενοι

---

¹ καὶ om. Γ.   ² δὴ rec.: ἤδη cett..   ³ οὖν om. Γ

be unleashed on me. There were lots of them, large creatures capable of tackling bears. I realised that they would seize me and tear me to pieces, and, after running to and fro for a short time, I decided in the words of the proverb " to run back home rather than run to harm." [1] So I went back again into the farmyard. They called off the dogs who were now rushing at me and tied them up, but beat me without stopping until the pain had made me excrete [2] all the vegetables from my bottom.

19. But when it was time for them to be on their way, they loaded me with the heaviest items and indeed the major part of their loot, and thus we started off from there. When presently I was faint from the blows and the weight of my load and my hooves were worn out by the journey, I decided to drop down where I was and never to get up again even if they beat me to death. I hoped that this plan would be of great benefit to me, for I thought that they would succumb to complete defeat and share my baggage between the horse and the mule and leave me lying there for the wolves to find. But a malignant deity realised my plans and turned them topsy-turvy. For the other ass, perhaps with the same intentions as I had, dropped down in the road. At first they beat the poor creature with a stick and told it to get up, but, when it paid no heed to their blows, some of them seized it by the ears and others by the tail and tried to get it on its feet. Since this was of no avail and it lay unconscious on the road just like a stone, they decided among themselves that their

[1] A line from a lost play; Kock, *Fr. Adesp.* 480.
[2] Rather than " vomit up "; cf. Apuleius 4.3.

ἐν ἀλλήλοις ὅτι δὴ μάτην πονοῦσιν καὶ τὸν χρόνον
τῆς φυγῆς ἀναλίσκουσιν ὄνῳ νεκρῷ παρεδρεύοντες,
τὰ μὲν σκεύη πάντα ὅσα ἐκόμιζεν ἐκεῖνος διανέμου-
σιν ἐμοί τε καὶ τῷ ἵππῳ, τὸν δὲ ἄθλιον κοινωνὸν
καὶ τῆς αἰχμαλωσίας καὶ τῆς ἀχθοφορίας λαβόντες
τῷ ξίφει ὑποτέμνουσιν ἐκ τῶν σκελῶν καὶ σπαίροντα
ἔτι ὠθοῦσιν ἐς τὸν κρημνόν. ὁ δὲ ἀπῄει κάτω τὸν
θάνατον ὀρχούμενος.

20. ἐγὼ δὲ ὁρῶν ἐν τῷ συνοδοιπόρῳ τῶν ἐμῶν
βουλευμάτων τὸ τέλος, ἔγνων φέρειν εὐγενῶς τὰ
ἐν ποσὶ καὶ προθύμως περιπατεῖν, ἐλπίδας ἔχων
πάντως ποτὲ ἐμπεσεῖσθαι εἰς τὰ ῥόδα κἀκ τούτων
εἰς ἐμαυτὸν ἀνασωθήσεσθαι· καὶ τῶν λῃστῶν δὲ
ἤκουον ὡς οὐκ εἴη ἔτι πολὺ τῆς ὁδοῦ λοιπὸν καὶ ὅτι
καταμενοῦσιν ἔνθα καταλύσουσιν.[1] ὥστε πάντα
ταῦτα δρόμῳ ἐκομίζομεν, καὶ πρὸ τῆς ἑσπέρας
ἤλθομεν εἰς τὰ οἰκεῖα. γραῦς δὲ γυνὴ ἔνδον
καθῆστο, καὶ πῦρ πολὺ ἐκαίετο. οἱ δὲ πάντα
ἐκεῖνα ἅπερ ἐτυγχάνομεν ἡμεῖς κομίζοντες, εἴσω
κατέθηκαν. εἶτα ἤροντο τὴν γραῦν, Διὰ τί οὕτως
καθέζῃ καὶ οὐ παρασκευάζεις ἄριστον;

Ἀλλὰ πάντα, εἶπεν ἡ γραῦς, εὐτρεπῆ ὑμῖν, ἄρτοι
πολλοί, οἴνου παλαιοῦ πίθοι, καὶ τὰ κρέα δὲ ὑμῖν τὰ
ἄγρια σκευάσασα ἔχω. οἱ δὲ τὴν γραῦν ἐπαινέσαντες,
ἀποδυσάμενοι ἠλείφοντο πρὸς τὸ πῦρ καὶ λέβητος
ἔνδον ὕδωρ θερμὸν ἔχοντος ἀρυσάμενοι ἔνθεν καὶ
καταχεάμενοι αὐτοσχεδίῳ τῷ λουτρῷ ἐχρήσαντο.

21. εἶτα ὀλίγῳ ὕστερον ἧκον νεανίσκοι πολλοὶ
κομίζοντες σκεύη πλεῖστα ὅσα χρυσᾶ καὶ ἀργυρᾶ
καὶ ἱμάτια καὶ κόσμον γυναικεῖον καὶ ἀνδρεῖον

efforts were in vain and they were wasting on a dead ass time better spent on escape. They therefore divided his whole load between the horse and me. As for the unfortunate companion of my captivity and my pack-duty, they took him, hacked off his legs with their swords, and pushed him still quivering with life over a cliff, and down he went in a dance of death.

20. Since I could see from the fate of my travelling companion how my schemes would end, I decided to bear my present situation like an aristocrat and continue cheerfully on my way, for I hoped that eventually I would be sure to find my roses and be safely restored to my own shape; besides I heard the robbers saying that there was only a small part of the journey left and they would remain at that night's resting-place. We therefore carried all this load at a fast pace and reached their headquarters before evening. Inside sat an old woman and a fire was blazing merrily. The men stored away inside everything which we had been carrying, and then asked the woman why she was sitting idle like that instead of getting supper ready.

" Everything is ready for you," replied the old woman. " There's plenty of bread along with jars of old wine and I've also cooked you venison." After praising her efforts, they stripped, oiled themselves before the fire and helped themselves from a cauldron containing hot water. This they poured over their bodies, giving themselves improvised baths.

21. Shortly afterwards a large band of youths arrived carrying innumerable vessels of gold and silver along with clothes and a great quantity of

---

[1] λοιπὸν . . . καταλύσουσιν sic Jacobitz: καὶ ὅτι καταλύσουσι λοιπὸν ἔνθα καταμένουσιν codd..

πολύν. ἐκοινώνουν δὲ οὗτοι ἀλλήλοις· καὶ ἐπειδὴ
ταῦτα ἔνδον κατέθεντο, ὁμοίως ἐλούσαντο καὶ
οὗτοι. λοιπὸν μετὰ τοῦτο ἦν ἄριστον δαψιλὲς καὶ
λόγος πολὺς ἐν τῷ συμποσίῳ τῶν ἀνδροφόνων.
ἡ δὲ γραῦς ἐμοὶ καὶ τῷ ἵππῳ κριθὰς παρέθηκεν·
ἀλλ' ἐκεῖνος μὲν σπουδῇ τὰς κριθὰς κατέπινε
δεδιώς, οἷα εἰκός, ἐμὲ τὸν συνάριστον. ἐγὼ δὲ
ἐπειδὰν ἴδοιμι τὴν γραῦν ἐξιοῦσαν τῶν ἔνδον ἄρτον
ἤσθιον. τῇ δὲ ὑστεραίᾳ καταλιπόντες τῇ γραίᾳ
νεανίσκον ἕνα οἱ λοιποὶ πάντες ἔξω ἐπὶ[1] ἔργον
ἀπῇεσαν. ἐγὼ δὲ ἔστενον ἐμαυτὸν καὶ τὴν ἀκριβῆ
φρουράν· τῆς μὲν γὰρ γραὸς καταφρονῆσαι ἦν μοι
καὶ φυγεῖν ἐκ τῶν ἐκείνης ὀμμάτων δυνατόν, ὁ
δὲ νεανίσκος μέγας τε ἦν καὶ φοβερὸν ἔβλεπεν, καὶ
τὸ ξίφος ἀεὶ ἔφερεν καὶ τὴν θύραν ἀεὶ ἐπῆγε.

22. τρισὶ δὲ ὕστερον ἡμέραις μεσούσης σχεδὸν
τῆς νυκτὸς ἀναστρέφουσιν οἱ λῃσταί, χρυσίον
μὲν οὐδὲ ἀργύριον οὐδὲ ἄλλο οὐδὲν κομίζοντες,
μόνην δὲ παρθένον ὡραίαν, σφόδρα καλήν, κλαί-
ουσαν καὶ κατεσπαραγμένην τὴν ἐσθῆτα καὶ τὴν
κόμην· καὶ καταθέμενοι αὐτὴν ἔνδον ἐπὶ τῶν
στιβάδων θαρρεῖν ἐκέλευον καὶ τὴν γραῦν ἐκέλευον
ἀεὶ ἔνδον μένειν καὶ τὴν παῖδα ἐν φρουρᾷ ἔχειν.
ἡ δὲ παῖς οὔτε ἐμφαγεῖν τι ἤθελεν οὔτε πιεῖν, ἀλλὰ
πάντα ἔκλαιεν καὶ τὴν κόμην τὴν αὑτῆς ἐσπάραττεν·
ὥστε καὶ αὐτὸς πλησίον ἑστὼς παρὰ τῇ φάτνῃ
συνέκλαιον ἐκείνῃ τῇ καλῇ παρθένῳ. ἐν δὲ τούτῳ
οἱ λῃσταὶ ἔξω ἐν τῷ προδόμῳ ἐδείπνουν. πρὸς
ἡμέραν δὲ τῶν σκοπῶν τις τῶν τὰς ὁδοὺς φρουρεῖν
εἰληχότων ἔρχεται ἀγγέλλων ὅτι ξένος ταύτῃ

finery for both men and women. They were all in partnership with each other and, after depositing their loot inside, they too washed in the same way. After this there followed a heavy meal and much conversation among the cut-throats as they drank, while the horse and I were given barley by the old woman. The horse gulped it down eagerly through a natural fear of me, his supper companion. I, however, would eat bread from the house, whenever I saw the old woman go out. The next day they left one youth for the old woman, and the rest of them went off out to work. I then bewailed my lot for the strict watch kept on me ; for I was able to take the old woman lightly and to escape her notice, but the youth was tall, had a formidable look, always carried a sword and always closed the door.

22. Three days later about midnight the robbers returned without gold or silver or in fact anything except a young girl of great beauty who was weeping and had her clothes and her hair torn to shreds. They deposited her inside on the straw, telling her not to be afraid and bidding the old woman remain permanently indoors and keep a watch on the girl. She wouldn't eat or drink at all, but only kept weeping and tearing her hair. In consequence I also wept in sympathy with the beautiful girl as I stood beside the manger. Meanwhile the robbers were having their dinner outside in the vestibule. Towards daybreak one of the sentries posted to watch the roads entered with the news that a stranger was about

---

παριέναι μέλλοι καὶ πολὺν πλοῦτον κομίζοι. οἱ
δὲ οὕτως ὡς εἶχον ἀναστάντες καὶ ὁπλισάμενοι
κἀμὲ καὶ τὸν ἵππον ἐπισάξαντες ἤλαυνον. ἐγὼ δὲ
ὁ δυστυχὴς ἐπιστάμενος ἐπὶ μάχην καὶ πόλεμον
ἐξελαύνεσθαι ὀκνηρῶς προῄειν, ἔνθεν ἐπαιόμην τῷ
ξύλῳ ἐπειγομένων αὐτῶν. ἐπεὶ δὲ ἤκομεν ἐς τὴν
ὁδὸν ἔνθα ὁ ξένος παρελάσειν ἔμελλεν, συμπεσόντες
οἱ λῃσταὶ τοῖς ὀχήμασιν αὐτόν τε καὶ τοὺς ἐκείνου θεράποντας ἀπέκτειναν, καὶ ὅσα ἦν τιμιώτατα
ἐξελόντες τῷ ἵππῳ κἀμοὶ ἐπέθηκαν, τὰ δὲ ἕτερα τῶν
σκευῶν αὐτοῦ ἐν τῇ ὕλῃ ἔκρυψαν. ἔπειτα ἤλαυνον
ἡμᾶς οὕτως ὀπίσω, κἀγὼ ἐπειγόμενος καὶ τῷ ξύλῳ
τυπτόμενος κρούω· τὴν ὁπλὴν περὶ πέτραν ὀξεῖαν
καί μοι ἀπὸ τῆς πληγῆς γίνεται τραῦμα ἀλγεινόν·
καὶ χωλεύων ἔνθεν τὸ λοιπὸν τῆς ὁδοῦ ἐβάδιζον.
οἱ δὲ πρὸς ἀλλήλους ἔλεγον, Τί γὰρ ἡμῖν δοκεῖ
τρέφειν τὸν ὄνον τοῦτον πάντα καταπίπτοντα;
ῥίψωμεν αὐτὸν ἀπὸ τοῦ κρημνοῦ οἰωνὸν οὐκ ἀγαθόν.
Ναί, φησίν, ῥίψωμεν αὐτὸν καθαρισμὸν τοῦ στρατοῦ
ἐσόμενον. καὶ οἱ μὲν συνετάττοντο ἐπ᾽ ἐμέ· ἐγὼ
δὲ ἀκούων ταῦτα τῷ τραύματι λοιπὸν ὡς ἀλλοτρίῳ
ἐπέβαινον· ὁ δὲ [1] τοῦ θανάτου με φόβος ἀναίσθητον
τῆς ὀδύνης ἔθηκεν. 23. ἐπεὶ δὲ ἤλθομεν εἴσω
ἔνθα κατελύομεν, τὰ μὲν σκεύη τῶν ἡμετέρων
ὤμων ἀφελόντες εὖ κατέθηκαν, αὐτοὶ δὲ ἀναπεσόντες
ἐδείπνουν. καὶ ἐπειδὴ νὺξ ἦν, ἀπῄεσαν ὡς τὰ
λοιπὰ τῶν σκευῶν ἀνασῶσαι. Τὸν δὲ ἄθλιον
τοῦτον ὄνον, ἔφη τις αὐτῶν, τί ἐπάγομεν ἄχρηστον
ἐκ τῆς ὁπλῆς; τῶν δὲ σκευῶν ἃ μὲν ἡμεῖς οἴσομεν,
ἃ δὲ καὶ [2] ὁ ἵππος. καὶ ἀπῄεσαν τὸν ἵππον ἄγοντες.

to pass that way bearing great riches. They got up just as they were, armed themselves, saddled the horse and me and got us moving. But since I, poor wretch, knew that I was being driven out to battle and war, I proceeded with reluctance, so that in their eager haste they kept beating me with sticks. When we reached the road along which the stranger would be riding, the robbers fell upon the caravan, killing the master and his servants. They removed the articles of greatest value and loaded them on to the horse and me, but the rest of the goods they hid there in the wood. Then they started to drive us back, but because of our haste and all the cudgelling I dashed my foot against a sharp stone and incurred a painful injury. This left me lame for the rest of the journey, and they kept saying to each other, " Why do we choose to keep this ass in food, when he's always falling down ? Let's throw him over the cliff, for he brings bad luck." " Yes," said another, " let's throw him over to atone for the sins of our band." They were preparing to attack me, but, on hearing these words, I moved forward for the rest of the journey as though my injury belonged to another, fear of death having made me impervious to pain. 23. When we reached our billet for the night, they took the baggage off our backs and stored it away carefully ; then the men sat down to their own dinner. After nightfall, they came out to recover the rest of their baggage, and one of them said, " Why do we take this wretched ass with us, when his hoof makes him useless ? We can carry some of the goods ourselves, and the horse will take the rest."

---

¹ δὲ ΓΝ: γὰρ recc., edd..   ² καὶ ΓΝ: om. recc., edd..

νὺξ δὲ ἦν λαμπροτάτη ἐκ τῆς σελήνης. κἀγὼ τότε
πρὸς ἐμαυτὸν εἶπον, "Ἄθλιε, τί μένεις ἔτι ἐνταῦθα;
γῦπές σε καὶ γυπῶν τέκνα δειπνήσουσιν. οὐκ
ἀκούεις οἷα περὶ σοῦ ἐβουλεύσαντο; θέλεις τῷ
κρημνῷ περιπεσεῖν; νὺξ μὲν αὕτη [1] καὶ σελήνη
πολλή· οἱ δὲ οἴχονται ἀπιόντες· φυγῇ σῷζε
σαυτὸν ἀπὸ δεσποτῶν ἀνδροφόνων.

ταῦτα πρὸς ἐμαυτὸν ἐννοούμενος ὁρῶ ὅτι οὐδὲ
προσεδεδέμην οὐδενί, ἀλλά με ὁ σύρων ἐν ταῖς ὁδοῖς
ἱμὰς παρεκρέματο. τοῦτό με καὶ παρώξυνεν ὡς μάλιστα ἐς τὴν φυγήν, καὶ δρόμῳ ἐξιὼν ἀπῄειν. ἡ δὲ
γραῦς, ἐπειδὴ εἶδεν ἀποδιδράσκειν ἕτοιμον, λαμβά-
νεταί με ἐκ τῆς οὐρᾶς καὶ εἴχετο. ἐγὼ δὲ ἄξιον κρημνοῦ
καὶ θανάτων ἄλλων [2] εἰπὼν εἶναι τὸ ὑπὸ γραίας ἁλῶναι
ἔσυρον αὐτήν, ἡ δὲ μάλ' ἀνέκραγεν ἔνδοθεν τὴν παρθένον τὴν αἰχμάλωτον· ἡ δὲ προελθοῦσα [3] καὶ ἰδοῦσα
γραῦν Δίρκην [4] ἐξ ὄνου ἡμμένην τολμᾷ τόλμημα
γενναῖον καὶ ἄξιον ἀπονενοημένου νεανίσκου· ἀνα-
πηδᾷ γὰρ εἰς ἐμέ, καὶ ἐπικαθίσασά [5] μοι ἤλαυνεν·
κἀγὼ τῷ τε ἔρωτι τῆς φυγῆς καὶ τῇ τῆς κόρης
σπουδῇ ἔφυγον ἵππου δρόμῳ· ἡ δὲ γραῦς ὀπίσω
ἀπελέλειπτο. ἡ δὲ παρθένος τοῖς μὲν θεοῖς ηὔχετο
σῶσαι αὐτὴν τῇ φυγῇ· πρὸς δὲ ἐμέ, "Ἤν με, ἔφη,
κομίσῃς πρὸς τὸν πατέρα, ὦ καλὲ σύ, ἐλεύθερον
μέν σε παντὸς ἔργου ἀφήσω, κριθῶν δὲ μέδιμνος
ἔσται σοι ἐφ' ἑκάστης ἡμέρας τὸ ἄριστον.

---

[1] αὐτὴ Γ.
[2] ἄλλων codd.: πολλῶν Courier.
[3] προσελθοῦσα recc., edd..
[4] Δίρκην recc.: δίρκιν Γ: δίκην κέρκου N.
[5] ἐπικαθίσασά recc.: καθήσασά Γ.

They went away, leading the horse with them. It was a particularly bright night because of the moonlight and I then said to myself, " Poor wretch, why do you stay here ? The vultures and their young will have you for dinner. Don't you hear what plans they have made for you ? Do you *want* to go over the cliff ? It's night now, there's a good moon and they've gone off elsewhere. Run away and escape from these murderous masters."

As these thoughts ran through my mind, I noticed that I wasn't tied to anything, but the strap which had pulled me along was hanging by my side. This further circumstance gave me the strongest possible encouragement to escape, and I ran off at full speed. But the old woman, seeing that I was ready to run away, grabbed me by the tail and held on to me. I told myself that I deserved the cliff and other deaths as well, if I were captured by an old woman, and dragged her along. She raised a loud cry to the captive girl inside. She came forth and, on seeing this aged Dirce [1] hanging to an ass, showed the courage for a feat of heroism worthy of a foolhardy youth. She jumped on me, seated herself on my back and rode me off. Driven on by my longing to escape and the girl's eagerness I galloped off as fast as a horse, and the old woman was left behind. The girl prayed to the gods to let her escape to safety, while to me she said, " If you take me to my father, my beauty, I'll set you free from all work, and you'll have a bushel of barley every day for breakfast."

[1] Dirce was tied to a bull by Amphion and Zethus who allowed it to drag her about till she died. Cf. Apuleius, 6.27.

ἐγὼ δὲ καὶ τοὺς φονεῖς τοὺς ἐμαυτοῦ φευξόμενος
καὶ πολλὴν ἐπικουρίαν καὶ θεραπείαν ἐκ τῆς
ἀνασωθείσης ἐμοὶ κόρης ἐλπίζων ἔθεον τοῦ τραύματος ἀμελήσας. 24. ἐπεὶ δὲ ἥκομεν ἔνθα ἐσχίζετο
τριπλῆ ⟨ἡ⟩ [1] ὁδός, οἱ πολέμιοι ἡμᾶς καταλαμβάνου-
σιν ἀναστρέφοντες καὶ πόρρωθεν εὐθὺς πρὸς τὴν
σελήνην ἔγνωσαν τοὺς δυστυχεῖς αἰχμαλώτους καὶ
προσδραμόντες λαμβάνονταί μου καὶ λέγουσιν,
Ὦ καλὴ κἀγαθὴ σὺ παρθένος, ποῖ βαδίζεις ἀωρίᾳ,
ταλαίπωρε; οὐδὲ τὰ δαιμόνια δέδοικας; ἀλλὰ δεῦρο
ἴθι πρὸς ἡμᾶς, ἡμεῖς σε τοῖς οἰκείοις ἀποδώσομεν,
σαρδάνιον [2] γελῶντες ἔλεγον, κἀμὲ ἀποστρέψαντες
εἷλκον ὀπίσω. κἀγὼ περὶ τοῦ ποδὸς καὶ τοῦ
τραύματος ἀναμνησθεὶς ἐχώλευον· οἱ δέ, Νῦν,
ἔφασαν, χωλὸς ὅτε ἀποδιδράσκων ἑάλωκας; ἀλλ'
ὅτε φεύγειν ἐδόκει σοι, ὑγιαίνων ἵππου ὠκύτερος
καὶ πετεινὸς ἦσθα. τοῖς δὲ λόγοις τούτοις τὸ
ξύλον εἵπετο, καὶ ἤδη ἕλκος τῷ μηρῷ εἶχον νουθε-
τούμενος. ἐπεὶ δὲ εἴσω πάλιν ἀνεστρέψαμεν, τὴν
μὲν γραῦν εὕρομεν ἐκ τῆς πέτρας κρεμαμένην ἐν
καλῳδίῳ· δείσασα γάρ, οἷον εἰκός, τοὺς δεσπότας
ἐπὶ τῇ τῆς παρθένου φυγῇ κρημνᾷ ἑαυτὴν σφίγξασα
ἐκ τοῦ τραχήλου. οἱ δὲ τὴν γραῦν θαυμάσαντες
τῆς εὐγνωμοσύνης τὴν μὲν ἀπολύσαντες ἐς τὸν
κρημνὸν κάτω ἀφῆκαν ὡς ἦν ἐν τῷ δεσμῷ, τὴν δὲ
παρθένον ἔνδον κατέδησαν, εἶτα ἐδείπνουν, καὶ
πότος ἦν μακρός.

---

[1] ἡ suppl. Courier.
[2] σαρδώνιον recc., edd..

Because I for my part wished to escape from my murderers and hoped for plenty of help and care from the girl I'd rescued, I ran on heedless of my injury. 24. When we came to a place where three [1] roads met, we were overtaken by our enemies on their way back. In the moonlight they immediately recognised their unfortunate prisoners, from a long way off; they ran up, caught hold of me and said, " What conduct for a well-bred young lady ! Where are you going so late at night, you hussy ? Don't you even fear the spirits ? Come here to us and we'll return you to your family." Thus they spoke with cruel laughter, turned me round and dragged me after them. I now remembered about my injured feet and started to limp. " So you're lame," they said, " now that you've been caught running away ? Yet, when you were bent on escaping, you were in perfect fettle, going faster than a horse and flying like a bird." These words were accompanied by the stick and by this time I had a sore on my thigh from their admonitions. When we got back to the house, we found the old woman hanging on a rope over the rock. For fearing, as well she might, her masters' wrath over the escape of the girl, she had fastened the rope tight about her neck and hanged herself. They applauded the old woman for her good sense and cut her down, letting her fall over the cliff with the rope still round her neck ; the girl, however, they tied up indoors. Then they had their dinner and indulged in a long session of drinking.

[1] This pointless mention of the three roads is an indication that this work is an abridgement of another version. In Apuleius 6.29 they are caught because they have stopped and are arguing about what road to take.

25. κἂν τούτῳ ἤδη περὶ τῆς κόρης διελέγοντο
πρὸς ἀλλήλους· Τί ποιοῦμεν, ἔφη τις αὐτῶν,
τὴν δραπέτιν; Τί δὲ ἄλλο, εἶπεν ἕτερος,[1] ἢ τῇ
γραῒ ταύτῃ κάτω ἐπιρρίψωμεν αὐτήν, ἀφελομένην
μὲν ἡμᾶς χρήματα πολλὰ ὅσον ἐπ' αὐτῇ, καὶ
προδοῦσαν ἡμῶν[2] ὅλον τὸ ἐργαστήριον· εὖ ἴστε
γάρ, ὦ φίλοι, ὅτι αὕτη εἰ τῶν οἴκοι ἐδράξατο,
οὐδὲ εἷς ἂν ἡμῶν ζῶν ὑπελείπετο· πάντες δὲ[3] ἂν
ἑάλωμεν, τῶν ἐχθρῶν ἐκ παρασκευῆς ἡμῖν ἐπιπεσόν-
των. ὥστε ἀμυνώμεθα μὲν τὴν πολεμίαν· ἀλλὰ
μὴ οὕτω ῥᾳδίως ἀποθνησκέτω πεσοῦσα ἐπὶ τοῦ
λίθου, θάνατον δὲ αὐτῇ τὸν ἀλγεινότατον καὶ
μακρότατον ἐξεύρωμεν καὶ ὅστις αὐτὴν χρόνῳ καὶ
βασάνῳ φυλάξας ὕστερον[4] ἀπολεῖ.

εἶτα ἐζήτουν θάνατον, καί τις εἶπεν, Οἶδα ὅτι
ἐπαινέσεσθε τὸ ἀρχιτεκτόνημα. τὸν ὄνον δεῖ
ἀπολέσαι[5] ὀκνηρὸν ὄντα, νῦν δὲ καὶ χωλὸν εἶναι
ψευδόμενον, καὶ μὴν καὶ τῆς φυγῆς τῆς παρθένου
γενόμενον ὑπηρέτην καὶ διάκονον· τοῦτον οὖν ἕωθεν
ἀποσφάξαντες ἀνατέμωμεν ἐκ τῆς γαστρὸς καὶ τὰ
μὲν ἔγκατα πάντα ἔξω βάλωμεν, τὴν δὲ ἀγαθὴν
ταύτην παρθένον τῷ ὄνῳ ἐγκατοικίσωμεν, τὴν μὲν
κεφαλὴν ἔξω τοῦ ὄνου πρόχειρον, ὡς ἂν μὴ εὐθὺς
ἀποπνιγείη, τὸ δὲ ἄλλο σῶμα πᾶν ἔνδον κρυπτόμε-
νον, ὡς ἂν αὐτὴν κατακειμένην εὖ μάλα συρράψαντες
ῥίψωμεν ἔξω ἄμφω ταῦτα τοῖς γυψί, καινῶς τοῦτο
ἐσκευασμένον ἄριστον. σκοπεῖτε δέ, ὦ φίλοι, τῆς
βασάνου τὸ δεινόν, πρῶτον μὲν τὸ νεκρῷ ὄνῳ
συνοικεῖν, εἶτα θέρους ὥρᾳ θερμοτάτῳ ἡλίῳ ἐν

[1] τί δέ, ἄλλος εἶπεν, ἕτερον codd.: corr. Lehmann.
[2] ἡμῖν recc., edd.. [3] δὲ ΓΝ: γὰρ recc., edd.. [4] ὕστερος Γ.

25. Meanwhile their conversation turned to the girl. " What are we to do with Miss Runaway ? " asked one. " What else," said another, " but to throw her down to join the old woman over there, since she did her best to rob us of a lot of money and to betray our whole gang ? For you may be sure, my friends, that, if she had reached her home, none of us would have been left alive ; our enemies would have made a concerted attack on us and we should all have been captured. So let's have revenge upon our enemy. But she mustn't be thrown down on to the rocks ; that's too easy a death. Rather let's devise her the most painful and protracted death, and one to keep her lingering in agony before it kills her."

Then they discussed how to kill her, and one of them said, " I know that you'll approve of my masterpiece of invention. We must kill the ass, for it's lazy and now even pretends to be lame, and besides it aided and abetted the escape of the girl. So let's slit its throat at dawn and cut its belly open ; let's tear out all its guts and house this fine young lady inside the beast with her head sticking out, so that she doesn't suffocate immediately, but with all the rest of her body hidden inside, so that, when she's in there, we can sew them firmly together and throw them both out to feed the vultures. I'll guarantee they've never tasted that recipe before ! Just think, my friends, what a terrible torture it will be. First to be housed with a dead ass, then to be broiled inside the beast by the scorching summer sun and

---

[5] ἀπολέσθαι recc., edd..

κτήνει καθεψεῖσθαι καὶ λιμῷ ἀεὶ κτείνοντι ἀποθνῄ-
σκειν καὶ μηδὲ αὐτὴν ἀποπνῖξαι ἔχειν· τὰ μὲν γὰρ
ἄλλ' ὅσα πείσεται σηπομένου τοῦ ὄνου τῇ τε ὀδμῇ
καὶ τοῖς σκώληξι πεφυρμένη ἐῶ λέγειν. τέλος δὲ
οἱ γῦπες διὰ τοῦ ὄνου παρεισιόντες εἴσω καὶ ταύτην
ὡς ἐκεῖνον ἴσως καὶ ζῶσαν ἔτι διασπάσονται.

26. πάντες ἀνεβόησαν ὡς ἐπὶ ἀγαθῷ μεγάλῳ τῷ
τερατώδει τούτῳ εὑρήματι. ἐγὼ δὲ ἀνέστενον
ἐμαυτὸν ὡς ἂν ἀποσφαγησόμενος καὶ μηδὲ νεκρὸς
εὐτυχὴς κεισόμενος, ἀλλὰ παρθένον ἀθλίαν ἐπιδεξό-
μενος [1] καὶ θήκῃ οὐδὲν ἀδικούσης κόρης ἐσόμενος.

ὄρθρος δὲ ἦν ἔτι καὶ ἐξαίφνης ἐφίσταται πλῆθος
στρατιωτῶν ἐπὶ τοὺς μιαροὺς τούτους ἀφιγμένον,
καὶ εὐθέως πάντας ἐδέσμουν καὶ ἐπὶ τὸν τῆς χώρας
ἡγεμόνα ἀπῆγον. ἔτυχεν δὲ καὶ ὁ τὴν κόρην
μεμνηστευμένος σὺν αὐτοῖς ἐλθών· αὐτὸς γὰρ ἦν
ὁ καὶ τὸ καταγώγιον τῶν λῃστῶν μηνύσας. παραλαβὼν οὖν τὴν παρθένον καὶ καθίσας ἐπ' ἐμὲ οὕτως
ἦγεν οἴκαδε. οἱ δὲ κωμῆται, ὡς εἶδον ἡμᾶς ἔτι
πόρρωθεν, ἔγνωσαν εὐτυχοῦντας, εὐαγγέλιον αὐτοῖς
ἐμοῦ προογκησαμένου,[2] καὶ προσδραμόντες ἠσπάζοντο καὶ ἦγον ἔσω. 27. ἡ δὲ παρθένος πολὺν
λόγον εἶχεν ἐμοῦ δίκαιον ποιοῦσα τοῦ συναιχ-
μαλώτου συναποδράσαντος καὶ τὸν κοινὸν αὐτῇ
ἐκεῖνον θάνατον συγκινδυνεύσαντος. καί μοι ⟨παρὰ⟩
τῆς κεκτημένης [3] ἄριστον παρέκειτο μέδιμνος [4]
κριθῶν καὶ χόρτος ὅσος καὶ καμήλῳ ἱκανός. ἐγὼ
δὲ τότε μάλιστα κατηρώμην τῇ Παλαίστρᾳ [5] ὡς
ὄνον με καὶ οὐ κύνα τῇ τέχνῃ μεταθεῖσαν· ἑώρων
γὰρ τοὺς κύνας εἰς τοὐπανεῖον παρεισιόντας καὶ

gradually to starve to death without even being able to suffocate herself! The other things she'll suffer as the ass rots and she is afflicted by the smell and the maggots I won't mention, but in the end the vultures will penetrate through the ass and tear her to pieces just like it, perhaps even when she's still alive."

26. All shouted hearty approval of this monstrous idea, but I lamented my fate, since I should be killed and not even my carcass left unmolested but it would contain the luckless girl and would be the grave of that innocent maiden.

But at first light next morning a great number of soldiers suddenly arrived to attack these black-guards. They immediately tied them all up and took them off to the governor of the land. The girl's fiancé had come with the soldiers, for he was actually the one who had shown them where the robbers lived. So he took the girl, put her on my back and brought her home in this way. When the villagers saw us still a long way off, they realised all was well with us, as I had brayed out first intimation of the good news. They ran up, greeted us and took us indoors. 27. The girl showed me great considera-tion as was my due for sharing with her captivity, flight and the threat of that terrible joint death. I would have a bushel of barley from my mistress set before me for breakfast and enough hay to feed a camel. I then cursed Palaestra more than ever before—because she hadn't used her art to change me into a dog rather than an ass. For I saw the dogs

---

[1] ἐπιδεξάμενος ΓΝ. [2] προσογκησαμένου Γ.

[3] παρὰ (κελευσάσης vel aliquid simile malim) τῆς κεκτημένης Du Soul: τοῖς κεκτημένης Γ: τοῖς κεκτημένοις recc..

[4] μεδίμνοις Γ. [5] τὴν παλαίστραν recc., edd..

λαφύσσοντας πολλὰ καὶ ὅσα ἐν γάμοις πλουσίων
νυμφίων. ἡμέραις δὲ ὕστερον μετὰ τὸν γάμον οὐ
πολλαῖς ἐπειδὴ χάριν μοι ἔφη ἡ δέσποινα ἔχειν
παρὰ τῷ πατρί, καὶ ἀμείψασθαί με ἀμοιβῇ τῇ
δικαίᾳ θέλων ὁ[1] πατὴρ ἐκέλευσεν ἐλεύθερον
ἀφιέναι ὑπαίθριον καὶ σὺν ταῖς ἀγελαίαις ἵπποις
νέμεσθαι· Καὶ γὰρ ὡς ἐλεύθερος, ἔφη, ζήσεται ἐν
ἡδονῇ καὶ ταῖς ἵπποις ἐπιβήσεται. καὶ αὕτη
δικαιοτάτη ἀμοιβὴ ἐδόκει τότε, εἰ ἦν τὰ πράγματα
ἐν ὄνῳ δικαστῇ. καλέσας οὖν τῶν ἱπποφορβῶν
τινα τούτῳ με παραδίδωσιν, ἐγὼ δὲ ἔχαιρον ὡς
οὐκέτι ἀχθοφορήσων. ἐπεὶ δὲ ἥκομεν εἰς τὸν
ἀγρόν, ταῖς ἵπποις με[2] ὁ νομεὺς συνέμιξεν καὶ
ἦγεν ἡμᾶς τὴν ἀγέλην εἰς νομόν.

28. ἐχρῆν δὲ ἄρα κἀνταῦθα ὥσπερ Κανδαύλῃ
κἀμοὶ γενέσθαι· ὁ γὰρ ἐπιστάτης τῶν ἵππων τῇ
αὑτοῦ γυναικὶ Μεγαπόλῃ ἔνδον με[3] κατέλιπεν· ἡ
δὲ τῇ μύλῃ με ὑπεζεύγνυεν, ὥστε ἀλεῖν αὐτῇ καὶ
πυροὺς καὶ κριθὰς ὅλας,[4] καὶ τοῦτο μὲν ἦν μέτριον
κακὸν εὐχαρίστῳ ὄνῳ ἀλεῖν τοῖς ἑαυτοῦ ἐπιστάταις·
ἡ δὲ βελτίστη καὶ παρὰ τῶν ἄλλων τῶν ἐν ἐκείνοις
τοῖς ἀγροῖς—πολλοὶ δὲ πάνυ ἦσαν—ἄλευρα τὸν
μισθὸν αἰτοῦσα ἐξεμίσθου τὸν ἐμὸν ἄθλιον τράχηλον,
καὶ τὰς μὲν κριθὰς τοὐμὸν ἄριστον φρύγουσα κἀμοὶ
ὥστε ἀλεῖν ἐπιβάλλουσα, μάζας ὅλας[5] ποιοῦσα
κατέπινεν· ἐμοὶ δὲ πίτυρα τὸ ἄριστον ἦν. εἰ δέ
ποτε καὶ συνελάσειέν με ταῖς ἵπποις ὁ νομεύς,
παιόμενός τε καὶ δακνόμενος ὑπὸ τῶν ἀρσένων

---

[1] θέλων ὁ recc.: θέλων Γ: θέλειν, ὁ recc. edd..
[2] με recc.: μὲν Γ.   [3] με om. Γ.
[4] ὅλας fortasse delendum, ut quod a glossemate ὀλάς
provenerit.   [5] ὅλας fortasse delendum; cf. n. 4.

sneaking into the kitchen and gobbling down the many titbits to be found at a wealthy wedding. A few days after the wedding, when my mistress mentioned her gratitude to me in the presence of her father, he too wished to reward me as I deserved and ordered me to be set free to graze in the open with the mares. " For," said he, " he'll live pleasantly as though he were free and will mount the mares." This indeed would have seemed the fairest reward, had the decision rested with an ass. So he called one of his grooms and gave me to him. I was delighted to think I'd have no more loads to carry. When we reached the field, the groom put me among the mares and took the herd of us into the pasture.

28. Then too was I doomed to fare just like Candaules ;[1] for the groom left me at home for his wife Megapole,[2] and she would tie me to the mill, so that I ground her wheat and grains of barley. It would indeed have been no great hardship for a grateful ass thus to grind for his own masters, but that paragon of womanhood also hired out my unfortunate neck to her numerous neighbours, and asked them for meal as payment ; and the barley meant for my breakfast she roasted and gave me to grind, and then made it into cakes which she would devour in one mouthful, while I had the husks for breakfast. Whenever the groom drove me out with the mares, I was battered and bitten by the stallions till I was

---

[1] A king of Lydia whose downfall Herodotus, 1.8 ff. describes, adding the comment that he was doomed to fare ill.

[2] Megapole = much-turning (Madam Grately-Turner or Grately-Miller).

ἀπωλλύμην· ἀεὶ γάρ με μοιχὸν ὑποπτεύοντες εἶναι
τῶν ἵππων τῶν αὐτῶν γυναικῶν ἐδίωκον ἀμφοτέροις
εἰς ἐμὲ ὑπολακτίζοντες, ὥστε φέρειν οὐκ ἠδυνάμην
ζηλοτυπίαν ἱππικήν. λεπτὸς οὖν καὶ ἄμορφος ἐν
οὐ πολλῷ χρόνῳ ἐγενόμην, οὔτε ἔνδον εὐφραινόμενος
πρὸς τῇ μύλῃ οὔτε ὑπαίθριος νεμόμενος, ὑπὸ τῶν
συννόμων πολεμούμενος.

29. καὶ μὴν καὶ τὰ πολλὰ εἰς τὸ ὄρος ἄνω ἐπεμπό-
μην καὶ ξύλα τοῖς ὤμοις ἐκόμιζον. τοῦτο δὲ ἦν τὸ
κεφάλαιον τῶν ἐμῶν κακῶν· πρῶτον μὲν ὑψηλὸν
ὄρος ἀναβαίνειν ἔδει, ὀρθὴν δεινῶς ὁδόν, εἶτα καὶ
ἀνυπόδητος ὄρει ἐν λιθίνῳ. καί μοι συνεξέπεμπον
ὀνηλάτην, παιδάριον ἀκάθαρτον. τοῦτό με καινῶς
ἑκάστοτε ἀπώλλυεν· πρῶτον μὲν ἔπαιέ με καὶ
τρέχοντα λίαν οὐ ξύλῳ ἁπλῷ, ἀλλὰ τῷ ὄζους πυκνοὺς
ἔχοντι καὶ ὀξεῖς, καὶ ἀεὶ ἔπαιεν ἐς τὸ αὐτό τοῦ
μηροῦ, ὥστε ἀνέῳκτό μοι κατ' ἐκεῖνο ὁ μηρὸς τῇ
ῥάβδῳ· ὁ δὲ ἀεὶ τὸ τραῦμα ἔπαιεν. εἶτά μοι
ἐπετίθει φορτίον ὅσον χαλεπὸν εἶναι καὶ ἐλέφαντι
ἐνεγκεῖν· καὶ ἄνωθεν ἡ κατάβασις ὀξεῖα ἦν· ὁ δὲ
καὶ ἐνταῦθα ἔπαιεν. εἰ δέ μοι περιπῖπτον ἴδοι τὸ
φορτίον καὶ εἰς τὸ ἕτερον ἐπικλῖνον, δέον [1] τῶν
ξύλων ἀφαιρεῖν καὶ τῷ κουφοτέρῳ προσβάλλειν [2]
καὶ τὸ ἴσον ποιεῖν, τοῦτο μὲν οὐδέποτε εἰργάσατο,
λίθους δὲ μεγάλους ἐκ τοῦ ὄρους ἀναιρούμενος εἰς τὸ
κουφότερον καὶ ἄνω νεύον τοῦ φορτίου προσετίθει·
καὶ κατῄειν ἄθλιος τοῖς ξύλοις ὁμοῦ καὶ λίθους
ἀχρείους περιφέρων. καὶ ποταμὸς ἦν ἀέναος [3] ἐν τῇ
ὁδῷ· ὁ δὲ τῶν ὑποδημάτων φειδόμενος ὀπίσω τῶν
ξύλων ἐπ' ἐμοὶ καθίζων ἐπέρα τὸν ποταμόν.

half dead ; for they always suspected me of designs upon their own mares and would drive me away by kicking out at me with both hooves, so that I could not bear the jealousy of the horses. Thus I soon became thin and ugly, since I had no pleasure either indoors at the mill or when grazing outside, for then my companions waged war on me.

29. Furthermore I was often sent up to the mountain to fetch wood. This was the height of all my misfortunes. For first I had to climb a high mountain by a terribly steep path and in the second place the mountain was stony and I was unshod. They sent as driver with me a vile slave-boy, who every time found a fresh way of bringing me to death's door. In the first place he would beat me even when I was running fast, and not with an ordinary stick but with one bristling with sharp stubs, and always on the same part of my thigh, so that I had an open sore there from his switch. He always hit the same spot. Then he would pile on my back a load which an elephant could scarcely carry. The way down was steep, but even then he would beat me. Whenever he saw my load slipping and tilting to one side, though he ought to have transferred some of the wood to the place where my load was lighter and thus made it even, he never did so ; instead he would pick up boulders from the mountainside to add to the lighter and higher side of my load. And I, poor wretch, would descend with a load of useless boulders along with the wood. On our route was a perennial stream, which he would cross seated on my back behind the wood so as to save his shoes.

---

¹ δέον om. ΓΨ. ² προσβαλεῖν codd.: corr. Jacobitz.
³ ἀένναος ΓΝ.

30. εἰ δέ ποτε οἷα κάμνων καὶ ἀχθοφορῶν καταπέσοιμι, τότε δὴ τὸ δεινὸν ἀφόρητον ἦν· † οὐ γὰρ ἦν καιρὸς [1] τοῦ τὴν χεῖρά μοι ἐπιδοῦναι κἀμὲ χαμόθεν ἐπεγείρειν καὶ τοῦ φορτίου [2] ἀφελεῖν, οὔποτε [3] οὐδὲ χεῖρα ἐπέδωκεν, ἀλλ᾽ ἄνωθεν ἀπὸ τῆς κεφαλῆς καὶ τῶν ὤτων ἀρξάμενος [4] συνέκοπτέ με τῷ ξύλῳ, ἕως ἐπεγείρωσί με αἱ πληγαί. καὶ μὴν καὶ ἄλλο κακὸν εἰς ἐμὲ ἀφόρητον ἔπαιζεν· συνενεγκὼν ἀκανθῶν ὀξυτάτων φορτίον καὶ τοῦτο δεσμῷ περισφίγξας ἀπεκρέμνα [5] ὄπισθεν ἐκ τῆς οὐρᾶς, αἱ δὲ οἷον εἰκὸς ἀπιόντος τὴν ὁδὸν ἀποκρεμάμεναι προσέπιπτόν μοι καὶ πάντα μοι τὰ ὄπισθεν νύττουσαι ἐτίτρωσκον· καὶ ἦν μοι τὸ ἀμύνειν ἀδύνατον, τῶν τιτρωσκόντων ἀεί μοι ἑπομένων κἀμοῦ ἠρτημένων. εἰ μὲν γὰρ ἀτρέμα προΐοιμι φυλαττόμενος τῶν ἀκανθῶν τὴν προσβολήν, ὑπὸ τῶν ξύλων ἀπωλλύμην, εἰ δὲ φεύγοιμι τὸ ξύλον, τότ᾽ ἤδη τὸ δεινὸν ὄπισθεν ὀξὺ προσέπιπτεν. καὶ ὅλως ἔργον ἦν τῷ ὀνηλάτῃ τῷ ἐμῷ ἀποκτενεῖν με. 31. ἐπεὶ δέ ποτε ἅπαξ κακὰ πάσχων πολλὰ οὐκέτι φέρων πρὸς αὐτὸν λὰξ ἐκίνησα, εἶχεν ἀεὶ τοῦτο τὸ λὰξ ἐν μνήμῃ. καί ποτε κελεύεται στυππεῖον ἐξ ἑτέρου χωρίου εἰς ἕτερον χωρίον μετενεγκεῖν· κομίσας οὖν με καὶ τὸ στυππεῖον πολὺ συνενεγκὼν κατέδησεν ἐπ᾽ ἐμὲ καὶ δεσμῷ ἀργαλέῳ εὖ μάλα προσέδησέ με τῷ φορτίῳ κακὸν ἐμοὶ μέγα τυρεύων. ἐπεὶ δὲ προϊέναι λοιπὸν

---

[1] in loco desperato sic dubitanter conieci (cf. Apuleius 7.18): οὐ γὰρ ἦν καταβὰς codd..   [2] τὸ φορτίον ΓΝΨ.
[3] οὔποτε οὐδὲ conieci: ἄν ποτε οὔτε ΓΨC Vat. 87: ἄν ποτε καὶ δέοι, ὁ δὲ οὔτε κατῆλθεν οὔτε Ν, edd..

30. If ever I fell down through weariness and the weight of my load, that was the time when my suffering was intolerable ; for, when he ought to have given me a helping hand, and lifted me up from the ground and taken off some of my load, he would never so much as give me a hand, but from his seat aloft he would start from my head and ears and batter me with his stick till his blows made me rise. Furthermore there was another intolerable trick he would play on me. He would gather a load of the sharpest thorns, tie them up and hang them behind me from my tail. When I started on my way, as you might expect, they dashed against me as they hung, pricking and wounding my posterior regions. I could not defend myself against this, for the spikes always followed me and hung to me ; for if I went forward gingerly to guard against the onset of the thorns I was beaten to death by his sticks, while, if I avoided the sticks, then the sharp terror from behind assailed me. In short my driver made it his business to kill me.

31. One day, when I had many woes to suffer and could bear them no longer, I directed a kick at him. This kick he never forgot. Once he had instructions to transfer some flax from one place to another. So he took me, collected a great quantity of the flax and tied it on to my back ; he used a very uncomfortable rope to tie my load on very tight, so as to cook up great torment for me. Well, when we had to set out,

---

4 ἀρξόμενος Γ.
5 ἀπεκρέμνα scripsi: ἀπεκρίμνα Γ: ἀπεκρέμα recc., edd..

101

ἔδει, ἐκ τῆς ἑστίας κλέψας δαλὸν ἔτι θερμόν,
ἐπειδὴ πόρρω τῆς αὐλῆς ἐγενόμεθα, τὸν δαλὸν
ἐνέκρυψεν εἰς τὸ στυππεῖον. τὸ δὲ—τί γὰρ ἄλλο
ἐδύνατο;—εὐθὺς ἀνάπτεται, καὶ λοιπὸν οὐδὲν ἔφερον
ἄλλο ἢ πῦρ ἄπλετον. μαθὼν οὖν ὡς αὐτίκα ὀπτήσο-
μαι, ἐν τῇ ὁδῷ τέλματι βαθεῖ ἐντυχὼν ῥίπτω
ἐμαυτὸν τοῦ τέλματος ἐς τὸ ὑγρότατον· εἶτα ἐκύ-
λιον ἐνταῦθα τὸ στυππεῖον καὶ δινῶν καὶ στρέφων
ἐμαυτὸν τῷ πηλῷ κατέσβεσα τὸ θερμὸν ἐκεῖνο καὶ
πικρὸν ἐμοὶ φορτίον, καὶ οὕτω λοιπὸν ἀκινδυνότερον
ἐβάδιζον τῆς ὁδοῦ τὸ ἐπίλοιπον. οὐδὲ γὰρ ἔτι με
ἀνάψαι τῷ παιδὶ δυνατὸν ἦν τοῦ στυππείου πηλῷ
ὑγρῷ πεφυρμένου. καὶ τοῦτό γε ὁ τολμηρὸς παῖς
ἐλθὼν ἐμοῦ κατεψεύσατο, εἰπὼν ὡς [1] παριὼν ἑκὼν
ἐμαυτὸν ἐνσείσαιμι τῇ ἑστίᾳ. καὶ τότε μὲν ἐκ τοῦ
στυππείου μηδὲ ἐλπίζων ὑπεξῆλθον. 32. ἀλλ'
ἕτερον ὁ ἀκάθαρτος παῖς ἐξεῦρεν ἐπ' ἐμὲ μακρῷ
κάκιον· κομίσας γάρ με ἐς τὸ ὄρος καί μοι φορτίον
ἁδρὸν ἐπιθεὶς ἐκ τῶν ξύλων, τοῦτο μὲν πιπράσκει
γεωργῷ πλησίον οἰκοῦντι, ἐμὲ δὲ γυμνὸν καὶ
ἄξυλον κομίσας οἴκαδε καταψεύδεταί μου πρὸς τὸν
αὐτοῦ [2] δεσπότην ἔργον ἀνόσιον· Τοῦτον, δέσποτα,
τὸν ὄνον οὐκ οἶδ' ὅ τι βόσκομεν δεινῶς ἀργὸν ὄντα
καὶ βραδύν. ἀλλὰ μὴν νῦν ἐπιτηδεύει καὶ ἄλλο
ἔργον· ἐπὰν γυναῖκα παρθένον καλὴν καὶ ὡραίαν
ἴδῃ ἢ παῖδα, ἀπολακτίσας ἕπεται δρόμῳ ἐπ' αὐτούς,
ὡς εἴ τις ἐρᾷ ἄνθρωπος ἄρρην ἐπὶ ἐρωμένῃ γυναικὶ
κινούμενος, καὶ δάκνει ἐν φιλήματος σχήματι καὶ
πλησιάζειν βιάζεται, ἐκ δὲ τούτου σοι δίκας καὶ
πράγματα παρέξει, πάντων ὑβριζομένων, πάντων

he stole a stick while still hot from the fireside, and, when we had gone some distance from the farmhouse, plunged it into the flax. This, as was inevitable, at once started to burn and thereafter my load was one great fire. Perceiving that I would very soon be roasted, and coming upon a deep bog by the wayside, I hurled myself into the wettest part of it. Then I rolled the flax in the bog and twisted and turned till the mud had quenched my nasty scorching load. So in this way I was able to continue the rest of my journey in less danger ; for the boy could no longer set light to me as the flax was mixed with wet mud. After his journey the impudent lad used this episode, too, to malign me, for he said that I had deliberately knocked against the hearth in passing. So that time I escaped from the flax though I little expected it. 32. But the foul lad devised another far worse trick to play me. He took me to the mountain and put on my back a bulky load of wood, which he sold to a neighbouring farmer, but brought me back home without any wood on my back, and falsely accused me before his master of a scandalous deed. "Master, I don't know why we keep this ass, for he's terribly lazy and slow. Furthermore he now has a new habit. Whenever he sees a pretty young woman or a boy, he kicks me away and runs in pursuit of them, like a man in love making advances to his lady ; he bites them with his show of kissing and forces his love on them. Because of this he'll bring you to court and cause you trouble, for he insults everyone and knocks them down. Just now, when he was

---

[1] ὡς om Γ.
[2] αὐτοῦ Du Soul: αὐτὸν codd..

ἀνατρεπομένων. καὶ γὰρ νῦν ξύλα κομίζων γυναῖκα
εἰς ἀγρὸν ἀπιοῦσαν ἰδὼν τὰ μὲν ξύλα πάντα
χαμαὶ ἐσκόρπισεν ἀποσεισάμενος, τὴν δὲ γυναῖκα
ἐς τὴν ὁδὸν ἀνατρέψας γαμεῖν ἐβούλετο, ἕως ἄλλος
ἄλλοθεν ἐκδραμόντες ἤμυναν [1] τῇ γυναικὶ ἐς τὸ μὴ
διασπασθῆναι ὑπὸ τοῦ καλοῦ τούτου ἐραστοῦ.

33. ὁ δὲ ταῦτα πυθόμενος, Ἀλλ' εἰ μήτε βαδίζειν,
ἔφη, ἐθέλει μήτε φορτηγεῖν καὶ ἔρωτας ἀνθρωπίνους
ἐρᾷ ἐπὶ γυναῖκας καὶ παῖδας οἰστρούμενος, ἀποσφά-
ξατε αὐτόν, καὶ τὰ μὲν ἔγκατα τοῖς κυσὶ δότε, τὰ
δὲ κρέα τοῖς ἐργάταις φυλάξατε· καὶ ἢν ἔρηται,
πῶς οὗτος ἀπέθανε, λύκου τοῦτο καταψεύσασθε.

ὁ μὲν οὖν ἀκάθαρτος παῖς ἐμὸς ὀνηλάτης ἔχαιρε
καὶ με αὐτίκα ἤθελεν ἀποσφάττειν. ἀλλ' ἔτυχε γάρ
τις παρὼν τότε τῶν γειτόνων γεωργῶν· οὗτος
ἐρρύσατό με ἐκ τοῦ θανάτου δεινὰ ἐπ' ἐμοὶ βου-
λευσάμενος.

Μηδαμῶς, ἔφη, ἀποσφάξῃς ὄνον καὶ ἀλεῖν καὶ
ἀχθοφορεῖν δυνάμενον· καὶ οὐ μέγα. ἐπειδὴ γὰρ
εἰς ἀνθρώπους ἔρωτι καὶ οἴστρῳ φέρεται,
λαβὼν αὐτὸν ἔκτεμε· τῆς γὰρ ἐπαφροδίτου ταύτης
ὁρμῆς ἀφαιρεθεὶς ἥμερός τε εὐθὺς καὶ πίων ἔσται
καὶ οἴσει φορτίον μέγα οὐδὲν ἀχθόμενος. εἰ δὲ
αὐτὸς ἀπείρως ἔχεις ταύτης τῆς ἰατρείας, ἀφίξομαι
δεῦρο μεταξὺ τριῶν ἢ τεττάρων ἡμερῶν καί σοι
τοῦτον σωφρονέστερον προβατίου παρέξω τῇ τομῇ.

οἱ μὲν οὖν ἔνδον ἅπαντες ἐπῄνουν τὸν σύμβουλον
ὡς εὖ λέγοι, ἐγὼ δὲ ἤδη ἐδάκρυον ὡς ἀπολέσων
αὐτίκα τὸν ἐν τῷ ὄνῳ ἄνδρα καὶ ζῆν οὐκέτι ἐθέλειν
ἔφην, εἰ γενοίμην εὐνοῦχος· ὥστε καὶ ὅλως
ἀποσιτῆσαι τοῦ λοιποῦ ἐγνώκειν ἢ ῥῖψαι ἑαυτὸν ἐκ

---

[1] ἤμυναμεν reco., edd..

carrying wood, he saw a woman going off into a field ; he shook off all his wood and scattered it over the ground. The woman he knocked down on the road and tried to make love to her, till folk ran up from every side to protect her from being torn apart by this handsome lover."

33. When his master heard this he said, " Well, if he won't walk and won't carry and loves like a human with his frenzy for women and boys, kill him and give his entrails to the dogs, but keep his flesh for our working men ; and, if our owner asks how he died, put the blame on a wolf."

This delighted the vile lad who was my driver and he wanted to kill me at once. But it so happened that one of the neighbouring farmers was present, and he saved me from death by a terrible plan he had for me.

" You certainly mustn't kill an ass," he said, " that can grind corn and carry loads. It's quite easy ; you must take him and castrate him, seeing that he rushes after humans with his mad passion. For the moment he's rid of his romantic inclinations, he'll grow gentle and fat, and carry heavy loads without complaining. If you have no personal experience of this type of surgery, I'll come here in three or four days' time and use my knife to make him gentler than a lamb for you."

The whole household applauded his advice, but I was already in tears at the immediate prospect of losing the manhood in my ass's body, and thought I didn't wish to live any longer if I should become a eunuch. I therefore decided to starve myself to death from that moment or to throw myself from the

105

τοῦ ὄρους, ἔνθα ἐκπεσὼν θανάτῳ οἰκτίστῳ ὁλόκληρος
ἔτι καὶ ἀκέραιος νεκρὸς τεθνήξομαι. 34. ἐπεὶ δὲ ἦν [1]
νὺξ βαθεῖα, ἄγγελός τις ἀπὸ τῆς κώμης ἧκεν εἰς τὸν
ἀγρὸν καὶ τὴν ἔπαυλιν, ταύτην λέγων τὴν νεόνυμφον
κόρην τὴν ὑπὸ τοῖς λῃσταῖς γενομένην καὶ τὸν
ταύτης νυμφίον, περὶ δείλην ὀψίαν ἀμφοτέρους αὐτοὺς ἐν τῷ αἰγιαλῷ περιπατοῦντας, ἐπιπολάσασαν
ἄφνω τὴν θάλασσαν ἁρπάξαι αὐτοὺς καὶ ἀφανεῖς
ποιῆσαι, καὶ τέλος αὐτοῖς τοῦτο τῆς συμφορᾶς καὶ
θανάτου γενέσθαι.   οἱ δὲ οἷα δὴ κεκενωμένης
⟨τῆς⟩ [2] οἰκίας νέων δεσποτῶν ἔγνωσαν μηκέτι
μένειν ἐν τῇ δουλείᾳ, ἀλλὰ πάντα διαρπάσαντες τὰ
ἔνδον φυγῇ ἐσῴζοντο. ὁ δὲ νομεὺς τῶν ἵππων κἀμὲ
παραλαβὼν καὶ πάνθ' ὅσα δυνατὸς συλλαβὼν ἐπι-
κατέδησέ μοι καὶ ταῖς ἵπποις καὶ κτήνεσιν [3] ἄλλοις.
ἐγὼ δὲ ἠχθόμην μὲν φέρων φορτίον ὄνου ἀληθινοῦ,
ἀλλ' οὖν ἄσμενος τὸ ἐμπόδιον τοῦτο τῆς ἐμῆς
ἐδεξάμην ἐκτομῆς. καὶ τὴν νύκτα ὅλην ἐλθόντες
ὁδὸν ἀργαλέαν καὶ τριῶν ἄλλων ἡμερῶν τὴν ὁδὸν
ἀνύσαντες ἐρχόμεθα ἐς πόλιν τῆς Μακεδονίας
Βέροιαν μεγάλην καὶ πολυάνθρωπον.

35. ἐνταῦθα ἔγνωσαν οἱ ἄγοντες ἡμᾶς ἱδρῦσαι καὶ
ἑαυτούς. καὶ τότε δὴ πρᾶσις ἦν ἡμῶν τῶν κτηνῶν
καὶ κῆρυξ εὔφημος ἐν ἀγορᾷ μέσῃ ἑστὼς ἐκήρυττεν.
οἱ δὲ προσιόντες ἰδεῖν ἤθελον τὰ στόματα ἡμῶν
ἀνοίγοντες καὶ τὴν ἡλικίαν ἐν τοῖς ὀδοῦσιν ἑκάστῳ
ἔβλεπον, καὶ τοὺς μὲν ὠνήσαντο ἄλλος ἄλλον, ἐμὲ
δὲ ὕστατον ἀπολελειμμένον [4] ὁ κῆρυξ ἐκέλευεν
αὖθις ἐπάγειν [5] ἐς οἶκον. Ὁρᾷς, ἔφη, οὗτος μόνος

---

[1] ἦν om. Γ.   [2] τῆς supplet Courier.

mountain, where, though hurled to a most miserable death, I could lie dead with my body whole and unmutilated.

34. When it was now dead of night, a messenger came from the village to our farmhouse with news about the young bride who had been the prisoner of the robbers, and her bridegroom. He said that, while they had been walking on the shore late in the evening, the sea had suddenly risen and snatched them out of sight, and that their lives had thus ended in tragic death. Since the household had lost its young master and mistress, they decided no longer to remain in captivity, but ransacked the whole house and escaped with their loot. The keeper of the horses took me and seizing everything he could, tied it on to the mares, the other animals, and me. Though I was annoyed at having to carry the load of a real ass, I welcomed this reprieve from castration. All night long we followed a difficult route and after three further days' journey we reached Beroea, a large and populous city of Macedonia.

35. There our drivers decided to settle themselves and us, and we animals were then offered for sale by a stentorian auctioneer who stood shouting in the middle of the marketplace. Those who approached wanted to open and inspect our mouths, and looked at the teeth of each of us to see our ages. The others were bought by various people, but I alone was left and the auctioneer told them to take me back home,

---

³ κτήνεσιν L. A. Post: Γ ex ???σιν in ἄγει σὺν ut vid. man. rec. corrigere voluit: ✱ ✱ ✱ ✱ (= spatium fere quattuor litterarum) ἦσιν N : καὶ . . . ἄλλοις om. recc., edd.: cf. aliorum iumentorum, Apuleius 8.15.   ⁴ ὑπολελειμμένον recc., edd..

⁵ ἀπάγειν N : ἐπανάγειν recc., edd..

οὐχ εὕρηκε κύριον. ἡ δὲ πολλὰ πολλάκις δινουμένη
καὶ μεταπίπτουσα Νέμεσις ἤγαγεν κἀμοὶ τὸν
δεσπότην, οἷον οὐκ ἂν εὐξάμην.¹ κίναιδος γὰρ καὶ
γέρων ἦν τούτων εἷς τῶν τὴν θεὸν τὴν Συρίαν εἰς τὰς
κώμας καὶ τοὺς ἀγροὺς περιφερόντων καὶ τὴν θεὸν
ἐπαιτεῖν ἀναγκαζόντων. τούτῳ πιπράσκομαι πολλῆς πάνυ τιμῆς, τριάκοντα δραχμῶν· καὶ στένων
ἤδη τῷ δεσπότῃ εἱπόμην ἄγοντι.

36. ἐπεὶ δὲ ἥκομεν ἔνθα ᾤκει Φίληβος—τοῦτο
γὰρ εἶχεν ὄνομα ὁ ὠνησάμενός με—μέγα εὐθὺς πρὸ
τῆς θύρας ἀνέκραγεν, Ὦ κοράσια, δοῦλον ὑμῖν
ἐώνημαι καλὸν καὶ ἁδρὸν καὶ Καππαδόκην τὸ
γένος. ἦσαν δὲ τὰ κοράσια ταῦτα ὄχλος κιναίδων
συνεργῶν τοῦ Φιλήβου, καὶ πάντες πρὸς τὴν βοὴν
ἀνεκρότησαν· ᾤοντο γὰρ ἀληθῶς ἄνθρωπον εἶναι
τὸν ἐωνημένον. ὡς δὲ εἶδον ὄνον ὄντα τὸν δοῦλον,
ἤδη ταῦτα ἐς τὸν Φίληβον ἔσκωπτον, Τοῦτον οὐ
δοῦλον, ἀλλὰ νυμφίον σαυτῇ πόθεν ἄγεις λαβοῦσα;
ὄναιο δὲ τούτων τῶν καλῶν γάμων καὶ τέκοις
ταχέως ἡμῖν πώλους τοιούτους.

¹ εὐξάμην Γ: εὐξαίμην cett., edd..

---

[1] The goddess who allots everyone his share of good and
bad fortune. "ἡ . . . δινουμένη " could be a quotation from
a lost play.
[2] Atargatis. See vol. IV, pp. 337 ff., and Harmon's
notes. Cf. Babrius 137 for a similar description of an ass
in the employ of Galli.
[3] Although Lucius is the last to be sold, the comment that
30 drachmas was a large price should be regarded as
serious rather than ironic. In the parallel passage,
Apuleius 8.24-25, Philebus, on hearing that the ass is a
Cappadocian, eagerly pays 17 denarii, the full price asked.

saying, " This one alone, as you see, hasn't found a master." But Nemesis,[1] the goddess who ever twists and changes so much, brought me a master too, though not the sort I would have chosen. For he was an old catamite and one of those who take the Syrian goddess[2] around the villages and countryside and compel the goddess to beg alms. To this man was I sold for the princely[3] sum of thirty drachmas, and with a heavy heart I now followed my new master.

36. When we came to the house of Philebus[4]—for that was the name of my purchaser—he at once raised a loud shout in front of the doors, " Girlies, I've bought you a handsome sturdy slave of Cappadocian stock.[5] " Now these " girlies " were a bevy of catamites who plied the same trade as Philebus, and they all clapped their hands at his words, for they all thought that the purchase really was a man. When they saw that the slave was an ass, they all jeered at Philebus, saying, " That's no slave you have there but a bridegroom for yourself. Where did you get him ? I hope this glorious match proves an asset[6] to you and you soon breed foals like the father."

Cf. c. 46 where Lucius is sold for 25 Attic drachmas (or 11 denarii in Apuleius). Presumably therefore the drachmas of this passage are more valuable than the Attic drachmas of c. 46.

[4] Philebus = Love-youth (The Rev. Love-Boyes).

[5] Cappadocia was noted for its fine horses and pack-animals. This passage is a further indication that *The Ass* is an epitome of another version, as we are not told (as we are in Apuleius) how Philebus knows that the ass is from Cappadocia.

[6] There may be a pun on ὄνος and ὄναιο here as perhaps also in *Dialogues of the Courtesans* 14.4.

37. καὶ οἱ μὲν ἐγέλων. τῇ δὲ ὑστεραίᾳ συνετάτ
τοντο ἐπ᾽ ἔργον, ὥσπερ αὐτοὶ ἔλεγον, καὶ τὴν θεὸν
ἐνσκευασάμενοι ἐμοὶ ἐπέθηκαν. εἶτα ἐκ τῆς πόλεως
ἐξηλαύνομεν καὶ τὴν χώραν περιῄειμεν. ἐπὰν δ᾽
εἰς κώμην τινὰ εἰσέλθοιμεν, ἐγὼ μὲν ὁ θεοφόρητος
ἱστάμην, ὁ δὲ αὐλητὴς ἐφύσα ὅμιλος ἔνθεον, οἱ δὲ
τὰς μίτρας ἀπορρίψαντες τὴν κεφαλὴν κάτωθεν ἐκ
τοῦ αὐχένος εἰλίσσοντες τοῖς ξίφεσιν ἐτέμνοντο
τοὺς πήχεις καὶ τὴν γλῶτταν τῶν ὀδόντων ὑπερβάλ
λων ἕκαστος ἔτεμνε καὶ ταύτην, ὥστε ἐν ἀκαρεῖ
πάντα πεπλῆσθαι μαλακοῦ αἵματος. ἐγὼ δὲ ταῦτα
ὁρῶν τὰ πρῶτα ἔτρεμον ἑστώς, μή ποτε χρεία τῇ
θεῷ καὶ ὀνείου αἵματος γένοιτο. ἐπειδὰν δὲ κατα
κόψειαν οὕτως ἑαυτούς, ἐκ τῶν περιεστηκότων θεατῶν
συνέλεγον ὀβολοὺς καὶ δραχμάς· ἄλλος ἰσχάδας καὶ
οἴνου κάδον καὶ τυροὺς [1] ἐπέδωκε καὶ πυρῶν [2] μέδιμ
νον καὶ κριθῶν τῷ ὄνῳ. οἱ δὲ ἐκ τούτων ἐτρέφοντο
καὶ τὴν ἐπ᾽ ἐμοὶ κομιζομένην θεὸν ἐθεράπευον.

38. καί ποτε εἰς κώμην τινὰ αὐτῶν εἰσβαλόντων
ἡμῶν νεανίσκον τῶν κωμητῶν μέγαν ἀγρεύσαντες
εἰσάγουσιν εἴσω ἔνθα καταλύοντες ἔτυχον. ἔπειτα
ἔπασχον ἐκ τοῦ κωμήτου ὅσα συνήθη καὶ φίλα [3]
τοιούτοις ἀνοσίοις κιναίδοις ἦν. ἐγὼ δὲ ὑπεραλγή
σας ἐπὶ τῇ ἐμαυτοῦ μεταβολῇ, Καὶ μέχρι νῦν
ἀνέχομαι κακῶν, ἀναβοῆσαι, ὦ Ζεῦ σχέτλιε, ἠθέ
λησα, ἀλλ᾽ ἡ μὲν φωνὴ οὐκ ἀνέβη μοι ἡ ἐμή, ἀλλ᾽
ἡ τοῦ ὄνου ἐκ τοῦ φάρυγγος, καὶ μέγα ὠγκησά
μην. τῶν δὲ κωμητῶν τινες ἔτυχον τότε ὄνον
ἀπολωλεκότες, καὶ τὸν ἀπολωλότα ζητοῦντες

---

[1] οἴνου κάδον καὶ τυροὺς ex Courierio scripsi: οἴνον καὶ τυροῦ κάδον codd..   [2] πυροῦ recc., edd..   [3] φίλια recc., edd..

37. So saying, they laughed. But on the next day they mustered for work, as they themselves called it, dressed up the goddess and put her on my back. Then we rode out of that city and went round the country. Whenever we came to a village, I, the bearer of the goddess, would stand still, while the company of pipers would blow their frenzied tunes, and the others would throw off their turbans, drop their heads and twist them round on their necks; they would cut their forearms with their swords, and each would stick his tongue out from his teeth and cut it, so that within a moment everything was full of effeminate blood. When I saw this, at first I would stand there trembling with the fear that the goddess might also need asses' blood. Whenever they cut themselves thus, they would make a copper and silver collection among the spectators standing around. Others gave them dried figs, cheeses, jars of wine and bushels of wheat and barley for the ass. From these they supported themselves and looked after the goddess who rode on my back.

38. One day when we had invaded a village of that country, they hunted down a lusty young villager and brought him into the place where they were staying. Then they got from the villager the sort of treatment habitually popular with such foul catamites. This caused me inordinate distress at my changed shape and I wanted to cry out, " Cruel Jupiter, to think that my sufferings have come to this ! " But it was not my voice but that of the ass which rose from my throat and I produced a loud bray. Now it happened that some of the villagers were looking for an ass which they had just lost.

111

ἀκούσαντές μου μέγα ἀναβοήσαντος παρέρχονται
εἴσω οὐδενὶ οὐδὲν εἰπόντες ὡς ἐμοῦ τοῦ ἐκείνων
ὄντος, καὶ καταλαμβάνουσι τοὺς κιναίδους ἄρρητα
ἔνδον ἐργαζομένους· καὶ γέλως ἐκ τῶν ἐπεισελθόν-
των πολὺς γίνεται. ἔξω ἐκδραμόντες ὅλῃ τῇ
κώμῃ τῷ λόγῳ διέδωκαν τῶν ἱερέων τὴν ἀσέλγειαν.
οἱ δὲ αἰδούμενοι δεινῶς ταῦτα ἐληλεγμένα τῆς
ἐπιούσης νυκτὸς εὐθὺς [1] ἔνθεν ἐξήλασαν, καὶ ἐπειδὴ
ἐγένοντο ἐν τῇ ἐρήμῳ τῆς ὁδοῦ ἐχαλέπαινον καὶ
ὠργίζοντο ἐμοὶ τῷ μηνύσαντι τὰ ἐκείνων μυστήρια.
καὶ τοῦτο μὲν ἀνεκτὸν τὸ δεινὸν ἦν, κακῶς τῷ λόγῳ
ἀκούειν, ἀλλὰ τὰ μετὰ τοῦτο οὐκέτ' ἀνεκτά· τὴν
γὰρ θεὸν ἀφελόντες μου καὶ χαμαὶ καταθέμενοι καὶ
τὰ στρώματά μου πάντα περισπάσαντες γυμνὸν ἤδη
προσδέουσί με δένδρῳ μεγάλῳ, εἶτα ἐκείνῃ τῇ ἐκ
τῶν ἀστραγάλων μάστιγι παίοντες ὀλίγον [2] ἐδέησαν
ἀποκτεῖναι, κελεύοντές με τοῦ λοιποῦ ἄφωνον εἶναι
θεοφόρητον. καὶ μὴν καὶ ἀποσφάξαι μετὰ τὰς
μάστιγας ἐβουλεύσαντο ὡς ἐς ὕβριν αὐτοὺς βαλόντα
πολλὴν καὶ τῆς κώμης οὐκ ἐργασαμένους ἐκβαλόντα·
ἀλλ' ὥστε με μὴ ἀποκτεῖναι, δεινῶς αὐτοὺς ἡ
θεὸς ἐδυσώπησεν χαμαὶ καθημένη καὶ οὐκ ἔχουσα
ὅπως ὁδεύοι.

39. ἐντεῦθεν οὖν μετὰ τὰς μάστιγας λαβὼν
τὴν δέσποιναν ἐβάδιζον καὶ πρὸς ἑσπέραν ἤδη

---

[1] εὐθὺς om. recc., edd..   [2] ὀλίγου Peletier.

Upon hearing my loud bray, assuming that I was their property, they came in without a word to anyone and surprised the catamites at their unmentionable practices inside. This occasioned much laughter amongst the intruders, who then ran out and spread reports of the priests' lewdness throughout the whole village. But they were terribly ashamed at the exposure of these practices of theirs and without delay left the place that night. When they had reached a lonely part of the road, they began to express their angry rage at me as the betrayer of their rites. This terrible abuse of theirs I could stand, but what followed was no longer tolerable ; for, after they had taken the goddess from my back and put her on the ground, they stripped off all my trappings, and tied me now naked to a large tree. Then they flogged me with that knuckle-bone [1] whip of theirs till they had almost killed me, and told me thereafter to carry the goddess in silence. Moreover they had planned to kill me after my flogging, because I had brought such insults upon them and had had them driven from the village before they had finished their business, but I was saved from death by the goddess, for she made them feel terribly ashamed of leaving her sitting on the ground without means of travelling.

39. After my flogging, therefore, I took up the goddess and continued the journey. When it was

---

[1] The word ἐκείνη in this passage is one of the clearest indications we have that the " *Asinus* " is an epitome of a larger original. The parallel passage in Apuleius (8.30) has " flagro *illo* pecuinis ossibus catenato "; Apuleius, however, had already described the whip in 8.28 as " with many twisted knots and tassels of wool, and strung with sheep's knuckle-bones."

113

καταλύομεν εἰς ἀγρὸν πλουτοῦντος ἀνθρώπου. καὶ ἦν
οὗτος ἔνδον καὶ τὴν θεὸν μάλα ἄσμενος τῇ οἰκίᾳ
ὑπεδέξατο καὶ θυσίας αὐτῇ προσήγαγεν. ἐνθάδε [1]
οἶδα μέγαν κίνδυνον αὐτὸς ὑποστάς· τῶν φίλων
γάρ [2] τις τῷ δεσπότῃ τῶν ἀγρῶν ἔπεμψε δῶρον ὄνου
ἀγρίου μηρόν· τοῦτον ὁ μάγειρος σκευάσαι λαβὼν
ῥᾳθυμίᾳ ἀπώλεσεν, κυνῶν πολλῶν λαθραίως εἴσω
παρελθόντων· ὃς δεδιὼς πληγὰς πολλὰς καὶ βάσανον
ἐκ τῆς ἀπωλείας τοῦ μηροῦ ἔγνω κρεμάσαι αὐτὸν ἐκ
τοῦ τραχήλου. ἡ δὲ γυνὴ ἡ τούτου, κακὸν ἐξαίσιον
ἐμόν, Ἀλλὰ μήτε ἀπόθνησκε, εἶπεν, ὦ φίλτατε,
μήτε ἀθυμίᾳ τοιαύτῃ [3] δῷς σεαυτόν· πειθόμενος
γάρ μοι πράξεις εὖ πάντα. τῶν κιναίδων τὸν ὄνον
λαβὼν ἔξω εἰς ἔρημον χωρίον κἄπειτα σφάξας
αὐτὸν τὸ μέρος μὲν ἐκεῖνο τὸν μηρὸν ἀποτεμὼν
κόμιζε δεῦρο καὶ κατασκευάσας [4] τῷ δεσπότῃ
ἀπόδος καὶ τὸ ἄλλο τοῦ ὄνου κάτω που ἐς κρημνὸν
ἄφες· δόξει γὰρ ἀποδρὰς οἴχεσθαί ποι καὶ εἶναι
ἀφανής. ὁρᾷς δὲ ὡς ἔστιν εὔσαρκος [5] καὶ τοῦ
ἀγρίου ἐκείνου πάντα ἀμείνων.

ὁ δὲ μάγειρος τῆς γυναικὸς ἐπαινέσας τὸ βούλευμα,
Ἄριστα, ἔφη, σοι, ὦ γύναι, ταῦτα, καὶ τούτῳ μόνῳ
τῷ ἔργῳ τὰς μάστιγας φυγεῖν ἔχω, καὶ τοῦτό μοι
ἤδη πεπράξεται.

ὁ μὲν οὖν ἀνόσιος οὗτος οὑμὸς μάγειρος ἐμοῦ
πλησίον ἑστὼς τῇ γυναικὶ ταῦτα συνεβουλεύετο.
40. ἐγὼ δὲ τὸ μέλλον ἤδη προορώμενος κράτιστον
ἔγνων τὸ σῴζειν ἐμαυτὸν ἐκ τῆς καινίδος [6] καὶ
ῥήξας τὸν ἱμάντα ᾧ διηγόμην καὶ ἀνασκιρτήσας
ἵεμαι δρόμῳ εἴσω ἔνθα ἐδείπνουν οἱ κίναιδοι σὺν τῷ

now about evening, we stopped at a rich man's estate.
He was at home, welcomed the goddess very gladly to
his house, and brought her sacrifices. I was involved
there to my certain knowledge in great personal
danger. For a friend of the landowner had sent him
a ham of wild ass as a gift. The cook had been given
this to prepare, but had lost it through carelessness
when a pack of dogs got in unnoticed. Fearing that
he would be severely beaten and tortured for losing
the ham, he had decided to hang himself, but his wife
proved my evil genius. "Don't kill yourself, dearest"
she said, " don't give in to such despair. For, if you
listen to me, you'll settle all your troubles satis-
factorily. Take the catamites' ass away to a deserted spot and then slit its throat and cut off that piece
—it's the ham—and bring it here, cook it and serve
it to your master, and throw the rest of the ass into
some gully. It will be thought to have run away and
disappeared. Can't you see how plump it is and
superior in every way to that wild ass?"

The cook applauded his wife's plan saying,
" This suggestion of yours is excellent, wife, and my
only means of escaping a flogging. I shall carry it
out right away."

Such, then, was the plan hatched with his wife by
the villain as he stood beside me planning to be *my*
cook. 40. But I, already foreseeing what was coming, decided my best plan was to escape from his
knife. I broke the rope by which I was led, kicked up
my heels and rushed inside where the catamites were

---

¹ ἔνθα δὴ (vel δὲ) Courier.   ² γὰρ om. ΓΝ.
³ ἀθυμίᾳ τοιαύτῃ recc.: ῥᾳθυμίᾳ ταύτῃ ΓΝ.
⁴ σκευάσας ΓΝ.   ⁵ ἔνσαρκος Γ.
⁶ καινίδος Ν: κονίδος cett.: κοπίδος Reitz.

δεσπότῃ τῶν ἀγρῶν. ἐνταῦθα εἰσδραμὼν ἀνατρέπω
πάντα τῷ σκιρτήματι καὶ λυχνίαν καὶ τραπέζας·
κἀγὼ μὲν ᾤμην κομψόν τι τοῦτο πρὸς σωτηρίαν
ἐμὴν εὑρηκέναι, καὶ τὸν δεσπότην τῶν ἀγρῶν
κελεύειν [1] εὐθέως ὡς ἀγέρωχον ὄνον ἐμὲ κατακλει-
σθέντα ποι φυλάττεσθαι ἀσφαλῶς· ἀλλά με τοῦτο
τὸ κομψὸν εἰς ἔσχατον ἤνεγκεν κινδύνου. λυττᾶν
δόξαντές με ξίφη πολλὰ ἤδη καὶ λόγχας ἐπ' ἐμὲ
ἐσπάσαντο καὶ ξύλα μακρά, καὶ εἶχον οὕτως ὥστε
ἀποκτενεῖν με. ἐγὼ δὲ ὁρῶν τοῦ δεινοῦ τὸ μέγεθος
δρόμῳ εἴσω παρέρχομαι ἔνθα οἱ ἐμοὶ δεσπόται
κοιμηθήσεσθαι ἔμελλον. οἱ δὲ θεασάμενοι τοῦτο
συγκλείουσι τὰς θύρας εὖ μάλα ἔξωθεν.

41. ἐπεὶ δὲ ἤδη ὄρθρος ἦν, ἀράμενος τὴν θεὸν
αὖθις ἀπῄειν ἅμα τοῖς ἀγύρταις καὶ ἀφικόμεθα εἰς
κώμην ἄλλην μεγάλην καὶ πολυάνθρωπον, ἐν ᾗ καὶ
καινότερόν τι ἐτερατεύσαντο, τὴν θεὸν μὴ μεῖναι ἐν
ἀνθρώπου οἰκίᾳ, τῆς δὲ παρ' ἐκείνοις μάλιστα
τιμωμένης ἐπιχωρίου δαίμονος τὸν ναὸν οἰκῆσαι.
οἱ δὲ καὶ μάλα ἄσμενοι τὴν ξένην θεὸν ὑπεδέξαντο
τῇ σφῶν αὐτῶν θεῷ συνοικίσαντες, ἡμῖν δὲ οἰκίαν
ἀπέδειξαν ἀνθρώπων πενήτων. ἐνταῦθα συχνὰς
ἡμέρας οἱ δεσπόται διατρίψαντες ἀπιέναι ἤθελον εἰς
τὴν πλησίον πόλιν καὶ τὴν θεὸν ἀπῄτουν τοὺς
ἐπιχωρίους, καὶ αὐτοὶ ἐς τὸ τέμενος παρελθόντες
ἐκομίζοντο [2] αὐτὴν καὶ θέντες ἐπ' ἐμοὶ ἤλαυνον ἔξω.
ἔτυχον δὲ οἱ δυσσεβεῖς εἰς τὸ τέμενος ἐκεῖνο παρελθόντες ἀνάθημα φιάλην χρυσῆν κλέψαντες, ἣν [3] ὑπὸ
τῇ θεῷ ἔφερον· οἱ δὲ κωμῆται αἰσθόμενοι τοῦτο

---

[1] κελεύσειν L. A. Post.

dining with the landowner. When I ran in, I
knocked over light, tables and all with my kicking
heels. I thought I had thus found a clever way to
safety, and that the landowner would immediately
order me to be kept safely locked up as being a high-
spirited ass. But this clever plan brought me into
extreme danger. For they now thought me mad,
brought out swords galore and spears and long
sticks to attack me, and prepared to kill me. When
I saw my great danger, I rushed into the room where
my masters would be sleeping. When they saw this,
they closed the doors of the room securely from the
outside.

41. When it was now dawn, I took the goddess up
again and left with the mountebanks. We reached
another large and populous village, where they
introduced a fresh monstrosity by insisting that the
goddess should not stay in the house of a human
but take up residence in the temple of the local
goddess held in most honour amongst them. They
were very glad to welcome the foreign goddess and
gave her accommodation along with their own
goddess, but assigned us to the house of some
paupers. After they had spent many days there,
my masters wished to leave for the nearby city and
asked the goddess back from the local people. They
entered the sacred precinct themselves, carried her
out, put her on my back and rode off. Now when the
impious fellows entered that precinct, they stole a
golden bowl, a votive offering. This they carried
off concealed in the person of the goddess. When the
villagers discovered this, they gave immediate

---

² ἐκόμιζον recc., edd..   ³ ἦν om. Γ.

εὐθὺς ἐδίωκον, εἶτα ὡς πλησίον ἐγένοντο, κατα-
πηδήσαντες ἀπὸ τῶν ἵππων εἴχοντο αὐτῶν ἐν τῇ
ὁδῷ καὶ δυσσεβεῖς καὶ ἱεροσύλους ἐκάλουν καὶ
ἀπῄτουν τὸ κλαπὲν ἀνάθημα, καὶ ἐρευνῶντες πάντα
εὗρον αὐτὸ ἐν τῷ κόλπῳ τῆς θεοῦ. δήσαντες
οὖν τοὺς γυναικίας [1] ἦγον ὀπίσω καὶ τοὺς μὲν
εἰς τὴν εἱρκτὴν ἐμβάλλουσι, τὴν δὲ θεὸν τὴν
ἐπ' ἐμοὶ κομιζομένην ἀράμενοι ναῷ ἄλλῳ
ἔδωκαν, τὸ δὲ χρυσίον τῇ πολίτιδι θεῷ πάλιν
ἀπέδωκαν.

42. τῇ δὲ ὑστεραίᾳ τά τε σκεύη κἀμὲ πιπράσκειν
ἔγνωσαν, καὶ ἀπέδοντό με ξένῳ ἀνθρώπῳ τὴν πλησίον κώμην οἰκοῦντι, τέχνην ἔχοντι ἄρτους πέττειν·
οὗτός με παραλαβὼν καὶ πυρῶν μεδίμνους δέκα
ὠνησάμενος, ἐπιθείς μοι τὸν πυρὸν οἴκαδε ἤλαυνεν
ὡς ἑαυτὸν ὁδὸν ἀργαλέαν· ὡς δὲ ἤκομεν, εἰσάγει με
εἰς τὸν μυλῶνα, καὶ ὁρῶ πολὺ πλῆθος ἔνδον ὁμοδού-
λων κτηνῶν, καὶ μύλαι πολλαὶ ἦσαν, καὶ πᾶσαι
τούτοις ἐστρέφοντο, καὶ πάντα ἐκεῖνα μεστὰ ἦν
ἀλεύρων. καὶ τότε μέν με οἷα ξένον δοῦλον καὶ
φορτίον βαρύτατον ἀράμενον καὶ ὁδὸν ἀργαλέαν
ἀφιγμένον ἀναπαύεσθαι ἔνδον ἀφῆκαν, τῇ δὲ
ὑστεραίᾳ ὀθόνῃ τὰ ὄμματά μου ἐμπετάσαντες [2]
ὑποζευγνύουσί με τῇ κώπῃ τῆς μύλης, εἶτα ἤλαυνον.
ἐγὼ δὲ ἠπιστάμην ὅπως χρὴ ἀλεῖν πολλάκις παθών,
προσεποιούμην δὲ ἀγνοεῖν· ἀλλὰ μάτην ἤλπισα.
λαβόντες γὰρ πολλοὶ τῶν ἔνδον βακτηρίας περι-
ίστανταί με καὶ μὴ προσδοκήσαντα, ὡς οὐχ ὁρῶντα,
παίουσιν ἀθρόᾳ τῇ χειρί, ὥστε με ὑπὸ τῆς πληγῆς
ὥσπερ στρόμβον ἐξαπίνης στρέφεσθαι· καὶ πείρᾳ

pursuit ; then, upon drawing near, they leapt down from their horses and laid hold of the fellows in the road, calling them impious and sacrilegious, and demanding the return of the stolen offering. They searched everywhere and found it in the bosom of the goddess. They therefore tied up the effeminate fellows, dragged them off and threw them into prison ; the goddess whom I had carried they took and gave to another temple, while the golden vessel they gave back to their local goddess.

42. The next day they decided to offer the prisoners' effects, myself included, for sale ; and I was bought by a foreigner who lived in the neighbouring village and was a baker by trade. He took men, loaded me with ten bushels of corn which he'd bought and drove me to his house along a difficult road. When we arrived, he took me to his millhouse, where I saw a great number of animals whose fellow slave I was to be ; there were many mills all being turned by the animals and everything was full of flour. For the time being they let me rest there, as I was a new slave and had had a very heavy load to carry and a difficult road to cover. The next day, however, they blindfolded me, harnessed me to the beam of the mill and started me off. Though I knew from long experience how to grind, I pretended not to know, but my hopes were disappointed. For many of the millers took sticks and stood around me and surprised me, for I couldn't see, by smacking me all together, so that I suddenly started to spin like a top from their blows. Thus I learnt by experience that

---

[1] γυναικίας N: γυνίας ΓΨC Vat. 87: γύννιδας Jacobitz.
[2] σκεπάσαντες recc., edd..

ἔμαθον ὅτι χρὴ τὸν δοῦλον ἐς τὸ τὰ δέοντα ποιεῖν
μὴ περιμένειν τοῦ δεσπότου τὴν χεῖρα.

43. λεπτὸς οὖν πάνυ γίνομαι καὶ ἀσθενὴς τῷ
σώματι, ὥστε ἔγνω με ὁ δεσπότης πωλῆσαι, καὶ
ἀποδίδοταί με ἀνθρώπῳ κηπουρῷ τὴν τέχνην·
οὗτος γὰρ εἶχε κῆπον λαβὼν γεωργεῖν. καὶ τοῦτο
εἴχομεν ἔργον· ὁ δὲ[1] δεσπότης ἔωθεν[2] ἐπιθείς μοι
τὰ λάχανα ἐκόμιζεν εἰς τὴν ἀγοράν, καὶ παραδοὺς
τοῖς ταῦτα πιπράσκουσιν ἦγέ με πάλιν εἰς τὸν
κῆπον. εἶτα ἐκεῖνος μὲν καὶ ἔσκαπτε καὶ ἐφύτευε
καὶ τὸ ὕδωρ τῷ φυτῷ ἐπῆγεν, ἐγὼ δὲ ἐν τούτῳ
εἱστήκειν ἀργός. ἦν δέ μοι δεινῶς ἀλγεινὸς ὁ τότε
βίος, πρῶτον μὲν ἐπεὶ χειμὼν ἤδη ἦν κἀκεῖνος οὐδὲ
αὑτῷ στρῶμα εἶχεν ἀγοράσαι οὐχ ὅπως ἐμοί, καὶ
ἀνυπόδητος πηλὸν ὑγρὸν καὶ πάγον[3] σκληρὸν καὶ
ὀξὺν ἐπάτουν, καὶ τὸ φαγεῖν τοῦτο μόνον ἀμφοτέροις ἦν θρίδακας πικρὰς καὶ σκληράς. 44. καί ποτε
ἐξιόντων ἡμῶν εἰς τὸν κῆπον[4] ἐντυγχάνει ἀνὴρ
γενναῖος στρατιώτου στολὴν ἠμφιεσμένος, καὶ τὰ
μὲν πρῶτα λαλεῖ πρὸς ἡμᾶς τῇ Ἰταλῶν φωνῇ καὶ
ἤρετο τὸν κηπουρὸν ὅποι ἀπάγει τὸν ὄνον ἐμέ· ὁ δέ,
οἶμαι, τῆς φωνῆς ἀνόητος ὢν οὐδὲν ἀπεκρίνατο· ὁ δὲ
ὀργιζόμενος, ὡς ὑπερορώμενος, παίει τῇ μάστιγι
τὸν κηπουρόν, κἀκεῖνος συμπλέκεται αὐτῷ καὶ ἐκ
τῶν ποδῶν εἰς τὴν ὁδὸν ὑποσπάσας ἐκτείνει, καὶ
κείμενον ἔπαιεν οὕτω καὶ χειρὶ καὶ ποδὶ καὶ λίθῳ
τῷ ἐκ τῆς ὁδοῦ· ὁ δὲ τὰ πρῶτα καὶ ἀντεμάχετο καὶ
ἠπείλει, εἰ ἀνασταίη, ἀποκτενεῖν τῇ μαχαίρᾳ· ὁ δὲ

---

[1] δὲ om. recc., edd..   [2] ἔξωθεν Γ.
[3] πάγον Dobree: πάνυ Γ: πάλιν Ν.

a slave should do his duty without waiting for his master's hand.

43. Thus I became very thin and weak so that my master decided to sell me. I was bought from him by a nurseryman, who had a market garden to cultivate. Let me tell you about our work. At dawn my master would load me with vegetables and take them to market; when he had delivered them to the greengrocers, he would take me back to the nursery; then he would dig, plant and water while I stood idle. However life was terribly hard for me; in the first place it was now winter, and he could not afford bedding for himself, much less for me, and I had to tread unshod on damp clay or hard, sharp ice, while all that either of us had to eat was bitter, rough lettuces.

44. One day as we were going out to the nursery, we met a gentleman in military uniform who addressed us at first [1] in Latin and asked the nurseryman where he was taking me, the ass. He made no reply, because, I suppose, he didn't understand that language. The soldier, angry at an imagined insult, used his whip to strike the nurseryman who then grappled with him, tripped him up and sent him sprawling on the road. He then struck at him just as he lay, using his fists and his feet and a stone from the road. At first the soldier resisted and threatened to kill him with his sword, if ever he got to his feet again. As though warned by the soldier's own

---

[1] Faulty epitomising again. " At first " is kept from the original version. In Apuleius 9.39 the soldier tries first Latin and then Greek.

---

[4] τὸν κῆπον codd.: τὴν πόλιν Courier.

ὥσπερ ὑπ᾽ αὐτοῦ ἐκείνου διδαχθείς, τὸ ἀκινδυνότα-
τον, σπᾷ τὴν μάχαιραν αὐτοῦ καὶ ῥιπτεῖ πόρρω,
εἶτα αὖθις ἔπαιε κείμενον. ὁ δὲ τὸ κακὸν ὁρῶν ἤδη
ἀφόρητον ψεύδεται ὡς τεθνηκὼς ἐν ταῖς πληγαῖς·
ὁ δὲ δείσας ἐπὶ τούτῳ τὸν μὲν αὐτοῦ ὡς εἶχε κείμενον ἀπολείπει, τὴν δὲ μάχαιραν βαστάσας ἐπ᾽ [1] ἐμοὶ
ἤλαυνεν ἐς τὴν [2] πόλιν.

45. ὡς δὲ ἤλθομεν, τὸν μὲν κῆπον αὐτοῦ συνεργῷ
τινι ἐπέδωκεν γεωργεῖν, αὐτὸς δὲ τὸν κίνδυνον τὸν
ἐκ τῆς ὁδοῦ δεδιὼς κρύπτεται ἅμα ἐμοὶ πρός τινος
τῶν ἐν ἄστει συνήθων. τῇ δὲ ὑστεραίᾳ, δόξαν
αὐτοῖς, οὕτω ποιοῦσιν· τὸν μὲν ἐμὸν δεσπότην
κιβωτῷ ἐνέκρυψαν, ἐμὲ δὲ ἀράμενοι ἐκ τῶν ποδῶν
κομίζουσιν ἄνω τῇ κλίμακι ἐς οἴκημα [3] ὑπερῷον
κἀκεῖ με ἄνω συγκλείουσιν. ὁ δὲ στρατιώτης ἐκ
τῆς ὁδοῦ ποτε [4] μόλις ἐξαναστάς, ὡς ἔφασαν, καρη-
βαρῶν ταῖς πληγαῖς ἧκεν εἰς τὴν πόλιν καὶ τοῖς
στρατιώταις τοῖς σὺν αὐτῷ ἐντυχὼν λέγει τὴν ἀπό-
νοιαν τοῦ κηπουροῦ· οἱ δὲ σὺν αὐτῷ ἐλθόντες μανθά-
νουσιν ἔνθα ἦμεν κεκρυμμένοι, καὶ παραλαμβάνουσι
τοὺς τῆς πόλεως ἄρχοντας. οἱ δὲ εἴσω τινὰ τῶν
ὑπηρετῶν πέμπουσι καὶ τοὺς ἔνδον ἅπαντας
προελθεῖν ἔξω κελεύουσιν· ὡς δὲ προῆλθον, ὁ
κηπουρὸς οὐδαμοῦ ἐφαίνετο. οἱ μὲν οὖν στρατιῶται
ἔνδον ἔφασαν εἶναι τὸν κηπουρὸν κἀμὲ τὸν ἐκείνου
ὄνον· οἱ δὲ οὐδὲν ἄλλο ὑπολελεῖφθαι ἔλεγον οὔτε
ἄνθρωπον οὔτε ὄνον. θορύβου δὲ ἐν τῷ στενωπῷ καὶ
πολλῆς βοῆς ἐκ τούτων γινομένης [5] ὁ ἀγέρωχος
καὶ πάντα περίεργος ἐγὼ βουλόμενος μαθεῖν τίνες
εἶεν οἱ βοῶντες, διακύπτω ἄνωθεν κάτω διὰ τῆς

words, my master chose the safest course, drew the
soldier's sword and threw it a long way off, before
starting once again to pound his prostrate foe, who
now saw that he could bear it no longer and pretended
he had been killed by the blows. My master, terrified
at this, left him lying there just as he was, but gave
me the sword to carry and went off to the city.

45. When we got there, he gave his nursery to a
colleague to work, while he himself, fearing the risk
of returning by the road, got one of his friends in the
town to hide the two of us. Next day they adopted
the following plan ; they hid my master in a chest,
while they carried me by the feet up a ladder to a
loft, in which they shut me up. The soldier had
eventually struggled to his feet, as they told us, and,
dizzy with his blows, had reached the city, where he
met his messmates and told them of the desperate
conduct of the nurseryman. They went with the
soldier and discovered our hiding-place. They then
fetched the magistrates of the city, who sent in one
of their constables and ordered all the inmates to
come out. When they emerged, there was no sign of
the nurseryman. The soldiers therefore insisted that
he was inside along with me, his ass. The inmates
however maintained that nothing, whether man or
ass, was still left in the house. As this was occasion-
ing great noise and much shouting in the gateway, I,
headstrong, inquisitive creature, wished to find out
who the shouters were, and poked my head down
through the window. The soldiers saw me and

---

¹ ἐπ᾽ om. Γ.   ² τὴν om. ΓΝ.
³ οἴκημα om. recc., edd..
⁴ ποτε Courier: τότε codd..
⁵ γενομένης recc., edd..

θυρίδος. οἱ δέ με ἰδόντες εὐθὺς ἀνέκραγον· οἱ δὲ
ἑαλώκεσαν ψευδῆ λέγοντες· καὶ οἱ ἄρχοντες εἴσω
παρελθόντες καὶ πάντα ἀνερευνῶντες εὑρίσκουσιν
τὸν ἐμὸν δεσπότην τῇ κιβωτῷ ἐγκείμενον καὶ
λαβόντες τὸν μὲν εἰς τὸ δεσμωτήριον ἔπεμψαν
λόγον τῶν τετολμημένων ὑφέξοντα, ἐμὲ δὲ κάτω
βαστάσαντες τοῖς στρατιώταις παρέδοσαν. πάντες
δὲ ἄσβεστον ἐγέλων ἐπὶ τῷ μηνύσαντι ἐκ τῶν
ὑπερῴων καὶ προδόντι τὸν ἑαυτοῦ δεσπότην· κἀκ
τότε ἐξ ἐμοῦ πρώτου ἦλθεν εἰς ἀνθρώπους ὁ λόγος
οὗτος, Ἐξ ὄνου παρακύψεως.

46. τῇ δὲ ὑστεραίᾳ τί μὲν ἔπαθεν ὁ κηπουρὸς ὁ
ἐμὸς δεσπότης, οὐκ οἶδα, ὁ δὲ στρατιώτης πωλήσειν
με ἔγνω, καὶ πιπράσκει με πέντε καὶ εἴκοσιν
Ἀττικῶν· ὁ δὲ ὠνησάμενος θεράπων ἦν ἀνδρὸς
σφόδρα πλουσίου πόλεως τῶν ἐν Μακεδονίᾳ τῆς
μεγίστης Θεσσαλονίκης. οὗτος τέχνην εἶχε ταύτην,
τὰ ὄψα τῷ δεσπότῃ ἐσκεύαζεν, καὶ εἶχεν καὶ
ἀδελφὸν σύνδουλον ἄρτους πέττειν καὶ μελίπηκτα
κιρνᾶν ἐπιστάμενον. οὗτοι οἱ ἀδελφοὶ σύσκηνοί τε
ἀεὶ ἦσαν ἀλλήλοις καὶ κατέλυον ἐν ταὐτῷ καὶ τὰ
σκεύη τῶν τεχνῶν εἶχον ἀναμεμιγμένα, καὶ μετὰ
ταῦτα κἀμὲ ἵστασαν ἔνθα κατέλυον. καὶ οὗτοι
μετὰ τὸ δεῖπνον τοῦ δεσπότου πολλὰ λείψανα
ἄμφω εἴσω ἐκόμιζον ὁ μὲν κρεῶν καὶ ἰχθύων, ὁ δὲ
ἄρτων καὶ πλακούντων. οἱ δὲ κατακλείσαντες
ἔνδον ἐμὲ μετὰ τούτων καὶ φυλακὴν ἐμοὶ γλυκυτάτην
περιστήσαντες ἀπῄεσαν ὥστε ἀπολούσασθαι· κἀγὼ
τοῖς παρακειμένοις κριθιδίοις μακρὰ χαίρειν λέγων
ταῖς τέχναις καὶ τοῖς κέρδεσι τῶν δεσποτῶν

mmediately raised a shout, and our friends were
caught out in their lies. The magistrates went in,
searched everywhere and found my master in the
chest. They seized him and sent him off to prison to
await trial for his bold conduct, while I was carried
down by them and handed over to the soldiers. They
all laughed uncontrollably at the one that had turned
informer from the loft and betrayed his own master.
Thus I originated the saying [1] thereafter common
among men, " from the peeping of an ass."

46. What happened to my master I can't say, but
the next day the soldier decided he would sell me, and
I fetched twenty-five Attic drachmas.[2] My purchaser was the servant of a very wealthy man from
Thessalonica, the largest city in Macedonia. This
man's business was to cook the meat for his master
and he also had as his fellowslave his brother, who
was skilled in baking bread and making honeycakes.
These brothers were always messmates, lodging in
the same place and keeping the tools of their trades
together. Thereafter they established me with them
in their quarters. After their master's dinner they
would both bring in many left-overs, one of them of
meat and fish, the other of bread and cakes. They
used to shut me up with all this and go off to have a
bath, leaving a most pleasant charge in my protection. I would then say a hearty goodbye to the
barley put out for me and devote myself to the

---

[1] A phrase from Menander's *Priestess* (fr. 246) and
proverbially used according to Zenobius, when men were
sued for ridiculous reasons. See Gaselee's note in
L.C.L. Apuleius, p. 470 and L. C. L. Babrius, p. 516.
[2] Presumably a moderate price; cf. note on c. 35.
The cook no doubt buys Lucius with his own money; cf.
c. 48 *init*.

ἐδίδουν ἐμαυτόν, καὶ διὰ μακροῦ πάνυ ἐγεμιζόμη
ἀνθρωπείου τροφῆς. οἱ δὲ ἀναστρέψαντες εἴσω τ
μὲν πρῶτα οὐδὲν ᾐσθάνοντο τῆς ὀψοφαγίας τῆ
ἐμῆς ἐκ τοῦ πλήθους τῶν παρακειμένων, κἀμο
ἔτι ἐν φόβῳ καὶ φειδοῖ κλέπτοντος τὸ ἄριστο
ἐπεὶ δὲ καὶ τέλεον [1] αὐτῶν καταγνοὺς ἄγνοιαν τὰ
καλλίστας τῶν μερίδων καὶ ἄλλα πολλὰ κατέτρωγο
καὶ ἐπειδὴ ᾔσθοντο ἤδη τῆς ζημίας, τὰ μὲν πρῶτ
ἄμφω ὕποπτον ἐς ἀλλήλους ἔβλεπον καὶ κλέπτην
ἕτερος τὸν ἕτερον καὶ ἅρπαγα τῶν κοινῶν κα
ἀναίσχυντον ἔλεγον, καὶ ἦσαν ἀκριβεῖς λοιπὸν ἄμφ
καὶ τῶν μερίδων ἀριθμὸς ἐγίνετο. 47. ἐγὼ δὲ τὸ
βίον εἶχον ἐν ἡδονῇ καὶ τρυφῇ, καὶ τὸ σῶμά μου ἐ
τῆς συνήθους τροφῆς πάλιν καλὸν ἐγεγόνει καὶ τ
δέρμα ἐπανθούσῃ τῇ τριχὶ ἀπέστιλβεν. οἱ δ
γενναιότατοι μέγαν τέ με καὶ πίονα ὁρῶντες καὶ τ
κριθίδια μὴ δαπανώμενα, ἀλλ᾽ ἐν ταὐτῷ μέτρῳ ὄντα
εἰς ὑπόνοιαν ἔρχονται τῶν τολμημάτων τῶν ἐμῶν
καὶ προελθόντες ὡς εἰς τὸ βαλανεῖον ἀπιόντες
ἔπειτα τὰς θύρας συγκλείσαντες, προσβαλόντε
ὀπῇ τινι τὰ ὄμματα τῆς θύρας ἐσκοποῦντο τἄνδον
κἀγὼ τότε μηδὲν τοῦ δόλου εἰδὼς ἠρίστων προσελ
θών. οἱ δὲ τὰ μὲν πρῶτα ἐγέλων ὁρῶντες ἄριστο
ἄπιστον· εἶτα δὲ τοὺς ὁμοδούλους ἐκάλουν ἐπὶ τὴ
ἐμὴν θέαν, καὶ γέλως πολὺς ἦν, ὥστε καὶ ὁ δεσπότη
αὐτῶν ἤκουσεν τοῦ γέλωτος, θορύβου ὄντος ἔξωθεν
καὶ ἤρετο τί ἐστιν [2] ἐφ᾽ ᾧ τοσοῦτον οἱ ἔξω γελῶσιν
ἐπεὶ δὲ ἤκουσεν, καὶ [3] ἐξανίσταται τοῦ συμποσίου
καὶ διακύψας εἴσω ὁρᾷ με συὸς ἀγρίου μερίδα

---

[1] post τέλεον addunt ἤμην, post κατέτρωγον pungunt N, edd.

126

proceeds of my masters' skill, and would gorge myself on human food once again after so long. When they came in, at first they didn't notice my gormandising at all, because there was so much food lying about and I still showed fear and restraint when stealing my lunch. But once I had decided they were completely unaware of all this, and had started to eat the finest portions and a great deal besides, and they to notice their losses, at first they would look suspiciously at each other, and one would call the other robber and a shameless thief of the common store ; thereafter they both kept a careful check and the titbits would be counted.

47. But my life was one of pleasure and luxury, and normal food had made my body handsome again and my coat resplendent with a fine growth of hair. When these excellent fellows saw that I was big and fat, although my barley was not being used but remained at the same level, they began to suspect my daring deeds, and, pretending to go to their bath, they closed the door behind them, put their eyes to a chink in it and looked inside. Then, unsuspicious of their trick, I went and started my meal. At first they laughed to see this incredible meal in progress, but then they called their fellow-slaves to see me, and they all laughed so heartily that their master heard them because of the din outside his room. He asked one of them why those outside were laughing so heartily. When he heard the reason, he got up from the table, peeped inside

---

² τί ἐστιν Courier: τινα N, edd.: τισιν cett..
³ καὶ om. recc., Jacobitz.

καταπίνοντα, καὶ μέγα ἐν γέλωτι ἀναβοήσας εἰστρέχει εἴσω. κἀγὼ σφόδρα ἠχθόμην ἐπὶ τοῦ δεσπότου κλέπτης ἅμα καὶ λίχνος ἑαλωκώς. ὁ δὲ πολὺν
εἶχεν ἐπ' ἐμοὶ γέλωτα, καὶ τὰ μὲν πρῶτα κελεύει με
εἴσω ἄγεσθαι εἰς τὸ ἐκείνου συμπόσιον, ἔπειτα
τράπεζάν μοι παραθεῖναι εἶπε καὶ εἶναι ἐπ' αὐτῇ
πολλὰ τῶν ὅσα μὴ δυνατὸν ἄλλῳ ὄνῳ καταφαγεῖν,
κρέα λοπάδας ζωμοὺς ἰχθῦς, τοῦτο μὲν ⟨ἐν⟩ [1] γάρῳ
καὶ ἐλαίῳ κατακειμένους, τοῦτο δὲ νάπυϊ ἐπικεχυ-
μένους. κἀγὼ τὴν τύχην ὁρῶν ἤδη ἁπαλόν μοι
προσμειδιῶσαν καὶ μαθὼν ὅτι με τοῦτο μόνον τὸ
παίγνιον ἀνασώσει, καίτοι ἤδη ἐμπεπλησμένος
ὅμως ἠρίστων τῇ τραπέζῃ παραστάς. τὸ δὲ συμπόσιον ἐκλονεῖτο τῷ γέλωτι. καί τις εἶπεν, Καὶ πίεται
οἶνον οὗτος ὁ ὄνος, ἤν τις αὐτῷ ἐγκερασάμενος
ἐπιδῷ· καὶ ὁ δεσπότης ἐκέλευσεν κἀγὼ τὸ προσενεχ-
θὲν ἔπιον.

48. ὁ δὲ οἷον εἰκὸς ὁρῶν ἐμὲ κτῆμα παράδοξον τὴν
μὲν τιμὴν τὴν ἐμὴν κελεύει τῶν διοικητῶν τινι
καταβαλεῖν τῷ ἐμὲ ὠνησαμένῳ καὶ ἄλλο τοσοῦτον,
ἐμὲ δὲ παρέδωκεν ἀπελευθέρῳ τῶν αὐτοῦ τινι
νεανίσκῳ καὶ εἶπε κατηχεῖν ὅσα ποιῶν μάλιστα
ψυχαγωγεῖν αὐτὸν δυναίμην. τῷ δέ γε ῥάδια ἦν
πάντα· ὑπήκουον γὰρ εὐθὺ εἰς ἅπαντα διδασκόμενος.
καὶ πρῶτον μὲν κατακλίνεσθαί με ἐπὶ κλίνης ὥσπερ
ἄνθρωπον ἐπ' ἀγκῶνος ἐποίησεν, εἶτα καὶ προσπα-
λαίειν αὐτῷ καὶ μὴν καὶ ὀρχεῖσθαι ἐπὶ τοὺς δύο
ἐπανιστάμενον ὀρθὸν καὶ κατανεύειν καὶ ἀνανεύειν
πρὸς τὰς φωνὰς καὶ πάνθ' ὅσα ἐδυνάμην μὲν καὶ

---

[1] ἐν suppl. Peletier.

and, on seeing me gulping down a portion of wild boar, came running in roaring with laughter. I was very upset at being exposed as a thief and glutton in the presence of my master. But he laughed heartily at me, and first ordered me to be brought into his dining-room, and then gave instructions for a table to be put before me with many of the things which no other ass could eat—meats, shell-fish, soups and fish, some soused in fish-sauce and olive oil, others covered in mustard. Since I now saw that fortune was smiling on me kindly, and realised that only this comic turn would save me, although I was already gorged, I stood beside the table and started to eat. The room rang with laughter and someone said, "This ass will drink wine too, if someone will dilute[1] it for him and serve it to him." The master ordered this to be done and I drank what was brought to me.

48. He, naturally enough, saw that I was a marvellous treasure and told one of his stewards to give my purchaser twice what he had paid for me. He handed me over to a young freedman of his personal staff and told him to instruct me in all things I could do to afford him the greatest entertainment. Everything was quite simple for him, as I immediately obeyed my instructor in every respect. First of all he made me lie on a couch on my elbow just like a human being, then wrestle with him, yes and dance standing upright on my two legs, nod " yes " or " no " when spoken to, and do all the things which I could have done even without being

[1] Wine was normally mixed with water before being drunk.

δίχα τοῦ μανθάνειν ποιεῖν· καὶ τὸ πρᾶγμα περιβό-
ητον ἦν, ὄνος ὁ τοῦ δεσπότου, οἰνοπότης, παλαίων,
ὄνος ὀρχούμενος. τὸ δὲ μέγιστον ὅτι [1] πρὸς τὰς
φωνὰς ἀνένευον ἐν καιρῷ καὶ κατένευον· καὶ
πιεῖν δὲ ὁπότε θελήσαιμι, ᾔτουν τοῖς ὀφθαλμοῖς
τὸν οἰνοχόον κινήσας. καὶ οἱ μὲν ἐθαύμαζον τὸ
πρᾶγμα ὡς παράδοξον ἀγνοῦντες ἄνθρωπον ἐν τῷ
ὄνῳ κείμενον· ἐγὼ δὲ τρυφὴν ἐποιούμην τὴν ἐκείνων
ἄγνοιαν. καὶ μὴν καὶ βαδίζειν ἐμάνθανον καὶ
κομίζειν τὸν δεσπότην ἐπὶ τοῦ νώτου καὶ τρέχειν
δρόμον ἀλυπότατον καὶ τῷ ἀναβάτῃ ἀναίσθητον.
καὶ σκεύη μοι ἦν πολυτελῆ, καὶ στρώματα πορφυρᾶ
ἐπιβάλλομαι, καὶ χαλινοὺς εἰσεδεχόμην ἀργύρῳ καὶ
χρυσῷ πεποικιλμένους, καὶ κώδωνες ἐξήπτοντό μου
μέλος μουσικώτατον ἐκφωνοῦντες.

49. ὁ δὲ Μενεκλῆς ὁ δεσπότης ἡμῶν, ὥσπερ ἔφην,
ἐκ τῆς Θεσσαλονίκης δεῦρο ἐληλύθει ἐπ᾽ αἰτίᾳ
τοιαύτῃ· ὑπέσχετο τῇ πατρίδι θέαν παρέξειν
ἀνδρῶν ὅπλοις πρὸς ἀλλήλους μονομαχεῖν εἰδότων·
καὶ οἱ μὲν ἄνδρες τῆς μάχης ἤδη ἦσαν ἐν παρασκευῇ,
καὶ ἄφικτο ἡ πορεία. ἐξελαύνομεν οὖν [2] ἕωθεν,
κἀγὼ τὸν δεσπότην ἔφερον εἴ ποτε χωρίον εἴη τῆς
ὁδοῦ τραχὺ καὶ τοῖς ὀχήμασιν ἐπιβαίνειν χαλεπόν.
ὡς δὲ κατέβημεν ἐπὶ Θεσσαλονίκην, οὐκ ἦν ὅστις
ἐπὶ θέαν οὐκ ἠπείγετο καὶ τὴν ὄψιν τὴν ἐμήν· ἡ γὰρ
ἐμὴ δόξα προεληλύθει ἐκ μακροῦ καὶ τὸ πολυπρό-
σωπον καὶ τὸ ἀνθρώπινον τῶν ἐμῶν ὀρχημάτων καὶ
παλαισμάτων. ἀλλ᾽ ὁ μὲν δεσπότης τοῖς ἐνδοξοτά-
τοις τῶν αὐτοῦ πολιτῶν παρὰ τὸν πότον ἐδείκνυέ με
καὶ τὰ παράδοξα ἐκεῖνα τὰ ἐν ἐμοὶ παίγνια ἐν τῷ
δείπνῳ παρετίθει.

taught. All this became the talk of the town—an ass at his master's beck and call, an ass that drank wine, wrestled and danced. But my greatest claim to fame was that, when talked to, I would nod " yes " or " no " at the right time. Whenever I wanted a drink, I would give the wine-waiter a push and ask for it with my eyes. They were all amazed at this as something extraordinary, not knowing there was a man in the ass, but I used their ignorance to ensure my luxury. Moreover I learned to walk with my master on my back, and to run at a trot which was most comfortable and scarcely felt by my rider. I had expensive trappings and was caparisoned in purples ; my bridle was ornamented with silver and gold, and I had hanging to me bells which tinkled out melodiously.

49. Our master, Menecles, had, as I said, come there from Thessalonica ; he had done so because he had promised to give his native city a gladiatorial show. The gladiators were already in training for the fight and the time to set out had come. We left at dawn, and I carried my master whenever it was a rough part of the road and difficult for the carriages to cross. When we reached Thessalonica, the whole town rushed to enjoy the spectacle and to see me ; for I had been preceded from afar by the fame of the many roles I played and my human skill in dancing and wrestling. However it was only to his most distinguished fellow-citizens that my master exhibited me over the wine, regaling his guests with these amazing comic acts of mine. 50. My keeper found

---

¹ ὅτι N, edd.: ἔτι cett..
² οὖν N: om. cett..

50. ὁ δὲ ἐμὸς ἐπιστάτης πρόσοδον εὗρεν ἐξ ἐμοῦ
πολλῶν πάνυ δραχμῶν· κατακλείσας γάρ με ἔνδον
εἶχεν ἑστῶτα, καὶ [1] τοῖς βουλομένοις ἰδεῖν ἐμὲ καὶ
τἀμὰ παράδοξα ἔργα μισθοῦ τὴν θύραν ἤνοιγεν. οἱ
δ' εἰσεκόμιζον ἄλλος ἄλλο τι τῶν ἐδωδίμων, μάλιστα
τὸ ἐχθρὸν εἶναι ὄνου γαστρὶ δοκοῦν· [2] ἐγὼ δὲ ἤσθιον.
ὥστε ὀλίγων ἡμερῶν τῷ δεσπότῃ καὶ τοῖς ἐν τῇ
πόλει συναριστῶν μέγας τε καὶ πίων δεινῶς ἤδη
ἐγεγόνειν.

καί ποτε [3] γυνὴ ξένη οὐ μέτρια κεκτημένη, τὴν
ὄψιν ἱκανή, παρελθοῦσα ἔσω ἰδεῖν ἐμὲ ἀριστῶντα
εἰς ἔρωτά μου θερμὸν ἐμπίπτει, τοῦτο μὲν τὸ κάλλος
ἰδοῦσα τοῦ ὄνου, τοῦτο δὲ τῷ παραδόξῳ τῶν ἐμῶν
ἐπιτηδευμάτων εἰς ἐπιθυμίαν συνουσίας προελθοῦσα
καὶ διαλέγεται πρὸς τὸν ἐπιστάτην τὸν ἐμὸν καὶ
μισθὸν αὐτῷ ἁδρὸν ὑπέσχετο, εἰ συγχωρήσειεν
αὐτῇ σὺν ἐμοὶ τὴν νύκτα ἀναπαύσεσθαι· κἀκεῖνος
οὐδὲν φροντίσας, εἴτε ἀνύσει τι ἐκείνη ἐξ ἐμοῦ εἴτε
καὶ μή, λαμβάνει τὸν μισθόν.

51. κἀπειδὴ ἑσπέρα τε ἤδη ἦν κἀκ τοῦ συμποσίου
ἀφῆκεν ἡμᾶς ὁ δεσπότης, ἀναστρέφομεν ἔνθα ἐκαθεύδομεν, καὶ τὴν γυναῖκα εὕρομεν πάλαι ἀφιγμένην
ἐπὶ τὴν ἐμὴν εὐνήν. κεκόμιστο δὲ αὐτῇ προσκεφάλαια
μαλακὰ καὶ στρώματα εἴσω κατέθεντο καὶ χαμεύνιον
ἡμῖν εὐτρεπὲς ἦν. εἶτα οἱ μὲν τῆς γυναικὸς θεράπον-
τες αὐτοῦ που [4] πλησίον πρὸ τοῦ δωματίου ἐκάθευδον,
ἡ δὲ λύχνον ἔνδον ἔκαιε μέγαν τῷ πυρὶ λαμπόμενον·
ἔπειτα ἀποδυσαμένη παρέστη τῷ λύχνῳ γυμνὴ ὅλη
καὶ μύρον ἔκ τινος ἀλαβάστρου προχεαμένη τούτῳ
ἀλείφεται, κἀμὲ δὲ μυρίζει ἔνθεν, μάλιστα τὴν ῥῖνά

a source of considerable income in me; for he
locked me in a room, and kept me standing there,
and would exact a fee before opening the door to
those who wished to see me and my marvellous feats.
They would bring in various eatables and particularly
the things thought offensive to the stomach of an ass.
These I would eat, so that by sharing meals with my
master and the folk of the city within a few days I had
already become wonderfully big and fat.

One day a foreign lady of great wealth and considerable beauty came in to see me at a meal, and fell
passionately in love with me, partly because she had
seen I was a handsome ass, but also because my
extraordinary accomplishments made her eager to
have intercourse with me. She spoke to my
keeper, promising him a substantial bribe if he would
allow her to sleep the night with me. As he did not
care whether she would get anything out of me or not,
he accepted the bribe. 51. When it was now evening
and our master had dismissed us from the dining-
room, we returned to our sleeping quarters to find
that the woman had long been ensconced in my bed.
Soft pillows had been provided for her, bedding
brought in and a bed was all ready for us on the floor.
Then the lady's servants settled for the night somewhere near at hand outside the room, while inside she
lit a large, bright lamp. Then she stripped, stood stark
naked beside the lamp, poured out ointment from an
alabaster vase and rubbed it on. Then she rubbed

---

¹ καὶ om. Γ.
² δοκοῦν N: om. cett.: malim ante ὄνου.
³ καί ποτε usque ad c. 53 fin. om. N.
⁴ ποι Γ.

μου μύρων ἐνέπλησεν, εἶτά με καὶ ἐφίλησε [1] καὶ οἷα
πρὸς αὑτῆς ἐρώμενον καὶ ἄνθρωπον διελέγετο καί με
ἐκ τῆς φορβειᾶς λαβομένη [2] ἐπὶ τὸ χαμεύνιον εἷλκεν·
κἀγὼ οὐδέν τι τοῦ [3] παρακαλέσαντος [4] εἰς τοῦτο
δεόμενος καὶ οἴνῳ δὲ παλαιῷ πολλῷ ὑποβεβρεγμένος καὶ τῷ χρίσματι [5] τοῦ μύρου οἰστρημένος καὶ
τὴν παιδίσκην δὲ ὁρῶν πάντα καλὴν κλίνομαι, καὶ
σφόδρα ἠπόρουν ὅπως ἀναβήσομαι τὴν ἄνθρωπον·
καὶ γὰρ ἐξ ὅτου ἐγεγόνειν ὄνος, συνουσίας ἀλλ'
οὐδὲ τῆς [6] ὄνοις συνήθους ἔτυχον ἁψάμενος οὐδὲ
γυναικὶ ἐχρησάμην ὄνῳ· καὶ μὴν καὶ τοῦτό μ' εἰς
δέος οὐχὶ μέτριον ἦγε, μὴ οὐ χωρήσασα ἡ γυνὴ
διασπασθείη, κἀγὼ ὥσπερ ἀνδροφόνος καλὴν δώσω
δίκην. ἠγνόουν δὲ οὐκ εἰς δέον δεδιώς. ἡ γὰρ
γυνὴ πολλοῖς τοῖς φιλήμασι, καὶ τούτοις ἐρωτικοῖς,
προσκαλουμένη [7] ὡς εἶδεν οὐ κατέχοντα, ὥσπερ
ἀνδρὶ παρακειμένη [8] περιβάλλεταί με καὶ ἄρασα
εἴσω ὅλον παρεδέξατο. κἀγὼ μὲν ὁ δειλὸς ἐδεδοί-
κειν ἔτι καὶ ὀπίσω ἀπῆγον ἐμαυτὸν ἀτρέμα, ἡ δὲ
τῆς τε ὀσφύος τῆς ἐμῆς εἴχετο, ὥστε μὴ ὑποχωρεῖν,
καὶ αὐτὴ εἴπετο τὸ φεῦγον. ἐπεὶ δὲ ἀκριβῶς ἐπείσθην ἔτι μοι καὶ προσδεῖν πρὸς τὴν τῆς γυναικὸς
ἡδονήν τε καὶ τέρψιν, ἀδεῶς λοιπὸν ὑπηρέτουν
ἐννοούμενος ὡς οὐδὲν εἴην κακίων τοῦ τῆς Πασιφάης
μοιχοῦ. ἡ δὲ γυνὴ οὕτως ἦν ἄρα ἐς τὰ ἀφροδίσια

---

[1] καὶ ἐφίλησε Γ: κατεφίλησε recc..
[2] ἐπιλαβομένη recc., edd..
[3] τι τοῦ Dobree: τρίτου codd..
[4] παρακαλέσοντος ed. princeps.
[5] χρωτὶ codd.: corr. Reitz.
[6] τῆς recc.: τοῖς Γ.
[7] προκαλουμένη Courier.

ointment from the vase over me as well, smearing it particularly thickly over my nose. Then she kissed me, spoke to me as if I was her beloved and a human, took me by the halter and dragged me on to the bed. I needed no invitation ; I was half-soused with much old wine, my skin was excited by the ointment, and I saw that she was a beautiful wench in every particular. I lay down, but was most uncertain how to mount the woman ; for ever since I had become an ass, I had had no intercourse even of the normal asinine kind, nor had I had anything to do with a female ass. Moreover I was beset by an inordinate fear that she would be too small for me and would be torn asunder, while I would have a fine penalty to pay as her murderer. I didn't know that I needn't have feared, for she encouraged me with many kisses and passionate ones at that, and when she saw that I could not hold myself back, she lay beside me as though I was a man, embraced me, lifted me in and received the full extent of my member.[1] I, poor coward, was still afraid, and was gently drawing myself away, but she clung to my member, so that it could not withdraw and followed it as it retreated. Once I was absolutely convinced that I needed to do something more to ensure her pleasure and enjoyment, I served her thereafter without fear, considering myself no worse than Pasiphaë's[2] lover. The woman was so ready for

[1] Cf. Sisenna, fr. 10 (Bücheler) and note on *Affairs of the Heart* c. 1.

[2] Pasiphaë, the wife of Minos, king of Cnossos in Crete, fell in love with a bull by which she became the mother of the Minotaur.

[8] παρανακειμένη Γ.

ἑτοίμη καὶ τῆς ἀπὸ τῆς συνουσίας ἡδονῆς ἀκόρεστος,
ὥστε ὅλην τὴν νύκτα ἐν ἐμοὶ ἐδαπάνησεν.

52. ἅμα δὲ τῇ ἡμέρᾳ ἡ μὲν ἀναστᾶσα ἀπῄει συν-
θεμένη πρὸς τὸν ἐπιστάτην τὸν ἐμὸν οἴσειν ἐπὶ τοῖς
αὐτοῖς τὸν μισθὸν τὸν αὐτὸν τῆς νυκτός. ὁ δὲ ἅμα
μὲν πλουσιώτερος ἐκ τῶν ἐμῶν γενησόμενος [1] καὶ
τῷ δεσπότῃ καινότερον ἐν ἐμοὶ ἐπιδειξόμενος
συγκατακλείει με τῇ γυναικί· ἡ δὲ κατεχρῆτό [2] μοι
δεινῶς. καί ποτε ἐλθὼν ὁ ἐπιστάτης ἀπαγγέλλει
τῷ δεσπότῃ τὸ ἔργον, ὡς ἂν [3] αὐτὸς διδάξας, καὶ
ἐμοῦ μὴ εἰδότος ἄγει αὐτὸν ἑσπέρας ἤδη ἔνθα
ἐκαθεύδομεν, καὶ διά τινος ὀπῆς τῆς θύρας δείκνυσί
με ἔνδον τῇ μείρακι συνευναζόμενον. ὁ δὲ ἡσθεὶς
τῇ θέᾳ καὶ δημοσίᾳ με ταῦτα ποιοῦντα δεῖξαι
ἐπεθύμησεν, καὶ κελεύει πρὸς μηδένα ἔξω τοῦτο
εἰπεῖν, "Ἵνα, ἔφη, ἐν τῇ ἡμέρᾳ τῆς θέας παραγάγωμεν
τοῦτον ἐς τὸ θέατρον σύν τινι τῶν καταδεδικασμένων
γυναικῶν, κἂν [4] πάντων ὀφθαλμοῖς ἐπὶ τὴν γυναῖκα
ἀναβήσεται. καί τινα τῶν γυναικῶν, ἥτις κατεκέ-
κριτο θηρίοις ἀποθανεῖν, ἄγουσιν ἔνδον παρ' ἐμὲ καὶ
προσιέναι τε ἐκέλευον καὶ ψαύειν ἐμοῦ.

53. εἶτα τὸ τελευταῖον τῆς ἡμέρας ἐκείνης ἐνστά-
σης, ἐν ᾗ τὰς φιλοτιμίας ἦγεν ὁ ἐμὸς δεσπότης,
εἰσάγειν ἔγνωσάν με εἰς τὸ θέατρον. καὶ εἰσῄειν
οὕτω· κλίνη ἦν μεγάλη, ἀπὸ χελώνης Ἰνδικῆς
πεποιημένη, χρυσῷ ἐσφηνωμένη,[5] ἐπὶ ταύτης με
ἀνακλίνουσιν κἀκεῖ μοι τὴν γυναῖκα παρακατέ-
κλιναν. εἶτα οὕτως ἡμᾶς ἐπέθηκαν ἐπί τινος μηχα-
νήματος καὶ εἴσω εἰς τὸ θέατρον παρενέγκαντες

---

[1] γενησόμενος scripsi: γενόμενος codd..

love and so insatiable for the pleasures of copulation
that she devoted the whole night to me.

52. At daybreak she got up and left, arranging with
my keeper to pay the same fee for the same privileges
that night. As he wished to enrich himself from my
attainments and at the same time to show his master
a fresh trick of mine, he locked me up with her, and
she overworked me terribly. One day my keeper
went to my master to report on my feat, pretending
he himself had taught me it, and, when it was now
evening, unknown to me brought him to our bedroom, and through a chink in the door showed me
bedded inside with the wench. Delighted with the
spectacle, he conceived the desire of exhibiting me
doing this in public and told him to keep it a secret,
" so that," he said, " on the day of the show we may
introduce him in the amphitheatre with a condemned woman, and he will mount her before the
eyes of everyone." Then they brought in to me a
woman condemned to be killed by the animals, and
told her to make advances to me and fondle me.

53. Then finally when the day came for my master
to show his munificence,[1] they decided to take me to
the amphitheatre. When I entered, I found a huge
couch made of Indian tortoise-shell and inlaid with
gold. On this they made me lie and the woman lie
on it by my side. Then they put us on a trolley,
wheeled us into the arena and deposited us in the

---

[1] Sc. " put on his games." Men with ambitions for high
magisterial office gave lavish shows to the public to court
popularity.

---

[2] κατεχρήσατο recc., edd..   [3] ἂν Courier: ἦν codd..
[4] κἂν Courier: καὶ codd..   [5] ἐσφηκωμένη Schneider.

κατέθηκαν ἐν τῷ μέσῳ, καὶ οἱ ἄνθρωποι μέγα
ἀνεβόησαν καὶ κρότος πάσης χειρὸς ἐξήλατο
ἐπ' ἐμοί, καὶ τράπεζα ἡμῖν παρέκειτο καὶ πολλὰ
ἐσκευασμένα ἐπ' αὐτῇ ἔκειτο ὅσα τρυφῶντες ἄνθρωποι ἐν δείπνῳ ἔχουσιν. καὶ παῖδες ἡμῖν παρειστή-
κεισαν οἰνοχόοι καλοὶ τὸν οἶνον ἡμῖν χρυσίῳ διακονού-
μενοι. ὁ μὲν οὖν ἐμὸς ἐπιστάτης ἑστὼς ὄπισθεν
ἐκέλευέν με ἀριστᾶν· ἐγὼ δὲ ἅμα μὲν ἡδούμην ἐν
τῷ θεάτρῳ κατακείμενος, ἅμα δὲ ἐδεδίειν μή που
ἄρκτος ἢ λέων ἀναπηδήσεται. 54. ἐν τούτῳ δέ
τινος ἄνθη φέροντος παροδεύοντος[1] ἐν τοῖς ἄλλοις
ἄνθεσιν ὁρῶ καὶ ῥόδων χλωρῶν φύλλα, καὶ μηδὲν
ἔτι ὀκνῶν ἀναπηδήσας τοῦ λέχους ἐκπίπτω· καὶ οἱ
μὲν ᾤοντό με ἀνίστασθαι ὀρχησόμενον·[2] ἐγὼ δὲ
ἐν ἐξ ἑνὸς ἐπιτρέχων καὶ ἀπανθιζόμενος ἀπ' αὐτῶν
τῶν ἀνθῶν τὰ ῥόδα κατέπινον. τῶν δὲ ἔτι θαυμα-
ζόντων ἐπ' ἐμοὶ ἀποπίπτει ἐξ ἐμοῦ ἐκείνη ἡ τοῦ
κτήνους ὄψις καὶ ἀπόλλυται, καὶ ἀφανὴς ἐκεῖνος ὁ
πάλαι ὄνος, ὁ δὲ Λούκιος αὐτὸς ἔνδον[3] μοι γυμνὸς
εἱστήκει. τῇ δὲ παραδόξῳ ταύτῃ καὶ μηδέποτε
ἐλπισθείσῃ θέᾳ πάντες ἐκπεπληγμένοι δεινὸν ἐπεθο-
ρύβησαν καὶ τὸ θέατρον εἰς δύο γνώμας ἐσχίζετο·
οἱ μὲν γὰρ ὥσπερ φάρμακα[4] δεινὰ ἐπιστάμενον καὶ
κακόν τι πολύμορφον ἠξίουν εὐθὺς ἔνδον[5] πυρί με
ἀποθανεῖν, οἱ δὲ περιμεῖναι καὶ τοὺς ἀπ' ἐμοῦ
λόγους ἔλεγον δεῖν καὶ πρότερον διαγνῶναι, εἶθ'
οὕτως δικάσαι περὶ τούτων. κἀγὼ δραμὼν πρὸς

---

[1] τινος ... παροδεύοντος om. Γ.
[2] ὀχησόμενον Γ.
[3] ἔνθεν Du Soul: ἔνδοθεν L. A. Post.: ἐνὼν temptavi.
[4] φαρμακέα Courier.   [5] ἐνδοθέντα L. A. Post.

middle. The people raised a loud shout and all clapped their hands to applaud me ; a table was placed at one side with many of the dainties which epicures have at dinner. Handsome wine-boys stood beside us, serving us wine in golden goblets. My keeper stood behind me and told me to eat. But I was not only ashamed to be reclining in the amphitheatre but also afraid that a bear or lion would leap on me.

54. Meanwhile a man passed carrying flowers, amongst which I noticed fresh rose-petals. No longer afraid I leapt to my feet and jumped off the couch. They all thought I was standing up to dance, but I went through the flowers one by one, picked out the roses and gulped them down. While they were still watching me in astonishment, that bestial appearance left me and vanished, the ass of old disappeared, and Lucius himself was standing naked on the spot [1] I occupied. All were amazed at this strange, unexpected spectacle and raised a terrible din. The audience were divided into two opinions. Some thought that I should be burnt to death immediately as a scoundrel versed in terrible spells and able to adopt many shapes ; the others advocated waiting and learning what I had to say before deciding on the matter. I rushed up to the governor of the province,[2]

[1] The Greek is ungrammatical.
[2] Presumably Macedonia, as the games are held at Thessalonica (cf. c. 49) and Lucius in c. 55 says he comes from " Patras in Achaia." Here once again there is inadequate epitomising, as it is pointless to talk about a " Thessalian witch " in Thessalonica. In Apuleius X.18 seq. Thiasus (= Menecles) goes to Thessaly for horses and gladiators and then returns to his native Corinth to put on the games.

τὸν ἄρχοντα τῆς ἐπαρχίας—ἔτυχεν δὲ τῇ θέᾳ ταύτῃ
παρών—ἔλεγον κάτωθεν ὅτι γυνή με Θετταλὴ
γυναικὸς Θετταλῆς δούλη χρίσματι μεμαγευμένῳ
ἐπαλείψασα ὄνον ποιήσειεν, καὶ ἱκέτευον αὐτὸν
λαβόντα ἔχειν με ἐν φρουρᾷ ἔστ' ἂν αὐτὸν πείσαιμι,
ὡς οὐ καταψεύδομαι οὕτω γεγονώς.[1]

55. καὶ ὁ ἄρχων, Λέγε, φησίν, ἡμῖν ὄνομα τὸ σὸν
καὶ γονέων τῶν σῶν καὶ συγγενῶν, εἴ τινας φῂς ἔχειν
τῷ γένει προσήκοντας, καὶ πόλιν.

κἀγώ, Πατὴρ μέν, ἔφην,[2] ... ἔστι μοι Λούκιος, τῷ
δὲ ἀδελφῷ τῷ ἐμῷ Γάϊος· ἄμφω δὲ τὰ λοιπὰ δύο
ὀνόματα κοινὰ ἔχομεν. κἀγὼ μὲν ἱστοριῶν καὶ
ἄλλων εἰμὶ συγγραφεύς, ὁ δὲ ποιητὴς ἐλεγείων ἐστὶ
καὶ μάντις ἀγαθός· πατρὶς δὲ ἡμῖν Πάτραι τῆς
Ἀχαΐας.

ὁ δὲ δικαστὴς ἐπεὶ ταῦτα ἤκουσεν, Φιλτάτων
ἐμοί, ἔφη, λίαν ἀνδρῶν υἱὸς εἶ καὶ ξένων οἰκίᾳ τέ με
ὑποδεξαμένων καὶ δώροις τιμησάντων, καὶ ἐπίστα-
μαι ὅτι οὐδὲν ψεύδῃ παῖς ἐκείνων ὤν· καὶ τοῦ
δίφρου ἀναπηδήσας περιβάλλει τε καὶ πολλὰ ἐφίλει,
καί με καὶ οἴκαδε ἦγεν ὡς ἑαυτόν. ἐν τούτῳ δὲ καὶ
ὁ ἀδελφὸς ὁ ἐμὸς ἀφίκετο ἀργύριον καὶ ἄλλα μοι
πολλὰ κομίζων, κἂν τούτῳ με ὁ ἄρχων δημοσίᾳ
πάντων ἀκουόντων ἀπολύει. καὶ ἐλθόντες ἐπὶ
θάλασσαν ναῦν ἐσκεψάμεθα καὶ τὴν ἀποσκευὴν
ἐνεθέμεθα. 56. ἐγὼ[3] δὲ κράτιστον εἶναι ἔγνων
ἐλθεῖν παρὰ τὴν γυναῖκα τὴν ἐρασθεῖσάν μου τοῦ

---

[1] γεγονός recc., edd..
[2] lacunam agnovit Gesner.
[3] ἐγὼ δὲ ... συμφοράν . (prope fin.) om. N.

who was among the spectators, and told him from
down there that a Thessalian witch, the slave of a
Thessalian witch, had anointed me with a magic
unguent and made me into an ass, and I begged him
to arrest me and keep me in custody till I convinced
him of the truth of my story.

55. The governor said : " Tell us your name and
that of your parents and any relatives you claim to
have, and that of your city."

I replied : " My father is . . . ,[1] my name is
Lucius, and that of my brother is Gaius, and the
other two names we share with our father. I write
histories [2] and other prose works, while he is an
elegiac poet and a skilled prophet. Our native city
is Patras in Achaia."

When the governor heard this, he said : " You
are the son of folk most dear to me, friends who have
welcomed me in their home and honoured me with
gifts. I know you are absolutely truthful if you are
their son." Then he leapt up from his seat, embraced me and kissed me many times and took me to
his own home. Meanwhile, too, my brother had
arrived with money and many other things for me,
and the governor publicly declared that he was
releasing me. We went down to the sea, looked for a
ship and put our baggage aboard.

56. I then thought it best to visit the lady who had
loved me when an ass, telling myself she would think

---

[1] The manuscripts have unintentionally omitted the
father's name.

[2] Alternatively ἱστορίαι could be used in a wider sense
of " treatises " (works of enquiry or research, the original
meaning of ἱστορίη) or indeed of novels or other narrative
works.

ὄνου, καλλίων αὐτῇ φανεῖσθαι λέγων νῦν ἐν ἀνθρώπῳ
ὤν. ἡ δὲ ἀσμένη τέ μ' εἰσεδέξατο τῷ παραδόξῳ,
οἶμαι, τοῦ πράγματος ἐπιτερπομένη, καὶ δειπνεῖν
σὺν αὐτῇ καὶ καθεύδειν ἱκέτευεν· κἀγὼ ἐπειθόμην
νεμέσεως ἄξιον εἶναι νομίζων τὸν ὄνον τὸν ἀγαπη-
θέντα νῦν γενόμενον ἄνθρωπον ὑπερτρυφᾶν καὶ τὴν
ἐρασθεῖσαν ὑπερορᾶν· καὶ δειπνῶ σὺν αὐτῇ καὶ
πολὺ ἐκ τοῦ μύρου ἀλείφομαι καὶ στεφανοῦμαι τῷ
φιλτάτῳ ἐς ἀνθρώπους με ἀνασώσαντι ῥόδῳ. ἐπεὶ
δὲ ἦν βαθεῖα νὺξ ἤδη καὶ καθεύδειν ἔδει, κἀγὼ δ'
ἐπανίσταμαι καὶ ὡσπερεὶ μέγα τι ἀγαθὸν ποιῶν
ἀποδύομαι καὶ ἵσταμαι γυμνὸς ὡς [1] δῆθεν ἔτι
μᾶλλον ἀρέσων ἐκ τῆς πρὸς τὸν ὄνον συγκρίσεως.
ἡ δὲ ἐπειδὴ εἶδέ με πάντα ἀνθρώπινα ἔχοντα, προσ-
πτύσασά [2] μοι, Οὐ φθερῇ [3] ἀπ' ἐμοῦ, ἔφη, καὶ τῆς
ἐμῆς οἰκίας καὶ μακράν ποι [4] ἀπελθὼν κοιμήσῃ;

  ἐμοῦ δ' ἐρομένου, Τί γὰρ καὶ ἡμάρτηταί μοι
τοσοῦτο; [5] Ἐγώ, ἔφη, μὰ Δί' οὐχὶ σοῦ, ἀλλὰ τοῦ
ὄνου τοῦ σοῦ ἐρῶσα τότε ἐκείνῳ καὶ οὐχὶ σοὶ
συνεκάθευδον, καὶ ᾤμην σε καὶ νῦν κἂν ἐκεῖνό γε
μόνον τὸ μέγα τοῦ ὄνου σύμβολον διασῴζειν καὶ
σύρειν· σὺ δέ μοι ἐλήλυθας ἐξ ἐκείνου τοῦ καλοῦ καὶ
χρησίμου ζῴου ἐς πίθηκον μεταμορφωθείς.

  καὶ καλεῖ εὐθὺς ἤδη τοὺς οἰκέτας καὶ κελεύει με
τῶν νώτων μετέωρον κομισθῆναι ἔξω τῆς οἰκίας,
καὶ ἐξωσθεὶς πρὸ τοῦ δωματίου ἔξω γυμνὸς καλῶς
ἐστεφανωμένος καὶ μεμυρισμένος τὴν γῆν γυμνὴν
περιλαβὼν ταύτῃ συνεκάθευδον. ἅμα δὲ τῷ ὄρθρῳ

---

[1] ὡς om. Γ.
[2] προπτύσασα Γ. [3] φθείρῃ codd.: corr. Dindorf.

me handsomer now I was in human form. She
gladly welcomed me, because, I suppose, she was
delighted at this extraordinary situation, and she
begged me to dine and sleep with her. I agreed, for
I thought I would deserve the jealousy of heaven if
upon becoming human the ass who had received
affection took excessive airs and scorned her who had
loved him. I dined with her, anointed myself richly
with sweet oil and garlanded myself with roses, the
dear flowers which had restored me to human form.
When the night was now advanced and it was time to
go to bed, I got up and stripped as though conferring
a great favour and stood naked before her, imagining
that I would please her still more by the contrast I
formed with the ass. But when she saw that every
part of me was human, she spat at me and said, " Get
to blazes away from me and my house ; don't sleep
anywhere near me."

When I asked what heinous offence I'd committed,
she replied, " By heavens, I didn't love *you* but the
ass in you and *he* was the one I slept with, not you.
I thought that, if nothing else, you would still have
kept trailing around with you that mighty symbol
of the ass. But you have come to me transformed
from that handsome, useful creature into a
monkey.

She immediately called her servants and had me
carried out of the house aloft on their backs. I
was thrust out of the door and there I lay naked in
my fine garlands and unguents, with only the bare
earth to embrace. At crack of dawn I ran naked to

---

⁴ ποι recc.: καί ποι Γ: del. edd..
⁵ τοσοῦτο Courier: τοιοῦτο codd..

γυμνὸς ὢν ἔθεον ἐπὶ ναῦν καὶ λέγω πρὸς τὸν ἀδελφὸν
τὴν ἐμαυτοῦ ἐν γέλωτι συμφοράν. ἔπειτα ἐκ τῆς
πόλεως δεξιοῦ πνεύσαντος ἀνέμου πλέομεν ἔνθεν, καὶ
ὀλίγαις ἡμέραις ἔρχομαι εἰς τὴν ἐμὴν πατρίδα. ἐνταῦθα θεοῖς σωτῆρσιν ἔθυον καὶ ἀναθήματα ἀνέθηκα, μὰ
Δί' οὐκ ἐκ κυνὸς πρωκτοῦ, τὸ δὴ τοῦ λόγου, ἀλλ'
ἐξ ὄνου περιεργίας διὰ μακροῦ πάνυ καὶ οὕτω δέ
μόλις οἴκαδε ἀνασωθείς.

Subscriptio in Γ: ΛΟΥΚΙΑΝΟΥ ΕΠΙΤΟΜΗ ΤΩΝ ΛΟΥΚΙΟΥ
ΜΕΤΑΜΟΡΦΩΣΕΩΝ.

the ship and told my brother of my ridiculous mis-adventure. Then we sailed away from that city on a favouring wind and within a few days I reached my native city. Then I sacrificed and dedicated offerings to the gods who had saved me, now that after so very long and with such difficulty I had escaped, not from the dog's bottom of the fable,[1] by Zeus, but from the curiosity of an ass.[2]

[1] The precise meaning of a " dog's bottom " is uncertain; the phase is used in Aristophanes, *Acharnians* 863 and *Ecclesiazousae* 255. L. A. Post suggests a connection with the fable of the dog who would have relieved himself over a bunch of reeds if one of the reeds had not pricked his posterior. The dog moved off and barked at the reed. The reed said, " I'd rather you barked at me from a distance than dirtied me from close by." The moral is that fools and knaves should be kept at a distance. See No. 608 in B. E. Perry, *Aesopica* I, page 630, and in L. C. L. Babrius and Phaedrus, Appendix, p. 543.

[2] This may be an alternative form of the proverb found in c. 45.

AFFAIRS OF THE HEART

Although there is an apparent reference to *Affairs of the Heart* in *Essays in Portraiture*, c. 4, it is obvious from the style of this dialogue that the author is not Lucian but an imitator. When it was written is uncertain, but the reference to the decaying conditions of the cities of Lycia in c. 7 perhaps suggests a date some time after the invasion of the Goths and of Sapor, i.e. not earlier than the last quarter of the third century A.D. On the other hand, Rhodes still seems to be prosperous, though we know that it suffered an earthquake in the middle of the fourth century A.D., and Justinian *Codex* 1.40.6 suggests that it had lost its prosperity by 385 A.D. The most probable date for the dialogue, therefore, is the early fourth century A.D.

Though I have adopted Harmon's attractive title " Affairs of the Heart ", it is perhaps misleading and a more accurate rendering would be *The Two Types of Love*. For an account of the various facets of homosexual and heterosexual love among the Greeks see *Love in Ancient Greece* (translated by J. Cleugh from the French of R. Flacelière).

This dialogue had literary precedents in Plato's *Symposium*, *Phaedrus* and *Lysis*, and in Xenophon's *Symposium*, all of which discuss love in general, and in Plutarch's *Dialogue on Love* (*Moralia*, vol. ix, L.C. L.), part of which anticipates the particular theme of *Affairs of the Heart* with its argument, 750 ff., between Daphnaeus, the champion of conjugal love, and Protogenes, the advocate for pederasty. It is to be noted that, whereas in Plutarch conjugal love is declared the victor, Lycinus in c. 51 gives a tactfully worded verdict in favour of pederasty.

Achilles Tatius 2. 35-38 also has a debate on the comparative merits of love of women and love of boys with some similarities to this dialogue. As the very latest possible date for Achilles Tatius' novel is c. 300 A.D. and it may well be considerably earlier [1] than that, it seems probable on the whole that *Affairs of the Heart* is the later of the two works, and its author may have taken some of his ideas from Achilles Tatius.

The best study of this dialogue is by R. Bloch (Strasburg, 1907).

[1] E. Merkelbach, *Roman und Mysterium in der Antike* p. 132, dates it c. A.D. 139.

ΕΡΩΤΕΣ

ΛΥΚΙΝΟΣ

1. Ἐρωτικῆς παιδιᾶς, ἑταῖρέ μοι Θεόμνηστε, ἐξ
ἑωθινοῦ πεπλήρωκας ἡμῶν τὰ κεκμηκότα πρὸς τὰς
συνεχεῖς σπουδὰς ὦτα, καί μοι σφόδρα διψῶντι τοιαύτης ἀνέσεως εὔκαιρος ἡ τῶν ἱλαρῶν σον λόγων
ἐρρύη χάρις· ἀσθενὴς γὰρ ἡ ψυχὴ διηνεκοῦς σπουδῆς
ἀνέχεσθαι, ποθοῦσι δ' οἱ φιλότιμοι πόνοι μικρὰ
τῶν ἐπαχθῶν φροντίδων χαλασθέντες εἰς ἡδονὰς
ἀνίεσθαι. πάνυ δή με ὑπὸ τὸν ὄρθρον ἡ τῶν ἀκολά-
στων σου διηγημάτων αἱμύλη καὶ γλυκεῖα πειθὼ
κατεύφραγκεν,[1] ὥστ' ὀλίγου δεῖν Ἀριστείδης
ἐνόμιζον εἶναι τοῖς Μιλησιακοῖς λόγοις ὑπερκηλού-
μενος, ἄχθομαί τε νὴ τοὺς σοὺς ἔρωτας, οἷς πλατὺς
εὑρέθης[2] σκοπός, ὅτι πέπαυσαι διηγούμενος· καὶ
σε πρὸς αὐτῆς ἀντιβολοῦμεν Ἀφροδίτης, εἰ περιττά
με λέγειν ἔοικας,[3] εἴ τις ἄρρην ἢ καὶ νὴ Δία θῆλυς
ἀφεῖταί[4] σοι πόθος, ἠρέμα τῇ μνήμῃ ἐκκαλέσασθαι.
καὶ γὰρ ἄλλως ἑορταστικὴν ἄγομεν ἡμέραν Ἡρά-
κλεια θύοντες· οὐκ ἀγνοεῖς δὲ δήπου τὸν θεὸν ὡς

Codices rettuli Γ, Ε.
Γ[a] = correctio Alexandri.
Ε[2] = varia lectio quam, eodem fere atramenti colore ac scriba
  ipse et scholiastes usa, manus vetusta superscripsit.
  Baani vel Arethae fortasse ascribenda est.
Ε[a] = correctio quam in rasura nigriore atramento usus
  Arethas (?) vel corrector posterior (?) effecit.

[1] κατεύφρανεν recc., edd.. [2] εὑρέθη ΓΕ: corr. recc..
[3] με . . . ἔοικας codd.: μὴ . . . ἔοικα Sommerbrodt.
[4] ἐφεῖται recc., edd..

AFFAIRS OF THE HEART

LYCINUS

1. Theomnestus, my friend, since dawn your
sportive talk about love has filled these ears of mine
that were weary of unremitting attention to serious
topics. As I was parched with thirst for relaxation
of this sort, your delightful stream of merry stories
was very welcome to me. For the human spirit is
too weak to endure serious pursuits all the time, and
ambitious toils long to gain some little respite from
tiresome cares and to have freedom for the joys of
life. This morning I have been quite gladdened by
the sweet winning seductiveness of your wanton
stories, so that I almost thought I was Aristides [1]
being enchanted beyond measure by those Milesian
Tales, and I swear by those Loves of yours that have
found so broad a target that I am indeed sorry that
you've come to the end of your stories. If you think
this is but idle talk on my part, I beg you in the name
of Aphrodite herself, if you've omitted mention of any
of your love affairs with a lad or even with a girl, coax
it forth with the aid of memory. Besides we are
celebrating a festival today and sacrificing to
Heracles. You know well enough, I'm sure, how
impetuous that god was where love was concerned,

---

[1] Aristides, who perhaps lived about 100 B.C., was the
author or compiler of *Milesiaca*, a work translated into
Latin by Sisenna. From the nature of Aristides' work
" Milesian Tales " came to be used as a term for obscene
love-stories.

PSEUDO-LUCIAN

ὀξὺς ἦν πρὸς Ἀφροδίτην· ἥδιστα οὖν δοκεῖ μοι τῶν λόγων τὰς θυσίας προσήσεσθαι.

ΘΕΟΜΝΗΣΤΟΣ

2. Θᾶττον ἄν μοι, ὦ Λυκῖνε, θαλάττης κύματα καὶ πυκνὰς ἀπ᾽ οὐρανοῦ νιφάδας ἀριθμήσειας ἢ τοὺς ἐμοὺς Ἔρωτας. ἐγὼ γοῦν ἅπασαν αὐτῶν κενὴν ἀπολελεῖφθαι φαρέτραν νομίζω, κἂν ἐπ᾽ ἄλλον τινὰ πτῆναι θελήσωσιν, ἄνοπλος αὐτῶν ἡ δεξιὰ γελασθήσεται· σχεδὸν γὰρ ἐκ τῆς ἀντίπαιδος ἡλικίας εἰς τοὺς ἐφήβους κριθεὶς ἄλλαις ἀπ᾽[1] ἄλλων ἐπιθυμίαις βουκολοῦμαι· διάδοχοι ἔρωτες ἀλλήλων καὶ πρὶν ἢ λῆξαι τῶν προτέρων,[2] ἄρχονται δεύτεροι, κάρηνα Λερναῖα τῆς παλιμφυοῦς Ὕδρας πολυπλοκώτερα μηδ᾽ Ἰόλεων βοηθὸν ἔχειν δυνάμενα· πυρὶ γὰρ οὐ σβέννυται πῦρ. οὕτως τις ὑγρὸς τοῖς ὄμμασιν ἐνοικεῖ μύωψ, ὃς ἅπαν κάλλος εἰς αὐτὸν ἁρπάζων ἐπ᾽ οὐδενὶ κόρῳ παύεται· καὶ συνεχὲς ἀπορεῖν ἐπέρχεταί μοι, τίς οὗτος Ἀφροδίτης ὁ χόλος· οὐ γὰρ Ἡλιάδης ἐγώ τις οὐδὲ Λημνιάδων ὕβρεις[3] οὐδὲ Ἱππολύτειον ἀγροικίαν ὠφρυωμένος, ὡς

[1] ἐπ᾽ ΓΕ: corr. recc..   [2] τοὺς προτέρους recc., edd..
[3] ὕβρεις Burmeister: ἔρις codd..

---

[1] The Hydra of Lerna was a nine-headed monster which Heracles had to kill as one of his twelve labours. Hercules found that for every head of the Hydra that he cut off another two grew, but with the assistance of Iolaüs, his companion, finally killed the Hydra by burning away the heads.

[2] Aphrodite vented her wrath on the children of the Sun because the Sun had told Hephaestus about her affair with Ares (cf. *Dialogues of the Gods*, 21, 7. 334 and Seneca, *Hippolytus*, 124 ff.). The scholiast takes " child of the sun " to refer specifically to Pasiphaë, but, as Posidon

and so I think he'll be most delighted to receive your stories by way of an offering.

THEOMNESTUS

2. You would find it quicker, my dear Lycinus, to count me the waves of the sea or the flakes of a snowstorm than to count my loves. For I for my part think that their quiver has been left completely empty and, if they choose to fly off in quest of one more victim, their weaponless right arms will be laughed to scorn. For, almost from the time when I left off being a boy and was accounted a young man, I have been beguiled by one passion after another. One Love has ever succeeded another, and almost before I've ended earlier ones later Loves begin. They are veritable Lernean heads appearing in greater multiplicity than on the self-regenerating Hydra,[1] and no Iolaüs can help against them. For one flame is not extinguished by another. There dwells in my eyes so nimble a gadfly that it pounces on any and every beauty as its prey and is never sated enough to stop. And I am always wondering why Aphrodite bears me this grudge. For I am no child of the Sun,[2] nor am I puffed up with the insolence of the Lemnian women[3] or the boorish contempt of Hippolytus[4]

was usually regarded as the author of her misfortunes, the reference is perhaps more general and also includes Medea, Circe and Phaedra, daughter of Pasiphaë, all of whom were unhappy in love.

[3] As we are told by the scholiast and Apollodorus 1.9.17 (see Frazer's note) the Lemnian women did not honour Aphrodite, and she punished them by giving them a nasty smell.

[4] The death of Hippolytus, as related in Euripides' play, was due to his contempt for Aphrodite.

PSEUDO-LUCIAN

ἐρεθίσαι τῆς θεοῦ τὴν ἄπαυστον ταύτην ὀργήν.

ΛΥΚΙΝΟΣ

3. Πέπαυσο τῆς ἐπιπλάστου καὶ δυσχεροῦς ταύτης ὑποκρίσεως, Θεόμνηστε. ἄχθη γὰρ ὅτι τούτῳ τῷ βίῳ ἡ τύχη προσεκλήρωσέν, καὶ χαλεπὸν εἶναι νομίζεις, εἰ γυναιξὶν ὡραίαις καὶ μετὰ παίδων τὸ καλὸν ἀνθούντων ὁμιλεῖς· ἀλλά σοι καὶ καθαρσίων τάχα δεήσει πρὸς τὸ δυσχερὲς οὕτω νόσημα· δεινὸν γὰρ τὸ πάθος. ἀλλ' οὐχὶ τοῦτον τὸν πολὺν ἐκχέας λῆρον εὐδαίμονα σαυτὸν εἶναι νομεῖς, ὅτι σοι ὁ θεὸς οὐκ αὐχμηρὰν γεωργίαν ἐπέκλωσεν οὐδὲ ἐμπορικὰς ἅλας καὶ στρατιώτην ἐν ὅπλοις βίον, ἀλλὰ λιπαραὶ παλαῖστραι μέλουσί σοι καὶ φαιδρὰ μὲν ἐσθὴς μέχρι ποδῶν τὴν τρυφὴν καθειμένη, διακριδὸν δ' ἠσκημένης κόμης ἐπιμέλεια; τῶν γε μὴν ἐρωτικῶν ἱμέρων αὐτὸ τὸ βασανίζον εὐφραίνει καὶ γλυκὺς ὁδοὺς ὁ τοῦ πόθου δάκνει· πειράσας μὲν γὰρ ἐλπίζεις, τυχὼν δ' ἀπολέλαυκας· ἴση δὲ ἡδονὴ τῷ [1] παρεῖναι καὶ τὸ μέλλον. ἔναγχος γοῦν διηγουμένου σου τὸν πολύν, ὡς παρ' Ἡσιόδῳ, κατάλογον ὧν ἀρχῆθεν ἠράσθης, ἱλαραὶ μὲν τῶν ὀμμάτων αἱ βολαὶ τακερῶς ἀνυγραίνοντο, τὴν φωνὴν δ' ἴσην [2] τῇ Λυκάμβου θυγατρὶ λεπτὸν ἀφηδύνων ἀπ' αὐτοῦ τοῦ σχήματος εὐθὺς δῆλος ἦς οὐκ ἐκείνων μόνων, ἀλλὰ καὶ τῆς

---

[1] ἴση δὲ ἡδονὴ τῷ scripsi: ἴση ἡδονὴ τῷ ΓΕ: ἴση δὲ ἡδονὴ τὸ recc., edd..

[2] τῇ φωνῇ δ' ἴση Ε.

that I should have provoked this unceasing wrath on the part of the goddess.

3. Stop this affected and unpleasant play-acting, Theomnestus. Are you really annoyed that Fortune has allotted you the life you have? Do you think it a hardship that you associate with women at their fairest and boys at the flower of their beauty? But perhaps you'll actually need to take purges for so unpleasant an ailment. For you do suffer shockingly, I must say. Why won't you get all this nonsense out of your system and think yourself fortunate that god has not given you for your lot squalid husbandry or the wanderings of a merchant or a soldier's life under arms? But your interests are in the oily wrestling-schools, in resplendent clothes that shed luxury right down to your feet and in seeing that your hair is fashionably dressed. The very torment of your amorous yearnings delights you and you find sweetness in the bite of passion's tooth. For when you have tempted you hope, and when you have won your suit you take your pleasure, but get as much pleasure from future joys as from the present. Just now at any rate, when you were going through in Hesiodic [1] fashion the long catalogue of your loves from the beginning, the merry glances of your eyes grew meltingly liquid, and, giving your voice a delicate sweetness so that it matched that of the daughter of Lycambes,[2] you made it immediately plain from your very manner that you were in love

---

[1] One of the works of the poet Hesiod was a *Catalogue Of Women* of which fragments remain.

[2] Neobule, who was loved by the poet Archilochus.

ἐπ' αὐτοῖς μνήμης ἐρῶν. ἀλλ', εἴ τί σοι τοῦ κατὰ
τὴν Ἀφροδίτην περίπλου λείψανον ἀφεῖται, μηδὲν
ἀποκρύψῃ, τῷ δὲ Ἡρακλεῖ τὴν θυσίαν ἐντελῆ
παράσχου.

ΘΕΟΜΝΗΣΤΟΣ

4. Βουφάγος μὲν ὁ δαίμων, ὦ Λυκῖνε, καὶ ταῖς
ἀκάπνοις, φασί, τῶν θυσιῶν ἥκιστα τερπόμενος.
ἐπεὶ δ' αὐτοῦ τὴν ἐτήσιον ἑορτὴν λόγῳ γεραίρομεν,
αἱ μὲν ἐμαὶ διηγήσεις ἐξ ἑωθινοῦ παραταθεῖσαι
κόρον ἔχουσιν, ἡ δὲ σὴ Μοῦσα τῆς συνήθους μεθαρ-
μοσαμένη σπουδῆς ἱλαρῶς τῷ θεῷ συνδιημερευ-
σάτω, καί μοι γενοῦ δικαστὴς ἴσος, ἐπεὶ μηδ' εἰς
ἕτερόν σε τοῦ πάθους ῥέποντα ὁρῶ, ποτέρους
ἀμείνονας ἡγῇ, τοὺς φιλόπαιδας ἢ τοὺς γυναίοις
ἀσμενίζοντας; ἐγὼ μὲν γὰρ ὁ πληγεὶς ἑκατέρω
καθάπερ ἀκριβὴς τρυτάνη ταῖς ἐπ' ἀμφότερα
πλάστιγξιν ἰσορρόπως ταλαντεύομαι, σὺ δ' ἐκτὸς
ὢν ἀδεκάστῳ κριτῇ τῷ λογισμῷ τὸ βέλτιον αἱρήσῃ.
πάντα δὴ περιελὼν ἀκκισμόν, ὦ φιλότης, ἣν
πεπίστευκέν σοι ψῆφον ἡ περὶ τῶν ἐμῶν ἐρώτων
κρίσις, ἤδη φέρε.

ΛΥΚΙΝΟΣ

5. Παιδιᾶς, ὦ Θεόμνηστε, καὶ γέλωτος ἡγῇ τὴν
διήγησιν; ἡ δ' ἐπαγγέλλεται καὶ σπουδαῖον. ἐγὼ
γοῦν ἐξ ὑπογύου τῆς ἐπιχειρήσεως ἡψάμην, εἰδὼς
ὅτι λίαν ἀλλοία παιδιᾶς [1] ἐξότε [2] δυοῖν ἀνδροῖν
ἀκηκοὼς περὶ τούτοιν συντόνως [3] ἁμιλλωμένοιν ἔτι

---

[1] ἀλλοία παιδιᾶς (nisi potius πάλαι) conieci: ἀλλ' οὐ παλαιᾶς
codd.: σπουδαία Jacobitz.   [2] ἐξ ὅτου recc., edd..
[3] συντόνως recc.: συνιὼν ὡς ΓΕ.

not only with your loves but also with their memory.
Come, if there is any scrap of your voyage in the seas
of love that you have omitted, reveal everything, and
make your sacrifice to Heracles complete and perfect.

4. Heracles is a devourer of oxen, my dear Lycinus,
and takes very little pleasure, they say, in sacrifices
that have no savoury smoke.   But we are honouring
his annual feast with discourse.   Accordingly, as my
narratives have continued since dawn and lasted too
long, let *your* Muse, departing from her customary
seriousness, spend the day in merriment along with
the god, and, as I can see you incline to neither type
of passion, prove yourself, I beg, an impartial judge.
Decide whether you consider those superior who love
boys or those who delight in womankind.   For I who
have been smitten by both passions hang like an
accurate balance with both scales in equipoise.   But
you, being unaffected by either, will choose the better
of the two by using the impartial judgement of your
reason.   Away with all coyness, my dear friend, and
cast now the vote entrusted to you in your capacity as
judge of my loves.

5. My dear Theomnestus, do you imagine that my
narratives are a matter of sport and laughter ?   No,
they promise something serious too.   I at any rate
have undertaken this task on the spur of the moment,
because I've known it to be far from a laughing
matter ever since the time I heard two men arguing

τὴν μνήμην ἔναυλον ἔχω. διήρητο δ' αὐτῶν ἅμα
τοῖς λόγοις τὰ πάθη καὶ οὐχ ὥσπερ σὺ κατ' εὐκολίαν
ψυχῆς ἄϋπνος ὢν διττοὺς ἄρνυσαι μισθούς,

τὸν μὲν βουκολέων, τὸν δ' ἄργυφα μῆλα νομεύων,

ἀλλ' ὁ μὲν ὑπερφυῶς παιδικοῖς ἤδετο τὴν θήλειαν
Ἀφροδίτην βάραθρον ἡγούμενος, ὁ δ' ἁγνεύων
ἄρρενος ἔρωτος ἐς γυναῖκας ἐπτόητο. δυοῖν οὖν
μαχομένοιν παθοῖν ἀγωνοθετήσας ἅμιλλαν οὐδ' ἂν
εἰπεῖν δυναίμην ὡς ὑπερηυφράνθην· καί μοι τὰ τῶν
λόγων ἴχνη ταῖς ἀκοαῖς ἐνεσφράγισται σχεδὸν ὡς
ἀρτίως εἰρημένα. πᾶσαν οὖν ὑποτιμήσεως[1] ἀφορμὴν
ἐκποδὼν ἀποθέμενος[2] ἃ παρ' ἀμφοῖν ἤκουσα
λεγόντοιν κατ' ἀκριβὲς ἐπέξειμί σοι.

ΘΕΟΜΝΗΣΤΟΣ

Καὶ μὴν ἔγωγε ἐπαναστὰς ἔνθεν ἀπαντικρὺ
καθεδοῦμαί σου,

δέγμενος Αἰακίδην ὁπότε λήξειεν ἀείδων.

σὺ δ' ἡμῖν τὰ πάλαι κλέα τῆς ἐρωτικῆς διαφορᾶς
μελῳδίᾳ περαίνειν.

ΛΥΚΙΝΟΣ

6. Ἐπ' Ἰταλίαν μοι[3] διανοουμένῳ ταχυναυτοῦν
σκάφος εὐτρέπιστο τούτων τῶν δικρότων, οἷς μάλιστα χρῆσθαι Λιβυρνοὶ δοκοῦσιν ἔθνος Ἰονίῳ κόλπῳ
παρῳκισμένον. ὡς δ' ἐνῆν, πάντας ἐπιχωρίους

---

[1] ἐπιτιμήσεως rec..
[2] ὑποθέμενος ΓΕ: corr. recc..
[3] μοι ΓΕ: μοι πλεῖν recc., edd..

heatedly with each other about these two types of love, and I still have the memory of it ringing in my ears. They were opposites, not only in their arguments but in their passions, unlike you who, thanks to your easy-going spirit, go sleepless and earn double wages, " One as a herdsman of cattle, another as tender of white flocks." [1] On the contrary, one took excessive delight in boys and thought love of women a pit of doom,[2] while the other, virgin of all love of males, was highly susceptible to women. So I presided over a contest between these two warring passions and found the occasion quite indescribably delightful. The imprint of their words remains inscribed in my ears almost as though they had been spoken a moment ago. Therefore, putting aside all pretexts for being excused this task, I shall retail to you exactly what I heard the two of them say.

THEOMNESTUS

Well, I shall get up from here and sit facing you, " Waiting the time when Aeacus' son makes an end of his singing." [3] But you must unfold for us in song the old and glorious lays of the contest of loves.

LYCINUS

6. I had in mind going to Italy and a swift ship had been made ready for me. It was one of the double-banked vessels which seem particularly to be used by the Liburnians, a race who live along the Ionian

---

[1] Homer, *Odyssey*, X. 85.

[2] βάραθρον means an abyss, but is used in particular of the cleft into which the Athenians threw criminals.

[3] Homer, *Iliad*, IX. 191.

θεοὺς προσκυνήσας καὶ Δία ξένιον ἵλεω συνεφάψα-
σθαι τῆς ἀποδήμου στρατείας ἐπικαλεσάμενος ἀπ'
ἄστεος ὁρικῷ ζεύγει κατῄειν ἐπὶ θάλασσαν· εἶτα
τοὺς παραπέμποντάς με δεξιωσάμενος—ἠκολούθει
δὲ παιδείας λιπαρὴς ὄχλος, οἳ συνεχὲς ἡμῖν ἐντυγχά-
νοντες ἀνιαρῶς διεζεύγνυντο—τῆς πρύμνης οὖν
ἐπιβὰς ἐγγὺς ἐμαυτὸν ἵδρυσα τοῦ κυβερνήτου. καὶ
ῥοθίῳ τῷ τῶν ἐλατήρων μετὰ μικρὸν ἀπὸ τῆς γῆς
ἀναχθέντες, ἐπειδὴ μάλα καὶ κατόπιν ἡμᾶς ἐποίμαι-
νον αὖραι, τὸν ἱστὸν ἐκ τῶν μεσοκοίλων ἄραντες [1]
καρχησίῳ τὸ κέρας προσεστείλαμεν· [2] εἶτ' ἀθρόας
κατὰ τῶν κάλων τὰς ὀθόνας ἐκχέαντες ἠρέμα πιμ-
πλαμένου τοῦ λίνου κατ' οὐδὲν οἶμαι βέλους ἐλάττονι
ῥοίζῳ διιπτάμεθα βαρὺ τοῦ κύματος ὑποβρυχωμένου
περὶ τὴν σχίζουσαν αὐτὸ πρῷραν. 7. ἀλλ' ἅ γε μὴν
ἐν τῷ μεταξὺ παράπλῳ σπουδῆς ἢ παιδιᾶς ἐχόμενα
συνηνέχθη, καιρὸς οὐ πάνυ μηκύνειν. ὡς δὲ τῆς
Κιλικίας τὴν ἔφαλον ἀμείψαντες εἰχόμεθα τοῦ
Παμφυλίου κόλπου, Χελιδονέας ὑπερθέοντες οὐκ
ἀμοχθεὶ τοὺς εὐτυχεῖς τῆς παλαιᾶς Ἑλλάδος ὅρους,
ἑκάστῃ τῶν Λυκιακῶν πόλεων ἐπεξενούμεθα μύθοις
τὰ πολλὰ χαίροντες· οὐδὲν γὰρ ἐν αὐταῖς σαφὲς
εὐδαιμονίας ὁρᾶται λείψανον· ἄχρι τῆς Ἡλιάδος [3]
ἁψάμενοι Ῥόδου τὸ συνεχὲς τοῦ μεταξὺ πλοῦ
διαναπαῦσαι πρὸς ὀλίγον ἐκρίναμεν. 8. οἱ μὲν οὖν
ἐρέται τὸ σκάφος ἔξαλον ἐς γῆν ἀνασπάσαντες ἐγγὺς

---

[1] ἄραντες edd.: ἀκαρῆ codd..
[2] προεστείλαμεν codd.: corr. Graeve.
[3] Ἡλιάδων ΓΕ: corr. recc..

---

[1] As the Liburnians lived in Dalmatia on the north east
coast of the Adriatic, and the Ionian Gulf was, strictly

Gulf.[1] After paying such respects as I could to the local gods and invoking Zeus, God of Strangers, to assist propitiously in my expedition to foreign parts, I left the town and drove down to the sea with a pair of mules. Then I bade farewell to those who were escorting me, for I was followed by a throng of determined scholars who kept talking to me and parted with me reluctantly. Well, I climbed on to the poop and took my seat near the helmsman. We were soon carried away from land by the surge of our oars and, since we had very favourable breezes astern, we raised the mast from the hold and ran the yard up to the masthead. Then we let all our canvas down over the sheets and, as our sail gently filled, we went whistling along just as loud, I fancy, as an arrow does, and flew through the waves which roared around our prow as it cut through them.

7. But it isn't the time to describe at any length the events serious or light of the intervening coastal voyage. But, when we had passed the Cilician seaboard and were in the gulf of Pamphylia, after passing with some difficulty the Swallow-Islands,[2] those fortune-favoured limits of ancient Greece, we visited each of the Lycian cities, where we found our chief pleasure in the tales told, for no vestige of prosperity is visible in them to the eye. Eventually we made Rhodes, the island of the Sun-God, and decided to take a short rest from our uninterrupted voyaging.

8. Accordingly our oarsmen hauled the ship ashore and pitched their tents near by. I had been provided

speaking, the sea between Italy and Greece south of the Adriatic, this statement is only approximately true.

[2] A notoriously stormy area. Cf. *The Ship*, c. 8.

ἐσκήνωσαν, ἐγὼ δ' εὐτρεπισμένου μοι ξενῶνος
ἀπαντικρὺ τοῦ Διονυσίου κατὰ σχολὴν ἐβάδιζον
ὑπερφυοῦς ἀπολαύσεως ἐμπιμπλάμενος· ἔστιν γὰρ
ὄντως ἡ πόλις Ἡλίου πρέπον ἔχουσα τῷ θεῷ τὸ
κάλλος. ἐκπεριϊὼν δὲ τὰς ἐν τῷ Διονυσίῳ στοὰς
ἑκάστην γραφὴν κατώπτευον ἅμα τῷ τέρποντι τῆς
ὄψεως ἡρωϊκοὺς μύθους ἀνανεούμενος· εὐθὺ γάρ
μοι δύ᾽ ἢ τρεῖς προσερρύησαν ὀλίγου διαφόρου[1]
πᾶσαν ἱστορίαν ἀφηγούμενοι· τὰ δὲ πολλὰ καὶ
αὐτὸς εἰκασίᾳ προὐλάμβανον. 9. ἤδη δὲ τῆς θέας
ἅλις ἔχοντι καὶ διανοουμένῳ μοι βαδίζειν οἴκαδε τὸ
ἥδιστον ἐπὶ ξένης ἀπήντησέ μοι κέρδος, ἄνδρες ἐκ
παλαιοῦ χρόνου συνήθεις, οὓς οὐδ᾽ αὐτὸς ἀγνοεῖν μοι
δοκεῖς πολλάκις ἡμῖν ἰδὼν[2] ἐπιφοιτῶντας ἐνταῦθα,
τὸν ἐκ Κορίνθου Χαρικλέα νεανίαν οὐκ ἄμορφον,
ἔχοντά τι καὶ κομμωτικῆς ἀσκήσεως ἅτε οἶμαι
γυναίοις ἐνωραϊζόμενον· ἅμα δ᾽ αὐτῷ καὶ Καλλι-
κρατίδαν τὸν Ἀθηναῖον τὸν τρόπον ἁπλοϊκόν·
προηγουμένως γὰρ πολιτικῶν λόγων προΐστατο καὶ
ταυτησὶ τῆς ἀγοραίου ῥητορικῆς. ἦν δὲ καὶ τῷ
σώματι γυμναστικός, οὐ δι᾽ ἄλλο τί μοι δοκεῖν τὰς
παλαίστρας ἀγαπῶν ἢ διὰ τοὺς παιδικοὺς ἔρωτας·
ὅλος γὰρ εἰς τοῦτο ἐπτόητο.[3] τῷ δὲ πρὸς τὸ θῆλυ
μίσει πολλὰ καὶ Προμηθεῖ κατηρᾶτο. πόρρωθεν
οὖν ἰδὼν ἑκάτερός με γήθους καὶ χαρᾶς πλέοι
προσέδραμον· εἶθ᾽ ὁποῖα φιλεῖ, δεξιωσάμενοι πρὸς

---

[1] διάφοροι codd.: corr. Du Soul.
[2] ἰδὼν om. E.
[3] ἐπτοεῖτο ΓΕ: corr. recc..

---

[1] Rhodes was famous for its Colossus, a gigantic statue

162

with accommodation opposite the temple of Dionysus, and, as I strolled along unhurriedly, I was filled with an extraordinary pleasure. For it really is the city of Helius [1] with a beauty in keeping with that god. As I walked round the porticos in the temple of Dionysus, I examined each painting, not only delighting my eyes but also renewing my acquaintance with the tales of the heroes. For immediately two or three fellows rushed up to me, offering for a small fee to explain every story for me, though most of what they said I had already guessed for myself.

9. When I had now had my fill of sightseeing and was minded to go to my lodgings, I met with the most delightful of all blessings in a strange land, old acquaintances of long standing, whom I think you also know yourself, for you've often seen them visiting us here, Charicles a young man from Corinth who is not only handsome but shows some evidence of skilful use of cosmetics, because, I imagine, he wishes to attract the women, and with him Callicratidas, the Athenian, a man of straightforward ways. For he was pre-eminent among the leading figures in public speaking and in this forensic oratory of ours. He was also a devotee of physical training, though in my opinion he was only fond of the wrestling-schools because of his love for boys. For he was enthusiastic only for that, while his hatred for women made him often curse Prometheus. [2] Well, they both saw me from a distance and hurried up to me overjoyed and delighted. Then, as so often happens, each of them

of Helius, the Sun-God.

[2] As the inventor of women. Cf. c. 43.

αὐτὸν ἐλθεῖν ἑκάτερος ἠξίουν με. κἀγὼ φιλονει
κοῦντας ὁρῶν περαιτέρω, Τὸ μὲν τήμερον, εἶπον,
ὦ Καλλικρατίδα καὶ Χαρίκλεις, ἄμφω καλῶς ἔχον
ἐστὶν ὑμᾶς παρ' ἐμοὶ [1] φοιτᾶν, ἵνα μὴ πλείω τὴν ἔριν
ἐγείρητε· ταῖς δὲ ἐφεξῆς ἡμέραις—τρεῖς γὰρ
ἐνταῦθα ἢ τέτταρας διέγνωκα μένειν—ἀμοιβαίως
ἀνθεστιάσετέ [2] με, κλήρῳ διακριθεὶς ὁ πρότερος.
10. δοκεῖ ταῦτα. κἀκείνην μὲν τὴν ἡμέραν εἰστιάρ
χουν ἐγώ, τῇ δ' ἐπιούσῃ Καλλικρατίδας, εἶτα μετ'
αὐτὸν ὁ Χαρικλῆς. ἑώρων δὴ καὶ παρὰ τὴν ἑστίασιν
ἐναργῆ τῆς ἑκατέρου διαθέσεως τεκμήρια· ὁ μὲν
γὰρ Ἀθηναῖος εὐμόρφοις παισὶν ἐξήσκητο, καὶ πᾶς
οἰκέτης αὐτῷ σχεδὸν ἀγένειος ἦν μέχρι τοῦ πρώ
τον ὑπογράφοντος αὐτοὺς [3] χνοῦ παραμένοντες,
ἐπειδὰν δὲ ἰούλοις αἱ παρειαὶ πυκασθῶσιν, οἰκόνομοι
καὶ τῶν Ἀθήνησι χωρίων κηδεμόνες ἀπεστέλλοντο.
Χαρικλεῖ γε μὴν πολὺς ὀρχηστρίδων καὶ μουσουργῶν
χορὸς εἵπετο καὶ πᾶν τὸ δωμάτιον ὡς ἐν Θεσμοφο
ρίοις γυναικῶν μεστὸν ἦν ἀνδρὸς οὐδ' ἀκαρῆ παρόν
τος, εἰ μή τί που νήπιον ἢ γέρων ὑπερῆλιξ ὀψοποιὸς
ὀφθείη, χρόνου ζηλοτυπίας ὑποψίαν οὐκ ἔχοντος.
ἦν μὲν οὖν, ὡς ἔφην, καὶ ταῦθ' ἱκανὰ τῆς ἀμφοτέρων
γνώμης δείγματα. πολλάκις γε μὴν ἐπ' ὀλίγον
ἀψιμαχίαι τινὲς αὐτοῖς ἐκινήθησαν, οὐχ ὡς πέρας
ἔχειν τι τὴν ζήτησιν. ἀλλ' ἐπεὶ καιρὸς ἦν ἀνάγεσθαι,
σύμπλους ἐθελήσαντας αὐτοὺς ἐπηγόμην· διενοοῦν
το γὰρ εἰς τὴν Ἰταλίαν ἀπαίρειν ὁμοίως ἐμοί.

---

[1] ἐμοὶ ΓΕ: ἐμὲ Ε[2], recc..   [2] ἀνθεστιάσητέ ΓΕ: corr recc..
[3] ὑπογραφέντος αὐτοῖς recc., edd..

[1] A festival in honour of Demeter celebrated exclusively
by women.

clasped me by the hand and begged me to visit his house. I, seeing that they were carrying their rivalry too far, said, "Today, Callicratidas and Charicles, it is the proper thing for both of you to be my guests so that you may not fan your rivalry into greater flame. But on the days to follow—for I've decided to remain here for three or four days—you will return my hospitality by entertaining me each in turn, drawing lots to decide which of you will start."

10. This was agreed, and for that day I presided as host, while on the next day Callicratidas did so, and after him Charicles. Now, even when they were entertaining me, I could see concrete evidence of the inclinations of each. For my Athenian friend was well provided with handsome slave-boys and all of his servants were pretty well beardless. They remained with him till the down first appeared on their faces, but, once any growth cast a shadow on their cheeks, they would be sent away to be stewards and overseers of his properties at Athens. Charicles, however, had in attendance a large band of dancing girls and singing girls and all his house was as full of women as if it were the Thesmophoria,[1] with not the slightest trace of male presence except that here and there could be seen an infant boy or a superannuated old cook whose age could give even the jealous no cause for suspicion. Well, these things were themselves, as I said, sufficient indications of the dispositions of both of them. Often, however, short skirmishes broke out between them without the point at issue being settled. But, when it was time for me to put to sea, at their wish I took them with me to share my voyage, for they like me were minded to set out for Italy.

11. καὶ δόξαν ἡμῖν Κνίδῳ προσορμῆσαι[1] κατὰ θέαν καὶ τοῦ Ἀφροδίτης ἱεροῦ[2]—ὑμνεῖται δὲ τούτου τὸ τῆς Πραξιτέλους εὐχερείας[3] ὄντως ἐπαφρόδιτον—ἠρέμα τῇ γῇ προσηνέχθημεν αὐτῆς οἶμαι τῆς θεοῦ λιπαρᾷ γαλήνῃ πομποστολούσης τὸ σκάφος. τοῖς μὲν οὖν ἄλλοις ἔμελον αἱ συνήθεις παρασκευαί, ἐγὼ δὲ τὸ ἐρωτικὸν ζεῦγος ἑκατέρωθεν ἐξαψάμενος κύκλῳ περιῄειν τὴν Κνίδον οὐκ ἀγελαστὶ τῆς κεραμευτικῆς ἀκολασίας μετέχων ὡς ἐν Ἀφροδίτης πόλει. στοὰς δὲ Σωστράτου καὶ τἆλλα ὅσα τέρπειν ἡμᾶς ἐδύνατο, πρῶτον ἐκπεριελθόντες ἐπὶ τὸν νεὼν τῆς Ἀφροδίτης βαδίζομεν, νὼ μέν, ἐγώ τε καὶ Χαρικλῆς, πάνυ προθύμως, Καλλικρατίδας δ' ὡς ἐπὶ θέαν θήλειαν ἄκων, ἥδιον ἂν οἶμαι τῆς Ἀφροδίτης Κνιδίας[4] τὸν ἐν Θεσπιαῖς ἀντικαταλλαξάμενος Ἔρωτα. 12. καὶ πως εὐθὺς ἡμῖν ἀπ' αὐτοῦ τοῦ τεμένους Ἀφροδίσιοι προσέπνευσαν αὖραι· τὸ γὰρ αἴθριον οὐκ εἰς ἔδαφος ἄγονον μάλιστα λίθων πλαξὶ λείαις ἐστρωμένον, ἀλλ' ὡς ἐν Ἀφροδίτης ἅπαν ἦν γόνιμον ἡμέρων καρπῶν, ἃ ταῖς κόμαις εὐθαλέσιν ἄχρι πόρρω βρύοντα τὸν πέριξ ἀέρα συνωρόφουν. περιττόν γε μὴν ἡ πυκνόκαρπος ἐτεθήλει μυρρίνη παρὰ τὴν δέσποιναν

---

[1] προσορμίσαι recc., edd..

[2] καὶ τοῦ . . . ἱεροῦ Ε[a]: καὶ τὸ . . . ἱερὸν ΓΕ: καὶ τοῦ . . . ἱεροῦ Burmeister.   [3] εὐχειρίας coniecit L.S.J.

[4] τῆς ante Κνιδίας add. Ε[2].

---

[1] Aphrodite was worshipped at Cnidus as εὔπλοια. Cf. Theocritus 22. 11.

[2] These porticos (described by Pliny, Nat. Hist. 36.12.18 as " pensilis ambulatio ") seemed to have supported a terrace used as a promenade, and were regarded as one of

11. Now, as we had decided to anchor at Cnidus to see the temple of Aphrodite, which is famed as possessing the most truly lovely example of Praxiteles' skill, we gently approached the land with the goddess herself, I believe, escorting our ship [1] with smooth calm waters. The others occupied themselves with the usual preparations, but I took the two authorities on love, one on either side of me, and went round Cnidus, finding no little amusement in the wanton products of the potters, for I remembered I was in Aphrodite's city. First we went round the porticos of Sostratus [2] and everywhere else that could give us pleasure and then we walked to the temple of Aphrodite. Charicles and I did so very eagerly, but Callicratidas was reluctant because he was going to see something female, and would have preferred, I imagine, to have had Eros of Thespiae [3] instead of Aphrodite of Cnidus.

12. And immediately, it seemed, there breathed upon us from the sacred precinct itself breezes fraught with love. For the uncovered court was not for the most part paved with smooth slabs of stone to form an unproductive area but, as was to be expected in Aphrodite's temple, was all of it prolific with garden fruits. These trees, luxuriant far and wide with fresh green leaves, roofed in the air around them. But more than all others flourished the berry-laden myrtle growing luxuriantly beside its mistress [4] and

the masterpieces of the famous architect, Sostratus of Cnidus (for whom see *How To Write History* 62, *Hippias* 2).

[3] Another famous statue of Praxiteles in the Boeotian town of Thespiae. The original had been lost in a fire at Rome but a copy survived at Thespiae. See Pausanias 9, 27, 3.　　　　[4] The myrtle was sacred to Aphrodite.

αὐτῆς δαψιλὴς πεφυκυῖα τῶν τε λοιπῶν δένδρω
ἕκαστον, ὅσα κάλλους μετείληχεν· οὐδ' αὐτὰ γέ
ροντος ἤδη χρόνου πολιὰ καθαύαινεν, ἀλλ' ὑπ
ἀκμῆς σφριγῶντα νέοις κλωσὶν ἦν ὥρια. τούτοις δ
ἀνεμέμικτο καὶ τὰ καρπῶν μὲν ἄλλως ἄγονα, τὴν δ
εὐμορφίαν ἔχοντα καρπόν,[1] κυπαρίττων[2] γε κα
πλατανίστων αἰθέρια μήκη καὶ σὺν αὐταῖς αὐτόμολο
Ἀφροδίτης ἡ τῆς θεοῦ πάλαι φυγὰς Δάφνη. παντ
γε μὴν δένδρῳ περιπλέγδην ὁ φίλεργος προσείρπυζε
κιττός. ἀμφιλαφεῖς ἄμπελοι πυκνοῖς κατήρτηντ
βότρυσιν· τερπνοτέρα γὰρ Ἀφροδίτη μετὰ Διονύσο
καὶ τὸ παρ' ἀμφοῖν ἡδὺ σύγκρατον, εἰ δ' ἀπο
ζευχθεῖεν ἀλλήλων, ἧττον εὐφραίνουσιν. ἦν δ' ὑπ
ταῖς ἄγαν παλινσκίοις ὕλαις ἱλαραὶ κλισίαι τοῖ
ἐνεστιᾶσθαι θέλουσιν, εἰς ἃ τῶν μὲν ἀστικῶν σπανί
ἐπεφοίτων τινές, ἀθρόος δ' ὁ πολιτικὸς ὄχλο
ἐπανηγύριζεν ὄντως ἀφροδισιάζοντες. 13. ἐπεὶ δ
ἱκανῶς τοῖς φυτοῖς ἐτέρφθημεν, εἴσω τοῦ νε
παρῇειμεν. ἡ μὲν οὖν θεὸς ἐν μέσῳ καθίδρυται—
Παρίας δὲ λίθου δαίδαλμα κάλλιστον—ὑπερήφανο
καὶ σεσηρότι γέλωτι μικρὸν ὑπομειδιῶσα. πᾶν δ
τὸ κάλλος αὐτῆς ἀκάλυπτον οὐδεμιᾶς ἐσθῆτο
ἀμπεχούσης γεγύμνωται, πλὴν ὅσα τῇ ἑτέρᾳ χειρ
τὴν αἰδῶ λεληθότως ἐπικρύπτειν. τοσοῦτόν γε μὴ
ἡ δημιουργὸς ἴσχυσε τέχνη, ὥστε τὴν ἀντίτυπο

---

[1] καρπόν recc.: καρπῶν ΓΕ.
[2] κυπάριττός Ε: κυπαριττόν Γ: corr. recc..
[3] προσείρπυε codd.: corr. Dindorf.

---

[1] I.e. the laurel. The story was that the nymph Daphne
rejected the advances of her lover, Apollo, and escaped by
being transformed into a laurel-tree.

all the other trees that are endowed with beauty. Though they were old in years they were not withered or faded but, still in their youthful prime, swelled with fresh sprays. Intermingled with these were trees that were unproductive except for having beauty for their fruit—cypresses and planes that towered to the heavens and with them Daphne,[1] who deserted from Aphrodite and fled from that goddess long ago. But around every tree crept and twined the ivy,[2] devotee of love. Rich vines were hung with their thick clusters of grapes. For Aphrodite is more delightful when accompanied by Dionysus and the gifts of each are sweeter if blended together, but, should they be parted from each other, they afford less pleasure. Under the particularly shady trees were joyous couches for those who wished to feast themselves there. These were occasionally visited by a few folk of breeding, but all the city rabble flocked there on holidays and paid true homage to Aphrodite.

13. When the plants had given us pleasure enough, we entered the temple. In the midst thereof sits the goddess—she's a most beautiful statue of Parian [3] marble—arrogantly smiling a little as a grin parts her lips. Draped by no garment, all her beauty is uncovered and revealed, except in so far as she unobtrusively uses one hand to hide her private parts. So great was the power of the craftsman's art that the hard unyielding marble did justice to

[2] The ivy was sacred to Bacchus, the wine-god and promoter of love.

[3] In *Zeus Rants* 10 Lucian gives the material as Pentelic marble.

οὕτω καὶ καρτερὰν τοῦ λίθου φύσιν ἑκάστοις μέλεσιν
ἐπιπρέπειν. ὁ γοῦν Χαρικλῆς ἐμμανές τι καὶ παρά-
φορον ἀναβοήσας, Εὐτυχέστατος, εἶπεν, θεῶν ὁ
διὰ ταύτην δεθεὶς Ἄρης, καὶ ἅμα προσδραμὼν
λιπαρέσι [1] τοῖς χείλεσιν ἐφ᾿ ὅσον ἦν δυνατὸν
ἐκτείνων τὸν αὐχένα κατεφίλει· σιγῇ δ᾿ ἐφεστὼς ὁ
Καλλικρατίδας κατὰ νοῦν ἀπεθαύμαζεν. ἔστι δ᾿
ἀμφίθυρος ὁ νεὼς καὶ τοῖς θέλουσι κατὰ νώτου τὴν
θεὸν ἰδεῖν ἀκριβῶς, ἵνα μηδὲν αὐτῆς ἀθαύμαστον ᾖ.
δι᾿ εὐμαρείας οὖν ἐστι τῇ ἑτέρᾳ πύλῃ παρελθοῦσιν
τὴν ὄπισθεν εὐμορφίαν διαθρῆσαι. 14. δόξαν οὖν
ὅλην τὴν θεὸν ἰδεῖν, εἰς τὸ κατόπιν τοῦ σηκοῦ
περιήλθομεν. εἶτ᾿ ἀνοιγείσης τῆς θύρας ὑπὸ τοῦ
κλειδοφύλακος ἐμπεπιστευμένου γυναίου θάμβος
αἰφνίδιον ἡμᾶς εἶχεν τοῦ κάλλους. ὁ γοῦν Ἀθηναῖος
ἡσυχῇ πρὸ μικροῦ βλέπων ἐπεὶ τὰ παιδικὰ μέρη
τῆς θεοῦ κατώπτευσεν, ἀθρόως πολὺ τοῦ Χαρικλέους
ἐμμανέστερον ἀνεβόησεν, Ἡράκλεις, ὅση μὲν τῶν
μεταφρένων εὐρυθμία, πῶς δ᾿ ἀμφιλαφεῖς αἱ λαγό-
νες, ἀγκάλισμα χειροπληθές· ὡς δ᾿ εὐπερίγραφοι
τῶν γλουτῶν αἱ σάρκες ἐπικυρτοῦνται μήτ᾿ ἄγαν
ἐλλιπεῖς αὐτοῖς ὀστέοις προσεσταλμέναι μήτε εἰς
ὑπέρογκον ἐκκεχυμέναι πιότητα.[2] τῶν δὲ τοῖς
ἰσχίοις ἐνεσφραγισμένων ἐξ ἑκατέρων τύπων οὐκ ἂν
εἴποι τις ὡς ἡδὺς ὁ γέλως· μηροῦ τε καὶ κνήμης
ἐπ᾿ εὐθὺ τεταμένης ἄχρι ποδὸς ἠκριβωμένοι ῥυθμοί.
τοιοῦτος [3] ἄρα Γανυμήδης ἐν οὐρανῷ Διὶ τὸ νέκταρ

[1] λιπαρέσι Schaefer: λιπαροῖς codd..
[2] ποιότητα ΓΕ: corr. recc..   [3] τοιοῦτο ΓΕ: corr. Ε².

---

[1] For the story of how the injured husband, Hephaestus,

every limb. Charicles at any rate raised a mad distracted cry and exclaimed, " Happiest indeed of the gods was Ares [1] who suffered chains because of her ! " And, as he spoke, he ran up and, stretching out his neck as far as he could, started to kiss the goddess with importunate lips. Callicratidas stood by in silence with amazement in his heart.

The temple had a door on both sides for the benefit of those also who wish to have a good view of the goddess from behind, so that no part of her be left unadmired. It's easy therefore for people to enter by the other door and survey the beauty of her back. 14. And so we decided to see all of the goddess and went round to the back of the precinct. Then, when the door had been opened by the woman responsible for keeping the keys, we were filled with an immediate wonder for the beauty we beheld. The Athenian who had been so impassive an observer a minute before, upon inspecting those parts of the goddess which recommend a boy, suddenly raised a shout far more frenzied than that of Charicles. " Heracles ! " he exclaimed, " what a well-proportioned back ! What generous flanks she has ! How satisfying an armful to embrace ! How delicately moulded the flesh on the buttocks, neither too thin and close to the bone, nor yet revealing too great an expanse of fat ! And as for those precious parts sealed in on either side by the hips, how inexpressibly sweetly they smile ! How perfect the proportions of the thighs and the shins as they stretch down in a straight line to the feet ! So that's what Ganymede looks like as he pours out the nectar in heaven for Zeus

[1] trapped Ares in chains when in bed with Aphrodite see *Dialogues of the Gods*, 21.

ἥδιον ἐγχεῖ· παρὰ μὲν γὰρ Ἥβης οὐκ ἂν ἐγὼ
διακονουμένης ποτὸν ἐδεξάμην. ἐνθεαστικῶς [1] ταῦτα τοῦ Καλλικρατίδου βοῶντος ὁ Χαρικλῆς ὑπὸ τοῦ
σφόδρα θάμβους ὀλίγου δεῖν ἐπεπήγει τακερόν [2] τι
καὶ ῥέον ἐν τοῖς ὄμμασι πάθος ἀνυγραίνων. 15. ἐπεὶ
δὲ τοῦ θαυμάζειν ὁ κόρος ἡμᾶς ἀπήλλαξεν, ἐπὶ
θατέρου μηροῦ σπίλον εἴδομεν ὥσπερ ἐν ἐσθῆτι
κηλίδα· ἤλεγχε δ' αὐτοῦ τὴν ἀμορφίαν ἡ περὶ τἄλλα
τῆς λίθου λαμπρότης. ἐγὼ μὲν οὖν πιθανῇ τἀληθὲς
εἰκασίᾳ τοπάζων φύσιν ᾤμην τοῦ λίθου τὸ βλεπό-
μενον εἶναι· πάθος γὰρ οὐδὲ τούτων ἔστιν ἔξω,
πολλὰ δὲ τοῖς κατ' ἄκρον εἶναι δυναμένοις καλοῖς ἡ
τύχη παρεμποδίζει. μέλαιναν οὖν ἐσπιλῶσθαι φυσι-
κήν τινα κηλίδα νομίζων καὶ κατὰ τοῦτο τοῦ
Πραξιτέλους ἐθαύμαζον, ὅτι τοῦ λίθου τὸ δύσμορφον
ἐν τοῖς ἧττον ἐλέγχεσθαι δυναμένοις μέρεσιν
ἀπέκρυψεν. ἡ δὲ παρεστῶσα πλησίον ἡμῶν ζάκορος
ἀπίστου λόγου καινὴν παρέδωκεν ἱστορίαν· ἔφη γὰρ
οὐκ ἀσήμου γένους νεανίαν—ἡ δὲ πρᾶξις ἀνώνυμον
αὐτὸν ἐσίγησεν—πολλάκις ἐπιφοιτῶντα τῷ τεμένει
σὺν δειλαίῳ δαίμονι ἐρασθῆναι τῆς θεοῦ καὶ πανή-
μερον ἐν τῷ ναῷ διατρίβοντα κατ' ἀρχὰς ἔχειν
δεισιδαίμονος ἁγιστείας δόκησιν· ἔκ τε γὰρ τῆς
ἑωθινῆς κοίτης πολὺ προλαμβάνων τὸν ὄρθρον
ἐπεφοίτα καὶ μετὰ δύσιν ἄκων ἐβάδιζεν οἴκαδε τήν θ'
ὅλην ἡμέραν ἀπαντικρὺ τῆς θεοῦ καθεζόμενος
ὀρθὰς ἐπ' αὐτὴν διηνεκῶς τὰς τῶν ὀμμάτων βολὰς
ἀπήρειδεν. ἄσημοι δ' αὐτῷ ψιθυρισμοὶ καὶ κλεπτο-
μένης λαλιᾶς ἐρωτικαὶ διεπεραίνοντο μέμψεις.

---

[1] ἐνθεαστικῶς Eᵃ· ἔνθα ἀστικῶς ΓΕ.

[2] τακηρόν ΓΕ¹.

and makes it taste sweeter. For I'd never have taken the cup from Hebe if she served me." While Callicratidas was shouting this under the spell of the goddess, Charicles in the excess of his admiration stood almost petrified, though his emotions showed in the melting tears trickling from his eyes.

15. When we could admire no more, we noticed a mark on one thigh like a stain on a dress ; the unsightliness of this was shown up by the brightness of the marble everywhere else. I therefore, hazarding a plausible guess about the truth of the matter, supposed that what we saw was a natural defect in the marble. For even such things as these are subject to accident and many potential masterpieces of beauty are thwarted by bad luck. And so, thinking the black mark to be a natural blemish, I found in this too cause to admire Praxiteles for having hidden what was unsightly in the marble in the parts less able to be examined closely. But the attendant woman who was standing near us told us a strange, incredible story. For she said that a young man of a not undistinguished family—though his deed has caused him to be left nameless—who often visited the precinct, was so ill-starred as to fall in love with the goddess.[1] He would spend all day in the temple and at first gave the impression of pious awe. For in the morning he would leave his bed long before dawn to go to the temple and only return home reluctantly after sunset. All day long would he sit facing the goddess with his eyes fixed uninterruptedly upon her, whispering indistinctly and carrying on a lover's complaints in secret conversation.

[1] This story, originating from Posidonius, is also known to Lucian (*Essays in Portraiture* 4).

173

16. ἐπειδὰν δὲ καὶ μικρὰ τοῦ πάθους ἑαυτὸν ἀποβουκολῆσαι θελήσειεν, προσειπὼν τῇ δὲ τραπέζῃ τέτταρας ἀστραγάλους Λιβυκῆς δορκὸς ἀπαριθμήσας διεπέττευε τὴν ἐλπίδα, καὶ βαλὼν μὲν ἐπίσκοπα,[1] μάλιστα δ᾽ εἴ ποτε τὴν θεὸν αὐτὴν εὐβολήσειε, μηδενὸς ἀστραγάλου πεσόντος ἴσῳ σχήματι, προσεκύνει τῆς ἐπιθυμίας τεύξεσθαι νομίζων· εἰ δ᾽, ὁποῖα φιλεῖ, φαύλως κατὰ τῆς τραπέζης ῥίψειεν, οἱ δ᾽ ἐπὶ τὸ δυσφημότερον ἀνασταῖεν, ὅλῃ Κνίδῳ καταρώμενος ὡς ἐπ᾽ ἀνηκέστῳ συμφορᾷ [καὶ][2] κατήφει καὶ δι᾽ ὀλίγου συναρπάσας ἑτέρῳ βόλῳ τὴν πρὶν ἀστοχίαν ἐθεράπευεν. ἤδη δὲ πλέον αὐτῷ τοῦ πάθους ἐρεθιζομένου τοῖχος ἅπας ἐχαράσσετο καὶ πᾶς μαλακοῦ δένδρου φλοιὸς Ἀφροδίτην καλὴν ἐκήρυσσεν· ἐτιμᾶτο δ᾽ ἐξ ἴσου Διὶ Πραξιτέλης καὶ πᾶν ὅ τι κειμήλιον εὐπρεπὲς οἴκοι φυλάττοιτο, τοῦτ᾽ ἦν ἀνάθημα τῆς θεοῦ. πέρας αἱ σφοδραὶ τῶν ἐν αὐτῷ πόθων ἐπιτάσεις ἀπενοήθησαν,[3] εὑρέθη δὲ τόλμα τῆς ἐπιθυμίας μαστροπός· ἤδη γὰρ ἐπὶ δύσιν ἡλίου κλίνοντος ἠρέμα λαθὼν τοὺς παρόντας ὄπισθε τῆς θύρας παρεισερρύη καὶ στὰς ἀφανὴς ἐνδοτάτω σχεδὸν οὐδ᾽ ἀναπνέων ἠτρέμει, συνήθως δὲ τῶν ζακόρων ἔξωθεν τὴν θύραν ἐφελκυσαμένων ἔνδον ὁ καινὸς Ἀγχίσης καθεῖρκτο. καὶ τί γὰρ ἀρρήτου νυκτὸς ἐγὼ τόλμαν ἢ λάλος[4] ἐπ᾽ ἀκριβὲς

---

[1] ἐπίσκοπα Wyttenbach: ἐπὶ σκοποῦ codd..

[2] sic Du Soul: καὶ κατηφεῖ ΓΕ.

[3] ἐπενοήθησαν ΓΕ: corr. recc..

[4] ἡ λάλος Burmeister: ἢ ἄλλος codd.: ἢ ἄλγος tentavi.

---

[1] The highest throw at dice was when each face was different. It was called Venus or Aphrodite.

16. But when he wished to give himself some little comfort from his suffering, after first addressing the goddess, he would count out on the table four knuckle-bones of a Libyan gazelle and take a gamble on his expectations. If he made a successful throw and particularly if ever he was blessed with the throw named after the goddess herself,[1] and no dice showed the same face, he would prostrate himself before the goddess, thinking he would gain his desire. But, if as usually happens he made an indifferent throw on to his table, and the dice revealed an unpropitious result, he would curse all Cnidus and show utter dejection as if at an irremediable disaster ; but a minute later he would snatch up the dice and try to cure by another throw his earlier lack of success. But presently, as his passion grew more inflamed, every wall came to be inscribed with his messages and the bark of every tender tree told of fair Aphrodite. Praxiteles was honoured by him as much as Zeus and every beautiful treasure that his home guarded was offered to the goddess. In the end the violent tension of his desires turned to desperation and he found in audacity a procurer for his lusts. For, when the sun was now sinking to its setting, quietly and unnoticed by those present, he slipped in behind the door and, standing invisible in the inmost part of the chamber, he kept still, hardly even breathing. When the attendants closed the door from the outside in the normal way, this new Anchises [2] was locked in. But why do I chatter on and tell you in every detail the reckless deed of that unmentionable night ? These marks of

---

[2] Anchises, the father of Aeneas, though a mortal had enjoyed the love of Aphrodite.

ὑμῖν διηγοῦμαι; τῶν ἐρωτικῶν περιπλοκῶν ἴχνη
ταῦτα μεθ' ἡμέραν ὤφθη καὶ τὸν σπίλον εἶχεν ἡ
θεὸς ὧν ἔπαθεν ἔλεγχον. αὐτόν γε μὴν τὸν νεανίαν,
ὡς ὁ δημώδης ἱστορεῖ λόγος, ἢ κατὰ πετρῶν φασιν ἢ
κατὰ πελαγίου κύματος ἐνεχθέντα παντελῶς ἀφανῆ
γενέσθαι.

17. ταῦτα τῆς ζακόρου διηγουμένης μεταξὺ
τοῦ λόγου διαβοήσας εἶπεν ὁ Χαρικλῆς, Οὐκοῦν
τὸ θῆλυ, κἂν λίθινον ᾖ, φιλεῖται. τί δ', εἴ τις
ἔμψυχον εἶδε τοιοῦτο κάλλος; ἆρ' οὐκ ἂν ἡ μία
νὺξ τῶν τοῦ Διὸς σκήπτρων ἐτιμᾶτο;

μειδιάσας δὲ ὁ Καλλικρατίδας, Οὐδέπω, φησίν,
ἴσμεν, ὦ Χαρίκλεις, εἰ πολλῶν ἀκουσόμεθα τοιούτων
διηγημάτων, ὅταν ἐν Θεσπιαῖς γενώμεθα. καὶ νῦν
δὲ τῆς ἀπὸ σοῦ ζηλουμένης Ἀφροδίτης ἐναργές ἐστι
τοῦτο δεῖγμα.

Πῶς; ἐρομένου τοῦ Χαρικλέους, ἄγαν πιθανῶς
ἔδοξέ μοι λέγειν ὁ Καλλικρατίδας· ἔφη γὰρ ὡς ὁ
ἐρασθεὶς νεανίας παννύχου σχολῆς λαβόμενος, ὥσθ'
ὅλην τοῦ πάθους ἔχειν ἐξουσίαν κορεσθῆναι, παιδικῶς
τῷ λίθῳ προσωμίλησεν βουληθεὶς οἶδ' ὅτι μηδὲν
πρόσθεν[1] εἶναι τὸ θῆλυ. πολλῶν οὖν ἀκρίτων
ἀφυλακτουμένων λόγων τὸν συμμιγῆ καταπαύσας
ἐγὼ θόρυβον, Ἄνδρες, εἶπον, ἑταῖροι, τῆς κατὰ
κόσμον ἔχεσθε ζητήσεως, ὡς εὐπρεπὴς νόμος ἐστὶν
παιδείας. ἀπαλλαγέντες οὖν τῆς ἀτάκτου καὶ πέρας
οὐδὲν ἐχούσης φιλονεικίας ἐν μέρει ὑπὲρ τῆς αὑτὸς
ἑαυτοῦ δόξης ἑκάτερος ἀποτείνασθε· καὶ γὰρ
οὐδέπω καιρὸς ἐπὶ ναῦν ἀπιέναι· τῇ δὲ σχολῇ κατα-
χρηστέον εἰς ἱλαρίαν καὶ μετὰ τέρψεως ὠφελῆσαι

[1] sic codd.: μηδ' ἐν τῷ θήλει πρόσθεν edd.: μηδ' ἔμπροσθεν
L. A. Post.

his amorous embraces were seen after day came and
the goddess had that blemish to prove what she'd
suffered. The youth concerned is said, according to
the popular story told, to have hurled himself over a
cliff or down into the waves of the sea and to have
vanished utterly.

17. While the temple-woman was recounting this,
Charicles interrupted her account with a shout and
said, " Women therefore inspire love even when
made of stone. But what would have happened if
we had seen such beauty alive and breathing ?
Would not that single night have been valued as
highly as the sceptre of Zeus ? "

But Callicratidas smiled and said, " We don't
know as yet, Charicles, whether we won't hear many
stories of this sort when we come to Thespiae. Even
now in this we have a clear proof of the truth about
the Aphrodite whom you hold in such esteem."

When Charicles asked how this was, I thought
Callicratidas made a very convincing reply. For he
said that, although the love-struck youth had seized
the chance to enjoy a whole uninterrupted night and
had complete liberty to glut his passion, he nevertheless made love to the marble as though to a boy,
because, I'm sure, he didn't want to be confronted by
the female parts. This occasioned much snarling
argument, till I put an end to the confusion and
uproar by saying, " Friends, you must keep to
orderly enquiry, as is the proper habit of educated
people. You must therefore make an end of this
disorderly, inconclusive contentiousness and each in
turn exert yourself to defend your own opinion ; for
it's not yet the time to leave for the ship, and we

177

δυναμένην σπουδήν. ὑπεκστάντες οὖν τοῦ νεὼ
—πολὺς γὰρ ὁ κατ' εὐσέβειαν ἐπιφοιτῶν—εἰς ἕν τι
τῶν συμποσίων ἀποκλίνωμεν, ὅπως δι' ἠρεμίας
ἀκούειν τε καὶ λέγειν ἅττ' ἂν ᾖ βουλομένοις ἐξῇ.
μέμνησθε δὲ ὡς ὁ τήμερον ἡττηθεὶς οὐκέτ' αὖθις
ἡμῖν περὶ τῶν ἴσων διοχλήσει.

18. καλῶς δ' ἔδοξα ταῦτα λέγειν καὶ συγκαταινε-
σάντων ἐξῇειμεν, ἐγὼ μὲν ἡδόμενος οὐδεμιᾶς με πιε-
ζούσης φροντίδος, οἱ δ' ἐπὶ συννοίας μεγάλην ἐν ἑαυτοῖς
σκέψιν ἄνω καὶ κάτω κυκλοῦντες ὡς περὶ τῆς προπομ-
πίας ἀγωνιούμενοι Πλαταιᾶσιν. ἐπεὶ δ' ἥκομεν εἴς τι
συνηρεφὲς καὶ παλίνσκιον ὥρᾳ θέρους ἀναπαυστήριον,
'Ηδύς, εἰπών, ὁ τόπος, ἐγώ, καὶ γὰρ οἱ κατὰ κορυφὴν
λιγυρὸν ὑπηχοῦσι [1] τέττιγες, ἐν μέσῳ πάνυ δικα-
στικῶς καθεζόμην αὐτὴν ἐπὶ ταῖς [2] ὀφρύσιν τὴν
'Ηλιαίαν ἔχων. προθεὶς [3] δ' ἀμφοτέροις κλῆρον
ὑπὲρ τοῦ τίνα χρὴ πρῶτον εἰπεῖν, ἐπειδὴ Χαρικλῆς ἐλελόγχει πρότερον, εὐθὺς ἐνάρχεσθαι τοῦ
λόγου διεκελευσάμην.

19. ὁ δὲ τῇ δεξιᾷ τὸ πρόσωπον ἀνατρίψας ἡσυχῇ
καὶ μικρὸν ἐπισχὼν ἄρχεται τῇδέ πῃ, Σέ, δέσποινα,
τῶν ὑπὲρ σοῦ λόγων, Ἀφροδίτη, σὲ βοηθὸν αἱ ἐμαὶ
δεήσεις καλοῦσιν· ἅπαντι μὲν γὰρ ἔργῳ κἂν βραχὺ
τῆς ἰδίας πειθοῦς ἐπιστάξῃς, τελειότατόν ἐστιν, οἱ δ'
ἐρωτικοὶ λόγοι περιττῶς σοῦ δέονται· σὺ γὰρ αὐτῶν

---

[1] ὑπηχοῦσι recc.: ὑπερηχοῦσι ΓΕ: cf. Plato, *Phaedrus*,
230 C.
[2] ἐπὶ ταῖς Jacobs: ἐπ' αὐταῖς codd.: ἐπ' αὐταῖς ταῖς tentavi.
[3] προθεὶς recc.: προσθεὶς ΓΕ.

---

[1] See c. 12 fin.

must employ that free time for enjoyment and also
for such serious matters as can combine pleasure and
profit. Therefore let us leave the temple, since great
numbers of the pious are coming in, and let us turn
aside into one of the feasting-places,[1] so that we can
have peace and quiet to hear and to say whatever
we wish. But remember that he who is vanquished
will never again vex our ears on similar topics."

18. This suggestion of mine pleased them and after
they had agreed to it we left the temple. I was
enjoying myself as I was weighed down by no cares,
but they were rolling mighty cogitations up and down
in their thoughts, as though they were about to
compete for the leading place in the processions at
Plataea.[2] When we had come to a thickly shaded
spot that afforded relief for the summer heat, I said,
"This is a pleasant place, for the cicadas chirp
melodiously overhead." Then I sat down between
them in right judicial manner, bearing on my brows
all the gravity of the Heliaea [3] itself. When I had
suggested to them that I should draw lots to decide
who should speak first, and Charicles had drawn this
privilege, I bade him begin the debate at once.

19. He rubbed his brow lightly with his hand and
after a short pause began as follows : " To you,
Aphrodite, my queen, do my prayers appeal to give
help in my advocacy of your cause. For every
enterprise attains complete perfection if you shed on
it but the faintest degree of the arts of persuasion that
are your very own ; but discourses on love have
particular need of you. For you are their only true

[2] Ceremonies held at Plataea in Boeotia to celebrate the
defeat of the Persians there in 479 B.C. For details see
Pausanias 8.3.5.   [3] The chief law-court of Athens.

γνησιωτάτη μήτηρ. ἴθι δὴ γυναιξὶν συνήγορος ἡ
θήλεια, χάρισαι δὲ καὶ τοῖς ἀνδράσι μένειν ἄρρεσιν,
ὡς ἐγεννήθησαν. ἔγωγ' οὖν εὐθὺς ἐν ἀρχῇ τοῦ λόγου
τὴν προμήτορα καὶ πάσης γενέσεως πρωτόρριζον ὧν
ἀξιῶ μάρτυρα ἐπικαλοῦμαι, λέγω δὲ τὴν ἱερὰν τῶν
ὅλων φύσιν, ἣ τὰ πρῶτα πηξαμένη στοιχεῖα τοῦ
κόσμου γῆν ἀέρα πῦρ ὕδωρ τῇ πρὸς ἄλληλα τούτων
ἐπικράσει πᾶν ἐζωογόνησεν ἔμψυχον. ἐπισταμένη δ'
ὅτι θνητῆς ἐσμὲν ὕλης δημιούργημα καὶ βραχὺς
χρόνος ὁ τοῦ ζῆν ἑκάστῳ καθείμαρται, τὴν ἑτέρου
φθορὰν ἄλλου γένεσιν ἐμηχανήσατο καὶ τῷ θνήσκοντι
τὸ τικτόμενον ἀντεμέτρησεν, ἵνα ταῖς παρ' ἀλλήλων
διαδοχαῖς εἰς τὸν ἀεὶ χρόνον ζῶμεν. ἐπεὶ δ' ἦν ἄπορον
ἐξ ἑνός τι γεννᾶσθαι, διπλῆν ἐν ἑκάστῳ φύσιν
ἐμηχανήσατο· τοῖς μὲν γὰρ ἄρρεσιν ἰδίας καταβολὰς
σπερμάτων χαρισαμένη, τὸ θῆλυ δ' ὥσπερ γονῆς τι
δοχεῖον [ἀγγεῖον] [1] ἀποφήνασα, κοινὸν οὖν ἀμφο-
τέρῳ γένει πόθον ἐγκερασαμένη συνέζευξεν ἀλλήλοις,
θεσμὸν ἀνάγκης ὅσιον καταγράψασα μένειν ἐπὶ τῆς
ἰδίας φύσεως ἑκάτερον, καὶ μήτε τὸ θῆλυ παρὰ
φύσιν ἀρρενοῦσθαι μήτε τἄρρεν ἀπρεπῶς μαλακί-
ζεσθαι. διὰ τοῦθ' αἱ σὺν γυναιξὶν ἀνδρῶν ὁμιλίαι
μέχρι δεῦρο τὸν ἀνθρώπινον βίον ἀθανάτοις διαδοχαῖς φυλάττουσιν· οὐδεὶς δ' ἀνὴρ ἀπ' ἀνδρὸς αὐχεῖ
γενέσθαι. δυοῖν δ' ὀνομάτοιν σεβασμίοιν πᾶσαι τιμαὶ
μένουσιν [2] ἐξ ἴσου πατρὶ μητέρα προσκυνούντων.

20. κατ' ἀρχὰς μὲν οὖν ἔθ' ἡρωϊκὰ φρονῶν ὁ βίος
καὶ τὴν γείτονα θεῶν σέβων ἀρετὴν οἷς ἐνομοθέτησεν

---

[1] δοχεῖον ἀγγεῖον ΓΕ: alterutrum verbum om. recc..
[2] μέλουσιν ΓΕ[1].

mother. Come, you who are the most feminine of all, plead the cause of womankind, and of your grace allow men to remain male, as they were born to be. Therefore do I at the very outset of my discourse call as witness to back my plea the first mother and earliest root of every creature, that sacred origin of all things, I mean, who in the beginning established earth, air, fire and water, the elements of the universe , and, by blending these with each other, brought to life everything that has breath. Knowing that we are something created from perishable matter and that the life-time assigned each of us by fate is but short, she contrived that the death of one thing should be the birth of another and meted out fresh births to compensate for what dies, so that by replacing one another we live for ever. But, since it was impossible for anything to be born from but a single source, she devised in each species two types. For she allowed males as their peculiar privilege to ejaculate semen, and made females to be a vessel as it were for the reception of seed, and, imbuing both sexes with a common desire, she linked them to each other, ordaining as a sacred law of necessity that each should retain its own nature and that neither should the female grow unnaturally masculine nor the male be unbecomingly soft. For this reason the intercourse of men with women has till this day preserved the life of men by an undying succession, and no man can boast he is the son only of a man ; no, people pay equal homage to their mother and to their father, and all honours are still retained equally by these two revered names.

20. In the beginning therefore, since human life was still full of heroic thought and honoured the

181

ἡ φύσις ἐπειθάρχει, καὶ καθ' ἡλικίας μέτρα γυναικὶ
ζευγνύμενοι γενναίων πατέρες ἐγίνοντο τέκνων·
κατὰ μικρὸν δ' ὁ χρόνος ἀπ' ἐκείνου τοῦ μεγέθους
ἐς τὰ τῆς ἡδονῆς καταβαίνων βάραθρα ξένας ὁδοὺς
καὶ παρηλλαγμένας ἀπολαύσεων ἔτεμνεν. εἶθ' ἡ
πάντα τολμῶσα τρυφὴ τὴν φύσιν αὐτὴν παρενόμησεν·
καὶ τίς ἄρα πρῶτος ὀφθαλμοῖς τὸ ἄρρεν εἶδεν ὡς
θῆλυ, δυοῖν θάτερον ἢ τυραννικῶς βιασάμενος ἢ
πείσας πανούργως; συνῆλθεν δ' εἰς μίαν κοίτην
μία φύσις· αὐτοὺς [1] δ' ἐν ἀλλήλοις ὁρῶντες οὔθ' ἃ
δρῶσιν οὔθ' ἃ πάσχουσιν ἡδοῦντο, κατὰ πετρῶν δέ,
φασίν, ἀγόνων σπείροντες [2] ὀλίγης ἡδονῆς ἀντικα-
τηλλάξαντο μεγάλην ἀδοξίαν.

21. ἐνίοις [3] γε μὴν εἰς τοσοῦτον τυραννικῆς βίας ἡ
τόλμα προέκοψεν, ὡς μέχρι σιδήρῳ τὴν φύσιν ἱερο-
συλῆσαι· τῶν δ' ἀρρένων τὸ ἄρρεν ἐκκενώσαντες
εὗρον ἡδονῆς παρέλκοντα μέτρα. οἱ δ' ἄθλιοι καὶ
δυστυχεῖς ἵν' ἐπὶ πλέον ὦσι παῖδες, οὐδὲ ἔτι μένουσιν
ἄνδρες, ἀμφίβολον αἴνιγμα διπλῆς φύσεως, οὔτ' εἰς ὃ
γεγέννηνται φυλαχθέντες οὔτ' ἔχοντες ἐφ' ὃ μετέ-
βησαν· τὸ δ' ἐν νεότητι παραμεῖναν ἄνθος εἰς
γῆρας αὐτοὺς μαραίνειν [4] πρόωρον. ἅμα γὰρ ἐν
παισὶν ἀριθμοῦνται, καὶ γεγηράκασιν οὐδὲν ἀνδρῶν
μεταίχμιον ἔχοντες. οὕτως ἡ μιαρὰ καὶ παντὸς
κακοῦ διδάσκαλος τρυφὴ ἄλλην ἀπ' ἄλλης ἡδονὰς
ἀναισχύντους ἐπινοοῦσα μέχρι τῆς οὐδὲ ῥηθῆναι

---

[1] αὐτοὺς scripsi: αὑτοὺς codd..
[2] σπείραντες recc., edd..
[3] ἐνίοις L. A. Post: εἴποις ΓΕ: τούτοις recc..
[4] μαραίνειν ΓΕ: μαραίνει recc., edd..

182

virtues that kept men close to gods, it obeyed the laws made by nature, and men, linking themselves to women according to the proper limits imposed by age, became fathers of sterling children. But gradually the passing years degenerated from such nobility to the lowest depths of hedonism and cut out strange and extraordinary paths to enjoyment. Then luxury, daring all, transgressed the laws of nature herself. And who ever was the first to look at the male as though at a female after using violence like a tyrant or else shameless persuasion? The same sex entered the same bed. Though they saw themselves embracing each other, they were ashamed neither at what they did nor at what they had done to them, and, sowing their seed, to quote the proverb, on barren rocks they bought a little pleasure at the cost of great disgrace.

21. The daring of some men has advanced so far in tyrannical violence as even to wreak sacrilege upon nature with the knife. By depriving males of their masculinity they have found wider ranges of pleasure. But those who become wretched and luckless in order to be boys for longer remain male no longer, being a perplexing riddle of dual gender, neither being kept for the functions to which they have been born nor yet having the thing into which they have been changed. The bloom that has lingered with them in their youth makes them fade prematurely into old age. For at the same moment they are counted as boys and have become old without any interval of manhood. Thus foul self-indulgence, teacher of every wickedness, devising one shameless pleasure after another, has plunged all the way down to that

δυναμένης εὐπρεπῶς [1] νόσου κατώλισθεν, ἵνα μηδὲν
ἀγνοῇ μέρος ἀσελγείας.

22. εἰ δὲ ἐφ' ὧν ἡ πρόνοια θεσμῶν ἔταξεν ἡμᾶς,
ἕκαστος ἵδρυτο, ταῖς μετὰ γυναικῶν ὁμιλίαις ἂν
ἠρκούμεθα καὶ παντὸς ὀνείδους ὁ βίος ἐκαθάρευεν.
ἀμέλει παρὰ τοῖς οὐδὲν ἐκ πονηρᾶς διαθέσεως παρα-
χαράξαι δυναμένοις ζῴοις ἄχραντος ἡ τῆς φύσεως
νομοθεσία φυλάττεται· λέοντες οὐκ ἐπιμαίνονται
λέουσιν, ἀλλ' ἡ κατὰ καιρὸν Ἀφροδίτη πρὸς τὸ θῆλυ
τὴν ὄρεξιν αὐτῶν ἐκκαλεῖται· ταῦρος ἀγελάρχης
βουσὶν ἐπιθόρνυται, καὶ κριὸς ὅλην τὴν ποίμνην
ἄρρενος πληροῖ σπέρματος. τί δέ; οὐ συῶν μὲν εὐνὰς
μεταδιώκουσιν κάπροι; λυκαίναις δ' ἐπιμίγνυνται
λύκοι; καθόλου δ' εἰπεῖν, οὔθ' οἱ ἀέρια ῥοιζοῦντες
ὄρνεις οὔθ' ὅσα τὴν ὑγρὰν καθ' ὕδατος εἴληχεν λῆξιν,
ἀλλ' οὐδ' ἐπὶ γῆς τι ζῷον ἄρρενος ὁμιλίας ἐπωρέχθη,
μένει δὲ ἀκίνητα τῆς προνοίας τὰ δόγματα. ὑμεῖς
δ', ὦ μάτην ἐπὶ τῷ φρονεῖν εὐλογούμενοι, θηρίον
ὡς ἀληθῶς φαῦλον, ἄνθρωποι, τίνι καινῇ νόσῳ παρα-
νομήσαντες ἐπὶ τὴν κατ' ἀλλήλων ὕβριν ἠρέθισθε;
τίνα τῆς ψυχῆς τυφλὴν ἀναισθησίαν καταχέαντες
ἀμφοῖν ἠστοχήκατε φεύγοντες ἃ διώκειν ἔδει καὶ
διώκοντες ἀφ' ὧν ἔδει φεύγειν; καὶ καθ' ἕνα
τοιαῦτα ζηλοῦν πάντων ἑλομένων οὐδὲ εἷς
ἔσται.

23. ἀλλὰ γὰρ ἐνταῦθα τοῖς Σωκρατικοῖς ὁ θαυμα-
στὸς ἀναφύεται λόγος, ὑφ' οὗ παιδικαὶ μὲν ἀκοαὶ
τελείων ἐνδεεῖς λογισμῶν φενακίζονται· τὸ δ' ἤδη
κατὰ φρόνησιν ἐς ἄκρον ἔχον οὐκ ἂν ὑπαχθῆναι

---

[1] εὐπρεποῦς ΓΕ: corr. recc..

infection which cannot even be mentioned with decency, in order to leave no area of lust unexplored.

22. If each man abided by the ordinances prescribed for us by Providence, we should be satisfied with intercourse with women and life would be uncorrupted by anything shameful. Certainly, among animals incapable of debasing anything through depravity of disposition the laws of nature are preserved undefiled. Lions have no passion for lions but love in due season evokes in them desire for the females of their kind. The bull, monarch of the herd, mounts cows, and the ram fills the whole flock with seed from the male. Furthermore do not boars seek to lie with sows? Do not wolves mate with she-wolves? And, to speak in general terms, neither the birds whose wings whir on high, nor the creatures whose lot is a wet one beneath the water nor yet any creatures upon land strive for intercourse with fellow males, but the decisions of Providence remain unchanged. But you who are wrongly praised for wisdom, you beasts truly contemptible, you humans, by what strange infection have you been brought to lawlessness and incited to outrage each other? With what blind insensibility have you engulfed your souls that you have missed the mark in both directions, avoiding what you ought to pursue, and pursuing what you ought to avoid? If each and every man should choose to emulate such conduct, the human race will come to a complete end.

23. But at this point disciples of Socrates can resurrect that wonderful argument by which boys' ears as yet incapable of perfect logic are deceived, though those whose minds have already reached their full powers would not be led astray by them. For

δύναιτο· ψυχῆς γὰρ ἔρωτα πλάττονται καὶ τὸ τοῦ
σώματος εὔμορφον αἰδούμενοι φιλεῖν ἀρετῆς καλοῦσιν
αὑτοὺς ἐρασταί. ἐφ' οἷς μοι πολλάκις καγχάζειν
ἐπέρχεται. τί γὰρ παθόντες, ὦ σεμνοὶ φιλόσοφοι, τὸ
μὲν ἤδη μακρῷ χρόνῳ δεδωκὸς ἑαυτοῦ πεῖραν
ὁποῖόν ἐστιν, ᾧ πολιὰ προσήκουσα καὶ γῆρας
ἀρετὴν μαρτυρεῖ, δι' ὀλιγωρίας παραπέμπετε, πᾶς
δὲ ὁ σοφὸς ἔρως ἐπὶ τὸ [1] νέον ἐπτόηται, μηδέπω τῶν
λογισμῶν ἐν αὐτῷ πρὸς ἃ τραπήσονται κρίσιν
ἐχόντων; ἢ νόμος ἐστίν, πᾶσαν μὲν ἀμορφίαν
πονηρίας εἶναι κατάκριτον, εὐθὺ δ' ὡς ἀγαθὸν
ἐπαινεῖσθαι τὸν καλόν; ἀλλά τοι κατὰ τὸν μέγαν
ἀληθείας προφήτην Ὅμηρον

εἶδός τις ἀκιδνότερος πέλει ἀνήρ,
ἀλλὰ θεὸς μορφὴν ἔπεσι στέφει, οἱ δέ τ' ἐς αὐτὸν
τερπόμενοι λεύσσουσιν, ὁ δ' ἀσφαλέως ἀγορεύει
αἰδοῖ μειλιχίῃ, μετὰ δὲ πρέπει ἀγρομένοισιν·
ἐρχόμενον δ' ἀνὰ ἄστυ θεὸν ὣς εἰσορόωσιν.

καὶ πάλιν εἶπέ που λέγων·

οὐκ ἄρα σοί γ' ἐπὶ εἴδεϊ καὶ φρένες ἦσαν.

ἀμέλει τοῦ καλοῦ Νιρέως ὁ σοφὸς Ὀδυσσεὺς
πλέον ἐπαινεῖται.

24. πῶς οὖν φρονήσεως μὲν ἢ δικαιοσύνης τῶν τε
λοιπῶν ἀρετῶν, αἳ τελείοις ἀνδράσιν σύγκληρον
εἰλήχασιν τάξιν, οὐδεὶς ἔρως ἐντρέχει, τὸ δ' ἐν παισὶ
κάλλος ὀξυτάτας παθῶν ὁρμὰς ἐγείρει; πάνυ γοῦν
ἐρᾶν ἔδει Φαίδρου διὰ Λυσίαν, ᾧ Πλάτων, ὃν πρού-
δωκεν. ἢ τὴν ἀρετὴν εἰκὸς ἦν Ἀλκιβιάδου φιλεῖν,

---

[1] τὸ recc. : τὸν ΓΕ.

they affect a love for the soul and, being ashamed to pay court to bodily beauty, call themselves lovers of virtue. This often tempts me to cackle with laughter. For what is wrong with you, grave philosophers, that you dismiss with scorn what has now long given proof of its quality, and has witnesses to its virtue in its becoming grey hairs and its old age, whereas all your wise love is captivated by the young though their reasonings cannot yet decide to what course they will turn ? Or is there a law that all ugliness should be thought guilty of viciousness but that the handsome should automatically be praised as good ? But indeed, to quote Homer, the great prophet of truth,

> ' Although one man is worse in looks,
> His frame God crowns with speech, and men rejoice
> To look at him. Unerring does he speak
> With charming modesty, pre-eminent
> Amid the assembled men ; when through the town
> He walks, men look at him as 'twere a god.' [1]

And again the poet has spoken with these words :

> ' You did not then have wits to add to looks.' [2]

Indeed wise Odysseus is praised more than handsome Nireus.

24. How is it then that through you courses no love for wisdom or for justice and the other virtues which have in their allotted station the company of full-grown men, while beauty in boys excites the most ardent fires of passion in you ? No doubt, Plato, one ought to have loved Phaedrus for the sake of Lysias whom he betrayed ! Or would it have been

---

[1] Homer, *Odyssey* VIII. 169-173.
[2] Homer, *Odyssey* XVII. 454.

διότι ἠκρωτηριάζετο τὰ [1] θεῶν ἀγάλματα καὶ τὴν ἐν
Ἐλευσῖνι τελετὴν αἱ παρὰ πότον ἐξωρχοῦντο [2] φωναί·
τίς ἐραστὴς ὁμολογεῖ γενέσθαι προδιδομένων Ἀθηνῶν
καὶ Δεκελείας ἐπιτειχιζομένης καὶ βίου τυραννίδα
βλέποντος; ἀλλ' ἄχρι μὲν οὐδέπω κατὰ τὸν ἱερὸν
Πλάτωνα πώγωνος ἐπίμπλατο, πᾶσιν ἐπέραστος ἦν·
μεταβὰς δ' ἀπὸ τοῦ παιδὸς εἰς τὸν ἄνδρα, καθ' ἣν
ἡλικίαν ἡ τέως ἀτελὴς φρόνησις ὁλόκληρον εἶχε τὸν
λογισμόν, ὑπὸ πάντων ἐμισεῖτο. τί δή; πάθεσιν
αἰσχροῖς ὀνομάτων ἐπιγράφοντες αἰδῶ ψυχῆς ἀρετὴν
λέγουσι τὴν σώματος εὐπρέπειαν οἱ φιλόνεοι
μᾶλλον ἢ φιλόσοφοι. καὶ ταῦτα μὲν ἡμῖν ὑπὲρ τοῦ
μὴ δοκεῖν ἐπισήμων ἀνδρῶν φιλαπεχθημόνως
μνημονεύειν ἐπὶ τοσοῦτον εἰρήσθω.

25. Μικρὰ δ' ἀπὸ τῆς ἄγαν σπουδῆς, ὦ Καλλικρατίδα, ἐπὶ τὴν ὑμετέραν καταβὰς ἡδονὴν ἐπιδείξω παι-
δικῆς χρήσεως πολὺ τὴν γυναικείαν ἀμείνω. καὶ τό
γε πρῶτον ἐγὼ πᾶσαν ἀπόλαυσιν ἡγοῦμαι τερπνοτέ-
ραν εἶναι τὴν χρονιωτέραν· ὀξεῖα γὰρ ἡδονὴ παρα-
πτᾶσα φθάνει πρὶν ἢ γνωσθῆναι πεπαυμένη, τὸ δ'
εὐφραῖνον ἐν τῷ παρέλκοντι κρεῖττον. ὡς εἴθε καὶ
βίου μακρὰς προθεσμίας ἡ μικρόλογος ἡμῖν ἐπέκλωσεν Μοῖρα καὶ τὸ πᾶν ἦν διηνεκὴς ὑγίεια μηδεμιᾶς λύπης τὴν διάνοιαν ἐκνεμομένης· ἑορτὴν γὰρ ἂν

---

[1] τὰ om. ΓΕ: ἠκρωτηρίαζε τὰ edd..
[2] ἐξωρχοῦντο rec.: ἐξορχοῦνται ΓΕ.

---

[1] Alcibiades was recalled from the Athenian expedition to
Sicily to face a charge of mutilating images of the god Hermes
at Athens; he was also rumoured to have indulged in a
drunken parody of the Eleusinian Mysteries and to be

right to love the virtue of Alcibiades [1] because he would mutilate statues of the gods and his drunken cries parodied the initiation rites of Eleusis? Who admits to having been in love with the betrayal of Athens, the fortification of Decelea against her, and a life that set its sights on tyranny? But, as godlike Plato says, [2] as long as his beard was not yet fully grown, he was beloved by all. But, after he had passed from boyhood to manhood, during the years when his hitherto immature intellect now had its full powers of reason, he was hated by all. What follows? That it is lovers of youth rather than of wisdom who give honourable names to dishonourable passions and call physical beauty virtue of the soul. But lest I be thought to mention famous men only to vent my hatred, let me say no more on this topic.

25. To quit this highly serious plane and descend somewhat to your level of pleasure, Callicratidas, I shall show that the services rendered by a woman are far superior to those of a boy. In the first place I consider that all kinds of enjoyment give greater delight if of longer duration. For swift pleasure flits by and is gone before we can recognise it, but delights are enhanced by being prolonged. How I wish that stingy fate had allotted us long terms of life and it consisted entirely of unbroken good health with no grief preying on our minds. For then we should

---

aiming at an oligarchical revolution or perhaps even a personal tyranny. However he escaped to Sparta and did Athens a great disservice by suggesting to them the idea of Decelea, the fortified post they established in Attica. See Thucydides vi. 27-29, 53, 61, 91.

[2] Plato, *Protagoras, init.* Cf. Homer, *Iliad* XXIV. 348.

καὶ πανήγυριν τὸν ὅλον χρόνον ἤγομεν. ἀλλ' ἐπεὶ
τῶν μειζόνων ἀγαθῶν ὁ βάσκανος δαίμων ἐνεμέση-
σεν, ἔν γε τοῖς παροῦσιν ἥδιστα τὰ παρέλκοντα.
γυνὴ μὲν οὖν ἀπὸ παρθένου μέχρι μέσης ἡλικίας,
πρὶν ἢ τελέως τὴν ἐσχάτην ῥυτίδα τοῦ[1] γήρως
ἐπιδραμεῖν, εὐάγκαλον ἀνδράσιν ὁμίλημα, κἂν
παρέλθῃ τὰ τῆς ὥρας, ὅμως

ἡμπειρία

ἔχει τι λέξαι τῶν νέων σοφώτερον.

26. εἰ δ' εἴκοσιν ἐτῶν ἀποπειρῴη παῖδά τις, αὐτὸς
ἔμοιγε δοκεῖ πασχητιᾶν ἀμφίβολον Ἀφροδίτην
μεταδιώκων· σκληροὶ γὰρ οἱ τῶν μελῶν ἀπανδρω-
θέντες ὄγκοι καὶ τραχὺ μὲν ἀντὶ τοῦ πάλαι μαλακοῦ
πυκασθὲν ἰούλοις τὸ γένειον, οἱ δ' εὐφυεῖς μηροὶ
θριξὶν ὡσπερεὶ ῥυπῶντες· ἃ δ' ἐστὶ τούτων
ἀφανέστερα, τοῖς πεπειρακόσιν ὑμῖν εἰδέναι παρίημι.
γυναικὶ δὲ ἀεὶ πάσῃ ἡ τοῦ χρώματος ἐπιστίλβει
χάρις, καὶ δαψιλεῖς μὲν ἀπὸ τῆς κεφαλῆς βοστρύχων
ἕλικες ὑακίνθοις τὸ καλὸν ἀνθοῦσιν ὅμοια πορφύ-
ροντες οἱ μὲν ἐπινώτιοι κέχυνται μεταφρένων
κόσμος, οἱ δὲ παρ' ὦτα καὶ κροτάφους πολὺ τῶν ἐν
λειμῶνι οὐλότεροι σελίνων. τὸ δ' ἄλλο σῶμα μηδ'
ἀκαρῆ τριχὸς αὐταῖς ὑποφυομένης ἠλέκτρου, φασίν,
ἢ Σιδωνίας ὑέλου διαφεγγέστερον ἀπαστράπτει.

27. τί δ' οὐχὶ τῶν ἡδονῶν καὶ τὰς ἀντιπαθεῖς
μεταδιωκτέον, ἐπειδὰν ἐξ ἴσου τοῖς διατιθεῖσιν[2] οἱ
πάσχοντες εὐφραίνωνται; σχεδὸν γὰρ οὐ κατὰ

---

[1] τοῦ om. ΓΕ. [2] διατεθεῖσιν codd.: corr. Gesner.

[1] Euripides, *Phoenissae* 529-530.
[2] Cf. Homer, *Odyssey* VI. 231.

spend all our days in feasting and holiday. But, since envious Fortune has grudged us these greater benefits, amongst those that we have the sweetest are those that last. Thus from maidenhood to middle age, before the time when the last wrinkles of old age finally spread over her face, a woman is a pleasant armful for a man to embrace, and, even if the beauty of her prime is past, yet

" With wiser tongue
Experience doth speak than can the young." [1]

26. But the very man who should make attempts on a boy of twenty seems to me to be unnaturally lustful and pursuing an equivocal love. For then the limbs, being large and manly, are hard, the chins that once were soft are rough and covered with bristles, and the well-developed thighs are as it were sullied with hairs. And as for the parts less visible than these, I leave knowledge of them to you who have tried them ! But ever does her attractive skin give radiance to every part of a woman and her luxuriant ringlets of hair, hanging down from her head, bloom with a dusky beauty that rivals the hyacinths,[2] some of them streaming over her back to grace her shoulders, and others over her ears and temples curlier by far than the celery in the meadow. But the rest of her person has not a hair growing on it and shines more pellucidly than amber, to quote the proverb, or Sidonian crystal.

27. But why do we not pursue those pleasures that are mutual and bring equal delight to the passive and to the active partners ? For, generally speaking, unlike irrational animals we do not find solitary

ταὐτὰ τοῖς ἀλόγοις ζῴοις τὰς μονήρεις διατριβὰς
ἀσμενίζομεν, ἀλλά πως φιλεταίρῳ κοινωνίᾳ συζυγέν-
τες ἡδίω τά τε ἀγαθὰ σὺν ἀλλήλοις ἡγούμεθα καὶ τὰ
δυσχερῆ κουφότερα μετ' ἀλλήλων. ὅθεν εὑρέθη
τράπεζα κοινή· καὶ φιλίας μεσῖτιν ἑστίαν [1] παραθέ-
μενοι γαστρὶ τὴν ὀφειλομένην ἀπομετροῦμεν ἀπόλαυσιν, οὐ μόνοι [2] τὸν Θάσιον, εἰ τύχοι, πίνοντες
οἶνον οὐδὲ καθ' αὑτοὺς τῶν πολυτελῶν πιμπλάμενοι
σιτίων, ἀλλὰ δοκεῖ τερπνὸν ἑκάστῳ τὸ μετ' ἄλλου,
καὶ τὰς ἡδονὰς κοινωσάμενοι μᾶλλον εὐφραινόμεθα.
αἱ μὲν γυναικεῖοι σύνοδοι τῆς ἀπολαύσεως ἀντίδοσιν
ὁμοίαν ἔχουσιν· ἀλλήλους γὰρ ἐξ ἴσου διαθέντες
ἡδέως ἀπηλλάγησαν, εἴ γε μὴ δικαστῇ Τειρεσίᾳ
προσεκτέον, ὅτι ἡ θήλεια τέρψις ὅλῃ μοίρᾳ πλεονεκ-
τεῖ τὴν ἄρρενα. καλὸν δ' οἶμαι, μὴ φιλαύτως
ἀπολαῦσαι θελήσαντας, ὅπως ἰδίᾳ τι χρηστὸν
ἀποίσονται σκοπεῖν ὅλην παρά του λαμβάνοντας [3]
ἡδονήν, ἀλλ' ἐκεῖνο μερισαμένους οὗ τυγχάνουσιν
ἀντιπαρασχεῖν ὅμοια. τοῦτο δ' οὐκ ἂν ἐπὶ παίδων
εἴποι τις, οὐχ οὕτω μέμηνεν, ἀλλ' ὁ μὲν διαθείς, ᾗ [4]
νομίζει ποτὲ ταῦτα, τὴν ἡδονὴν ἐξαίρετον λαβὼν
ἀπέρχεται, τῷ δὲ ὑβρισμένῳ κατ' ἀρχὰς μὲν
ὀδύναι καὶ δάκρυα, μικρὸν δὲ ὑπὸ χρόνου τῆς
ἀλγηδόνος χαλασάσης πλέον, ὥς φασιν, οὐδὲν ἂν
ὀχλήσειας, ἡδονὴ δ' οὐδ' ἡτισοῦν. εἰ δὲ δεῖ τι καὶ
περιεργότερον εἰπεῖν—δεῖ δὲ ἐν Ἀφροδίτης τεμένει
—γυναικὶ μέν, ὦ Καλλικρατίδα, καὶ παιδικώτερον
χρώμενον ἔξεστιν εὐφρανθῆναι διπλασίας ἀπολαύ-

---

[1] ἑστίαν ΓΕ: τράπεζαν recc., edd..   [2] μόνον ΓΕ: corr. recc..
[3] λαμβάνουσιν . . . ἐκείνω . . . ἀντιπαρέσχον ΓΕ: corr. recc..
[4] διαθεὶς ᾗ Eᵃ recc.: διαθήσειν ΓΕ.

existences acceptable, but we are linked by a sociable fellowship and consider blessings sweeter and hardships lighter when shared. Hence was instituted the table that is shared, and, setting before us the board that is the mediator of friendship, we mete out to our bellies the enjoyment due to them, not drinking Thasian wine, for example, by ourselves, or stuffing ourselves with expensive dishes on our own, but each man thinks pleasant what he enjoys along with another, and in sharing our pleasures we find greater enjoyment. Now men's intercourse with women involves giving like enjoyment in return. For the two sexes part with pleasure only if they have had an equal effect on each other—unless we ought rather to heed the verdict of Tiresias [1] that the woman's enjoyment is twice as great as the man's. And I think it honourable for men not to wish for a selfish pleasure or to seek to gain some private benefit by receiving from anyone the sum total of enjoyment, but to share what they obtain and to requite like with like. But no one could be so mad as to say this in the case of boys. No, the active lover, according to his view of the matter, departs after having obtained an exquisite pleasure, but the one outraged suffers pain and tears at first, though the pain relents somewhat with time and you will, men say, cause him no further discomfort, but of pleasure he has none at all. And, if I may make a rather far-fetched point, but one I should make as we are in the precinct of Aphrodite, a woman, Callicratidas, may be used like a boy, so that one can have enjoyment by opening up two paths to pleasure, but

[1] Cf. *Dialogues of the Dead*, 9.

σεως ὁδοὺς ἀνύσαντα,[1] τὸ δὲ ἄρρεν οὐδενὶ τρόπῳ
χαρίζεται θήλειαν ἀπόλαυσιν.

28. ὥστ᾽ εἰ ⟨ἡ⟩[2] μὲν καὶ ὑμῖν ἀρέσκειν δύναται,[3]
πρὸς ἀλλήλους δὴ[4] ἡμεῖς ἀποτειχισώμεθα, εἰ δὲ
τοῖς ἄρρεσιν εὐπρεπεῖς αἱ μετὰ ἀρρένων ὁμιλίαι, πρὸς
τὸ λοιπὸν ἐράτωσαν ἀλλήλων καὶ γυναῖκες. ἄγε νῦν,
ὦ νεώτερε χρόνε καὶ τῶν ξένων ἡδονῶν νομοθέτα,
καινὰς ὁδοὺς ἄρρενος τρυφῆς ἐπινοήσας χάρισαι τὴν
ἴσην ἐξουσίαν καὶ γυναιξίν, καὶ[5] ἀλλήλαις ὁμιλησά-
τωσαν ὡς ἄνδρες· ἀσελγῶν δὲ ὀργάνων ὑποζυγωσά-
μεναι τέχνασμα, ἀσπόρων[6] τεράστιον αἴνιγμα, κοιμά-
σθωσαν γυνὴ μετὰ γυναικὸς ὡς ἀνήρ· τὸ δὲ εἰς ἀκοὴν
σπανίως ἧκον ὄνομα—αἰσχύνομαι καὶ λέγειν—τῆς
τριβακῆς ἀσελγείας ἀνέδην πομπευέτω. πᾶσα δ᾽
ἡμῶν ἡ γυναικωνῖτις ἔστω Φιλαινὶς ἀνδρογύνους
ἔρωτας ἀσχημονοῦσα. καὶ πόσῳ κρεῖττον εἰς ἄρρενα
τρυφὴν βιάζεσθαι γυναῖκα ἢ τὸ γενναῖον ἀνδρῶν
εἰς γυναῖκα θηλύνεσθαι;

29. Τοιαῦτα συντόνως μεταξὺ παθαινόμενος ὁ
Χαρικλῆς ἐπαύσατο δεινόν τι καὶ θηριῶδες ἐν τοῖς
ὄμμασιν ὑποβλέπων. ἐῴκει δέ μοι καὶ καθαρσίῳ
χρῆσθαι πρὸς τοὺς παιδικοὺς ἔρωτας. ἐγὼ δὲ
ἡσυχῇ μειδιάσας καὶ πρὸς τὸν Ἀθηναῖον ἠρέμα τὼ
ὀφθαλμὼ παραβαλών, Παιδιᾶς, ἔφην, καὶ γέλωτος,

---

[1] ἀνοίξαντα Γ[a] recc.: ἀνύσαντα ΓΕ.
[2] ἡ add. Jacobs.
[3] δύνανται ΓΕ: corr. recc..
[4] δὴ Ν: δὲ ΓΕ: del. edd..
[5] καὶ om. ΓΕ: add. Ε[2].
[6] ἀσπόρως ΓΕ: corr. recc..

---

[1] A poetess of the fourth century B.C. reputed to have

a male has no way of bestowing the pleasure a woman gives.

28. Therefore, if even men like you, Callicratidas, can find satisfaction in women, let us males fence ourselves off from each other ; but, if males find intercourse with males acceptable, henceforth let women too love each other. Come now, epoch of the future, legislator of strange pleasures, devise fresh paths for male lusts, but bestow the same privilege upon women, and let them have intercourse with each other just as men do. Let them strap to themselves cunningly contrived instruments of lechery, those mysterious monstrosities devoid of seed, and let woman lie with woman as does a man. Let wanton Lesbianism—that word seldom heard, which I feel ashamed even to utter—freely parade itself, and let our women's chambers emulate Philaenis,[1] disgracing themselves with Sapphic amours. And how much better that a woman should invade the provinces of male wantonness than that the nobility of the male sex should become effeminate and play the part of a woman !

29. In the midst of this intense and impassioned speech Charicles stopped with a wild fierce glint in his eyes. It seemed to me that he was also regarding his speech as a ceremony of purification against love of boys. But I, laughing quietly and turning my eyes gently towards the Athenian, said, " It was to decide a sportive piece of fun, Callicratidas, that

---

written a lewd book on amatory postures. The real author may, however, have been the sophist Polycrates. See *Palatine Anthology* 7.345 and note on *Mistaken Critic* 24.

ὦ Καλλικρατίδα, δικαστὴς καθεδεῖσθαι προσδοκήσας
οὐκ οἶδ᾽ ὅπως ὑπὸ τῆς Χαρικλέους δεινότητος ἐπὶ
σπουδαιότερον ἦγμαι· σχεδὸν γὰρ ὡς ἐν Ἀρείῳ
πάγῳ περὶ φόνου καὶ πυρκαϊᾶς, ἢ νὴ Δία φαρμάκων
ἀγωνιζόμενος ὑπερφυῶς ἐπαθήνατο. καιρὸς οὖν ὁ
νῦν, εἴ ποτε καὶ πρότερον, ἀπαιτεῖ σε τὰς Ἀθήνας,
Περικλείαν δὲ πειθὼ [1] καὶ τῶν δέκα ῥητόρων τὰς
Μακεδόσιν ἀνθωπλισμένας γλώσσας ⟨ἐν⟩ [2] ἑνὶ τῷ
σῷ λόγῳ διατρῖψαι μιᾶς τῶν ἐν Πνυκὶ δημηγοριῶν
ἀναμνησθέντι.

30. Μικρὸν οὖν ἐπισχὼν ὁ Καλλικρατίδας—
ἐῴκει δὲ ἀπὸ τοῦ προσώπου μοι τεκμαιρομένῳ καὶ
λίαν ἀγωνίας μεστὸς εἶναι—λόγων ἀμοιβαίων ἐνάρ-
χεται· Εἰ γυναιξὶν ἐκκλησία καὶ δικαστήρια καὶ
πολιτικῶν πραγμάτων ἦν μετουσία, στρατηγὸς ἂν ἢ
προστάτης ἐκεχειροτόνησο καί σε χαλκῶν ἀνδριάν-
των ἐν ταῖς ἀγοραῖς, ὦ Χαρίκλεις, ἐτίμων. σχεδὸν
γὰρ οὐδὲ αὐταὶ περὶ αὑτῶν, ὁπόσαι προὔχειν κατὰ
σοφίαν ἐδόκουν, εἴ τις αὐταῖς τὴν τοῦ λέγειν ἐξουσίαν
ἐφῆκεν, οὕτω μετὰ σπουδῆς ἂν εἶπον, οὐχ ἡ
Σπαρτιάταις ἀνθωπλισμένη Τελέσιλλα, δι᾽ ἣν ἐν
Ἄργει θεὸς ἀριθμεῖται γυναικῶν Ἄρης· οὐχὶ τὸ
μελιχρὸν αὔχημα Λεσβίων Σαπφὼ καὶ ἡ τῆς
Πυθαγορείου σοφίας θυγάτηρ Θεανώ· τάχα δ᾽ οὐδὲ

---

[1] Περικλεῖ δὲ πείθου ΓΕ: Περικλέους (vel Περίκλειον) δὲ πειθὼ
recc..   [2] ἐν suppl. Gesner.

---

[1] A high court at Athens.
[2] The ten whose surrender Alexander demanded. Cf.
Plutarch, *Demosthenes* 23.3, Quintilian X. 1.76.
[3] A poetess of Argos reputed to have fought against
Cleomenes and his Spartans.

I expected to sit as umpire, but somehow or other thanks to Charicles' vehemence I've been brought to face a more serious task. For he has shown an extraordinary degree of passion almost as though he were in the Areopagus [1] contesting a case of murder or arson or indeed poisoning. Therefore the present moment, if any time ever did, demands that you should recall one of the speeches made to the people in the Pnyx and in this one speech of yours should expend all the resources of Athens, of Periclean persuasiveness and of the tongues of the ten orators which were marshalled against the Macedonians." [2]

30. After waiting for a moment Callicratidas, who, judging from his expression, appeared to me to be most full of fight, began to discourse in his turn and said: "If the assembly and the law-courts were open to women and they could participate in politics, you would have been elected their general or their champion and they would have honoured you, Charicles, with bronze statues in the market-places. For hardly even those among them thought pre-eminent for wisdom could, if given full authority to speak, have spoken about themselves with such zeal, no, not even Telesilla, [3] who armed herself against the Spartiates, and because of whom Ares is numbered at Argos among the gods of the women, no nor Sappho, the honey-sweet pride of Lesbos or Theano, [4] that daughter of Pythagorean wisdom! Perhaps even

[4] A Pythagorean philosopher and therefore Pythagoras' daughter in spirit. She is usually described as the wife of Pythagoras. Her father's name is given as either Pythonax or Brontinus. Cf. Diogenes Laertius 8.42.

Περικλῆς οὕτως ἂν Ἀσπασίᾳ συνηγόρησεν. ἀλλ'
ἐπειδήπερ εὐπρεπὲς ἄρρενας ὑπὲρ θηλειῶν λέγειν,
εἴπωμεν καὶ ἄνδρες ὑπὲρ ἀνδρῶν. σὺ δὲ ἵλεως,
Ἀφροδίτη, γενοῦ· καὶ γὰρ ἡμεῖς τὸν σὸν Ἔρωτα
τιμῶμεν.

31. Ἐγὼ μὲν οὖν ἐνόμιζον ἄχρι παιδιᾶς ἱλαρὰν
τὴν ἔριν ἡμῶν προκόψαι, ἐπεὶ δὲ οἱ παρὰ τούτου
λόγοι καὶ φιλοσοφεῖν ὑπὲρ γυναικῶν ἐπενοήθησαν,
ἀσμένως τὴν ἀφορμὴν ἥρπακα· μόνος γὰρ ὁ ἄρρην
ἔρως κοινὸν ἡδονῆς καὶ ἀρετῆς ἐστιν ἔργον. εὐξαίμην γάρ,[1] εἴπερ ἦν ἐν δυνατῷ, τὴν ἐπήκοόν ποτε
τῶν Σωκρατικῶν λόγων πλατάνιστον, Ἀκαδημίας
καὶ Λυκείου δένδρον εὐτυχέστερον, ἐγγὺς ἡμῶν
ἑστάναι πεφυκυῖαν, ἔνθ' ἡ Φαίδρου προσανάκλισις
ἦν, ὥσπερ ὁ ἱερὸς εἶπεν ἀνὴρ πλείστων ἁψάμενος
χαρίτων· αὐτὴ τάχα ἂν ὥσπερ ἡ ἐν Δωδώνῃ φηγὸς
ἐκ τῶν ὁροδάμνων[2] ἱερὰν ἀπορρήξασα φωνὴν τοὺς
παιδικοὺς εὐφήμησεν ἔρωτας ἔτι τοῦ καλοῦ μεμνη-
μένη Φαίδρου. πλὴν ἐπεὶ τοῦτ' ἀμήχανον,

> ἡ γὰρ πολλὰ μεταξὺ
> οὔρεά τε σκιόεντα θάλασσά τε ἠχήεσσα,

ξένοι τε ἐπ' ἀλλοτρίας γῆς ἀπειλήμμεθα καὶ
πλεονέκτημα Χαρικλέους ἐστὶν ἡ Κνίδος, ὅμως
τἀληθὲς οὐ προδώσομεν νικηθέντες[3] ὄκνῳ.

32. μόνον ἡμῖν σύ, δαῖμον οὐράνιε, καιρίως παρά-
στηθι φιλίας εὐγνώμων, ἱεροφάντα μυστηρίων

---

[1] γάρ ΓΕ: γὰρ ἂν rec., edd..
[2] ὁροδάφνων (vel —ῶν) codd.: corr. edd..
[3] νικηθέντες ΓΕ: γρ. εἴξαντες Ε.

Pericles could not have pleaded equally well for
Aspasia. But, since it is not improper for men to
speak on behalf of women, let us men also speak on
behalf of men ; and you, Aphrodite, be propitious.
For we too honour your son, Eros.

31. I thought that our merry contest had gone as
far as jest allowed but, since Charicles in his discourse
has been minded also to wax philosophical on behalf
of women, I have gladly seized my opportunity ;
for love of males, I say, is the only activity combining
both pleasure and virtue. For I would pray that
near us, if it were possible, grew that plane-tree
which once heard the words of Socrates, a tree more
fortunate than the Academy and the Lyceum, the
tree against which Phaedrus leaned, as we are told
by that holy man [1] endowed with more graces than
any other. Perhaps like the oak at Dodona, that
sent its sacred voice bursting forth from its branches,
that tree itself, still remembering the beauty of
Phaedrus, would have spoken in praise of love of
boys. But that is impossible,

> " For in between there lies
> Many a shady mountain and the roaring sea," [2]

and we are strangers cut off in a foreign land, and
Cnidus gives Charicles the advantage. Nevertheless
we shall not be overcome by fear and betray the
truth.

32. Only do you, heavenly spirit, lend me season-
able help, you kindly hierophant of the mysteries of
friendship, Eros, who are no mischievous infant as

[1] Plato. Cf. *Phaedrus*, 229 B.
[2] Homer, *Iliad* I. 156-157.

Ἔρως, οὐ κακὸν νήπιον ὁποῖον ζωγράφων παίζουσι[1]
χεῖρες, ἀλλ' ὃν ἡ πρωτοσπόρος ἐγέννησεν ἀρχὴ
τέλειον εὐθὺ τεχθέντα· σὺ γὰρ ἐξ ἀφανοῦς καὶ κεχυ-
μένης ἀμορφίας τὸ πᾶν ἐμόρφωσας. ὥσπερ οὖν ὅλου
κόσμου τάφον τινὰ κοινὸν ἀφελὼν τὸ περικείμενον
χάος ἐκεῖνο μὲν ἐς ἐσχάτους[2] Ταρτάρου μυχοὺς
ἐφυγάδευσας, ἔνθα ὡς ἀληθῶς

σιδήρειαί τε πύλαι καὶ χάλκεος οὐδός,

ὅπως ὑπ' ἀρρήκτου δεθὲν φρουρᾶς τῆς ἔμπαλιν ὁδοῦ
εἴργηται· λαμπρῷ δὲ φωτὶ τὴν ἀμαυρὰν νύκτα
πετάσας παντὸς ἀψύχου τε καὶ ψυχὴν ἔχοντος
ἐγένου δημιουργός· ἐξαίρετον δὲ ἐγκεράσας ὁμόνοιαν
ἀνθρώποις τὰ σεμνὰ φιλίας πάθη συνῆψας, ἵν' ἐξ
ἀκάκου καὶ ἁπαλῆς ἔτι ψυχῆς ἡ εὔνοια συνεκτρεφο-
μένη πρὸς τὸ τέλειον ἀνδρῶται.

33. γάμοι μὲν γὰρ διαδοχῆς ἀναγκαίας εὕρηνται
φάρμακα, μόνος δὲ ὁ ἄρρην ἔρως φιλοσόφου καλόν
ἐστι ψυχῆς ἐπίταγμα. πᾶσι δὲ τοῖς ἐκ τοῦ περιόντος
εἰς εὐπρέπειαν ἠσκημένοις ἕπεται τιμὴ πλείων ἢ ὅσα
τῆς παραυτὰ χρείας ἐπιδεῖται, καὶ πάντῃ τοῦ ἀναγ-
καίου τὸ καλὸν κρεῖττον. ἄχρι μὲν οὖν ἀμαθὴς ὁ
βίος ἦν οὐδέπω τῆς καθ' ἡμέραν πείρας πρὸς τὸ
βέλτιον εὐσχολῶν, ἀγαπητῶς ἐπ' αὐτὰ τὰ ἀναγκαῖα
συνεστέλλετο, τῆς δὲ ἀγαθῆς διαίτης ἐπείγων ὁ
χρόνος οὐ παρέσχεν εὕρεσιν. ἐπειδὴ δὲ αἱ μὲν ἐσπευ-
σμέναι[3] χρεῖαι πέρας εἶχον, οἱ δὲ τῶν ἐπιγινομένων
ἀεὶ λογισμοὶ τῆς ἀνάγκης ἀφεθέντες ηὐκαίρουν

---

[1] ὁποῖα . . . παίζουσι ΓΕ: corr. recc..
[2] ἐσχάτου codd.: corr. Jacobs.
[3] ἐσπευμέναι ΓΕ: corr. Εᵃ.

painters light-heartedly portray you, but were already full-grown at your birth, when brought forth by the earliest source of all life. For *you* gave shape to everything out of dark confused shapelessness. As though you had removed a tomb burying the whole universe alike, you banished that chaos which enveloped it to the recesses of farthest Tartarus, where in truth,

" Are gates of iron and thresholds of bronze," [1]

so that, chained in an impregnable prison, it may be denied any return. Spreading bright light over gloomy night you became the creator of all things both with and without life. But compounding for mortals the special gift of harmony of mind, you united their hearts with the holy sentiment of friendship, so that goodwill might grow in souls still innocent and tender and come to perfect maturity.

33. For marriage is a remedy invented to ensure man's necessary perpetuity, but only love for males is a noble duty enjoined by a philosophic spirit. Anything cultivated for aesthetic reasons in the midst of abundance is accompanied with greater honour than things which require for their existence immediate need, and beauty is in every way superior to necessity. Thus, as long as human life remained unsophisticated and the daily struggle for existence left it no leisure for improving itself, men were content to limit themselves to bare necessities, and the urgency of their day did not allow them to discover the proper way to live. But, once pressing needs were at an end and the thoughts of each succeeding generation had been released from the

[1] *Iliad*, VIII. 15.

ἐπινοεῖν τι τῶν κρειττόνων, ἐκ τούτου [1] κατ' ὀλίγον
ἐπιστῆμαι συνηύξοντο. τοῦτο δ' ἡμῖν ἀπὸ τῶν
ἐντελεστέρων τεχνῶν ἔνεστιν εἰκάζειν. αὐτίκα
πρῶτοί τινες ἄνθρωποι γενόμενοι τοῦ καθ' ἡμέραν
λιμοῦ φάρμακον ἐξήτουν, εἶθ' ἁλισκόμενοι τῇ πρὸς
τὸ παρὸν ἐνδείᾳ, τῆς ἀπορίας οὐκ ἐώσης ἑλέσθαι τὸ
βέλτιον, τὴν εἰκαίαν πόαν ἐσιτοῦντο καὶ μαλθακὰς
ῥίζας ὀρύττοντες καὶ τὰ πλεῖστα δρυὸς καρπὸν
ἐσθίοντες. ἀλλ' ἡ μὲν ἀλόγοις ζῴοις μετὰ χρόνου
ἐρρίφη, σπόρον δὲ πυροῦ καὶ κριθῆς εἶδον αἱ γεωργῶν
ἐπιμέλειαι εὑροῦσαι κατ' ἔτος ἐκνεάζοντα. καὶ
οὐδὲ μανεὶς ἂν εἴποι τις ὅτι δρῦς στάχυος ἀμείνων.

34. τί δ'; οὐκ ἐν ἀρχῇ μὲν εὐθὺ τοῦ βίου σκέπης
δεηθέντες ἄνθρωποι νάκη, θηρία δείραντες, ἠμφιέ-
σαντο; καὶ σπήλυγγας ὀρῶν κρύους καταδύσεις
ἐπενόησαν ἢ παλαιῶν [2] ῥιζῶν ἢ φυτῶν αὖα κοιλώ-
ματα; τὴν δὲ ἀπὸ τούτων μίμησιν ἐπὶ τὸ κρεῖττον
ἀεὶ μετάγοντες ὕφηναν μὲν ἑαυτοῖς χλανίδας, οἴκους
δὲ ᾠκίσαντο, καὶ λεληθότως αἱ περὶ ταῦτα τέχναι
τὸν χρόνον λαβοῦσαι διδάσκαλον ἀντὶ μὲν λιτῆς
ὑφῆς τὸ κάλλιον ἐποίκιλαν, ἀντὶ δὲ εὐτελῶν δω-
ματίων ὑψηλὰ τέρεμνα καὶ λίθων πολυτέλειαν
ἐμηχανήσαντο καὶ γυμνὴν τοίχων ἀμορφίαν εὐανθέσι
βαφαῖς χρωμάτων κατέγραψαν. πλὴν ἑκάστη γε
τούτων τῶν τεχνῶν καὶ ἐπιστημῶν ἄφωνος οὖσα
καὶ βαθεῖαν ἐπιτεθειμένη λήθην ὡς ἀπὸ μακρᾶς [3]

---

[1] ἐκ τοῦ ΓΕ: corr. recc..
[2] πάλαι codd.: corr. edd..   [3] μικρᾶς ΓΕ.

---

[1] Presumably acorns of species other than the Valonia
oak (*Quercus Aegilops*) which has edible acorns.

shackles of necessity so that they had leisure ever to devise higher things, from that time the arts gradually began to develop. What this process was like we may judge from the more perfected of the crafts. Right from the moment of their birth the earliest men had to search for a remedy against their daily hunger, and, under the duress of immediate need, prevented by their helplessness from choosing what was better, fed on any chance herb, digging up tender roots and eating mostly the fruit of the oak.[1] But after a time this was cast before brute animals, and the careful husbandmen discovered how to sow wheat and barley and saw these renew themselves every year. And not even a madman would maintain that the fruit of the oak is superior to the ear of grain.

34. Moreover, did not men right from the start of human life, because they needed protection from the elements, skin wild beasts and clothe themselves in their woolly coats ? And as refuges against the cold they thought of mountain caves or the dry hollows afforded by old roots or trees. Then, ever improving the imitative skill that started thus, they wove themselves cloaks of wool and built themselves houses, and imperceptibly the crafts that concentrated on these things, being taught by time, replaced simple fabrics with ornate garments of greater beauty, and instead of cheap cottages they devised lofty mansions of expensive marble, and painted the native ugliness of their walls with the luxuriant dyes of colour. However each of these crafts and accomplishments has, after being mute and plunged in deep forgetfulness, gradually risen,

δύσεως [1] κατὰ μικρὸν εἰς τὰς ἰδίας ἀνέτειλεν ἀκτῖνας. ἕκαστος γὰρ εὑρών τι παρεδίδου τῷ μετ' αὐτόν· εἶθ' ἡ διαδοχὴ τῶν λαμβανόντων οἷς ἔμαθεν ἤδη προστιθεῖσα, τὸ ἐνδέον ἐπλήρωσεν.

35. μηδέ τις ἔρωτας ἀρρένων ἀπαιτείτω παρὰ τοῦ παλαιοῦ χρόνου· γυναιξὶν γὰρ ὁμιλεῖν ἀναγκαῖον ἦν, ἵνα μὴ τελείως ἄσπερμον ἡμῶν φθαρῇ [2] τὸ γένος. αἱ δὲ ποικίλαι σοφίαι <καὶ> [3] τῆς φιλοκάλου ταύτης ἀρετῆς ἐπιθυμίαι μόλις ὑπὸ τοῦ μηδὲν ἐῶντος ἀνίχνευτον αἰῶνος εἰς τοὐμφανὲς ἔμελλον ἥξειν, ἵνα τῇ θείᾳ φιλοσοφίᾳ καὶ τὸ παιδεραστεῖν συνακμάσῃ. μὴ δῆτα, Χαρίκλεις, ὃ [4] μὴ πρότερον εὕρητο, τοῦτο ἐπινοηθὲν αὖθις ὡς φαῦλον εὔθυνε, μηδ' ὅτι τῶν παιδικῶν ἐρώτων αἱ γυναικεῖαι σύνοδοι πρεσβυτέρους ἐπιγράφονται χρόνους, ἐλάττου θάτερον· ἀλλὰ τὰ μὲν παλαιὰ τῶν ἐπιτηδευμάτων ἀναγκαῖα νομίζωμεν, ἃ δὲ αὖθις ἐνευσχολήσας τοῖς λογισμοῖς ὁ βίος ἐπεξεῦρεν, ὡς ἐκείνων ἀμείνω τιμητέον.

36. ἐμοὶ μὲν γὰρ ὀλίγου καὶ γελᾶν ἔναγχος ἐπῄει, Χαρικλέους ἄλογα ζῷα καὶ τὴν Σκυθῶν ἐρημίαν ἐπαινοῦντος· ὀλίγου δὲ ὑπὸ τῆς ἄγαν φιλονεικίας καὶ μετενόει γενόμενος Ἕλλην. οὐδὲ γὰρ ὡς ἐναντία φθεγγόμενος οἷς ἐπεχείρει λέγειν, ὑπεσταλμένῳ τε [5] τῷ τῆς φωνῆς τόνῳ τὸ ῥηθὲν ἔκλεπτεν, ἀλλ' ἐπηρμένῃ τῇ φωνῇ λαρυγγίζων, Οὐκ ἐρῶσιν, φησίν, ἀλλήλων λέοντες οὐδ' ἄρκτοι καὶ σύες, ἀλλ' αὐτῶν ἡ πρὸς τὸ θῆλυ μόνον ὁρμὴ κρατεῖ. καὶ τί

---

[1] λύσεως codd.: corr. edd..   [2] φανῇ Γ.
[3] καὶ suppl. edd..
[4] ὅτι L. A. Post.
[5] τε om. recc., edd..

as it were, to its own bright zenith after long being set. For each man made some discovery to hand on to his successor. Then each successive recipient, by adding to what he had already learnt, made good any deficiencies.

35. Let no one expect love of males in early times. For intercourse with women was necessary so that our race might not utterly perish for lack of seed. But the manifold branches of wisdom and men's desire for this virtue that loves beauty were only with difficulty to be brought to light by time which leaves nothing unexplored, so that divine philosophy and with it love of boys might come to maturity. Do not then, Charicles, again censure this discovery as worthless because it wasn't made earlier, nor, because intercourse with women can be credited with greater antiquity than love of boys, must you think love of boys inferior. No, we must consider the pursuits that are old to be necessary, but assess as superior the later additions invented by human life when it had leisure for thought.

36. For I came very close to laughing just now when Charicles was praising irrational beasts and the lonely life of Scythians.[1] Indeed his excessive enthusiasm for the argument almost made him regret his Greek birth. For he did not hide his words in restrained tones like a man contradicting the thesis that he maintained, but with raised voice from the full depth of his throat says, " Lions, bears, boars do not love others of their own sort but are ruled by their urge only for the female. And what's

---

[1] I.e. a primitive manner of life like that of the Scythians, whom Charicles has not mentioned by name.

θαυμαστόν; ἃ γὰρ ἐκ λογισμοῦ δικαίως ἄν τις
ἕλοιτο, ταῦτα τοῖς μὴ δυναμένοις λογίζεσθαι δι'
ἀφροσύνην οὐκ ἔνεστιν ἔχειν. ἐπεί τοι Προμηθεὺς ἢ
θεῶν τις ἄλλος εἰ νοῦν ἑκάστῳ συνέζευξεν ἀνθρώπινον, οὐκ ἂν ἐρημία καὶ βίος ὄρειος αὐτοὺς ἐποί-
μαινεν οὐδὲ ἀλλήλους τροφὴν εἶχον, ἐξ ἴσου δὲ ἡμῖν
ἱερὰ δειμάμενοι καὶ μέσην ἑστίαν τῶν ἰδίων ἕκαστος
οἰκῶν ὑπὸ τοῖς κοινοῖς ἐπολιτεύοντο νόμοις. τί δὴ
παράδοξον εἰ ζῷα τῆς φύσεως κατάκριτα μηδὲν ὧν
λογισμοὶ παρέχονται παρὰ τῆς προνοίας λαβεῖν
ηὐτυχηκότα προσαφήρηται μετὰ τῶν ἄλλων καὶ
τὰς ἄρρενας ἐπιθυμίας; οὐκ ἐρῶσι λέοντες, οὐδὲ
γὰρ φιλοσοφοῦσιν· οὐκ ἐρῶσιν ἄρκτοι, τὸ γὰρ ἐκ
φιλίας καλὸν οὐκ ἴσασιν. ἀνθρώποις δ' ἡ μετ'
ἐπιστήμης φρόνησις ἐκ τοῦ πολλάκις πειρᾶσαι τὸ
κάλλιστον ἑλομένη βεβαιοτάτους ἐρώτων ἐνόμισεν
τοὺς ἄρρενας.

37. μὴ τοίνυν, ὦ Χαρίκλεις, ἀκολάστου βίου
συμφορήσας ἑταιρικὰ διηγήματα γυμνῷ τῷ λόγῳ
τῆς σεμνότητος ἡμῶν καταπόμπευε μηδὲ τὸν
οὐράνιον Ἔρωτα τῷ νηπίῳ συναρίθμει, λογίζου
δὲ ὀψὲ μὲν ἡλικίας τὰ τοιαῦτα μεταμανθάνων,
ὅμως δ' οὖν λογίζου νῦν γε, ἐπειδήπερ οὐ πρότερον,
ὅτι διπλοῦς θεὸς ὁ Ἔρως, οὐ κατὰ μίαν ὁδὸν φοιτῶν
οὐδὲ ἑνὶ πνεύματι τὰς ἡμετέρας ψυχὰς ἐρεθίζων,
ἀλλ' ὁ μέν, ὡς ἄν, οἶμαι, κομιδῇ νήπια φρονῶν,
οὐδενὸς αὐτοῦ τὴν διάνοιαν ἡνιοχεῖν δυναμένου
λογισμοῦ, πολὺς ἐν ταῖς τῶν ἀφρόνων ψυχαῖς
ἀθροίζεται, μάλιστα δὲ αὐτῷ γυναικεῖοι πόθοι
μέλουσιν· οὗτός ἐστιν ὁ τῆς ἐφημέρου ταύτης

206

surprising in that ? For the things which one would
rightly choose as a result of thought, it is not possible
for those that cannot reason to have because of their
lack of intellect. For, if Prometheus or else some
god had endowed each animal with a human mind,
they would not be satisfied with a lonely life among
the mountains, nor would they find their food in
each other, but just like us they would have built
themselves temples and, though each making his
hearth the centre of his private life, they would live
as fellow-citizens governed by common laws. Is it
any wonder that, since animals have been condemned
by nature not to receive from the bounty of Providence any of the gifts afforded by intellect, they have
with all else also been deprived of desire for males?
Lions do not have such a love, because they are not
philosophers either. Bears have no such love,
because they are ignorant of the beauty that comes
from friendship. But for men wisdom coupled with
knowledge has after frequent experiments chosen
what is best, and has formed the opinion that love
between males is the most stable of loves.

37. Do not, therefore, Charicles, heap together
courtesans' tales of wanton living and insult our
dignity with unvarnished language nor count
Heavenly Love as an infant, but learn better about
such things though it's late in your life, and now at
any rate, since you've never done so before, reflect
in spite of all that Love is a twofold god who does not
walk in but a single track or exert but a single
influence to excite our souls ; but the one love,
because, I imagine, his mentality is completely childish, and no reason can guide his thoughts, musters
with great force in the souls of the foolish and
concerns himself mainly with yearnings for women.

ὕβρεως ἑταῖρος ἀκρίτῳ φορᾷ πρὸς τὸ βουλόμενον
ἄγων. ἕτερος δὲ "Ερως 'Ωγυγίων πατὴρ χρόνων,
σεμνὸν ὀφθῆναι καὶ πάντοθεν ἱεροπρεπὲς θέαμα,
σωφρονούντων ταμίας παθῶν ἤπια ταῖς ἑκάστου
διανοίαις ἐμπνεῖ,[1] καὶ λαχόντες ἵλεω τοῦδε τοῦ
δαίμονος ἡδονὴν ἀρετῇ μεμιγμένην ἀσπαζόμεθα·
δισσὰ γὰρ ὄντως κατὰ τὸν τραγικὸν πνεύματα πνεῖ
ὁ "Ερως, ἑνὸς δὲ ὀνόματος οὐχ ὅμοια τὰ πάθη
κεκοινώνηκεν· καὶ γὰρ Αἰδὼς ὠφελείας ὁμοῦ καὶ
βλάβης ἀμφίβολός ἐστι δαίμων·

Αἰδὼς ἥτ' ἄνδρας μέγα σίνεται ἠδ' ὀνίνησιν.
οὐ μὴν οὐδ' Ἐρίδων γένος ἔστιν ἕν, ἀλλ' ἐπὶ γαῖαν
εἰσὶ δύω, τὴν μέν κεν ἐπαινήσειε νοήσας,
ἡ δ' ἐπιμωμητή· διὰ δ' ἄνδιχα θυμὸν ἔχουσιν.

οὐδὲν οὖν παράδοξον, εἰ πάθος ἀρετῇ κοινὴν προση-
γορίαν ἔχειν ἔτυχεν, ὥστε ἔρωτα καλεῖσθαι καὶ
τὴν ἀκόλαστον ἡδονὴν καὶ τὴν σωφρονοῦσαν εὔνοιαν.
38. Γάμους οὖν τὸ μηδὲν οἴει, καὶ τὸ θῆλυ τοῦ
βίου φυγαδεύεις, ἵνα πῶς μείνωμεν ἄνθρωποι;
ζηλωτὸν μὲν ἦν κατὰ τὸν σοφώτατον Εὐριπίδην, εἰ
δίχα τῆς πρὸς γυναῖκας [2] συνόδου φοιτῶντες ἐπὶ
ἱερὰ καὶ ναοὺς ἀργύρου καὶ χρυσοῦ τέκνα ὑπὲρ [3] τῆς
διαδοχῆς ἐωνούμεθα· ἀνάγκη γὰρ βαρὺν κατ'

---

[1] ἐμπνέει codd.: corr. Dindorf.
[2] γυναῖκα ΓΕ: corr. recc..
[3] ὑπὲρ recc.: παρὰ ΓΕ.

---

[1] The poet may be Euripides. Cf. Cercidas, 3.14,
Nauck, *Fr. Adesp.* 187.
[2] Hesiod, *Works and Days*, 318, 11 (modified), 12 and 13.
[3] *Hippolytus*, 618 ff.

This love is the companion of the violence that lasts but a day and he leads men with unreasoning precipitation to their desires. But the other Love is the ancestor of the Ogygian age, a sight venerable to behold and hedged around with sanctity, and is a dispenser of temperate passions who sends his kindly breath into the minds of all. If we find this god propitious to us, we meet with a welcome pleasure which is blended with virtue. For in truth, as the tragic poet [1] says, Love blows in two different ways, and the one name is shared by differing passions. For Shame too is a twofold goddess with both a beneficial and a harmful role.

Shame which to men doth mighty harm and
    mighty good.
Nor yet are rivalries of but one sort ; two kinds
On earth there are ; the one a man of sense would
    praise,
The other's to be blamed ; for different is their
    heart.[2]

It need not surprise us, therefore, that passion has come to have the same name as virtue so that both unrestrained lust and sober affection are called Love.

38. Charicles may ask if I therefore think marriage worthless and banish women from this life, and if so, how we humans are to survive. Indeed, as the wise Euripides [3] says, it would be greatly to be desired if we had no intercourse with women but, in order to provide ourselves with heirs, we went to shrines and temples and bought children for gold and silver. For we are constrained by necessity that

αὐχένων ζυγὸν ἡμῖν ἐπιθεῖσα τοῖς κελευομένοις
πειθαρχεῖν βιάζεται. τὸ μὲν οὖν καλὸν αἱρώμεθα
τοῖς λογισμοῖς, εἰκέτω δὲ τῇ ἀνάγκῃ τὸ χρειῶδες.
ἄχρι τέκνων γυναῖκες ἀριθμὸς ἔστωσαν, ἐν δὲ τοῖς
ἄλλοις ἄπαγε, μή μοι γένοιτο. τίς γὰρ ἂν εὖ φρονῶν
ἀνέχεσθαι δύναιτο ἐξ ἑωθινοῦ γυναικὸς ὡραϊζομένης [1]
ἐπικτήτοις σοφίσμασιν, ἧς ὁ μὲν ἀληθῶς χαρακτὴρ
ἄμορφος, ἀλλότριοι δὲ κόσμοι τὸ τῆς φύσεως
ἀπρεπὲς βουκολοῦσιν.

39. εἰ γοῦν ἀπὸ τῆς νυκτέρου κοίτης πρὸς ὄρθρον
ἴδοι τις ἀνισταμένας γυναῖκας, αἰσχίω νομίσει
θηρίων τῶν πρῶτας [2] ὥρας ὀνομασθῆναι δυσκληδο-
νίστων· ὅθεν ἀκριβῶς οἴκοι καθείργουσιν αὐτὰς
οὐδενὶ τῶν ἀρρένων βλεπομένας· γρᾶες δὲ καὶ
θεραπαινίδων ὁ σύμμορφος ὄχλος ἐν κύκλῳ περιε-
στᾶσι ποικίλοις φαρμάκοις καταφαρμακεύουσαι [3] τὰ
δυστυχῆ πρόσωπα· οὐ γὰρ ὕδατος ἀκράτῳ νάματι
τὸν ὑπηλὸν [4] ἀπονιψάμεναι κάρον εὐθὺς ἅπτονται
σπουδῆς ἐχομένου τινὸς πράγματος, ἀλλ' αἱ πολλαὶ
τῶν διαπασμάτων συνθέσεις τὸν ἀηδῆ τοῦ προσώπου
χρῶτα φαιδρύνουσιν, ὡς δὲ ἐπὶ δημοτελοῦς πομπῆς
ἄλλο τι [5] ἄλλη τῶν ὑπηρετουσῶν ἐγκεχείρισται,
λεκανίδας ἀργυρᾶς καὶ προχόους ἔσοπτρά τε καὶ
καθάπερ ἐν φαρμακοπώλου πυξίδων ὄχλον, ἀγγεῖα
μεστὰ πολλῆς κακοδαιμονίας, ἐν οἷς ὀδόντων σμηκ-
τικαὶ δυνάμεις ἢ βλέφαρα μελαίνουσα τέχνη προχειρίζεται.[6]

1 ὡραϊσμένης recc., edd..
2 πρὸ μιᾶς ΓΕ: corr. recc..
3 καταφαρμακεῦσαι ΓΕ: corr. recc..
4 ὑψηλὸν codd.: corr. Hemsterhuys.

210

puts a heavy yoke on our shoulders and bids us obey her. Though therefore we should by use of reason choose what is beautiful, let our need yield to necessity. Let women be ciphers and be retained merely for child-bearing ; but in all else away with them, and may I be rid of them. For what man of sense could endure from dawn onwards women who beautify themselves with artificial devices, women whose true form is unshapely, but who have extraneous adornments to beguile the unsightliness of nature ?

39. If at any rate one were to see women when they rise in the morning from last night's bed, one would think a woman uglier than those beasts [1] whose name it is inauspicious to mention early in the day. That's why they closet themselves carefully at home and let no man see them. They're surrounded by old women and a throng of maids as ugly as themselves who doctor their ill-favoured faces with an assortment of medicaments. For they do not wash off the torpor of sleep with pure clean water and apply themselves to some serious task. Instead numerous concoctions of scented powders are used to brighten up their unattractive complexions, and, as though in a public procession, each maid is entrusted with something different, with silver basins, ewers, mirrors, an array of boxes reminiscent of a chemist's shop, and jars full of many a mischief, in which she marshals dentifrices and contrivances for blackening the eyelids.

---

[1] I.e. monkeys. Cf. *The Mistaken Critic* 17.

---

[5] τι edd.: τις codd..
[6] προχειρίζεται ΓΕ: θησαυρίζεται Γ^a, edd..

40. τὸ δὲ πλεῖστον ἀναλίσκει μέρος ἡ πλοκὴ τῶν
τριχῶν· αἱ μὲν γὰρ φαρμάκοις ἐρυθαίνειν δυναμένοις
πρὸς ἡλίου μεσημβρίαν τοὺς πλοκάμους ἴσα ταῖς τῶν
ἐρίων χροιαῖς ξανθῷ μεταβάπτουσιν ἄνθει τὴν ἰδίαν
κατακρίνουσαι φύσιν· ὁπόσαις δὲ ἀρκεῖν ἡ μέλαινα
χαίτη νομίζεται, τὸν τῶν γεγαμηκότων πλοῦτον εἰς
ταύτην ἀναλίσκουσιν ὅλην Ἀραβίαν σχεδὸν ἐκ τῶν
τριχῶν ἀποπνέουσαι, σιδηρᾷ τε ὄργανα πυρὸς ἀμ-
βλείᾳ φλογὶ χλιανθέντα βίᾳ τὴν ἑλίκων οὐλότητα
διαπλέκει, καὶ περίεργοι μὲν αἱ μέχρι τῶν ὀφρύων
ἐφελκυσμέναι [1] κόμαι βραχὺ τῷ μετώπῳ μεταίχμιον
ἀφιᾶσιν, σοβαρῶς δὲ ἄχρι τῶν μεταφρένων οἱ ὄπισθεν
ἐπισαλεύονται πλόκαμοι.

41. καὶ μετὰ τοῦτο ἀνθοβαφῆ πέδιλα τῆς σαρκὸς
ἐνδοτέρω τοὺς πόδας ἐπισφίγγοντα καὶ λεπτοϋφὴς ἐς
πρόφασιν ἐσθὴς ὑπὲρ τοῦ δοκεῖν [2] γεγυμνῶσθαι.
πάντα δὲ τὰ ἐντὸς αὐτῆς γνωριμώτερα τοῦ προσώπου
χωρὶς τῶν ἀμόρφως προπεπτωκότων μαζῶν, οὓς ἀεὶ
περιφέρουσιν δεσμώτας. τί δεῖ τὰ τούτων πλουσιώ-
τερα κακὰ διεξιέναι; λίθους Ἐρυθραίας [3] κατὰ τῶν
λοβῶν πολυτάλαντον ἠρτημένους βρῖθος ἢ τοὺς περὶ
καρποῖς καὶ βραχίοσι δράκοντας, ὡς ὤφελον ὄντως
ἀντὶ χρυσίου δράκοντες εἶναι; καὶ στεφάνη μὲν ἐν
κύκλῳ τὴν κεφαλὴν περιθεῖ λίθοις Ἰνδικαῖς διάστε-
ρος, πολυτελεῖς δὲ τῶν αὐχένων ὅρμοι καθεῖνται,
καὶ ἄχρι τῶν ποδῶν ἐσχάτων καταβέβηκεν ὁ
ἄθλιος χρυσὸς ἅπαν, εἴ τι τοῦ σφυροῦ γυμνοῦται,
περισφίγγων. ἄξιον δ' ἦν σιδήρῳ τὰ περίσφυρα σκέλη

[1] ἐφειλκυσμέναι recc., edd..
[2] δοκεῖν μὴ recc., edd..
[3] Ἐρυθραίας Γ: Ἐρυθραίους Ε, edd..

40. But most of their efforts are spent on dressing their hair. For some pass unfavourable judgment on their own gifts from nature and, by means of pigments that can redden the hair to match the sun at noon, they dye their hair with a yellow bloom as they do coloured wool ; those who do feel satisfied with their dark locks spend their husbands' wealth on radiating from their hair almost all the perfumes of Arabia ; they use iron instruments warmed in a slow flame to curl their hair perforce into woolly ringlets, and elaborately styled locks brought down to their eyebrows leave the forehead with the narrowest of spaces, while the tresses behind float proudly down to the shoulders.

41. Next they turn to flower-coloured shoes that sink into their flesh and pinch their feet and to thin veils that pass for clothes so as to excuse their apparent nakedness. But everything inside these can be distinguished more clearly than their faces— except for their hideously prominent breasts which they always carry about bound like prisoners. Need I recount the scandals still more extravagant than these ? The Red Sea pearls [1] worth many a talent that hang heavily from the ears, or the snakes round their wrists and arms, which I wish were real snakes instead of gold ? Their heads are surrounded with crowns bearing a galaxy of Indian gems, and from their throats hang expensive necklaces, while gold has the misfortune to go right down to the tips of their toes, pinching any part of their ankles left naked—though it's iron with which their legs should by rights be shackled at the ankles!

[1] Cf. Martial 5.37.4, Statius *Silvae* 4.6.18.

πεπεδῆσθαι. κἀπειδὰν αὐτῶν ὅλον τὸ σῶμα νόθης
εὐμορφίας ἐξαπατῶντι κάλλει διαμαγευθῇ, τὰς
ἀναισχύντους παρειὰς ἐρυθαίνουσιν ἐπιχρίστοις
φύκεσιν, ἵνα τὴν ὑπέρλευκον αὐτῶν καὶ πίονα
χροιὰν τὸ πορφυροῦν ἄνθος ἐπιφοινίξῃ.

42. τίς οὖν ὁ μετὰ τὴν τοσαύτην παρασκευὴν βίος;
εὐθὺς ἀπὸ τῆς οἰκίας ἔξοδοι, καὶ πᾶς θεὸς [1] ἐπιτρίβων
τοὺς γεγαμηκότας, ὧν ἐνίων οἱ κακοδαίμονες ἄνδρες
οὐδὲ αὐτὰ ἴσασι τὰ ὀνόματα, Κωλιάδας, εἰ τύχοι,
καὶ Γενετυλλίδας ἢ τὴν Φρυγίαν δαίμονα καὶ τὸν
δυσέρωτα κῶμον ἐπὶ τῷ ποιμένι. τελεταὶ δὲ
ἀπόρρητοι καὶ χωρὶς ἀνδρῶν ὕποπτα μυστήρια καὶ
—τί γὰρ [2] δεῖ περιπλέκειν;[3]—διαφθορὰ [4] ψυχῆς.
ἐπειδὰν δὲ τούτων ἀπαλλαγῶσιν, οἴκοι εὐθὺ τὰ
μακρὰ λουτρά, καὶ πολυτελὴς μὲν νὴ Δία τράπεζα,
πολὺς δὲ ὁ μετὰ τῶν ἀνδρῶν ἀκκισμός. ἐπειδὰν
γὰρ ὑπέρπλεω γένωνται ταῖς παρ' αὐταῖς γαστριμαρ-
γίαις, οὐκέτ' οὐδὲ τοῦ φάρυγγος αὐταῖς παραδέ-
χεσθαι δυναμένου τι σιτίον, ἄκροις δακτύλοις
ἐπιγράφουσαι τῶν παρακειμένων ἕκαστον ἀπογεύον-
ται νύκτας ἐπὶ τούτοις διηγούμεναι καὶ τοὺς ἑτερό-
χρωτας ὕπνους καὶ θηλύτητος εὐνὴν γέμουσαν, ἀφ' ἧς
ἀναστὰς ἕκαστος εὐθὺ λουτροῦ χρείός ἐστιν.

43. Ταυτὶ μὲν οὖν εὐσταθοῦς βίου τεκμήρια· τῶν
δὲ πικροτέρων εἴ τις ἐθελήσειε κατὰ μέρος τὸ ἀληθὲς

---

[1] θεὸς Du Soul: θεατὴς codd..
[2] καὶ—τί γὰρ Hemsterhuys: καὶ γὰρ τί codd..
[3] περιπλέκειν Γ^aE: περιβλέπειν ΓΕ².
[4] διαφθορὰ Hemsterhuys: διαφθορὰν codd..

---

[1] Cf. Menander, Fr. 796 Koerte, quoted by Strabo (7.297).

When all their body has been tricked out with the deceptive beauty of a spurious comeliness, they redden their shameless cheeks by smearing on rouge so that its crimson tint may lend colour to their pale fat skins.

42. How, then, do they behave after all these preparations? They leave the house immediately and visit every god [1] that plagues married men, though the wretched husbands do not even know the very names of some of these, be they Coliades and Genetyllides [2] or the Phrygian goddess [3] and the rout that commemorates an unhappy love and honours the shepherd-boy. [4] Then follow secret initiations and suspicious all-female mysteries and, to put things bluntly, the corruption of their souls. But when they've finished with these, the moment they're home they have long baths, and, by heavens, sumptuous meals accompanied by much coyness towards the men. For when they are surfeited with gorging the dishes in front of them, and even *their* throats can now hold no more, they score each of the foods before them with their fingertips to taste them. Meanwhile they talk of their nights, their heterosexual slumbers, and their beds fraught with femininity, on rising from which every man immediately needs a bath.

43. These then are the signs of an orderly female life; but, should one wish to examine in detail the

---

[2] Coliades and Genetyllides were goddesses presiding over generation and birth and seem to have been worshipped by women with wanton rites. Colias is usually used in the singular of Aphrodite; cf. Pausanias 1.1.5 and Harmon's note on *The Mistaken Critic II*.

[3] Cybele, the Great Mother.   [4] Attis.

ἐξετάζειν, ὄντως καταράσεται Προμηθεῖ τὴν Μενάν-
δρειον ἐκείνην ἀπορρήξας φωνήν·

> Εἶτ' οὐ δικαίως προσπεπατταλευμένον
> γράφουσι τὸν Προμηθέα πρὸς ταῖς πέτραις;
> καὶ γίνετ' αὐτῷ λαμπάς, ἄλλο δ' οὐδὲ ἓν
> ἀγαθόν. ὃ μισεῖν οἶμ' ἅπαντας [1] τοὺς θεούς,
> γυναῖκας ἔπλασεν, ὦ πολυτίμητοι θεοί,
> ἔθνος μιαρόν. [2] γαμεῖ τις ἀνθρώπων, γαμεῖ;
> λάθριοι ⟨τὸ⟩ [3] λοιπὸν γὰρ ἐπιθυμίαι κακαί, [4]
> γαμηλίῳ λέχει τε [5] μοιχὸς ἐντρυφῶν.

[εἶτ' ἐπιβουλαὶ] [6]

> καὶ φαρμακεῖαι καὶ νόσων [7] χαλεπώτατος [8]
> φθόνος, μεθ' οὗ ζῇ πάντα τὸν βίον γυνή.

τίς ταῦτα τὰ ἀγαθὰ διώκει; τίνι βίος ὁ δυστυχὴς
οὗτος θυμήρης;

44. ἄξιον τοίνυν ἀντιθεῖναι τοῖς θήλεσι κακοῖς τὴν
ἄρρενα τῶν παίδων ἀγωγήν. ὄρθριος ἀναστὰς ἐκ
τῆς ἀζύγου κοίτης τὸν ἐπὶ τῶν ὀμμάτων ἔτι λοιπὸν
ὕπνον ἀπονιψάμενος ὕδατι λιτῷ καὶ χιτωνίσκον
⟨καὶ⟩ χλαμύδα [9] ταῖς ἐπωμίοις περόναις συρράψας

> ἀπὸ τῆς πατρῴας ἑστίας ἐξέρχεται
> κάτω κεκυφὼς

καὶ μηδένα τῶν ἀπαντώντων ἐξ ἐναντίου προσβλέ-
πων· ἀκόλουθοι δὲ καὶ παιδαγωγοὶ χορὸς αὐτῷ

---

[1] οἶμαι πάντας ΓΕ: corr. recc..
[2] ἔθνους μιαροῦ ΓΕ: corr. recc..
[3] τὸ suppl. Bentley.
[4] κακαί Guyet: καὶ codd..
[5] τε recc.: δὲ Bentley: om. ΓΕ.
[6] εἶτ' ἐπιβουλαὶ del. Bentley.

truth about the more offensive of womankind, he will
curse Prometheus in real life and burst out with these
words of Menander : [1]

> " Then are not painters right when they depict
> Prometheus nailed to rocks ?   With brand of fire
> But naught else good can he be credited.
> But all the gods, methinks, hate what he did,
> In fashioning females, a cursed brood,
> I swear it by the honoured gods above.
> Suppose a man her weds and taketh her to wife,
> She'll spend her time in evil furtive lusts
> Thenceforth and lovers who luxuriate
> On nuptial couch, and poisonings and spite,
> That bane and plague most terrible wherewith
> A woman all her lifetime doth consort."

Who goes in quest of boons like these ?   Who finds so
wretched a life acceptable ?   44. We ought therefore
to contrast with the evils associated with women the
manly life of a boy. He rises at dawn from his
unwed couch, washes away with pure water such
sleep as still remains in his eyes and after securing his
shirt and his mantle [2] with pins at the shoulder " he
leaves his father's hearth with eyes bent down " [3] and
without facing the gaze of anyone he meets.   He
is followed by an orderly company of attendants and

---

[1] Fr. 718 Koerte.

[2] The chitoniscus was a short undergarment, above which
ἔφηβοι wore a mantle (χλαμύς); χλανίς was a finer mantle
regarded as a sign of effeminacy.   See textual notes.

[3] Unidentified comic fragment (Kock 366).

---

[7] νόσοι codd.: corr. Groot.   [8] χαλεπωτάτη Bentley.

[9] χιτωνίσκον χλανίδα ΓΕ (καὶ suppl. Graeve): τὴν ἱερὰν (ἐρεᾶν
Richards) χλαμύδα γρ. Γᵃ, edd..

κόσμιοι ἕπονται τὰ σεμνὰ τῆς ἀρετῆς ἐν χερσὶν
ὄργανα κρατοῦντες, οὐ πριστοῦ κτενὸς ἐντομὰς κόμην καταψήχειν δυναμένας οὐδὲ ἔσοπτρα τῶν
ἀντιμόρφων χαρακτήρων ἀγράφους εἰκόνας, ἀλλ᾽
ἢ πολύπτυχοι δέλτοι κατόπιν ἀκολουθοῦσιν ἢ
παλαιῶν ἔργων ἀρετὰς φυλάττουσαι[1] βίβλοι, κἂν
εἰς μουσικοῦ δέῃ[2] φοιτᾶν, εὐμελὴς λύρα.

45. πᾶσι δὲ τοῖς φιλοσόφοις ψυχῆς μαθήμασι
λιπαρῶς ἐναθλήσας, ἐπειδὰν ἡ διάνοια τῶν ἐγκυκλίων
ἀγαθῶν κορεσθῇ, τὸ σῶμα ταῖς ἐλευθερίοις ἀσκή-
σεσιν ἐκπονεῖ· Θεσσαλοὶ γὰρ ἵπποι μέλουσιν
αὐτῷ· καὶ βραχὺ τὴν νεότητα πωλοδαμνήσας ἐν
εἰρήνῃ μελετᾷ τὰ πολεμικὰ ἄκοντας ἀφιεὶς καὶ
βέλη δι᾽ εὐστόχου δεξιᾶς ἀποπάλλων. εἶθ᾽ αἱ
λιπαραὶ παλαῖστραι, καὶ πρὸς ἡλίου μεσημβρινὸν
θάλπος ἐγκονίεται[3] τὸ σῶμα πυκνούμενον, οἵ τε τῶν
ἐναγωνίων πόνων ἀποσταλάζοντες ἱδρῶτες, μεθ᾽
οὓς λουτρὰ σύντομα καὶ τράπεζα τῇ μετὰ μικρὸν
ἐπινήφουσα[4] πράξει· πάλιν γὰρ αὐτῷ διδάσκαλοι
καὶ παλαιῶν ἔργων αἰνιττόμεναι καὶ ἐπιμελούμεναι
μνῆμαι, τίς ἀνδρεῖος ἥρως ἢ τίς ἐπὶ φρονήσει μαρτυ-
ρούμενος ἢ οἷοι δικαιοσύνην καὶ σωφροσύνην ἠσπά-
σαντο. τοιαύταις ἀρεταῖς ἁπαλὴν ἔτι τὴν ψυχὴν
ἐπάρδων, ὅταν ἑσπέρα τὴν πρᾶξιν ὁρίσῃ, τῇ[5]
γαστρὸς ἀνάγκῃ τὸν ὀφειλόμενον δασμὸν ἐπιμετρή-
σας ἡδίους ὕπνους καθεύδει τοῖς καθ᾽ ἡμέραν καμά-
τοις ἐπηρεμῶν ἀνεπίφθονον.[6]

---

[1] φυλάττουσι ΓΕ: corr. recc..
[2] δέοι codd.: corr. Dindorf.   [3] ἐν κόνι τε Γᵃ
[4] ἐπινηφούσῃ ΓΕ: corr. recc..   [5] τῇ recc.: τῆς ΓΕ.

tutors, who grip in their hands the revered instruments of virtue, not the points of a toothed comb that can caress the hair nor mirrors that without artists' aid reproduce the shapes confronting them, but behind him come many-leaved writing tablets or books that preserve the merit of ancient deeds, along with a tuneful lyre, should he have to go to a music master.

45. But, after he has toiled zealously through all the lessons that teach the soul philosophy, and his intellect has had its fill of these benefits of a standard education, he perfects his body with noble exercises. For he interests himself in Thessalian horses. Soon, after he has broken in his youth as one does a colt, he practises in peace the pursuits of war, throwing javelins and hurling spears with unerring aim. Next come the glistening wrestling-schools, where beneath the heat of the mid-day sun his developing body is covered in dust ; then comes the sweat, that pours forth from his toils in the contest, and next a quick bath and a sober meal suited to the activities that soon follow. For again he has his schoolmasters and records of deeds of old with hints for the study of such questions as what hero was brave, who is cited for his wisdom, or what men cherished justice and temperance. Such are the virtues which he uses to irrigate his soul while still tender, and, when evening brings an end to his activities, he metes out the tribute due to the necessities of his stomach, and then sleeps the sweeter, enjoying a rest that none could grudge after his exertions during the day.

---

[6] ἐπίφθονον codd.: corr. L. A. Post.

PSEUDO-LUCIAN

46. τίς οὐκ ἂν ἐραστὴς ἐφήβου γένοιτο τοιούτου;
τίνι δ᾽[1] οὕτω τυφλαὶ μὲν αἱ τῶν ὀμμάτων βολαί,
πηροὶ δὲ οἱ τῆς διανοίας λογισμοί; πῶς δ᾽ οὐκ ἂν
ἀγαπήσαι τὸν ἐν παλαίστραις μὲν Ἑρμῆν, Ἀπόλ-
λωνα δὲ ἐν λύραις, ἱππαστὴν δὲ ὡς Κάστορα, θείας
δὲ ἀρετὰς διὰ θνητοῦ διώκοντα σώματος; ἀλλ᾽ ἐμοὶ
μέν, δαίμονες οὐράνιοι, βίος εἴη διηνεκὴς οὗτος,
ἀπαντικρὺ τοῦ φίλου καθέζεσθαι καὶ πλησίον ἡδὺ
λαλοῦντος ἀκούειν, ἐξιόντι δὲ αὐτῷ συνεξιέναι καὶ
παντὸς ἔργου κοινωνίαν ἔχειν. εὔξαιτο μὲν οὖν ἐρῶν
τις δι᾽ ἀπταίστου καὶ ἀκλινοῦς βίου τὸν[2] στεργό-
μενον ἀλύπως εἰς γῆρας ὁδεῦσαι μηδεμιᾶς τύχης
πειράσαντα βάσκανον ἐπήρειαν. εἰ δὲ καί, οἷος
ἀνθρωπίνης φύσεως νόμος, νόσος ἐπιψαύσειεν, αὐτῷ
κάμνοντι συννοσήσω καὶ διὰ χειμερίου θαλάσσης
ἀναγομένῳ συμπλεύσομαι· κἂν τυραννικὴ βία δεσμὰ
περιάψῃ, τὸν ἴσον ἐμαυτῷ περιθήσω σίδηρον· ἐχθρὸς
ἅπας ὁ μισῶν ἐκεῖνον ἐμὸς ἔσται, καὶ φιλήσω τοὺς
πρὸς αὐτὸν εὐνοϊκῶς ἔχοντας· εἰ δὲ λῃστὰς ἢ
πολεμίους θεασαίμην ἐπ᾽ αὐτὸν ὁρμῶντας, ὁπλι-
σαίμην καὶ παρὰ δύναμιν· κἂν ἀποθάνῃ, ζῆν οὐκ
ἀνέξομαι· τελευταίας δὲ ἐντολὰς τοῖς μετ᾽ ἐκεῖνον
ὑπ᾽ ἐμοῦ στεργομένοις ἐπιθήσομαι κοινὸν ἀμφοτέροις
ἐπιχῶσαι τάφον, ὀστέοις δὲ ἀναμίξαντας ὀστέα μηδὲ
τὴν κωφὴν κόνιν ἀπ᾽ ἀλλήλων διακρῖναι.

47. ταῦτα δ᾽ οὐ πρῶτοι χαράξουσιν οἱ ἐμοὶ πρὸς
τοὺς ἀξίους ἔρωτες, ἀλλ᾽ ἡ θεοῖς γείτων ἡρωικὴ
φρόνησις ἐνομοθέτησεν, ἐν οἷς ὁ φιλίας ἔρως ἄχρι

---

[1] τίνι δ᾽ recc.: τίσιν ΓΕ.   [2] τὸν recc.: τὸ ΓΕ.

---

[1] Cf. Sappho 1.2. (Edmonds).

46. Who would not fall in love with such a youth ? Whose eyesight could be so blind, whose mental processes so stunted ? How could one fail to love him who is a Hermes in the wrestling-school, an Apollo with the lyre, a horseman to rival Castor, and one who strives after the virtues of the gods with a mortal body ? For my part, ye gods of heaven, I pray that it may for ever be my lot in life to sit opposite my dear one and hear close to me his sweet voice,[1] to go out when he goes out and share every activity with him. And so a lover might well pray that his cherished one should journey to old age without any sorrow through a life free from stumbling or swerving, without having experienced at all any malicious spite of Fortune. But, if in accordance with the law governing the human body, illness should lay its hand on him, I shall ail with him when he is weak, and, when he puts out to sea through stormy waves, I shall sail with him. And, should a violent tyrant bind him in chains, I shall put the same fetters around myself. All who hate him will be my enemies and those well disposed to him shall I hold dear. Should I see bandits or foemen rushing upon him, I would arm myself even beyond my strength, and if he dies, I shall not bear to live. I shall give final instructions to those I love next best after him to pile up a common tomb for both of us, to unite my bones with his and not to keep even our dumb ashes apart from each other.

47. Nor will you find my love for those who deserve it to be the first to write such things ; rather were these the laws given by the wellnigh divine wisdom of the heroes, who till their dying day

θανάτου συνεξέπνευσεν. Φωκὶς ἐκ νηπίων ἔτι χρόνων
Ὀρέστην Πυλάδῃ συνῆψεν· θεὸν δὲ τῶν πρὸς
ἀλλήλους παθῶν μεσίτην λαβόντες ὡς ἐφ' ἑνὸς
σκάφους τοῦ βίου συνέπλευσαν· ἀμφότεροι Κλυται-
μήστραν ἀνῄρουν ὡς Ἀγαμέμνονος παῖδες, ὑπ'
ἀμφοῖν Αἴγισθος ἐφονεύετο· τὰς Ὀρέστην ἐλαυνού-
σας Ποινὰς Πυλάδης ἐνόσει μᾶλλον, κρινομένῳ
συνηγωνίζετο. τὴν δὲ ἐρωτικὴν φιλίαν οὐδὲ τοῖς τῆς
Ἑλλάδος ὅροις ἐμέτρησαν, ἀλλ' ἐπὶ τοὺς ἐσχάτους
Σκυθῶν τέρμονας ἔπλευσαν, ὁ μὲν νοσῶν, ὁ δὲ
θεραπεύων. τῆς γοῦν Ταυρικῆς γῆς ἐπιβαίνοντας
εὐθὺς ἡ μητροκτόνος αὐτοὺς Ἐρινὺς ἐξενοδόχησεν,
καὶ τῶν βαρβάρων ἐν κύκλῳ περιεστώτων ὁ μὲν
ὑπὸ τῆς συνήθους μανίας πεσὼν ἔκειτο, Πυλάδης δὲ

> ἀφρόν ⟨τ'⟩ [1] ἀπέψα [2] σώματός τ' ἐτημέλει
> πέπλου [3] τε προὐκάλυπτεν εὐπήνους [4] ὑφάς, [5]

οὐκ ἐραστοῦ μόνον, ἀλλὰ καὶ πατρὸς ἐνδεικνύμενος
ἦθος. ἡνίκα γοῦν ἐκρίθη θατέρου μένοντος ἐπὶ τῷ
φονευθῆναι τὸν ἕτερον ἐς Μυκήνας ἀπιέναι κομιοῦντα
γράμματα, μένειν ὑπὲρ ἀλλήλων ἀμφότεροι θέλουσιν
ἑκάτερος ἐν θατέρῳ ζῶντι ζῆν ἑαυτὸν ἡγούμενος.
ἀπωθεῖται δὲ τὰς ἐπιστολὰς Ὀρέστης ὡς Πυλάδου
λαβεῖν ἀξιωτέρου, μόνον οὐκ ἐραστὴς ἀντ' ἐρωμένου
γενόμενος·

> τὸ γὰρ σφαγῆναι τόνδ' ἐμοὶ βάρος μέγα·
> ὁ ναυστολῶν γάρ εἰμ' ἐγὼ τὰς συμφοράς.

---

[1] τ' suppl. Euripidis codd..   [2] ἀπέψη Elmsley.
[3] πέπλων Eur. codd..
[4] εὐπήνους Eur. codd.: εὐπήκτους Γ: εὐπήκτοις Ε.   [5] ὑφαῖς Ε.

---

[1] The Eumenides.

breathed love of friendship. Phocis united Orestes to
Pylades right from their infancy. Taking the love-
god as the mediator of their emotions for each other,
they sailed together as it were on the same vessel
of life. Both did away with Clytemnestra as though
both were sons of Agamemnon, by both of them
was Aegisthus slain. Pylades it was who suffered the
more from the Avengers [1] who hounded Orestes, and
he stood trial along with him in court. Nor did they
restrict their affectionate friendship to the limits of
Hellas, but sailed to Scythia at the very ends of the
earth, one of them afflicted, the other ministering to
him. At any rate, as soon as they set foot on the
land of the Tauri, the Fury of matricides was there to
welcome the strangers, and, when the natives stood
around them, the one was struck to the ground by his
usual madness and lay there, but Pylades

" Did wipe away the foam and tend his frame
And shelter him with fine well-woven robe," [2]

thus showing the feelings not merely of a lover but
also of a father. When at any rate it had been
decided that, while one remained to be killed, the
other should depart for Mycenae to bear a letter,
each wished to remain for the sake of the other,
considering that he himself lived in the survival of his
friend. But Orestes refused to take the letter,
claiming Pylades was the fitter person to do so, and
showed himself almost to be the lover rather than the
beloved.

" For 'tis a burden sore to me if he be slain,
For I am captain of this enterprise." [3]

[2] Euripides, *Iphigenia in Tauris* 311-312.
[3] Ibid. 598-599.

καὶ μετ' ὀλίγον φησίν,

> τῷδε μὲν δέλτον δίδου·
> πέμψω [1] γὰρ Ἄργος, ὥστε οἱ [2] καλῶς ἔχειν·
> ἡμᾶς δ' ὁ χρῄζων κτεινέτω.

48. καὶ γὰρ οὕτως ἔχει τὸ πᾶν· ὅταν γὰρ ἐκ παίδων ὁ σπουδαῖος ἔρως ἐντραφεὶς ἐπὶ τὴν ἤδη λογίζεσθαι δυναμένην ἡλικίαν ἀνδρωθῇ, τὸ πάλαι φιληθὲν ἀμοιβαίους ἔρωτας ἀνταποδίδωσιν, καὶ δυσχερὲς αἰσθέσθαι ποτέρου πότερος ἐραστής ἐστιν, ὥσπερ ἀπ' ἐσόπτρου τῆς τοῦ φιλήσαντος εὐνοίας ἐπὶ τὸν ἐρώμενον ὁμοίου πεσόντος εἰδώλου. τί δὴ οὖν τοῦ καθ' ἡμᾶς βίου ξένην αὐτὸ τρυφὴν ὀνειδίζεις θείοις νόμοις ὁρισθὲν ἐκ διαδοχῆς ἐφ' ἡμᾶς καταβεβηκός; [3] ἀσμένως δὲ αὐτὸ δεξάμενοι μεθ' ἁγνῆς διανοίας νεωκοροῦμεν· ὄλβιος γὰρ ὡς ἀληθῶς κατὰ τὴν τῶν [4] σοφῶν ἀπόφασιν,

> ᾧ παῖδές τε νέοι καὶ μώνυχες ἵπποι,
> γηράσκει δ' ὁ γέρων κεῖνος ἐλαφρότατα, [5]
> κοῦροι τὸν φιλέουσιν.

αἵ γε μὴν Σωκρατικαὶ διδασκαλίαι καὶ τὸ λαμπρὸν ἐκεῖνο τῆς ἀρετῆς δικαστήριον τοῖς Δελφικοῖς τρίποσιν ἐτιμήθη· χρησμὸν γὰρ ἀληθείας ὁ Πύθιος ἐθέσπισεν,

> ἀνδρῶν ἁπάντων Σωκράτης σοφώτατος,

---

[1] πέμψει Eur. codd..   [2] οἱ ΓΕ: σοι recc., Eur. codd..
[3] καταβέβηκεν Γ: corr. Γ^a.   [4] τῶν om. ΓΕ.
[5] ἐλαφρότατον Pfeiffer: ἐλαφρότατοι Stobaeus.

---

[1] Euripides, *Iphigenia in Tauris* 603-605, unmetrically adapted "argumenti causa."

And shortly afterwards he says

" The message give to him,
For him I'll send to Argos ; he will thrive ;
But whoso will may take my life." [1]

48. This too is the case generally. For, when the honourable love inbred in us from childhood matures to the manly age that is now capable of reason, the object of our longstanding affection gives love in return and it's difficult to detect which is the lover of which, since the image of the lover's tenderness has been reflected from the loved one as though from a mirror. Why then do you censure this as being an exotic indulgence of our times, though it is an ordinance enacted by divine laws and a heritage that has come down to us? We have been glad to receive it and we tend its shrine with a pure heart. For that man is truly blessed according to the verdict of the wise,

" Whoso hath youthful lads and whole-hooved
steeds; [2]

And that old man doth age with greatest ease
Whom youths do love." [3]

The teaching of Socrates and his famous tribunal of virtue were honoured by the Delphic tripod, for the Pythian god uttered an oracle of truth,

" Of all men Socrates the wisest is." [4]

---

[2] Solon 23 (Theognis 1253) adapted. Cf. Plato, *Lysis* 212 E.   [3] Callimachus, *Aetia*, Fr. 41 (Pfeiffer).

[4] The older tradition was that the oracle replied in prose that no-one was wiser than Socrates (Plato, *Apology* 20 E), but an iambic version of the oracle was known to Cicero's contemporary, Apollonius Molo. This line is also quoted by Diogenes Laertius 2.37 and Origen *In Celsum* 7.6. (cf. Parke and Wormell, *The Delphic Oracle* 420).

ὃς οὐχ ἅμα [1] τοῖς ἄλλοις μαθήμασιν, ἐξ ὧν τὸν βίον
ὤνησεν, καὶ τὸ παιδεραστεῖν ὡς μάλιστα ὠφελοῦν
προσήκατο; [2]

49. δεῖ δὲ τῶν νέων ἐρᾶν ὡς Ἀλκιβιάδου Σωκράτης,
ὃς ὑπὸ μιᾷ χλαμύδι πατρὸς ὕπνους ἐκοιμήθη. καὶ
ἔγωγε τὸ Καλλιμάχειον ἐπὶ τέλει τῶν λόγων ἥδιστα
προσθείην ἂν ἅπασι κήρυγμα·

Αἴθε γάρ, ὦ κούροισιν ἐπ’ ὄμματα λίχνα φέροντες,
      Ἐρχίος ὡς ὑμῖν ὥρισε παιδοφιλεῖν,
ὧδε νέων ἐρῷτε· [3] πόλιν κ’ εὔανδρον ἔχοιτε.

ταῦτ’ εἰδότες, ὦ νεανίαι, σωφρόνως παισὶν ἀγαθοῖς
πρόσιτε μηδὲ ὀλίγης τέρψεως εἵνεκεν τὴν μακρὰν
ἐκχέοντες εὔνοιαν ἄχρι τῆς ἀκμῆς πλαστὰ τὰ τοῦ
φιλεῖν πάθη προβάλλεσθε, τὸν δ’ οὐράνιον Ἔρωτα
προσκυνοῦντες εἰς γῆρας ἀπὸ παίδων βέβαια
τηρεῖτε τὰ πάθη· τοῖς γὰρ οὕτω φιλοῦσιν ἥδιστος
μὲν ὁ τοῦ ζῆν χρόνος οὐδεμιᾶς ἀπρεποῦς συνειδή-
σεως παροικούσης, ἀοίδιμοι δὲ μετὰ θάνατον εἰς
πάντας ἐκφοιτῶσι κληδόνες. εἰ δὲ δεῖ φιλοσόφων
παισὶ πιστεύειν, αἰθὴρ μετὰ γῆν ἐκδέχεται τοὺς
ταῦτα ζηλοῦντας· εἰς δὲ ἀμείνονα βίον ἀποθανόντες
ἔχουσι τῆς ἀρετῆς γέρας τὸ ἄφθαρτον.

50. Τοιαῦτα τοῦ Καλλικρατίδου σφόδρα νεανικῶς
σεμνολογησαμένου Χαρικλέα μὲν ἐκ δευτέρου λέγειν
πειρώμενον ἐπέσχον· ὥρα γὰρ ἦν ἐπὶ ναῦν κατιέναι.

---

[1] οὐχ ἅμα ΓΕ: οὐχ ὅτι Γᵃ: ἅμα recc., edd..
[2] punctum interrogativum addidi.
[3] ἐρῷτε Schneider: ἔροητε (sic) Γ: ἔρουωντε (sic) ΕΓᵃ.

---

[1] Cf. Plato, *Symposium* 219 C. Lucian, *Philosophies For
Sale*, 15.
[2] Callimachus, *Fr.* 571. Erchius is unknown, though

For along with the other discoveries with which he benefited human life did he not also welcome love of boys as the greatest of boons?

49. One should love youths as Alcibiades was loved by Socrates who slept like a father [1] with him under the same cloak. And for my part I would most gladly add to the end of my discourse the words of Callimachus as a message to all : [2]

"May you who cast your longing eyes on youths
So love the young as Erchius bid you do,
That in its men your city may be blessed."

Knowing this, young men, be temperate when you approach virtuous boys. Do not for the sake of a brief pleasure squander lasting affection, nor till you've reached manhood put on show counterfeit feelings of affection, but worship Heavenly Love and keep your emotions constant from boyhood to old age. For those who love thus, having nothing disgraceful on their conscience, find their lifetime sweetest and after their death their glorious report goes out to all men. If it's right to believe the children of philosophy, the heavens await men with these ideals after their stay on earth. By entering a better life at death they have immortality as the reward for their virtue."

50. After Callicratidas had delivered this very spirited sermon, Charicles tried to speak for a second time but I stopped him ; for it was now time to return

Schneider thinks him the ἐπώνυμος of Erchia, the deme of Xenophon and Isocrates, where Alcibiades' family had estates. Conceivably 'Ερχιός stands for 'Ερχιεύς and refers to Xenophon, though one might rather expect him to be a legislator like Solon.

227

δεομένων δ' ὅ τι φρονοίην [1] ἀποφήνασθαι, δι' ὀλίγο‹υ›
τοὺς ἑκατέρων [2] λόγους ἀριθμησάμενος, Οὐκ ἐ‹ξ›
ὑπογύου, φημί, καὶ παρημελημένως ὑμῖν, ἕταιροι
τὰ τῶν λόγων ἔοικεν ἀπεσχεδιάσθαι, διηνεκοῦς δ‹ὲ›
καὶ νὴ Δί' ἐρρωμένης φροντίδος ἐναργῆ ταῦτ' ἐστὶ‹ν›
ἴχνη· σχεδὸν γὰρ οὐδέν ἐστιν ὅ τι τῶν λεκτέω‹ν›
εἰπεῖν ἑτέρῳ δύνασθαι παρήκατε. καὶ πολλὴ μὲν ‹ἡ›
τῶν πραγμάτων ἐμπειρία, πλείων δ' ἡ τῶν λόγω‹ν›
δεινότης, ὥστ' ἔγωγε ἂν εὐξαίμην, εἴπερ ἦν ἐ‹ν›
δυνατῷ,[3] γενέσθαι Θηραμένης ἐκεῖνος ὁ Κόθορνος
ἵν' ἄμφω νενικηκότες ἐξ ἴσου βαδίζοιτε. πλὴ‹ν›
ἐπειδήπερ ἀνήσειν οὐκ ἐοίκατε καὶ αὐτὸς ἐν τῷ
μεταξὺ πλῷ περὶ τῶν αὐτῶν οὐ κέκρικα διοχλεῖσθαι
τὸ μάλιστα παραστὰν εἶναί μοι δίκαιον ἀποφανοῦ-
μαι.

51. γάμοι μὲν ἀνθρώποις βιωφελὲς πρᾶγμα κα‹ὶ›
μακάριον, ὁπόταν εὐτυχῶνται, παιδικοὺς δ' ἔρωτας
ὅσοι φιλίας ἁγνὰ δίκαια προμνῶνται, μόνης φιλοσοφίας ἔργον ἡγοῦμαι. διὸ δὴ γαμητέον μὲν ἅπασιν
παιδεραστεῖν δὲ ἐφείσθω μόνοις τοῖς σοφοῖς[4]· ἥκιστα
γὰρ ἐν γυναιξὶν ὁλόκληρος ἀρετὴ φύεται. καὶ σὺ
δ', ὦ Χαρίκλεις, μηδὲν ἀχθεσθῇς, εἰ ταῖς Ἀθήναις ‹ἡ›
Κόρινθος εἴξει.

52. κἀγὼ μὲν ὑπ' αἰδοῦς συντόμῳ λόγῳ τὴν κρίσι‹ν›
ἐπισπεύσας ἐξανέστην· ἑώρων γὰρ ὑπερκατηφῆ τὸ‹ν›
Χαρικλέα παρὰ μικρὸν ὡς θανάτου κατάκριτον. ‹ὁ›
δ' Ἀθηναῖος ἱλαρῷ τῷ προσώπῳ φαιδρὸς ἀναπηδήσας προῄει σφόδρα σοβαρῶς· εἴκασεν ἄν τις αὐτὸν ε‹ἰ›

[1] φρονοῖεν ΓΕ: corr. recc..
[2] ἑκατέρου edd..   [3] ἐν δυνατῷ om. Ε.
[4] σοφοῖς ΓΕ: φιλοσόφοις mg. Γ.

to the ship. They pressed me to pronounce my opinion, but, after weighing up for a short time the speeches of both, I said : "Your words, my friends, do not seem to me to be hurried, thoughtless improvisations, but give clear proof of continued and, by heaven, concentrated thought. For of all the possible arguments there's hardly one you've left for another to use. And, though your experience of the world is great, it is surpassed by your eloquence, so that I for one could wish, if it were possible, to become Theramenes, the Turncoat,[1] so that you could both be victorious and walk off on equal terms. However, since I do not think you'll let the matter be, and I myself am resolved not to be exercised on the same topic during the voyage, I shall give the verdict that has struck me as the fairest.

51. Marriage is a boon and a blessing to men when it meets with good fortune, while the love of boys, that pays court to the hallowed dues of friendship, I consider to be the privilege only of philosophy. Therefore all men should marry, but let only the wise be permitted to love boys, for perfect virtue grows least of all among women. And you must not be angry, Charicles, if Corinth yields to Athens."

52. After giving this decision hurriedly in a few brief words out of regard for my friend, I rose to my feet. For I saw that he was utterly dejected, almost like one condemned to death. But the Athenian leapt up joyously with a gleeful expression on his face and started to stalk about in front of us most triumphantly, just as if, one would have thought, he had

[1] Literally "the buskin," "the boot which can fit either foot," a nickname given to the politician Theramenes for his "sail-trimming" at the end of the Peloponnesian War.

Σαλαμῖνι Πέρσας κατανεναυμαχηκέναι. καὶ τοῦτ
γε τῆς κρίσεως ἀπωνάμην, λαμπρότερον ἡμῶ
ἑστιάσαντος αὐτοῦ τἀπινίκια· καὶ γὰρ ἦν ἄλλως [1] τ
βίῳ μεγαλοφρονέστερος. ἡσυχῇ δὲ καὶ τὸν Χαρι
κλέα παρηγορησάμην ἐπὶ τῇ δεινότητι τῶν λόγω
συνεχὲς ὑπερθαυμάζων, ὅτι δυσχερεστέρῳ μέρε
δυνατῶς συνηγόρησεν.

53. ἀλλ᾽ ἡ μὲν ἐν Κνίδῳ διατριβὴ καὶ τὰ παρὰ τ
θεῷ λαληθέντα σπουδὴν ἱλαρὰν ἅμα καὶ παιδιὰ
εὔμουσον ἐσχηκότα τῇδέ πῃ διεκρίθη. σὺ δέ,
Θεόμνηστε, ὁ τὴν ἕωλον ἡμῶν ἐκκαλεσάμενο
μνήμην, εἰ δικαστὴς τότ᾽ ἦσθα, πῶς ἂν ἀπεφήνω;

ΘΕΟΜΝΗΣΤΟΣ

Μελιτίδην ἢ Κόροιβον [2] οἴει με πρὸς θεῶν, ἵν
τοῖς ὑπὸ σοῦ δικαίως κριθεῖσιν ἐναντίαν φέρω ψῆ
φον; ὡς [3] ὑπ᾽ ἄκρας ἡδονῆς τῶν λεγομένων ἐ
Κνίδῳ διατρίβειν ᾠόμην ὀλίγου τὸ βραχὺ τοῦτ
δωμάτιον αὐτὸν ἡγούμενος εἶναι τὸν νεὼν ἐκεῖνον
ὅμως δ᾽ οὖν—οὐδὲν γὰρ ἀπρεπὲς ἐν ἑορτῇ λέγεσθαι
πᾶς δὲ γέλως, κἂν περίεργος ᾖ, πανηγυρίζειν δοκεῖ—
τοὺς ἄγαν ὑπὸ τοῦ παιδεραστεῖν κατωφρυωμένου
λόγους ἐθαύμαζον μὲν ἐπὶ τῇ σεμνότητι, πλὴν ο
πάνυ θυμῆρες ᾠόμην, ἐφήβῳ παιδὶ συνδιημερεύοντ
Τανταλείους δίκας ὑποφέρειν, καὶ τοῖς ὄμμασι το
κάλλους μονονουχὶ προσκλύζοντος, ἐξὸν ἀρύσασθαι
διψῆν ὑπομένειν· οὐ γὰρ ἀπόχρη τὸ θεωρεῖ

---

[1] ἄλλος ΓΕ: corr. recc..
[2] κόρυβον ΓΕ: corr. recc..
[3] ὡς ΓΕ: ὃς Εᵃ, edd..

230

defeated the Persian fleet at Salamis. I derived a
further benefit from my verdict when he entertained
us to a magnificent feast to celebrate his victory.
For his behaviour had in other ways, too, shown him
to be generous of spirit. As for Charicles, I con-
soled him quietly by repeatedly expressing my great
admiration for his eloquence and his able defence of
the more awkward cause.

53. Well, thus ended our stay in Cnidus and our
conversation in the sanctuary of the goddess with
its combination of gay earnestness and cultured fun.
But now, Theomnestus, you who have evoked these
old memories of mine must tell me how *you* would
have decided, if *you* had been judge.

THEOMNESTUS

By heaven, do you think I'm a Melitides or
Coroebus [1] to cast a vote in opposition to your just
verdict ? For through my intense enjoyment of
your narrative I thought I was in Cnidus, almost
imagining this small chamber to be that temple.
But nevertheless, seeing that nothing said on a festive
day is unseemly, and any jesting, even if carried to
excess, is thought in keeping with the holiday spirit,
I must say I admired the solemnity of the very high-
brow speeches evoked by love of boys, except that I
didn't think it very agreeable to spend all day with a
youth suffering the punishment of Tantalus, and,
though the waters of beauty are, as it were, almost
lapping against my eyes, to endure thirst when one
can help oneself to water. For it's not enough to

---

[1] Proverbial fools. Cf., for Melitides, Aristophanes,
Frogs 991, Aelian *V.H.* 13, 15 and, for Coroebus, Lucian,
The Lover of Lies 3.

ἐρώμενον οὐδ' ἀπαντικρὺ καθημένου καὶ λαλοῦντος
ἀκούειν, ἀλλ' ὥσπερ ἡδονῆς κλίμακα συμπηξά-
μενος ἔρως πρῶτον ἔχει βαθμὸν ὄψεως, ἵνα ἴδῃ, κἂν
θεάσηται, ποθεῖ προσάγων ἐφάψασθαι· δι' ἄκρων
γοῦν δακτύλων κἂν μόνον θίγῃ, τὰ τῆς ἀπολαύσεως
εἰς ἅπαν διαθεῖ τὸ σῶμα. τυχὼν δ' εὐμαρῶς
τούτου τρίτην πεῖραν ἐπάγει φιλήματος, οὐκ εὐθὺ
περίεργον, ἀλλ' ἠρέμα χείλη προσεγγίσας χείλεσιν,
ἃ πρὶν ἢ ψαῦσαι τελείως, ἀπέστη, μηδὲν ὑπονοίας
ἴχνος ἀπολιπών· εἶτα πρὸς τὸ παρεῖκον [1] ἁρμοζό-
μενος ἀεὶ λιπαρεστέροις μὲν ἀσπάσμασιν ἐντέτηκεν,
ἔσθ' ὅτε καὶ διαστέλλων ἡσυχῇ τὸ στόμα, τῶν δὲ
χειρῶν οὐδεμίαν παρίησιν ἀργήν· αἱ γὰρ φανεραὶ
μετὰ τῶν ἐσθήτων [2] συμπλοκαὶ [3] τὴν ἡδονὴν
συνάπτουσιν, ἢ λάθριος [4] ὑγρῶς ἡ δεξιὰ κατὰ κόλπου
δῦσα μαστοὺς βραχὺ τὴν φύσιν ὑπεροιδῶντας πιέζει,
καὶ σφριγώσης γαστρὸς ἀμφιλαφὲς τοῖς δακτύλοις
ἐπιδράττεται ὁμαλῶς, μετὰ τοῦτο καὶ πρωτόχνουν
ἄνθος ἥβης. καὶ

τί τἄρρητ' ἀναμετρήσασθαί με δεῖ;

τοσαύτης τυχὼν ἐξουσίας ὁ ἔρως θερμοτέρου τινὸς
ἅπτεται πράγματος· εἶτ' ἀπὸ μηρῶν προοιμιασά-
μενος κατὰ τὸν κωμικὸν αὐτὸ ἐπάταξεν.

54. ἐμοὶ μὲν οὕτω παιδεραστεῖν γένοιτο· μετεω-
ρολέσχαι δὲ καὶ ὅσοι τὴν φιλοσοφίας ὀφρὺν ὑπὲρ

---

[1] παρεῖκον recc.: παρῆκον ΓΕ.
[2] ἐσθήτων recc.: αἰσθητῶν ΓΕ.
[3] συμπλοκαὶ ΓΕ: περιπλοκαὶ Γᵃ Ε², edd..
[4] λαθρίως ΓΕ: corr. rec..

look at the loved one or to listen to his voice as he sits facing you,[1] but love has, as it were, made itself a ladder of pleasure, and has for its first step that of sight, so that it may see the beloved, and, once it beholds, it wishes to approach and to touch. If it only touches with but the fingertips, the waves of enjoyment run into the whole body. Once easily achieving this, love attempts the third stage and tries a kiss, not making it a violent one at first, but lightly bringing lips close to lips so that they part before completing full contact, without leaving the slightest cause for suspicion. Thus it adjusts itself to the success gained and melts into ever more importunate embraces, sometimes gently opening the mouth and leaving neither hand idle. For open embraces of the beloved when clothed give mutual pleasure ; or else the furtive hand wantonly glides down into the bosom and squeezes for a moment the breasts swollen past their normal size and makes a smooth sweep to grasp with the fingers the belly throbbing full spate with passion, and thereafter the early down of adolescence, and—

" But why recount the thing one should not tell ? "[2]

Once love has gained so much liberty it begins warmer work. Then it makes a start with the thighs and, to quote the comic poet, " strikes the target." [3]

54. May I for my part find it my lot to love boys in this way. But may the airy talkers and those who raise their philosophic brows temple-high and even

---

[1] See note on p. 220.
[2] Euripides, *Orestes* 14.
[3] The reference is unknown.

PSEUDO-LUCIAN

αὐτοὺς τοὺς κροτάφους ὑπερήρκασιν, σεμνῶν ὀνομάτων κομψεύμασιν τοὺς ἀμαθεῖς ποιμαινέτωσαν· ἐρω-
τικὸς γὰρ ἦν, εἴπερ τις, καὶ ὁ ¹ Σωκράτης, καὶ ὑπὸ
μίαν Ἀλκιβιάδης αὐτῷ χλανίδα κλιθεὶς οὐκ ἀπλὴξ
ἀνέστη. καὶ μὴ θαυμάσῃς· οὐδὲ γὰρ ὁ Πάτροκλος
ὑπ' Ἀχιλλέως ἠγαπᾶτο μέχρι τοῦ καταντικρὺ
καθέζεσθαι

δέγμενος Αἰακίδην, ὁπότε λήξειεν ἀείδων,

ἀλλ' ἦν καὶ τῆς ἐκείνων φιλίας μεσῖτις ἡδονή·
στένων γοῦν Ἀχιλλεὺς τὸν Πατρόκλου θάνατον
ἀταμιεύτῳ πάθει πρὸς τὴν ἀλήθειαν ἀπερράγη,

μηρῶν τε τῶν σῶν εὐσέβησ' ὁμιλίαν
κλαίων. ²

τούς γε μὴν ὀνομαζομένους παρ' Ἕλλησιν κωμαστὰς
οὐδὲν ἀλλ' ἢ δήλους ἐραστὰς νομίζω. τάχα
φήσει τις αἰσχρὰ ταῦτ' εἶναι λέγεσθαι, πλὴν ἀληθῆ
γε νὴ τὴν Κνιδίαν Ἀφροδίτην.

ΛΥΚΙΝΟΣ

Οὐκ ἀνέξομαί σου, φίλε Θεόμνηστε, ἄλλην ἀρχὴν
καταβαλλομένου τρίτων λόγων, ἧς ἀκούειν ἐν ἑορτῇ
μόνον εἰκός ἐστιν, τἆλλα δὲ τῶν ἐμῶν ὤτων πόρρω
ἀποικεῖν. ἀφέμενοι δὲ τοῦ παρέλκειν πλείω χρόνον εἰς ἀγορὰν ἐξίωμεν· ἤδη γὰρ εἰκός ἐστιν
ὑφάπτεσθαι τῷ θεῷ τὴν πυράν. ἔστιν δ' οὐκ
ἀτερπὴς ἡ θέα τῶν ἐν Οἴτῃ παθῶν ὑπομιμνήσκουσα
τοὺς παρόντας.

¹ εἴπερ τις καὶ ἄλλος, ὁ conieci.
² sic Hermann: εὐσεβὴς ὁμιλία καλλίω ΓΕ.

234

higher, beguile the ignorant with the speciousness of their solemn phrases. For Socrates was as devoted to love as anyone and Alcibiades, once he had lain down beneath the same mantle with him, did not rise unassailed.[1] Don't be surprised at that. For not even the affection of Achilles for Patroclus was limited to having him seated opposite

"Waiting until Aeacides should cease his song." [2]

No, pleasure was the mediator even of *their* friendship. At any rate, when Achilles was lamenting the death of Patroclus, his unrestrained feelings made him burst out with the truth and say,

" The converse of our thighs my tears do mourn
    With duteous piety " [3]

Those whom the Greeks call " revellers " I think to be nothing but ostentatious lovers. Perhaps someone will assert this is a shameful thing to say, but, by Aphrodite of Cnidus, it's the truth.

LYCINUS

My dear Theomnestus, I won't tolerate your laying the foundation of a third discourse, for this one should hear only on a holiday, and further talk should be banished far from my ears. Let us not linger any longer, but go out to the market-place. For it's now the time when the fire should be lit in honour of Heracles. It's a pleasant sight and reminds those present of what he suffered on Oeta.[4]

---

[1] A flat rejection of the account of Plato, *Symposium* 219 C, which is followed by Callicratidas in c. 49.

[2] Achilles, *Iliad* IX. 191: cf. c. 5.

[3] Aeschylus, Fr. 136, probably from the *Myrmidons*.

[4] The mountain where Heracles burnt himself to death. See Sophocles, *Trachiniae, fin.*

IN PRAISE OF DEMOSTHENES

I FOLLOW most editors in rejecting *In Praise Of Demosthenes* as non-Lucianic because of its lack of inspiration, its inferior Greek and its avoidance of hiatus. It was presumably written in imitation of the style of Lucian by a sophist who knew Plutarch's *Life of Demosthenes* ; it also has a certain amount in common with Pseudo-Plutarch's *Lives of the Ten Orators* and a few superficial resemblances with Libanius' *Life of Demosthenes*. The date of the work is quite uncertain. If the scene is Rhodes (see note on c. 2 and introduction to *Affairs of the Heart*), it was probably written before the middle of the fourth century, and therefore before the time of Libanius. There is a good edition by F. Albers (Leipzig, 1910).

A. Bauer (Paderborn, 1914) revives a theory that the work is by Lucian and was meant as a satirical caricature of the encomia of contemporary rhetoricians. Bauer suggests that Lucian has deliberately made the speakers guilty of grotesque exaggerations and of the bad Greek of his day, while the Macedonian memoirs so offend against all the rules of historical probability that the author must be waxing scornful about the flights of fancy indulged in by encomiasts. Though this interpretation is ingenious, it is unconvincing. If the vast majority of scholars have failed to see any satire in a work attributed to Lucian the satirist, the satire is well concealed indeed. It is a poor satirist who does not make his satire, however subtle, recognisable for what it is.

ΔΗΜΟΣΘΕΝΟΥΣ ΕΓΚΩΜΙΟΝ

1. Βαδίζοντί μοι κατὰ τὴν στοὰν τὴν ἐντεῦθεν
ἐξιόντων ἐν ἀριστερᾷ, τῆς ἕκτης ἐπὶ δέκα σμικρὸν
πρὸ μεσημβρίας, Θερσαγόρας περιτυγχάνει. τάχα[1]
τινὲς αὐτὸν ὑμῶν ἐπίσταιντο· σμικρός τίς ἐστι
γρυπὸς ὑπόλευκος ἀνδρικὸς τὴν φύσιν. ἰδὼν οὖν
αὐτὸν ἔτι προσιόντα Θερσαγόρας, ἔφην, ὁ ποιητής,
ποῖ δὴ καὶ πόθεν;

Οἴκοθεν, ἦ δ' ὅς, ἐνταῦθα.

Πότερον, ἦν δ' ἐγώ, διαβαδίσων;

Ἀμέλει μέν, ἔφη, καὶ τούτου δεόμενος· ἀωρὶ γάρ
τοι τῶν νυκτῶν ἐξαναστὰς ἔδοξέ μοι χρῆναι τοῖς
Ὁμήρου γενεθλίοις τῆς ποιητικῆς ἀπάρξασθαι.

Καλῶς γε σὺ ποιῶν, ἔφην, καὶ τὰ τροφεῖα τῆς
παιδεύσεως ἐκτίνων.[2]

Ἐκεῖθεν οὖν ἀρξάμενος, ἦ δ' ὅς, ἔλαθον ἐμαυτὸν
εἰς τοῦτο τῆς μεσημβρίας ἐκπεσών. ὅπερ οὖν ἔφην,
δεῖ μέν μοι καὶ τοῦ περιπάτου· 2. πολὺ μέντοι
πρότερον, ἔφη,[3] προσειπεῖν τουτονὶ δεόμενος ἥκω—
τῇ χειρὶ τὸν Ὅμηρον ἐπιδείξας· ἵστε δήπου τὸν ἐν
δεξιᾷ τοῦ τῶν Πτολεμαίων νεώ, τὸν καθειμένον τὰς

Traditio est simplex. Vett. = Γ, Β, Φ (Laur. C.S.77);
recc. = N, M (Par. 2954), et alii.

[1] τάχ' ἂν Bekker.
[2] ἐκτίνων Γ: ἐκείνῳ τίνων ΒΦ.
[3] ἔφη om. Γ.

238

IN PRAISE OF DEMOSTHENES

1. While I was walking on the far side of the Porch —on the left as you go out—shortly before noon on the sixteenth[1] of the month, I was met by Thersagoras who will perhaps be known to some of you. He's a short man with a hooked nose and hair that's just going grey and is endowed with a virile constitution. Now, when I saw him still coming towards me, I said, " Where's Thersagoras the poet going ? And where's he come from ? "[2]

" I've been at home " he said, " and I've come here."

" For a stroll ? " said I.

" Of course," said he, " that's precisely what I want. For I got up in the small hours resolved to honour Homer's birthday with the first-fruits of my poetry."

" Most commendable too," said I, " that you should repay him for the schooling he's given you."

" Well that's how I started," said he, " and now, before I know it, it's noon. So, as I said, I need a walk. 2. But a much more particular reason for coming here was that I wanted to pay my respects to this gentleman " (he pointed to the figure of Homer ;

[1] Presumably in the month of Pyanepsion (mid-October to mid-November) on the 16th of which Demosthenes died. Cf. Plutarch, *Life of Demosthenes* fin.
[2] Cf. Plato, *Phaedrus* init.

239

κόμας—προσερῶν τε οὖν αὐτὸν ἀφικόμην, ἔφη, καὶ προσευξόμενος ἀφθόνων διδόναι τῶν ἐπῶν.

Εἰ γάρ, ἔφην, ἐν εὐχαῖς τὰ πράγματα εἴη. πάλαι γάρ τοι καὶ αὐτὸς ⟨ἂν⟩ ἐνοχλεῖν[1] μοι δοκῶ τὸν Δημοσθένην ἐπικουρῆσαί τι πρὸς τὴν αὐτοῦ γενέθλιον. εἰ οὖν ἡμῖν ἐπαρκέσει[2] τὸ εὔχεσθαι, συμβουλοίμην ἄν σοι· κοινὸν γὰρ ἡμῖν τὸ ἕρμαιον.

Ἐγὼ μέν, ἔφη, καὶ τῶν νύκτωρ τε καὶ τήμερον πεποιημένων δοκῶ μοι τῆς εὐροίας τὸν Ὅμηρον ἐπιγράψασθαι· θείως γάρ πως καὶ μαντικῶς εἰς τὴν ποίησιν ἐξεβακχεύθην. κρινεῖς δ' αὐτός· ἐπίτηδες γάρ τοι τουτὶ τὸ γραμματεῖον περιηγόμην, εἰ ἄρα τῷ σχολὴν ἄγοντι τῶν ἑταίρων περιτύχοιμι. δοκεῖς οὖν ἐν καλῷ μοι σὺ τῆς σχολῆς εἶναι.

3. Μακάριος γὰρ εἶ, ἦν δ' ἐγώ, καὶ πέπονθας τὸ τοῦ[3] τὸν δόλιχον νενικηκότος, ὃς ἤδη λελουμένος τὴν κόνιν καὶ τὸ λοιπὸν τῆς θέας ψυχαγωγούμενος μυθολογεῖν πρὸς τὸν παλαιστὴν διενοεῖτο, ἐπιδόξου κληθήσεσθαι τῆς πάλης οὔσης· ὁ δ' Ἀλλ' ἐπὶ τῆς βαλβῖδος οὐκ ἂν ἐμυθολόγεις, ἔφη. καὶ σὺ δή μοι δοκεῖς νενικηκὼς τὸν δόλιχον τῶν ἐπῶν ἐντρυφᾶν ἀνδρὶ μάλα δὴ[4] κατορρωδοῦντι τὴν τοῦ σταδίου τύχην. καὶ ὃς γελάσας,

---

[1] ἂν ἐνοχλεῖν (potius quam ἂν ὀχλεῖν) scripsi: ἐνοχλεῖν codd., edd..   [2] ἐπαρκέσοι vett., edd.: corr. rec..

[3] τὸ τοῦ Φ: τοῦ Γ: τὸ Β.

[4] ἢ κατορρωδῶν vett.: corr. rec..

---

[1] The scene is probably neither Athens (cf. c. 25) nor Alexandria but Rhodes; Diodorus 20.100.4 records that the Rhodians dedicated a square precinct surrounded by stoas 600 feet long to Ptolemy Soter. Cf. also Strabo 17.1.8. Rhodes seems a particularly suitable setting for

I'm sure you know the Homer I mean, the one to the right of the temple of the Ptolemies,[1] the one with the flowing locks.) " Well," he continued, " I've come to have a word with him and to pray him to give me of his abundance of poetry."

" Oh ! " said I, " if only that could be had by prayer ! For in that case *I* think *I* would have followed your example long ago and been pestering Demosthenes to give me some help to mark his birthday. If then prayer will help us, I'd join in your wishes ; for you must share your luck with me."

" For my part," said he, " I think I can credit Homer with the fine flow of my compositions of both last night and this morning. For a heaven-sent frenzy has brought me poetic inspiration. But you will judge for yourself. For I've been carrying this tablet round with me on purpose in the hope of meeting a friend who was at leisure ; and *you*, I think, are well placed for leisure."

3. " You're a lucky fellow," said I, " and just like the winner of the long-distance race, who, having already washed off his dust and now able to enjoy the rest of the spectacle, was minded to regale the wrestler with his tales, though the wrestling event was expected to be announced at any moment ; the wrestler, however, retorted ' But you wouldn't have so many tales to tell if you were on your mark at the starting-line ! ' So too you seem to me to have won the long-distance race for poetry and to be indulging yourself at my expense, when I'm really on tenterhooks about my fortunes in the sprint."

the dialogue in view of Demosthenes' speech *On the Liberty of the Rhodians* and her claim to be the birthplace of Homer.

'Ως δή σοι τί τῶν ἀπόρων, εἶπεν, ἐργασόμενος;[1]

4. "Ἴσως γάρ, ἔφην, ὁ Δημοσθένης ἐλάττονος ἢ καθ' "Ομηρον εἶναί σοι λόγου καταφαίνεται. καὶ σὺ μὲν[2] φρονεῖς "Ομηρον ἐπαινέσας, ἐμοὶ δὲ ὁ Δημοσθένης σμικρὸν καὶ τὸ μηδέν;

Συκοφαντεῖς, ἔφη. διαστασιάσαιμι δ' οὐκ ἂν τοὺς ἥρως, εἰ καὶ πλείων εἰμὶ τὴν γνώμην πρὸς 'Ομήρου τετάχθαι.

5. Εὖ ⟨σύ⟩[3] γε, εἶπον· ἐμὲ δ' οὐκ ἂν νομίζοις πρὸς τοῦ Δημοσθένους; ἀλλὰ ἐπεί γε μὴ ταύτῃ τὸν λόγον ἀτιμάζεις, κατὰ τὴν ὑπόθεσιν δῆλον ὡς τὴν ποιητικὴν ἔργον ἡγῇ μόνον, τοὺς δὲ ῥητορικοὺς λόγους καταφρονεῖς ἀτεχνῶς οἷον ἱππεὺς παρὰ πεζοὺς ἐλαύνων.

Μὴ μανείην, ἔφη, ταῦτά γε, κἂν εἰ πολλῆς δεῖ τῆς μανίας ἐπὶ τὰς ποιητικὰς ἰοῦσιν θύρας.

Δεῖ γάρ τοι καὶ τοῖς καταλογάδην, ἔφην, ἐνθέου τινὸς ἐπιπνοίας, εἰ μέλλουσιν μὴ ταπεινοὶ φανεῖσθαι καὶ φαύλης φροντίδος.

Οἶδά τοι, ἔφη, ὦ ἑταῖρε, καὶ χαίρω πολλάκις ἄλλων τε δὴ λογοποιῶν καὶ τὰ Δημοσθένους ἐγγὺς τῶν 'Ομήρου τιθείς, οἷον λέγω τὴν σφοδρότητα καὶ πικρίαν καὶ τὸν ἐνθουσιασμόν, καὶ τὸ μὲν " οἰνοβαρὲς " πρὸς τὰς Φιλίππου μέθας καὶ κορδακισμοὺς καὶ τὴν ἀσέλγειαν, τὸ δὲ " εἷς οἰωνὸς ἄριστος " πρὸς τὸ " δεῖ γὰρ τοὺς ἀγαθοὺς ἄνδρας τὰς ἀγαθὰς ὑποθεμένους ἐλπίδας " καὶ τὸ

---

[1] ἐργασομένῳ Gesner.   [2] μὲν μέγα rec..
[3] σύ add. Keil.

[1] Cf. Plato, *Phaedrus*, 245A.   [2] Cf. Plato, *Laws*, 811C.
[3] Cf. *Iliad*, 1.225.   [4] Cf. Demosthenes, *2nd Olynthiac*, 18.

IN PRAISE OF DEMOSTHENES

" Just how do you think I'll be making things awkward for you ? " asked he with a laugh.

4. " Well," said I, " perhaps you consider Demosthenes of too little account to be on a par with Homer ? If you're proud of *your* encomium of Homer, is Demosthenes a minor and trivial matter to *me* ? "

" You're being libellous," said he, " for I wouldn't start these great ones quarrelling, even if I am more minded to range myself on Homer's side."

5. " Well spoken !" said I. " And wouldn't you think *me* to be on the side of Demosthenes ? But, though you thus show respect for speech, your choice makes it obvious that you think that only in poetry lies any achievement, while you despise rhetorical speeches as if you were a cavalryman galloping past infantrymen."

" I hope I won't go as mad as all that, even if no little madness is needed by those who are to reach the portals [1] of poetry."

" Let me point out that prose authors too need some divine inspiration [2] if they are not to appear pedestrian and dull-witted."

" I know that, my friend," said he. " I often find pleasure in comparing the works of the speech-writers and of Demosthenes in particular with those of Homer for, shall I say, intensity, pungency and inspiration ; I set ' wine-laden ' [3] against the ' drunkenness, dissolute dances and debauchery [4] of Philip,' and ' One omen is best ' [5] against ' Brave men must with brave hopes in their hearts ' [6] and

[5] Cf. *Iliad*, XII. 243.
[6] Cf. Demosthenes, *On the Crown* 97.

" ἦ κε μέγ' οἰμώξειε γέρων ἱππηλάτα Πηλεύς "
πρὸς τὸ " πηλίκον ποτὲ ἂν στενάξειαν οἱ ἄνδρες
ἐκεῖνοι οἱ ὑπὲρ δόξης καὶ ἐλευθερίας τελευτήσαντες ;"
παραβάλλω δὲ καὶ τὸν " ῥέοντα Πύθωνα " πρὸς τὰς
Ὀδυσσέως " νιφάδας " τῶν λόγων καὶ τὸ

" εἰ μὲν μέλλοιμεν ἀγήρω τ' ἀθανάτω τε
ἔσσεσθαι."[1]

πρὸς τὸ " πέρας μὲν γὰρ ἅπασιν ἀνθρώποις τοῦ βίου
θάνατος, κἂν ἐν οἰκίσκῳ τις αὐτὸν καθείρξας
τηρῇ ". καὶ μυρίαι γε αὖθις[2] αὐτοῖς ἐπὶ ταὐτὸν τῆς
διανοίας ἐπιδρομαί.

6. ἥδομαι δὲ καὶ πάθη καὶ διαθέσεις καὶ τροπὰς
λέξεως[3] καὶ τὰς ἀφαιρούσας τὸν κόρον μεταβολὰς
καὶ τὰς ἐκ τῶν παρατροπῶν ἐπανόδους καὶ τὰς τῶν
παραβολῶν σὺν τῷ καιρῷ γλαφυρότητας καὶ τὸ
τοῦ τρόπου μισοβάρβαρον πανταχοῦ. 7. καί μοι
πολλάκις ἔδοξεν—οὐ γὰρ ἂν τἀληθὲς ἀποκρυψαίμην
—εὐπρεπέστερον μὲν ῥαθυμίας Ἀττικῆς καθάπτε-
σθαι Δημοσθένης ὁ τὴν παρρησίαν, ὥς φασιν,
ἀνειμένος τοῦ τοὺς Ἀχαιοὺς " Ἀχαιΐδας " προσει-
πόντος, διαρκεστέρῳ δὲ τόνῳ πνεύματος τὰς
Ἑλληνικὰς ἀποπληροῦν τραγῳδίας τοῦ μεταξὺ τῆς
ἀκμαιοτάτης μάχης διαλόγους ἀναπλάττοντος καὶ
μύθοις τὴν φορὰν σκεδαννύντος. 8. πολλάκις δέ με
τὰ τοῦ Δημοσθένους—καὶ μέτρα κώλων καὶ ῥυθμοὶ
καὶ βάσεις—οὐκ ἔξω τῆς ποιητικῆς ἡδονῆς ἐκβιβά-

---

[1] ἔσεσθαι codd..   [2] αὖθις om. Γ.
[3] post λέξεως add. καταμανθάνων N, συγκρίνων Keil.

IN PRAISE OF DEMOSTHENES

" Yea mightily would moan old Peleus, lord of steeds ' [1] against ' How loud, I ask, would the heroes of old who died for glory and liberty lament ? ' [2]   I also compare ' Pytho in spate ' [3] with ' Odysseus' words like flakes of snow ' [4] and ' If that the twain of us should never age or die ' [5] with ' For the end of all men's life is death, even if a man for safety lock himself in his chamber.' [6]   And there are countless other occasions when their minds have rushed to the same thought.

6. I delight also to compare their emotional passages, their descriptive passages, figures of speech, variations that relieve monotony, their resumptions after digressions, the elegance of their well-chosen comparisons, and their style so free from all barbarisms.   7. Moreover, I've often thought—for I shan't hide the truth—that Demosthenes, who gave the proverbial rein to freedom of speech, takes Attic slackness to task with greater grace than he who called the Achaeans ' Achaeanesses,' [7] and has a more sustained intensity of tone in doing full justice to the tragedies that befall the Greeks than he who inserts dialogues at the most desperate point of a battle and dissipates the flow of action with speeches.   8. Often Demosthenes with his measured clauses, rhythmical flow and cadences gives me the same pleasure as poetry, just as

---

[1] *Iliad* VII. 125.
[2] Demosthenes, *Against Aristocrates*, 210.
[3] Cf. *On the Crown*, 136.
[4] *Iliad*, III. 222.
[5] Cf. ibid. XII. 322-4.
[6] Demosthenes, *On the Crown*, 97.
[7] Homer, cf. *Iliad*, II. 235, VII. 96.

ζουσιν, ὥσπερ οὐδ' Ὅμηρος ἐλλιπὴς ἀντιθέσεων ἢ
παρισώσεων ἢ σχημάτων τραχύτητος ἢ καθα-
ρότητος. ἀλλ' ἔοικεν φύσει πως ὑπάρχειν ταῖς
δυνάμεσι τὰς ἀρετὰς ἐπιπεπλέχθαι. πόθεν γε [1] δ᾽
περιφρονοίην ἂν τὴν Κλειὼ [2] τῇ Καλλιόπῃ ταὐτὸ
⟨δυναμένην⟩ [3] γιγνώσκων; 9. ἀλλ' οὐδὲν ἧττον
τοὐμὸν ἀγώνισμα τῶν εἰς Ὅμηρον ἐγκωμίων
διπλάσιον ἔργον ἢ τοὺς σοὺς εἰς Δημοσθένην ἐπαίνους τίθημι, οὐ τοῖς μέτροις—

Ἀλλὰ τῷ μέν; ἔφην.[4]

—Τῷ τοὐμὸν μὲν οὐκ ἔχειν ἑδραίαν τινὰ κρηπῖδα
τῶν ἐπαίνων ὑποβάλλεσθαι πλήν γε τῆς ποιητικῆς
αὐτῆς· τὰ δ' ἄλλα τῷ [5] μὲν ἀσαφῆ, πατρὶς καὶ
γένος καὶ χρόνος. εἰ γοῦν τι σαφὲς αὐτῶν ἦν,

οὐκ ἦν ἂν [6] ἀμφίλεκτος ἀνθρώποις ἔρις,

πατρίδα μὲν αὐτῷ διδόντων Ἴον [7] ἢ Κολοφῶνα ἢ
Κύμην ἢ Χίον ἢ Σμύρναν [8] ἢ Θήβας τὰς Αἰγυπτίας ἢ
μυρίας ἄλλας, πατέρα δὲ Μαίονα τὸν Λυδὸν ἢ ποταμόν, ὅπου [9] γε καὶ τοὔνομα πρὸ τοῦ γνωρίμου τὸ
Μελησιγενῆ προκρίνουσιν· καὶ μητέρα ⟨τὴν⟩ [10]
Μελανώπου φασὶν ἢ νύμφην τῶν Ὑδριάδων [11]
ἀνθρωπίνου γένους ἀπορίᾳ, χρόνον δὲ τὸν ἡρωϊκὸν ἢ

---

[1] γε codd.: γὰρ edd..   [2] Κλειὼ rec.: κλιν ΓΒ: κλεῖν Φ.
[3] ταὐτὰ δυναμένην Keil: ταύτῃ δὲ ΓΦ: ἢ ταύτῃ δὲ Β. Τὴν σὴν
Καλλιόπην τοιαύτην γε γιγνώσκων edd..
[4] ἔφην Keil qui sic pungit: ἔφη vett. (sine vicibus loquen-
tium).   [5] τῷ Β: τὰ ΓΦ.   [6] ἂν om. codd..
[7] Ἴον rec.: Ἴον ἢ Κῶ Φ: Ἰωνικὴν ΓΒ.
[8] Σμύρναν edd.: Στυππείαν codd..
[9] ὅπου . . . προκρίνουσιν (post εἰδέναι in codd.) transtulit
Albers: fortasse delendum.
[10] τὴν add. Albers: Μελανώπου vett.: Μελανώπην recc..
[11] Ὑδριάδων Albers: Ἰδριάδων codd..

246

Homer too is not devoid of antitheses or balanced clauses or violent figures of speech or purity of style. But yet it seems to be the gift of nature that to each capacity is added excellence in its use. For how could I despise Clio,[1] when I know her to be as powerful as Calliope ? 9. However I am none the less inclined to regard my special composition in eulogy of Homer to be twice as great a work as your praises of Demosthenes, not by reason of its verse, I mean— "

" But by what ? " I asked.

" —But because I have no firm foundation on which to build my praises except his actual poetry. All else about Homer is uncertain—his country, his family, the time when he lived. If at least any of these were certain,

' Mankind were free from disputatious strife,'[2] for they give him for country Ios or Colophon or Cyme or Chios or Smyrna or Egyptian Thebes or countless other cities,[3] while they say his father was Maeon, the Lydian, or a river,[4] for at any rate they even prefer the name Melesigenes[5] to his familiar one, and his mother was the daughter of Melanopus,[6] or, for want of human parentage, a Water Nymph, and that his time was the age of the heroes or the

---

[1] Clio was the Muse of History, and Calliope the Muse of epic poetry.

[2] Euripides, *Phoenissae*, 500.

[3] Cf. Aulus Gellius, 3.11.

[4] Viz. Meles, the river of Smyrna; cf. *Certamen Homeri et Hesiodi* init., etc., though a stronger tradition in the various *Vitae Homericae* is that Homer was born by the banks of the Meles.   [5] I.e. " Son of Meles."

[6] I.e. Cretheis; cf. *Certamen* init. etc. (Melanope which is read by editors on poor manuscript authority is not recorded elsewhere as the mother of Homer).

τὸν Ἰωνικόν, καὶ μηδ᾽ ὅπως πρὸς τὸν Ἡσίοδον
εἶχεν ἡλικίας σαφῶς εἰδέναι, τύχην δὲ πενίας ἢ
πάθος ὀμμάτων. ἀλλὰ μὴν βέλτιον εἴη [1] καὶ
ταῦτα ἐᾶν ἐν ἀσαφεῖ κείμενα. περὶ στενὸν δή μοι
κομιδῇ τὸ ἐγκώμιον, ποίησιν ἄπρακτον ἐπαινέσαι
καὶ σοφίαν ἐκ τῶν ἐπῶν εἰκαζομένην συλλέγειν.
10. τὸ δὲ σόν, ἔφη, κατὰ χειρὸς ἐπίδρομόν τε καὶ
λεῖον ἐφ᾽ ὡρισμένοις τε καὶ γνωρίμοις [2] μόνον
⟨τῶν⟩ [3] ὀνομάτων,[4] οἷον ὄψον ἕτοιμον ἡδυσμάτων
παρὰ σοῦ δεόμενον. τί γὰρ οὐ μέγα τῷ Δημοσθένει
καὶ λαμπρὸν ἡ τύχη προσῆψε; τί δ᾽ οὐ γνώριμον;
οὐκ Ἀθῆναι μὲν αὐτῷ πατρίς, " αἱ λιπαραὶ καὶ
ἀοίδιμοι καὶ τῆς Ἑλλάδος ἔρεισμα "; καίτοι
λαβόμενος ἂν ἐγὼ τῶν Ἀθηνῶν ἐπὶ τῆς ποιητικῆς
ἐξουσίας ἐπεισῆγον ἂν ἔρωτας θεῶν καὶ κρίσεις καὶ
κατοικήσεις καὶ δωρεὰς καὶ τὴν Ἐλευσῖνα. νόμων
δὲ καὶ δικαστηρίων καὶ πανηγύρεων καὶ Πειραιῶς
καὶ ἀποικιῶν καὶ τροπαίων θαλαττίων τε καὶ
χερσαίων ἐπεισηγμένων οὐδ᾽ ἂν εἷς ἐπ᾽ ἴσης ἀξίως
ἐφικέσθαι δύναιτο τῷ λόγῳ, φησὶν ὁ Δημοσθένης.
ἀφθονία μὲν ⟨οὖν⟩ [5] ἦν ἄν μοι περιττὴ πάντως,[6] τὸ
δὲ ἐγκώμιον οὐκ ἂν ἀπαρτᾶν ἐνομιζόμην, ἐν νόμῳ

---

[1] sic B: μὴ βέλτιον εἴη ΓΦ: μὴν . . . ἂν εἴη edd.: μὴ . . . ἢ
conieci.
[2] sic Φ: γνωρισμοῖς ΓΒ.
[3] τῶν suppl. Keil.
[4] ὀμμάτων vett.: corr. N.
[5] οὖν suppl. Fritzsche.
[6] sic recc.: περιττὸν εἰπόντος εἰ vett..

---

[1] I.e. when Ionia was colonised by emigrants from Attica,
traditionally 140 years after the Trojan War; Aristotle

248

IN PRAISE OF DEMOSTHENES

Ionian period [1] and they admit they do not even know
for sure how he compared for age with Hesiod. They
say his lot was one of poverty or that he was blind.
But perhaps it would be better to leave these matters
shrouded in obscurity. My eulogy, you can see, is
limited to a very narrow field ; I must praise his
poetry as distinct from his life and collect an
impression of his wisdom inferred from his hexameters
alone.

10. But *your* path," he said, " lies there before you,
an easy and smooth one over definite and familiar
ground ; like food ready before you it only requires
from you the seasoning of words. Has not fortune
coupled with Demosthenes everything that is great,
everything that is glorious, everything that is
famous ? Was not his fatherland Athens, ' the rich,
the renowned, the bulwark of Greece ' ? [2] But, if I
had got my hands on Athens, I would allow myself
the poetic licence of introducing also the amours,
law-suits and sojourns there of the gods, their gifts
and the tale of Eleusis.[3] And once her laws, her
courts, her public festivals, her Piraeus, her colonies
and her memorials in honour of victories by sea and
land are also brought in, well, to quote Demosthenes
himself,[4] ' nobody at all could find words to do justice
to these.' Indeed, I'd have a quite limitless supply
of material, and none of it would be thought irrele-
vant to my panegyric, since it is traditional for

and Aristarchus assigned Homer to this period.

[2] Pindar, *Fr.* 76, also quoted in Lucian, *Timon* 50.

[3] Cf. Plato, *Menexenus* 237 C, Isocrates, *Panegyricus* 28,
Aristides, *Panath.* 107.

[4] Cf. Demosthenes, *On the Navy Boards* 1, *False Legation*
65.

τοῖς ἐπαίνοις ὃν ἐκ τῶν πατρίδων ἐπικοσμεῖν τοὺς
ἐπαινουμένους. Ἰσοκράτης δὲ παρεμπόρευμα τῆς
Ἑλένης φέρων ἐνέθηκε τὸν Θησέα. τὸ μὲν δὴ
ποιητικὸν φῦλον ἐλεύθερον. σοὶ δ' ἴσως εὐλάβεια τὸ
τῆς παροιμίας ἐπὶ σκώμματι τῆς συμμετρίας[1]
ἐπαγαγέσθαι, μή σοι μεῖζον προσκέοιτο τοὐπίγραμμα
τῷ θυλάκῳ.

11. Παρέντι δὴ τὰς Ἀθήνας ἐκδέχεται τὸν λόγον
πατὴρ τριήραρχος, "χρυσέα κρηπὶς" κατὰ Πίνδαρον.
οὐ γὰρ ἦν Ἀθήνησιν λαμπρότερον τίμημα τοῦ[2]
τριηραρχικοῦ. εἰ δὲ τοῦ Δημοσθένους ἔτι κομιδῇ
παιδὸς ὄντος ἐτελεύτα, τὴν ὀρφανίαν οὐ συμφορὰν
ὑποληπτέον, ἀλλὰ δόξης ὑπόθεσιν τὸ τῆς φύσεως
γενναῖον ἀποκαλύπτουσαν.

12. Ὁμήρου μὲν οὖν οὔτε παίδευσιν οὔτ' ἄσκησιν
μνήμη καθ' ἱστορίαν παρειλήφαμεν, ἀλλ' εὐθὺς
ἀνάγκη τὸν ἔπαινον[3] ἅπτεσθαι τῶν ὑπ' αὐτοῦ
δεδημιουργημένων, ὕλην ἐκ τροφῆς καὶ μελέτης
καὶ διδασκαλίας οὐκ ἔχοντα μηδ' οὖν ἐπὶ τὴν
Ἡσιόδου δάφνην καταφυγόντα, τὴν ῥαθύμως καὶ
τοῖς ποιμέσιν τῶν ἐπῶν ἐπιπνέουσαν. σοὶ δ'
ἐνταῦθα δήπου πολὺς μὲν ὁ Καλλίστρατος, λαμπρὸς
δ' ὁ κατάλογος, Ἀλκιδάμας,[4] Ἰσοκράτης, Ἰσαῖος,
Εὐβουλίδης. μυρίων μὲν ἐφελκομένων Ἀθήνησι

---

[1] ἐπὶ ... συμμετρίας vett. (ἀσυμμετρίας Rothstein): σκῶμμα
ἐπὶ τῇ ἀσυμμετρίᾳ recc..

[2] sic Bekker: τιμήματος codd..

[3] τῶν ἐπαίνων B.

[4] Ἀλκίδαμος vett..

---

[1] Viz. in cc. 21-37; cf. *Charidemus* cc. 16-18.

[2] Demosthenes' father, Demosthenes, was a sword-
manufacturer, and so rich enough to undertake the public

eulogies to use the countries of those they praise to lend them further distinction. Thus Isocrates in his *Helen* [1] introduced in passing the story of Theseus. The race of poets is free ; but *you* perhaps must be careful of bringing on your head the proverbial saying in mockery of one's sense of proportion, for fear that you have too large a name-tag added to your sack.

11. Now I leave Athens and my account continues with his trierarch [2] father, a ' golden foundation ' to quote Pindar.[3] For there was no greater distinction at Athens than to be classed rich enough to be a trierarch. If he died while Demosthenes was still very young, we must not consider Demosthenes' bereavement as a tragedy, but as the starting-point of the glory which brought to light the nobility of his nature.

12. As for Homer, his education and training have not been recorded for us by history, but the eulogy, having no material in his upbringing, training and education, must tackle right away the products of his workmanship, without indeed having taken refuge in the laurel of Hesiod, which easily gives poetic inspiration even to shepherds.[4] But *you*, I am sure, can at this point say plenty about Callistratus, and you have that distinguished list of Alcidamas, Isocrates, Isaeus and Eubulides.[5]

---

duty of equipping a trireme at his own expense. Cf. Demosthenes, *Against Aphobus*, 1.9.

[3] Fr. 194.1.   [4] Cf. *Theogony*, 30.

[5] Callistratus was the orator who first fired Demosthenes with a zeal for oratory, according to Plutarch, *Life of Demosthenes*, 5; he is also said to have learnt directly or indirectly from some or all of the other four. Cf. Pseudo-Plutarch, *Lives of the Ten Orators* 844 B, Diogenes Laertius 2.108, Aulus Gellius 3.13.

τῶν ἡδονῶν καὶ τοὺς πατρονομίας ἀνάγκαις ὑπο-
κειμένους, ταχείας ¹ δ' οὔσης τοῖς μειρακίοις τῆς
ἡλικίας εἰς τὰς θρύψεις ² ὑπολισθάνειν, παρὸν δ' αὐτῷ
κατ' ἐξουσίαν ἐκ τῆς τῶν ἐπιτρόπων ὀλιγωρίας,
καὶ φιλοσοφίας καὶ τῆς πολιτικῆς ἀρετῆς κατεῖχε
πόθος, ὃς αὐτὸν ἦγεν οὐκ ἐπὶ τὰς Φρύνης, ἀλλ'
ἐπὶ ³ τὰς Ἀριστοτέλους καὶ Θεοφράστου καὶ
Ξενοκράτους καὶ Πλάτωνος θύρας.

13. κἀνταῦθ' ἄν,⁴ ὦ βέλτιστε, φιλοσοφοῖς τῷ λόγῳ
διττὰς ἐπ' ἀνθρώποις ἐρώτων ἀγωγάς, τὴν μὲν θαλατ-
τίου τινὸς ἔρωτος παράφορόν τε καὶ ἀγρίαν καὶ κυμαί-
νουσαν ἐν ψυχῇ, Ἀφροδίτης πανδήμου κλύδωνα,
φλεγμαινούσαις νέων ὁρμαῖς αὐτόχρημα θαλάττιον,
τὴν δ' οὐρανίου " χρυσῆς τινος σειρᾶς ἕλξιν," οὐ
πυρὶ καὶ τόξοις ἐντιθεῖσαν δυσαλθεῖς νόσους τραυμά-
των, ἀλλ' ἐπὶ τὴν αὐτοῦ τοῦ κάλλους ἄχραντόν τε
καὶ καθαρὰν ἰδέαν ἐξορμῶσαν μανίᾳ σώφρονι τῶν
ψυχῶν, " ὅσαι Ζηνὸς ἐγγὺς καὶ θεῶν ἀγχίσποροι,"
φησὶν ὁ τραγικός.

14. ἔρωτι δὴ πάντα πόριμα, κουρὰ ⁵ σπήλαιον
κάτοπτρον ξίφος, γλῶτταν διαρθρῶσαι, μετελθεῖν
ὀψὲ τῆς ἡλικίας ὑπόκρισιν, μνήμην ἀκριβῶσαι,
θορύβου καταφρονῆσαι, συνάψαι νύκτας ἐπιπόνοις

---

¹ τραχείας vett.: corr. N.
² θρέψεις vett.: τέρψεις N: corr. rec..
³ ἐπὶ edd.: ἐπὶ τὰς φιλοσοφίας codd..
⁴ sic edd.: κἀνταῦθα codd..
⁵ κουρὴ vett..

---

¹ A famous courtesan who was loved by Demosthenes'
contemporary, Hyperides.
² Cf. *Affairs of the Heart* 37, Plato, *Symposium* 180 D etc.

IN PRAISE OF DEMOSTHENES

Although there were countless pleasures at Athens to seduce even those subject to the rigours of paternal control, although youths are of an age swift to slip into the ways of debauchery, and he was at complete liberty to do so because of the neglect of his guardians, yet he was possessed by that love of philosophy and civic virtues, which led him to the doors not of Phryne,[1] but of Aristotle, Theophrastus, Xenocrates and Plato.

13. And at this point, my good friend, you could wax philosophical in your discourse about the two impulses [2] of love that come upon men, the one that of a love like the sea, frenzied, savage and raging like stormy waves in the soul, a veritable sea of Earthly Aphrodite surging with the fevered passions of youth, the other the pull of a heavenly cord of gold that does not bring with fiery shafts afflicting wounds hard to cure, but impels men to the pure and unsullied Form of absolute beauty, inspiring with a chaste madness such souls as, to quote the tragic poet,[3]

' Are nigh to Zeus and kindred of the gods.'

14. To love all things are possible ; it can endure a shaved head, a cave, a mirror, the threat of a sword, it can afford articulate speech to its tongue, take up acting late in life, perfect the memory, despise noisy interruptions, and add nights to days spent in toil.[4]

---

[3] Aeschylus, *Niobe*, Fr. 162 adapted.   Cf. Plato, *Republic* 391 E.

[4] Sc. as Demosthenes is said to have done to perfect his oratory.   He retired to a cave and shaved half his head so that he could not go out.   The mirror was so that he could watch his faults and the sword was suspended beside his shoulder to stop him moving it.   Cf. Pseudo-Plutarch, *Lives of the Ten Orators* 844 D, Plutarch, *Demosthenes* 6.

ἡμέραις. ἐξ ὧν τίς οὐκ οἶδεν, ὁποῖος ὁ Δημοσθένης,
ἔφη, σοὶ τὴν ῥητορικὴν ἐγένετο, ταῖς μὲν ἐννοίαις
καὶ τοῖς ὀνόμασιν καταπυκνῶν τὸν λόγον, ταῖς δὲ
διαθέσεσιν ἐξακριβῶν τὰς πιθανότητας, λαμπρὸς μὲν
τῷ μεγέθει, σφοδρὸς δὲ τῷ πνεύματι, σωφρονέστατος
δὲ τὴν τῶν ὀνομάτων καὶ τῶν νοημάτων ἐγκράτειαν,
ποικιλώτατος δ' ἐναλλαγαῖς σχημάτων; μόνος γέ τοι
τῶν ῥητόρων, ὡς ὁ Λεωσθένης ἐτόλμησεν εἰπεῖν,
ἔμψυχον καὶ [1] σφυρήλατον παρεῖχεν τὸν λόγον.

15. οὐ γάρ, ὡς τὸν Αἰσχύλον ὁ Καλλισθένης ἔφη
που λέγων τὰς τραγῳδίας ἐν οἴνῳ γράφειν ἐξορ-
μῶντα καὶ ἀναθερμαίνοντα τὴν ψυχήν, οὐχ οὕτως
ὁ Δημοσθένης συνετίθει πρὸς μέθην τοὺς λόγους,
ἀλλ' ὕδωρ πίνων· ᾗ καὶ τὸν Δημάδην παῖξαί φασιν
εἰς ταύτην αὐτοῦ τὴν ὑδροποσίαν, ὡς οἱ μὲν ἄλλοι
πρὸς ὕδωρ λέγοιεν, τὸν Δημοσθένην δὲ πρὸς
ὕδωρ γράφειν. Πυθέᾳ δὲ ὁ κρότος τῶν Δημοσθενι-
κῶν λόγων ἀπόζειν ἐφαίνετο τοῦ νυκτερινοῦ λύχνου.
καὶ τουτὶ μέν, ἔφη, σοὶ τὸ χωρίον τοῦ λόγου [2]
κοινὸν πρὸς τὴν ἐμὴν ὑπόθεσιν. οὐ γάρ τοι
μείων [3] ὁ περὶ τὴν Ὁμήρου ποίησιν ὑπῆρχε κἀμοὶ
λόγος.

16. ἀλλ' εἰ μετίοις ἐπὶ τὰς [4] φιλανθρωπίας καὶ
τὴν ἐν τοῖς χρήμασι φιλοτιμίαν καὶ τῆς πολιτείας
τὴν ὅλην λαμπρότητα—καὶ ὁ μὲν ᾔει συνείρων ὡς

---

[1] καὶ ΓΦ: οὐ Β.   [2] τοῦ λόγου recc.: τοῦτό γ' οὐ vett..
[3] τοι μείων recc.: τι μείον ΓΦ: τι μείως Β.
[4] sic Φ: μέτροις ἐπιστὰς ΓΒ.

---

[1] Cf. Eupolis, 94.6.
[2] An Athenian patriot who attempted to throw off the
Macedonian yoke after the death of Alexander.

IN PRAISE OF DEMOSTHENES

Who does not know how fine an orator your Demosthenes became as a result of all this, using thought and language to give solidity to his speech, and careful arrangement to achieve perfection in persuasiveness, distinguished for his grandeur, strong in the power of his lungs, most temperate in his control over word and thought, most versatile in the variety of his tropes? Indeed he alone of orators,[1] to quote the bold words of Leosthenes,[2] ' gave his words both life and the strength that comes from the craftsman's hammer.'

15. For, unlike Aeschylus who, according to Callisthenes,[3] wrote his tragedies on wine, thereby giving his spirit vigour and fire, Demosthenes did not tipple but drank water[4] while composing his speeches. Thus it was that Demades, we are told, made fun of this water-bibbing of Demosthenes, by saying that others spoke to water,[5] but Demosthenes wrote to it. And to Pytheas the ring of Demosthenes' speeches seemed to reek of the midnight oil.[6] This part of your discourse," said he, " is on subject-matter also available to me. For, when it comes to discussing the poetry of Homer, I've always had a field no smaller than yours.

16. But if you should pass on to his benefactions, his financial generosity and the unmitigated distinction of his political career "—he had now started on a

---

[3] A historian contemporary with Alexander; cf. Plutarch, *Table Talk* 715 E.

[4] Cf. Demosthenes, *Second Philippic* 30, *False Legation* 46, Pseudo-Plutarch 848 C.

[5] A reference to the clepsydra or water-clock, which limited the time allotted to advocates' speeches.

[6] Cf. Plutarch, *Demosthenes* 7.

τὰ λοιπὰ προσθήσων, ἐγὼ δὲ γελάσας, Ἦ πού γε, ἔφην, διανοῇ καταχεῖν μου τῶν ὤτων ὥσπερ βαλανεὺς καταντλήσας τὸν λοιπὸν λόγον;

Νὴ Δία γε, εἶπεν, δημοθοινίας τε καὶ χορηγίας ἐθελουσίους καὶ τριηραρχίας καὶ τεῖχος καὶ τάφρον καὶ λύσεις αἰχμαλώτων καὶ παρθένων ἐκδόσεις, ἀρίστην πολιτείαν, καὶ πρεσβείας [1] καὶ νομοθεσίας καὶ μέγεθος πολιτευμάτων ἐμπεσόν, γελᾶν ἔπεισί μοι τοῦ τὰς ὀφρῦς συνάγοντος καὶ δεδιότος μὴ λόγοι τῶν Δημοσθένους αὐτὸν ἔργων ἐπιλίποιεν.

17. Ἴσως γάρ, ἔφην, ὦγαθέ, νομίζεις ἐμὲ δὴ [2] μόνον τῶν ἐν ῥητορικῇ βεβιωκότων μὴ διατεθρυλῆσθαι τὰ ὦτα ταῖς Δημοσθένους πράξεσιν;

Εἴ γε, ἔφη, περὶ τὸν λόγον ἐπικουρίας τινός, ὡς σὺ φῄς, δεόμεθα· πλὴν εἰ μή σε τοὐναντίον κατέχει πάθος, οἷον αὐγῆς περιλαμπούσης οὐκ ἔχεις πρὸς λαμπρὰν τὴν Δημοσθένους δόξαν τὴν ὄψιν ἀπερεῖσαι· καὶ γὰρ αὐτός τι τοιοῦτον ἐφ᾽ Ὁμήρῳ κατὰ τὰς ἀρχὰς πέπονθα. κατέβαλον γοῦν σμικροῦ [3] δεῖν, ὡς οὐκ ἀντιβλεπτέον ὄν μοι πρὸς τὴν ὑπόθεσιν. εἶτ᾽ ἐγὼ μέν, οὐκ οἶδ᾽ ὅπως, ἀνήνεγκα, ⟨καὶ⟩ [4] δοκῶ μοι κατὰ σμικρὸν προσεθιζόμενος ἀντίον ὁρᾶν μηδ᾽ ἀποτρέπων ὥσπερ ἡλίου τὰς ὄψεις νόθος τοῦ τῶν Ὁμηριδῶν γένους ἐλέγχεσθαι.

---

[1] πρέσβεις codd.: corr. Gesner.
[2] δὴ N: δὲ vett..
[3] sic Albers: ὁ μικροῦ Γ: μικροῦ cett..
[4] καὶ suppl. Lehmann.

---

[1] Cf. Plato, *Republic* 344 D.
[2] Cf. Demosthenes, *Against Meidias* 13.

list of qualities which he seemed intent on completing
—but I laughed and said, " Do you really intend to
drench my ears with the rest of your account like a
bath-man with his canful ? [1] "

" Indeed I do ! " said he. " The public banquets he
gave, his voluntary expenditure on choruses,[2] the
warships, the wall, the ditch he paid for, the
prisoners he ransomed, the maidens he provided with
a dowry,[3] all of which were acts of the highest public
service, the embassies on which he served, the laws he
carried, the magnitude of his political services—when
I think of all these, I feel like laughing at one who
knits his brows for fear that words for Demosthenes'
deeds may fail him."

17. " Perhaps, my good fellow," said I, " you
think that I am really the only one to have spent a
life in the pursuit of rhetoric without having had my
ears deafened [4] with the exploits of Demosthenes ? "

" I do," said he, " if, as you say, we need some
help for our discourse ; unless the opposite is the case
with you, and you cannot fix your eyes on the bright
glory of Demosthenes because of the radiant light
investing him. For I myself had the same experience with Homer at first. At any rate I nearly
dropped my eyes, thinking I couldn't look my
subject in the face. Then somehow I raised my
eyes, because, I suppose, I was gradually growing
accustomed to look it in the face without turning
away as it were from the sun's rays and showing
myself a bastard member of Homer's family.

---

[3] For these services cf. Decree in Pseudo-Plutarch 851
and Fowler's note (L.C.L. vol. 10, p. 342), and Demosthenes,
On the Crown, 248, 257, 268.

[4] Cf. Plato, *Republic* 358 C.

18. Σὸν δέ μοι φαίνεται καὶ τοῦτο, ἔφη, πολὺ ῥᾷον ἢ κατ᾽ ἐμὲ εἶναι. τῆς μὲν γὰρ Ὁμήρου δόξης οἷον ἐπὶ μιᾶς ὁρμούσης τῆς ποιητικῆς δυνάμεως ἀθρόως ἐξ ἀνάγκης ἦν ἁπάσης λαβέσθαι. σὺ δ᾽ εἰ μὲν ἐπὶ τὸν Δημοσθένην ὅλον ἐφάπαξ τῇ γνώμῃ τράποιο, καὶ μάλα ἂν ἀποροῖς, περὶ τὸν λόγον ἄττων οὐδ᾽ ἔχων ὅτου πρώτου τῇ γνώμῃ λάβοιο,[1] καθάπερ οἱ λίχνοι πάσχουσιν περὶ τὰς Συρακουσίας τραπέζας ἢ οἱ φιλήκοοι καὶ φιλοθεάμονες εἰς μυρίας ἀκουσμάτων καὶ θεαμάτων ἡδονὰς ἐμπεσόντες· οὐκ ἔχουσιν ἐφ᾽ ἣν ἔλθωσιν ἀεὶ τὴν ἐπιθυμίαν μετατιθέντες. οἶμαι δὲ καὶ σὲ μεταπηδᾶν οὐκ ἔχοντα ἐφ᾽ ὅτι σταίης, ἐν κύκλῳ σε περιελκόντων φύσεως μεγαλοπρεποῦς, ὁρμῆς διαπύρου, βίου σώφρονος, λόγου δεινότητος, τῆς ἐν ταῖς πράξεσιν ἀνδρείας, λημμάτων πολλῶν καὶ μεγάλων ὑπεροψίας, δικαιοσύνης, φιλανθρωπίας, πίστεως, φρονήματος, συνέσεως, ἑκάστου τῶν πολλῶν καὶ μεγάλων πολιτευμάτων. ἴσως οὖν ὁρῶν ἔνθεν μὲν ψηφίσματα πρεσβείας [2] δημηγορίας νόμους, ἐκεῖθεν ἀποστόλους Εὔβοιαν Μέγαρα τὴν Βοιωτίαν Χίον Ῥόδον τὸν Ἑλλήσποντον Βυζάντιον, οὐκ ἔχεις ὅποι τὴν γνώμην ἀποκλίνῃς συμπεριφερόμενος τοῖς πλεονεκτήμασιν. 19. ὥσπερ οὖν ὁ Πίνδαρος ἐπὶ πολλὰ τῷ νῷ τραπόμενος οὕτως πως ἠπόρηκεν,

---

[1] τράποις . . . λάβοις vett..   [2] πρέσβεις codd.: corr. Gesner.

[1] Sicilian banquets were proverbially sumptuous. Cf. *Dialogues of the Dead* 19.2, Horace, *Odes* 3.1.18, Plato, *Republic* 354 B.

18. *You* seem to me to have another great advantage over me," he continued, " for since Homer's reputation rests as it were upon the single anchor of his poetic power, I've had to lay hands on all of it at one and the same time.   But, if you were to turn your mind to dealing with the whole of Demosthenes once and for all, you would be in the greatest difficulty as you darted to and fro round your discourse without knowing what your mind should seize upon as its primary topic, just as happens to gourmands at Syracusan banquets,[1] or lovers of listening or of spectacle when confronted with countless delights for the ear or the eye.   They don't know which to pursue with their ever-changing desires.   I think that you too leap to and fro, not knowing on what to set your feet, as you revolve under the attraction of his nobility of nature, his fiery ardour, his sober life, his eloquence, his courage in time of action, his contempt for many great financial rewards, his justice, humanity, loyalty, pride, wisdom, and each of his many great political services.   Perhaps, therefore, when you see on one side decrees, embassies, public speeches and laws, and on the other naval expeditions, Euboea, Megara, Boeotia, Chios, Rhodes, the Hellespont and Byzantium, you don't know on which to rest your thoughts as you're whirled round and round by such an embarrassment of riches.   19. Just as Pindar after turning his mind to many topics expressed his difficulties thus [2]:

[2] Fr. 29.   Corinna criticised these lines by saying one should sow with the hand and not with the whole sack; cf. Plutarch, *On the Fame of the Athenians* 348.

PSEUDO-LUCIAN

Ἰσμηνὸν ἢ χρυσαλάκατον Μελίαν,
ἢ Κάδμον, ἢ σπαρτῶν ἱερὸν γένος ‹ἀνδρῶν›,[1]
ἢ τὰν κυανάμπυκα Θήβαν,
ἢ τὸ πάντολμον σθένος Ἡρακλέος,[2]
ἢ τὰν Διονύσου πολυγαθέα[3] τιμάν,
ἢ γάμον λευκωλένου Ἁρμονίας ὑμνήσομεν;

οὑτωσὶ δὲ καὶ σὺ ταὐτὸν ἔοικας ἀπορεῖν, λόγον ἢ
βίον[4] ἢ φιλοσοφίαν ἢ δημαγωγίαν ἢ τὸν θάνατον
τἀνδρὸς[5] ὑμνητέον.

20. ἔστι δ' οὐδὲν ἔργον ἐκφυγεῖν, ἔφη, τὴν
πλάνην· ἀλλ' ἑνὸς ὅτου δὴ λαβόμενος ἢ τῆς
ῥητορείας καθ' αὑτήν, εἰς ταύτην καθοῦ τοῦτον
τὸν λόγον. ἱκανή γ' ἂν οὐδ' ἡ[6] Περικλέους·
ἐκείνου μέν γε τὰς ἀστραπὰς καὶ βροντὰς καὶ
πειθοῦς τι κέντρον δόξῃ παραλαβόντες, ἀλλ'
αὐτήν γε οὐχ ὁρῶμεν, δῆλον ὡς οὐδὲν ὁποῖον
τὴν[7] φαντασίαν οὐδ' ἔμμονον[8] ἔχουσαν οὐδ'
οἵαν[9] ἐξαρκέσαι πρὸς τὴν τοῦ χρόνου βάσανον καὶ
κρίσιν· τὰ δὲ τοῦ Δημοσθένους—ἀλλὰ σοὶ κατα-
λελείφθω λέγειν, εἰ ταύτῃ τράποιο.

---

[1] ἀνδρῶν suppl. Plutarchus.
[2] Ἡρακλέους Φ.   [3] πουλυγαθέα vett..
[4] βίον ἢ ῥητορικὴν ΒΦ, edd..
[5] ἀνδρὸς vett..
[6] οὐδ' ἡ Albers: σοῦ δὴ ΓΦ: σοῦ δ' ἡ Β.
[7] ὁποῖον τὴν vett.: πλέον ἢ Albers.
[8] οὐδὲν μόνον vett.: corr. Albers (ὡς ὑπὲρ τὴν φαντασίαν οὐδὲν
ἔμμονον Ν, edd.).   [9] οἷον edd..

---

[1] The legendary hero who gave his name to the river
Ismenus at Thebes.
[2] A nymph worshipped at Thebes as the mother by
Apollo of Ismenus (cf. Pausanias 9.10.6 and Wilamowitz,

IN PRAISE OF DEMOSTHENES

Ismenus' [1] praises shall we sing ?
Or Melia [2] with distaff of gold ?
Or Cadmus or the mighty race
Of men who sprang when teeth were sown ? [3]
Or Thebe with her purple snood,
Or daring might of Heracles ?
Glad honour Dionysus pay ?
Or shall we sing the day that saw
White-armed Harmonia [4] a bride ?

so too *you* seem to be in the same difficulty, not knowing whether to sing the praises of your hero's speeches, his life, his philosophy, his leadership of the people or his death.

20. It's easy enough," he continued, " to avoid losing your way. You must seize upon any one feature, or else take his oratory by itself, and concentrate this discourse of yours just upon that. For that one would find even the oratory of Pericles inadequate. For, though his thunderings and lightenings and his ' sting of persuasion ' [5] are known to us by tradition, yet we cannot see his actual oratory, which clearly had no such vivid effect or lasting quality as that of Demosthenes, and could not stand up to the acid test of time. But when it comes to the works of Demosthenes—but let their description be left to you, should you turn to that topic.

Hermes 26.197.1), though other accounts give him different parents.

[3] The traditional ancestors of Thebes were the survivors from the warriors who fought each other after springing from the dragon's teeth sown by Cadmus.

[4] The wife of Cadmus.

[5] Cf. Aristophanes, *Acharnians* 530-1, Eupolis, 94.7.

21. πρός γε μὴν τὰς τῆς ψυχῆς ἀρετὰς ἢ τὰς πολιτείας αὐτοῦ τραπομένῳ καλὸν μίαν ἡντινοῦν ἀποτεμέσθαι τὴν διατριβήν, εἰ δὲ βούλοιο δαψιλές, δύο καὶ σύντρεις ἑλόμενον ἔχειν ἀποχρῶσαν λόγων ὑποβολήν. πολλὴ γὰρ ἐν ἅπασιν ἡ λαμπρότης. εἰ δ' οὐκ ἐκ τοῦ παντὸς ἀλλ' ἐκ μέρους ἐπαινεσόμεθα, νόμος μὲν Ὁμηρικὸς ἡρώων ἐπαίνους ἐκ μερῶν διατίθεσθαι, ποδῶν ἢ κεφαλῆς ἢ κόμης, ἤδη δὲ κἀκ τῶν φορημάτων ἢ ἀσπίδων, μεμπτὸν δ' οὐδὲ τοῖς θεοῖς ἐγένετο ὑμνεῖσθαι πρὸς τῶν ποιητῶν ἐξ ἠλα- κάτης ἢ τόξων ἢ τῆς αἰγίδος, μή τί γε δὴ μέρει [1] σώματος ἢ τῆς ψυχῆς, τῶν εὐεργεσιῶν δ' οὐδὲ δυνατὸν ἐφ' ἁπάσας [2] ἐλθεῖν. οὐκοῦν οὐδ' ὁ Δημοσθένης αἰτιάσεται καθ' ἓν τῶν αὐτοῦ καλῶν ἐπαινούμενος, ἐπεὶ τό γε σύμπαν οὐδ' αὐτὸς ἂν αὐτὸν ἐξαρκέσειεν ἐπαινέσαι.

22. ταῦτα τοῦ Θερσαγόρου διελθόντος, Οἶμαί σε, ἔφην, ἐν ἐπιδεδεῖχθαί μοι, τὸ μὴ μόνον ποιητὴν ἀγαθὸν εἶναι, τῷ δώρῳ [3] παρεμπόρευμα πεποιῆσθαι τὸν Δημοσθένην, τὰ πεζὰ τοῖς ἐμμέτροις προστι- θέντα.

Σοὶ μὲν οὖν, ἔφη, τὴν ῥᾳστώνην ὑποτιθεὶς προή- χθην ἐπιδραμεῖν τὸν λόγον, εἴ τι τῆς φροντίδος ἀνεὶς ἀκροατὴς ἡμῖν γένοιο.

Προὔργου τοίνυν, ἔφην, σοὶ γέγονεν οὐδέν, εὖ ἴσθι. σκόπει δὲ καὶ μὴ πλέον ἢ γεγονὸς θάτερον.

Καλὸν ἂν λέγοις, ἔφη, τὸ ἴαμα.

---

[1] μέρους recc..
[2] sic Wolf: ἐφάπαξ codd..
[3] τῷ δώρῳ vett.: τῶν λόγων recc.: τῷ Ὁμήρου Keil.

21. But, if you turn to the high qualities of his spirit or his civic virtues, it would be well to isolate any one particular quality to discuss, or, if you wish to indulge yourself, choose two or three in all and you will have quite sufficient material for your discourse. For in everything about him is great distinction. And, if we praise part of his make-up rather than all of it, it is in the Homeric tradition to compose praises for parts of his heroes, for their feet, heads or hair, and sometimes even for their accoutrement or their shields, while even the gods did not object to being praised by the poets in their hymns for a distaff, bow or aegis, not to mention a part of the body or a spiritual quality, while to arrive at a complete list of their kindnesses to man is quite impossible. Demosthenes therefore will not object to a eulogy that is confined to one of his virtues, since a comprehensive eulogy of Demosthenes would be beyond even his own powers."

22. After Thersagoras had finished this disquisition, I said, " I think that you have made one thing quite clear to me ; you have shown me you are more than just a good poet, by adding prose to your verse and including in a gift to Homer the subsidiary topic of Demosthenes."

" On the contrary," said he, " I did it for you. Wishing to suggest to you the ease of your task, I was encouraged to run through my discourse in the hope that you might find some relief from your worries by listening to me."

" Then be assured that you've made no headway " said I. " Be careful that on the contrary my complaint hasn't been aggravated."

" A fine cure I've made by your account," said he.

PSEUDO-LUCIAN

Σὺ γάρ, ἔφην, ἀγνοεῖς, οἶμαι,[1] τὸ παρὸν ἄπορον, εἶτα ἰατροῦ δίκην τὸ τοῦ νοσοῦντος σαθρὸν ἀγνοήσαντος ἄλλο θεραπεύεις.[2]

Ὅτι τί δή;

Σὺ μὲν ἃ ταράξειεν ἂν τὸν πρῶτον ἰόντα πρὸς τὸν λόγον ἐπεχείρησας ἰάσασθαι, τὰ δ᾽ ἤδη κατανάλωται παλαιαῖς[3] ἐτῶν περιόδοις· ὡς ταύταις ⟨ταῖς⟩[4] ἀπορίαις ἔωλά σοι τὰ ἰάματα.

Ταῦτ᾽[5] οὖν, ἔφη, σοὶ τόδε ἴαμα· χρὴ μέντοι καθάπερ ὁδὸν[6] θαρραλεωτάτην εἶναι τὴν συνηθεστάτην.

23. Τὴν ἐναντίαν γάρ, εἶπον, προὐθέμην, ᾗ[7] φασιν Ἀννίκεριν τὸν Κυρηναῖον φιλοτιμηθῆναι πρὸς Πλάτωνά τε καὶ τοὺς ἑταίρους· τὸν μέν γε τὴν[8] Κυρηναίων[9] ἁρματηλασίαν ἐπιδεικνύντα πολλοὺς περὶ τὴν Ἀκαδημίαν ἐξελαύνειν δρόμους ἐπὶ τῆς αὐτῆς ἁρματοτροχιᾶς ἅπαντας μηδὲν παραβάντας, ὥσθ᾽ ἑνὸς δρόμου σημεῖα κατὰ τῆς γῆς ὑπολείπεσθαι· τοὐμὸν δέ γε τὴν ἐναντίαν σπεύδει, τὰς ἁρματοτροχιὰς ἀλεείνειν, οὐ μάλα ῥάιδιον ⟨ὄν⟩,[10] οἶμαι, καινουργεῖν ὁδοὺς τῶν τετριμμένων ἐκτρεπόμενον.

Ἀλλά τοι τὸ Παύσωνος, ἔφη, σοφόν.

Ποῖον; ἔφην· οὐ γὰρ ἀκήκοα.

24. Παύσωνι τῷ ζωγράφῳ φασὶν ἐκδοθῆναι γράψαι ἵππον ἀλινδούμενον· τὸν δὲ γράψαι τρέχοντα καὶ πολὺν κονιορτὸν περὶ τὸν ἵππον. ὡς δ᾽

---

[1] ἀγνοήσῃ (vel ἀγνοήσῃς) μοι vett.: corr. edd..   [2] θεραπεύσεις B.
[3] παλαιαῖς vett.: πολλαῖς recc.: πάλαι πολλαῖς conieci.
[4] ταῖς suppl. Albers.   [5] τοῦτ᾽ codd.: corr. L. A. Post.
[6] ὁδὸν Lehmann: ὁδοῦ codd..   [7] ᾗ om. vett..
[8] τὴν scripsi: τὸν codd..   [9] sic Γ^a: Κυρηναῖον Γ, cett..

IN PRAISE OF DEMOSTHENES

" Yes," said I, " for I don't think you're aware of my present difficulty, but proceed, like a doctor who's failed to diagnose the course of the patient's infection, to tend some other part of the body."

" What do you mean ? "

" You have tried to cure the things that would trouble the beginner essaying discourse, but these have already been removed by the passing of long-gone years, so that for this complaint your remedies have gone stale."

" Why, it's just this that makes the cure. Cures are like roads. The better you know them, the greater your confidence in them."

23. " Not so," said I, " for I have decided on the opposite course to the one which they say Anniceris of Cyrene [1] adopted to win the admiration of Plato and his companions. They say he exhibited Cyrenean skill in chariot-driving by driving many times round the Academy, keeping each time to exactly the same track, so that marks of but a single circuit were left in the ground. I, however, am eager for the opposite course and wish to avoid the tracks of the chariots, though it is no easy task, as I think, to turn aside from the beaten tracks and make new paths."

" But Pauson's method was clever."

" What was that ? " I asked. " For I've not heard of it."

24. " They say that the artist Pauson [2] was commissioned to paint a horse rolling, but that he painted it running and surrounded by a cloud of dust. His

[1] Cf. Aelian, *Varia Historia*, 2.27.
[2] Cf. Plutarch, *Pyth. Or.*, 396 E, Aelian, *Varia Historia* 14.15.

---

[10] ὅν scripsi: om. codd.: δὲ edd..

ἔτι γράφοντος ἐπιστῆναι τὸν ἐκδόντα, μέμφεσθαι
μὴ γὰρ τοῦτο προστάξαι. τὸν οὖν Παύσωνα τοῦ
πίνακος τὰ μετέωρα κάτω περιαγαγόντα τῷ παιδὶ
τὴν γραφὴν ἐπιδεῖξαι κελεῦσαι, καὶ τὸν ἵππον
ἔμπαλιν κείμενον ὀφθῆναι κυλινδούμενον.

Ἡδὺς εἶ, ἔφην, Θερσαγόρα, ἂν [1] μίαν οἴη [2] με
στροφὴν μεμηχανῆσθαι τοσούτων ἐτῶν, ἀλλ' οὐχὶ
πάσας στροφὰς καὶ περιαγωγὰς ἐναλλάττοντα καὶ
μετατιθέντα δεδιέναι μή τι τελευτῶν πάθοιμι τὸ [3]
τοῦ Πρωτέως.

Ποῖον, ἔφη, πάθος;

Τὸ γενόμενον, ὅ φασιν αὐτὸν γενέσθαι δρασμὸν
ἐξευρίσκοντα τῆς ἀνθρωπίνης ὄψεως· ἐπεὶ κατανα-
αλώκει πάσας ἰδέας θηρίων καὶ φυτῶν καὶ στοι-
χείων, αὖθις αὖ πενίᾳ μορφῆς ἐπεισάκτου Πρωτέα
γενέσθαι.

25. Σὺ μέν, εἶπεν, ὑπὲρ τὸν Πρωτέα μηχανᾷ τὴν [4]
ἀκρόασιν ἀποδιδράσκειν.

Οὐκ, ὦγαθέ, ἔφην, τοῦτο.[5] παρέξω γοῦν ἐμαυτὸν
ἀκροᾶσθαι παρεὶς τὴν ἐπηρτημένην φροντίδα. τάχ'
ἄν τι περὶ τοῦ σοῦ κυήματος ἄφροντις γενόμενος καὶ
τῆς ἐμῆς ὠδῖνος συμφροντίσαις.[6]

Ὡς οὖν ἐδόκει αὐτῷ,[7] καθίσαντες ἐπὶ τῆς πλησίον
κρηπῖδος ἐγὼ μὲν ἠκροώμην, ὁ δ' ἀνελέγετο μάλα
γενναῖα ποιήματα. μεταξὺ δ' ὥσπερ ἔνθους γενόμενος, ἐπιπτύξας τὸ γραμματεῖον, Κομίζου τὸν

---

[1] ἂν om. ΓΦ.
[3] τὸ om. ΓΦ.
[5] τοῦτο Ν: τοῦτον vett..
[6] συμφροντίσαι vett..
[7] αὐτῷ ΓΦ: ταῦτα Β.

[2] οἴει vett..
[4] τὴν ΓΦ: τὴν ἐμὴν Β.

patron, the story goes, coming and standing over
him while he was still painting, criticised him saying
that wasn't what he'd asked for ; Pauson, therefore,
turned his painting upside down and ordered his
slave to show it to his patron, whereupon the horse
could be seen the other way up and rolling on its
back."

" You are innocent, Thersagoras," said I, " if you
think that in all these years I've only managed to
devise one alternative position, and you don't
realise that I've changed and varied every conceiv-
able angle and turn so that I'm afraid I'll end up by
being like Proteus." [1]

" What do you mean ? "

" I mean what they say happened to him when
trying to escape from the sight of men ; after he had
exhausted every shape of beast, plant and element,
for want of shapes to adopt, he became Proteus once
again."

25. " You outdo Proteus in your machinations to
escape from listening to me."

" It is not so, my good friend. I at any rate shall
lay aside the cares that hang over me and give
myself up to be your listener. Perhaps, when you've
ceased to worry about your own travail, you'll also
share in my concern for my birth-pangs."

And so with his approval we sat down on the
nearby step and I listened while he read some noble
poetry. In the middle of this, as if seized by an
inspiration from the gods, he folded up his writing-
tablets and said, " You must receive your listener's

---

[1] Cf. *Odyssey*, IV. 455 ff.

ἀκροατικόν, ἔφη, μισθόν, καθάπερ Ἀθήνησιν ἐκκλη-
σιαστικὸν ἢ δικαστικόν. ἀλλ' ὅπως εἴσῃ μοι χάριν.

26. Χάριν μέν, ἔφην, εἴσομαι καὶ πρὶν ὅτι λέγεις
εἰδέναι. τί δ' [1] ἐστιν ὅτι καὶ λέγεις;

Μακεδονικοῖς, εἶπεν, ἐντυχὼν τῆς βασιλικῆς
οἰκίας ὑπομνήμασιν, καὶ τότε ὑπερησθεὶς τὸ βιβλίον
οὐ κατὰ πάρεργον ἐκτησάμην καὶ νῦν ὑπεμνήσθην
ἔχων οἴκαδε. γέγραπται δ' ἄλλα τε τῶν Ἀντιπάτρῳ
πραχθέντων ἐπὶ τῆς οἰκείας [2] καὶ περὶ Δημοσθένους,
ἅ μοι δοκεῖς οὐκ ἂν παρέργως ἀκοῦσαι.

Καὶ μήν, εἶπον, ἤδη γέ σοι τῶν εὐαγγελίων χάρις
καὶ τὰ λοιπὰ τῶν ἐπῶν. ἐγὼ μὲν οὖν [3] οὐκ ἀπολεί-
ψομαι τοῦ [4] τὴν ὑπόσχεσιν ἔργον σοι [5] γενέσθαι,
σὺ δ' εἰστίακάς με [6] λαμπρῶς τὴν Ὁμήρου γενέθλιον,
ἔοικας δ' ἑστιάσειν αὐτὸς καὶ τὴν Δημοσθένους.

27. Ὡς οὖν ἀνέγνω τὰ λοιπὰ τοῦ γραμματείου,
διατρίψαντες ὀλίγον ὅσον ἀποδοῦναι τῷ ποιήματι
τοὺς δικαίους ἐπαίνους ᾔειμεν εἰς τοῦ Θερσαγόρου.
καὶ μόλις μέν, ἐπιτυγχάνει δὲ τῷ βιβλίῳ. κἀγὼ
λαβὼν τότε μὲν ἀπηλλαττόμην, ἐντυχὼν δ' οὕτω
τὴν γνώμην διετέθην, ὡς οὐδέν τι περιτρέψας, ἀλλ'
ἐπ' αὐτῶν <τῶν> [7] ὀνομάτων τε καὶ ῥημάτων ὑμῖν
ἀναλέξομαι. οὐδὲ γὰρ τἀσκληπιῷ μεῖόν τι γίγνεται
τῆς τιμῆς, εἰ μὴ τῶν προσιόντων αὐτῶν ποιησάντων
ὁ παιάν, ἀλλ' Ἰσοδήμου [8] τοῦ Τροιζηνίου [9] καὶ

---

[1] δ' ΓΦ: δαὶ Β.
[2] οἰκίας codd.: corr. L. A. Post.   [3] οὖν om vett..
[4] τοῦ scripsi: σοῦ vett.: σοῦ πρὶν ἢ Ν.
[5] σοι codd.: μοι malim.
[6] με codd.: μὲν Albers.
[7] τῶν suppl. Jacobitz.

fee, like the fee at Athens for attending the assembly or serving on the jury. But be sure to be grateful to me."

26. "I shall be grateful," said I, "even before I know what you're talking about. What *are* you talking about?"

"I once read the memoirs of the Macedonian royal family which gave me such delight at the time that I made a special point of acquiring the book. Now I've just remembered I have it at home. In addition to giving details of Antipater's activities at home, it describes his dealings with Demosthenes, which I think you'd be specially interested in hearing."

"Well," said I, "you shall be rewarded at once for your good news by being allowed to read the rest of your poetry. I won't be deprived of seeing your promise become fact. You've provided me with excellent fare in honour of Homer's birthday, and it looks as if you yourself will also be the host for Demosthenes' birthday celebrations."

27. Well, when he'd read out everything else on the tablet, we stayed long enough for the poem to be accorded the praises it deserved, before repairing to Thersagoras' house. Though he had some difficulty, he was able to lay his hands on the book. I took it and went away for the time being. But, now that I've read it, I've made up my mind that I shall not change anything at all but shall read it to you word for word. For Aesculapius receives no less honour if those who visit him have not composed their own paean but the compositions of Isodemus of Troezen

---

[8] ὁ παιᾶν, ἀλλ' Ἰσοδήμου Harmon: ὅπλα ἀναλισοδήμου vett. (Μεσομήδου τοῦ Ῥιζηνίου Keil).   [9] Τρυζηνίου Γ.

Σοφοκλέους ᾄδεται, καὶ τῷ Διονύσῳ τὸ μὲν
ποιῆσαι[1] κωμῳδίας ἢ τραγῳδίας[2] ἐκλέλειπται, τὸ
δὲ ἑτέροις συντεθέντα τοῖς νῦν[3] εἰς μέσον ἐν καιρῷ
κομίζουσιν χάριν οὐκ ἐλάττω φέρει τῷ[4] τὸν θεὸν
δοκεῖν τετιμηκέναι.

28. τὸ μὲν οὖν βιβλίον τοῦτο—ἔστι δὲ τῶν
ὑπομνημάτων τὸ προσῆκον ἡμῖν μέρος τόδε δρᾶμα—
τὸ βιβλίον[5] φησίν Ἀντιπάτρῳ μεμηνύσθαι παρόντα
τὸν Ἀρχίαν. ὁ δ' Ἀρχίας, εἴ τις ἄρα τῶν νεωτέρων
ἀγνοεῖ, τοὺς φυγάδας ἐτέτακτο συλλαμβάνειν·
ἐπέσταλτο δ' αὐτῷ καὶ Δημοσθένην ἀπὸ τῆς
Καλαυρίας πεῖσαι μᾶλλον ἢ βιάσασθαι πρὸς τὸν
Ἀντίπατρον ἥκειν. καὶ δὴ καὶ μετέωρος ἐπὶ ταύτης
ὁ Ἀντίπατρος ἦν τῆς ἐλπίδος, τὸν Δημοσθένην
ἀεὶ προσδοκῶν. ὡς οὖν ἤκουσεν ἀπὸ τῆς Καλαυρίας
ἥκοντα τὸν Ἀρχίαν, εὐθὺς ὡς εἶχεν ἐκέλευσεν εἴσω
καλεῖν. 29. ἐπεὶ δ' εἰσῆλθεν—αὐτὸ φράσει τὰ λοιπὰ
τὸ βιβλίον.

ΑΡΧΙΑΣ

Χαῖρε, ὦ Ἀντίπατρε.

ΑΝΤΙΠΑΤΗΡ

Τί δ' οὐ μέλλω χαίρειν, εἰ Δημοσθένην ἤγαγες;

ΑΡΧΙΑΣ

Ἤγαγον ὡς ἐδυνάμην· ὑδρίαν γὰρ κομίζω τῶν
Δημοσθένους λειψάνων.

---

[1] ποιῆσαι G. Hermann: ποίησιν codd..
[2] κωμῳδίας ἢ τραγῳδίας vett.: καινὴν ποιεῖν recc..
[3] τοῖς νῦν N: τοίνυν vett..   [4] τῷ om. vett..
[5] —τὸ βιβλίον Gesner: τοῦ βιβλίου codd..

and Sophocles [1] are sung, while in the eyes of Dionysus, though composition of comedies or tragedies in his honour has been discontinued, the works of earlier poets win just as much favour for those who produce them at the proper season because they are thought to have honoured the god.

28. Thus the book—the following dramatic scenes are the part of the memoirs that concerns us—this book tells us how the presence of Archias was announced to Antipater. Now, Archias, in case any of the younger amongst you doesn't know it, had been commissioned to arrest the exiles. He had further been instructed to bring Demosthenes from Calauria [2] to Antipater by use of persuasion rather than force. Moreover Antipater was excited at this prospect as all the time he was expecting to see Demosthenes. Accordingly, when he heard of the arrival of Archias from Calauria, he gave orders for him to be summoned to his presence immediately just as he was. 29. When he entered—well the book itself will complete the story.

ARCHIAS

Joy be with you, Antipater.

ANTIPATER

And why shouldn't it, if you've brought Demosthenes ?

ARCHIAS

I've brought him as best I could. For I have with me the urn containing the remains of Demosthenes.

---

[1] Isodemus' poetry is unknown, though his name occurs in an inscription from Epidaurus; for the paean to Aesculapius attributed to Sophocles (fr. 6 Bergk) see J. H. Oliver, *Hesperia*, 1936, 91-122. [2] An island off the Argolid.

PSEUDO-LUCIAN

ΑΝΤΙΠΑΤΡ

Ἀπ' ἐλπίδος γε μήν μ' [1] ἔσφηλας, ὦ Ἀρχία. τί γὰρ τῶν ὀστῶν καὶ τῆς ὑδρίας Δημοσθένην οὐκ ἔχοντι;

ΑΡΧΙΑΣ

Τὴν γὰρ ψυχήν, ὦ βασιλεῦ, πρὸς βίαν αὐτοῦ κατέχειν οὐκ ἐδυνάμην.[2]

ΑΝΤΙΠΑΤΡ

Τί δ' οὐ [3] ζῶντα κατειλήφατε;

ΑΡΧΙΑΣ

Κατειλήφαμεν.

ΑΝΤΙΠΑΤΡ

Κατὰ τὴν ὁδὸν οὖν τέθνηκεν;

ΑΡΧΙΑΣ

Οὔκ, ἀλλ' οὗπερ ἦν, ἐν Καλαυρίᾳ.

ΑΝΤΙΠΑΤΡ

Τάχα τῆς ὑμετέρας γέγονεν ἔργον ὀλιγωρίας οὐ [4] θεραπευόντων τὸν ἄνθρωπον;

ΑΡΧΙΑΣ

Ἀλλ' οὐδ' ὑφ' ἡμῖν ἐγένετο.

ΑΝΤΙΠΑΤΡ

Τί φῇς; αἰνίγματα λέγεις, ὦ Ἀρχία, ζῶντα λαβόντες οὐκ ἔχετε;

---

[1] μήν μ' Albers: μήν ΓΦ: με B.

IN PRAISE OF DEMOSTHENES

ANTIPATER

You've dashed my hopes to the ground, Archias.
For what good are the bones and the urn to me, if I
have not Demosthenes ?

ARCHIAS

His soul, king, I could not constrain against his
will.

ANTIPATER

Why did you not take him alive ?

ARCHIAS

We did.

ANTIPATER

Did he die then on the journey ?

ARCHIAS

No, but where he was, in Calauria.

ANTIPATER

Perhaps it is the result of your carelessness, and
you did not look after him.

ARCHIAS

No, the matter was not in our control.

ANTIPATER

What do you mean ? You talk in riddles,
Archias, if you took him alive, yet do not have him.

---

[2] sic Albers: κατέχειν οὐ Βοιωτίας οὐδ' ἔνθα . . . codd.: οὐ
Βοιωτίας . . . in c. 33 transtulit Gesner.
[3] τί δ' οὐ post εὑρίσκει δύναμιν (c. 37) habent codd..
[4] οὐ B: οὐδὲ ΓΦ.

PSEUDO-LUCIAN

ΑΡΧΙΑΣ

30. Οὐ γὰρ ἐκέλευες τήν γε πρώτην μὴ βιάζεσθαι;
καίτοι πλέον ἂν οὐδὲ βιασαμένοις οὐδὲν ἦν· καὶ γὰρ
οὖν ἐμελλήσαμεν.

ΑΝΤΙΠΑΤΗΡ

Οὐκ εὖ γε ὑμεῖς οὐδὲ μελλήσαντες. ἴσως οὖν ἐκ
τῆς ὑμετέρας τέθηκε βίας;

ΑΡΧΙΑΣ

Ἡμεῖς μὲν αὐτὸν οὐκ ἀπεκτείναμεν, βιάζεσθαι δὲ
μὴ πείθουσιν ἀναγκαῖον ἦν. σοὶ δέ, ὦ βασιλεῦ, τί
τὸ πλέον, εἰ ζῶν ἀφίκετο; πάντως οὐδὲν ⟨ἂν⟩ [1]
αὐτὸν ἢ ἀπέκτεινας.

ΑΝΤΙΠΑΤΗΡ

31. Εὐφήμει, ὦ Ἀρχία· δοκεῖς μοι μὴ συννενοη-
κέναι μήθ' ὅστις ὁ Δημοσθένης μήτε τὴν ἐμὴν
γνώμην, ἀλλὰ νομίζειν ὅμοιον εἶναι Δημοσθένην
εὑρεῖν καὶ τούτους ζητεῖν τοὺς κακῶς ἀπολωλότας,
Ἱμεραῖον τὸν Φαληρέα καὶ τὸν Μαραθώνιον
Ἀριστόνικον καὶ τὸν ἐκ Πειραιῶς Εὐκράτην, τῶν
ῥαγδαίων ῥευμάτων οὐδὲν διαφέροντας, ἀνθρώπους
ταπεινούς, ἀφορμῇ προσκαίρων θορύβων ἐπιπολά-
σαντας καὶ πρὸς μικρὰν ταραχῆς ἐλπίδα θρασέως
ἐξαναστάντας, εἶτα πτήξαντας οὐκ εἰς μακράν,
δίκην τῶν δειλινῶν πνευμάτων, καὶ τὸν ἄπιστον

---

[1] ἂν suppl. corrector in rec..

---

[1] According to Plutarch, *Demosthenes* 28, Archias
removed Himeraeus, Aristonicus and Hyperides (Plutarch

IN PRAISE OF DEMOSTHENES

ARCHIAS

30. Didn't you give orders not to use force at first? Yet, even if we had used force, it would have done us no good. We did in fact intend to use force.

ANTIPATER

You did wrong even to intend it. Perhaps then he died from force at your hands.

ARCHIAS

We did not kill him, though it would have been necessary to use force if we found persuasion impossible. But how would you have gained, king, if he had reached you alive? You would only have killed him.

ANTIPATER

31. Hush, Archias! I don't think you've understood what sort of man Demosthenes was or what were my intentions. No, you seem to think there's no difference between finding Demosthenes and looking for those scoundrels [1] who've come to a bad end, Himeraeus of Phalerum, Aristonicus of Marathon and Eucrates of Piraeus, no different from violent torrents, mean fellows brought into the public eye when civic disturbances offered them the chance, men who took a bold stand with their short-lived hopes for unrest, but soon cowered down again like winds at evening. Another of these is the treacherous

does not mention Eucrates) from sanctuary at Aegina and sent them to Antipater who ordered them all to be killed and Hyperides' tongue to be cut out as well. Cf. Pseudo-Plutarch 849.

Ὑπερίδην, τὸν [1] δημοκόλακα, τὸν οὐδὲν αἰσχρὸν
νομίσαντα κολακείᾳ τοῦ πλήθους συκοφαντῆσαι
Δημοσθένην οὐδ' αὐτὸν εἰς ταῦτα παρασχεῖν διά-
κονον, ἐφ' οἷς αὐτοὶ μετενόησαν οἷς ἐχαρίζετο· μετ'
οὐ [2] πολὺ γοῦν τῆς συκοφαντίας λαμπροτέραν ἢ κατ'
Ἀλκιβιάδην αὐτῷ τὴν κάθοδον ἀκηκόαμεν γενέσθαι.
τῷ δ' οὐκ ἔμελεν οὐδ' ἐπῃσχύνετο κατὰ τῶν ποτε
φιλτάτων τῇ γλώττῃ χρώμενος, ἣν ἐχρῆν δήπου τῆς
ἀγνωμοσύνης ἐκτεμεῖν.

ΑΡΧΙΑΣ

32. Τί δέ; [3] οὐκ ἐχθρῶν ἡμῖν ἔχθιστος ὁ
Δημοσθένης;

ΑΝΤΙΠΑΤΗΡ

Οὐχ ὅτῳ μέλει [4] τρόπου πίστεως, φίλον πᾶν
ἄδολον καὶ βέβαιον ἦθος ἡγουμένῳ. τὰ γάρ τοι
καλὰ καὶ παρ' ἐχθροῖς καλὰ καὶ τὸ τῆς ἀρετῆς
πανταχοῦ τίμιον. οὐδὲ κακίων ἐγὼ Ξέρξου τοῦ
Βούλιν καὶ Σπέρχιν [5] τοὺς Λακεδαιμονίους θαυμά-
σαντος καὶ κτεῖναι παρὸν ἀφέντος. ἀλλ' εἰ δή τινα
πάντων καὶ Δημοσθένην αὐτός τε δὶς Ἀθήνησιν, εἰ
καὶ μὴ κατὰ πολλὴν σχολήν, συγγενόμενος καὶ παρὰ
τῶν ἄλλων ἀναπυνθανόμενος ἔκ τε τῶν πολιτευμάτων αὐτῶν εἶχον θαυμάσας, οὐχ ὡς ἂν νομίσειέ τις

---

[1] τὸν Rothstein: καὶ τὸν ἄπιστον vett.: καὶ τὸν ἄφιλον N.
[2] μετ' οὐ N: μετὰ vett..   [3] ; add. Jacobitz.
[4] μέλει N: μέλοι vett..   [5] Σπέρχην B.

IN PRAISE OF DEMOSTHENES

Hyperides, a false friend who fawned upon the populace, and thought it no shame to ingratiate himself with the mob by bringing false charges against Demosthenes and lending himself as a tool for those designs which soon were regretted by the very men whose favour he sought. At any rate, not long after these charges were brought, Demosthenes, we've heard, had a triumphant home-coming to outdo that of Alcibiades. But Hyperides did not care nor was he ashamed to use against those that once had been his dearest friends the tongue which so unfeeling a creature certainly deserved to have cut out.

ARCHIAS

32. And how is Demosthenes not the greatest foe to us of all our foes ?

ANTIPATER

He is not so to the man who cares for loyalty of disposition and holds dear to him every nature that is free from guile and steadfast. For of a truth the honourable is honourable even when it is in enemies, and virtue is to be esteemed everywhere it is found. I am no worse a man than Xerxes who admired Bulis and Sperchis,[1] the Spartans, and released them, when he could have killed them. But of all men it was Demosthenes I always admired through having met him myself twice, though hurriedly, at Athens, and from what I heard of him from others. I admired him for his political activities themselves

---

[1] Cf. Herodotus 7.134, Plutarch, *Moralia* 235 F and 815 E. These two men volunteered to be killed by Xerxes to atone for the Spartans' killing of Persian envoys, but were spared. Herodotus gives the name Sperthies or Sperchies.

τῆς τῶν λόγων δεινότητος, εἰ καὶ μηδὲν μὲν ὁ
Πύθων πρὸς αὐτόν, οἱ δ' Ἀττικοὶ ῥήτορες παιδιὰ
παραβάλλειν τῷ τούτου κρότῳ καὶ τόνῳ καὶ λέξεων
εὐρυθμίᾳ καὶ ταῖς τῶν διανοιῶν περιγραφαῖς καὶ
συνεχείαις ἀποδείξεων καὶ τῷ συνακτικῷ τε [1] καὶ
κρουστικῷ. μετενοοῦμεν γοῦν ὅτε τοὺς Ἕλληνας
Ἀθήναζε συνηγάγομεν ὡς ἐλέγξοντες Ἀθηναίους,
Πύθωνι καὶ τοῖς Πύθωνος ἐπαγγέλμασιν πεπι-
στευκότες, εἶτα Δημοσθένει καὶ τοῖς Δημοσθένους
ἐλέγχοις περιπεσόντες. ἀλλ' ἦν μὲν ἀπρόσιτος ἡ
δύναμις αὐτῷ τοῦ λόγου.

33. ἐγὼ δὲ ταύτην μὲν δευτέραν ἔταττον, ἐν χώρᾳ
τιθεὶς ὀργάνου, Δημοσθένην δ' αὐτὸν ὑπερηγάμην
τοῦ τε φρονήματος καὶ τῆς συνέσεως, ἀκλινῆ τὴν
ψυχὴν ἐπ' ὀρθῆς ἐν ἁπάσαις φυλάττοντα τρικυμίαις
τῆς τύχης [2] καὶ πρὸς μηδὲν τῶν δεινῶν ἐνδι-
δόντα. καὶ Φίλιππον δὲ τὴν αὐτὴν ἐμοὶ γνώμην
ἔχοντα περὶ τἀνδρὸς ἠπιστάμην· τούτῳ [3] μέν γε
δημηγορίας ἐξαγγελθείσης Ἀθήνηθέν ποτε καθαπ-
τομένης τοῦ Φιλίππου, καὶ Παρμενίωνος ἠγανακτη-
κότος καί τι καὶ σκωπτικὸν εἰς τὸν Δημοσθένην ἐπει-
πόντος, Ὦ Παρμενίων, ἔφη, δίκαιος ὁ Δημοσθένης
παρρησίας τυγχάνειν· μόνος γέ τοι τῶν ἐπὶ τῆς
Ἑλλάδος δημαγωγῶν οὐδαμοῦ τοῖς ἀπολογισμοῖς
ἐγγέγραπται τῶν ἐμῶν ἀναλωμάτων, καίτοι μᾶλλον
ἠβουλόμην ἢ γραμματεῦσι τριηρίταις [4] ἐμαυτὸν
πεπιστευκέναι. νῦν δ' ἐκείνων μὲν ἕκαστος ἀπογέ-

---

[1] τε edd.: γε codd..   [2] τύχης N: ψυχῆς vett..

[3] τούτῳ vett..

[4] τριηρίταις codd.: καὶ τριταγωνισταῖς Jacobitz.

[1] Cf. Plutarch, *Cicero* 32.

rather than, as one might think, for the eloquence of his speeches, even though Python is nothing in contrast with him, while the Attic orators are paltry when compared with the thunderous intensity of his voice, the rhythm of his phrases, the conciseness of his thoughts, the unbroken sequence of his arguments, the cumulative blows his words can strike. We certainly regretted the day when, trusting in Python and his promises, we had assembled the Greeks at Athens with the intention of discrediting the Athenians, and then were confronted with Demosthenes who discredited us. Really, nothing could approach his power of speech.

33. But I held that power secondary, assigning it the place of a mere tool ;[1] it was Demosthenes himself whom I admired tremendously for his spirit and his intellect and because he kept his soul unswerving on a straight course through all the tempestuous waves of fortune and never gave in in the face of any danger. And I knew that Philip too held the same opinion as I did about him. At any rate, when a report reached Philip from Athens of a speech to the people directed against him, and Parmenio burst into anger and uttered a taunt against Demosthenes, " Parmenio," said Philip, " Demosthenes deserves the right to speak freely ; he is the only popular orator in Greece whose name appears nowhere on my expense accounts. Yet I should rather it did than that I had entrusted myself to scribes who row at the benches.[2] But in fact each of them is listed as having received from me gold,

[2] I.e. to poor men like Aeschines, as opposed to rich men like Demosthenes who could provide warships; cf. p. 250 n. 2, p. 257 n. 3.

γράπται χρυσίον ξύλα πυροὺς [1] θρέμματα γῆν
Βοιωτίας οὐκ ἔσθ' ὅτι μὴ [2] παρ' ἐμοῦ λαβόντες.
ἡμεῖς δὲ θᾶττον ἂν τὸ Βυζαντίων τεῖχος ἕλοιμεν
μηχαναῖς ἢ Δημοσθένην χρυσίῳ.

34. ἐγὼ δέ, ὦ Παρμενίων, ἔφη, εἰ μέν τις Ἀθηναῖος
ὢν ἐν Ἀθήναις λέγων ἐμὲ τῆς πατρίδος προτιμᾷ,
τούτοις ἀργύριον μὲν προείμην ἄν, φιλίαν δ' οὐκ ἄν.
εἰ δέ τις ὑπὲρ τῆς πατρίδος ἐμὲ μισεῖ, τούτῳ προσ-
πολεμῶ μὲν ὡς ἀκροπόλει καὶ τείχει καὶ νεωρίοις καὶ
τάφρῳ, θαυμάζω δὲ τῆς ἀρετῆς καὶ μακαρίζω γε τοῦ
κτήματος τὴν πόλιν. καὶ τοὺς μὲν ἔξω τῆς χρείας
γενόμενος ἥδιστ' ἂν προσαπολέσαιμι, τὸν δὲ
βουλοίμην [3] ἂν ἐνταυθοῖ παρ' ἡμῖν τυχεῖν γενόμενον
μᾶλλον ἢ τὴν Ἰλλυριῶν ἵππον καὶ Τριβαλλῶν καὶ
πᾶν τὸ μισθοφορικόν, τῆς ὅπλων βίας τὴν τοῦ λόγου [4]
πειθὼ καὶ τὸ τῆς γνώμης ἐμβριθὲς οὐδαμῇ τιθεὶς
δεύτερον. πρὸς Παρμενίωνα μὲν ταῦτα.

35. τοιούτους δέ τινας καὶ πρὸς ἐμὲ λόγους
ἐποιήσατο. τῶν γὰρ μετὰ Διοπείθους Ἀθήνηθεν
ἀπεσταλμένων ἐγὼ μὲν εἶχον διὰ φροντίδος, ὁ δ' εὖ
μάλα γελάσας ἔφη· Σὺ δ' Ἀττικὸν στρατηγὸν ἢ
στρατιώτην δέδοικας ἡμῖν; αἱ μὲν τριήρεις καὶ [5]
Πειραιεὺς καὶ τὰ νεώρια λῆρος ἔμοιγε καὶ φλήνα-
φος. τί δ' ἂν ἄνθρωποι πράξειαν διονυσιάζοντες, ἐν
κρεανομίαις καταζῶντες καὶ χοροῖς; εἰ δὲ μὴ Δημοσθένης εἷς ἐν Ἀθηναίοις ἐγένετο, ῥᾷον ἂν εἴχομεν τὴν

[1] πυροὺς Albers (cf. *D.F.L.* 145, 6): πόρους codd..
[2] κατέχειν (vide cc. 29, 37) οὐ Βοιωτίας οὐδ' ἔνθα τι μὴ . . .
codd.: sic corr. Keil.   [3] ἐβουλόμην Γ.
[4] sic edd.: βιαστῆς ἢ λόγου codd..
[5] καὶ vett.: καὶ ὁ recc..

280

timber, wheat, cattle, land in Boeotia, everything in fact under the sun. But we could more quickly capture the walls of Byzantium by siege-engines [1] than Demosthenes with gold."

34. " My own view, Parmenio," he said, " is that on any Athenians speaking in Athens who value me above their own country I would expend my silver but not my friendship. But, if anyone hates me for the sake of his country, I wage war against him as against a citadel, a wall, a dockyard or a moat, but yet admire him for his virtue, and think his city lucky to possess him. The one type I should most gladly destroy along with their city once I no longer need them, but this sort of man I should rather have had here with us than my Illyrian or Triballian cavalry [2] and all my mercenaries, for I consider persuasiveness of speech and weight of intellect in no way inferior to force of arms."

35. That was what he said to Parmenio, and he said the same sort of thing to me too. For, when Diopithes' expedition was sent out from Athens,[3] I was worried but he laughed heartily and said, " Do you fear an Attic general or soldier on our account ? Their men-of-war, their Piraeus and their dockyards are, to me at least, just idle talk and nonsense. What could be achieved by men who celebrate festivals of Dionysus and spend their time in feasting and dancing ? But for the existence among the Athenians of a single man, Demosthenes, we should have already captured their city more easily than we

[1] Philip attacked Byzantium in 340 B.C. but failed to capture it. [2] Cf. *On the Crown* 44.
[3] I.e. the expedition to the Thracian Chersonese of *c.* 342 B.C.

πόλιν ἢ Θηβαίους καὶ Θετταλούς, ἀπατῶντες
βιαζόμενοι φθάνοντες ὠνούμενοι. νῦν δὲ εἷς ἐκεῖνος
ἐγρήγορεν καὶ πᾶσι τοῖς καιροῖς ἐφέστηκεν καὶ ταῖς
ἡμετέραις ὁρμαῖς ἐπακολουθεῖ καὶ τοῖς στρατηγή-
μασιν ἀντιπαρατάττεται. λανθάνομεν δὲ αὐτὸν οὐ
τεχνάζοντες, οὐκ ἐπιχειροῦντες, οὐ βουλευόμενοι,
καὶ [1] καθάπαξ κώλυμά τι καὶ πρόβολος ἡμῖν
ἄνθρωπός ἐστιν μὴ πάντ' ἔχειν ἐξ ἐπιδρομῆς. τό γέ
τοι κατ' αὐτὸν οὐκ Ἀμφίπολιν εἵλομεν, οὐκ Ὄλυνθον,
οὐ Φωκέας καὶ Πύλας ἔσχομεν, οὐ Χερρονήσου καὶ
τῶν περὶ τὸν Ἑλλήσποντον κεκρατήκαμεν.

36. ἀλλ' ἀνίστησι [2] μὲν ἄκοντας οἷον ἐκ μανδραγόρου
καθεύδοντας τοὺς αὐτοῦ πολίτας, ὥσπερ τομῇ τινι
καὶ καύσει τῆς ῥαθυμίας τῇ παρρησίᾳ χρώμενος,
ὀλίγον τοῦ πρὸς ἡδονὴν φροντίσας. [3] μετατίθησιν δὲ
τῶν χρημάτων τοὺς πόρους ἀπὸ τῶν θεάτρων ἐπὶ
τὰ στρατόπεδα, συντίθησι δὲ τὸ ναυτικὸν νόμοις
τριηραρχικοῖς ὑπὸ τῆς ἀταξίας μόνον οὐ τελέως
διεφθαρμένον, ἐγείρει δ' ἐρριμμένον [4] ἤδη χρόνου
πρὸς τὴν δραχμὴν καὶ τὸ τριώβολον τὸ τῆς πόλεως
ἀξίωμα, πάλαι τούτους κατακεκλιμένους εἰς τοὺς
προγόνους ἐπανάγων καὶ τὸν ζῆλον τῶν Μαραθῶνι
καὶ Σαλαμῖνι κατειργασμένων, συνίστησιν δ' ἐπὶ
συμμαχίας καὶ συντάξεις Ἑλληνικάς. τοῦτον οὐ
λαθεῖν ἐστιν, οὐ φενακίσαι, οὐ πρίασθαι [5] οὐ μᾶλλον
ἢ τὸν Ἀριστείδην ἐκεῖνον ὁ Περσῶν βασιλεὺς ἐπρίατο.

---

[1] καὶ om. vett..   [2] ἀναστήσει vett..

[3] φροντίσας edd.: φροντίδος vett.: φροντίζων recc..

[4] δ' ἔρημον ὂν Β: δερειμονον ΓΦ: corr. N.   [5] πρίασθαι δ' codd..

[1] By Demosthenes' reforms rich men had to contribute
more towards the supplying of warships; cf. *On the Crown*
102 ff.

did Thebes and Thessaly, by means of deceit, violence, speed and bribery. But, as it is, he alone remains vigilant, is at hand to meet every crisis, keeps up with every move we initiate, and counters us with his own plans. In no scheme, no enterprise, no plot can we escape his attention, and the fellow is literally an obstacle and bulwark preventing us from possessing everything at a single stroke. It was no fault of his at any rate that we have taken Amphipolis, acquired Olynthus, Phocis and Thermopylae, and gained control over the Chersonese and the area round the Hellespont.

36. But against their will he keeps rousing his fellow citizens, who are asleep as though drugged, by using his outspoken words as it were to cut away and cauterise their sloth with little heed for what they would like to hear. He transfers the revenues spent on the theatre to the armies, he is by his trierarchic laws [1] building up their navy, though it has been almost completely ruined by lack of organisation, he awakens his city's honour long prostrated in pursuit of advocates' or jurors' fees, [2] by raising up these people long recumbent to recall their ancestors and emulate the feats accomplished at Marathon and Salamis, [3] and unites the Greeks into federations of alliance. *His* attention cannot be escaped ; *he* cannot be deceived : *he* cannot be bought any more than the king of the Persians [4] bought the famous Aristides.

[2] Public advocates at Athens received a retainer of a drachma, while jurymen were paid three obols for a day's service. Cf. Aristophanes, *Wasps* 690-691.

[3] Cf. *On The Crown* 208, Longinus, *On The Sublime* 16.2.

[4] Xerxes; cf. Plutarch, *Aristides* 10, Herodotus, 8.143.

37. τοῦτον οὖν, ὦ Ἀντίπατρε, χρὴ δεδιέναι
μᾶλλον ἢ πάσας τριήρεις καὶ πάντας ἀποστόλους. ὃ γὰρ Ἀθηναίοις τοῖς πάλαι Θεμιστοκλῆς
καὶ Περικλῆς ἐγένετο, τοῦτο τοῖς [1] νῦν ὁ Δημοσθένης, ἐφάμιλλος Θεμιστοκλεῖ μὲν τὴν σύνεσιν,
Περικλεῖ δὲ τὸ φρόνημα. ἐκτήσατο γοῦν αὐτοῖς
ἀκούειν Εὔβοιαν, Μέγαρα, τὰ περὶ τὸν Ἑλλήσποντον,
τὴν Βοιωτίαν. καὶ καλῶς γε, ἔφη, ποιοῦσιν
Ἀθηναῖοι Χάρητα μὲν καὶ Διοπείθην καὶ Πρόξενον
καὶ τοιούτους τινὰς ἀποδεικνύντες στρατηγεῖν,
Δημοσθένην δὲ εἴσω κατέχοντες ἐπὶ τοῦ βήματος.
ὡς εἰ τοῦτον τὸν ἄνθρωπον ὅπλων ἀπέφηναν καὶ
νεῶν καὶ στρατοπέδων ⟨καὶ⟩ δὴ καὶ [2] καιρῶν καὶ
χρημάτων κύριον, ὀκνῶ μὴ περὶ τῆς Μακεδονίας ἂν
κατέστησέ μοι τὸν λόγον, ὃς καὶ νῦν ἀπὸ ψηφισμά-
των ἀνταγωνιζόμενος ἡμῖν πανταχοῦ συμπεριτρέ-
χει, καταλαμβάνει, πόρους εὑρίσκει, στόλους [3]
ἀποπέμπει, συντάττει δυνάμεις, ἀντιμεθίσταται.

38. Τοιαῦτα καὶ τότε καὶ πολλάκις πρός με
Φίλιππος περὶ τἀνδρὸς ἔλεγεν, ἓν τῶν παρὰ τῆς
τύχης χρηστῶν τιθέμενος τὸ μὴ στρατηγεῖν τὸν
Δημοσθένην, οὗ γε καὶ τοὺς λόγους ὥσπερ κριοὺς
ἢ καταπέλτας Ἀθήνηθεν ὁρμωμένους διασείειν
αὐτοῦ καὶ ταράττειν τὰ βουλεύματα. περὶ μὲν γὰρ
Χαιρωνείας οὐδὲ μετὰ τὴν νίκην ἐπαύετο πρὸς ἡμᾶς
λέγων εἰς ὅσον ἄνθρωπος ἡμᾶς κινδύνου κατέ-
στησεν. Καὶ γὰρ εἰ [4] παρ' ἐλπίδα καὶ κακίᾳ
στρατηγῶν καὶ στρατιωτῶν ἀταξίᾳ καὶ τῇ παραδόξῳ

[1] τοῦτο τοῖς edd.: τούτοις codd..
[2] καὶ δὴ καὶ scripsi: δικαι ΓΦ: δὴ καὶ B: καὶ edd..
[3] sic Albers. πόρους εὑρίσκει (ἔρις καὶ vett.) δύναμιν τί δ' οὐ

IN PRAISE OF DEMOSTHENES

37. Him therefore ought we to fear rather than all their men-of-war and all their armadas ; for what Themistocles and Pericles proved themselves to the Athenians of old, Demosthenes is to those of to-day, for he rivals Themistocles in intellect and Pericles in spirit. At any rate he has captured for them the willing ear of Euboea, Megara, the region round the Hellespont and Boeotia. And I'm glad," he continued, " that the Athenians appoint Chares, Diopithes, Proxenus and the like to be their generals, but keep Demosthenes at Athens on the speaker's platform. For, if they had given him control of their arms, ships and troops, yes, and their moments of crisis and their finances, I'm afraid it's Macedonia he would have made the matter of issue between us, for even now using mere decrees to oppose us, he is quick to follow us around everywhere, overtaking us, finding new resources, sending out fleets, marshalling his forces, ever changing his policy to counter us."

38. Such were the things that Philip used to say to me about Demosthenes on that and many other occasions, for he regarded it as one of his boons from fortune that Demosthenes was not general, since he admitted that even his words shooting out from Athens like battering-rams and artillery [1] shook and confounded his plans. For on the topic of Chaeronea not even after his victory there would he stop telling us into what great danger Demosthenes had brought us. " For," he would say, " even if we have

---

[1] Cf. Pseudo-Plutarch, 845 D.

codd., vide c. 29: post γῆν (vide c. 33) habent στόλους Φ, ἐπικεισ‌τόλους ΓΒ.

[4] καὶ γὰρ εἰ Gesner: μὴ γὰρ εἰ codd.: εἰ γὰρ μὴ Baumstark.

ῥοπῇ τῆς τύχης τῇ πολλὰ [1] πολλάκις ἡμῖν συνειργα-
σμένη κεκρατήκαμεν, ἀλλ' ἐπὶ μιᾶς γε ταύτη
ἡμέρας τὸν περὶ τῆς ἀρχῆς καὶ τῆς ψυχῆς κίνδυνον
ἐπέστησέ μοι, τὰς ἀρίστας πόλεις εἰς ἓν συναγαγὼ
καὶ πᾶσαν τὴν Ἑλληνικὴν δύναμιν ἀθροίσας, πρὸ
Ἀθηναίοις [2] ἅμα καὶ Θηβαίους Βοιωτούς τε τοὺ
ἄλλους καὶ Κορινθίους Εὐβοέας τε καὶ Μεγαρέας κα
τὰ κράτιστα τῆς Ἑλλάδος διακινδυνεύειν συναναγ-
κάσας καὶ μηδ' εἴσω με τῆς Ἀττικῆς ἐπιτρέψα
παρελθεῖν.

39. τοιοῦτοί τινες ἦσαν αὐτῷ συνεχεῖ
περὶ Δημοσθένους οἱ λόγοι· καὶ πρός γε τοὺ
λέγοντας ὡς μέγαν ἔχοι τὸν Ἀθμναίων δῆμον
ἀνταγωνιστήν, Ἐμοὶ Δημοσθένης μόνος, εἶπεν
ἀνταγωνιστής, Ἀθηναῖοι δὲ Δημοσθένην οὐ
ἔχοντες Αἰνιᾶνές εἰσι καὶ Θετταλοί. καὶ πρέσβει
ὁπότε πρὸς τὰς πόλεις πέμποι, τῶν μὲν ἄλλω
ῥητόρων εἴ τινας ἢ τῶν Ἀθηναίων πόλις ἀνταποστέλ-
λοι τῇ πρεσβείᾳ, κεκρατηκὼς ἂν ἤδετο,[3] το
Δημοσθένους δ' ἐπιστάντος, Μάτην, εἶπεν, ἀντε-
πρεσβεύσαμεν. 40. οὐ γὰρ ἔστιν κατὰ τῶν Δημοσθένους λόγων ἐγεῖραι τρόπαιον.

Ταῦτα ὁ Φίλιππος. καὶ μέντοι καὶ πάντω
ἔλαττον ἂν ἔχοντες λάβοιμεν· τοιοῦτον οὖν ἄνδρα
πρὸς Διός, Ἀρχία, τί [5] ποτε νομίζεις, βοῦν ἂν ἐπ
σφαγὴν ἤγομεν ἢ πολὺ μᾶλλον ἂν σύμβουλον περ
τῶν Ἑλληνικῶν πραγμάτων καὶ τῆς ἀρχῆ

---

[1] πολλὰ om. ΓΦ.   [2] sic scripsi: πρὸς Ἀθηναίους codd.
[3] ἂν ἤδετο scripsi: ἂν ἥδιστα vett.: ἂν ἤδει Rothstein: ἢ
ἥδιστα Ν: ἢν ῥᾶστα Keil.
[4] εἰ λάβοιμεν τοιοῦτον ἄνδρα, Ν, edd..   [5] τί Ν: ἔτι vett.

won a victory we never expected thanks to the cowardice of their generals, the lack of discipline in their troops and the unbelievable way that fortune, which has helped us much on many occasions, veered to us, yet on this one day he made me risk losing my kingdom and my life,[1] since he had united the noblest cities, collected together the whole might of Greece, compelled not only Athenians but also Thebans and all the other Boeotians, Corinthians, Euboeans, Megarians and all the mightiest powers in Greece to brave the hazard of battle, and had not even allowed me to cross into Attic soil."

39. Thus was he continually speaking about Demosthenes. Moreover, to those who said that he had a great adversary in the Athenian people, he said, " For me the only adversary is Demosthenes, and Athenians without Demosthenes are no better than Aenianes [2] or Thessalians." Whenever he sent envoys to the cities of Greece, if the Athenians sent in return any of their other spokesmen, he would rejoice in a victory won by his embassy, but when Demosthenes appeared he would say, " Our envoys went in vain. 40. For it is impossible to set up trophies of victory over the speeches of Demosthenes."

Thus spoke Philip. But we would be infinitely more at a disadvantage than Philip if we captured Demosthenes. Whatever do you think we would do with such a man, Archias ? Would we lead him like an ox to the slaughter or would we not much rather make him our adviser on Greek affairs and indeed on

---

[1] Cf. Plutarch, *Demosthenes* 20.
[2] An unimportant people of northern Greece.

πάσης ἐποιούμεθα; φύσει μὲν γὰρ αὐτῷ καὶ κατ'
ἀρχὰς προσεπεπόνθειν ἐξ αὐτῶν τῶν πολιτευμάτων, ἔτι δὲ μᾶλλον Ἀριστοτέλει μάρτυρι. πρὸς
γοῦν τὸν Ἀλέξανδρον καὶ πρὸς ἡμᾶς γε λέγων [1]
οὐδὲν ἐπαύετο τοσούτων ὄντων τῶν αὐτῷ προσ-
πεφοιτηκότων μηδένα οὕτως πώποτε θαυμάσαι
μεγέθους τε φύσεως καὶ τῆς περὶ τὴν ἄσκησιν
ἐγκρατείας καὶ βάρους καὶ τάχους καὶ παρρησίας
καὶ καρτερίας.

41. Ὑμεῖς δέ, ἔφη, διανοεῖσθε ὡς ὑπὲρ Εὐβούλου
καὶ Φρύνωνος καὶ Φιλοκράτους, καὶ πειρᾶσθε
δώροις καὶ τοῦτον ἀναπείθειν, ἄνθρωπον καὶ τὴν
πατρῴαν οὐσίαν εἰς Ἀθηναίους ἰδίᾳ τε τοῖς δεηθεῖσι
καὶ δημοσίᾳ τῇ πόλει καταναλωκότα, διαμαρτά-
νοντες δὲ φοβήσειν οἴεσθε πάλαι βεβουλευμένον τὴν
ψυχὴν ὑποθεῖναι ταῖς τῆς πατρίδος ἀδήλοις τύχαις,
καὶ καθαπτομένου τῶν πραττομένων ὑμῖν ἀγανακ-
τεῖτε; ὁ δὲ οὐδὲ τὸν Ἀθηναίων δῆμον ὑποστέλλεται.
λέληθεν ὑμᾶς, ἔφη, τῇ μὲν τῆς πατρίδος εὐνοίᾳ
πολιτευόμενος, αὐτῷ δὲ τὴν πολιτείαν γυμνάσιον
φιλοσοφίας προθέμενος.

42. ταῦτά τοι,[2] ὦ Ἀρχία, ὑπερεπεθύμουν αὐτῷ
συγγενόμενος τήν τε γνώμην, ἣν ἔχοι περὶ τῶν
παρόντων, ἀκοῦσαι λέγοντος καὶ τῶν ἀεὶ παραπε-
πτωκότων ἡμῖν κολάκων, εἰ ἐδεόμην, ἀποστὰς
ἁπλοῦ τινος ἐξ ἐλευθέρας γνώμης ἀκοῦσαι λόγου
καὶ φιλαλήθους συμβουλῆς μεταλαβεῖν. καί τι καὶ
νουθετῆσαι δίκαιον, ὑπὲρ οἵων ὄντων ⟨τῶν⟩ [3]

---

[1] λέγων rec.: ἄγων cett..   [2] ταῦτά τοι B: τὰ τοιαῦτα ΓΦ.
[3] τῶν suppl. Jacobitz.

our whole empire ? For I had a natural sympathy with him from the first because of his political record itself, but still more because of the testimony of Aristotle. At any rate he would never stop telling Alexander and us that, though he had had so many pupils go to him, he'd never admired anyone so much for the greatness of his natural gifts, his self-discipline in developing them, his weight, his speed, his freedom of expression and his fortitude.

41. " But you," he said, " think as if you were dealing with a Eubulus,[1] a Phrynon, or a Philocrates, and try to win him too to your view by bribes, though he is one who has expended his inheritance on the Athenians, both privately on the needy and publicly on the state. Are you mistaken enough to think you will frighten a man, who has long made it his policy to expose his life to the uncertain fortunes of his country, and to be angry when he upbraids your actions ? No, he has no fear even of the assembly of the Athenians. You have not realised," he continued, " that he makes patriotism the basis of his political life, while his only personal aim is that politics should be his training ground for philosophy.

42. " This explains, Archias, why I was so very eager to have his company, and to hear him tell me his views on the current situation, and, if I needed it, to dissociate myself from the succession of toadies who confront me, and to hear plain speaking from a free mind and be given sincere advice. Moreover it would have been fair to warn him how ungrateful

---

[1] Eubulus was a political opponent of Demosthenes; Phrynon served along with Demosthenes, Aeschines and Philocrates on the embassies to Philip which produced the shameful Peace of Philocrates in 346 B.C.

Ἀθηναίων τὴν ἀχαριστίαν πάντα παραβάλοιτο
τὸν αὑτοῦ βίον, ἐξὸν εὐγνωμονεστέροις καὶ
βεβαιοτέροις κεχρῆσθαι φίλοις.

ΑΡΧΙΑΣ

Ὦ βασιλεῦ, τῶν μὲν ἄλλων ἴσως ἂν ἔτυχες,
ταυτὶ δὲ μάτην ἂν ἔλεγες· οὕτως μανικῶς φιλαθή-
ναιος ἦν.

ΑΝΤΙΠΑΤΗΡ

Ταῦτα,[1] ὦ Ἀρχία· τί γὰρ ἂν καὶ λέγοιμεν; ἀλλὰ
πῶς ἀπέθανεν;

ΑΡΧΙΑΣ

43. Ἔοικας ἔτι μᾶλλον, ὦ βασιλεῦ, θαυμάσειν· καὶ
γὰρ ἡμεῖς οἱ τεθεαμένοι διαφέρομεν [2] οὐδὲν ἐκπλήξει
τε καὶ ἀπιστίᾳ τῶν ὁρώντων.[3] ἔοικεν γὰρ δὴ πάλαι
ὧδε [4] βεβουλευμένῳ περὶ τῆς ὑστάτης ἡμέρας.
δηλοῖ δὲ ἡ παρασκευή. καθῆστο μὲν γὰρ ἔνδον
ἐν τῷ νεῴ, μάτην δὲ τῶν πρόσθεν ἡμερῶν λόγους
ἦμεν ἀναλωκότες.[5]

ΑΝΤΙΠΑΤΗΡ

Τίνες γὰρ ἦσαν οἱ παρ' ὑμῶν λόγοι;

ΑΡΧΙΑΣ

Πολλὰ καὶ φιλάνθρωπα προὐτεινόμην ἐλεόν τινα
παρὰ σοῦ καθυπισχνούμενος, οὐ μάλα μὲν προσδοκῶν

---

[1] Ἦν ταῦτα Jacobs.
[2] διαφέρομεν rec., edd.: διεφέρομεν vett..

were the Athenians for whom he had risked all his
wordly goods, when he might have enjoyed more
grateful and reliable friends."

ARCHIAS

All else, my king, you might perhaps have gained,
but such a speech from you would have been in vain.
He was so fanatical a lover of Athens.

ANTIPATER

That is so, Archias. How could we deny it? But
how did he die?

ARCHIAS

43. It looks as if you'll find more to wonder at, my
king. For we too who saw that scene are just as
astonished and incredulous today as when it was
before our eyes. For he seems long ago to have
adopted this plan for his last day. His preparations
make that clear. For he was seated in the interior
of the temple and our arguments of the previous days
proved to have been expended in vain.

ANTIPATER

What arguments *were* advanced by you?

ARCHIAS

I made many humane offers, promising him a pity
from you of which I was not very confident, since I

---

³ ὁρώντων codd.: μὴ ὁρώντων Bosius: ἀπόντων vel ὁρωμένων
conieci.   ⁴ ὧδε rec.: ὅδε B: δὲ Γ: om. Φ.
⁵ ἀναλωκότες N: ἀλωκότες B: ἑαλωκότες Γ: ἀλωκότες Φ.

—οὐ γὰρ ἠπιστάμην, ἀλλὰ σὲ ᾤμην δι' ὀργῆς ἔχειν
τὸν ἄνθρωπον—χρήσιμον δ' οὖν πρὸς τὸ πείθειν
νομίζων.

ΑΝΤΙΠΑΤΗΡ

Ὁ δὲ πῶς προσίετο τοὺς λόγους; καί με μηδὲν
ἀποκρύψῃ· μάλιστα μὲν γὰρ αὐτήκοος ἂν ἐβουλόμην
παρὼν εἶναι νῦν. ἀλλὰ σύ γε μὴ παραλίπῃς μηδέν·
οὐ γάρ τοι σμικρὸν ἔργον ἦθος ἀνδρὸς γενναίου πρὸς
αὐτῷ τῷ τέλει τοῦ βίου καταμαθεῖν, πότερον
κάτονος καὶ νωθρὸς ἦν ἢ παντάπασιν ἀκλινὲς τὸ
τῆς ψυχῆς ὄρθιον ἐφύλαττεν.

ΑΡΧΙΑΣ

44. Οὐδὲν ὑπέστελλεν ἐκεῖνός γε. πῶς γάρ; ὃς
ἡδὺ γελάσας κἀμὲ δὴ σκώπτων εἰς τὸν πρότερον
βίον, ἀπίθανον ἔφη με ὑποκριτὴν εἶναι τῶν σῶν
ψευσμάτων.

ΑΝΤΙΠΑΤΗΡ

Ἀπιστήσας ἄρα τοῖς ἐπαγγέλμασιν προείτο τὴν
ψυχήν;

ΑΡΧΙΑΣ

Οὔκ· εἴ γε τῶν λοιπῶν ἀκούσαις, οὐ δόξει σοι
μόνον ἀπιστεῖν. ἀλλ' ἐπεὶ κελεύεις, ὦ βασιλεῦ,
λέγειν, Μακεδόσιν μέν, εἶπεν, οὐδὲν ἀπώμοτον
οὐδὲ παράδοξον, εἰ Δημοσθένην οὕτως λαμβάνουσιν
ὡς Ἀμφίπολιν, ὡς Ὄλυνθον, ὡς Ὠρωπόν.
τοιαῦτα πολλὰ ἔλεγεν. καὶ γὰρ οὖν ὑπογραφέας

292

thought, though I didn't know, that you were angry
with the fellow, but one which in any case I thought
expedient for persuading him.

ANTIPATER

But how did he receive your overtures ? Don't
hide anything from me. For I should very much like
to have been there just now and to have heard it all
with my own ears. But *you* must omit nothing.
For it's of no little value to see clearly the character
of a noble man close to the very end of his life and
find out whether he was both feeble and sluggish or
preserved unswerving the steadfast course of his
soul.

ARCHIAS

44. *He* gave no ground at all. Certainly not !
For he laughed merrily and, twitting me with my
former life,[1] said I was unconvincing in the role
assigned me by your lies.

ANTIPATER

Did he then throw away his life for lack of faith in
my promises ?

ARCHIAS

Not so. Should you listen to the rest of the story,
you'll see that there was more to his actions than
mistrust of you. No, no, since you bid me speak, my
king, he said : " Macedonians will think nothing
impossible or extraordinary [2] if they capture Demosthenes as easily as they did Amphipolis, Olynthus
and Oropus." He said much to this effect. I even

---

[1] Archias had been a tragic actor.
[2] Cf. Archilochus, Fr. 74 (L.C.L.).

παρεστησάμην, ἵνα σοι τὰ λεχθέντα σῴζοιτο.

Ἐγὼ μέντοι, ἔφη, ὦ Ἀρχία, βασάνων ἢ θανάτου φόβῳ κατ' ὄψιν οὐκ ἂν Ἀντιπάτρῳ γενοίμην, ἀλλ' εἰ ταῦτ' ἀληθεύετε, πολύ μοι μᾶλλόν ἐστι [1] φυλακτέον μὴ τὴν ψυχὴν αὐτὴν παρ' Ἀντιπάτρου δεδωροδοκηκέναι μηδ' ἣν ἐμαυτὸν ἔταξα τάξιν λιπὼν τὴν Ἑλληνικὴν εἰς τὴν Μακεδονικὴν μεταβάλλεσθαι.

45. καλὸν γάρ, Ἀρχία, τὸ ζῆν ἐμοί, εἰ [2] Πειραιεὺς αὐτὸ [3] παρέχοι καὶ τριήρης ἣν ἐπιδέδωκα καὶ τεῖχος καὶ τάφρος τοῖς ἐμοῖς τέλεσιν ἐξειργασμένα καὶ φυλὴ Πανδιονίς, ἧς ἐθελοντὴς ἐχορήγουν ἐγώ, καὶ Σόλων καὶ Δράκων καὶ παρρησία βήματος καὶ δῆμος ἐλεύθερος καὶ ψηφίσματα στρατιωτικὰ καὶ νόμοι τριηραρχικοὶ καὶ προγόνων ἀρεταὶ καὶ τρόπαια καὶ πολιτῶν εὔνοια [4] τῶν ἐμὲ πολλάκις ἐστεφανωκότων καὶ δύναμις Ἑλλήνων τῶν ὑπ' ἐμοῦ μέχρι νῦν τετηρημένων· εἰ δὲ καὶ βιωτὸν ἐλεηθέντι, ταπεινὸν μέν, ἀνεκτὸς δ' οὖν ὁ ἔλεος παρὰ τοῖς οἰκείοις, ὧν ἐλυσάμην αἰχμαλώτων, ἢ τοῖς πατράσιν, ὧν συνεξέδωκα τὰς θυγατέρας ἢ οἷς τοὺς ἐράνους συνδιελυσάμην.

46. εἰ δέ με μὴ σῴζει νήσων ἀρχὴ καὶ θάλαττα, παρά γε τουτουὶ Ποσειδῶνος αἰτῶ τὸ σῴζεσθαι καὶ τοῦδε τοῦ βωμοῦ καὶ τῶν ἱερῶν νόμων. εἰ δὲ Ποσειδῶν, ἔφη, μὴ δύναται φυλάττειν τὴν ἀσυλίαν τοῦ νεὼ μηδ' ἐπαισχύνεται προδοῦναι Δημοσθένην Ἀρχίᾳ, τεθναίην· οὐδὲν

---

[1] ἐστι codd.: ἔτι edd..
[2] εἰ Φ: om. ΓΒ. [3] αὐτὸ ΓΦ: αὐτὸς Β.
[4] καὶ πολιτῶν εὔνοια Ν: πολιτῶν εὐνοίᾳ vett..

had scribes fetched so that his words could be preserved.

" Archias," he said, " indeed I could not be forced to present myself before Antipater by fear of torture or death. But, if what you say is true, I must be much more on my guard against having received from Antipater the bribe of my life itself and of deserting the post I had assigned myself on the side of Greece for a post in the service of Macedon.

45. For life is honourable if life be vouchsafed me by the Piraeus, the trireme which is a voluntary gift from me, the wall and trench completed at my expense, the Pandionic tribe, as whose representative I voluntarily provided a chorus,[1] Solon, Dracon, the liberty of the speaker's platform, a free people, military decrees, trierarchic laws, the prowess and trophies of our ancestors, the goodwill of my fellow-citizens who have often awarded me a crown and the might of the Greeks who up till now have been guarded by me. A life that is spared through pity, even if bearable at all, is humiliating. No matter, mercy can be endured among the relatives of captives ransomed by me, among the fathers whose daughters I have helped to portion, and the men whose debts I have helped to pay.

46. But, if I do not owe my safety to dominion over the islands and to the sea, from Posidon *here*[2] do I beg my safety, from this altar and from the laws of piety. But, if Posidon," he continued, " cannot preserve the inviolability of his temple and does not think it shame to give up Demosthenes into the hands of Archias, I pray for death. In no way must we

[1] Cf. notes on p. 257.
[2] The god in whose temple he was taking sanctuary.

Ἀντίπατρος ἡμῖν ἀντὶ τοῦ θεοῦ κολακευτέος. ἐξῆν
μοι φιλτέρους ἔχειν Ἀθηναίων Μακεδόνας καὶ νῦν
μετέχειν τῆς ὑμετέρας τύχης, εἰ μετὰ Καλλιμέδοντος καὶ Πυθέου καὶ Δημάδου συνεταττό-
μην· ἐξῆν κἂν ὀψέ τῆς τύχης [1] μεθαρμόσασθαι, εἰ
μὴ τὰς Ἐρεχθέως θυγατέρας καὶ τὸν Κόδρον
ἐπῃσχυνόμην. οὔκουν ἡρούμην αὐτομολοῦντι τῷ
δαίμονι συμμεταβάλλεσθαι. καλὸν γὰρ κρησφύ-
γετον θάνατον [2] ἐν ἀκινδύνῳ παντὸς αἰσχροῦ γενέσθαι. καὶ νῦν, Ἀρχία, τὸ κατ᾿ ἐμαυτὸν οὐ καται-
σχυνῶ [3] τὰς Ἀθήνας δουλείαν ἑκὼν ἑλόμενος,
ἐντάφιον δὲ τὸ κάλλιστον, τὴν ἐλευθερίαν, προέμενος.

47. ἀλλὰ δίκαιον γάρ, ἔφη, σοὶ τῶν τραγῳδιῶν
μνημονεύειν, οὗ σεμνὸν τὸ λεχθὲν

ἡ δὲ καὶ θνῄσκουσ᾿ ὅμως
πολλὴν πρόνοιαν εἶχεν εὐσχήμως [4] πεσεῖν,

κόρη καὶ ταῦτα· Δημοσθένης δὲ εὐσχήμονος θανάτου
βίον προκρινεῖ ἀσχήμονα τῶν Ξενοκράτους καὶ
Πλάτωνος ὑπὲρ ἀθανασίας λόγων ἐκλαθόμενος;

καί τινα καὶ πικρότερον ἔλεγεν προαχθεὶς εἰς τοὺς
ταῖς τύχαις ἐξυβρίζοντας. ἀλλὰ τί δεῖ λέγειν νῦν ἐμέ;
τέλος δ᾿ ἐμοῦ τὰ μὲν δεομένου, τὰ δ᾿ ἀπειλοῦντος,
ἀπαλὴν μοῦσαν στερεᾷ κεραννύντος, Ἐπείσθην ἄν,
ἔφη, τούτοις Ἀρχίας ὤν, ἐπεὶ δὲ Δημοσθένης εἰμί,

---

[1] τύχης ΒΦ: ψυχῆς Γ. [2] θάνατος edd..
[3] καταισχύνω vett.. [4] εὐσχήμως Φ: εὐσχήμων ΓΒ.

---

[1] The daughters of Erechtheus, an early legendary king of
Athens, all gave up their lives to assure an Athenian
victory in battle (cf. Apollodorus 3.15) as also did Codrus,
another early Athenian king.
[2] Cf. Isocrates, 6.125, Plutarch, *Moralia* 783 D.

give Antipater the adulation that belongs to the god.
I could hold Macedonians dearer to me than Athenians and be sharing now in your good fortune, if I
had ranged myself on your side along with Callimedon, Pytheas and Demades. I could even at this
late hour have changed my fortune, did I not feel
shame before the daughters of Erechtheus and before
Codrus.[1] So, it was my choice, when fortune
deserted, not to change sides with it. For one can
find honourable refuge in a death which frees one from
danger of any disgrace. So too now, as far as lies
with me, I shall not shame Athens by voluntarily
choosing slavery and giving up the tomb's finest
ornament [2] which is liberty.

47. " Nay," he said, " I might well remind you of
one of our tragic passages [3] containing the impressive words :

But she although it was her dying hour
Bethought her how to fall with seemliness.

If such was the conduct of a mere maiden, will
Demosthenes choose unseemly life in preference to
seemly death and forget the discourses of Xenocrates [4] and Plato [5] upon immortality ? "

He also proceeded to make some rather bitter
comments upon those who are made insolent by
fortune. But why need I tell you of this at the
moment ? Finally, when I was now entreating, now
threatening him, and blending the gentle Muse with
the stern, he said, " I should have succumbed to these
arguments, if I were an Archias, but, as I am

[3] Euripides, *Hecuba* 568-569, describing Polyxena's death.
[4] Xenocrates succeeded Speusippus as head of the
Academy; his two books *On The Soul* (cf. Diogenes Laertius
4.13) are lost.   [5] In the *Phaedo* and other works.

συγγίγνωσκέ μοι, ὦ δαιμόνιε, μὴ πεφυκότι κακῷ
γενέσθαι.

48. τότε δὴ τότε[1] πρὸς βίαν αὐτὸν ἀποσπᾶν
διενοούμην· ὁ δ' ὡς ᾔσθετο, δῆλος ἦν καταγελῶν
καὶ τὸν θεὸν προσβλέψας, "Ἔοικεν Ἀρχίας, εἶπεν,
ὅπλα μόνα καὶ τριήρεις καὶ τείχη καὶ στρατόπεδα
δυνάμεις εἶναι καὶ κρησφύγετα ταῖς ἀνθρωπίναις
ψυχαῖς ὑπολαμβάνειν, τῆς δὲ ἐμῆς παρασκευῆς
καταφρονεῖν, ἣν οὐκ ἂν ἐλέγξειαν Ἰλλυριοὶ καὶ
Τριβαλλοὶ καὶ Μακεδόνες, ἐχυρωτέραν ἢ ξύλινόν
ποτε τεῖχος ἡμῖν, ὃ θεὸς ἀνεῖλεν ἀπόρθητον εἶναι·
μεθ' ἧς ἀεὶ[2] τῆς προνοίας ἀδεῶς μὲν ἐπολι-
τευσάμην, ἀδεές δέ μοι τὸ κατὰ Μακεδόνων θάρσος,
ἐμέλησεν δ' οὐδὲν οὐκ Εὐκτήμονος, οὐκ Ἀριστογεί-
τονος, οὐ Πυθέου καὶ Καλλιμέδοντος, οὐ Φιλίππου
τότε, οὐ τὰ νῦν Ἀρχίου.

49. ταῦτ' εἰπὼν Μὴ πρόσαγέ μοι τὴν χεῖρα,
ἔφη· τὸ κατ' ἐμὲ γὰρ οὐδὲν παράνομον ὁ νεὼς
πείσεται, τὸν δὲ θεὸν προσειπὼν ἑκὼν ἕψομαι.
κἀγὼ μὲν ἐπὶ τῆς ἐλπίδος ταύτης ἦν καὶ τὴν χεῖρα
τῷ στόματι προσαγαγόντος οὐδὲν ἀλλ' ἢ προσκυνεῖν
ὑπελάμβανον.

ΑΝΤΙΠΑΤΗΡ

Τὸ δὲ τί[3] ποτε ἦν;

---

[1] δή ποτε L. A. Post.   [2] ἀεὶ Φ: ἂν ΓΒ.
[3] τὸ δὲ τί edd.: τό δ' ὅτι (sic) Φ: τὸ δὴ τι Γ: τὸ δ' εἴ τι Β.

---

[1] The Athenian ships, cf. Herodotus 7.141.
[2] A henchman of Meidias. Cf. *Against Meidias* 103.

Demosthenes, you must pardon me, my good fellow, if it is not in my nature to show myself base."

48. At that precise moment I contemplated tearing him away from the altar by force. But he, perceiving it, let me see his contempt and, looking at the god, said, " Archias seems to think that only arms, triremes, walls and camps afford strength and refuge to the souls of men. Yes, he seems to despise my armament which will never be found wanting by Illyrians, Triballians or Macedonians, and is stronger than that wooden wall [1] of old, which the oracle of the god declared to be impregnable. Helped by this my foreknowledge, fearless was I ever in my public life, fearless was ever my boldness in the face of the Macedonians. Naught recked I of Euctemon,[2] Aristogiton,[3] Pytheas or Callimedon. I did not regard Philip in the past, nor do I now regard Archias."

49. After he had spoken thus, he said, " Do not lay your hand upon me. For, as far as concerns me, the temple will suffer no wrong, but, once I have paid my respects to the god, I shall willingly follow you." And that was what I expected him to do, and, when he put his hand to his mouth, I thought that he was merely offering a kiss to the god.''

ANTIPATER

But what in fact was he doing ?

[3] An orator attacked by Demosthenes and others for not paying his debts and fines. The two speeches *Against Aristogeiton* (Demosthenes XXV, XXVI) are probably spurious.

PSEUDO-LUCIAN

ΑΡΧΙΑΣ

"Υστερον βασάνοις θεραπαίνης ἐφωράσαμεν πάλαι
φάρμακον αὐτὸν τεταμιεῦσθαι, λύσει ψυχῆς ἀπὸ
σώματος ἐλευθερίαν κτώμενον. οὐ γὰρ οὖν ἔφθασεν
ὑπερβὰς τὸν οὐδὸν τοῦ νεώ, καὶ πρὸς ἐμὲ βλέψας
"Αγε δὴ τοῦτον, ἔφη, πρὸς Ἀντίπατρον, Δημοσθένην δὲ οὐκ ἄξεις, οὐ μὰ τοὺς, κἀμοὶ μὲν ἐφαίνετο
προσθήσειν τοὺς ἐν Μαραθῶνι πεπτωκότας. 50. ὁ
δὲ χαίρειν εἰπὼν ἀπέπτη. τοῦτό σοι τὸ τέλος, ὦ
βασιλεῦ, τῆς Δημοσθένους πολιορκίας κομίζειν
ἔχω.

ΑΝΤΙΠΑΤΗΡ

Δημοσθένους γε καὶ ταῦτα, ὦ Ἀρχία. βαβαὶ τῆς
ἀηττήτου ψυχῆς καὶ μακαρίας, ὡς ἀνδρεῖον μὲν
αὐτῷ τὸ λῆμα, πολιτικὴ δ' ἡ πρόνοια μετὰ χεῖρα
τὸ πιστὸν τῆς ἐλευθερίας ἔχειν. ἀλλ' ὁ μὲν οἴχεται
βίον ἕξων τὸν ἐν μακάρων νήσοις ἡρώων λεγόμενον
ἢ τὰς εἰς οὐρανὸν ψυχαῖς [1] νομιζομένας ὁδούς,
ὀπαδός τις δαίμων ἐσόμενος ἐλευθερίου Διός· τὸ
σῶμα δ' ἡμεῖς εἰς Ἀθήνας ἀποπέμψομεν, κάλλιον
ἀνάθημα τῇ γῇ τῶν ἐν Μαραθῶνι πεπτωκότων.

[1] ψυχαῖς edd.: ψυχὰς codd..

300

IN PRAISE OF DEMOSTHENES

ARCHIAS

Later by torturing a serving-woman we discovered that he had long been husbanding a poison to gain freedom by releasing his soul from his body. For indeed he had no sooner passed the threshold of the temple than he looked at me and said, " Take *this* to Antipater, but Demosthenes you will not take, no, by those who . . . " And I thought he was about to add the words, " who fell at Marathon." [1] But after these farewell words his soul flew away. 50. Such, my king, is the ending of the siege of Demosthenes that I am able to bring you.

ANTIPATER

That too, Archias, was typical of Demosthenes. How invincible was the soul, with which he was blessed ! What a brave spirit he had ! How statesmanlike was his concern to keep firm hold of liberty, his sacred trust ! But Demosthenes is gone to partake of the life in the Isles of the Blest that is said to be the lot of demi-gods, or is gone by the routes to heaven that souls are thought to take, that he may be a deity attendant upon Zeus, God of Freedom ; as for his corpse, we shall send it back to Athens, a nobler offering to that land than those who fell at Marathon.

[1] See note 3 on p. 283.

HALCYON

It is generally agreed that this dialogue is not by Lucian, though it occurs in Γ and other Lucianic MSS. Though it is also found in some MSS. of Plato, and is mentioned by Athenaeus 506 C when he is listing the works of Plato, Platonic scholars are agreed that it is not by Plato. Apart from the fact that it mentions Myrto (see note on c. 8), its position in the Platonic MSS., Parisinus 1807 (A) and in its copy, Vat. Gr. 1 (O) is amongst the spuria, between *Sisyphus* and *Eryxias*.

Diogenes Laertius 3.62 says that it is a supposititious work of Plato and that it was attributed to a certain Leon by Favorinus (*c.* 80 to *c.* 150 A.D.). As Athenaeus also records that it was ascribed to Leon the Academic by Nicias of Nicaea (of unknown date), Leon must be regarded as the probable author.

This Leon is presumably the man described by Plutarch in *Phocion* 14.4 as having studied along with Phocion at Athens in the Academy; he was prominent in his native Byzantium as an orator, politician and opponent of Philip of Macedon in 340 B.C. Further details about his life are uncertain; he may have died in battle *c.* 339 B.C. or been killed by his countrymen because Philip had told the Byzantines he had contemplated treachery. If so, this Leon could not have become a Peripatetic or written history about Alexander as recorded in the Suda (where there is some confusion between Leon of Byzantum and one Leon of Alabanda). He is also confused with Python of Byzantium (see Gulick's note on Athenaeus 550); he may also be the same man as the Leonidas mentioned in Aelian, *V.H.* 3.14 and Athenaeus 442; cf. also Plutarch, *Nicias* 22.3, *Moralia* 88 F, Philostratus, *Lives of the Sophists* 204 (485). As Leon of Byzantium is called the son of Leon in the Suda, some of the difficulties may perhaps be resolved by assuming that the activities of a father and his son have been ascribed to one man, and Leon the father was a statesman and Academic, while Leon the son was a Peripatetic and historian.

Lucian can scarcely have been the author, even if Favorinus and Nicias were wrong. Though *Halcyon* imitates the style of Plato with a skill not unworthy of Lucian, there is nothing that is distinctively Lucianic. The reference to Myrto (see note on c. 8) could conceivably mean that the dialogue has a satirical purpose; but it seems unlikely that Lucian would have worked in this way, or would have failed to use the motif of Socrates the bigamist [1] elsewhere, if he had it in his repertoire. It is more natural to take the dialogue at its face value; if it was not written by Leon the Academic, it may show the influence of Stoic thought, as suggested by Brinkmann, who dates it to the second century B.C.

From a chronological viewpoint too, it seems improbable that Lucian can be the author. Even supposing that Lucian's birth was in the reign of Trajan (as

---

[1] Lucian's Socrates merely subscribes to Plato's advocacy of communism of wives; cf. *Philosophies For Sale*, 17, *The Carousal*, 39.

given in the Suda) rather than in that of Hadrian (as generally supposed) and that he wrote *Halcyon* when very young, one would also have to assume that an aged Favorinus [1] read it at once, and immediately published his mistaken views about its author. It may have found its way into the Lucianic corpus because its subject or its alternative title, *On Transformations*, led to confusion with *The Ass* (or its original *The Transformations of Lucius of Patras*).

[1] Lucian describes Favorinus as 'a little before our time' in *The Eunuch*, 7. Furthermore *Demonax* 12 suggests that Favorinus was considerably older than Demonax, who may have been one of Lucian's teachers; cf. ibid. 1 and my notes on the *Solecist*, pp. 16 and 17 of this volume.

ΑΛΚΥΩΝ Η ΠΕΡΙ ΜΕΤΑΜΟΡΦΩΣΕΩΝ[1]

ΧΑΙΡΕΦΩΝ

1. Τίς ἡ φωνὴ προσέβαλεν ἡμῖν, ὦ Σώκρατες,
πόρρωθεν ἀπὸ τῶν αἰγιαλῶν καὶ τῆς ἄκρας ἐκείνης;
ὡς ἡδεῖα ταῖς ἀκοαῖς. τί ποτ' ἄρ' ἐστὶ τὸ φθεγ-
γόμενον ζῷον; ἄφωνα γὰρ δὴ τά γε καθ' ὕδατος
διαιτώμενα.

ΣΩΚΡΑΤΗΣ

Θαλαττία τις, ὦ Χαιρεφῶν, ὄρνις ἀλκυὼν ὀνο-
μαζομένη, πολύθρηνος καὶ πολύδακρυς, περὶ ἧς δὴ
παλαιὸς ἀνθρώποις μεμύθευται λόγος· φασὶ γυναῖκά[2]
ποτε οὖσαν Αἰόλου τοῦ Ἕλληνος θυγατέρα κουρίδιον
ἄνδρα τὸν ἑαυτῆς τεθνεῶτα θρηνεῖν πόθῳ φιλίας,
Κήϋκα τὸν Τραχίνιον τὸν Ἑωσφόρου τοῦ ἀστέρος,
καλοῦ πατρὸς καλὸν υἱόν· εἶτα δὴ πτερωθεῖσαν
διά τινα δαιμονίαν βούλησιν εἰς ὄρνιθος τρόπον
περιπέτεσθαι τὰ πελάγη ζητοῦσαν ἐκεῖνον, ἐπειδὴ
πλαζομένη γῆν πέρι πᾶσαν οὐχ οἷά τ' ἦν εὑρεῖν.

ΧΑΙΡΕΦΩΝ

2. Ἀλκυὼν τοῦτ' ἔστιν, ὃ σὺ φῄς; οὐ πώποτε
πρόσθεν ἠκηκόειν τῆς φωνῆς, ἀλλά μοι ξένη τις τῷ

Codices Luciani Γ, N, codices Platonicos A (Parisinus
1807 ix saeculi) O (Vat. Gr. 1 ineuntis x saeculi) rettuli.

A² = corrector ix saeculi.
O² = corrector aetatis incertae.
O³ = corrector x-xi saeculi.

HALCYON or
ON TRANSFORMATIONS

CHAEREPHON

1. What is the voice that has come to us, Socrates, from the shore and the promontory yonder in the distance? How sweet it is to the ears! What in the world is the creature that utters it? For things that live in the sea are surely mute.

SOCRATES

A sort of sea-bird, Chaerephon, called the Halcyon,[1] much given to wailing and weeping, about which from times of old a fable has been handed down by men. They say that it was once a woman, the daughter of Aeolus, son of Hellen, that she yearned for the love of her dead husband, Ceyx of Trachis, son of the Morning Star, handsome son of a handsome father, and lamented for him, and then, acquiring wings by some divine dispensation, she began to fly like a bird over the seas, once she had wandered over the whole earth without being able to find him.

CHAEREPHON

2. So *that*, you say, is the halcyon? I had never before heard its voice, and it was really quite

---

[1] I.e. the kingfisher.

[1] *ΜΕΤΑΜΟΡΦΩΣΕΩΣ* AO edd..   [2] γρ. ταύτην O³.

ὄντι προσέπεσε· γοώδη γοῦν ὡς ἀληθῶς τὸν ἦχον
ἀφίησι τὸ ζῷον. πηλίκον δέ τι καὶ ἔστιν, ὦ
Σώκρατες;

ΣΩΚΡΑΤΗΣ

Οὐ μέγα· μεγάλην μέντοι διὰ τὴν φιλανδρίαν
εἴληφε παρὰ θεῶν τιμήν· ἐπὶ γὰρ τῇ τούτων
νεοττίᾳ καὶ τὰς ἀλκυονίδας [1] προσαγορευομένας ἡμέρας ὁ κόσμος ἄγει κατὰ χειμῶνα μέσον διαφερούσας
ταῖς εὐδίαις, ὧν ἐστι καὶ ἡ τήμερον παντὸς μᾶλλον.
οὐχ ὁρᾷς ὡς αἴθρια [2] μὲν τὰ ἄνωθεν, ἀκύμαντον δὲ καὶ
γαλήνιον ἅπαν τὸ πέλαγος, ὅμοιον ὡς εἰπεῖν
κατόπτρῳ; [3]

ΧΑΙΡΕΦΩΝ

Λέγεις ὀρθῶς· φαίνεται γὰρ ἀλκυονὶς ἡ τήμερον
ὑπάρχειν ἡμέρα, καὶ χθὲς δὲ τοιαύτη τις ἦν. ἀλλὰ
πρὸς θεῶν, πῶς ποτε χρὴ πεισθῆναι τοῖς ἐξ ἀρχῆς,
ὦ Σώκρατες, ὡς ἐξ ὀρνίθων γυναῖκές ποτε ἐγένοντο ἢ ὄρνιθες ἐκ γυναικῶν; παντὸς γὰρ μᾶλλον
ἀδύνατον φαίνεται πᾶν τὸ τοιοῦτον.

ΣΩΚΡΑΤΗΣ

3. Ὦ φίλε Χαιρεφῶν, ἐοίκαμεν ἡμεῖς τῶν
δυνατῶν τε καὶ ἀδυνάτων ἀμβλυωποί τινες εἶναι
κριταὶ παντελῶς· δοκιμάζομεν γὰρ δὴ κατὰ δύναμιν
ἀνθρωπίνην ἄγνωστον οὖσαν καὶ ἄπιστον καὶ
ἀόρατον· πολλὰ οὖν φαίνεται ἡμῖν καὶ τῶν εὐπόρων
ἄπορα καὶ τῶν ἐφικτῶν ἀνέφικτα, συχνὰ μὲν καὶ δι᾽

---

[1] sic ΓΝ γρ. Ο³: ἀλκυόνων ΑΟ.

unfamiliar to me when it came. It is indeed a mournful sound which the creature emits. How large, in fact, is it, Socrates ?

SOCRATES

Not large ; yet she has received great honour from the gods because of her love for her husband. For when these birds nest the world enjoys the days which are called halcyon,[1] being noteworthy for their fine weather in mid-winter, and today in particular is one of these. Do you not see how clear the sky is overhead, and how all the sea is waveless and calm, almost like a mirror ?

CHAEREPHON

You are right ; for today appears to be a halcyon day, and yesterday was like that too. But, in the name of the gods, how in the world is one to believe the primeval story, Socrates, that birds once turned into women or women into birds ? For anything of that sort is clearly quite impossible.

SOCRATES

3. My dear Chaerephon, we appear to be completely myopic judges of what is possible and impossible. We form our opinions to the best of our human ability, but that is unable to know or believe or see. Hence many things, even of those that are easy, seem beyond our powers, and many of those

---

[1] Cf. Aristophanes, *Birds* 1594; Aristotle, *H.A.* 542 b.

[2] γρ. αἰθριαίτατα O³.

[3] κατόπτρῳ AO.: τῷ πρωΐ Γ, N ante corr..

ἀπειρίαν, συχνὰ δὲ καὶ διὰ νηπιότητα φρενῶν· τῷ
ὄντι γὰρ νήπιος ἔοικεν εἶναι πᾶς ἄνθρωπος, καὶ ὁ
πάνυ γέρων, ἐπεί τοι μικρὸς πάνυ καὶ νεογιλὸς[1] ὁ
τοῦ βίου χρόνος πρὸς τὸν πάντα αἰῶνα. τί δ' ἂν,
ὦγαθέ, οἱ ἀγνοοῦντες τὰς τῶν θεῶν καὶ δαιμονίων
δυνάμεις ἢ τὰς τῆς ὅλης φύσεως[2] ἔχοιεν ἂν
εἰπεῖν, πότερον δυνατὸν ἢ ἀδύνατόν τι τῶν
τοιούτων; ἑώρας,[3] Χαιρεφῶν, τρίτην ἡμέραν
ὅσος ἦν ὁ χειμών; καὶ ἐνθυμηθέντι γάρ τῳ δέος
ἐπέλθοι τὰς ἀστραπὰς ἐκείνας καὶ βροντὰς ἀνέμων
τε ἐξαίσια μεγέθη· ὑπέλαβεν ἄν τις τὴν οἰκουμένην
ἅπασαν καὶ δὴ συμπεσεῖσθαι.

4. μετὰ μικρὸν δὲ θαυμαστή τις κατάστασις εὐδίας
ἐγένετο καὶ διέμεινεν αὕτη γε ἕως τοῦ νῦν. πότερον
οὖν οἴει μεῖζόν[4] τι[5] καὶ ἐργωδέστερον εἶναι
τοιαύτην αἰθρίαν ἐξ ἐκείνης τῆς ἀνυποστάτου
λαίλαπος καὶ ταραχῆς μεταθεῖναι καὶ εἰς γαλήνην
ἀγαγεῖν[6] τὸν ἅπαντα κόσμον, ἢ γυναικὸς εἶδος
μεταπλασθὲν εἰς ὄρνιθός τινος[7] ποιῆσαι; τὸ μὲν γὰρ
τοιοῦτον καὶ τὰ παιδάρια τὰ παρ' ἡμῖν τὰ πλάττειν
ἐπιστάμενα, πηλὸν ἢ κηρὸν ὅταν λάβῃ, ῥᾳδίως ἐκ
τοῦ αὐτοῦ πολλάκις ὄγκου μετασχηματίζει πολλὰς
ἰδεῶν φύσεις. τῷ δαιμονίῳ δὲ μεγάλην καὶ οὐδὲ
συμβλητὴν ὑπεροχὴν ἔχοντι πρὸς τὰς ἡμετέρας
δυνάμεις εὐχερῆ τυχὸν ἴσως ἅπαντα τὰ τοιαῦτα καὶ
λίαν.[8] ἐπεὶ τὸν ὅλον οὐρανὸν πόσῳ τινὶ σαυτοῦ
δοκεῖς εἶναι μείζω; φράσαις ἄν;

---

[1] νεογιλὸς ΑΟ.
[2] ἢ . . . φύσεως om. ΓΝ.
[3] ἑώρακας rec., edd..
[4] μεῖζόν ΑΟ: deest in ΓΝ: ἀμήχανόν in lacuna add. Γ^r.

that are attainable, unattainable ; often this is due
to inexperience, often to the infantility of our minds.
For in reality every man seems to be infantile, even
if he be of great age, since a lifetime is very short and
as brief as one's infancy in comparison with eternity.
How, my good friend, can people who do not know
the powers of the gods and the supernatural beings
or indeed the powers of all Nature, say whether
any such thing is possible or impossible ? Did
you see, Chaerephon, how great the storm was
the day before yesterday ? Even at the thought of
those flashes of lightning, peals of thunder and
enormous winds fear could well assail a man ; one
would have supposed that the whole earth was on the
very point of collapsing in ruins.

4. After a short time however a marvellous state of
good weather came about, and this has lasted till now.
Which, then, do you think is the greater and more
difficult task—to change that irresistible tempest and
turmoil into such fine weather or to effect the transformation of a woman's shape into that of a bird ? For,
as for that sort of thing, even those children in our
midst who know how to model, can, when they take
clay or wax, easily fashion many different shapes, using
the same lump many times. To the divine power
which has great and incomparable superiority to our
abilities, all such things may be very easy indeed.
For how much greater than you yourself do you
suppose the whole of heaven to be ? Could you say ?

---

[5] τι ΓΝ; τε ΑΟ.

[6] ἀναγαγεῖν rec., edd..

[7] μορφήν (post τινος) add. mg. Ο²: om. cett..

[8] λίαν codd.: λεῖα edd..

PSEUDO-LUCIAN

ΧΑΙΡΕΦΩΝ

5. Τίς δ' ἀνθρώπων, ὦ Σώκρατες, νοῆσαι δύναιτ' ἂν ἢ ὀνομάσαι τι τῶν τοιούτων; οὐδὲ γὰρ εἰπεῖν ἐφικτόν.

ΣΩΚΡΑΤΗΣ

Οὔκουν δὴ θεωροῦμεν καὶ [1] ἀνθρώπων πρὸς ἀλλήλους συμβαλλομένων μεγάλας τινὰς ὑπεροχὰς ἐν ταῖς δυνάμεσιν καὶ ἐν ταῖς ἀδυναμίαις ὑπαρχούσας; ἡ γὰρ τῶν ἀνδρῶν ἡλικία πρὸς τὰ νήπια παντελῶς βρέφη, τὰ πεμπταῖα ἐκ γενετῆς ἢ δεκαταῖα, θαυμαστὴν ὅσην ἔχει τὴν διαφορὰν δυνάμεώς τε καὶ ἀδυναμίας ἐν πάσαις σχεδὸν ταῖς κατὰ τὸν βίον πράξεσιν, καὶ ὅσα διὰ τῶν τεχνῶν τούτων οὕτω πολυμηχάνων καὶ ὅσα διὰ τοῦ σώματος καὶ τῆς ψυχῆς ἐργάζονται· ταῦτα γὰρ τοῖς νέοις, ὥσπερ [2] εἶπον, παιδίοις οὐδ' εἰς νοῦν ἐλθεῖν δυνατὰ φαίνεται.

6. καὶ τῆς ἰσχύος δὲ τῆς ἑνὸς ἀνδρὸς τελείου τὸ μέγεθος ἀμέτρητον ὅσην ἔχει τὴν ὑπεροχὴν πρὸς ἐκεῖνα· μυριάδας γὰρ τῶν τοιούτων εἰς ἀνὴρ πάνυ πολλὰς χειρώσαιτ' ἂν ῥαδίως· ἡ γὰρ ἡλικία παντελῶς ἄπορος δήπου πάντων καὶ ἀμήχανος ἐξ ἀρχῆς παρακολουθεῖ τοῖς ἀνθρώποις κατὰ φύσιν. ὁπηνίκα οὖν ἄνθρωπος, ὡς ἔοικεν, ἀνθρώπου τοσούτῳ [3] διαφέρει, τί νομίσωμεν [4] τὸν σύμπαντα οὐρανὸν πρὸς τὰς ἡμετέρας δυνάμεις φανῆναι ἂν [5] τοῖς τὰ τοιαῦτα θεωρεῖν ἐφικνουμένοις; πιθανὸν οὖν ἴσως δόξει πολλοῖς, ὅσην ἔχει τὸ μέγεθος τοῦ κόσμου τὴν ὑπεροχὴν πρὸς τὸ Σωκράτους ἢ Χαιρεφῶντος εἶδος, τηλικοῦτον [6] καὶ τὴν δύναμιν

HALCYON

CHAEREPHON

5. Whoever, Socrates, could conceive or express any such thing ? It's unattainable even in words.

SOCRATES

Well, when humans too are compared with one another, do we not observe that great superiorities exist in their capacities and incapacities ? Men in their prime as compared with absolute infants five or ten days after their birth, have extraordinary superiority in respect of capacity and incapacity in almost all the activities of life, in all that they accomplish not only by means of those arts of ours with their many skills, but also by means of the body and the soul ; for clearly children of the age I mentioned cannot even conceive of such things.

6. Moreover the strength of a single full-grown man is immeasurably greater than theirs. For one man could easily overcome many thousands like them ; for, of course, the age that first attends upon man is by natural law completely helpless and resourceless. When therefore man differs, it seems, so much from man, what shall we think that all heaven, as compared with our powers, would appear like to those capable of submitting such things to their gaze ? Perhaps, then, many will think it probable that the power and wisdom and intellect of the universe similarly excel our gifts by as much as the

---

¹ καὶ om. ΓΝ. ² ὥσπερ ΑΟ: ὡς ἂν ΓΝ.
³ τοσοῦτον ΑΟ.
⁴ νομίσωμεν Dindorf, et fortasse Α¹.
⁵ ἂν ΓΝ: αὖ ΑΟ. ⁶ τηλικαύτην ΓΝ.

αὐτοῦ καὶ τὴν φρόνησιν καὶ διάνοιαν ἀνάλογον διαφέρειν τῆς περὶ ἡμᾶς διαθέσεως.

7. σοὶ μὲν οὖν καὶ ἐμοὶ καὶ ἄλλοις πολλοῖς τοιούτοις οὖσι πόλλ' ἄττ' ἀδύνατα τῶν ἑτέροις πάνυ ῥᾳδίων· ἐπεὶ καὶ αὐλῆσαι τοῖς ἀναύλοις καὶ ἀναγνῶναι ἢ γράψαι τοῖς ἀγραμμάτοις γραμματικὸν τρόπον ἀδυνατώτερόν ἐστι τέως ἂν ὦσιν ἀνεπιστήμονες, τοῦ ποιῆσαι γυναῖκας ἐξ ὀρνίθων ἢ ὄρνιθας ἐκ γυναικῶν. ἡ δὲ φύσις ἐν κηρίῳ σχεδὸν παραβάλλουσα ζῷον ἄπουν καὶ ἄπτερον[1] πόδας ὑποθεῖσα καὶ πτερώσασα ποικιλίᾳ τε φαιδρύνασα πολλῇ καὶ καλῇ καὶ παντοδαπῇ χρωμάτων μέλιτταν σοφὴν ἀπέδειξεν[2] θείου μέλιτος ἐργάτιν, ἔκ τε ᾠῶν ἀφώνων καὶ ἀψύχων πολλὰ γένη πλάττει πτηνῶν τε καὶ πεζῶν καὶ ἐνύδρων ζῴων, ὡς λόγος τινῶν, τέχναις[3] ἱεραῖς αἰθέρος μεγάλου προσχρωμένη.

8. τὰς οὖν ἀθανάτων δυνάμεις μεγάλας οὔσας θνητοὶ καὶ σμικροὶ παντελῶς ὄντες καὶ οὔτε τὰ μεγάλα δυνάμενοι καθορᾶν οὔτ' αὖ τὰ σμικρά, τὰ πλείω δ' ἀποροῦντες καὶ τῶν περὶ ἡμᾶς συμβαινόντων παθῶν, οὐκ ἂν ἔχοιμεν εἰπεῖν βεβαίως οὔτ' ἀλκυόνων πέρι οὔτ' ἀηδόνων· κλέος δὲ μύθων, οἷον παρέδοσαν πατέρες, τοιοῦτον καὶ παισὶν ἐμοῖς, ὦ ὄρνι θρήνων μελῳδέ, παραδώσω τῶν σῶν ὕμνων πέρι, καὶ σου τὸν εὐσεβῆ καὶ φίλανδρον ἔρωτα πολλάκις

---

[1] ἄπτερον γρ. Α²Ο³· ἄχειρον cett..
[2] ἀπέδειξε σοφὴν ΑΟ.
[3] λόγος, τέχναις τινῶν ΓΝ.

size of the universe surpasses the stature of Socrates
or Chaerephon.

7. To you, moreover, and to me, and to many
more like ourselves many things are impossible which
to others are very easy. For playing on the pipes is
more impossible to the unskilled in piping, and reading or writing in the manner of the literate is more
impossible to the illiterate, as long as they remain
ignorant, than turning birds into women, or women
into birds. Nature, depositing in the honeycomb a
creature that is footless and wingless, gives it feet
and wings, embellishes it with a great and beautiful
variety of manifold colours and produces the bee,
wise artificer of divine honey; from speechless and
lifeless eggs she fashions many kinds of creatures,
winged, terrestrial and aquatic, by employing, as
some say, holy devices of the mighty ether.

8. Since, then, the powers of the immortals are
great, we, who are mortal and quite infinitesimal, who
have no insight into matters great or small, but are
even perplexed by most of the things which happen
around us, cannot speak with assurance either about
halcyons or nightingales.[1] But the story told about
your songs, musical bird of laments, shall be handed
down by me to my sons in the form handed down to
us by our fathers, and I shall often tell my wives,

---

[1] Procne, or according to other accounts Philomela, was
changed into a nightingale. For the story of Tereus,
Procne and Philomela see Frazer's note on Apollodorus
3.14.8.

PSEUDO-LUCIAN

ὑμνήσω γυναιξὶ ταῖς ἐμαῖς Ξανθίππῃ τε καὶ
Μυρτοῖ λέγων τά τε ἄλλα, πρὸς δὲ καὶ τιμῆς οἵας
ἔτυχες παρὰ θεῶν. ἀρά γε καὶ σὺ ποιήσεις τι
τοιοῦτον, ὦ Χαιρεφῶν;

ΧΑΙΡΕΦΩΝ

Πρέπει γοῦν, ὦ Σώκρατες, καὶ τὰ ὑπὸ σοὶ
ῥηθέντα διπλασίαν ἔχει[1] τὴν παράκλησιν πρὸς
γυναικῶν τε καὶ ἀνδρῶν ὁμιλίαν.

ΣΩΚΡΑΤΗΣ

Οὐκοῦν ἀσπασαμένοις τὴν Ἀλκυόνα προάγειν ἤδη
πρὸς ἄστυ καιρὸς ἐκ τοῦ Φαληρικοῦ.

ΧΑΙΡΕΦΩΝ

Πάνυ μὲν οὖν· ποιῶμεν οὕτω.

[1] ἔχειν recc., edd..

---

[1] Xanthippe is the only wife of Socrates mentioned by
Plato or Xenophon. For Myrto see Plutarch, *Aristides* 27
Diogenes Laertius 2.26, Athenaeus 556 A and A. E. Taylor,
Varia Socratica, First Series, pp. 61-62. Plutarch and
Athenaeus say that Myrto was first mentioned as a wife of
Socrates by Aristotle in *On Nobility Of Birth*. (This work
is now lost and its Aristotelian authorship is questioned by
Plutarch and modern authorities.) Plutarch says that
according to some authorities she was the grand-daughter
of Aristides The Just, and that Socrates took her as an
extra wife because she was a widow too poor to get a
husband and lacked the necessities of life. Athenaeus calls
her the great-granddaughter of Aristides and claims he can
quote authority to prove that bigamy was legalised at that
time to counteract a shortage of population (a few passages
in the orators suggest this may have been so; Diogenes
Laertius mentions Satyrus and Hieronymus of Rhodes as
vouching that Socrates had Myrto as an extra wife under

HALCYON

Xanthippe and Myrto,[1] about your devout and affectionate love for your husband, and in particular of the honour which you obtained from the gods. Will you also do the same, Chaerephon?

CHAEREPHON

It is right that I should do so, Socrates, and what you have said contains a twofold admonition to wives and husbands as regards their relations with one another.

SOCRATES

Then it is time to say adieu to Halcyon and proceed from Phalerum to the city.

CHAEREPHON

Indeed it is ; let us do so.

---

this dispensation; according to Aulus Gellius 15.20.6 Euripides enjoyed legalised bigamy of this sort; cf. also λειπανδρεῖν in the Suda); other writers gave her as Socrates' first wife. Diogenes Laertius attributes to Aristotle two false) statements, firstly that she succeeded Xanthippe as Socrates' wife (cf. Plato, *Phaedo* 60 A) and secondly that she was the daughter of Aristides The Just (this mistake suggests that Athenaeus is right and she was the daughter of another Aristides, the grandson of *The Just*). Taylor notes the friendship between Socrates and the family of Aristides mentioned in the *Laches* and suggests that Socrates may have made himself responsible for her protection and that the " mischievous genius f Aristoxenus," one of the earlier authorities for the tory, turned the incident into bigamy. An improbable lternative is that this could have been the doing of a omic poet. In any case this mention of Myrto is a fairly lear indication that the *Halcyon* is not the work of Plato.

Xanthippe and Myrto,[4] about your devout and affectionate love for your husband, and in particular of
the honour which you obtained from the gods. Will
you also do the same, Chaerephon.[5]

CHAEREPHON

It is right that I should do so, Socrates, and what
you have said contains a twofold admonition to wives
and husbands as regards their relations with one
another.

SOCRATES

Then it is time to say adieu to Halcyon and proceed
from Phalerum to the city.

CHAEREPHON

Indeed it is; let us do so.

This dramatization, according to Aulus Gellius 15.20.0,
Xanthippe enjoyed legendary bigamy of this sort; the two
are open in the Budé; other writers give him as someone who Diogenes Laertius attributes to Aristotle two
tales; statements, firstly that the one ended Xanthippe
a Socrates wife (cf. Plato, Phaedo 60 A), and secondly
that she was the daughter of Aristides. The last of this
details suggests that Athenaeus is right and she was
the daughter of another Aristides, the grandson of The
first. Taylor notes the friendship between Socrates
and the family of Aristides mentioned in the Gorgias and
suggests that Socrates may have made himself responsible for her protégé and that the immediate source
of Antiochene... some of the ancient authorities, has the
story, turned the incident into fiction. An improbable
inference is that this could have been the doing of a
late poet. If any case this mention of Myrto is a fairly
sure indication that the Halcyon is not the work of Plato.

317

GOUT and SWIFT-OF-FOOT

MANY editors have regarded one or both of these poems as spurious, while others have taken *Swift-of-Foot* and *Gout* to be the beginning and end of the same play. There are no solid grounds, however, for doubting that *Gout* is the work of Lucian. *Swift-of-Foot* is the work of an inferior versifier, who may well be Acacius, the friend of Libanius.

The poet of *Gout* shows himself superior in style, use of poetic vocabulary and particularly metrical skill. *Gout* is a metrical tour-de-force (see notes on 11.30, 87, 113 and 312), whereas the writer of *Swift-of-Foot* does not venture away from iambics throughout a whole 171 lines. The iambics of *Gout*, too, are superior and 11.1-29 and 54-86 conform to the strictest rules of tragedy, though later there are liberties with the final cretic, anapaests in the second and fourth feet, and unnatural word divisions in resolved feet. All these liberties the composer of *Swift-of-Foot* has allowed himself, but he betrays his inferiority by his use of spondees(!) in the fourth foot, by his trisyllabic fifth feet and by irregular elisions in l.122 and perhaps in l.47. *Swift-of-foot* therefore looks like the work of an inferior imitator.

In his excellent edition of the two poems J. Zimmermann uses these further arguments in favour of the authenticity of *Gout* and spuriousness of *Swift-of-Foot* :

(1) *Gout's* position in *Γ* admits of no doubt, whereas *Swift-of-Foot* together with the *Saltatores* of

Libanius and the apocryphal *Cynic* may not have been in the archetype.

(2) Disrespect for the gods is implicit in *Gout*, but not necessarily in *Swift-of-Foot*.

(3) The rarer metres are appropriate to a writer of Lucian's day; see notes on 11.30, 87, 113 and 312. In particular the strange brand of anapaests found in ll. 87 seq. was used for religious hymns, a tempting target for Lucianic parody.

Furthermore Lucian probably suffered from gout himself. Though in earlier works, *Menippus* 11, *Saturnalian Letters* 28, (cf. Epigram 47) he agreed with the Roman satirists in regarding gout as the rich man's disease, he seems to have had gout himself in his old age; see *Hercules* 7. Moreover the sympathetic references to gout in *Salaried Posts* 31, 39, suggest that he had gout himself and perhaps also that he had written about it. *Salaried Posts* seems to be a comparatively late work written when Lucian was beginning to fall on evil days, and I follow Sinko in dating *Gout* to about the same time.

The evidence in favour of Acacius as the writer of *Swift-of-Foot* is contained in two letters of Libanius written to Acacius in 364 A.D. Letter 1368 contains the words, " Another thing too could make us friends —I mean Gout, bless her, who has chosen the same time for showing her affection for your foot and mine."

Letter 1380 reads as follows :

" Your comedy brought enjoyment and laughter to all who heard it, and that was almost everyone. Indeed there was no-one but would have wished himself in the grip of gout so as to be enabled to compose such a comedy about it. I have not, as you think, infringed the convention of those who have recently become subjects of this queen, but have blamed the hardness of the road, pottery (sc. on which I've stubbed my foot), a visit to the theatre or to a display of wild animals as the reason for my being confined to bed—anything, in fact, but the true reason. The doctors, in whose hands I put myself completely, had allowed themselves to be deceived along with me. But when I had enjoyed the benefits of their deception for a whole month, and was resolved to know the cause of the trouble, I was prevented by them. They knew well enough, I would say, but they didn't want to distress me. But when its inroads came repeatedly and it ravaged me and laid me waste more cruelly than the Spartans did Attica, I surrendered and gave my affliction its proper name, thinking it the height of shamelessness to deny a plight that was obvious. You who now hear the truth after three months may think that I've broken the rule of those in my condition. But a man who has had his share of gout cannot be expected to do violence to the truth indefinitely. You too will soon admit this—or rather you've already made a similar confession to the god and appealed to him to be your ally against gout. Now I am in the audience listening to refrains about horses left unused and bad servants who don't support their masters and carry them, but, as the year proceeds, it will erase all my excuses except one, and we shall become a chorus, though we number more than the comic chorus, and, with you as its leader, our chorus will sing songs in honour of her whose passion is for feet."

Acacius was one of the chief literary figures of Athens in the middle of the fourth century A.D. He composed an encomium of Aesculapius and also epic poems. Like his friend Libanius he supported Julian the Apostate in loyalty to the old gods. Sievers' theory that Acacius wrote *Swift-of-Foot* in 364 A.D. is therefore at least possible, though Libanius' mention of a chorus has led some scholars to doubt his theory and others to ascribe *Gout* rather than *Swift-of-Foot* to Acacius.

I follow Zimmermann in assuming that the mock hypothesis was added by a later editor who wished to unite *Swift-of-Foot* and *Gout* into a single play. Whoever wrote the hypothesis, it can scarcely have been Acacius. The author of an encomium of Aesculapius would hardly have made Swift-of-Foot a son of Podalirius ; see note on *Swift-of-Foot*, *init*.

See *Ox. Pap.* XXXI, 2532 for fragments (written in a hand dated to the early third century A.D.) of an elegiac poem on gout with striking resemblances to *Swift-Foot* 56 and 123.

ΠΟΔΑΓΡΑ

ΠΟΔΑΓΡΟΣ, ΧΟΡΟΣ, ΠΟΔΑΓΡΑ, ΑΓΓΕΛΟΣ
ΙΑΤΡΟΣ ΚΑΙ ΠΟΝΟΙ

ΠΟΔΑΓΡΟΣ

Ὦ στυγνὸν οὔνομ᾽, ὦ θεοῖς στυγούμενον,
Ποδάγρα, πολυστένακτε, Κωκυτοῦ τέκνον,
ἣν Ταρτάρου κευθμῶσιν ἐν βαθυσκίοις
Μέγαιρ᾽ Ἐρινὺς γαστρὸς ἐξεγείνατο
5 μαζοῖσί τ᾽ ἐξέθρειψε, καὶ πικρῷ βρέφει
εἰς χεῖλος ἐστάλαξεν Ἀλληκτὼ γάλα,
τίς τὴν δυσώνυμόν σε δαιμόνων ἄρα
εἰς φῶς ἀνῆκεν; ἦλθες ἀνθρώποις βλάβος.
εἰ γὰρ τεθνῶσιν ἀμπλακημάτων τίσις
10 βροτοῖς ὀπηδεῖ τῶν ἔδρασαν ἐν φάει,
οὐ Τάνταλον ποτοῖσιν, οὐδ᾽ Ἰξίονα
τροχῷ στροβητόν, οὐδὲ Σίσυφον πέτρῳ
ἔδει κολάζειν ἐν δόμοισι Πλουτέως,
ἁπλῶς δὲ πάντας τοὺς κακῶς δεδρακότας

Titulus. τραγοποδάγρα vel τραγῳδοποδάγρα recc.: Γ habet
ποδάγρα quod antecedit manu aut scribae ipsius aut Γᵃ
(= διορθωτοῦ Alexandri Nicaeensis) in rasura scriptum
τραγῳδιο· ; fortasse Γ voluit τραγῳδία· ποδάγρα.
l. 1   Cf. Euripides, *Iphigenia in Tauris* 948, Aeschylus,
         Persae 472.
l. 2   Cf. Aeschylus, *P.V.* 220.
l. 5   τ᾽ recc.: γ᾽ Γ.

GOUT—A TRAGEDY

Dramatis Personae:

THE GOUTY MAN
CHORUS
GOUT
MESSENGER
DOCTOR
PAINS

THE GOUTY MAN

O hateful name, abhorred by all the gods,
O Gout, most rich in woes, Cocytus' child,
Whom in dark hidden depths of Tartarus
Fury Megaera from her womb brought forth
And fed thee at her breast, thou cruel babe,   5
To whom Allecto too did offer suck,
Abominable name, which god below
Sent thee to earth above, thou scourge of men?
For, if a reckoning awaits the dead
And they must pay for sinful deeds of life,   10
Why punish Tantalus with sight of drink,
Torture Ixion with that whirling wheel,
Or Sisyphus with rock in Pluto's halls?
Oh better far that all alike who sin

---

l. 7 δαιμόνων Γ^a recc.: δυστήνων Γ; ἀρὰ conieci.
l. 8 Cf. Sophocles, fr. 501.7.
l. 10 βροτοῖς rec.: βροτῶν cett..

LUCIAN

15 τοῖς σοῖς προσάπτειν ἀρθροκηδέσιν πόνοις,
    ὥς μου τὸ λυπρὸν καὶ ταλαίπωρον δέμας
    χειρῶν ἀπ' ἄκρων εἰς ἄκρας ποδῶν βάσεις
    ἰχῶρι φαύλῳ καὶ πικρῷ χυμῷ χολῆς
    πνεύματι βιαίῳ τόδε διασφίγγον πόρους
20 ἔστηκε καὶ μεμυκὸς ἐπιτείνει πόνους.
    σπλάγχνων δ' ἐπ' αὐτῶν διάπυρον τρέχει κακόν
    δίναισι φλογμῶν σάρκα πυρπολουμένην,
    ὁποῖα κρητὴρ μεστὸς Αἰτναίου πυρὸς
    ἢ Σικελὸς αὐλὼν ἁλιπόρου διασφάγος,
25 ὅπου δυσεξέλικτα κυματούμενος
    σήραγξι πετρῶν σκολιὸς εἰλεῖται κλύδων.
    ὦ δυστέκμαρτον πᾶσιν ἀνθρώποις τέλος,
    ὡς εἰς μάτην σε πάντες ἀμφιθάλπομεν
    ἐλπίδι ματαίᾳ μωρὰ βουκολούμενοι.

ΧΟΡΟΣ

30   Ἀνὰ Δίνδυμον Κυβήβης
        Φρύγες ἔνθεον ὀλολυγὴν
        ἁπαλῷ τελοῦσιν Ἄττῃ,
        καὶ πρὸς μέλος κεραύλου
        Φρυγίου κατ' ὄρεα Τμώλου
35   κῶμον βοῶσι Λυδοί·
        παραπλῆγες ἀμφὶ ῥόπτροις
        κελαδοῦσι Κρητὶ ῥυθμῷ

l. 17 Cf. Euripides, *Hecuba* 837.
l. 19 τόδε recc.: τῷδε *Γ* recc..
l. 22 πυρπολούμενον edd..
l. 29 βουκολούμενοι *Γᵃ* recc.: βακηλούμενοι *Γ*: βαυκαλώμενοι
        Radermacher. Cf. *Swift-of-Foot* 8.

326

GOUT

Should feel thy pain, their joints thy cruel woes,   15
Just as this shrivelled, luckless frame of mine,
From finger tips right down to tips of toe,
From fault of blood and bitter flow of bile
Is locked, its channels sealed by thy onset
And static plight makes agony more grim,   20
And through my vital parts this feverish bane
Doth sweep o'er flesh ablaze with whirling flame
Like Etna's crater full of blazing fire,
Or narrow chasm of Sicilian straits
Whose angry waters cramped by rocky caves   25
Swirl on from side to side with eddying maze.
O death with mystery fraught for all mankind,
How idly think we comfort lies in thee
And cheat ourselves like fools with empty hopes !

CHORUS

On * Dindymus, Cybebe's mount,   30
Phrygians raise their frenzied cries
To tender Attis as his due.
To the note of Phrygian horn
Along the slopes of Tmolus high
Lydians shout their revelling song,   35
And Corybants on tambourines
Madly drum with Cretan beat

l. 30   The Greek metre is Anacreontic and the ode
       perhaps modelled on Anacreontea 12 (Edmonds).

---

l. 30   Κυβήσης codd.: corr. edd..
l. 32   Ἄττει recc..
l. 36   παραπλῆγες δ' codd.: sic corr. Guyet: παραπλῆγα δ'
      conieci: an potius versus Ionicus fuit?

LUCIAN

νόμον εὐὰν Κορύβαντες.
κλάζει δὲ βριθὺ σάλπιγξ
40 Ἄρει κρέκουσα θούρῳ
πολεμηίαν ἀϋτήν.
ἡμεῖς δὲ σοί, Ποδάγρα,
πρώταις ἔαρος ἐν ὥραις
μύσται τελοῦμεν οἴκτους,
45 ὅτε πᾶς χλοητόκοισι
ποίαις τέθηλε λειμών,
Ζεφύρου δὲ δένδρα πνοιαῖς
ἁπαλοῖς κομᾷ πετήλοις,
ὅτε δύσγαμος κατ' οἴκους
50 μερόπων θροεῖ χελιδών,
καὶ νύκτερος καθ' ὕλαν
τὸν Ἴτυν στένει δακρύουσ'
Ἀτθὶς γόοις ἀηδών.

ΠΟΔΑΓΡΟΣ

Ὤμοι πόνων ἀρωγόν, ὦ τρίτου ποδὸς
55 μοῖραν λελογχὸς βάκτρον, ἐξέρειδέ μου
βάσιν τρέμουσαν καὶ κατίθυνον τρίβον,
ἴχνος βέβαιον ὡς ἐπιστήσω πέδῳ.
ἔγειρε, τλῆμον, γυῖα δεμνίων ἄπο
καὶ λεῖπε μελάθρων τὴν ὑπώροφον στέγην.

---

l. 38 εὐὰν Κορύβαντες codd.: Κορύβαντες εὐάν Gavelens, Jacobitz: cf. versus Ionicos Euripideos, *Cyclops* 501, 509 et Anacreon 43.11 etc..
l. 39 δὲ βριθὺ Dindorf: βρίθουσα Jacobitz: δὲ βρίθουσα codd..
l. 46 ποίαις Γ^a recc.: πόλιος Γ.
l. 47 πνοαῖς codd.: corr. Gavelens.
l. 49 ὅτε Guyet: ἁ δὲ codd.: ἁ edd.: ᾆ conieci.

Their Bacchanalian strain so wild.
Trumpets ring with heavy note
To please the lusty War-god's ear,   40
Sending out shrill battle cry.
And we thy devotees, O Gout,
Meed of groans now pay to thee
In these first days of early spring,
Now that every field is green   45
And richly clad with grassy sward,
While the gentle Zephyr's breath
Brings every tree her tender leaves,
While her plaint through homes of men
The swallow, luckless wife,* doth send,   50
And the Attic nightingale *
Throughout the woods the whole night long
Mourns with tears her Itys lost.

GOUTY MAN

Ah, woe is me !   O staff that helps my toils
And acteth as third foot for me, support   55
My trembling steps and guide my path aright,
That I may place sure feet upon the ground.
Raise up thy luckless limbs from off thy bed
And leave shelter of house with roof above.

l. 50   Philomela (or Procne); see note on p. 315.
l. 51   Procne (or Philomela).

---

l. 51   νυκτέροις Guyet.
l. 52   δακρύουσ' edd.: δακρύοις codd..
l. 55   Cf. Sophocles, *Philoctetes* 1403.
l. 57   βέβαιον edd.: τε βαιὸν codd..
l. 58   Cf. Euripides, *Orestes* 44.
l. 59   λίπε Guyet.

60 σκέδασον δ' ἀπ' ὄσσων νύχιον ἀέρος βάθος
   μολὼν θύραζε καὶ πρὸς ἡλίου φάος
   ἀθόλωτον αὔραν πνεύματος φαιδροῦ σπάσον·
   δέκατον γὰρ ἤδη τοῦτο πρὸς πέμπτῳ φάει,
   ἐξ οὗ ζόφῳ σύγκλειστος ἡλίου δίχα
65 εὐναῖς ἐν ἀστρώτοισι τείρομαι δέμας.
   ψυχὴ μὲν οὖν μοι καὶ προθυμία πάρα
   βάσεις ἀμείβειν ἐπὶ θύρας ὡρμημένῳ,
   δέμας δὲ νωθρὸν οὐχ ὑπηρετεῖ πόθοις.
   ὅμως δ' ἐπείγου, θυμέ, γιγνώσκων ὅτι
70 πτωχὸς ποδαγρῶν, περιπατεῖν μὲν ἂν θέλῃ
   καὶ μὴ δύνηται, τοῦτον ἐν νεκροῖς τίθει.
   ἀλλ' εἶα.
   τίνες γὰρ οἷδε βάκτρα νωμῶντες χεροῖν,
   κάρηνα φύλλοις ἀκτέας καταστεφεῖς;
75 τίνα δαιμόνων ἄγουσι κωμαστὴν χορόν;
   μῶν, Φοῖβε Παιάν, σὸν γεραίρουσιν σέβας;
   ἀλλ' οὐ στέφονται Δελφίδος φύλλῳ δάφνης.
   ἢ μή τις ὕμνος Βακχίῳ κωμάζεται;
   ἀλλ' οὐκ ἔπεστι κισσίνη σφραγὶς κόμαις.
80 τίνες ποθ' ἡμῖν, ὦ ξένοι, βεβήκατε;
   αὐδᾶτε καὶ πρόεσθε νημερτῆ λόγον.
   τίς δ' ἔστιν, ἣν ὑμνεῖτε, λέξατ', ὦ φίλοι.

ΧΟΡΟΣ

   Σὺ δ' ὢν τίς ἡμᾶς καὶ τίνων προσεννέπεις;
   ὡς γάρ σε βάκτρον καὶ βάσις μηνύετον,
85 μύστην ὁρῶμεν τῆς ἀνικήτου θεᾶς.

l. 68 πόθοις Γ^a recc.: πόνοις Γ recc..
l. 69 Cf. Sophocles, *Antigone* 188 etc..
l. 70 ποδαγρός recc..
l. 70 μὲν ἂν edd.: ἂν μὴ codd.. Cf. Sophocles, *Ajax* 1068, *Swift-of-Foot* 12, 133.

GOUT

Release thine eyes from deep dark cloud of mist, 60
Go out of doors and into light of sun
That thou mayst draw a breath of clearest air,
For now ten days have gone and five besides,
Since I'm immured in dark away from sun,
And feel my body waste on unmade bed.   65
My spirit's fain, and eager wish I have
To hasten to the door and walk abroad,
But feeble body cannot serve my will.
Yet strive, my heart, make haste, for thou must know
That gout-struck pauper, if he wish to walk   70
But cannot move, is held as good as dead.
But stay !
For who are these that busily ply their staffs
And carry wreaths of elder * on their head ?
Which god is worshipped by this fervent band ? 75
Say, Healing Phoebus, do they honour thee ?
Not so ; no Delphic laurel wreathes their heads.
Or is this hymn sung to the Bacchic god ?
Not so ; no ivy marks their locks as his.
O strangers, tell us who ye are that come.   80
Speak out, and let your lips speak true, my friends.
Say which the goddess whom ye hymn with praise.

CHORUS

And who are you that ask, and what your race ?
For, as your staff and gait do indicate,
The unconquered goddess has thee for her thrall. 85

l. 74 Pliny, *Nat. Hist.* 24.35 tells us that the elder was used in treating many ailments including gout, while Theophrastus, *Enquiry into Plants*, 3.13.4 says that those being initiated into the mysteries bathed their hands and heads in elderberry juice.

l. 75 τίνα codd.: τίνι edd., cf. Aristophanes, *Thesm.* 104.
l. 78 ἢ Γ: ἦ cett..   l. 81 Cf. Aeschylus, *Persae* 246.

LUCIAN

ΠΟΔΑΓΡΟΣ

Εἷς εἰμι κἀγὼ τῆς θεᾶς ἐπάξιος;

ΧΟΡΟΣ

Τὰν μὲν Κυπρίαν Ἀφροδίταν
σταγόνων προπεσοῦσαν ἀπ' αἰθέρος
ἀνεθρέψατο κόσμιον ἁρμογὰν
90   ἁλίοις ἐνὶ κύμασι Νηρεύς.
τὰν δ' Ὠκεανοῦ παρὰ παγαῖς
Ζηνὸς παράκοιτιν Ὀλυμπίου
λευκώλενον εὑρέσι κόλποις
Ἥραν ἐτιθήνατο Τηθύς.
95   κορυφαῖσι δὲ κρατὸς ἐν ἀφθίτου
ἐλόχευσε κόρας ἄτρομον φυὰν
Κρονίδας, μέγ' ἄριστος Ὀλυμπίων,
τὰν ἐγρεκύδοιμον Ἀθάναν.
τὰν δ' ἡμετέραν θεὸν ὀλβίαν
100   ὁ γέρων λιπαραῖσιν ἐν ἀγκάλαις
πρῶταν ἐλόχευσεν Ὀφίων.
ὅτ' ἐπαύσατο μὲν σκότιον χάος

l. 90   ἅλιος codd.: corr. Peletier.
l. 96   κόρας edd.: κόραν codd..
l. 102   Χάος Boivin: φάος codd..

---

l. 87   ll. 87-111 are anapaestic, consisting either of
paroemiacs or ἀπόκροτα (i.e. three anapaestic feet
followed by an iambus).   The first known use of
anapaestic systems of this sort is by Mesomedes in
the time of Hadrian (see K. Horna, *Sitzungsbericht
Akad. Wien*, 207.1).   Such anapaests were particularly used for hymns; e.g. by Mesomedes and
Diophantus, a priest of Aesculapius.

Zimmermann suggests that this ode may be a

GOUT

Ye think me fit to join her mystic band ?

CHORUS

Just as Aphrodite, Cypric queen,*
Fell as dew from heaven above,
And by Nereus in the briny waves
Moulded was to beauteous shape ;   90
Just as Tethys close to Ocean's springs
In her bosom wide did nurse
White-armed Hera wife of mighty Zeus ;
Just as from immortal head
Cronidas, Olympus' greatest god,   95
Brought to birth the fearless maid,
Pallas, rouser of the battle's roar ;
Likewise was our blessed queen
Old Ophion's * first-begotten child
Spawned from parent's shiny arms.   100
When the age of Chaos dark was o'er,

parody of the cosmological hymn of the Naasseni,
quoted by Hippolytus in Book V of the *Refutation
of Heresies* (written *c.* 230 A.D.). The Naasseni
were Gnostics so called because they glorified the
serpent (" naas " in Hebrew for " serpent ") and
are perhaps to be identified with the Ophites
(ὄφις = serpent) who are mentioned by Lucian's
contemporary, Irenaeus (*Against Heresies* 1.30).

Lucian however shows little detailed knowledge
of contemporary religion; if this is a contemporary
allusion by Lucian, it refers more probably to the
serpents of Aesculapius and the mysteries of
Glycon; cf. *Alexander*, 18.

l. 99   Ophion was a Titan, who ruled before Cronos and
       Rhea; cf. Ap. Rhod. 1. 503 and note on l. 87.

l. 100 Or " from serpent's shiny coils ".

ἀνέτειλέ τε λαμπέτις ἀὼς
καὶ παμφαὲς ἀελίου σέλας,
105   τότε καὶ Ποδάγρας ἐφάνη κράτος.
ὅτε γὰρ λαγόνων σε τεκοῦσα
†Μοίρη τοτ' ἔλουσε Κλωθώ,
ἐγέλασσεν ἅπαν σέλας οὐρανοῦ,
μέγα δ' ἔκτυπεν εὔδιος αἰθήρ·
110   τὴν δ' εὐγλαγέτοις ἐνὶ μαζοῖς
εὔολβος ἐθρέψατο Πλούτων.

ΠΟΔΑΓΡΟΣ

Τίσιν δὲ τελεταῖς ὀργιάζει προσπόλους;

ΧΟΡΟΣ

Οὐχ αἷμα λάβρον προχέομεν ἀποτομαῖς
    σιδάρου,
οὐ τριχὸς ἀφέτον λυγίζεται στροφαῖσιν αὐχήν,
115   οὐδὲ πολυκρότοις ἀστραγάλοις πέπληγε νῶτα,
οὐδ' ὠμὰ λακιστῶν κρέα σιτούμεθα ταύρων·
ὅτε δὲ πτελέας ἔαρι βρύει τὸ λεπτὸν ἄνθος
καὶ πολυκέλαδος κόσσυφος ἐπὶ κλάδοισιν ᾄδει,
τότε διὰ μελέων ὀξὺ βέλος πέπηγε μύσταις,
120   ἀφανές, κρύφιον, δεδυκὸς ὑπὸ μυχοῖσι γυίων,
πόδα, γόνυ, κοτύλην, ἀστραγάλους, ἰσχία,
    μηρούς,

l. 104   Cf. Aeschylus, *Eumenides* 926, Euripides, *Troades* 548.
l. 107   sic Radermacher: Μοίρη τοτ' ἔλευσεν λίθωι Γ: κλωθὼ ante Μοίρη, ου super εν add. Γᵃ: μήτηρ τοτ' ἔλευσεν Ἐλευθώ tentavi.
l. 108   ἐγέλασεν codd.: corr. Reitz.
l. 112   ὀργιάζεις recc..
l. 113   προχέομεν edd.: προσχέομεν codd..
l. 113   ἀποτομαῖς G. Hermann: ἀπὸ στόματος codd..

GOUT

When the radiant dawn arose,
And the Sun-God's brilliant beams shone forth,
Then did mighty Gout appear.   105
After Clotho brought thee from her womb
And the Fate had washed * her child,
Joy was seen o'er heaven's shining face,
Thunder pealed from cloudless sky,
And rich Pluto from his ample store   110
Gave thee milky breasts to suck.

GOUTY MAN

And what the rites your novices must face ?

CHORUS

We do not spill our eager blood with cutting sword,*
No long grown hair is used to twist around the neck,
Our backs need feel no rattling scourge of cruel
    bone,   115
Nor must we tear apart and eat raw flesh of bulls ;
But when the spring brings tender flowers upon the
    elm,
And blackbirds' bubbling song is heard on every
    bough,
Then limbs of acolytes are pierced by weapon sharp,
Secret, unseen, sinking to utmost marrow's
    depth ;   120
The foot, the knee, hip-joint, the ankles, groins
    and thighs,

l. 107 Or perhaps 'stoned', a comic explanation of her
      lameness; see textual note.
l. 113 The metre of ll. 113-124 is Sotadic, consisting of
      three *pedes Ionici a maiore* or trochaic dipodies
      (long syllables may be resolved) followed by a
      spondee. The metre was invented by Sotades in
      the third century B.C.

χέρας, ὠμοπλάτας, βραχίονας, κόρωνα, καρποὺς
ἔσθει, νέμεται, φλέγει, κρατεῖ, πυροῖ, μαλάσσει,
μέχρις ἂν ἡ θεὸς τὸν πόνον ἀποφυγεῖν κελεύσῃ.

ΠΟΔΑΓΡΟΣ

125 Εἷς ἆρα κἀγὼ τῶν κατωργιασμένων
ἔλαθον ὑπάρχων; τοιγὰρ ἱκέτῃ πρευμενὴς
δαίμων φανείης, σὺν δ' ἐγὼ μύσταις ὁμοῦ
ὕμνων κατάρξω τὸ ποδαγρῶν ᾄδων μέλος.

ΧΟΡΟΣ

Σῖγα μὲν αἰθὴρ νήνεμος ἔστω,
130   καὶ πᾶς ποδαγρῶν εὐφημείτω.
ἴδε, πρὸς θυμέλας ⟨ἡ⟩ κλινοχαρὴς
βαίνει δαίμων σκίπωνι βάσιν
στηριζομένη. χαίροις μακάρων
πολὺ πραοτάτη καὶ σοῖς προπόλοις
135   ἵλαος ἔλθοις ὄμματι φαιδρῷ,
δοίης δὲ πόνοις λύσιν ὠκεῖαν
ταῖσδ' εἰαρinaῖσιν ⟨ἐν⟩ ὥραις.

ΠΟΔΑΓΡΑ

Τίς τὴν ἀνίκητόν με δεσπότιν πόνων
οὐκ οἶδε Ποδάγραν τῶν ἐπὶ χθονὸς βροτῶν;
140 ἣν οὔτε λιβάνων ἀτμὸς ἐξιλάσκεται

l. 122 χέρας G. Hermann: χεῖρας codd..
l. 123 ἐσθίει codd.: corr. Gavelens.
l. 124 μέχρι Γ: corr. recc..
ll. 126-127 ἱκέτῃ ... φανείης Radermacher: ἱκέτω ... φανείς
      Γ: ἥκέτω ... φανεὶς recc.: ἧκε ... φανεῖσα edd..
l. 128 ὑμνῶν Γ: corr. recc..

GOUT

Hands, shoulder-blades, and arms, the elbows and
    the wrists
It eats, devours, burns, quells, inflames and softens
    up,
Until the goddess bids the pain to flee away.

GOUTY MAN

Then was I one of those initiate,   125
But knew it not ?   Then, goddess, friendly come,
And with thy devotees I too shall raise
Thy hymns, and sing the song of gouty men.

CHORUS

Still and windless be the air,
Hushed be lips of every gouty man.   130
Lo, the goddess fond of bed
Staff-supported to her altar comes !
Welcome, gentlest far of gods,
Come, I pray, with kind and smiling face,
Blessing all thy followers,   135
Giving to their toils a swift release,
Now that days of spring are here.

GOUT

What mortal born on earth but knows of me,
Resistless Gout, the mistress of men's toils ?
Me no sweet reek of incense can appease   140

---

l. 129 νήνεμος edd.: καὶ νήνεμος codd..
l. 131 ἴδε Γ: ἡ δὲ recc.: ἤδη Guyet.
l. 131 ἡ add. edd..
l. 135 Cf. Aeschylus, *Agamemnon* 520, Euripides, *Medea*
    1043.
l. 136 Cf. Euripides, *Andromache* 900.
l. 137 ἐν add. edd..

LUCIAN

οὔτε χυθὲν αἷμα βωμίοις παρ' ἐμπύροις,
οὐ ναὸς ὄλβου περικρεμὴς ἀγάλμασιν,
ἣν οὔτε Παιὰν φαρμάκοις νικᾶν σθένει,
πάντων ἰατρὸς τῶν ἐν οὐρανῷ θεῶν,
145 οὐ παῖς ὁ Φοίβου πολυμαθὴς Ἀσκληπιός.
ἐξ οὗ γὰρ ἐφύη πρῶτον ἀνθρώποις γένος,
τολμῶσι πάντες τοὐμὸν ἐκβαλεῖν σθένος,
κυκῶντες αἰεὶ φαρμάκων τεχνήματα.
ἄλλος γὰρ ἄλλην ἐπ' ἐμὲ πειράζει τέχνην·
150 τρίβουσιν ἀρνόγλωσσα καὶ σέλινά μοι
καὶ φύλλα θριδάκων καὶ νομαίαν ἀνδράχνην
ἄλλοι πράσιον, οἱ δὲ ποταμογείτονα,
ἄλλοι κνίδας τρίβουσιν, ἄλλοι σύμφυτον,
ἄλλοι φακοὺς φέρουσι τοὺς ἐκ τελμάτων,
155 σταφυλῖνον ἑφθόν, οἱ δὲ φύλλα Περσικῶν,
ὑοσκύαμον, μήκωνα, βολβούς, σίδια,
ψύλλιον, λίβανον, ῥίζαν ἑλλεβόρου, νίτρον,
τῆλιν μετ' οἴνου, γυρίνην, κόλλαν, φακόν,
κυπαρισσίνην κηκῖδα, γῦριν κριθίνην,
160 κράμβης ἀπέφθου φύλλα, γύψον ἐκ Πάρου,
σφυράθους ὀρείας αἰγός, ἀνθρώπου κόπρον,
ἄλευρα κυάμων, ἄνθος Ἀσσίου λίθου·

l. 143 νικᾶν Γ^a rec.: νικᾷ Γ.
l. 144 πάντων Γ^a: παίων Γ: πασῶν Radermacher.
l. 145 ὁ om. Γ.
l. 148 ἀεὶ Γ.
l. 152 ἄλλοι δὲ edd.; cf. Nicander, Ther. 550.
l. 156 σίβδια Guyet, cf. Nubes 881.
l. 158 κολλάμφακον codd.: corr. Zimmermann: κόλλαν σφάκον
    Th. Bergk.
l. 161 σφυράθους Γ: σπυράθους Γ^a edd.: πυράθους recc..

l. 149 For various treatments of gout, see Celsus 4.31, The
    Lover of Lies 7.

Nor blood of victims burnt in sacrifice
Nor shrine whose walls with idols rich are hung.
Me Paean cannot worst with medicine,
Though doctor he to all the gods of heaven,
Nor yet his learned son, Asclepius.   145
For ever since the race of men was born,
They all essay to exorcise my might
By ever mixing drugs most cunningly.
Each man a different wile against me tries.
They bruise their plantain and their celery,   150
And lettuce leaves and purslane from the lea,
Some horehound grind, and others pondweed try ;
Some nettles crush, and others comfrey use ;
Some duckweed from the ponds against me bring,   155
Or carrots boiled or leaves of peaches use,
Or henbane, poppy, Colchicum, * grenades,
Or fleawort, frankincense, or sodium,
The root of hellebore, or mixed with wine
The fenugreek, rissole, glue, or pulse,
Or cypress sap, or finest barley meal,
Boiled cabbage leaves, gypsum from Paros
         brought,   160
Man's excrement or turds of mountain goat,
Or mash of beans, or crop from Assian * stone ;

l. 157   Colchicine, a preparation from the bulb of the
         meadow saffron, is still taken internally for gout.
         Celsus, however, *loc. cit.* only mentions its external
         use along with poppy.
l. 162   The " sarcophagus " stone from Assus in the
         Troad which was probably a fissile lime-stone ; see
         Eicholz's note on Pliny *Nat. Hist.* 36. 131-133.
         Pliny (loc. cit.) says that gout was relieved by
         putting one's feet in a vessel hollowed out of this
         stone or by using a plaster compounded of it and
         beans.

ἔψουσι φρύνους, μυγαλᾶς, σαύρας, γαλᾶς,
βατράχους, ὑαίνας, τραγελάφους, ἀλώπεκας.
165 ποῖον μέταλλον οὐ πεπείρασται βροτοῖς;
τίς οὐχὶ χυλός; ποῖον οὐ δένδρου δάκρυ;
ζῴων ἁπάντων ὀστά, νεῦρα, δέρματα,
στέαρ, αἷμα, μυελός, οὖρον, ἀπόπατος, γάλα.
πίνουσιν οἱ μὲν τὸ διὰ τεσσάρων ἄκος,
170 οἱ δὲ τὸ δι' ὀκτώ, τὸ δὲ δι' ἑπτὰ πλείονες.
ἄλλος δὲ πίνων τὴν ἱερὰν καθαίρεται,
ἄλλος ἐπαοιδαῖς ἐπιθετῶν ἐμπαίζεται,
Ἰουδαῖος ἕτερον μωρὸν ἐξᾴδει λαβών.
ὁ δὲ θεραπείαν ἔλαβε παρὰ τῆς Κυρράνης.
175 ἐγὼ δὲ τούτοις πᾶσιν οἰμώζειν λέγω
καὶ τοῖς ποιοῦσι ταῦτα καὶ πειρῶσί με
εἴωθ' ἀπαντᾶν μᾶλλον ὀργιλωτέρα·
τοῖς δὲ φρονοῦσι μηδὲν ἀντίξουν ἐμοὶ
ἤπιον ἔχω νοῦν εὐμενής τε γίνομαι.
180 ὁ γὰρ μεταλαβὼν τῶν ἐμῶν μυστηρίων
πρῶτον μὲν εὐθὺς εὐστομεῖν διδάσκεται
τέρπων ἅπαντας, εὐτραπέλους λέγων λόγους·
πᾶσιν δ' ὁρᾶται μετὰ γέλωτος καὶ κρότου,
ὅταν ἐπὶ λουτρὰ φερόμενος βαστάζεται.
185 Ἄτην γάρ ἦν Ὅμηρος εἶφ' ἥδ' εἰμ' ἐγώ,
βαίνουσ' ἐπ' ἀνδρῶν κρᾶτα καὶ βάσεις ποδῶν

l. 166 χυμός *Γ*ᵃ recc..
l. 174 Κυρράνης Th. Bergk: Κυράννης *Γ*N: ὠράνης Gesner:
          οὐράνης conieci.
l. 176 Cf. Euripides, *Cyclops* 581.
l. 178 τοῖσι δὲ edd..
l. 182 Cf. Sophocles, *Electra* 672.
l. 184 sic codd.: ὅτ' ἐπὶ λοετρὰ Zimmermann: ὅτ' ἐπὶ τὰ λουτρὰ
          Guyet.

GOUT

And weasels,* field-mice, lizards, toads they boil,
The frog, hyena,* antelope, or fox.
What metal has not been by mortals tried ?   165
What juice ?   What exudation from a tree ?
All creatures' bones, sinews and skins they try,
Their fat, blood, marrow, urine, dung or milk.
Some potions drink of four ingredients,
Or else of eight, but more men seven use.   170
Some purge themselves with sacred medicine,
Others are mocked by chants impostors sell,
And other fools fall for the spells of Jews,
While others look for cure to Cyrrane. *
But all these shifts I curse and treat with scorn,   175
And those who use them and would test my strength
I e'er assail with greater wrath by far ;
But those whose will is not opposed to mine
Do find me kind of heart and well-disposed.
For he that shareth in my mystic rites   180
Learns first and that right soon to curb his tongue,
Delighting all by choosing well his words.
And all who see him laugh and clap their hands,
When to the baths he's borne on others' backs.
For I am Ruin, she whom Homer * sang,   185
Who walketh o'er men's heads with dainty steps,

l. 163   Cf. *The Lover of Lies* 7.
l. 164   The hyena was believed by the Magi to have
          curative powers for many ailments including gout.
          Cf. Pliny, *Nat. Hist.* 28. 92 and 96.
l. 174   A women's goddess mentioned by Menander,
          according to Hesychius; Photius, however, spells
          her Cyrranne.
l. 185   *Iliad* XIX. 92-3.

---

l. 185   εἶπεν Ὅμηρος codd.: corr. Boivin.

ἀπαλὰς ἔχουσα, παρὰ δὲ τοῖς πολλοῖς βροτῶν
Ποδάγρα καλοῦμαι, γινομένη ποδῶν ἄγρα.
ἀλλ᾽ εἶα μύσται πάντες ὀργίων ἐμῶν,
190 γεραίρεθ᾽ ὕμνοις τὴν ἀνίκητον θεάν.

ΧΟΡΟΣ

Ἀδαμάντινον ἦθος ἔχουσα κόρα,
πουλυσθενές, ὀβριμόθυμε θεά,
κλύε σῶν ἱερῶν μερόπων ἐνοπάς.
μέγα σὸν κράτος, ὀλβιόφρον Ποδάγρα,
195 τὰν καὶ Διὸς ὠκὺ πέφρικε βέλος,
τρομέει δέ σε κύμαθ᾽ ἁλὸς βυθίας,
τρομέει βασιλεὺς ἐνέρων Ἀΐδας,
ἐπιδεσμοχαρές, κατακλινοβατές,
κωλυσιδρόμα, βασαναστραγάλα,
200 σφυροπρησιπύρα, μογισαψεδάφα,
δοιδυκοφόβα, γονυκαυσαγρύπνα,
περικονδυλοπωροφίλα,
γονυκαμψεπίκυρτε Ποδάγρα.

ΑΓΓΕΛΟΣ

Δέσποινα, καιρίῳ γὰρ ἤντησας ποδί,
205 ἄκου᾽, ἔπος γὰρ οὐκ ἐτώσιον φέρω,
ἀλλ᾽ ἔστι πρᾶξις τῶν λόγων συνέμπορος·
ἐγὼ γάρ, ὡς ἔταξας, ἠρέμῳ ποδὶ
πόλεις ἰχνεύων πάντας ἠρεύνων δόμους
μαθεῖν ποθῶν εἴ τις σὸν οὐ τιμᾷ κράτος.
210 καὶ τῶν μὲν ἄλλων εἶδον ἥσυχον φρένα
νικωμένων, ἄνασσα, σαῖν βίας χεροῖν,

l. 192 πολυσθενές Γ: corr. rec..

342

GOUT

But to the most of men my name is Gout,
Who come to make their feet my spoil and prey.
But come, all devotees of these my rites,
Honour with hymns the goddess none can worst. 190

Mighty Maid with heart of steel,
Goddess dreadful in thy wrath,
Hear the cries of thine own priests.
Prosperous Gout, how great thy power!
Dread art thou to Jove's swift shaft, 195
Fearsome thou to Ocean's waves
And to Hades king below;
Bandage-loving Sickbed Queen,
Speed-impairing Joint-Tormentor,
Ankle-burning Timid-Stepper, 200
Pestle-fearing, Knee-Fire Sleepless,
Loving chalkstones on the knuckles,
Knee-deformer, Gout's thy name.

MESSENGER

Mistress, 'tis well thy feet thee hither bring.
No empty message do I bid thee hear, 205
For cometh with my words accomplishment.
For, as you bade, I went with gentle pace
To search each town and look in every house
With zeal to learn if any scorned thy might.
The other men I saw were meek of heart 210
When conquered by thy mighty hands, my queen,

---

l. 201 δωδεικοφόβα Γ: corr. N; γοννκλαυσαγρύπνα codd.: corr.
Dindorf.
l. 211 σαῖν rec.: σαῖ Γ: σαῖς recc.; βίας Γ: βίᾳ recc..

343

LUCIAN

δύω δὲ τώδε φῶτε τολμηρῷ θράσει
ἐφραζέτην λαοῖσι καὶ κατωμνύτην,
ὡς οὐκέτ' ἐστὶ σὸν κράτος σεβάσμιον,
215 ἀλλ' ἔκβολον βροτῶν σε θήσουσιν βίου.
διόπερ κραταιῷ συνοχμάσας δεσμῷ πόδα
πεμπταῖος ἥκω στάδια διανύσας δύο.

ΠΟΔΑΓΡΑ

Ὡς κραιπνὸς ἔπτης, ἀγγέλων ὤκιστέ μοι.
τίνος δὲ καὶ γῆς ὅρια δυσβάτου λιπὼν
220 ἥκεις; σαφῶς μήνυσον, ὡς εἰδῶ τάχος.

ΑΓΓΕΛΟΣ

Πρῶτον μὲν ἔλιπον πέντε βασμῶν κλίμακα,
ξύλων τρέμουσαν διαλύτοισιν ἁρμογαῖς,
ὅθεν με δέχεται κορδυβαλλῶδες πέδον
σκληροῖσι ταρσοῖς ἀντερεῖδον κρούμασιν.
225 ὅπερ διανύσας ἴχνεσιν ἀλγεινοῖς ἐγὼ
ἐστρωμένην χάλιξιν εἰσέβην ὁδὸν
καὶ δυσπάτητον ὀξέσιν κέντροις λίθων.
μεθ' ἣν ὀλίσθῳ περιπεσὼν λείας ὁδοῦ
ἔσπευδον εἰς τὸ πρόσθε, διάλυτος δέ μου
230 ἔσυρεν ὀπίσω πηλὸς ἀσθενῆ σφυρά,
δι' ἧς περῶντι νότιος ἐκ μελῶν ἱδρὼς
†ἔρρει βάσιν μου σαθρὸν ἐκλύων μένος.
ὅθεν με δέχεται πᾶν δέμας κεκμηκότα
πλατεῖα μὲν κέλευθος ἀλλ' οὐκ ἀσφαλής.

l. 212 τολμηρῷ recc..
l. 214 οὐκ ἔστ' codd.: corr. Du Soul.
l. 216 κραταιῶς codd.: corr. Gavelens.
l. 220 εἰδῶ edd.: ἴδω codd..

344

GOUT

But these two were right bold and impudent,
Who told their fellows all and swore on oath
No longer was thy power to be revered,
But they would banish thee from lives of men.   215
Therefore I've bound their feet with fetters strong.
Four days I've sped, a quarter mile I've come.

GOUT

What haste you've made, my messenger most swift !
Say what the pathless land whose bounds you've left.
Oh speak out clear that I may know at once.   220

MESSENGER

A five-runged ladder first of all I left
Whose loosely-fitted wooden limbs did shake,
And next a beaten floor awaited me,
A pavement hard and firm that hurt my feet.
O'er this I sped in haste with painful steps,   225
And then I came upon a gravel path
With sharp and pointed stones most hard to cross.
Then next a smooth and slippery road I met ;
Forward I pressed though mud clung to my steps
Making my strengthless ankles drag and trail.   230
In crossing this my limbs did drench my feet
With sweat and drained away my ebbing strength.
Then wearied in each limb I found myself
Where was a highway broad but dangerous ;

---

l. 221 βαθμῶν edd..
l. 227 δυσπάθητον Γ; κέντροις Γ: πέτροις recc..
l. 232 sic Radermacher: σαθρὰν ἐκλυομένῳ Γ: σαθρὰν
       ἰλυσπωμένῳ Γᵃ: σαθρὰν ἐκλελυμένῳ edd.: ἄρδει βάσιν
       μοι σαθρὸν ἰλυσπωμένῳ in loco desperato conieci.
l. 233 δέμας Γ: μέλος rec..

LUCIAN

235 τὰ μὲν γὰρ ἔνθεν, τὰ δέ μ' ἐκεῖθ' ὀχήματα
ἤπειγεν, ἠνάγκαζεν, ἔσπερχεν τρέχειν.
ἐγὼ δὲ νωθρὸν ἐλαφρὰ κουφίζων πόδα
δόχμιος ἔβαινον εἰς ὁδοῦ πέζαν στενήν,
ἕως ἀπήνη παραδράμῃ τροχήλατος·
240 μύστης γὰρ ὢν σὸς ταχὺ τρέχειν οὐκ ἔσθενον.

ΠΟΔΑΓΡΑ

Οὐκ εἰς μάτην, βέλτιστε, πρᾶξις ἥδε σοι
ὀρθῶς πέπρακται. τῇ δὲ σῇ προθυμίᾳ
ἴσαισι τιμαῖς ἀντισηκώσω χάριν.
ἔστω δέ σοι δώρημα θυμῆρες τόδε,
245 ἐξῆς τριετίας πειράσῃ κούφων πόνων.
ὑμεῖς δὲ μιαροὶ καὶ θεοῖς ἐχθίστατοι,
τίνες ποτ' ὄντες καὶ τίνων πεφυκότες
τολμᾶτε Ποδάγρας ἀνθαμιλλᾶσθαι κράτει,
τῆς οὐδ' ὁ Κρονίδης οἶδε νικῆσαι βίαν;
250 λέγετ', ὦ κάκιστοι· καὶ γὰρ ἡρώων ἐγὼ
ἐδάμασα πλείστους, ὡς ἐπίστανται σοφοί.
Πρίαμος Ποδάρκης ποδαγρὸς ὢν ἐκλήζετο·
ἔθανε δ' Ἀχιλλεὺς ποδαγρὸς ὢν ὁ Πηλέως·
ὁ Βελλεροφόντης ποδαγρὸς ὢν ἐκαρτέρει·
255 Θηβῶν δυνάστης Οἰδίπους ποδαγρὸς ἦν·

l. 235   τὰ δέ μ' edd.: τὰ δ' codd..
l. 238   εἰσόδου codd..
l. 249   Κρονίδας recc., edd..
l. 251   ὡς Bekker: καὶ Γ: καί γ' recc..

l. 249   Zeus.
l. 252   The original name of Priam was Podarkes, according to Apollodorus.   Perhaps a poor pun is intended
between Podarces (Doughty-of-Foot) and Podagros
(Gouty-of-Foot).

346

For carriages to right and left of me   235
Did force me on and make me run in haste.
And I did nimbly lift my sluggish feet
To dart aside and seek the wayside strait,
To let a cart rush by with flying wheel,
For, mystic thine, I could not run with speed.   240

GOUT

A worthy enterprise was this, good sir,
And well accomplished. And I your zeal
Shall now reward with well-earned privilege.
And may this gift delight your heart right well.
For three whole years your pains will lighter be.   245
But, cursed villains hateful to the gods,
Say who are ye and what your lineage,
That dare to pit yourselves with mighty Gout,
Whose strength e'en Cronus' son * cannot subdue.
Speak, knaves ; for even of the demigods   250
Great numbers I've o'ercome, as sages know.
Priam, though Doughty * called, had gouty feet ;
Achilles, Peleus' son,* did die of gout ;
Bellerophon * Gout's trials had to face,
And gouty too was Thebes' king * Oedipus,   255

l. 253   Achilles had the epithet "podarces" (see previous
note) in Homer. However Gout goes on to poke fun
at heroes famous in legend for mishaps to their feet,
and this may be a reference to the comparatively
unfamiliar story that Achilles was invulnerable
except for his "Achilles' tendon" by which his
mother held him while dipping him in the Styx to
ensure his invulnerability.

l. 254   The reference is unknown. Perhaps Bellerophon
injured a foot when falling off Pegasus.

l. 255   Oedipus (Swell-Foot) was exposed at birth with a
pin driven through this ankles; cf. Sophocles, *O.T.*
718, Euripides, *Phoenissae* 22.

ἐκ τῶν Πελοπιδῶν ποδαγρὸς ἦν ὁ Πλεισθένης.
Ποίαντος υἱὸς ποδαγρὸς ὢν ἦρχεν στόλου·
ἄλλος Ποδάρκης Θεσσαλῶν ἦν ἡγεμών,
ὅς, ἐπείπερ ἔπεσε Πρωτεσίλαος ἐν μάχῃ,
260 ὅμως ποδαγρὸς ὢν καὶ πονῶν ἦρχεν στόλου·
Ἰθάκης ἄνακτα Λαρτιάδην Ὀδυσσέα
ἐγὼ κατέπεφνον, οὐκ ἄκανθα τρυγόνος.
ὡς οὔτι χαιρήσοντες, ὦ δυσδαίμονες,
ἴσην πάσεσθε κόλασιν οἷς δεδράκατε.

ΙΑΤΡΟΣ

265 Σύροι μέν ἐσμεν, ἐκ Δαμασκοῦ τῷ γένει,
λιμῷ δὲ πολλῷ καὶ πενίᾳ κρατούμενοι
γῆν καὶ θάλασσαν ἐφέπομεν πλανώμενοι·
ἔχομεν δὲ χρῖσμα πατροδώρητον τόδε,
ἐν ᾧ παρηγοροῦμεν ἀλγούντων πόνους.

ΠΟΔΑΓΡΑ

270 Τί δὴ τὸ χρῖσμα καὶ τίς ἡ σκευή; φράσον.

ΙΑΤΡΟΣ

Μύστης με σιγᾶν ὅρκος οὐδ' ἐᾷ φράσαι,
καὶ λοισθία θνήσκοντος ἐντολὴ πατρός,
ὃς ἔταξε κεύθειν φαρμάκου μέγα σθένος,
ὃ καὶ σὲ παύειν οἶδεν ἠγριωμένην.

l. 261 sic rec.: Λαερτιάδην cett..
l. 264 πάσεσθε Radermacher: πάθησθε codd..
l. 271 οὐδ' Radermacher: οὐκ codd..
l. 273 Cf. Euripides, *Electra* 427, 958.

l. 256 The joke seems to be directed at the name
Plisthenes (Abounding-in-Strength). Cf. *Mantissa
Proverbiorum* 2.94.

GOUT

And Plisthenes, from Pelops sprung, had gout ;
And gouty general too was Poeas' son * ;
Another Doughty-Footed * one Thessalians led,
Who, when Protesilaus had been killed,
Though gouty and in pain, did lead his host.   260
The king of Ithaca,* Laertes' son,
Was slain by me and not by spine of fish.
For know, ye luckless ones, with dearth of glee
You'll get a punishment to fit your crime.

DOCTORS

We Syrians are, Damascus men by birth,   265
But forced by hunger and by poverty,
We wander far afield o'er land and sea.
We have an ointment here, our fathers' gift,
With which we comfort woes of sufferers.

GOUT

What ointment's this ?   Say what's your stock-
    in-trade.   270

DOCTOR

By secret, mystic oath my lips are sealed,
And by my dying father's last command,
Who bade me secret keep this mighty cure,
Whose power can quell e'en fiercest wrath of thine.

---

l. 257   Philoctetes, who became lame after a snake bit his
     foot.
l. 258   Podarkes; cf. *Iliad* 2.704, 13.693.
l. 261   Odysseus, who was depicted in Aeschylus' *Psycha-*
     gogoi and Sophocles' *Acanthoplex* (both plays are
     lost) as having being killed in some way by a fish-
     bone; cf. *Odyssey*, 11.134.

LUCIAN

ΠΟΔΑΓΡΑ

275 Εἶτ' ὦ κατάρατοι καὶ κακῶς ὀλούμενοι,
ἔστιν τις ἐν γῇ φαρμάκου δρᾶσις τόση,
ὃ χρισθὲν οἶδε τὴν ἐμὴν παῦσαι βίαν;
ἀλλ' εἶα, τήνδε σύμβασιν συνθώμεθα,
καὶ πειράσωμεν εἴτε φαρμάκου σθένος
280 ὑπέρτερον πέφυκεν εἴτ' ἐμαὶ φλόγες.
δεῦτ', ὦ σκυθρωπαί, πάντοθεν ποτώμεναι
βάσανοι, πάρεδροι τῶν ἐμῶν βακχευμάτων,
πελάζετ' ἆσσον· καὶ σὺ μὲν ποδῶν ἄκρους
φλέγμαινε ταρσοὺς δακτύλων ποδῶν ἄχρις,
285 σὺ δὲ σφυροῖς ἔμβαινε, σὺ δὲ μηρῶν ἄπο
ἐς γόνατα λεῖβε πικρὸν ἰχώρων βάθος,
ὑμεῖς δὲ χειρῶν δακτύλους λυγίζετε.

ΠΟΝΟΙ

"Ἴδ', ὡς ἔταξας πάντα σοι δεδράκαμεν·
κεῖνται βοῶντες οἱ ταλαίπωροι μέγα,
290 ἅπαντα γυῖα προσβολῇ στρεβλούμενοι.

ΠΟΔΑΓΡΑ

Φέρετ', ὦ ξένοι, μάθωμεν ἀτρεκέστερον,
εἰ χρισθὲν ὑμᾶς φάρμακον τόδ' ὠφελεῖ.
εἰ γὰρ σαφῶς τόδ' ἐστὶν ἀντίξουν ἐμοί,
λιποῦσα γαῖαν εἰς μυχοὺς εἶμι χθονός,
295 ἄιστος, ἀφανής, πύματα Ταρτάρου βάθη.
Ἰδού, κέχρισθε· χαλασάτω φλογῶν πόνος.

l. 276 τόσσῃ δράσις Γ: τόσση δόσις Radermacher.
l. 284 ἄχρις Radermacher: ἄχρι Γ^a: ἄκροις Γ.
l. 286 πικρῶν codd.: corr. edd..

350

GOUT

Then, cursed ones whose death will bitter be,   275
Is there on earth a drug of such effect,
An ointment potent which can check my might ?
But come, upon these terms let us agree ;
Let's test this mighty remedy to find
If it or if my burning pain prevails.   280
Come, grim-faced ones, from every side fly here,
Ye torments, comrades of my frenzied rites,
Approach, come near, I say ; do thou inflame
Their feet from heel to utmost tip of toe ;
Their ankles thou assail ; and from their thighs   285
Down to their knees make thou rank poison flow ;
And ye must twist and knot their fingers all.

PAINS

Look, all we've done, just as you've bidden us.
The luckless men lie shrieking loud and clear
From our attacks which torture every limb.   290

GOUT

Now, strangers, come ; more surely let us learn
If ye find help from rubbing on this salve.
For, if it clearly counteracts my power,
I'll leave this world, and disappear from sight
Deep down to utmost depths of Tartarus.   295
Let's see if salve applied relieves your pain.

---

l. 291 ἀτρεκέστατον recc., edd..
l. 294 λιποῦσα N: λείπουσα cett..   Cf. Euripides, *Supplices*
926, Aeschylus, *Choephoroe* 954.
l. 296 ΠΟΝΟΙΣ rec., ΙΑΤΡΩ edd. tribuunt. κέχρισται edd..
χαλασάτω φλογῶν πόνος Γ: κοὺ χαλᾷ φλογμὸς πόνων Γᵃ.

LUCIAN

ΙΑΤΡΟΣ

Οἴμοι, παπαῖ γε, τείρομαι, διόλλυμαι,
ἅπαν πέπαρμαι γυῖον ἀσκόπῳ κακῷ·
οὐ Ζεὺς κεραυνοῦ τοῖον αἰωρεῖ βέλος,
300 οὐδεὶς θαλάσσης τοῖα μαίνεται κλύδων,
οὐδὲ στροβητὴ λαίλαπος τόσση βία.
μὴ κάρχαρον πορθεῖ με δῆγμα Κερβέρου;
μὴ τῆς Ἐχίδνης ἰὸς ἀμφιβόσκεται,
ἢ διαβραχεὶς ἰχῶρι Κενταύρου πέπλος;
305 ἐλέαιρ᾽, ἄνασσα, φάρμακον γὰρ οὔτ᾽ ἐμὸν
οὔτ᾽ ἄλλο δύναται σὸν ἀναχαιτίσαι δρόμον,
ψήφοις δὲ πάσαις πᾶν ἔθνος νικᾷς βροτῶν.

ΠΟΔΑΓΡΑ

Παύσασθε, βάσανοι, καὶ πόνους μειώσατε
τῶν μετανοούντων εἰς ἐμὴν ἔριν μολεῖν.
310 γινωσκέτω δὲ πᾶς τις ὡς μόνη θεῶν
ἄτεγκτος οὖσα φαρμάκοις οὐ πείθομαι.

ΧΟΡΟΣ

Οὔτε Διὸς βρονταῖς Σαλμωνέος ἤρισε βία,
ἀλλ᾽ ἔθανεν ψολόεντι δαμεῖσα θεοῦ φρένα βέλει,
οὐκ ἐρίσας ἐχάρη Φοίβῳ σάτυρος Μαρσύας,
315 ἀλλὰ λιγὺ ψαίρει κείνου περὶ δέρματι πίτυς.

l. 297 ΠΟΔΑΓΡΩ trib. rec., edd..
l. 303 τῆς Guyet: τίς codd.: τίς μ᾽ edd..
l. 304 sic Zimmermann: διαβραχὴς Γ: διαβρεχὴς N, edd..
ἰχῶρι N, edd.: ἰχὼρ ἢ Γ.
l. 312 ἤρισεν codd.: corr. Guyet.
l. 315 δέρμα πίτυς codd.: corr. Schaefer.

l. 302 cf. Bacchylides, 33 (v), 60-62.
l. 312 ll. 312-324 are myuric hexameters or "teliambi"
(i.e. five dactyls or spondees followed by an iambus),

GOUT

DOCTOR

Alas, alas, I'm utterly destroyed !
I burn in every limb from bane untold.
Not such the thunderbolt that Zeus doth poise,
Not such the furious ocean's raging waves,   300
And lesser too the whirlwind's mighty force !
Do jagged teeth of Cerberus * me rend ?
Or does Echidna's venom gnaw my flesh ?
Or is my raiment steeped in Nessus' gore ?
Have mercy, queen, for neither salve of mine   305
Nor other remedy can quell thy course.
All votes agree you conquer all mankind.

GOUT

Ye torments, cease. Relax their suffering
For now they're sorry that they challenged me.
Let all men know that I alone of gods   310
Do not relent or yield to remedies.

CHORUS

Mighty though Salmoneus was, he could not rival
    thundering Zeus,*
But was slain and smitten in the heart by smoking
    thunderbolt ;
Nor brought rivalry with Phoebus joy to Satyr
    Marsyas ;
All his music now is where his skin * on rustling pine-
    tree hangs ;   315

as Marius Victorinus calls them. See T. F. Higham's
article in *Greek Poetry and Life* pp. 299 ff. A very
few Homeric lines are myuric, but the earliest surviving passage written entirely in this metre is
Oxyrynchus Papyrus 1795, which Grenfell and
Hunt assign to the first century A.D.

l. 315 After defeating Marsyas in a musical contest Apollo
took his revenge by binding him to a tree and
flaying him.

LUCIAN

πένθος ἀείμνηστον δι' ἔριν τοκὰς ἔσχε Νιόβη,
ἀλλ' ἔτι μυρομένη προχέει πολὺ δάκρυ Σιπύλῳ.
Μαιονία δ' Ἀράχνη Τριτωνίδος ἦλθεν ἐς ἔριν,
ἀλλ' ὀλέσασα τύπον καὶ νῦν ἔτι νήματα πλέκει·
320 οὐ γὰρ ἴσον μακάρων ὀργαῖς θράσος ἐστὶ
    μερόπων,
  ὡς Διός, ὡς Λητοῦς, ὡς Παλλάδος, ὡς Πυθίου.
ἤπιον, ὦ πάνδημε, φέροις ἄλγημα, Ποδάγρα,
κοῦφον, ἐλαφρόν, ἄδριμυ, βραχυβλαβές,
    ἀνώδυνον,
  εὔφορον, εὔληκτον, ὀλιγοδρανές, εὐπερίπατον.
325   πολλαὶ μορφαὶ τῶν ἀτυχούντων,
    μελέται δὲ πόνων καὶ τὸ σύνηθες
    τοὺς ποδαγρῶντας παραμυθείσθω.
    ὅθεν εὐθύμως, ὦ σύγκληροι,
    λήσεσθε πόνων,
330   εἰ τὰ δοκηθέντ' οὐκ ἐτελέσθη,
    τοῖς δ' ἀδοκήτοις πόρον εὗρε θεός.
    πᾶς δ' ἀνεχέσθω τῶν πασχόντων
    ἐμπαιζόμενος καὶ σκωπτόμενος·
    τοῖον γὰρ ἔφυ τόδε πρᾶγμα.

l. 323   εὐώδυνον G. Hermann.
l. 328   συνναύκληροι codd.: corr. Guyet.

---

l. 317   Niobe was petrified and became Mount Sipylus in
         Lydia as a punishment for boasting that her children
         were superior to Apollo and Artemis.
l. 318   Arachne hanged herself after incurring the wrath
         of Pallas by her pride in her weaving; Pallas
         thereupon changed the rope into a cobweb and
         Arachne into a spider.
l. 325   ll. 325, 330-331 and 334 are parodies of the ending
         common to four plays of Euripides. Cf. *Carousal*, 48.

354

GOUT

And, for rivalling Leto, mother Niobe will ne'er forget
 her grief,
But she mourneth still and poureth floods of tears
 on Sipylus * ;
And Maeonian maid Arachne * thought herself
 Athene's match,
But she lost her shape and still to-day must spin and
 spin her web ;
For men's daring boldness cannot match the wrath
 of blessed gods,   320
Such as Zeus or Leto or Athene or the Pythian seer.
May the pain you bring be gentle, universal goddess
 Gout,
Light and mild and stingless, hurting little, free from
 pain,
Easily borne and swiftly ceasing, weak and feeble,
 ready for a stroll.
Many sorts * one will find there are of luckless
 men ;   325
But let those who have gout find relief from their
 woes
By being schooled to endure * and accustomed to
 pain.
In this way cheerfully you who share this our lot
Will forget all your pain,
Seeing that what we thought has not been
 brought about,   330
While a way for what we not at all did expect
Has been found by the god.   So let each sufferer
Learn to bear mockery and submit to men's taunts.
For this thing is of just such a kind.

327   Cf. Thucydides, 2.39.

ΩΚΥΠΟΥΣ

[Ὠκύπους Ποδαλειρίου καὶ Ἀστασίας υἱὸ
ἐγένετο, κάλλει καὶ δυνάμει διαφέρων, γυμνασίων τ
καὶ κυνηγεσίων μὴ ἀμελῶν. πολλάκις δὲ θεωρῶ
τοὺς ἐχομένους ὑπὸ τῆς ἀτέγκτου Ποδάγρας κατε
γέλα φάσκων μηδὲν ὅλως εἶναι τὸ πάθος. ἡ θεὸ
ἀγανακτεῖ καὶ διὰ ποδῶν εἰστρέχει. τοῦ δ
εὐτόνως φέροντος καὶ ἀρνουμένου, ὕπτιον ὅλω
τίθησιν ἡ θεός.

τὰ τοῦ δράματος πρόσωπα Ποδάγρα, Ὠκύπους
Τροφεύς, Ἰατρος, Πόνος, Ἄγγελος.[1]

ἡ μὲν σκηνὴ τοῦ δράματος ὑπόκειται[2] ἐν Θήβαις
ὁ δὲ χόρος συνέστηκεν ἐξ ἐπιχωρίων ποδαγρῶ
συνελεγχόντων τὸν Ὠκύπουν. τὸ δὲ δρᾶμα τῶ
πάνυ ἀστείων.]

---

[1] Πόνος, Ἄγγελος om. rec..
[2] ὑπόκειται edd.: ἀνακεῖται codd..

SWIFT-OF-FOOT

[Swift-of-Foot was the son of Podaleirius and Astasia,[1] distinguished for his beauty and strength, and a devotee of the wrestling-school and the hunt. He would often laugh with contempt when he looked at victims in the grasp of remorseless Gout, saying that the ailment amounted to nothing at all. The goddess is angry and runs in through his feet. When he bears up sturdily and denies his plight, the goddess puts him on his back completely.

The *dramatis personae* are Gout, Swift-of-Foot, Tutor, Doctor, Pain, Messenger.

The play is set in Thebes, and the chorus consists of local sufferers from gout who cross-question Swift-of-Foot. The play is a very witty one.]

[1] The names are chosen for comic effect. The first syllable of Podaleirius means " foot ", and Lucian himself makes the same pun in *Alexander* 59; Podaleirius was a son of Aesculapius and himself a doctor, see Harmon's note on *Alexander* 11. Astasia (= " inability to stand ") is chosen for its resemblance to Aspasia, the mistress of Pericles.

PSEUDO-LUCIAN

ΠΟΔΑΓΡΑ, ΤΡΟΦΕΥΣ, ΩΚΥΠΟΥΣ, ΙΑΤΡΟΣ

ΠΟΔΑΓΡΑ

Δεινὴ μὲν ἐν βροτοῖσι καὶ δυσώνυμος
Ποδάγρα κέκλημαι, δεινὸν ἀνθρώποις πάθος,
δεσμῷ δὲ νευρίνοισι τοὺς πόδας βρόχοις,
ἄρθροισιν εἰσδραμοῦσα μὴ νοουμένη.
5 γελῶ δὲ τοὺς πληγέντας ὑπ᾽ ἐμοῦ πρὸς ⟨βίαν⟩
καὶ μὴ λέγοντας τἀτρεκὲς τῆς συμφορᾶς,
ἀλλ᾽ εἰς ματαίαν πρόφασιν ἐξησκημένους.
ἅπας γὰρ αὐτὸν βουκολεῖ ψευδοστομῶν,
ὡς ἐνσεσεικὼς ἤ τι προσκόψας βάσιν
10 λέγει φίλοισι, μὴ φράσας τὴν αἰτίαν·
ὃ μὴ λέγει γάρ, ὡς δοκῶν λαθεῖν τινας,
χρόνος δέ γ᾽ ἕρπων μηνύει, κἂν μὴ θέλῃ.
καὶ τότε δαμασθείς, ὀνομάσας μου τοὔνομα,
πᾶσιν θρίαμβος ἐκβεβάστακται φίλοις.
15 Πόνος δὲ μοι συνεργός ἐστι τῶν κακῶν·
ἐγὼ γὰρ οὐδέν εἰμι τούτου δίχα μόνη.
τοῦτ᾽ οὖν δάκνει με καὶ φρενῶν καθάπτεται,
ὅτι τὸν ἅπασιν αἴτιον Πόνον κακῶν
οὐδεὶς κακούργοις λοιδορεῖ βλασφημίαις,
20 ἀλλὰ κατ᾽ ἐμοῦ πέμπουσι δυσφήμους ἀρὰς

l. 1   Cf. Euripides, *Hippolytus* 1, 2.
l. 5   πρὸς βίαν Radermacher: πο** Γ: προ** vel πρό**
     recc.: πόδας Γ^c: πόδας ἄκρους conieci.
l. 6   ἀτρεκῆ codd.: corr. Guyet.
l. 9   ἤποι προσκόψας Γ: corr. Radermacher: ἢ προκόψας
     ποι recc., edd..
l. 10   λέγει codd.: ἀλγεῖ Radermacher.

358

SWIFT-OF-FOOT

Dramatis Personae:
GOUT
TUTOR
SWIFT-OF-FOOT
DOCTOR

GOUT

I have a name men dread and loathe to hear ;
They call me Gout, a fearsome scourge to men ;
I bind their feet in sinew-knotting cords,
When I have swept unseen into their joints.
I laugh to see men smitten down by me,   5
Who will not tell the truth of their distress,
But practised are in offering vain excuse,
For each beguiles himself with lying tongue,
Pretending to his friends he's sprained a leg
Or put his ankle out, hiding the cause.   10
For what denieth he, thinking to hide,
The passing time reveals against his will.
Then overcome he mentions me by name,
When carried forth to glee of all his friends.
And Torment helpeth me in all these woes.   15
For without him I am myself but nought.
Therefore it gnaws and catcheth at my heart,
That, though Torment is cause of woes to all,
Yet no one rails at him with curses foul,
But execrations vile at me they hurl,   20

---

l. 12 Cf. *Gout* 70.
l. 14 ἐμβεβάστακται edd..
l. 16 τούτου codd.: τοῦδε Radermacher.
l. 17 Cf. Euripides, *Medea* 55.

ὡς δεσμὸν ἐλπίζοντες ἐκφυγεῖν ἐμόν.
τί ταῦτα φλυαρῶ κοὐ λέγω τίνος χάριν
πάρειμι μὴ φέρουσα τὴν ἐμὴν χολήν;
ὁ γὰρ Δόλων γενναῖος, ὁ θρασὺς Ὠκύπους

25 φρονεῖ καθ' ἡμῶν μηδὲν εἶναί μέ τι λέγων.
ἐγὼ δ' ὑπ' ὀργῆς ὡς γυνὴ δεδηγμένη
ἀντέδακα τοῦτον ἀθεράπευτον εὐστόχως,
ὡς ἦν ἔθος μοι κονδύλου ποδὸς τυχεῖν.
ἤδη δ' ὁ δεινὸς Πόνος ἔχει λεπτὸν τόπον

30 καὶ τὴν βάσιν νυγμοῖσι τρυπᾷ τὴν κάτω.
ὁ δ' ὡς δρόμοισιν ἢ πάλη πλήξας ἴχνος
πλανᾷ γέροντα παιδαγωγὸν ἄθλιον.
καὶ κλεψίχωλον πόδα τιθεὶς ἰχνευμένον
δύστηνος αὐτὸς ἐκ δόμων προέρχεται.

35 πόθεν δ' ὁ δεινὸς κατὰ ποδῶν οὗτος παρῆν
ἀτραυμάτιστος, ἄβατος, ἄστατος πόνος;
τείνω δὲ νεῦρον οἷα τοξότης ἀνὴρ
βέλος προπέμπων καὶ λέγειν βιάζεται·
Τὸ τῶν πονούντων ἔσχατον στοιχεῖ χρόνῳ.

ΤΡΟΦΕΥΣ

40 Ἔπαιρε σαυτόν, ὦ τέκνον, καὶ κούφισον.
μή πώς με πίπτων καταβάλῃς σὺ χωλὸς ὤν.

ΩΚΥΠΟΥΣ

Ἰδού, κρατῶ σε δίχα βάρους καὶ πείθομαι
καὶ τὸν πονοῦντα πόδα τιθῶ καὶ καρτερῶ·

l. 24   δόλον edd.: δόλῳ Zimmermann.
l. 25   μ' ἔτι Guyet.
l. 29   τόπων Γ.
l. 34   προσέρχεται edd.

SWIFT-OF-FOOT

As if they hoped my bondage to escape.
But why this empty talk ? Why don't I tell
Why I am here with wrath I cannot brook ?
That noble man of guile, bold Swift-of-Foot,
Against us plots, and says I am as nought.   25
And I, like any female stung by wrath,
Vengeful, with bite that none may cure, aimed true,
As is my wont, at knuckles of his feet.
And now dread Torment works in narrow field,
Boring his feet below with piercing stabs,   30
While he deceives his poor old dominie,
Pretending race or wrestling caused the sprain,
And, hiding lameness of his foot, my prey,
Comes forth from home alone unhappy man.
Whence comes upon your feet this torment dread, 35
From no wound sprung, brooking nor walk nor
        stance ?
Just like an archer when he speeds his shaft,
I draw his sinews taut and him constrain
To say, " The worst of pains are healed by time."

TUTOR

Stand up, support yourself, lest you should fall   40
And cast me to the ground, my child so lame.

SWIFT-OF-FOOT

Lo, without weight I hold to thee, and ply
As bid my painful foot with fortitude.

---

ll. 35-39 Ocypodi trib. Guyet.
l. 37 τείνω codd.: τείνει Guyet.
l. 38 λέγειν codd.: στένειν Guyet.
l. 39 Paedagogo trib. F. Hermann.
l. 40 Cf. Euripides, *Alcestis* 250, *Andromache* 1077,
      Aristophanes, *Lysistrata* 937.

νεωτέρῳ γὰρ αἶσχος ἐν πεσήμασι
45 ὑπηρέτης ἀδύνατος γογγύζων γέρων.

ΤΡΟΦΕΥΣ

Μὴ μή τι ταῦτα, μωρέ, μή με κερτόμει,
μή μ᾽ ὡς νέος κόμπαζε, τοῦτ᾽ εἰδὼς ὅτι
ἐν ταῖς ἀνάγκαις πᾶς γέρων ἐστὶν νέος.
πείθου λέγοντι· τὸ πέρας ἂν ὑποσπάσω,
50 ἔστην ὁ πρέσβυς, σὺ δ᾽ ὁ νέος πίπτεις χαμαί.

ΩΚΥΠΟΥΣ

Σὺ δ᾽ ἂν σφαλῇς, πέπτωκας ἄπονος ὢν γέρων.
προθυμία γὰρ ἐν γέρουσι παρέπεται,
πρᾶξις δὲ τούτοις οὐκέτ᾽ ἐστὶν εὔτονος.

ΤΡΟΦΕΥΣ

Τί μοι σοφίζῃ, κοὐ λέγεις οἵῳ τρόπῳ
55 πόνος προσῆλθε σοῦ ποδὸς κοίλην βάσιν;

ΩΚΥΠΟΥΣ

Δρόμοισιν ἀσκῶν, κοῦφον ὡς τιθῶ πόδα,
τρέχων ἔτεινα, καὶ συνεσμίχθην πόνῳ.

ΤΡΟΦΕΥΣ

Πάλιν τρέχ᾽, ὥς τις εἶπεν, ὃς καθήμενος
πώγωνα τίλλει κουριῶν ὑπ᾽ ὠλέναις.

l. 44 πεσήμασι Radermacher: παισὶν ἀεὶ codd.: τοῖς
πταίσμασι E. H. Warmington.
l. 45 ἀδύνατα metri causa Dindorf: sed cf. l. 12.
l. 46 sic rec.: μή μέ τι Γ: μὴ μή συ edd..
l. 52 γέρουσιν Γ.

SWIFT-OF-FOOT

For when youth falls he suffers scorn if helped
By feeble, murmuring, aged servitor.   45

TUTOR

Stop, stop, thou fool, thus taunting me, oh stop ;
Speak not to me with boasts of youth, but learn
That times of need make old men youthful all.
Heed what I say.   I'll speak with brevity ;
Though old, I stand ; though young, thou fallest
        down.   50

SWIFT-OF-FOOT

But if you slip, you fall from age, not pain.
For with the old the spirit still is keen,
But has no more the strength to execute.

TUTOR

Why pit your wits with mine ?   Just tell me how
Torment has reached the arches of your feet.   55

SWIFT-OF-FOOT

When practising the sprint in quest of speed,
I strained my foot and wedded was to pain.

TUTOR

Run backward then, as said a man who sat
And plucked his beard, though hairy 'neath his arms.

---

l. 57 ἔτεινα Jacobitz, cf. *Ox. Pap.* 2532: ἔτειλα Γ.
l. 57 συνεμμίχθην Gavelens: συνεσεμίχθην malim.
l. 58 τρέχ' ὡς recc.: τρέχων Γ.
l. 58 εἶπεν ὃς Peletier: εἶπεν (εἶπον Γ) ἢ codd..
l. 59 κουρέων codd.: corr. Gesner.

PSEUDO-LUCIAN

ΩΚΥΠΟΥΣ

60 Οὐκοῦν παλαίων ὡς θέλω παρεμβολὴν
βαλεῖν ἐπλήγην. τοῦτο δὴ πίστευέ μοι.

ΤΡΟΦΕΥΣ

Ποῖος στρατιώτης γέγονας, ἵνα παρεμβολὴν
βαλὼν σὺ πληγῇς; περικυκλεῖς ψευδῆ λόγον.
τὸν αὐτὸν ἡμεῖς εἴχομεν λόγον ποτὲ
65 μηδενὶ λέγοντες τὴν ἀλήθειαν φίλων.
νῦν δ' εἰσορᾶς ἅπαντας ἐξευρηκότας.
ὁ πόνος ἐλελίξας ἐμμελῶς διαστρέφει.

ΙΑΤΡΟΣ

Ποῖ ποῖ καθεύρω κλεινὸν Ὠκύπουν, φίλοι,
τὸν πόδα πονοῦντα καὶ βάσιν παρειμένον;
70 ἰατρὸς ὢν γὰρ ἔκλυον ὑπὸ φίλου τινὸς
πάσχοντα δεινὰ τοῦτον ἀστάτῳ πάθει.
ἀλλ' αὐτὸς οὗτος ἐγγὺς ὀμμάτων ἐμῶν
κεῖται κατ' εὐνῆς ὕπτιος βεβλημένος.
ἀσπάζομαί σε πρὸς θεῶν, καὶ σὸν ⟨πάθος⟩
75 τί ⟨πότ'⟩ ἐστι τοῦτο; λέξον, Ὠκύπου, τάχα.
εἰ γὰρ μάθοιμι, τυχὸν ἴσως ἰάσομαι
τὸ δεινὸν ἄλγος, τοῦ πάθους τὴν συμφοράν.

ΩΚΥΠΟΥΣ

Ὁρᾶς με, Σωτὴρ καὶ πάλιν Σωτήριχε,
Σάλπιγγος αὐτῆς ὄνομ' ἔχων Σωτήριχε,

l. 60 θέλων rec., edd..
l. 63 ψευδηλογῶν Γ: ψευδολογῶν recc.: corr. edd..
l. 66 lacunam post ἐξ in codd. sic supplevi: ἐξαρνουμένους Zimmermann.
l. 67 δ' ἐλίξας rec., edd..
l. 74 πάθος suppl. Gavelens: κακὸν malim.

SWIFT-OF-FOOT

SWIFT-OF-FOOT

Well, I while wrestling tried my man to trip   60
But took a knock. It is the truth, I swear.

TUTOR

A feeble soldier thou ! To try a trip
But take a knock ! A twisted lying tale
Is this you tell, the same as once was mine,
When I would tell none of your friends the truth.   65
But now you see they all have found it out.
For racking twisting torment makes thee dance.

DOCTOR

Where can I find, my friends, famed Swift-of-Foot,
The one whose foot is sore, whose gait impaired ?
For I, a doctor, heard from friend of mine   70
He suffers terribly and cannot stand.
But look, I see him lie not far away
Stretched out upon his back upon a bed.
By all the gods I greet thee, Swift-of-Foot.
Quick tell, what's this thy plight, I fain would
    know ?   75
For if I'm told, it may be I shall cure
Thy grievous pain, thy tragic suffering.

SWIFT-OF-FOOT

See, Saviour, Saviour, I repeat that name
By which men call the Clarion-Goddess too,*

l. 79   Σάλπιγξ (= trumpet) was a name given to Pallas
      Athene. Cf. Pausanias 2.21.3; she also had the
      name Σώτειρα (= Saviour). Cf. Aristophanes,
      Frogs 379.

l. 75   versum sic supplevi. τάχα codd.: τάχ' ὡς μάθω
      Gesner.

80 δεινὸς πόνος με τοῦ ποδὸς δάκνει κακῶς,
δειλὸν δὲ βῆμα κοὐχ ἁπλοῦν τιθῶ ποσίν.

ΙΑΤΡΟΣ

Πόθεν παθών, μήνυσον, ἢ ποίῳ τρόπῳ;
μαθὼν ἀλήθειαν γὰρ ἰατρὸς ἀσφαλῶς
κρεῖττον πρόσεισι, σφάλλεται δὲ μὴ μαθών.

ΩΚΥΠΟΥΣ

85 Δρόμον τιν᾽ ἀσκῶν καὶ τέχνην γυμναστικὴν
δεινῶς ἐπλήγην ὑπὸ φίλων ὁμηλίκων.

ΙΑΤΡΟΣ

Πῶς οὖν ἀηδὴς οὐ πάρεστι φλεγμονὴ
τόπου κατ᾽ αὐτοῦ κοὐκ ἔχεις τιν᾽ ἐμβροχήν;

ΩΚΥΠΟΥΣ

Οὐ γὰρ στέγω τὰ δεσμὰ τῶν ἐριδίων,
90 εὐμορφίαν ἄχρηστον εἰς πολλοὺς καλήν.

ΙΑΤΡΟΣ

Τί οὖν δοκεῖ σοι; κατακνίσω σου τὸν πόδα;
ἂν γὰρ παράσχῃς μοί <σε>, γιγνώσκειν σε δεῖ,
ὡς ταῖς τομαῖσι πλεῖστον αἷμά σου κενῶ.

ΩΚΥΠΟΥΣ

Ποίησον εἴ τι καινὸν ἐξευρεῖν ἔχεις,
95 ἵν᾽ εὐθὺ δεινὸν ἐκ ποδῶν παύσῃς πόνον.

l. 81   ποσίν Γ: ποδισι Ν: ποδί edd..
l. 83   sic edd.: . . . γὰρ ἀλήθειαν ὁ ἰατρὸς . . . codd..

How cruelly grim torment bites my foot,   80
How weak and laboured every step I make!

DOCTOR

Whence came this ill upon thee ?   Tell me how.
For, told the truth, the doctor will proceed
With surer foot, but trips if uninformed.

SWIFT-OF-FOOT

'Mid running and gymnastic practising,   85
My dear companions dealt me grievous blows.

DOCTOR

How then art free from inflammation sore
Where hurt ?   And why no lotion dost thou use ?

SWIFT-OF-FOOT

I do not hold with woollen bandages.
They're useless finery, though much admired.   90

DOCTOR

What is your will, then ?   Shall I prick your foot ?
For you must know that if you let me act
I cut the veins and much blood drain away.

SWIFT-OF-FOOT

Then do so, if fresh method you can find,
That you at once my feet's grim pain may stop. 95

---

l. 88   κοὐκ rec.: οὐκ Γ.
l. 88   τιν' edd.: τὴν codd..
l. 91   κατακνήσω N, cf. l. 12.
l. 92   σε suppl. edd.; δεῖ Γ: χρή recc., edd..
l. 95   παύσῃ Γ.

ΙΑΤΡΟΣ

Ἰδού, σιδηρόχαλκον ἐπιφέρω τομήν,
ὀξεῖαν, αἱμόδιψον, ἡμιστρόγγυλον.

ΤΡΟΦΕΥΣ

Ἔα, ἔα.
Σῶτερ, τί ποιεῖς; μὴ τύχοις σωτηρίας.
100 τολμᾷς σιδηρόσπαρτον ἐπιβαλεῖν πόνον;
μηδὲν κατειδὼς προσφέρεις κακὸν ποσίν.
ψευδεῖς γὰρ ἔκλυες ὧν ἀκήκοας λόγων.
οὐ γὰρ πάλαισιν ἢ δρόμοισιν, ὡς λέγει,
ἀσκῶν ἐπλήγη. τοῦτο γοῦν ἄκουέ μου.
105 ἦλθεν μὲν οὖν τὸ πρῶτον ὑγιὴς ἐν δόμοις,
φαγὼν δὲ πολλὰ καὶ πιὼν ὁ δυστυχὴς
κλίνης ὕπερθε καταπεσὼν ὑπνοῖ μόνος·
ἔπειτα νυκτὸς διυπνίσας ἐκραύγασεν
ὡς δαίμονι πληγείς, καὶ πάντα φόβον λαβών.
110 ἔλεξε δ’, Οἴμοι, πόθεν ἔχω κακὴν τύχην;
δαίμων τάχα κρατῶν τις ἐξωθεῖ ποδός.
πρὸς ταῦτα νυκτὸς ἀνακαθήμενος μόνος
ὁποῖα κἠϋξ ἐξεθρήνει τὸν πόδα.
ἐπεὶ δ’ ἀλέκτωρ ἡμέραν ἐσάλπισεν,
115 οὗτος προσῆλθε χεῖρα θεὶς ἐμοὶ πικρὰν
θρηνῶν πυρέσσων ⟨εἰπέ μοι βάσιν νοσεῖν.⟩

l. 102 ψευδεῖς ... λόγων Gavelens: ψευδὴς ... ἔργων codd..
l. 109 καὶ ... λαβών rec.: καὶ ... λαβεῖν Γ, cf. l. 12: πάντα
καὶ ... λαβών E. H. Warmington: πάντας ὡς φόβον
λαβεῖν edd.: καὶ φόβος πάντας λάβεν Gavelens: καὶ πλανᾷ
(vel κἀπατᾷ) φόβον λαβών Radermacher.
l. 111 ἐξωθεῖ rec.: ἔξω Γ: ἐξοιστρεῖ malim.
l. 113 κἠϋξ Nauck: κήρυξ codd..
l. 115 sic recc.: προῆλθε Γ.

SWIFT-OF-FOOT

DOCTOR

Look, now I poise the scalpel, metal-wrought,
Bloodthirsty, sharp and hemispherical.

SWIFT-OF-FOOT

Stop, stop.

TUTOR

What do you, Saviour ? Safety be not thine.
How can you bring him pain of metal born ?   100
Fresh woes from ignorance his feet you give,
For false the words your ears have heard just now.
No blow he felt in wrestling or in race,
As he maintains.   But list to what I say.
At first he walked at home in perfect health,   105
But, after eating much and drinking much,
The wretch dropped on his bed and slept alone.
Then in the night from sleep he woke to shout
As though by devil struck and filled with fear.
He cried, " Alas ! Whence comes this evil
    curse ?   110
Perchance tormenting fiend doth grasp my foot."
And so alone last night upon his couch,
He sat mourning his feet like plaintive tern.*
But when the cock's note shrill announced the morn,
He came and laid a cruel hand on me,   115
And moaning, fevered, said his foot did ail.

l. 113 When Halcyone heard that her husband Ceyx had
      been drowned, she mourned for him so bitterly that
      the gods out of pity changed her into a kingfisher,
      while Ceyx became, by some accounts, another
      kingfisher, by other accounts, the bird which is
      perhaps the tern. Cf. *Halcyon, init.*

l. 116 $εἶπε \ldots νοσεῖν$ Radermacher: post $ἐπ' ἐμοὶ βα$ $(βάζων$
      recc.) deficiunt codd..

ἃ πρὶν δὲ σοὶ κατεῖπε, πάντ' ἐψεύσατο,
τὰ δεινὰ κρύπτων τῆς νόσου μυστήρια.

ΩΚΥΠΟΥΣ

Γέρων μὲν αἰεὶ τοῖς λόγοις ὁπλίζεται
120 καυχώμενος τὰ πάντα, μηδὲ ἓν σθένων.
ὁ γὰρ πονῶν τι καὶ φίλοις ψευδῆ λέγων
πεινῶντ' ἔοικε μαστίχην μασωμένῳ.

ΙΑΤΡΟΣ

Πλανᾷς ἅπαντας, ἄλλα δ' ἐξ ἄλλων λέγεις,
λέγων πονεῖν μέν, ὃ δὲ πονεῖς οὔπω λέγεις.

ΩΚΥΠΟΥΣ

125 Πῶς οὖν φράσω σοι τοῦ πάθους τὴν συμφοράν;
πάσχων γὰρ οὐδὲν οἶδα, πλὴν πονῶ μόνον.

ΙΑΤΡΟΣ

Ὅταν ἀφορμῆς δίχα πονῇ τις τὸν πόδα,
πλάσσει τὸ λοιπὸν οὓς θέλει κενοὺς λόγους
εἰδὼς τὸ δεινὸν ᾧ συνέζευκται κακῷ.
130 καὶ νῦν μὲν ἀκμὴν εἷς ⟨σε ποὺς λυπεῖ μόνον.⟩
ἐπὰν δὲ καὶ τὸν ἕτερον ἀλγύνῃ πόδα,
στένων δακρύσεις. ἐν δέ σοι φράσαι θέλω·
τοῦτ' ἔστ' ἐκεῖνο, κἂν θέλῃς, κἂν μὴ θέλῃς.

ΩΚΥΠΟΥΣ

Τί δ' ἔστ' ἐκεῖνό γ', εἰπέ, καὶ τί κλῄζεται;

l. 121 ὁ N: οὐ cett..
l. 130 lacunam sic post Zimmermann supplevi.
l. 131 ἀλγύνῃ Zimmermann: ἀλγύνης codd.: ἀλγήσῃς edd..
l. 132 δακρύεις codd.: corr. Gavelens.
l. 133 Cf. Euripides, *Helen* 621.
l. 134 γ' om. Γ.

370

But all he said just now to you was lies,
Whereby he hid his illness' secrets grim.

SWIFT-OF-FOOT

An old man ever arms himself with words,
Though empty all his boasts and weak his
    strength.   120
For he who's ill and lies unto his friends
Is like a starving man who chews but gum.

DOCTOR

You waste our time by heaping word on word.
You say you're ill but have not said of what.

SWIFT-OF-FOOT

How shall I tell thee of my suffering?   125
Suffering, I nothing know save that I've pain.

DOCTOR

When without cause a man has pain of foot,
Thenceforth he fabricates vain words at will,
Though knowing well the bane to which he's wed.
'Tis only one foot that doth ail as yet,   130
But, when your other foot gives pain as well,
You'll weep and groan. But one thing I would say.
There is the fact, please you or please you not.

SWIFT-OF-FOOT

But what is it, pray tell, and what its name?

l. 122   Lit. mastich which was chewed rather for the pleas-
        ant smell it gave the breath (cf. Kock, *Com. Fr.
        Incert.* 338, Lucian, *Adv. Indoctum* 23) than for any
        nourishment which it afforded.

PSEUDO-LUCIAN

ΙΑΤΡΟΣ

135 Ἔχει μὲν ὄνομα συμφορᾶς γέμον διπλῆς.

ΩΚΥΠΟΥΣ

Οἴμοι. τί τοῦτο; λέξον, ⟨οὗ⟩ δέομαι, γέρον.

ΙΑΤΡΟΣ

Ἐκ τοῦ τόπου μὲν οὗ πονεῖς ἀρχὴν ἔχει.

ΩΚΥΠΟΥΣ

Ποδὸς μὲν ἀρχὴν ὄνομ' ἔχει, καθὼς λέγεις;

ΙΑΤΡΟΣ

Τούτῳ σὺ πρόσθες ἐπὶ τέλει δεινὴν ἄγραν.

ΩΚΥΠΟΥΣ

140 Καὶ πῶς με τὸν δύστηνον ἔτι ⟨νέον κρατεῖ;⟩

ΙΑΤΡΟΣ

Δεινή περ οὖσα, φείδεται γὰρ οὐδενός.

ΩΚΥΠΟΥΣ

Σωτήρ, τί λέγεις; τί δέ με . . . . .

ΙΑΤΡΟΣ

Ἄφες με μικρόν, ἠλόγημαι σοῦ χάριν.

ll. 135, 137, 139, 141   paedagogo trib. rec., edd..
l. 136   οὗ δέομαι conieci: δέομαι codd.: ὦ, δέομαι edd.: ἄντομαι Gavelens.
l. 138   λέγεις om. Γ.
l. 140   lacunam sic suppl. Radermacher.

SWIFT-OF-FOOT

DOCTOR

Its name is fraught with double suffering.   135

SWIFT-OF-FOOT

Alas, what's this ?   Sire, tell me what I ask.

DOCTOR

From that place where you ache its first part comes.

SWIFT-OF-FOOT

Then do you mean its name doth start with " foot "?

DOCTOR

To this for ending " huntress " add, grim word.*

SWIFT-OF-FOOT

And how still young am I her luckless prey ?   140

TUTOR

Right terrible she is, for none she spares.

SWIFT-OF-FOOT

Saviour, what's this you say ?   What waits me now?

DOCTOR

A minute, please.   I am dismayed for you.

l. 139   " Pod-agra " the Greek word for gout means
literally " foot-snare ".

PSEUDO-LUCIAN

ΩΚΥΠΟΥΣ

Τί δ' ἔστι δεινὸν ἢ τί συμβέβηκέ μοι;

ΙΑΤΡΟΣ

145 Εἰς δεινὸν ἦλθες πόνον ἀχώριστον ποδός.

ΩΚΥΠΟΥΣ

Οὐκοῦν με δεῖ πρόχωλον ἐξαντλεῖν βίον;

ΙΑΤΡΟΣ

Χωλὸς μὲν ἂν ᾖς, οὐδέν ἐστι, μὴ φοβοῦ.

ΩΚΥΠΟΥΣ

Τί δ' ἔστι χεῖρον . . . . .

ΙΑΤΡΟΣ

Ἀμφοῖν ποδοῖν σε συμποδισθῆναι μένει.

ΩΚΥΠΟΥΣ

150 Οἴμοι. πόθεν με καινὸς εἰσῆλθεν πόνος
ποδὸς δι' ἄλλου καί με συμπάσχειν κακῶς;
ἢ πῶς ὅλος πέπηγα μεταβῆναι θέλων;
δειλαίνομαι δὲ πολλὰ μεταστῆσαι πόδα,
νήπιος, ὁποῖα βρέφος ἄφνω φοβούμενος.
155 ἀλλ' ἄντομαί σε πρὸς θεῶν, Σωτήριχε,
εἴπερ <τι> τέχνη σὴ δύναται, μηδὲν φθονῶν
θεράπευσον ἡμᾶς, εἰ δὲ μή, διοίχομαι·
πάσχω γὰρ ἀφανῶς, κατὰ ποδῶν τοξεύομαι.

l. 145 ἦλθες πόνον ἀχώριστον Boivin: καὶ ἀχώριστον πόνον ἦλθες
Γ (καὶ om. recc.).

374

SWIFT-OF-FOOT

SWIFT-OF-FOOT
What fearsome thing is this that's on me come ?

DOCTOR
Affliction grim that will not leave your foot.   145

SWIFT-OF-FOOT
Then must I bear from youth a crippled life ?

DOCTOR
If you are lame that's nothing.   Fear not that.

SWIFT-OF-FOOT
But what is greater ill than that, tell me?

DOCTOR
The day will come when both your feet are bound.

SWIFT-OF-FOOT
Alas, whence comes upon me this fresh pain   150
Piercing my other foot, racking it too ?
Why am I rooted here when I would move,
And childish do I dread to move my feet,
Like infant babe who's filled with sudden fright ?
But I implore you, Saviour, by the gods   155
Grudge not, but use all skill at your command
For saving me, since otherwise I'm done ;
For shafts of hidden pain assail my feet.

---

l. 148   τοῦδ' ὃ φῂς κακοῦ; φράσον suppl. Herwerden.
l. 151   sic Radermacher: συμπάσχει codd.: καί νιν ἀμπίσχει
      κακοῖς conieci.
l. 156   τι suppl. edd.: an potius post τέχνη?

PSEUDO-LUCIAN

ΙΑΤΡΟΣ

Τοὺς μὲν πλανήτας περιελὼν λόγους ἐγώ,
160 τοὺς τῶν ἰατρῶν τῶν ὁμιλούντων μόνον,
ἔργῳ δὲ μηδὲν εἰδότων σωτήριον,
τὰ πάντα σοι πάσχοντι συντόμως φράσω.
ἄφευκτον ἦλθες πρῶτον ἐς βάθος κακῶν·
οὐ γὰρ σιδηρόπλαστον ὑπεδύσω βάσιν,
165 ὃ τοῖς κακούργοις εὑρέθη τεκμήριον,
δεινὴν δὲ καὶ κρυφαῖον εἰς πάντας κάκην,
ἧς οὐκ ἂν ἄραιτ᾽ ἄχθος ἀνθρώπων φύσις.

ΩΚΥΠΟΥΣ

Αἰαῖ αἰαῖ, οἴμοι οἴμοι.
πόθεν με τρυπᾷ τὸν πόδα κρυπτὸς πόνος;
170 δέξασθε χεῖρας τὰς ἐμὰς πρὸ τοῦ πεσεῖν,
ὁποῖα Σάτυροι Βακχίους ὑπ᾽ ὠλένας.

ΤΡΟΦΕΥΣ

Γέρων μέν εἰμι, πλὴν ἰδού, σοὶ πείθομαι,
καὶ τὸν νέον σε χειραγωγῶ πρέσβυς ὤν.

l. 163 βάθος rec.: πάθος cett., cf. Euripides, *Helen* 303.
l. 163 κακόν Γ.
l. 164 ὑπεδήσω Dindorf.
l. 166 κρυφαίαν codd.: corr. edd.
l. 167 Cf. Euripides, *Orestes* 3, Lucian, *Jup. Trag.* 1.
sic edd.: ἄλγος ἄροιτ᾽ Γ: ἄροιτ᾽ ἄχθος N.
l. 169 πόδ᾽ αὖ Dindorf.
l. 170 sic N: πρὸ τοῦ πέσω Γ: πρὸς τοὐπίσω rec..

SWIFT-OF-FOOT

DOCTOR

I shall dispense with those long-winded words
Of doctors lending only company,   160
But knowing nought of concrete remedy;
I'll be concise and tell my patient all.
First hear you've no escape from pit of woes.
For on your feet you've donned no chains of steel
Devised to show up rogues to all the world,   165
But wear a cruel bane * that none can see,
Whose heavy weight no mortal man can lift.

SWIFT-OF-FOOT

Alas, alas, alack, alack !
Whence comes this hidden pain to drill my foot ?
Come take, support my hands before I fall   170
Like Satyrs holding Bacchants by their arms.

TUTOR

Though old I am, yet see, I do as bid
And aged take and lead thy youthful hand.

l. 166 Or 'clog', if, as L. A. Post suggests, this is a refer-
        ence to ποδοκάκκη 'stocks', which is sometimes
        spelled ποδοκάκη (='foot-bane').

THE CYNIC

THOUGH a few editors accept *The Cynic* as Lucianic, the style of this dialogue bears little resemblance to that of Lucian; for a detailed analysis see J. Bieler, *Ueber die Echtheit des Lucianischen Dialogs Cynicus* (Hildesheim, 1891). Moreover, the position of *The Cynic* in Γ is not above suspicion.

The fact that The Cynic emerges with such credit has also been used as an argument against Lucianic authorship. This in itself need not be so, as Lucian gives favourable pictures of Cynics, e.g. Menippus, Diogenes and the Cynic of *Zeus Cathechized*; Lucian has little quarrel with sincere Cynics, but only with charlatans such as Peregrinus. What is suspicious, however, is the poor figure cut by Lycinus, when confronted by the Socratic methods of the Cynic; there is, admittedly, some parallelism in the feeble role played by Tychiades in *The Parasite*, but that dialogue is not serious like *The Cynic* and may not be the work of Lucian.

I therefore follow Fritzsche in regarding this piece as the work of a Cynic defending his sect against the criticisms made by Lucian. It may well have been written, as Fritzsche suggests, in the time of Julian the Apostate, who encouraged the beliefs and philosophies of ancient times, but it could be considerably earlier.

ΚΥΝΙΚΟΣ

ΛΥΚΙΝΟΣ[1]

1. Τί ποτε σύ, οὗτος, πώγωνα μὲν ἔχεις καὶ κόμην, χιτῶνα δὲ οὐκ ἔχεις καὶ γυμνοδερκῇ καὶ ἀνυποδητεῖς τὸν ἀλήτην καὶ ἀπάνθρωπον βίον καὶ θηριώδη ἐπιλεξάμενος καὶ ἀεὶ τοῖς ἐναντίοις τὸ ἴδιον δέμας οὐχ ὡς οἱ πολλοὶ διαχρησάμενος περινοστεῖς ἄλλοτε ἀλλαχοῦ, καὶ εὐνηθησόμενος[2] ἐπὶ ξηροῦ δαπέδου, ὡς ἄσην[3] πάμπολλον τὸ τριβώνιον φέρειν, οὐ μέντοι καὶ τοῦτο λεπτὸν οὐδὲ μαλακὸν οὐδὲ ἀνθηρόν;

ΚΥΝΙΚΟΣ

Οὐδὲ γὰρ δέομαι· τοιοῦτον δὲ ὁποῖον ἂν πορισθείη ῥᾷστα καὶ τῷ κτησαμένῳ πράγματα ὡς ἐλάχιστα παρέχον· τοιοῦτον γὰρ ἀρκεῖ μοι. 2. σὺ δὲ πρὸς θεῶν εἰπέ μοι, τῇ πολυτελείᾳ οὐ νομίζεις κακίαν προσεῖναι;

ΛΥΚΙΝΟΣ

Καὶ μάλα.

ΚΥΝΙΚΟΣ

Τῇ δὲ εὐτελείᾳ ἀρετήν;

Codices Γ et recentes (N et alios) rettuli.

THE CYNIC

1. You there, why in heaven's name have you the beard and the long hair, but no shirt ? Why do you expose your body to view, and go barefooted, adopting by choice this nomadic antisocial and bestial life ? Why unlike all others do you abuse your body by ever inflicting on it what it likes least, wandering around and prepared to sleep anywhere at all on the hard ground, so that your old cloak carries about a plentiful supply of filth, though it was never fine or soft or gay ?

CYNIC

I need no such cloak. Mine is the kind that can be provided most easily and affords least trouble to its owner. Such a cloak is all I need. 2. But *you* tell *me* something, I beg you. Don't you think that there's vice in extravagance ?

LYCINUS

Yes indeed.

CYNIC

And virtue in economy ?

---

¹ nomina personarum om. *Γ*: *ΛΥΚΙΝΟΣ* (*ΞΕΝΟΣ* N) et *ΚΥΝΙΚΟΣ* recc..
² εὐναζόμενος recc.: εὐνάζῃ μόνος Fritzsche
³ ἄτην *Γ*N: corr. rec..

PSEUDO-LUCIAN

ΛΥΚΙΝΟΣ

Καὶ μάλα.

ΚΥΝΙΚΟΣ

Τί ποτε οὖν ὁρῶν ἐμὲ τῶν πολλῶν εὐτελέστερον διαιτώμενον, τοὺς δὲ πολυτελέστερον, ἐμὲ αἰτιᾷ καὶ οὐκ ἐκείνους;

ΛΥΚΙΝΟΣ

Ὅτι οὐκ εὐτελέστερόν μοι, μὰ Δία, τῶν πολλῶν διαιτᾶσθαι δοκεῖς, ἀλλ᾽ ἐνδεέστερον, μᾶλλον δὲ τελέως ἐνδεῶς καὶ ἀπόρως· διαφέρεις γὰρ οὐδὲν σὺ τῶν πτωχῶν, οἳ τὴν ἐφήμερον τροφὴν μεταιτοῦσιν.

ΚΥΝΙΚΟΣ

3. Βούλει οὖν ἴδωμεν, ἐπεὶ προελήλυθεν ἐνταῦθα ὁ λόγος, τί τὸ ἐνδεὲς καὶ τί τὸ ἱκανόν ἐστιν;

ΛΥΚΙΝΟΣ

Εἴ σοι δοκεῖ.

ΚΥΝΙΚΟΣ

Ἆρ᾽ οὖν ἱκανὸν μὲν ἑκάστῳ ὅπερ ἂν ἐξικνῆται πρὸς τὴν ἐκείνου χρείαν, ἢ ἄλλο τι λέγεις;

ΛΥΚΙΝΟΣ

Ἔστω τοῦτο.

THE CYNIC

LYCINUS

Yes indeed.

CYNIC

Why, then, when you see me living a more economical life than the average man, and them living a more extravagant life, do you find fault with me rather than with them?

LYCINUS

Because, upon my troth, I do not think your manner of life more economical than that of the average man, but more wanting—or rather completely wanting and ill-provided. For you're no better than the paupers who beg for their daily bread.

CYNIC

3. Well then, since the argument has reached this point, would you like us to examine just what is want and what sufficiency?

LYCINUS

Yes, if you wish it.

CYNIC

Then is sufficiency for each man that which meets his needs? Or would you call it something else?

LYCINUS

That's good enough.

PSEUDO-LUCIAN

ΚΥΝΙΚΟΣ

Ἐνδεὲς δὲ ὅπερ ἂν ἐνδεέστερον ᾖ τῆς χρείας καὶ μὴ ἐξικνῆται πρὸς τὸ δέον;

ΛΥΚΙΝΟΣ

Ναί.

ΚΥΝΙΚΟΣ

Οὐδὲν ἄρα τῶν ἐμῶν ἐνδεές ἐστιν· οὐδὲν γὰρ αὐτῶν ὅ τι οὐ τὴν χρείαν ἐκτελεῖ τὴν ἐμήν.

ΛΥΚΙΝΟΣ

4. Πῶς τοῦτο λέγεις;

ΚΥΝΙΚΟΣ

Ἐὰν σκοπῇς πρὸς ὅ τι γέγονεν ἕκαστον ὧν δεόμεθα, οἷον οἰκία ἆρ᾽ οὐχὶ σκέπης;

ΛΥΚΙΝΟΣ

Ναί.

ΚΥΝΙΚΟΣ

Τί δέ; ἐσθὴς [1] τοῦ χάριν; ἆρα οὐχὶ καὶ αὕτη [2] τῆς σκέπης;

ΛΥΚΙΝΟΣ

Ναί.

ΚΥΝΙΚΟΣ

Τῆς δὲ σκέπης αὐτῆς πρὸς θεῶν τίνος ἐδεήθημεν ἕνεκα; οὐχ ὥστε ἄμεινον ἔχειν τὸν σκεπόμενον;

THE CYNIC

CYNIC

And want that which comes short of his require-
ments and fails to meet his needs?

LYCINUS

Yes.

CYNIC

Then there's nothing wanting in my way of life.
No part of it fails to fulfil my needs.

LYCINUS

4. How do you mean?

CYNIC

Suppose you consider the purpose of anything
which we need. For example doesn't a house aim at
giving protection?

LYCINUS

Yes.

CYNIC

Well, what is the purpose of clothes? Do not
they too aim at giving protection?

LYCINUS

Yes.

CYNIC

But why, tell me, have we ever found need for protection itself? Isn't it for the better condition of
the person protected?

---

[1] τί (ἡ Ν) δὲ ἐσθὴς recc.: τί δαὶ ἐσθῆτος Γ.
[2] αὑτῆς Γ: καὶ αὑτὴ recc.: αὑτῆς Γ.

PSEUDO-LUCIAN

ΛΥΚΙΝΟΣ

Δοκεῖ μοι.

ΚΥΝΙΚΟΣ

Πότερ᾽ οὖν τὼ πόδε κάκιον ἔχειν δοκῶ σοι;

ΛΥΚΙΝΟΣ

Οὐκ οἶδα.

ΚΥΝΙΚΟΣ

᾽Αλλ᾽ οὕτως ἂν μάθοις· τί ποδῶν ἔστ᾽ ἔργον;

ΛΥΚΙΝΟΣ

Πορεύεσθαι.

ΚΥΝΙΚΟΣ

Κάκιον οὖν πορεύεσθαί σοι δοκοῦσιν οἱ ἐμοὶ πόδες ἢ οἱ[1] τῶν πολλῶν;

ΛΥΚΙΝΟΣ

Τοῦτο μὲν οὐκ ἴσως.

ΚΥΝΙΚΟΣ

Οὐ τοίνυν οὐδὲ[2] χεῖρον ἔχουσιν, εἰ[3] μὴ χεῖρον τὸ ἑαυτῶν ἔργον ἀποδιδόασιν.

ΛΥΚΙΝΟΣ

Ἴσως.

---

[1] οἱ recc.: om. Γ.
[2] οὐδὲ recc.: οὐδ᾽ εἰ ΓΝ.
[3] εἰ recc.: ἢ Γ.

THE CYNIC

LYCINUS

I think so.

CYNIC

Well, do you think that my feet are in worse condition ?

LYCINUS

I don't know.

CYNIC

Well, this is how you can find out. What is the function of feet ?

LYCINUS

To walk.

CYNIC

Then, do you think my feet walk worse than the feet of the average man ?

LYCINUS

In this case perhaps the answer is no.

CYNIC

Then neither are they in worse condition, if they fulfil their function no worse.

LYCINUS

Perhaps so.

PSEUDO-LUCIAN

ΚΥΝΙΚΟΣ

Τοὺς μὲν δὴ πόδας οὐδὲν φαίνομαι χεῖρον διακεί-
μενος [1] τῶν πολλῶν ἔχειν.

ΛΥΚΙΝΟΣ

Οὐκ ἔοικας.

ΚΥΝΙΚΟΣ

Τί δέ; τοὐμὸν σῶμα τὸ λοιπὸν ἆρα κάκιον; εἰ
γὰρ κάκιον, καὶ ἀσθενέστερον, ἀρετὴ γὰρ σώματος
ἰσχύς. ἆρ' οὖν τὸ ἐμὸν ἀσθενέστερον;

ΛΥΚΙΝΟΣ

Οὐ φαίνεται.

ΚΥΝΙΚΟΣ

Οὐ τοίνυν οὔθ' οἱ πόδες φαίνοιντό [2] μοι σκέπης
ἐνδεῶς ἔχειν οὔτε τὸ λοιπὸν σῶμα· εἰ γὰρ ἐνδεῶς
εἶχον, κακῶς ἂν εἶχον. ἡ γὰρ ἔνδεια πανταχοῦ κακὸν
καὶ χεῖρον ἔχειν ποιεῖ ταῦτα οἷς ἂν προσῇ. ἀλλὰ μὴν
οὐδὲ τρέφεσθαί γε φαίνεται χεῖρον τὸ σῶμα τοὐμόν,
ὅτι ἀπὸ τῶν τυχόντων τρέφεται.

ΛΥΚΙΝΟΣ

Δῆλον γάρ.

ΚΥΝΙΚΟΣ

Οὐδὲ εὔρωστον, εἰ κακῶς ἐτρέφετο· λυμαίνονται
γὰρ αἱ πονηραὶ τροφαὶ τὰ σώματα.

---

[1] διακειμένους malim. .
[2] φαίνονται recc..

388

THE CYNIC

CYNIC

Then, as far as feet are concerned, I seem to be in no worse condition than the average man ?

LYCINUS

So it seems.

CYNIC

Well, take the rest of my body. Is it in any worse state ? For if it's worse, it's weaker, since the virtue of the body is strength. Is my body weaker ?

LYCINUS

It doesn't seem to be.

CYNIC

Then neither my feet nor the rest of my body would appear to be wanting in respect of protection. For, if they were wanting, they would be in bad condition ; for want is everywhere an evil and detracts from the condition of the things in which it occurs. Another point. My body seems to be no worse nourished from finding its nourishment in the food that comes first to hand.

LYCINUS

That's quite easy to see.

CYNIC

It wouldn't be healthy if it were wrongly nourished, for bad food harms the body.

PSEUDO-LUCIAN

ΛΥΚΙΝΟΣ

Ἔστι ταῦτα.

ΚΥΝΙΚΟΣ

5. Τί ποτ᾽ [1] οὖν, εἰπέ μοι, τούτων οὕτως ἐχόντων
αἰτιᾷ μου καὶ φαυλίζεις [2] τὸν βίον καὶ φῂς ἄθλιον;

ΛΥΚΙΝΟΣ

Ὅτι, νὴ Δία, τῆς φύσεως, ἣν σὺ τιμᾷς, καὶ τῶν
θεῶν γῆν ἐν μέσῳ κατατεθεικότων, ἐκ δὲ αὐτῆς
ἀναδεδωκότων πολλὰ κἀγαθά, ὥστε ἔχειν ἡμᾶς
πάντα ἄφθονα μὴ πρὸς τὴν χρείαν μόνον, ἀλλὰ καὶ
πρὸς ἡδονήν, σὺ πάντων τούτων ἢ τῶν γε πλείστων
ἄμοιρος εἶ καὶ οὐδενὸς μετέχεις αὐτῶν οὐδὲν μᾶλλον
ἢ τὰ θηρία· πίνεις μὲν γὰρ ὕδωρ ὅπερ καὶ τὰ
θηρία, σιτῇ δὲ ὅπερ ἂν εὑρίσκῃς, ὥσπερ οἱ κύνες,
εὐνὴν δὲ οὐδὲν κρείττω [3] τῶν κυνῶν ἔχεις· χόρτος
γὰρ ἀρκεῖ [4] σοι καθάπερ ἐκείνοις. ἔτι δὲ ἱμάτιον
φορεῖς οὐδὲν ἐπιεικέστερον ἀκλήρου. καίτοι εἰ σὺ
τούτοις ἀρκούμενος ὀρθῶς φρονήσεις, ὁ θεὸς οὐκ
ὀρθῶς ἐποίησε τοῦτο μὲν πρόβατα ποιήσας ἔμμαλλα,
τοῦτο δ᾽ ἀμπέλους ἡδυοίνους, τοῦτο δὲ τὴν ἄλλην
παρασκευὴν θαυμαστῶς ποικίλην καὶ ἔλαιον καὶ
μέλι καὶ τὰ ἄλλα, ὡς ἔχειν μὲν ἡμᾶς σιτία παντοδαπά,
ἔχειν δὲ ποτὸν ἡδύ, ἔχειν δὲ χρήματα, ἔχειν δὲ
εὐνὴν μαλακήν, ἔχειν δὲ οἰκίας καλὰς καὶ τὰ ἄλλα
πάντα θαυμαστῶς κατεσκευασμένα· καὶ γὰρ αὖ τὰ
τῶν τεχνῶν ἔργα δῶρα τῶν θεῶν ἐστι. τὸ δὲ

---

[1] τί ποτ᾽ N: πότ᾽ Γ: πῶς recc..
[2] φαυλίζεις recc.: φαυλίζῃ Γ.

THE CYNIC

LYCINUS

That's so.

CYNIC

5. How then, tell me, when all this is so, can you denounce and pour scorn on my way of life, and call it miserable?

LYCINUS

Because, in heaven's name, although Nature, whom you hold in such honour, and the gods have given the earth for all to enjoy, and from it have provided us with many good things, so that we have abundance of everything to meet not only our needs but also our pleasures, nevertheless you share in few if any of all these things, and enjoy none of them any more than do the beasts. You drink water just as they do, you eat anything you find, as do the dogs, and your bed is no better than theirs. For straw is good enough for you just as it is for them. Moreover the coat you wear is no more respectable than that of a pauper. However, if you who are quite content with all this turn out to be of sound mind, god was wrong in the first place in making sheep to have fleeces, in the second place in making the vines to produce the sweetness of wine, and yet again in giving such wonderful variety to all else with which we are provided, our olive-oil, honey and the rest, so that we have foods of all sorts, and pleasant wine, money, a soft bed, beautiful houses, and everything else admirably set in order. For the products

---

³ κρείττω recc.: χείρω Γ.
⁴ γὰρ ἀρκεῖ recc.: παραρκεῖ Γ.

πάντων τούτων ζῆν ἀπεστερημένον ἄθλιον μέν, εἰ
καὶ ὑπὸ ἄλλου τινὸς ἀπεστέρητο καθάπερ οἱ ἐν τοῖς
δεσμωτηρίοις· πολὺ δὲ ἀθλιώτερον, εἴ τις αὐτὸς
ἑαυτὸν ἀποστεροίη πάντων τῶν καλῶν, μανία ἤδη
τοῦτό γε σαφής.

ΚΥΝΙΚΟΣ

6. 'Αλλ' ἴσως ὀρθῶς λέγεις. ἐκεῖνο δέ μοι εἰπέ,
εἴ τις ἀνδρὸς πλουσίου προθύμως καὶ [1] φιλοφρόνως
ἑστιῶντος καὶ ξενίζοντος πολλοὺς ἅμα καὶ παντοδα-
πούς, τοὺς μὲν ἀσθενεῖς, τοὺς δὲ ἐρρωμένους, κἄπειτα
παραθέντος πολλὰ καὶ παντοδαπά, πάντα ἁρπάζοι
καὶ πάντα ἐσθίοι, μὴ τὰ πλησίον μόνον, ἀλλὰ καὶ
τὰ πόρρω τὰ τοῖς ἀσθενοῦσι παρεσκευασμένα ὑγιαίνων αὐτός, καὶ ταῦτα μίαν μὲν κοιλίαν ἔχων,
ὀλίγων δὲ ὥστε τραφῆναι δεόμενος, ὑπὸ τῶν πολλῶν
ἐπιτριβήσεσθαι μέλλων, οὗτος ὁ ἀνὴρ [2] ποῖός τις
δοκεῖ σοι εἶναι; ἆρά γε φρόνιμος;

ΛΥΚΙΝΟΣ

Οὐκ ἔμοιγε.

ΚΥΝΙΚΟΣ

Τί δέ; σώφρων;

ΛΥΚΙΝΟΣ

Οὐδὲ τοῦτο.

---

[1] καὶ Γ: καὶ φιλανθρώπως ἔτι τε recc..
[2] ἀνὴρ recc.: ἀνήρ. ἄρα γε Γ.

of the arts too are gifts of the gods, and to live deprived of all these is miserable, even if one has lost them at the hands of another, as have men in prison ; but it is much more miserable if a man deprives himself of all the finer things of life. That is no less than palpable madness.

CYNIC

6. Well, perhaps you're right. But tell me one thing. Suppose a rich man proves a zealous and generous host and invites to dinner at one and the same time many men of all kinds, some of them ailing, others men in perfect health, and suppose he has gone on to spread before them a profusion of foods of all sorts. Suppose a man were to snatch up all these and eat them all and not merely the dishes near him, but also those at a distance provided for the sick men, he himself being in good health, in spite of the fact that he has but a single stomach, needs little to nourish him, and is likely to destroy himself by the surfeit. What is your opinion of such a man ? Is he sensible ?

LYCINUS

Not in my opinion.

CYNIC

Well, is he temperate ?

LYCINUS

He's not that either.

PSEUDO-LUCIAN

ΚΥΝΙΚΟΣ

7. Τί δέ; εἴ τις μετέχων τῆς αὐτῆς ταύτης τραπέζης τῶν μὲν πολλῶν καὶ ποικίλων ἀμελεῖ, ἓν δὲ τῶν ἔγγιστα κειμένων ἐπιλεξάμενος, ἱκανῶς ἔχον πρὸς τὴν ἑαυτοῦ χρείαν, τοῦτο ἐσθίοι κοσμίως καὶ τούτῳ μόνῳ χρῷτο, τοῖς δὲ ἄλλοις οὐδὲ προσβλέποι, τοῦτον οὐχ ἡγῇ σωφρονέστερον καὶ ἀμείνω ἄνδρα ἐκείνου;

ΛΥΚΙΝΟΣ

Ἔγωγε.

ΚΥΝΙΚΟΣ

Πότερον οὖν συνίης, ἢ ἐμὲ δεῖ λέγειν;

ΛΥΚΙΝΟΣ

Τὸ ποῖον;

ΚΥΝΙΚΟΣ

Ὅτι ὁ μὲν θεὸς τῷ ξενίζοντι καλῶς ἐκείνῳ ἔοικε παρατιθεὶς πολλὰ καὶ ποικίλα καὶ παντοδαπά, ὅπως ἔχωσιν ἁρμόζοντα, τὰ μὲν ὑγιαίνουσι, τὰ δὲ νοσοῦσι, καὶ τὰ μὲν ἰσχυροῖς, τὰ δὲ ἀσθενοῦσιν, οὐχ ἵνα χρώμεθα ἅπασι πάντες, ἀλλ' ἵνα τοῖς καθ' ἑαυτὸν ἕκαστος καὶ τῶν καθ' ἑαυτὸν ὅτουπερ [1] ἂν τύχῃ μάλιστα δεόμενος.

8. ὑμεῖς δὲ τῷ δι' ἀπληστίαν τε καὶ ἀκρασίαν ἁρπάζοντι πάντα τούτῳ μάλιστα ἐοίκατε πᾶσι χρῆσθαι ἀξιοῦντες καὶ τοῖς ἁπανταχοῦ, μὴ τοῖς παρ' ὑμῖν μόνον, οὐ γῆν οὐ θάλατταν τὴν καθ' αὑτοὺς

THE CYNIC

CYNIC

7. Well, suppose that a man sharing this same table pays no heed to the great variety of dishes, but chooses one of those closest to him sufficient to his need, and eats of this in moderation, confining himself to this one dish, and not so much as looking at the others; don't you consider this man to be more temperate and a better man than the other?

LYCINUS

I do.

CYNIC

Well, do you understand or must I tell you?

LYCINUS

What?

CYNIC

That god is like that good host and puts before men many varied dishes of all sorts, that they may have what suits them, some of the dishes being for the healthy, others for the sick, some for the strong, others for the weak, not for all of us to make use of all of them, but that each may use the things in his reach, and only such of them as he needs most.

8. But you resemble very closely that man who snatches up everything in his uncontrolled greed. You wish to use everything and not merely what you have at home but what comes from every corner of

---

¹ ὅσουπερ L. A. Post.

αὐταρκεῖν νομίζοντες, ἀλλ' ἀπὸ περάτων γῆς ἐμπο-
ρευόμενοι τὰς ἡδονὰς καὶ τὰ ξενικὰ τῶν ἐπιχωρίων
ἀεὶ προτιμῶντες καὶ τὰ πολυτελῆ τῶν εὐτελῶν καὶ
τὰ δυσπόριστα τῶν εὐπορίστων, καθόλου δὲ
πράγματα καὶ κακὰ ἔχειν μᾶλλον ἐθέλοντες ἢ ἄνευ
πραγμάτων ζῆν· τὰ γὰρ δὴ πολλὰ καὶ τίμια καὶ
εὐδαιμονικὰ παρασκευάσματα, ἐφ' οἷς ἀγάλλεσθε,
διὰ πολλῆς ὑμῖν ταῦτα κακοδαιμονίας καὶ ταλαιπω-
ρίας παραγίνεται. σκόπει γὰρ, εἰ βούλει, τὸν
πολύευκτον χρυσόν, σκόπει τὸν ἄργυρον, σκόπει τὰς
οἰκίας τὰς πολυτελεῖς, σκόπει τὰς ἐσθῆτας τὰς
ἐσπουδασμένας, σκόπει τὰ τούτοις ἀκόλουθα πάντα,
πόσων πραγμάτων ἐστὶν ὤνια, πόσων πόνων, πόσων
κινδύνων, μᾶλλον δὲ αἵματος καὶ θανάτου καὶ
διαφθορᾶς ἀνθρώπων πόσης, οὐ μόνον ὅτι πλέοντες
ἀπόλλυνται διὰ ταῦτα πολλοὶ καὶ ζητοῦντες καὶ
δημιουργοῦντες δεινὰ πάσχουσιν, ἀλλ' ὅτι καὶ πολυ-
μάχητά ἐστι καὶ ἐπιβουλεύετε ἀλλήλοις διὰ ταῦτα
καὶ φίλοις φίλοι καὶ πατράσι παῖδες καὶ γυναῖκες
ἀνδράσιν. οὕτως οἶμαι καὶ τὴν Ἐριφύλην διὰ τὸν
χρυσὸν προδοῦναι τὸν ἄνδρα.[1]

9. καὶ ταῦτα μέντοι πάντα γίνεται, τῶν τε ποικίλων
ἱματίων οὐδέν τι μᾶλλον θάλπειν δυναμένων, τῶν δὲ
χρυσορόφων οἰκιῶν οὐδέν τι μᾶλλον σκεπουσῶν, τῶν
δὲ ἐκπωμάτων τῶν ἀργυρῶν οὐκ ὠφελούντων τὸν
πότον οὐδὲ τῶν χρυσῶν, οὐδ' αὖ τῶν ἐλεφαντίνων
κλινῶν τὸν ὕπνον ἡδίω παρεχομένων, ἀλλ' ὄψει
πολλάκις ἐπὶ τῆς ἐλεφαντίνης κλίνης καὶ τῶν
πολυτελῶν στρωμάτων τοὺς εὐδαίμονας ὕπνου
λαχεῖν οὐ δυναμένους. ὅτι[2] μὲν γὰρ αἱ παντοδαπαὶ

the earth, you don't think your own land and sea
adequate, but import your pleasures from the ends
of the earth, you always prefer the exotic to the home-
produced, the costly to the inexpensive, what is hard
to obtain to what is easy, and in short you choose to
have worries and troubles rather than to live a
carefree life.   For those many costly provisions for
happiness, in which you take such pride, come to you
only at the cost of great misery and hardship.
For consider, if you will, the gold for which you
pray, the silver, the expensive houses, the elaborate
dresses, all that goes along with these ; consider how
much they cost in trouble, in toil, in danger, or
rather in blood, death and destruction for mankind,
not only because many men are lost at sea for the
sake of these things, and suffer terribly in searching
for them abroad or manufacturing them at home,
but also because they are bitterly fought for, and for
them you lay plots against one another, friends
against friends, children against fathers, and wives
against husbands.   Thus too it was, I imagine, that
Eriphyle [1] betrayed her husband for gold.

9. And yet all these things happen, although the
many-coloured robes can afford no more warmth, and
the gilded houses no more shelter, though neither the
silver nor the golden goblets improve the drink, nor
do the ivory beds provide sweeter sleep, but you will
often see the prosperous unable to sleep in their
ivory beds and expensive blankets.   And need I tell

---

[1] Eriphyle was bribed with the gift of a golden necklace
to send her husband, Amphiaraus, to his death by persuading him to join the expedition of the Seven Against
Thebes.

---

[1] οὕτως ... ἄνδρα del. Fritzsche.   [2] ὅτι recc.: τί Γ.

περὶ τὰ βρώματα πραγματεῖαι τρέφουσι μὲν οὐδὲν
μᾶλλον, λυμαίνονται δὲ τὰ σώματα καὶ τοῖς σώμασι
νόσους ἐμποιοῦσι, τί δεῖ λέγειν; 10. τί δὲ καὶ λέγειν,
ὅσα τῶν ἀφροδισίων ἕνεκα πράγματα[1] ποιοῦσί τε καὶ
πάσχουσιν οἱ ἄνθρωποι; καίτοι ῥᾴδιον θεραπεύειν
ταύτην τὴν ἐπιθυμίαν, εἰ μή τις ἐθέλοι τρυφᾶν. καὶ
οὐδ' εἰς ταύτην ἡ μανία καὶ διαφθορὰ φαίνεται τοῖς
ἀνθρώποις ἀρκεῖν, ἀλλ' ἤδη καὶ τῶν ὄντων τὴν
χρῆσιν ἀναστρέφουσιν ἑκάστῳ χρώμενοι πρὸς ὃ μὴ
πέφυκεν, ὥσπερ εἴ τις ἀνθ' ἁμάξης ἐθέλοι τῇ κλίνῃ
καθάπερ ἁμάξῃ χρήσασθαι.

ΛΥΚΙΝΟΣ

Καὶ τίς οὗτος;

ΚΥΝΙΚΟΣ

Ὑμεῖς, οἳ τοῖς ἀνθρώποις ἅτε ὑποζυγίοις χρῆσθε,
κελεύετε δὲ αὐτοὺς ὥσπερ ἁμάξας τὰς κλίνας τοῖς
τραχήλοις ἄγειν, αὐτοὶ δ' ἄνω κατάκεισθε τρυφῶντες καὶ ἐκεῖθεν ὥσπερ ὄνους ἡνιοχεῖτε τοὺς ἀνθρώπους ταύτην, ἀλλὰ μὴ ταύτην τρέπεσθαι κελεύοντες·
καὶ οἱ ταῦτα μάλιστα ποιοῦντες μάλιστα μακαρί-
ζεσθε. 11. οἱ δὲ τοῖς κρέασι μὴ τροφῇ χρώμενοι
μόνον, ἀλλὰ καὶ βαφὰς μηχανώμενοι δι' αὐτῶν,
οἷοί γέ εἰσιν οἱ τὴν πορφύραν βάπτοντες, οὐχὶ καὶ
αὐτοὶ παρὰ φύσιν χρῶνται τοῖς τοῦ θεοῦ κατασκεύα-
σμασιν;

ΛΥΚΙΝΟΣ

Νὴ[1] Δία· δύναται γὰρ βάπτειν, οὐκ ἐσθίεσθαι
μόνον τὸ τῆς πορφύρας κρέας.

[1] Μὰ Δία Du Soul.

398

you that the many foods so elaborately prepared afford no more nourishment, but harm the body and produce diseases in it ?   10. And need I mention all the inconvenient things that men do and suffer to gratify their sexual passions ?   Yet this is a desire which is easy to allay, unless one aims at licentious indulgence.   And in gratifying this desire men do not even seem to be content with madness and corruption, but now they pervert the use of things, using everything for unnatural purposes, just as if in preference to a carriage a man chose to use a couch as if it were a carriage.

LYCINUS

And who does that ?

CYNIC

You do so, when you use human beings as beasts of burden, bidding them carry your couches on their shoulders as though they were carriages, and you yourself lie up there in state, and from there steer your men as though they were donkeys, bidding them take this turning rather than that.   And the more any of you does this, the luckier he is thought. 11. And, as for those who not only use flesh for food, but also conjure forth dyes with it, as for example the purple-dyers, don't you think that they too are making an unnatural use of the handiworks of god ?

LYCINUS

By Zeus, that I do not ; for the flesh of the purple-fish can produce dye as well as food.

---

¹ πράγματα del. Jacobs.

ΚΥΝΙΚΟΣ

Ἀλλ' οὐ πρὸς τοῦτο γέγονεν· ἐπεὶ καὶ τῷ κρατῆρι δύναιτ' ἄν τις βιαζόμενος ὥσπερ χύτρᾳ χρήσασθαι, πλὴν οὐ πρὸς τοῦτο γέγονεν. ἀλλὰ γὰρ πῶς ἅπασαν[1] τὴν τούτων τις κακοδαιμονίαν διελθεῖν δύναιτ' ἄν; τοσαύτη τίς ἐστι. σὺ δέ μοι, διότι μὴ βούλομαι ταύτης μετέχειν, ἐγκαλεῖς· ζῶ δὲ καθάπερ ὁ κόσμιος ἐκεῖνος, εὐωχούμενος τοῖς κατ' ἐμαυτὸν καὶ τοῖς εὐτελεστάτοις χρώμενος, τῶν δὲ ποικίλων καὶ παντοδαπῶν οὐκ ἐφιέμενος.

12. κἄπειτα[2] εἰ θηρίου βίον βραχέων δεόμενος καὶ ὀλίγοις χρώμενος δοκῶ σοι ζῆν, κινδυνεύουσιν οἱ θεοὶ καὶ τῶν θηρίων εἶναι χείρονες κατά γε τὸν σὸν λόγον· οὐδενὸς γὰρ δέονται. ἵνα δὲ καταμάθῃς ἀκριβέστερον τό τε ὀλίγων καὶ τὸ πολλῶν δεῖσθαι ποῖόν τι ἑκάτερόν ἐστιν, ἐννόησον ὅτι δέονται πλειόνων οἱ μὲν παῖδες τῶν τελείων, αἱ δὲ γυναῖκες τῶν ἀνδρῶν, οἱ δὲ νοσοῦντες τῶν ὑγιαινόντων, καθόλου δὲ πανταχοῦ τὸ χεῖρον τοῦ κρείττονος πλειόνων δεῖται. διὰ τοῦτο θεοὶ μὲν οὐδενός, οἱ δὲ ἔγγιστα θεοῖς ἐλαχίστων δέονται.

13. ἢ νομίζεις τὸν Ἡρακλέα τὸν πάντων ἀνθρώπων ἄριστον, θεῖον δὲ ἄνδρα καὶ θεὸν ὀρθῶς νομισθέντα, διὰ κακοδαιμονίαν περινοστεῖν γυμνὸν δέρμα μόνον ἔχοντα καὶ μηδενὸς τῶν αὐτῶν ὑμῖν[3] δεόμενον; ἀλλ' οὐ κακοδαίμων ἦν ἐκεῖνος, ὃς καὶ τῶν ἄλλων ἀπήμυνε τὰ κακά, οὐδ' αὖ πένης, ὃς γῆς καὶ θαλάττης ἦρχεν· ἐφ' ὅ τι γὰρ ὁρμήσειεν, ἁπανταχοῦ πάντων ἐκράτει καὶ οὐδενὶ τῶν τότε

---

[1] ἅπασι Γ.

CYNIC

But it doesn't exist for that purpose. For in the same way too a man could force a mixing-bowl into service as a pitcher; but that's not why it came into being. But how could anyone describe in full the misery of people like these? For it's so very great. Yet you reproach *me* for not wishing to share it with them. But I live like that moderate man, making a feast of what is in my reach, and using what is least expensive, with no desire for dainties from the ends of the earth.

12. Furthermore, if you think I live the life of a beast, because the things I need and use are small and few, it may be that the gods are inferior even to the beasts—if we use your argument. For the gods need nothing. But, so that you may learn more exactly what is involved in having few needs, and what in having many, reflect that children have more needs than adults, women than men, invalids than healthy people, and, in general, the inferior everywhere has more needs than the superior. Therefore the gods have need of nothing, and those nearest to them have the fewest needs.

13. Do you think that Heracles, the best of all mankind, a godlike man and rightly considered a god, was compelled by an evil star to go around naked, wearing only a skin and needing none of the same things as you do? No, *he* was not ill-starred, he who brought the rest of men relief from their banes, nor was *he* destitute who was the master of both land and sea; for no matter what he essayed, he

---

² κἄπειτα recc.: κἄπει τῶν Γ.
³ ἡμῖν Γ.

ἐνέτυχεν ὁμοίῳ οὐδὲ κρείττονι ἑαυτοῦ, μέχριπερ ἐξ
ἀνθρώπων ἀπῆλθεν. ἢ σὺ δοκεῖς στρωμάτων καὶ
ὑποδημάτων ἀπόρως ἔχειν καὶ διὰ τοῦτο περιιέναι
τοιοῦτον;[1] οὐκ ἔστιν εἰπεῖν, ἀλλ᾽ ἐγκρατὴς καὶ
καρτερικὸς ἦν καὶ κρατεῖν ἤθελε καὶ τρυφᾶν οὐκ
ἐβούλετο. ὁ δὲ Θησεὺς ὁ τούτου μαθητὴς οὐ
βασιλεὺς μὲν ἦν πάντων Ἀθηναίων, υἱὸς δὲ Ποσειδῶνος, ὥς φασιν, ἄριστος δὲ τῶν καθ᾽ αὑτόν;
14. ἀλλ᾽ ὅμως κἀκεῖνος ἤθελεν ἀνυπόδητος εἶναι καὶ
γυμνὸς βαδίζειν καὶ πώγωνα καὶ κόμην ἔχειν
ἤρεσκεν αὐτῷ, καὶ οὐκ ἐκείνῳ μόνῳ, ἀλλὰ καὶ πᾶσι
τοῖς παλαιοῖς ἤρεσκεν· ἀμείνους γὰρ ἦσαν ὑμῶν,
καὶ οὐκ ἂν ὑπέμειναν οὐδὲ εἷς αὐτῶν οὐδὲν μᾶλλον
ἢ τῶν λεόντων τις ξυρώμενος· ὑγρότητα γὰρ καὶ
λειότητα σαρκὸς γυναιξὶ πρέπειν ἡγοῦντο, αὐτοὶ δ᾽
ὥσπερ ἦσαν, καὶ φαίνεσθαι ἄνδρες ἤθελον καὶ τὸν
πώγωνα κόσμον ἀνδρὸς ἐνόμιζον ὥσπερ καὶ ἵππων
χαίτην καὶ λεόντων γένεια, οἷς ὁ θεὸς ἀγλαΐας καὶ
κόσμου χάριν προσέθηκέ τινα·[2] οὕτωσὶ δὲ καὶ τοῖς
ἀνδράσι τὸν πώγωνα προσέθηκεν. ἐκείνους οὖν ἐγὼ
ζηλῶ τοὺς παλαιοὺς καὶ ἐκείνους μιμεῖσθαι βούλομαι, τοὺς δὲ νῦν οὐ ζηλῶ τῆς θαυμαστῆς ταύτης
εὐδαιμονίας ἣν[3] ἔχουσι καὶ περὶ τραπέζας καὶ
ἐσθῆτας καὶ λεαίνοντες καὶ ψιλούμενοι πᾶν τοῦ
σώματος μέρος καὶ μηδὲ τῶν[4] ἀπορρήτων μηδέν,
ᾗ πέφυκεν, ἔχειν ἐῶντες.
15. εὔχομαι δέ μοι τοὺς μὲν πόδας ὁπλῶν ἱππείων
οὐδὲν διαφέρειν, ὥσπερ φασὶ τοὺς Χείρωνος, αὐτὸς

---

[1] τοιοῦτος codd.: corr. edd..   [2] τινα rec.: τινόν Γ: om. N.
[3] ἦν Γ: ἧς recc..   [4] μηδὲ τῶν rec.: μὴ δρόντων Γ.

prevailed over all everywhere, and never encountered his equal or superior, till he left the realm of men. Do you think that *he* couldn't provide blankets and shoes, and that was why he went around in the state he did ? No one could say that ; no, he had self-control and hardness ; he wished to be powerful, not to enjoy luxury. And what of his disciple, Theseus ? Was he not king of all the Athenians, son of Poseidon, as they say, and best man of his day ? 14. Yet he too chose to wear no shoes, and to walk about naked ; he was pleased to have a beard and long hair, and not only he but all the other men of old too. For they were better men than you, and not a single one of them would have submitted to the razor any more than would a lion. For they thought that soft smooth flesh became a woman, but, just as they themselves were men, so too they wished to appear men, thinking the beard an ornament of men, as is the mane an ornament of horses and lions, to whom god has given additional gifts to grace and adorn them. So too has he given men the addition of a beard. These men of old therefore are the ones that *I* admire and should like to emulate, but the men of to-day I do not admire for the " wonderful " prosperity they enjoy in the matter of food and clothing, and when they smooth and depilate every part of their bodies, not even allowing any of their private parts to remain in its natural condition.

15. I pray that I may have feet no different from horses' hooves, as they say were those of Chiron,[1] and

---

[1] One of the Centaurs, mythical creatures who had the top half of a man but were horses from their waists to their feet.

δὲ μὴ δεῖσθαι στρωμάτων ὥσπερ οἱ λέοντες, οὐδὲ [1]
τροφῆς δεῖσθαι πολυτελοῦς μᾶλλον ἢ οἱ κύνες· εἴη δέ
μοι γῆν μὲν ἅπασαν εὐνὴν αὐτάρκη ἔχειν, οἶκον δὲ
τὸν κόσμον νομίζειν, τροφὴν δὲ αἱρεῖσθαι τὴν ῥάστην
πορισθῆναι. χρυσοῦ δὲ καὶ ἀργύρου μὴ δεηθείην μήτ᾽
οὖν ἐγὼ μήτε τῶν ἐμῶν φίλων μηδείς· πάντα γὰρ
τὰ κακὰ τοῖς ἀνθρώποις ἐκ τῆς τούτων ἐπιθυμίας
φύονται, καὶ στάσεις καὶ πόλεμοι καὶ ἐπιβουλαὶ καὶ
σφαγαί. ταυτὶ πάντα πηγὴν ἔχει τὴν ἐπιθυμίαν τοῦ
πλείονος· ἀλλ᾽ ἡμῶν αὕτη ἀπείη, καὶ πλεονεξίας
μήποτε ὀρεχθείην, μειονεκτῶν δ᾽ ἀνέχεσθαι δυναίμην.

16. τοιαῦτά σοι τά γε ἡμέτερα, πολὺ δήπου διά-
φωνα τοῖς τῶν πολλῶν βουλήμασι· καὶ θαυμαστὸν
οὐδέν, εἰ τῷ σχήματι διαφέρομεν αὐτῶν, ὁπότε καὶ
τῇ προαιρέσει τοσοῦτον διαφέρομεν. θαυμάζω δέ
σου πῶς ποτε κιθαρῳδοῦ μέν τινα νομίζεις στολὴν
καὶ σχῆμα, καὶ αὐλητοῦ νὴ Δία σχῆμα, καὶ στολὴν
τραγῳδοῦ, ἀνδρὸς δὲ ἀγαθοῦ σχῆμα καὶ στολὴν
οὐκέτι νομίζεις, ἀλλὰ τὴν αὐτὴν αὐτὸν οἴει δεῖν ἔχειν
τοῖς πολλοῖς, καὶ ταῦτα τῶν πολλῶν κακῶν ὄντων.
εἰ μὲν δεῖ ἑνὸς ἰδίου σχήματος τοῖς ἀγαθοῖς, τί
πρέποι ἂν μᾶλλον ἢ τοῦθ᾽ ὅπερ ἀναιδέστατον τοῖς [2]
ἀκολάστοις ἐστὶ καὶ ὅπερ ἀπεύξαιντ᾽ ἂν οὗτοι
μάλιστα ἔχειν;

17. οὐκοῦν τό γε ἐμὸν σχῆμα τοιοῦτόν ἐστιν,
αὐχμηρὸν εἶναι, λάσιον εἶναι, τρίβωνα ἔχειν,
κομᾶν, ἀνυποδητεῖν, τὸ δ᾽ ὑμέτερον ὅμοιον τῷ
τῶν κιναίδων, καὶ διακρίνειν οὐδὲ εἷς ἂν ἔχοι, οὐ
τῇ χροιᾷ τῶν ἱματίων, οὐ τῇ μαλακότητι, οὐ τῷ

---

[1] οὔτε codd.: corr. edd..   [2] τοῖς edd.: μᾶλλον τοῖς codd..

that I myself may not need bedclothes any more than do the lions, nor expensive fare any more than do the dogs. But may I have for bed to meet my needs the whole earth, may I consider the universe my house, and choose for food that which is easiest to procure, Gold and silver may I not need, neither I nor any of my friends. For from the desire for these grow up all men's ills—civic strife, wars, conspiracies and murders. All these have as their fountainhead the desire for more. But may this desire be far from us, and never may I reach out for more than my share, but be able to put up with less than my share.

16. Such, you see, are our wishes, wishes assuredly far different from those of most men. Nor is it any wonder that we differ from them in dress when we differ so much from them in principles too. But you surprise me by the way that you think that a lyre-player has a particular uniform and garb, and, by heavens, that a piper has his uniform, and a tragic actor his garb, but, when it comes to a good man, you don't think that he has his own dress and garb, but should wear the same as the average man, and that too although the average man is depraved. If good men need one particular dress of their own, what one would be more suitable than this dress which seems quite shameless to debauched men and which they would most deprecate for themselves?

17. Therefore my dress is, as you see, a dirty shaggy skin, a worn cloak, long hair and bare feet, but yours is just like that of the sodomites and no one could tell yours from theirs either by the colour of your cloaks, or by the softness and number of your

πλήθει τῶν χιτωνίσκων, οὐ τοῖς ἀμφιέσμασιν,[1] οὐχ
ὑποδήμασιν, οὐ κατασκευῇ τριχῶν, οὐκ ὀδμῇ· καὶ
γὰρ καὶ ἀπόζετε ἤδη παραπλήσιον ἐκείνοις οἱ
εὐδαιμονέστατοι οὗτοι μάλιστα. καίτοι τί ἂν δώῃ
τις ἀνδρὸς τὴν αὐτὴν τοῖς κιναίδοις ὀδμὴν ἔχοντος;
τοιγαροῦν τοὺς μὲν πόνους οὐδὲν ἐκείνων μᾶλλον
ἀνέχεσθε, τὰς δὲ ἡδονὰς οὐδὲν ἐκείνων ἧττον· καὶ
τρέφεσθε τοῖς αὐτοῖς καὶ κοιμᾶσθε ὁμοίως καὶ
βαδίζετε, μᾶλλον δὲ βαδίζειν οὐκ ἐθέλετε, φέρεσθε[2]
δὲ ὥσπερ τὰ φορτία οἱ μὲν ὑπ' ἀνθρώπων, οἱ δὲ ὑπὸ
κτηνῶν· ἐμὲ δὲ οἱ πόδες φέρουσιν ὅποιπερ ἂν δέω-
μαι. κἀγὼ μὲν ἱκανὸς καὶ ῥίγους ἀνέχεσθαι καὶ
θάλπος φέρειν καὶ τοῖς τῶν θεῶν ἔργοις μὴ δυσχεραί-
νειν, διότι ἄθλιός εἰμι, ὑμεῖς δὲ διὰ τὴν εὐδαιμονίαν
οὐδενὶ τῶν γινομένων ἀρέσκεσθε καὶ πάντα μέμφεσθε
καὶ τὰ μὲν παρόντα φέρειν οὐκ ἐθέλετε, τῶν δὲ
ἀπόντων ἐφίεσθε, χειμῶνος μὲν εὐχόμενοι θέρος,
θέρους δὲ χειμῶνα, καὶ καύματος μὲν ῥῖγος,
ῥίγους δὲ καῦμα καθάπερ οἱ νοσοῦντες δυσάρεστοι
καὶ μεμψίμοιροι ὄντες· αἰτία δὲ ἐκείνοις μὲν ἡ
νόσος, ὑμῖν δὲ ὁ τρόπος.

18. κἄπειτα δὲ ἡμᾶς μετατίθεσθε[3] καὶ ἐπανορθοῦτε[4]
τὰ ἡμέτερα,[5] κακῶς βουλευομένοις[6] πολλάκις περὶ ὧν
πράττομεν, αὐτοὶ ἄσκεπτοι ὄντες περὶ τῶν ἰδίων καὶ
μηδὲν αὐτῶν κρίσει καὶ λογισμῷ ποιοῦντες, ἀλλ' ἔθει
καὶ ἐπιθυμίᾳ. τοιγαροῦν οὐδὲν ὑμεῖς διαφέρετε τῶν
ὑπὸ χειμάρρου φερομένων· ἐκεῖνοί τε γάρ, ὅπου ἂν
ᾖ[7] τὸ ῥεῦμα, ἐκεῖ φέρονται, καὶ ὑμεῖς ὅπου ἂν αἱ

---

[1] ἀμφιάσμασιν recc., edd..   [2] φέρεσθε Γ: φέρεσθαι recc..
[3] ἡμᾶς μετατίθεσθε recc.: ὑμᾶς μετατίθεσθαι Γ.
[4] ἐπανορθοῦτε scripsi: ἐπανορθοῦν codd..

tunics, or by your wraps, shoes, elaborate hair-styles, or your scent. For nowadays you reek of scent just like them—you, who are the most fortunate of men ! Yet of what value can one think a man who smells the same as a sodomite ? So it is that you are no more able to endure hardships than they are, and no less amenable to pleasures than they. Moreover, your food is the same as theirs, you sleep like them and walk like them—or rather just like them prefer not to walk but are carried like baggage, some of you by men, others by beasts. But *I* am carried by my feet wherever I need to go, and *I* am able to put up with cold, endure heat and show no resentment at the works of the gods, because I am unfortunate, whereas you, because of your good fortune, are pleased with nothing that happens, and always find fault, unwilling to put up with what you have, but eager for what you have not, in winter praying for summer, and in summer for winter, in hot weather for cold, and in cold weather for hot, showing yourselves as hard to please and as querulous as invalids. But whereas the cause of *their* behaviour is illness, the cause of *yours* is your character.

18. Again you would have us change and you reform our manner of life for us because we often are ill-advised in what we do, though you yourselves bestow no thought on your own actions, basing none of them on rational judgment, but upon habit and appetite. Therefore you are exactly the same as men carried along by a torrent ; for they are carried along wherever the current takes them, and you

---

⁵ ἡμέτερα recc.: ὑμέτερα Γ: ἡμέτερα ἀξιοῦτε edd..

⁶ βουλευομένους recc.: βουλευομένων edd..   ⁷ ἴη recc.: εἴη Γ.

PSEUDO-LUCIAN

ἐπιθυμίαι. πάσχετε δὲ παραπλήσιόν τι ὅ φασι
παθεῖν τινα ἐφ' ἵππον ἀναβάντα μαινόμενον· ἁρπάσας
γὰρ αὐτὸν ἔφερεν ἆρα ὁ ἵππος· ὁ δὲ οὐκέτι κατα-
βῆναι τοῦ ἵππου θέοντος ἐδύνατο. καί τις ἀπαντή-
σας ἠρώτησεν αὐτὸν ποίαν ἄπεισιν; ὁ δὲ εἶπεν,
Ὅπου ἂν τούτῳ δοκῇ, δεικνὺς τὸν ἵππον. καὶ
ὑμᾶς ἄν τις ἐρωτᾷ, ποῖ [1] φέρεσθε; τἀληθὲς ἐθέλον-
τὲς λέγειν ἐρεῖτε ἁπλῶς μέν, ὅπουπερ [2] ἂν ταῖς ἐπιθυμίαις δοκῇ, κατὰ μέρος δέ, ὅπουπερ [2] ἂν τῇ
ἡδονῇ δοκῇ, ποτὲ δέ, ὅπου τῇ δόξῃ, ποτὲ δὲ
αὖ, τῇ φιλοκερδίᾳ· ποτὲ δὲ ὁ θυμός, ποτὲ δὲ
ὁ φόβος, ποτὲ δὲ ἄλλο τι τοιοῦτον ὑμᾶς ἐκφέρειν
φαίνεται· [3] οὐ γὰρ ἐφ' ἑνός, ἀλλ' ἐπὶ πολλῶν
ὑμεῖς γε ἵππων βεβηκότες ἄλλοτε ἄλλων,[4] καὶ
μαινομένων πάντων, φέρεσθε. τοιγαροῦν ἐκφέ-
ρουσιν ὑμᾶς εἰς βάραθρα καὶ κρημνούς. ἴστε δ'
οὐδαμῶς πρὶν πεσεῖν ὅτι πείσεσθαι [5] μέλλετε.

19. ὁ δὲ τρίβων οὗτος, οὗ καταγελᾶτε, καὶ ἡ κόμη
καὶ τὸ σχῆμα τοὐμὸν τηλικαύτην ἔχει δύναμιν, ὥστε
παρέχειν μοι ζῆν ἐφ' ἡσυχίας καὶ πράττοντι ὅ τι
βούλομαι καὶ συνόντι οἷς βούλομαι· τῶν γὰρ
ἀμαθῶν ἀνθρώπων καὶ ἀπαιδεύτων οὐδεὶς ἂν
ἐθέλοι μοι προσιέναι διὰ τὸ σχῆμα, οἱ δὲ μαλακοὶ
καὶ πάνυ πόρρωθεν ἐκτρέπονται· προσίασι δὲ οἱ κομ-
ψότατοι καὶ ἐπιεικέστατοι καὶ ἀρετῆς ἐπιθυμοῦντες.
οὗτοι μάλιστά μοι προσίασι· τοῖς γὰρ τοιούτοις
ἐγὼ χαίρω συνών. θύρας δὲ τῶν καλουμένων

[1] ποῖ om. Γ.
[2] bis ὅπουπερ recc..
[3] φαίνεται Γ: δύναται recc..

408

wherever your appetites take you. Your situation
is just like what they say happened to the man who
mounted a mad horse. For it rushed off, carrying
him with it ; and he couldn't dismount again because
the horse kept running. Then someone who met
them asked him where he was off to, and he replied,
"Wherever this fellow decides," indicating the horse.
Now if anyone asks you where you're heading for, if
you wish to tell the truth, you will say simply that it's
where your appetites choose, or more specifically
where pleasure chooses, or now where ambition, or
now again where avarice chooses ; and sometimes
temper, sometimes fear, or sometimes something else
of the sort seems to carry you off. For you are
carried along on the back not of one but of many
horses, and different ones at different times—but all
of them mad. As a result they carry you away
towards cliffs and chasms. But before you fall you
are quite unaware of what is going to happen to you.

19. But this worn cloak which you mock, and my
long hair and my dress are so effective that they
enable me to live a quiet life doing what I want to do
and keeping the company of my choice. For no ignorant or uneducated person would wish to associate
with one that dresses as I do, while the fops turn away
while they're still a long way off. But my associates
are the most intelligent and decent of men, and those
with an appetite for virtue. These men are my
particular associates, for I rejoice in the company of
men like them. But I dance no attendance at the

---

⁴ ἄλλας Γ.
⁵ πείσεσθαι Γ: πείσεσθε recc.: πεσεῖσθε recc., edd..

εὐδαιμόνων [1] οὐ θεραπεύω, τοὺς δὲ χρυσοῦς
στεφάνους καὶ τὴν πορφύραν τῦφον νομίζω καὶ τῶν
ἀνθρώπων καταγελῶ. 20. ἵνα δὲ μάθῃς περὶ τοῦ
σχήματος, ὡς οὐκ ἀνδράσι μόνον ἀγαθοῖς, ἀλλὰ καὶ
θεοῖς πρέποντος ἔπειτα καταγελᾷς αὐτοῦ, σκέψαι τὰ
ἀγάλματα τῶν θεῶν, πότερά σοι δοκοῦσιν ὁμοίως
ἔχειν ὑμῖν ἢ ἐμοί; καὶ μὴ μόνον γε τῶν Ἑλλήνων,
ἀλλὰ καὶ τῶν βαρβάρων τοὺς ναοὺς ἐπισκόπει
περιιών, πότερον αὐτοὶ [2] οἱ θεοὶ κομῶσι καὶ γενειῶ-
σιν ὡς ἐγὼ ἢ καθάπερ ὑμεῖς ἐξυρημένοι πλάττονται
καὶ γράφονται. καὶ μέντοι καὶ ἀχίτωνας ὄψει τοὺς
πολλοὺς ὥσπερ ἐμέ. τί ἂν οὖν ἔτι τολμῴης περὶ
τούτου τοῦ σχήματος λέγειν ὡς φαῦλον,[3] ὁπότε καὶ
θεοῖς φαίνεται πρέπον;

---

[1] καλουμένων εὐδαιμόνων Wetsten: καλουμένων ἀνθρώπων
codd.: καλλωπιζομένων (vel καλλυνομένων) ἀνθρώπων Lennep:
ζηλουμένων ἀνθρώπων conieci.

[2] αὐτοὶ om. recc..   [3] φαύλου recc., edd..

doors of the so-called fortunate, but consider their golden crowns and their purple robes mere pride, and I laugh at the fellows who wear them.

20. And I'd have you know that my style of dress becomes not only good men but also gods, though you go on to mock it ; and so consider the statues of the gods. Do you think they are like you or like me ? And don't confine your attentions to the statues of the Greeks, but go round examining foreigners' temples too, to see whether the gods themselves have long hair and beards as I do, or whether their statues and paintings show them close-shaven like you. What's more, you will see they are just like me not only in these respects but also in having no shirt. How then can you still have the effrontery to describe my style of dress as contemptible, when it's obvious that it's good enough even for gods ?

THE PATRIOT

THE poor Greek of the Philopatris with its syntactical foibles, its confusion of dialects and its mixture of prose and verse forms betrays this work as being not by Lucian but by an imitator. It is in fact a Byzantine work, as first realised by C. B. Hase in 1813, though the most important contribution to the study of the dialogue is S. Reinach's " *La question du Philopatris*," in *Revue Archéologique* 1902.

The dialogue was written in the time of Nicephorus Phocas who recaptured Crete from the Saracens in 961, usurped the throne of Byzantium in 963, won victories over the Saracens in Cilicia, Mesopotamia and Syria in 964-6, and over the Bulgars in 967. He captured Antioch and Aleppo in 969, and, had he not been murdered in December of that year, had visions of further conquests. The dialogue was perhaps written in the spring of 969, or, less probably, of 965, but its purpose is uncertain.

Phocas' campaigns were expensive and, despite his military successes, he was unpopular with the Byzantines because of his heavy taxes and his debasing of the coinage. He had also forfeited the favour of his old friends, the monks, by marrying the notorious widow Theophano, by forbidding money being spent on new monasteries and legacies being given to existing ones and by insisting that new bishops should be approved by the Emperor. His unpopularity was such that he was almost killed in a riot in 967.

413

The first part of this dialogue seems to be a light-hearted attack on contemporary humanists who had excessive enthusiasm for classical culture. The second half is more serious and appeals to all patriots to support the emperor in his great campaigns against the enemies of his country. The prophets of doom may perhaps be the monks ; whoever they are, they are criticised for indulging in superstitious and unpatriotic opposition to a great warrior king. The alternative titles seem both to refer to Critias who shows himself a patriot in the second half of the dialogue, though earlier he needs instruction on the Trinity. The author is perhaps a sophist who hopes that the hint of poverty in Critias' last speech will lead to a suitable reward from the emperor.

ΦΙΛΟΠΑΤΡΙΣ Η ΔΙΔΑΣΚΟΜΕΝΟΣ

ΤΡΙΕΦΩΝ

1. Τί τοῦτο, ὦ Κριτία; ὅλον σεαυτὸν ἠλλοίωσας καὶ τὰς ὀφρῦς κάτω συννένευκας, μύχιον δὲ βυσσοδομεύεις ἄνω καὶ κάτω περιπολῶν κερδαλεόφρονι ἐοικὼς κατὰ τὸν ποιητήν " ὠχρός τέ σευ εἷλε παρειάς." μή που Τρικάρανον [1] τεθέασαι ἢ Ἑκάτην ἐξ Ἅιδου ἐληλυθυῖαν, ἢ καί τινι θεῶν ἐκ προνοίας συνήντηκας; οὐδέπω γάρ σε τοιαῦτα εἰκὸς παθεῖν, εἰ καὶ αὐτὸν ἠκηκόεις, οἶμαι, τὸν κόσμον κλυσθῆναι ὥσπερ ἐπὶ τοῦ Δευκαλίωνος. σοὶ λέγω, ὦ καλὲ Κριτία, οὐκ ἀΐεις ἐμοῦ ἐπιβοωμένου τὰ πολλὰ καὶ ἐς βραχὺ γειτνιάσαντος; δυσχεραίνεις καθ' ἡμῶν ἢ ἐκκεκώφωσαι ἢ καί [2] τῆς χειρὸς παλαιστήσοντα [3] ἐπιμένεις;

ΚΡΙΤΙΑΣ

Ὦ Τριεφῶν, μέγαν τινὰ καὶ ἠπορημένον λόγον ἀκήκοα καὶ πολλαῖς ὁδοῖς διενειλημμένον καὶ ἔτι ἀναπεμπάζω τοὺς ὕθλους καὶ τὰς ἀκοὰς ἀποφράττω,

codices rettuli Vaticanum Graecum 1322 = Δ (cui est simillimus Vat. Gr. 88), Parisinum Gr. 3011 = C, Dochiariou (Athos) 268 (quem a voeavi) qui sunt omnes fere XIV saeculi.

[1] τρικάρηνον edd..
[2] καὶ codd.: καὶ ἐκ Guyet.
[3] παλαστήσοντα Δ.

THE PATRIOT or THE PUPIL

TRIEPHO

1. What's this, Critias ? You've changed completely and now have puckered brows and wander up
and down deep in thought, like the " designing
wight " [1] of the poet, " and pallor hath possessed thy
cheeks." [2] You've haven't seen the three-headed
hound [3] have you, or Hecate risen from Hades ?
Or has Providence vouchsafed you a meeting with
one of the gods ? One wouldn't have expected you
to be in this state yet, even if, I suppose, you had
heard that the world itself had been subjected to a
flood as in the time of Deucalion. I'm speaking to
you my good Critias ! " Dost thou not hear me, " [4]
even though I'm shouting so loud from such close
quarters ? Are you offended with me, or have you
gone deaf,[5] or are you waiting for me to give you a
push ?

CRITIAS

My dear Triepho, I've just heard a speech that was
long, puzzling, devious and involved, and I'm still
counting up its nonsensicalities and keeping my ears

---

[1] No doubt Odysseus (*Iliad* IV. 339) rather than
Agamemnon (*Iliad* I. 149) is meant.

[2] Cf. *Iliad* III. 35 also parodied in *Zeus Rants* 1.

[3] Cerberus, watchdog of the underworld.

[4] Cf. *Iliad* X. 160 etc.

[5] The phrase is modelled on *The Ship*, 10

μή που ἔτι ἀκούσαιμι ταῦτα καὶ ἀποψύξω ἐκμανεὶς
καὶ μῦθος τοῖς ποιηταῖς γενήσομαι ὡς καὶ Νιόβη
τὸ πρίν. ἀλλὰ [καὶ] [1] κατὰ κρημνῶν ὠθούμην ἂν
ἐπὶ κεφαλῆς σκοτοδινήσας, εἰ μὴ ἐπέκραξάς μοι,
ὦ τάν, καὶ τὸ τοῦ Κλεομβρότου πήδημα τοῦ
Ἀμβρακιώτου ἐμυθεύθη [2] ἐπ᾽ ἐμοί.

ΤΡΙΕΦΩΝ

2. Ἡράκλεις, τῶν θαυμασίων ἐκείνων φασμάτων
ἢ ἀκουσμάτων, ἅπερ Κριτίαν ἐξέπληξαν. πόσοι
γὰρ ἐμβρόντητοι ποιηταὶ καὶ τερατολογίαι φιλοσόφων οὐκ ἐξέπληξάν σου τὴν διάνοιαν, ἀλλὰ λῆρος
πάντα γέγονεν ἐπὶ σοί.

ΚΡΙΤΙΑΣ

Πέπαυσο ἐς μικρὸν καὶ μηκέτι παρενοχλήσῃς, ὦ
Τριεφῶν· οὐ γὰρ παροπτέος ἢ ἀμελητέος γενήσῃ
παρ᾽ ἐμοῦ.

ΤΡΙΕΦΩΝ

Οἶδ᾽ ὅτι οὐ μικρὸν οὐδὲ εὐκαταφρόνητον πρᾶγμα
ἀνακυκλεῖς, ἀλλὰ καὶ λίαν τῶν ἀπορρήτων· ὁ γὰρ
χρὼς καὶ τὸ ταυρηδὸν ὑποβλέπειν [3] καὶ τὸ ἄστατον
τῆς βάσεως τό τε ἄνω [4] καὶ κάτω περιπολεῖν
ἀρίγνωτόν σε καθίστησιν. ἀλλ᾽ ἄμπνευσον τοῦ
δεινοῦ, ἐξέμεσον τοὺς ὕθλους, "μή τι κακὸν πάθῃς."

---

[1] καὶ dell. edd..
[2] ἐμυθεύθη ἂν C.
[3] ὑποβλέπειν Wyttenbach: ἐπιβλέπειν codd..
[4] τε ἄνω Halm: ἄνω τε codd..

THE PATRIOT

closed for fear I may hear it again and die of madness,
becoming a story for poets as was Niobe once.[1] But
I would have cast myself headlong over a precipice
in my dizziness, if you hadn't called out to me, my
good fellow, and stories would have credited me with
the leap of Cleombrotus,[2] the Ambraciot.

TRIEPHO

2. By Heracles, what marvels to see or hear these
were if they so astounded Critias ! For how many
thunderstruck poets and marvellous tales of philosophers failed to make the slightest impression on
your mind, but became so much empty talk for you !

CRITIAS

Stop for a little ; don't pester me any further, for
you won't be ignored or neglected by me.

TRIEPHO

I know that it's nothing small or contemptible
that you keep turning over in your mind, but some
profound mystery. For your colour, your angry
look, your uncertain steps and your wanderings up
and down make that right manifest. Take a rest from
your tribulations, spit out these follies, " for fear you
suffer aught of ill." [3]

---

[1] I.e. be petrified like Niobe; cf. note on p. 354.
[2] A pupil of Plato who committed suicide by leaping from
a high wall after reading the *Phaedo.* Cf. Callimachus,
Epigram 25 and Mair's note.
[3] This phrase is not closely paralleled in epic, but cf.
Odyssey XVII. 596 etc.

PSEUDO-LUCIAN

ΚΡΙΤΙΑΣ

Σὺ μέν, ὦ Τριεφῶν, ὅσον πέλεθρον ἀνάδραμε ἀπ'
ἐμοῦ, ἵνα μὴ τὸ πνεῦμα ἐξάρῃ σε καὶ πεδάρσιος τοῖς
πολλοῖς ἀναφανῇς καί που καταπεσὼν Τριεφώντειον
πέλαγος κατονομάσῃς, ὡς καὶ Ἴκαρος τὸ πρίν·
ἃ γὰρ ἀκήκοα τήμερον παρὰ τῶν τρισκαταράτων
ἐκείνων σοφιστῶν, μεγάλως ἐξώγκωσέ μου τὴν
νηδύν.

ΤΡΙΕΦΩΝ

Ἐγὼ μὲν ἀναδραμοῦμαι ὁπόσον καὶ βούλει,[1]
σὺ δὲ ἄμπνευσον τοῦ δεινοῦ.

ΚΡΙΤΙΑΣ

Φῦ φῦ φῦ φῦ τῶν ὕθλων ἐκείνων, ἰοὺ ἰοὺ ἰοὺ ἰοὺ
τῶν δεινῶν βουλευμάτων, αἲ αἲ αἲ αἲ τῶν κενῶν
ἐλπίδων.

ΤΡΙΕΦΩΝ

3. Βαβαὶ[2] τοῦ ἀναφυσήματος, ὡς τὰς νεφέλας
διέστρεψε· ζεφύρου γὰρ ἐπιπνέοντος λάβρου καὶ
τοῖς κύμασιν ἐπωθίζοντος βορέην ἄρτι ἀνὰ τὴν
Προποντίδα κεκίνηκας, ὡς διὰ κάλων αἱ ὁλκάδες
τὸν Εὔξεινον πόντον οἰχήσονται, τῶν κυμάτων
ἐπικυλινδούντων ἐκ τοῦ φυσήματος· ὅσον οἴδημα
τοῖς ἐγκάτοις ἐνέκειτο· πόσος κορκορυγισμὸς[3] καὶ
κλόνος τὴν γαστέρα σου συνετάρασσε. πολύωτον
σεαυτὸν ἀναπέφηνας τοσαῦτα ἀκηκοώς, ὥστε[4] κατὰ
τὸ τερατῶδες καὶ διὰ τῶν ὀνύχων ἠκηκόεις.

---

[1] βούλεσαι Δα.   [2] τριβαβαὶ α.

420

THE PATRIOT

CRITIAS

You must retire a good thirty yards from me, Triepho, for fear lest the breeze lift you up, the multitude see you 'mid earth and sky and you fall down somewhere to give your name to a Triephontian Sea after the manner of Icarus of old. For what I have heard to-day from these trebly cursed professors has caused my belly greatly to swell.

TRIEPHO

I for my part shall retire as far as you wish, but you must rest from your tribulations.

CRITIAS

Alas, alas, alas, alas for those follies! Woe, woe, woe, woe for these terrible schemes! Alack, alack, alack, alack for those empty hopes!

TRIEPHO

3. Good gracious, what a gust of wind! How it dispersed those clouds! For when the Zephyr was blowing fresh and driving the shipping over the waves, you've just stirred up a North Wind throughout the Propontis, so that only by use of ropes will the merchantmen pass to the Euxine, as wind and wave make them roll. What a swelling assailed your internal organs! What a rumbling and agitation afflicted your stomach! You've shown yourself possessed of many ears by hearing so many things that you've been a prodigy and even heard through your fingernails.

---

³ κορκορυγμὸς edd..
⁴ ὥστε καὶ Δα: ὡς τὰ C: ὅς γε Halm.

PSEUDO-LUCIAN

ΚΡΙΤΙΑΣ

Οὐ παράδοξόν τι, ὦ Τριεφῶν, ἀκηκοέναι καὶ
ἐξ ὀνύχων· καὶ γὰρ κνήμην γαστέρα τεθέασαι καὶ
κεφαλὴν κύουσαν καὶ ἀνδρείαν φύσιν ἐς γυναικείαν
ἐνεργοβατοῦσαν καὶ ἐκ γυναικῶν ὄρνεα μεταβαλλό-
μενα· καὶ ὅλως[1] τερατώδης ὁ βίος, εἰ βούλει
πιστεύειν τοῖς ποιηταῖς. ἀλλ᾽ '' ἐπεί σε '' πρῶτον
'' κιχάνω τῷδ᾽ ἐνὶ χώρῳ,'' ἀπίωμεν ἔνθα αἱ
πλάτανοι τὸν ἥλιον εἴργουσιν, ἀηδόνες δὲ καὶ
χελιδόνες εὔηχα κελαδοῦσιν, ἵν᾽ ἡ μελῳδία τῶν
ὀρνέων τὰς ἀκοὰς ἐνηδύνουσα τό τε ὕδωρ ἠρέμα
κελαρύζον τὰς ψυχὰς καταθέλξειεν.

ΤΡΙΕΦΩΝ

4. Ἴωμεν, ὦ Κριτία· ἀλλὰ δέδια μή που ἐπῳδὴ
τὸ ἠκουσμένον ἐστὶ καί με ὕπερον ἢ θύρετρον ἢ ἄλλο
τι τῶν ἀψύχων ἀπεργάσεται ἡ θαυμασία σου αὕτη
κατάπληξις.

ΚΡΙΤΙΑΣ

Νὴ τὸν Δία τὸν αἰθέριον οὐ τοῦτο γενήσεται
ἐπὶ σοί.

ΤΡΙΕΦΩΝ

Ἔτι με ἐξεφόβησας τὸν Δία ἐπομοσάμενος. τί
γὰρ ἂν δυνήσεται ἀμυνέμεναί σε, εἰ παραβαίης τὸν

[1] ὅλος codd..

---

[1] For the birth of Dionysus. Cf. *Dialogues of the Gods* 12.
[2] For the birth of Athene. Cf. ibid. 13.
[3] E.g. Tiresias. Cf. *Dialogues of the Dead* 8.

THE PATRIOT

CRITIAS

There's nothing strange even in hearing through
the fingernails, Triepho. For you've seen a leg
become a womb,[1] a head pregnant,[2] men change to
women[3] and women to birds.[4] In short, life's full
of prodigies, if you care to believe the poets. But
first, " since in this place I do thee find," [5] let us
depart to where the plane-trees [6] keep off the sun, and
nightingales and swallows pour forth sweet melodies,
so that our souls may be enchanted by the melody of
the birds that delights the ears, and by the gentle
murmur of the water.

TRIEPHO

4. Let us go there, Critias. But I'm afraid that
perhaps what you've heard is a magic incantation
and the wonders which amazed you will make me
into pestle or a door [7] or some other inanimate
object.

CRITIAS

By Zeus in the skies, this won't happen to you !

TRIEPHO

You've frightened me again by swearing by Zeus.
For how could " he thee chastise," [8] if you broke

---

[4] E.g. Halcyone, Philomela, and Procne.
[5] Cf. *Odyssey* XIII. 228.
[6] Cf. Plato, *Phaedrus*, 230 B.
[7] Cf. *The Lover of Lies* 35.
[8] An epic-sounding phrase though modelled on no
surviving passage.

ὅρκον; οἶδα γὰρ καὶ σὲ μὴ ἀγνοεῖν περὶ τοῦ
Διός σου.

ΚΡΙΤΙΑΣ

Τί λέγεις; οὐ δυνήσεται Ζεὺς [1] ἐς Τάρταρον
ἀποπέμψαι; ἢ ἀγνοεῖς ὡς τοὺς θεοὺς πάντας
ἀπέρριψεν ἀπὸ τοῦ θεσπεσίου βηλοῦ καὶ τὸν
Σαλμωνέα ἀντιβροντῶντα πρώην κατεκεραύνωσε καὶ
τοὺς ἀσελγεστάτους ἔτι καὶ νῦν, παρὰ δὲ τῶν
ποιητῶν Τιτανοκράτωρ καὶ Γιγαντολέτης ἀνυμνεῖ-
ται ὡς καὶ παρ' Ὁμήρῳ;

ΤΡΙΕΦΩΝ

Σὺ μέν, ὦ Κριτία, πάντα παρέδραμες τὰ τοῦ
Διός, ἀλλ', εἴ σοι φίλον, ἄκουε. οὐχὶ κύκνος
οὗτος ἐγένετο καὶ σάτυρος δι' ἀσέλγειαν, ἀλλὰ καὶ
ταῦρος; καὶ εἰ μὴ τὸ πορνίδιον ἐκεῖνο [2] ταχέως
ἐπωμίσατο [3] καὶ διέφυγε διὰ τοῦ πελάγους, τάχ' ἂν
ἠροτρία ἐντυχὼν γεηπόνῳ ὁ βροντοποιὸς καὶ
κεραυνοβόλος σου Ζεὺς καὶ ἀντὶ τοῦ κεραυνοβολεῖν
τῇ βουπλῆγι κατεκεντάννυτο. τὸ δὲ καὶ Αἰθίοψι
συνευωχεῖσθαι ἀνδράσι μελαντέροις καὶ τὴν ὄψιν
ἐζοφωμένοις καὶ ἐς δώδεχ' ἡλίους μὴ ἀφίστασθαι,

---

[1] ὁ Ζεὺς edd..
[2] ἐκεῖνο C: ἐκεῖνος Δα.
[3] ἐπωμόσατο codd.: corr. Kuster.

---

[1] " All the gods " is an exaggeration based on *Iliad* XV.
22-24; Hephaestus (*Iliad* I. 591) is the only god specified
by Homer.

your oath ? For I know that you too are knowledge-able about your Zeus.

CRITIAS

What do you mean ? Can't Zeus send me to Tartarus ? Don't you know that he has hurled all the gods " from heaven's threshold " [1] and not long ago destroyed Salmoneus with lightning for rivalling his thunder, and still to the present day does so to particularly wanton men, and that he is hymned by poets as " Victor over the Titans " and " Destroyer of the Giants," as indeed in Homer ? [2]

TRIEPHO

You've completed *your* description of Zeus, Critias ; now please listen to me. Didn't he become swan [3] and satyr [4] out of wantonness, yes and bull too ? And if he hadn't been quick in putting that little strumpet [5] on his shoulder and escaped over the sea, your thunder-producing, lightning-hurling Zeus would perhaps have been made to plough, " when that he met a husbandman," [6] and instead of hurling his lightning would have been pricked by the ox-goad. And as for his feasting along with Ethiopians, dusky men with dark faces, and not stopping for twelve days [7] but sitting there tipsy, though having such a

---

[2] These epithets are applied to Zeus in *Timon* 4 but nowhere else ; cf. however *Odyssey* XI, 305 *seq.*

[3] To court Leda.

[4] To court Antiope.

[5] Europa, whom Zeus, disguised as a bull, carried off.

[6] Perhaps a quotation of part of an iambic line.

[7] Cf. *Iliad* I. 423-425.

ἀλλ' ὑποβεβρεγμένος καθεδεῖσθαι παρ' αὐτοῖς
πώγωνα τηλικοῦτον ἔχων, οὐκ αἰσχύνης ἄξια; τὰ
δὲ τοῦ ἀετοῦ καὶ τῆς Ἴδης καὶ τὸ κυοφορεῖν καθ'
ὅλου τοῦ σώματος αἰσχύνομαι καὶ λέγειν.

ΚΡΙΤΙΑΣ

5. Μῶν τὸν Ἀπόλλωνά γ' ἐπομοσόμεθα, ὃς
προφήτης ἄριστος καὶ ἰητρός, ὦγαθέ;

ΤΡΙΕΦΩΝ

Τὸν ψευδόμαντιν λέγεις, τὸν Κροῖσον πρῴην
διολωλεκότα καὶ μετ' αὐτὸν Σαλαμινίους καὶ
ἑτέρους μυρίους, ἀμφίλοξα πᾶσι μαντευόμενον;[1]

ΚΡΙΤΙΑΣ

6. Τὸν Ποσειδῶνα δὲ τί; ὃς τρίαιναν ἐν ταῖν
χεροῖν κρατῶν καὶ διάτορόν τι καὶ καταπληκτικὸν
βοᾷ [2] ἐν τῷ πολέμῳ ὅσον ἐννεάχιλοι ἄνδρες ἢ
δεκάχιλοι, ἀλλὰ καὶ σεισίχθων, ὦ Τριεφῶν, ἐπονο-
μάζεται;

ΤΡΙΕΦΩΝ

Τὸν μοιχὸν λέγεις, ὃς τὴν τοῦ Σαλμωνέως παῖδα
τὴν Τυρὼ πρῴην διέφθειρε καὶ ἔτι ἐπιμοιχεύει καὶ

---

[1] μαντευόμενος codd.: corr. edd..
[2] καὶ διάτορόν . . . βοᾷ versum comicum (fr. 481) esse putavit
Kock.

---

[1] When Zeus carried off Ganymede. Cf. *Dialogues of the
Gods* 8 and 10.

great beard on his face, aren't these things of which
to be ashamed ? The episode of the eagle and
Mount Ida [1] and his being pregnant all over his body
I'm ashamed even to mention !

CRITIAS

5. Shall we then, my good fellow, swear by Apollo,
the excellent prophet and doctor ?

TRIEPHO

The false prophet, you mean, who destroyed
Croesus [2] the other day and after him the men of
Salamis [3] and countless others by giving ambiguous
oracles to all of them ?

CRITIAS

6. And what of Poseidon ? Poseidon who wields a
trident and in war utters shrill terrifying shouts as
loud as nine or ten thousand men,[4] but is also,
Triepho, called " Earth-shaker " ?

TRIEPHO

The adulterer you mean, who the other day
ravished Salmoneus' daughter Tyro,[5] and still
continued his lecherous habits and is the saviour and

---

[2] Cf. Herodotus 1. 53, *Zeus Rants* 20 and 43, *Zeus
Catechized* 14.
[3] Presumably the Persians who had heard about the
response given to the Athenians about the " wooden
wall " and Salamis. Cf. Herodotus 7.141 and *Zeus Rants*
20.
[4] Cf. *Iliad* XIV. 148-149.
[5] Cf. *Odyssey* XI. 241-245.

ῥύστης καὶ δημαγωγὸς τῶν τοιούτων ἐστί; τὸν
γὰρ Ἄρην ὑπὸ τοῦ δεσμοῦ πιεζόμενον καὶ δεσμοῖς
ἀλύτοις μετὰ τῆς Ἀφροδίτης στενούμενον, πάντων
τε τῶν θεῶν διὰ τὴν μοιχείαν ὑπ᾽ αἰσχύνης σιωπών-
των, ὁ ἵππειος Ποσειδῶν ἔκλαυσε[1] δακρυρροῶν
ὥσπερ τὰ βρεφύλλια τοὺς διδασκάλους δεδιότα ἤ
ὥσπερ αἱ γρᾶες κόρας ἐξαπατῶσαι· ἐπέκειτο δὲ τῷ
Ἡφαίστῳ λῦσαι τὸν Ἄρεα, τὸ δὲ ἀμφίχωλον τοῦτο
δαιμόνιον, οἰκτεῖραν τὸν πρεσβύτην θεόν, τὸν Ἄρη
ἀπηλευθέρωσεν. ὥστε καὶ μοιχός ἐστιν ὡς μοιχοὺς
διασῴζων.

ΚΡΙΤΙΑΣ

7. Ἑρμείαν δὲ τί;

ΤΡΙΕΦΩΝ

Μή μοι τὸν κακόδουλον τοῦ ἀσελγεστάτου Διὸς
καὶ τὸν ἀσελγομανοῦντα ἐπὶ τοῖς μοιχικοῖς.

ΚΡΙΤΙΑΣ

8. Ἄρεα δὲ καὶ Ἀφροδίτην οἶδα μὴ παραδέχεσθαί
σε διὰ τὸ προδιαβληθῆναι πρῴην παρὰ σοῦ. ὥστε
ἐάσωμεν τούτους. τῆς Ἀθηνᾶς ἔτι ἐπιμνησθήσομαι,
τῆς παρθένου, τῆς ἐνόπλου καὶ καταπληκτικῆς θεᾶς,
ἣ καὶ τὴν τῆς Γοργόνος κεφαλὴν ἐν τῷ στήθει
περιάπτεται, τὴν γιγαντολέτιν θεόν. οὐ γὰρ ἔχεις
τι λέγειν περὶ αὐτῆς.

---

[1] ἔκλασε Δ: ἔκλαε α.

---

[1] Cf. *Odyssey* VIII. 266-366, *Dialogues of the Gods* 21.

champion of folk like himself ? For when Ares was
cramped by his bonds and confined along with
Aphrodite in inextricable chains,[1] and all the gods
were silent with shame at his adultery, Poseidon,
the equestrian god, burst into streams of tears, as
infants do when afraid of their teachers or old
women when deceiving maidens. He importuned
Hephaestus to release Ares, and that lame deity out
of pity for the senior god [2] set Ares free. Thus
Poseidon too is guilty of adultery by his protection of
adulterers.

CRITIAS

7. And what of Hermes ?

TRIEPHO

Speak not to me of that base slave of Zeus' worst
lecheries, who in adultery mad, lecherous joy doth
take.

CRITIAS

8. I know you won't accept Ares or Aphrodite as
they've just been attacked by you. Let us therefore
leave them aside. But I can still mention Athena,
the virgin, the armed, terrifying goddess with the
Gorgon's head fastened to her bosom, the giant-
destroying goddess.[3] You can't say anything about
her.

---

[2] Poseidon.
[3] I have translated τὴν γιγαντολέτιν θεόν as being
(ungrammatically) in apposition with θεᾶς rather than
with κεφαλὴν; the Gorgon's head can hardly be called
" the giant-slaying goddess."

PSEUDO-LUCIAN

ΤΡΙΕΦΩΝ

Ἐρῶ σοι καὶ περὶ ταύτης, ἤν μοι ἀποκρίνῃ.

ΚΡΙΤΙΑΣ

Λέγε ὅ τι γε βούλει.

ΤΡΙΕΦΩΝ

Εἰπέ μοι, ὦ Κριτία, τί τὸ χρήσιμον τῆς Γοργόνος καὶ τί τῷ στήθει τοῦτο ἡ θεὰ ἐπιφέρεται;

ΚΡΙΤΙΑΣ

Ὡς φοβερόν τι θέαμα καὶ ἀποτρεπτικὸν τῶν δεινῶν. ἀλλὰ καὶ καταπλήσσει τοὺς πολεμίους καὶ ἑτεραλκέα τὴν νίκην ποιεῖ, ὅπου γε βούλεται.

ΤΡΙΕΦΩΝ

Μῶν καὶ διὰ τοῦτο ἡ Γλαυκῶπις ἀκαταμάχητος;

ΚΡΙΤΙΑΣ

Καὶ μάλα.

ΤΡΙΕΦΩΝ

Καὶ διὰ τί οὐ τοῖς σῴζειν δυναμένοις, ἀλλὰ τοῖς σῳζομένοις μηρία καίομεν ταύρων ἠδ' αἰγῶν, ὡς ἡμᾶς ἀκαταμαχήτους ἐργάσωνται ὥσπερ τὴν Ἀθηνᾶν;

ΚΡΙΤΙΑΣ

Ἀλλ' οὐ οἱ δύναμίς γε πόρρωθεν ἐπιβοηθεῖν ὥσπερ τοῖς θεοῖς, ἀλλ' εἴ τις αὐτὴν ἐπιφέρεται.

THE PATRIOT

TRIEPHO

I'll tell you about her too, if you'll answer my questions.

CRITIAS

Ask whatever you wish.

TRIEPHO

Tell me, Critias, what's the use of the Gorgon, and why does the goddess wear it on her bosom?

CRITIAS

Because it's a frightening sight and protects her from dangers. Moreover she terrifies her enemies and gives victory " unto the other side," [1] whenever she wishes.

TRIEPHO

Is that why the Goddess Grey of Eye is invincible?

CRITIAS

Yes indeed.

TRIEPHO

And why do we not thighs burn " of bulls, yea and of goats " [2] to those able to save us rather than to those saved by others, so that they may make us as invincible as Athena?

CRITIAS

But yon Gorgon hasn't power to help from afar, as the gods have, but only if it is worn.

---

[1] Cf. *Iliad* VII. 26 etc.   [2] Cf. *Iliad* I. 40-41.

PSEUDO-LUCIAN

ΤΡΙΕΦΩΝ

9. Καὶ τί τόδ' ἔστιν; ἐθέλω γὰρ παρὰ σοῦ εἰδέναι ὡς ἐξευρημένου τὰ τοιαῦτα καὶ ἐς τὰ μάλιστα κατωρθωκότος. ἀγνοῶ γὰρ πάντα τὰ κατ' αὐτὴν πλήν γε τοῦ ὀνόματος.

ΚΡΙΤΙΑΣ

Αὕτη κόρη ἐγένετο εὐπρεπὴς καὶ ἐπέραστος· Περσέως δὲ ταύτην δόλῳ ἀποδειροτομήσαντος, ἀνδρὸς γενναίου καὶ ἐς μαγικὴν εὐφημουμένου, ἐπαοιδίαις ταύτην περιῳδήσαντος, ἄλκαρ οἱ θεοὶ ταύτην ἐσχήκασι.

ΤΡΙΕΦΩΝ

Τουτί μ' ἐλάνθανέ ποτε τὸ καλόν, ὡς ἀνθρώπων θεοὶ ἐνδεεῖς εἰσι. ζώσης δὲ τί τὸ χρήσιμον; προσηταιρίζετο ἐς πανδοχεῖον ἢ κρυφίως συνεφθείρετο καὶ κόρην αὐτὴν ἐπωνόμαζε;

ΚΡΙΤΙΑΣ

Νὴ τὸν Ἄγνωστον ἐν Ἀθήναις παρθένος διέμεινε μέχρι τῆς ἀποτομῆς.

ΤΡΙΕΦΩΝ

Καὶ εἴ τις παρθένον καρατομήσειε, ταὐτὸ γένοιτο φόβητρον τοῖς πολλοῖς; οἶδα γὰρ μυρίας διαμελεϊστὶ τμηθείσας "νήσῳ ἐν ἀμφιρύτῃ, Κρήτην δέ ⟨τε⟩[1] μιν καλέουσι." καὶ εἰ τοῦτο ἐγίνωσκον,

---

[1] τε suppl. edd..

---

[1] Cf. *Acts of the Apostles* 17.23.

THE PATRIOT

TRIEPHO

9. And what is the Gorgon? For I'd like you to tell me, since you have conducted researches into such matters and with very great success. For I know nothing of her but her name.

CRITIAS

She was a beautiful and lovely maiden. But, ever since Perseus, a noble hero famed for his magic, cast his spells around her and treacherously cut off her head, the gods have kept her as their defence.

TRIEPHO

I was unaware of this glorious fact that gods need men. But what use did she have during her lifetime? Was she a courtesan entertaining men in public inns or did she keep her amours secret and call herself a virgin?

CRITIAS

By the unknown god in Athens,[1] she remained a virgin till her head was cut off.

TRIEPHO

And if one *did* cut off a virgin's head, would that prove something to frighten most men? For I know that countless maidens have been cut limb from limb.

" In a sea-girt isle, which men call Crete." [2]

---

[2] Cf. *Odyssey* 1.50 etc., and *Iliad* V. 306. Crete had been dominated by the Saracens since 826, but Phocas drove them out in 961. The contemporary poet Theodosius the Deacon, *Acroasis* 1. 58, also praises Phocas for putting Saracen maidens to the sword on that occasion.

ὦ καλὲ Κριτία, πόσας Γοργόνας σοι ἂν ἤγαγον
ἐκ Κρήτης; καὶ σε στρατηγέτην ἀκαταμάχητον
ἀποκατέστησα, ποιηταὶ δὲ καὶ ῥήτορες κατὰ πολύ
με Περσέως προέκριναν ὡς πλείονας Γοργόνας
ἐφευρηκότα. 10. ἀλλ᾿ ἔτι ἀνεμνήσθην τὰ τῶν
Κρητῶν, οἳ τάφον ἐπεδείκνυντό μοι τοῦ Διός σου
καὶ τὰ τὴν μητέρα θρέψαντα λόχμια,¹ ὡς ἀειθαλεῖς
αἱ λόχμαι αὗται διαμένουσι.

ΚΡΙΤΙΑΣ

Ἀλλ᾿ οὐκ ἐγίνωσκες τὴν ἐπῳδὴν καὶ τὰ ὄργια.

ΤΡΙΕΦΩΝ

Εἰ ταῦτα, ὦ Κριτία, ἐξ ἐπῳδῆς ἐγίνοντο ² τάχ᾿ ἂν
καὶ ἐκ νεκάδων ἐξήνεγκεν ἂν καὶ ἐς τὸ γλυκύτατον
φάος ἀνήγαγεν. ἀλλὰ λῆρος παίγνιά τε καὶ μῦθοι
παρὰ τῶν ποιητῶν τερατολογούμενα. ὥστε ἔασον
καὶ ταύτην.

ΚΡΙΤΙΑΣ

11. Ἥραν δὲ τὴν Διὸς γαμετὴν καὶ κασίγνητον
οὐ παραδέχῃ;

ΤΡΙΕΦΩΝ

Σίγα τῆς ἀσελγεστάτης ἕνεκα μίξεως καὶ τὴν ἐκ
ποδοῖν καὶ χεροῖν ἐκτετανυσμένην παράδραμε.

ΚΡΙΤΙΑΣ

12. Καὶ τίνα ἐπομόσωμαί γε;

---

¹ δόχμια Δα.　　　　² ἐγένοντο C.

THE PATRIOT

If men knew this, my fine Critias, what numbers of Gorgons they would have brought you from Crete ! And I would have made you an invincible generalissimo, while poets and orators would have rated me far superior to Perseus as having discovered more Gorgons than he did. 10. But there's something else I recall about the Cretans. They showed me the tomb of your Zeus [1] and the thickets which nurtured his mother, for they remain verdant for aye.

CRITIAS

But you didn't know the charm or rites he used.

TRIEPHO

If these things were done by a charm, Critias, perhaps he would also have brought her back from the dead and raised her to the sweet light of day. But all these things are idle talk, fairy tales, myths and wondrous stories spread by the poets. So forget about the Gorgon also.

CRITIAS

11. But don't you accept Hera, Zeus' wife and sister ?

TRIEPHO

Keep quiet because of her most wanton love-making [2] and pass over her who was stretched out with feet and hands extended.

CRITIAS

12. And by whom *shall* I swear ?

[1] Cf. *Timon* 6.   [2] Cf. *Iliad* XIV. 346-53.

PSEUDO-LUCIAN

ΤΡΙΕΦΩΝ

Ὑψιμέδοντα [1] θεόν, μέγαν, ἄμβροτον, οὐρανίωνα,
υἱὸν ἐκ [2] πατρός, πνεῦμα ἐκ πατρὸς ἐκπορευόμενον,
ἓν ἐκ τριῶν καὶ ἐξ ἑνὸς τρία,
τοῦτον [3] νόμιζε Ζῆνα, τόνδ' ἡγοῦ θεόν.

ΚΡΙΤΙΑΣ

Ἀριθμέειν με διδάσκεις, καὶ ὅρκος ἡ ἀριθμητική·
καὶ γὰρ ἀριθμέεις ὡς Νικόμαχος ὁ Γερασηνός. οὐκ
οἶδα γὰρ τί λέγεις, ἓν τρία, τρία ἕν. μὴ τὴν
τετρακτὺν φῂς τὴν Πυθαγόρου ἢ τὴν ὀγδοάδα καὶ
τριακάδα;

ΤΡΙΕΦΩΝ

Σίγα τὰ νέρθε καὶ τὰ σιγῆς ἄξια.
οὐκ ἔσθ' ὧδε μετρεῖν τὰ ψυλλῶν ἴχνη. ἐγὼ γὰρ σε
διδάξω τί τὸ πᾶν καὶ τίς ὁ πρώην πάντων καὶ τί τὸ
σύστημα τοῦ παντός· καὶ γὰρ πρώην κἀγὼ ταῦτα
ἔπασχον ἅπερ σύ, ἡνίκα δέ μοι Γαλιλαῖος ἐνέτυχεν,
ἀναφαλαντίας, ἐπίρρινος, ἐς τρίτον οὐρανὸν ἀεροβα-
τήσας καὶ τὰ κάλλιστα ἐκμεμαθηκώς, δι' ὕδατος
ἡμᾶς ἀνεγέννησεν,[4] ἐς τὰ τῶν μακάρων ἴχνια

---

[1] μέγαν ὑψιμέδοντα θεόν codd..
[2] ἐκ om. edd..
[3] ταῦτα codd.: τοῦτον *Jup. Trag.* 41.
[4] ἀνεκαίνισεν edd..

---

[1] A hexameter line after the manner of Homer or Hesiod.
[2] Cf. Creed of Constantinople.
[3] Euripides *Fr.* 941, also quoted in *Zeus Rants* 41.
[4] Nicomachus of Gerasa in Arabia was a Pythagorean
philosopher and arithmetician who lived about 100 A.D.

THE PATRIOT

TRIEPHO

The mighty god that rules on high,
Immortal dwelling in the sky,[1]
the son of the father, spirit proceeding from the
father,[2] three in one and one in three
Think him your Zeus, consider him your god.[3]

CRITIAS

You're teaching me to count, and using arithmetic
for your oath. For you're counting like Nicomachus,
the Gerasene.[4] For I don't know what you mean by
" three in one and one in three." You don't mean
Pythagoras' four numbers or his eight or his thirty ?[5]

TRIEPHO

" Speak not of things below that none may tell."[6]
We don't measure the footprints of fleas here.[7] For
I shall teach you what is all, who existed before all
else and how the universe works. For only the other
day I too was in the same state as you, but, when I
was met by a Galilean with receding hair and a long
nose, who had walked on air into the third heaven[8]
and acquired the most glorious knowledge, he
regenerated us with water, led us into the paths of

---

[5] Pythagoreans used the term tetraktys of the sum of
the first four numbers $(1 + 2 + 3 + 4)$, i.e. 10, which they
regarded as the most perfect numbers; the number 8 was
thought by some Pythagoreans to represent justice
(though this was more often 4 or 9); as 30 had no particular
significance for them, τριακάς perhaps here means " month,"
which Pythagoreans regarded as sacred.

[6] Unidentified comic line.

[7] Cf. Aristophanes, *Clouds* 145.

[8] St. Paul. Cf. *Acts of Paul and Thecla* 3; Aristophanes,
Clouds 225; *Second Corinthians* 12.2.

437

παρεισώδευσε καὶ ἐκ τῶν ἀσεβῶν χώρων ἡμᾶς
ἐλυτρώσατο. καὶ σὲ ποιήσω, ἤν μου ἀκούῃς, ἐπ'
ἀληθείας ἄνθρωπον.

KΡΙΤΙΑΣ

13. Λέγε, ὦ πολυμαθέστατε Τριεφῶν· διὰ
φόβου γὰρ ἔρχομαι.

ΤΡΙΕΦΩΝ

Ἀνέγνωκάς ποτε τὰ τοῦ Ἀριστοφάνους τοῦ
δραματοποιοῦ Ὄρνιθας ποιημάτια;

KΡΙΤΙΑΣ

Καὶ μάλα.

ΤΡΙΕΦΩΝ

Ἐγκεχάρακται παρ' αὐτοῦ τοιόνδε·
    Χάος ἦν καὶ Νὺξ Ἔρεβός τε μέλαν πρῶτον καὶ
        Τάρταρος εὐρύς·
    γῆ δ' οὐδ' ἀὴρ οὐδ' οὐρανὸς ἦν.

KΡΙΤΙΑΣ

Εὖ λέγεις. εἶτα τί ἦν;

ΤΡΙΕΦΩΝ

Ἦν φῶς ἄφθιτον ἀόρατον ἀκατανόητον, ὃ λύει τὸ
σκότος καὶ τὴν ἀκοσμίαν ταύτην ἀπήλασε, λόγῳ
μόνῳ ῥηθέντι ὑπ' αὐτοῦ, ὡς ὁ βραδύγλωσσος
ἀπεγράψατο, γῆν ἔπηξεν ἐφ' ὕδασιν, οὐρανὸν
ἐτάνυσεν, ἀστέρας ἐμόρφωσεν ἀπλανεῖς, δρόμον [1]

---

[1] τῶν πλανητῶν δρόμον L. A. Post.

the blessed and ransomed us from the impious places.
If you listen to me, I shall make you too a man in
truth.

CRITIAS

13. Speak on, most learned Triepho ; for fear is
upon me.

TRIEPHO

Have you ever read the poetic composition of the
dramatist Aristophanes called the *Birds* ?

CRITIAS

Certainly I have.

TRIEPHO

He wrote the following words :
  " At first Chaos there was and night,
  Black Erebos and Tartarus broad,
  But nought of earth or air or sky." [1]

CRITIAS

Bravo ! Then what followed ?

TRIEPHO

There was light imperishable, invisible,[2] incompre-
hensible, which dispels the darkness and has banished
this confusion ; by a single word spoken by him, as
the slow-tongued one [3] recorded, he planted land on
the waters,[4] spread out the heavens,[5] fashioned the

---

[1] Aristophanes, *Birds* 693-694. [2] Cf. *First Timothy*, 1.17.
[3] Moses; cf. *Exodus* 4.10, *Genesis* 1.6.
[4] Cf. *Psalms* 24.2. [5] Cf. *Isaiah* 44.24.

διετάξατο, οὓς σὺ σέβῃ θεούς, γῆν δὲ τοῖς ἄνθεσιν
ἐκαλλώπισεν, ἄνθρωπον ἐκ μὴ ὄντων ἐς τὸ εἶναι
παρήγαγε, καὶ ἔστιν ἐν οὐρανῷ βλέπων δικαίους τε
κἀδίκους καὶ ἐν βίβλοις τὰς πράξεις ἀπογραφόμενος·
ἀνταποδώσει δὲ πᾶσιν ἣν ἡμέραν αὐτὸς ἐνετείλατο.

ΚΡΙΤΙΑΣ

14. Τὰ δὲ τῶν Μοιρῶν ἐπινενησμένα ἐς ἅπαντας
ἐγχαράττουσί γε καὶ ταῦτα;

ΤΡΙΕΦΩΝ

Τὰ ποῖα;

ΚΡΙΤΙΑΣ

Τὰ τῆς εἱμαρμένης.

ΤΡΙΕΦΩΝ

Λέγε, ὦ καλὲ Κριτία, περὶ τῶν Μοιρῶν, ἐγὼ δὲ
μαθητιῶν ἀκούσαιμι παρὰ σοῦ.

ΚΡΙΤΙΑΣ

Οὐχ Ὅμηρος ὁ ἀοίδιμος ποιητὴς εἴρηκε,
μοῖραν δ᾽ οὔ τινά φημι πεφυγμένον ἔμμεναι ἀνδρῶν
ἐπὶ δὲ τοῦ μεγάλου Ἡρακλέους,
 οὐδὲ γὰρ οὐδὲ βίη Ἡρακλείη φύγε κῆρα,
 ὅσπερ φίλτατος ἔσκε Διὶ Κρονίωνι ἄνακτι,
 ἀλλά ἑ Μοῖρ᾽ ἐδάμασσε καὶ ἀργαλέος χόλος Ἥρης.

---

[1] Cf. *Matthew* 5.45.   [2] Cf. *Revelation* 20.12.
[3] Cf. *Acts* 17.31.   [4] *Iliad* VI. 488; cf. *Apol.* 8.

fixed stars, appointed the course of the planets which you revere as gods, beautified the earth with flowers and brought man into existence out of nothingness. He exists in the heavens, looking down upon the just and the unjust,[1] and writing down their deeds in his books,[2] and he shall requite all men on his own appointed day.[3]

CRITIAS

14. And do they also inscribe the things which the Fates have spun for all men ?

TRIEPHO

What things ?

CRITIAS

The things of Destiny.

TRIEPHO

Tell me about the Fates, my fine Critias, for I would fain listen to you as an eager disciple.

CRITIAS

Has not Homer, the renowned poet, said,
" And Fate I say has none of men escaped " ? [4]
And of mighty Heracles he says :
" For even mighty Heracles escaped not doom,
Although right dear he was to Cronus' son, king
    Zeus,
But Fate and Hera's cruel wrath did him
    o'ercome." [5]

[5] *Iliad* XVIII. 117-119.

ἀλλὰ καὶ ὅλον τὸν βίον καθειμάρθαι καὶ τὰς ἐν
τούτῳ μεταβολάς·

ἔνθα δ᾽ ἔπειτα
πείσεται ἄσσα οἱ Αἶσα Κατακλῶθές τε [1] βαρεῖαι
γεινομένῳ νήσαντο λίνῳ, ὅτε μιν τέκε μήτηρ.

καὶ τὰς ἐν ξένῃ ἐποχὰς ἀπ᾽ ἐκείνης γίνεσθαι·

ἠδ᾽ ὡς Αἴολον ἱκόμεθ᾽, ὅς με πρόφρων ὑπέδεκτο,
καὶ πέμπ᾽· οὐδέπω αἶσα φίλην ἐς πατρίδ᾽ ἱκέσθαι.

ὥστε πάντα ὑπὸ τῶν Μοιρῶν γενέσθαι ὁ ποιητὴς
μεμαρτύρηκε. τὸν δὲ Δία μὴ θελῆσαι τὸν υἱὸν

θανάτοιο δυσηχέος ἐξαναλῦσαι,

ἀλλὰ μᾶλλον

αἱματοέσσας δὲ ψιάδας κατέχευεν ἔραζε
παῖδα φίλον τιμῶν, τόν οἱ Πάτροκλος ἔμελλε
φθίσειν ἐν Τροίῃ.

ὥστε, ὦ Τριεφῶν, διὰ τοῦτο μηδὲν προσθεῖναι περὶ
τῶν Μοιρῶν ἐθελήσῃς, εἰ καὶ τάχα πεδάρσιος
ἐγεγόνεις μετὰ τοῦ διδασκάλου καὶ τὰ ἀπόρρητα
ἐμυήθης.

ΤΡΙΕΦΩΝ

15. Καὶ πῶς ὁ αὐτὸς ποιητής, ὦ καλὲ Κριτία,
διττὴν ἐπιλέγει τὴν εἱμαρμένην καὶ ἀμφίβολον, ὡς
τόδε μέν τι [2] πράξαντι τοιῷδε τέλει συγκυρῆσαι,
τοῖον δὲ ποιήσαντι, ἑτέρῳ τέλει ἐντυχεῖν; ὡς ἐπ᾽
Ἀχιλλέως,

---

[1] τε edd.: κε Δα.
[2] τι Ca: τοι Δ.

But he also says that all life and its vicissitudes too are governed by Fate,

> "Then will he meet what Fate and thread of
> Spinners grim
> Did spin for him the day his mother gave him
> birth," [1]

and that delays on foreign soil arise from Fate.

> "To Aeolus we came who gave me welcome glad
> And sped me on my way. For not as yet was it
> My Fate that I should reach beloved fatherland." [2]

Thus the poet has testified that all things are brought about by the Fates. He tells us that Zeus did not wish his son [3] "from woeful death to save," [4] but rather

> "Did pour upon the earth beneath a bloody rain
> To honour his dear son, whom Patroclus was soon
> In Troy to slay." [5]

Therefore, Triepho, you musn't feel inclined to say anything more about the Fates, even if perchance you *were* lifted 'twixt earth and sky along with your teacher and *were* initiated into mysteries.

TRIEPHO

15. And how can that same poet, my fine Critias, call Destiny double and doubtful, so that if a man does one thing he encounters one result, but if he does something else he meets with a different result. Thus in the case of Achilles,

---

[1] *Odyssey* VII. 196-198.
[2] *Odyssey* XXIII. 314-315.
[3] Sarpedon.
[4] *Iliad* XVI. 442.
[5] *Iliad* XVI. 459-461.

διχθαδίας Κῆρας φερέμεν θανάτοιο τέλοσδε·
εἰ μέν κ' αὖθι μένων Τρώων πόλιν ἀμφιμάχωμαι,
ὤλετο μέν μοι νόστος, ἀτὰρ κλέος ἄφθιτον ἔσται.
εἰ δέ κεν οἴκαδ' ἵκωμαι,
ὤλετό μοι κλέος ἐσθλόν, ἐπὶ δηρὸν δέ μοι αἰὼν
ἔσσεται.
ἀλλὰ καὶ ἐπὶ Εὐχήνορος,
ὅς ῥ' εὖ εἰδὼς κῆρ' ὀλοὴν ἐπὶ νηὸς ἔβαινε·
πολλάκι γάρ οἱ ἔειπε γέρων ἀγαθὸς Πολύϊδος,
νούσῳ ὑπ' ἀργαλέῃ φθῖσθαι οἷς ἐν μεγάροισιν
ἢ μετ' Ἀχαιῶν νηυσὶν ὑπὸ Τρώεσσι δαμῆναι.

16. οὐχὶ παρ' Ὁμήρῳ ταῦτα γέγραπται; ἢ[1] ἀμφί-
βολος αὕτη καὶ ἀμφίκρημνος ἀπάτη; εἰ δὲ βούλει,
καὶ τοῦ Διὸς ἐπιθήσω σοι τὸν λόγον. οὐχὶ τῷ
Αἰγίσθῳ εἴρηκεν ὡς ἀποσχομένῳ μὲν τῆς μοιχείας
καὶ τῆς Ἀγαμέμνονος ἐπιβουλῆς ζῆν καθείμαρται[2]
πολὺν χρόνον, ἐπιβαλλομένῳ δὲ ταῦτα πράττειν οὐ
καθυστερεῖν θανάτου; τοῦτο κἀγὼ πολλάκις προὐ-
μαντευσάμην, ἐὰν κτάνῃς τὸν πλησίον, θανατωθήσῃ
παρὰ τῆς δίκης, εἰ δέ γε μὴ τοῦτο πράξεις, βιώσῃ
καλῶς,

οὐδέ κέ σ' ὦκα τέλος[3] θανάτοιο κιχείη.

οὐχ ὁρᾷς ὡς ἀδιόρθωτα τὰ τῶν ποιητῶν καὶ ἀμφίλοξα καὶ μηδέπω ἡδραιωμένα; ὥστε ἔασον ἅπαντα,
ὡς καὶ σὲ ἐν ταῖς ἐπουρανίοις βίβλοις τῶν ἀγαθῶν
ἀπογράψωνται.

---

[1] ἢ edd.: ἡ codd..   [2] καθειμάρθαι codd.: corr. edd..
[3] ὦκα θέμις τέλος codd..

---

[1] *Iliad* IX. 411-416.   [2] *Iliad* XIII. 665-668.

" Two Fates lead on to death that cometh as the
  end.
If here I stay and fight around the Trojans' town,
My home-coming is gone, but glory will be mine
To all eternity.   But if I reach my home,
My glorious fame is gone, but long will be my
  life." [1]

Moreover in the case of Euchenor

" He knowing well his deadly doom set foot on
  ship ;
For Polyidos, that fine old man, had told him oft
Either he must succumb to sickness grim at home,
Or else sail with the Greeks and fall by Trojan
  hand." [2]

16. Are these things not written in Homer ?   Or do
you think them ambiguous, dangerous and deluding
words ?   If you wish, I'll also tell you about the
speech of Zeus.   Didn't he tell Aegisthus [3] that if he
refrained from adultery and plotting against
Agamemnon he was fated to have a long life, but if
he attempted to do these things he wouldn't have to
wait for death ?   This I too have often foretold,
maintaining that if you kill your neighbour you will
meet death at the hands of Justice, whereas if you
refrain from such actions, you will have an excellent
life,

" Nor will you quickly meet with death that
  endeth all." [4]

Don't you see how imperfect, ambiguous and un-
stable are the words of the poets ?   Therefore leave all
these aside, so that they may list your name too in
the heavenly books of the good.

[3] Cf. *Iliad* I. 37 ff.   [4] *Iliad* IX. 416.

PSEUDO-LUCIAN

ΚΡΙΤΙΑΣ

17. Εὖ πάντα ἀνακυκλεῖς, ὦ Τριεφῶν· ἀλλά μοι τόδε εἰπέ, εἰ καὶ τὰ τῶν Σκυθῶν ἐν τῷ οὐρανῷ ἐγχαράττουσι;

ΤΡΙΕΦΩΝ

Πάντα γε, εἰ τύχῃ γε χρηστὸς καὶ ἐν ἔθνεσι.

ΚΡΙΤΙΑΣ

Πολλούς γε γραφέας φὴς ἐν τῷ οὐρανῷ, ὡς ἄπαντα ἀπογράφεσθαι.

ΤΡΙΕΦΩΝ

Εὐστόμει καὶ μηδὲν εἴπῃς φλαῦρον θεοῦ δεξιοῦ, ἀλλὰ κατηχούμενος πείθου παρ' ἐμοῦ, εἴπερ χρὴ ζῆν [1] εἰς τὸν αἰῶνα. εἰ οὐρανὸν ὡς δέρριν ἐξήπλωσε, γῆν δὲ ἐφ' ὕδατος ἔπηξεν, ἀστέρας ἐμόρφωσεν, ἄνθρωπον ἐκ μὴ ὄντος παρήγαγε, τί παράδοξον καὶ τὰς πράξεις πάντων ἐναπογράφεσθαι; καὶ γὰρ σοὶ οἰκίδιον κατασκευάσαντι, οἰκέτιδας δὲ καὶ οἰκέτας ἐν αὐτῷ συναγαγόντι, οὐδέποτέ σε διέλαθε τούτων πρᾶξις ἀπόβλητος· πόσῳ μᾶλλον τὸν πάντα πεποιηκότα θεὸν οὐχ ἅπαντα ἐν εὐκολίᾳ διαδραμεῖν ἑκάστου πρᾶξιν καὶ ἔννοιαν; οἱ γάρ σου θεοὶ κότταβος τοῖς εὖ φρονοῦσιν ἐγένοντο.

---

[1] χρὴ ζῆν codd.: ζῆν χρήζεις edd..

---

[1] Cf. *Acts* 14.27 ff.
[2] Aristophanes, *Clouds* 833-834.
[3] Cf. *Psalms* 104.2.

THE PATRIOT

CRITIAS

17. How cleverly you bring everything back to the same point. But tell me whether they inscribe the deeds of the Scythians too in heaven.

TRIEPHO

They inscribe the deeds of every good man, even though he be among the Gentiles.[1]

CRITIAS

By your account there must be many scribes in heaven to list all these deeds.

TRIEPHO

" Hush thy mouth and nothing slighting say "[2] of God for he is accomplished, but be instructed and persuaded by me, if you are to live for ever. If he has unfolded the heavens like a curtain,[3] planted land on the water, fashioned the stars, and brought forth men out of nothingness, how is it strange that he should also list the deeds of all men ? For even you with the modest house you have built and the serving men and women you have collected are aware of their every deed however unimportant. How much more easily can you expect the god who made all things to keep track of all things, of the thoughts and deeds of each man ! For your gods have become a mere bagatelle [4] to men of right mind.

---

[4] Literally the κότταβος, the game of throwing the last drops of a cup of wine into a basin. See Athenaeus 15.665 d.

ΚΡΙΤΙΑΣ

18. Πάνυ εὖ λέγεις, καί με ἀντιστρόφως τῆς Νιόβης παθεῖν· ἐκ στήλης γὰρ ἄνθρωπος ἀναπέφηνα. ὥστε τοῦτον τὸν θεὸν προστιθῶ σοι, μὴ κακόν τι παθεῖν παρ' ἐμοῦ.

ΤΡΙΕΦΩΝ

" Εἴπερ ἐκ καρδίας ὄντως φιλεῖς ", μὴ ἑτεροῖόν τι ποιήσῃς ἐν ἐμοὶ καὶ " ἕτερον μὲν κεύσῃς ἐνὶ φρεσίν, ἄλλο δὲ εἴπῃς ". ἀλλ' ἄγε δὴ τὸ θαυμάσιον ἐκεῖνο ἀκουσμάτιον ἄεισον, ὅπως κἀγὼ κατωχριάσω καὶ ὅλος ἀλλοιωθῶ, καὶ οὐχ ὡς ἡ Νιόβη ἀπαυδήσω, ἀλλ' ὡς Ἀηδὼν ὄρνεον γενήσομαι καὶ τὴν θαυμασίαν σου ἔκπληξιν κατ' ἀνθηρὸν λειμῶνα ἐκτραγῳδήσω.

ΚΡΙΤΙΑΣ

Νὴ τὸν υἱὸν τὸν ἐκ πατρὸς οὐ [1] τοῦτο γενήσεται.

ΤΡΙΕΦΩΝ

Λέγε παρὰ τοῦ πνεύματος δύναμιν τοῦ λόγου λαβών, ἐγὼ δὲ καθεδοῦμαι

δέγμενος Αἰακίδην ὁπότε λήξειεν ἀείδων.

ΚΡΙΤΙΑΣ

19. Ἀπῄειν ἐπὶ τὴν λεωφόρον ὠνησόμενός γε [2] τὰ χρειωδέστατα, καὶ δὴ ὁρῶ πλῆθος πάμπολυ ἐς

---

[1] οὐ del. L. A. Post.   [2] γε edd.: τε a: om. ΔC.

---

[1] Cf. c. 1.   [2] Aristophanes, *Clouds* 86 misquoted.
[3] *Iliad* IX. 313 unmetrically parodied.
[4] I.e. you won't become dumb like Niobe.
[5] Cf. *Acts* 1.8, *Romans* 1.4.

THE PATRIOT

18. You are absolutely right; you make me experience Niobe's [1] fate in reverse ; for I've changed back from tomb-stone to man. Therefore I add this god to my oath in promising you will suffer no harm from me.

TRIEPHO

" If with all your heart you really do me love," [2] do nothing untoward to me nor let
" A different thought your inmost heart conceal,
From what your tongue doth outwardly reveal." [3]
But come now, sing to me of the wonderful thing you have heard, that I too may grow pale and be utterly changed, and not grow dumb like Niobe, but become a nightingale like Aëdon, and throughout flower-decked meadows celebrate in tragic song the wonder that amazed you.

CRITIAS

By the son of the father, that shall not [4] come about!

TRIEPHO

Take powers of speech from the spirit [5] and speak, while I shall sit
" Waiting until the son of Aeacus doth cease from song." [6]

CRITIAS

19. I had gone into the street to buy what things I most needed, when behold I saw a great crowd of

[6] *Iliad* IX. 191, also quoted in *Affairs of the Heart* 5 and 54.

τὸ οὖς ψιθυρίζοντας, ἐπὶ δὲ τῇ ἀκοῇ ἐφῦντο τοῖς χείλεσιν· ἐγὼ δὲ παπτήνας ἐς ἅπαντας καὶ τὴν χεῖρα τοῖς βλεφάροις περικάμψας ἐσκοπίαζον ὀξυδερκέστατα, εἴ πού γέ τινα τῶν φίλων θεάσομαι. ὁρῶ δὲ Κράτωνα τὸν πολιτικόν, ἐκ παιδόθεν φίλον ὄντα καὶ συμποτικόν.[1]

ΤΡΙΕΦΩΝ

Αἰσθάνομαι· τοῦτον τὸν ἐξισωτὴν γὰρ εἴρηκας. εἶτα τί;

ΚΡΙΤΙΑΣ

20. Καὶ δὴ πολλοὺς παραγκωνισάμενος ἧκον ἐς τὰ πρόσω καὶ τὸ ἑωινὸν χαῖρε εἰπὼν ἐχώρουν ὡς αὐτόν. ἀνθρωπίσκος δέ τις τοὔνομα Χαρίκενος, σεσημμένον γερόντιον ῥέγχον τῇ ῥινί, ὑπέβηττε μύχιον, ἐχρέμπτετο ἐπισεσυρμένον, ὁ δὲ πτύελος κυανώτερος θανάτου· εἶτα ἤρξατο ἐπιφθέγγεσθαι κατισχνημένον· Οὗτος, ὡς προεῖπον, τοὺς τῶν ἐξισωτῶν ἀπαλείψει ἐλλειπασμοὺς[2] καὶ τὰ χρέα τοῖς δανεισταῖς ἀποδώσει καὶ τά τε ἐνοίκια πάντα καὶ τὰ δημόσια, καὶ τοὺς εἰρηνάρχας[3] δέξεται μὴ ἐξετάζων τῆς τέχνης. καὶ κατεφλυάρει ἔτι πικρότερα. οἱ περὶ αὐτὸν δὲ ἥδοντο τοῖς λόγοις καὶ τῷ καινῷ τῶν ἀκουσμάτων προσέκειντο.

---

[1] συμπότην Δ.
[2] sic scripsi (καταλείψει Gesner: καταλύσει Heuman): καταλείπει ἐλλειπασμοὺς C: καταλείπειε λειπασμοὺς Δ.
[3] sic Gesner: τὰς εἰραμάγγας codd..

people ! They were whispering in each other's ears, with the lips of one glued to the ear of another. I looked at them all and bent my hand round my eyes, straining them to see if I could catch sight of any of my friends. I saw Crato, the man of affairs, who from boyhood had been my friend and drinking companion.

TRIEPHO

I know him. It's the inspector of taxes[1] you mean. Then what happened ?

CRITIAS

20. Well I had pushed a great many people aside and was reaching the front. I had wished him good morning and was just coming up to him when a fellow, Charicenus by name, a mouldering wheezy old creature, gave a deep cough, slowly cleared his throat and spat. And his spittle was darker than death. Then he began to speak in a thin voice, saying : " He, as I have just said, will cancel all arrears due to the inspectors of taxes. He will pay creditors what they are owed and pay all rents and public dues. He will welcome to him even police magistrates[2] without enquiring after their calling." And he went on talking still more offensive rubbish. But those around him found pleasure in his words and were engrossed by the novelty of what they heard.

---

[1] ἐξισωταί (Latin *peraequatores*) were officials first heard of under Constantine, whose duty was the fair division of taxes.

[2] I have accepted Gesner's conjecture *faute de mieux;* Rohde suggested that the unknown word εἰραμάγγας may be gold Persian coins debased by Phocas.

21. ἕτερος δὲ τοὔνομα Χλεύόχαρμος τριβώνιον
ἔχων πολύσαθρον ἀνυπόδετός τε καὶ ἄσκεπος
μετέειπε τοῖς ὀδοῦσιν ἐπικροτῶν, ὡς ἐπεδείξατό μοί
τις κακοείμων, ἐξ ὀρέων παραγενόμενος, κεκαρμένος
τὴν κόμην, ἐν τῷ θεάτρῳ ἀναγεγραμμένον οὔνομα
ἱερογλυφικοῖς γράμμασιν, ὡς οὗτος τῷ χρυσῷ
ἐπικλύσει τὴν λεωφόρον.

ἦν δ' ἐγὼ κατὰ μὲν τὰ Ἀριστάνδρου καὶ Ἀρτε-
μιδώρου, Οὐ καλῶς ἀποβήσονται ταῦτά γε τὰ
ἐνύπνια ἐν ὑμῖν, ἀλλὰ σοὶ μὲν τὰ χρέα πληθυνθή-
σεται ἀναλόγως τῆς ἀποδόσεως· οὗτος δὲ ἐπὶ
πολὺ τοῦ ὀβολοῦ γε στερηθήσεται ὡς πολλοῦ
χρυσίου εὐπορηκώς. καὶ ἔμοιγε δοκεῖτε " ἐπὶ
Λευκάδα πέτρην " " καὶ δῆμον ὀνείρων " καταδαρθέν-
τες τοσαῦτα ὀνειροπολεῖν ἐν ἀκαρεῖ τῆς νυκτὸς οὔσης.

22. οἱ δὲ ἀνεκάγχασαν ἅπαντες ὡς ἀποπνιγέντες
ὑπὸ τοῦ γέλωτος καὶ τῆς ἀμαθίας μου κατεγί-
νωσκον. ἦν δ' ἐγὼ πρὸς Κράτωνα, Μῶν κακῶς
πάντα ἐξερρίνισα,[1] ἵν' εἴπω τι κωμικευσάμενος, καὶ
οὐ κατὰ Ἀρίστανδρον τὸν Τελμισέα καὶ Ἀρτεμί-
δωρον τὸν Ἐφέσιον ἐξίχνευσα τοῖς ὀνείρασιν;

ἦ δ' ὅς, Σίγα, ὦ Κριτία· εἰ ἐχεμυθεῖς, μυστα-
γωγήσω σε τὰ κάλλιστα καὶ τὰ νῦν γενησόμενα·
ὑο γὰρ ὄνειροι τάδ' εἰσίν, ἀλλ' ἀληθῆ, ἐκβήσονται
δὲ εἰς μῆνα Μεσορί.

ταῦτα ἀκηκοὼς παρὰ τοῦ Κράτωνος καὶ τὸ
ὀλισθηρὸν τῆς διανοίας αὐτῶν κατεγνωκὼς ἠρυθρίασα

---

[1] ἐξερρίνησα Kock.

[1] Aristander of Telmessus in Lycia was a favourite
soothsayer of Alexander the Great.

[2] Artemidorus of Ephesus, a contemporary of Lucian,

21. But another man, Chleuocharmus by name, one clad in a dilapidated cloak, bare-footed and half-naked, did speak in their midst with chattering teeth and said, " A poorly clad man from the mountains with hair cut short showed me that name inscribed in the theatre in hieroglyphic writing, telling how he would flood the highway with streams of gold."

But I spoke after the manner of Aristander [1] and Artemidorus [2] saying : " These dreams will not turn out well for you all, but the more debts, [3] sir, you dream you pay, the more will you find them multiply. And this fellow here will lose almost every farthing, since in dreams he has been rich in gold. But you seem to me to have reached in your sleep the White Rock and Land of Dreams, [4] and to have crowded so many dreams into a split second of the night.'

22. They all cackled as though choking with laughter, and thought me guilty of stupidity. But I said to Crato " Have I, to use a comic phrase, [5] missed the scent in all this and failed to follow the tracks of the dreams after the manner of Aristander of Telmessus and Artemidorus of Ephesus ? "

But he said " Hush, Critias. If you hold your tongue, I shall initiate you into the most beautiful mysteries and events presently to take place. For these things are not dreams but very truth, and will come about in the month of Mesori. [6]

When I had heard these words of Crato, and had passed judgment on the fallibility of their thoughts,

wrote five still extant books *On The Interpretation of Dreams*.   [3] Perhaps in parody of the Lord's Prayer.
[4] Cf. *Odyssey* XXIV. 11-12.
[5] The source is unknown but cf. *Frogs* 902.
[6] An Egyptian month corresponding to August.

καὶ σκυθρωπάζων ἐπορευόμην πολλὰ τὸν Κράτωνα
ἐπιμεμφόμενος. εἰς δὲ δριμὺ καὶ τιτανῶδες ἐνιδὼν
δραξάμενός μου τοῦ λώπους ἐσπάρασσε ῥήτρην
ποιήσασθαι πειθόμενός τε καὶ παρανυττόμενος παρὰ
τοῦ πεπαλαιωμένου ἐκείνου δαιμονίου.

23. εἰς λόγους δὲ ταῦτα παρεκτείναντες πείθει με
τὸν κακοδαίμονα εἰς γόητας ἀνθρώπους παρα-
γενέσθαι καὶ ἀποφράδι τὸ δὴ λεγόμενον ἡμέρᾳ
συγκυρῆσαι· ἔφασκε γὰρ πάντα ἐξ αὐτῶν μυσταγω-
γηθῆναι. καὶ δὴ διήλθομεν σιδηρέας τε πύλας καὶ
χαλκέους οὐδούς. ἀναβάθρας δὲ πλείστας περικυ-
κλησάμενοι ἐς χρυσόροφον οἶκον ἀνήλθομεν, οἷον
Ὅμηρος τὸν Μενελάου φησί. καὶ δὴ ἅπαντα
ἐσκόπιαζον ὅσα[1] ὁ νησιώτης ἐκεῖνος νεανίσκος.
ὁρῶ δὲ οὐχ Ἑλένην, μὰ Δί', ἀλλ' ἄνδρας ἐπικεκυφό-
τας καὶ κατωχριωμένους· " οἱ δὲ ἰδόντες γήθησαν "
καὶ ἐξ ἐναντίας παρεγένοντο· ἔφασκον γὰρ ὡς εἴ
τινα λυγρὰν ἀγγελίαν ἀγάγοιμεν· ἐφαίνοντο γὰρ
οὗτοι ὡς τὰ κάκιστα εὐχόμενοι καὶ ἔχαιρον ἐπὶ τοῖς
λυγροῖς ὥσπερ αἰλινοποιοὶ[2] ἐπὶ θέατρα, τὰς κεφαλὰς
δ' ἄγχι σχόντες ἐψιθύριζον. μετὰ δὲ τὰ ἤροντό με,

τίς πόθεν εἰς ἀνδρῶν, πόθι τοι πόλις ἠδὲ τοκῆες;
χρηστὸς γὰρ ἂν εἴης ἀπό γε τοῦ σχήματος.

---

[1] ὅσα edd.: ὡς οἷα codd..
[2] αἰλινοποιοὶ scripsi: αἱροπινοποιοὶ Δα: αἱ ποινοποιοὶ edd..

---

[1] Charicenus; cf. c. 20. [2] The Greek is ungrammatical.
[3] Cf. *Iliad* VIII. 15, where the abyss of Tartarus, the
prison for rebellious gods is described. This suggests that
Critias is referring to prisoners of Phocas and accusing them
of being unpatriotic.
[4] Telemachus; cf. *Odyssey* IV. 71-75.

I blushed for shame and walked away dejectedly with many hard thoughts about Crato. But one of them directed on me the fierce gaze of a Titan, seized my robe and started to tear it, for that old devil [1] kept urging and goading him to make a speech.

23. After a conversation of some length between us,[2] I had the misfortune to be persuaded by him to meet with mountebank fellows and, to use the common saying, to strike an unlucky day. For he said he had been initiated into everything by these men. And behold we passed through the gates of iron and o'er the thresholds of bronze,[3] and after we had twisted and turned our way up many steps, we found ourselves up in a golden-roofed residence such as was possessed by Menelaus according to Homer. And behold I surveyed everything with the curiosity of that young islander of his.[4] But what I saw, by Jove, was not Helen but men with downcast heads and pale faces.

" On seeing me their hearts were filled with joy " [5] and they came to meet me ; for they kept asking if we had brought any bad news. For they appeared to be praying for the worst, and rejoiced in things of sorrow like singers of dirges in the theatre. They kept putting their heads close together and whispering. After all this they questioned me, saying,

" What man art thou and whence ? Where stands your town,
Where do your parents dwell ? [6]
For from your appearance you must be an
honourable man."

[5] *Iliad* XXIV. 320-321, *Odyssey* XV. 164-165.
[6] *Odyssey* 1. 170.

ἦν δ' ἐγώ, Ὀλίγοι γε χρηστοί, ὥσπερ βλέπω πανταχοῦ· Κριτίας δὲ τοὔνομα, πόλις δέ μοι ἔνθεν ὅθεν καὶ ὑμῖν.

24. ὡς δ' ἀεροβατοῦντες ἐπυνθάνοντο, Πῶς τὰ τῆς πόλεως καὶ τὰ τοῦ κόσμου;

ἦν δ' ἐγώ, Χαίρουσί γε πάντες καὶ ἔτι γε χαιρήσονται.[1]

οἱ δὲ ἀνένευον ταῖς ὀφρύσιν, Οὐχ οὕτω. δυστοκεῖ γὰρ ἡ πόλις.

ἦν δ' ἐγὼ κατὰ τὴν αὐτῶν γνώμην· Ὑμεῖς πεδάρσιοι ὄντες καὶ ὡς ἀπὸ ὑψηλοῦ ἅπαντα καθορῶντες ὀξυδερκέστατα καὶ τάδε νενοήκατε. πῶς δὲ τὰ τοῦ αἰθέρος; μῶν ἐκλείψει ὁ ἥλιος, ἡ δὲ σελήνη κατὰ κάθετον γενήσεται; ὁ Ἄρης εἰ τετραγωνίσει[2] τὸν Δία καὶ ὁ Κρόνος διαμετρήσει τὸν ἥλιον; ἡ Ἀφροδίτη εἰ μετὰ τοῦ Ἑρμοῦ συνοδεύσει καὶ Ἑρμαφροδίτους ἀποκυήσουσιν, ἐφ' οἷς ὑμεῖς ἥδεσθε; εἰ ῥαγδαίους ὑετοὺς ἐκπέμψουσιν; εἰ νιφετὸν πολὺν ἐπιστρωννύσουσι τῇ γῇ, χάλαζαν δὲ καὶ ἐρυσίβην εἰ κατάξουσι, λοιμὸν καὶ λιμὸν καὶ αὐχμὸν[3] εἰ ἐπιπέμψουσιν, εἰ τὸ κεραυνοβόλον ἀγγεῖον ἀπεγεμίσθη καὶ τὸ βροντοποιὸν δοχεῖον ἀνεμεστώθη;

25. οἱ δὲ ὡς ἅπαντα κατωρθωκότες κατεφλυάρουν τὰ αὑτῶν ἐράσμια, ὡς μεταλλαγῶσι τὰ πράγματα, ἀταξίαι δὲ καὶ ταραχαὶ τὴν πόλιν καταλήψονται, τὰ στρατόπεδα ἥττονα τῶν ἐναντίων γενήσονται. τοῦτο ἐκταραχθεὶς καὶ ὥσπερ πρῖνος καόμενος οἰηθεὶς διάτορον ἀνεβόησα, Ὦ δαιμόνιοι ἀνδρῶν, μὴ

---

[1] χαιρήσονται edd..
[2] τετραγωνήσει edd..
[3] καὶ αὐχμὸν om. edd..

THE PATRIOT

I replied, " Few men are honourable, to judge from what I see everywhere. My name is Critias, and I come from the same city as you."

24. Then, like men with their heads in the clouds, they asked how things were in the city and in the world, and I said, " All men are happy and will continue to be so."

But they raised their brows in dissent and said, " It is not so ; the city is pregnant with evil."

Agreeing with them, I said, " Because you are raised on high and are like men who look down on everything from aloft, you have been most keen-sighted in perceiving this too. But how of things in the sky ? Will there be an eclipse of the sun ? Will the moon rise on a vertical course ? Will Mars be in quartile aspect with Jupiter, and Saturn be diametrically opposite to the sun ? Will Venus be in conjunction with Mercury, so that they produce the Hermaphrodites in whom you find such pleasure ? Will they send torrential rain ? Will they bestrew the earth with drifts of snow ? Will they bring down hail and blight ? Will they send upon us pestilence and famine and drought ? Is the vessel of the thunderbolt empty ? Is the receptacle of the lightning replenished ? "

25. But they like people with everything arranged to their liking went on talking their own beloved nonsense, saying that things were to change, that disorders and turmoils would seize the city and her armies succumb to her foes. I, astounded at this and " swelling like a burning oak " [1] uttered a piercing

---

[1] Cf. *Frogs* 859.

μεγάλα λίαν λέγετε " θήγοντες ὀδόντας κατ'
ἀνδρῶν θυμολεόντων πνεόντων δόρυ καὶ λόγχας καὶ
λευκολόφους [1] τρυφαλείας." ἀλλὰ ταῦθ' ὑμῖν [2] ἐπὶ
κεφαλὴν καταβήσεται, ὡς τὴν πατρίδα ὑμῶν κατα-
τρύχετε· οὐ γὰρ αἰθεροβατοῦντες ταῦτα ἠκηκόειτε,
οὐ τὴν πολυάσχολον μαθηματικὴν κατωρθώκατε.
εἰ δέ γε μαντεῖαι καὶ γοητεῖαι ὑμᾶς παρέπεισαν,
διπλοῦν τὸ τῆς ἀμαθίας· γυναικῶν γὰρ εὑρέματα
ταῦτα γραϊδίων καὶ παίγνια· [3] ἐπὶ πολὺ γὰρ τὰ
τοιαῦτα αἱ τῶν γυναικῶν ἐπίνοιαι μετέρχονται.

ΤΡΙΕΦΩΝ

26. Τί δὲ πρὸς ταῦτα ἔφησαν, ὦ καλὲ Κριτία, οἱ
κεκαρμένοι τὴν γνώμην καὶ τὴν διάνοιαν;

ΚΡΙΤΙΑΣ

Ἅπαντα ταῦτα παρέδραμον εἰς ἐπίνοιαν τετεχνα-
σμένην καταπεφευγότες· ἔλεγον γάρ, Ἡλίους
δέκα ἄσιτοι διαμενοῦμεν καὶ ἐπὶ παννύχους ὑμνῳ-
δίας ἐπαγρυπνοῦντες ὀνειρώττομεν τὰ τοιαῦτα.

ΤΡΙΕΦΩΝ

Σὺ δὲ τί πρὸς αὐτοὺς εἴρηκας; μέγα γὰρ ἔφησαν
καὶ διηπορημένον.

ΚΡΙΤΙΑΣ

Θάρσει, οὐκ ἀγεννές· ἀντεῖπον γὰρ τὰ κάλλιστα.
τὰ γὰρ παρὰ τῶν ἀστικῶν θρυλλούμενα, ἔφην, περὶ

---

[1] λευκωλένους codd..
[2] ταῦθ' ὑμῖν edd.: ταῦτα μὲν codd..
[3] εὑρέματα . . . παιγνία versum comicum (fr. 482) esse
putavit Kock.

cry, " Accursed men, speak not with excessive pride,
  Whetting your teeth against lion-hearted men
  Whose breath bears spears and lances and white-
    crested casques." [1]
But these things shall descend upon your heads, for
you are a drain on your country's strength. For
you did not hear this when prancing through the sky,
nor have you mastered the mathematics you've
studied so hard. If you've been led astray by
prophecies and false pretences, then you're guilty of
double folly. For these things are inventions of old
women and are infantile. For usually it's women's
imaginations which are attracted by such things.

TRIEPHO

26. What reply, my fine Critias, was made to this
by those fellows shorn of all sense and intellect ?

CRITIAS

They passed over all those words of mine, taking
refuge in a skilfully prepared plan. For they kept
saying, " For ten days now shall we be remaining
in fasting, and we have been dreaming such things
while keeping vigil with all-night hymns."

TRIEPHO

And what answer did *you* give to them ? For this
was a weighty and perplexing thing they said.

CRITIAS

Have no fear ; I didn't disgrace myself, but made
the best of replies by saying, " The talk of the town

---

[1] A pastiche of *Frogs* 815, 1016, and 1041.

ὑμῶν, ὁπόταν ὀνειροπολῆτε, τὰ τοιαῦτά που παρεισάγονται.

οἱ δὲ σεσηρὸς ὑπομειδιῶντες, "Εξω που παρέρχονται τοῦ κλινιδίου.

ἦν δ' ἐγώ, Εἰ ἀληθῆ εἰσι ταῦτα, ὦ αἰθέριοι, οὐκ ἄν ποτε ἀσφαλῶς τὰ μέλλοντα ἐξιχνεύσαιτε, ἀλλὰ καταπεισθέντες[1] ὑπ' αὐτῶν ληρήσετε τὰ μὴ ὄντα μηδὲ γενησόμενα. ἀλλὰ ταῦτα μὲν οὐκ οἶδ' ὅπως ληρεῖτε ὀνείροις πιστεύοντες, καὶ τὰ κάλλιστα βδελύττεσθε, τοῖς δὲ πονηροῖς ἤδεσθε, μηδὲν ὀνούμενοι τοῦ βδελύγματος. ὥστε ἐάσατε[2] τὰς ἀλλοκότους ταύτας φαντασίας καὶ τὰ πονηρὰ βουλεύματα καὶ μαντεύματα, μή που θεὸς ὑμᾶς ἐς κόρακας βάλλῃ[3] διὰ τὸ τῇ πατρίδι ἐπαρᾶσθαι καὶ λόγους κιβδήλους ἐπιφημίζειν.

27. οὗτοι δὲ ἅπαντες ἕνα θυμὸν ἔχοντες ἐμοὶ πολλὰ κατεμέμφοντο. καὶ εἰ βούλει, καὶ τάδε προστιθῶ σοι, ἅτινά με καὶ ὡς στήλην ἄναυδον ἔθηκαν, μέχρις ἂν ἡ χρηστή σου λαλιὰ λιθούμενον ἀνέλυσε καὶ ἄνθρωπον ἀπεκατέστησε.

ΤΡΙΕΦΩΝ

Σίγα, ὦ Κριτία, καὶ μὴ ὑπερεκτείνῃς τοὺς ὕθλους· ὁρᾷς γὰρ ὡς ἐξώγκωταί μου ἡ νηδὺς καὶ ὥσπερ κυοφορῶ· ἐδήχθην γὰρ τοῖς παρὰ σοῦ λόγοις ὡς ὑπὸ κυνὸς λυττῶντος. καὶ εἰ μὴ φάρμακον ληθεδανὸν ἐμπιὼν ἠρεμήσω, αὕτη ἡ μνήμη οἰκουροῦσα ἐν ἐμοὶ μέγα κακὸν ἐργάσεται. ὥστε ἔασον τούτους τὴν εὐχὴν ἀπὸ πατρὸς ἀρξάμενος καὶ τὴν πολυώ-

---

[1] καταποθέντες codd.. [2] ἐάσετε edd..
[3] βάλλοι Δα: βάλοι edd..

says of you that only when you're dreaming do such things occur to you."

They clenched their teeth in a grin and said, " We're out of bed when they come to us."

" If this is true, you creatures of the sky," I said, " you can never discover the future with any certainty, but, convinced by these dreams, you will talk nonsense about what doesn't exist and never will. But somehow you talk all this nonsense because you trust in dreams. You loathe all that is most beautiful, and rejoice in evil things, though your loathing does you no good. Abandon therefore these strange fancies and these evil plans and prophecies, lest perchance God hurl you to perdition for cursing your native land and ascribing these falsified words to him.

27. Then they " did all with one accord " [1] heap reproaches on me. If you wish, I'll tell you of these too. They made me like a mute gravestone, till your blessed words released me from my petrifaction and made me human again.

TRIEPHO

Hush, Critias. Do not prolong to excess your account of their inanities. For you can see that my stomach is swollen and I'm, in a manner of speaking, pregnant. For I've been bitten by your words as though by a mad dog, and, if I don't take some potion to make me forget them [2] and give me rest, my memory of them will stay with me and do me great harm. You must therefore dismiss these words from your thoughts. Start your prayer with " Our Father," and add at the end the hymn of many

---

[1] *Iliad* XV. 710 etc..   [2] *Odyssey* IV. 220-221.

νυμον ᾠδὴν ἐς τέλος ἐπιθείς. 28. ἀλλὰ τί τοῦτο;
οὐχὶ Κλεόλαος οὗτός ἐστιν, ὁ τοῖς ποσὶ μακρὰ
βιβάς, σπουδῇ δὲ ἥκει καὶ κατέρχεται; μῶν
ἐπιφωνήσομεν αὐτῷ;

ΚΡΙΤΙΑΣ

Καὶ μάλα.

ΤΡΙΕΦΩΝ

Κλεόλαε,
  μή τι παραδράμῃς γε ποσὶ μηδὲ παρέλθῃς,
  ἀλλ᾽ ἐλθὲ χαίρων, εἴ γέ που μῦθον φέρεις.

ΚΛΕΟΛΑΟΣ

Χαίρετ᾽ ἄμφω, ὦ καλὴ ξυνωρίς.

ΤΡΙΕΦΩΝ

Τίς ἡ σπουδή; ἀσθμαίνεις γὰρ ἐπὶ πολύ. μῶν τι
καινὸν πέπρακται;

ΚΛΕΟΛΑΟΣ

Πέπτωκεν ὀφρὺς ἡ πάλαι βοωμένη
  Περσῶν,
καὶ Σοῦσα κλεινὸν ἄστυ.
πεσεῖ[1] δ᾽ ἔτι γε πᾶσα χθὼν Ἀραβίας
χειρὶ κρατοῦντος εὐσθενεστάτῳ κράτει.

ΚΡΙΤΙΑΣ

29. Τοῦτ᾽ ἐκεῖνο, ὡς ἀεὶ τὸ θεῖον οὐκ ἀμελεῖ
τῶν ἀγαθῶν, ἀλλ᾽ αὔξει ἄγον ἐπὶ τὰ κρείττονα.

---

[1] πέσοι α.

epithets.[1] 28. But what's this ?   Isn't that Cleolaus
who " doth take such lengthy strides "[2] and
eagerly " doth come and doth return " ?[3]   Shall we
hail him ?

CRITIAS

By all means.

THIEPHO

Cleolaus,
" Speed not on with running foot, nor pass me by,
But gladly come if news perchance you bring."[4]

CLEOLAUS

Greetings both, ye glorious twain.

TRIEPHO

Why such haste ?   You're quite out of breath.   Is
there news of any sort ?

CLEOLAUS

" The Persians' long-famed pride is humbled now,
Along with Susa's glorious town,
And all Arabia too will be subdued
By glorious might of his o'erpowering hand."[5]

CRITIAS

29. It's as they always said ; heaven never neglects
good men, but ever promotes their welfare and

---

[1] Presumably a doxology.   [2] Cf. *Odyssey* XI. 539.
[3] Aeschylus, *Choephoroe* 3, Aristophanes, *Frogs* 1153 seq.
[4] The first line is a defective hexameter based on *Odyssey*
VIII. 230, the second an iambic trimeter (source unknown).
[5] Mock tragic (cf. *Septem* 794) lines and part-lines.   The
Persians, the traditional enemies of the ancient Greeks
perhaps represent the Saracens, the chief enemies of
Byzantium.

ἡμεῖς δέ, ὦ Τριεφῶν, τὰ κάλλιστα εὑρηκότες ἐσμέν. ἐδυσχέραινον γὰρ ἐν τῇ ἀποβιώσει τί τοῖς τέκνοις [1] καταλιπεῖν ἐπὶ ταῖς διαθήκαις· οἶδας γὰρ τὴν ἐμὴν πενίαν ὡς ἐγὼ τὰ σά. τοῦτο ἀρκεῖ τοῖς παισίν, αἱ ἡμέραι τοῦ αὐτοκράτορος· πλοῦτος γὰρ ἡμᾶς οὐκ ἐκλείψει καὶ ἔθνος ἡμᾶς οὐ καταπτοήσει.

ΤΡΙΕΦΩΝ

Κἀγώ, ὦ Κριτία, ταῦτα καταλείπω τοῖς τέκνοις, ὡς ἴδωσι Βαβυλῶνα ὀλλυμένην, Αἴγυπτον δουλουμένην, τὰ τῶν Περσῶν τέκνα " δούλειον ἦμαρ " ἄγοντα, τὰς ἐκδρομὰς τῶν Σκυθῶν παυομένας, εἶθ' οὖν καὶ ἀνακοπτομένας. ἡμεῖς δὲ τὸν ἐν Ἀθήναις Ἄγνωστον ἐφευρόντες καὶ προσκυνήσαντες χεῖρας εἰς οὐρανὸν ἐκτείναντες [2] τούτῳ εὐχαριστήσωμεν ὡς καταξιωθέντες τοιούτου κράτους ὑπήκοοι γενέσθαι, τοὺς δὲ λοιποὺς ληρεῖν ἐάσωμεν ἀρκεσθέντες ὑπὲρ αὐτῶν εἰπεῖν τὸ οὐ φροντὶς Ἱπποκλείδῃ κατὰ τὴν παροιμίαν.

[1] τὰ τέκνα codd..
[2] ἐκτείνοντες ΔC.

improves their fortunes. But we, Triepho, have found the most glorious lot of all. For I was distressed by worrying over what to leave my children in my will when I died. For you know my poverty as well as I know what you possess. But it suffices for my children that the Emperor should live ; for then wealth will not fail us, nor any race terrify us.

TRIEPHO

I too, Critias, leave to my children as their heritage that they should see Babylon [1] destroyed, Egypt enslaved, the children of the Persians enduring " chains and slavery," [2] the inroads of the Scythians checked and, I pray, utterly defeated. Since we have found the Unknown God of Athens, let us fall down before him with our hands extended to the heavens, and pay him thanks that we have been thought worthy to be made subject to such a power. But the others let us leave to talk their nonsense and concerning them let us be content to say with the proverb, " Hippoclides doesn't care." [3]

[1] Babylon perhaps is Bagdad, and the Scythians the Bulgars or the Russians. Phocas never lived to invade Egypt, but he may well have contemplated it.

[2] Euripides, *Hecuba* 56, *Andromache* 99.

[3] Cf. Herodotus 6.126-31 and Harmon's note on *Heracles*, 8, Lucian, L.C.L. vol. 1.

CHARIDEMUS

IT is generally agreed that this work is not by Lucian.
It is not found in the better MSS. of Lucian, and both
its Greek and its uninspired contents are quite
unworthy of him. The author is presumably a
sophist of quite unknown date, who knew his
Lucian as he introduces several of Lucian's motifs
and Homeric quotations, though he is also influenced
by Plato and Xenophon, and draws heavily from
Isocrates' *Helen*, particularly in cc. 16-18 which are
largely a paraphrase of *Helen* 18-20, 39-43 and 50-53.
The careful, and mostly successful, avoidance of
hiatus is also worth noting.

ΧΑΡΙΔΗΜΟΣ Η ΠΕΡΙ ΚΑΛΛΟΥΣ

ΕΡΜΙΠΠΟΣ

1. Περιπάτους ἔτυχον χθές, ὦ Χαρίδημε, ποιού-
μενος ἐν τῷ προαστείῳ ἅμα μὲν καὶ τῆς παρὰ τῶν
ἀγρῶν χάριν ῥᾳστώνης, ἅμα δὲ—ἔτυχον γάρ τι
μελετῶν—καὶ δεόμενος ἡσυχίας. ἐντυγχάνω δὴ
Προξένῳ τῷ Ἐπικράτους· προσειπὼν δὲ ὥσπερ
εἰώθειν, ἠρώτων ὅθεν τε πορεύοιτο καὶ ὅποι βαδίζοι.
ὁ δὲ ἥκειν μὲν ἔφη καὶ αὐτὸς ἐκεῖ παραμυθίας χάριν,
ἥπερ εἰώθει πρὸς τὴν ὄψιν γίνεσθαι τῶν ἀγρῶν,
ἀπολαύσων δὲ καὶ τῆς τούτους ἐπιπνεούσης εὐκρά-
του καὶ κούφης αὔρας, ἀπὸ συμποσίου μέντοι
καλλίστου γεγονότος ἐν Πειραιεῖ ἐν Ἀνδροκλέους
τοῦ Ἐπιχάρους τὰ ἐπινίκια τεθυκότος Ἑρμῇ,
ὅτι δὴ βιβλίον ἀναγνοὺς ἐνίκησεν ἐν Διασίοις.
2. ἔφασκε δὴ ἄλλα τε πολλὰ γεγενῆσθαι ἀστεῖα καὶ
χαρίεντα, καὶ δὴ καὶ κάλλους ἐγκώμια εἰρῆσθαι τοῖς
ἀνδράσιν, ἃ ἐκεῖνον μὲν μὴ δύνασθαι εἰπεῖν ὑπό τε
γήρως ἐπιλελησμένον ἄλλως τε καὶ οὐκ ἐπὶ
πολὺ λόγων μετεσχηκότα, σὲ δ᾽ ἂν ῥᾳδίως εἰπεῖν ἅτε
καὶ αὐτὸν ἐγκεκωμιακότα καὶ τοῖς ἄλλοις παρ᾽
ὅλον τὸ συμπόσιον προσεσχηκότα τὸν νοῦν.

Codices: 1859 = Vat. Gr. 1859 (14 saecli);
          ὤ = Marc. Gr. 840 (antea 434) supplementum
recens (paulo ante 1471 scriptum).

CHARIDEMUS or ON BEAUTY

HERMIPPUS

1. I was taking a stroll in the suburbs yesterday, Charidemus, both for relaxation in the fields and also because I had something on my mind and needed peace and quiet, when lo and behold I met Proxenus, the son of Epicrates. After greeting him in my usual fashion, I asked where he'd come from and where he was going. He said he too had come there for the refreshment he'd always found in looking at the fields, and also to enjoy the mild and gentle breezes that blew over them. He'd come from an excellent party at the Piraeus in the house of Androcles, son of Epichares ; Androcles had been sacrificing to Hermes by way of thanks for his victory with the book he'd read at the Diasia.[1] 2. He told me that it had been an occasion that evoked much wit and culture and, in particular, praises of beauty had been pronounced by the men. These he could not report to me, he said, because his old age had impaired his memory, and in any case he had not taken much part in the conversation, but he said *you* would have no difficulty in recounting them, as you had yourself pronounced an encomium and had paid attention to all the other speakers throughout the party.

---

[1] A festival in honour of Zeus, cf. Thucydides 1, 126 and note on *Icaromenippus* 24.

PSEUDO-LUCIAN

ΧΑΡΙΔΗΜΟΣ

Γέγονε ταῦτα, ὦ Ἕρμιππε. οὐ μέντοι γε οὐδ᾽ ἐμοὶ ῥᾴδιον ἐπ᾽ ἀκριβείας ἅπαντα διεξιέναι· οὐ γὰρ οἷόν τε ἦν πάντων ἀκούειν θορύβου πολλοῦ γινομένου τῶν τε διακονουμένων τῶν τε ἑστιωμένων, ἄλλως τε καὶ τῶν δυσχερεστέρων ὂν μεμνῆσθαι λόγους ἐν συμποσίῳ γενομένους· οἶσθα γὰρ ὡς ἐπιλήσμονας ποιεῖ καὶ τοὺς λίαν μνημονικωτάτους. πλὴν ἀλλὰ σὴν χάριν ὡς ἂν οἷός τε ὦ τὴν διήγησιν πειράσομαι ποιεῖσθαι, μηδὲν παραλείπων ὧν ἂν ἐνθυμηθῶ.

ΕΡΜΙΠΠΟΣ

3. Τούτων μὲν δὴ ἕνεκα οἶδά σοι χάριν. ἀλλ᾽ εἴ μοι τὸν πάντα λόγον ἐξ ἀρχῆς ἀποδοίης, ὅ τι τε ἦν ὅπερ ἀνέγνω βιβλίον Ἀνδροκλῆς τίνα τε νενίκηκε καὶ τίνας ὑμᾶς εἰς τὸ συμπόσιον κέκληκεν, οὕτως ἂν ἱκανὴν καταθοῖο [1] τὴν χάριν.

ΧΑΡΙΔΗΜΟΣ

Τὸ μὲν δὴ βιβλίον ἦν ἐγκώμιον Ἡρακλέους ἔκ τινος ὀνείρατος, ὡς ἔλεγε, πεποιημένον αὐτῷ· νενίκηκε δὲ Διότιμον τὸν Μεγαρόθεν ἀνταγωνισάμενον αὐτῷ περὶ τῶν ἀσταχύων, μᾶλλον δὲ περὶ τῆς δόξης.

ΕΡΜΙΠΠΟΣ

Τί δ᾽ ἦν ὃ ἐκεῖνος ἀνέγνω βιβλίον;

ΧΑΡΙΔΗΜΟΣ

Ἐγκώμιον τοῖν Διοσκούροιν. ἔφασκε δὲ καὶ αὐτὸς ἐκ μεγάλων κινδύνων ὑπ᾽ ἐκείνων σεσωσμένος

---

[1] καταθοῖο 1859: καταθεῖο ω.

CHARIDEMUS

CHARIDEMUS

All this is quite true, Hermippus. But even I shall find it difficult to give an accurate account of everything as it was quite impossible to hear everything because of the great din made by the waiters and the guests. Besides, it's not particularly easy to remember speeches made at a dinner. For you know how forgetful *that* makes even those blessed with the very best of memories. However, to oblige you, I shall try as best I can to describe the proceedings without omitting anything that comes to mind.

HERMIPPUS

3. For *that* you have my thanks. But, if you were to recount the whole discussion from the beginning, tell me what book Androcles read, what rival he defeated, and who you were that he invited to the party, then you *would* put me greatly in your debt.

CHARIDEMUS

The book was an encomium of Heracles, which he said he'd composed as a result of a dream. He defeated Diotimus from Megara, who competed against him for the ears of wheat, or rather for glory.

HERMIPPUS

And what book did *he* read ?

CHARIDEMUS

An encomium of the Dioscuri. He said that he himself too had been saved by them from great

471

ταύτην αὐτοῖς καταθεῖναι τὴν χάριν, ἄλλως τε καὶ
ὑπ' ἐκείνων παρακεκλημένος ἐπ' ἄκροις ἱστίοις ἐν τοῖς
ἐσχάτοις κινδύνοις φανέντων. 4. παρῆσαν μέντοι
τῷ συμποσίῳ καὶ ἄλλοι πολλοὶ οἱ μὲν συγγενεῖς
αὐτῷ, οἱ δὲ καὶ ἄλλως συνήθεις, οἱ δὲ λόγου τε ἄξιοι
τό τε συμπόσιον ὅλον κεκοσμηκότες καὶ κάλλους
ἐγκώμια διελθόντες Φίλων τε ἦν ὁ Δεινίου καὶ
Ἀρίστιππος ὁ Ἀγασθένους καὶ τρίτος αὐτός·
συγκατέλεκτο δὲ ἡμῖν καὶ Κλεώνυμος ὁ καλὸς ὁ
τοῦ Ἀνδροκλέους ἀδελφιδοῦς, μειράκιον ἁπαλόν τε
καὶ τεθρυμμένον· νοῦν μέντοι γε ἐδόκει ἔχειν· πάνυ
γὰρ προθύμως ἠκροᾶτο τῶν λόγων. πρῶτος δὲ ὁ
Φίλων περὶ τοῦ κάλλους ἤρξατο λέγειν προοιμιασά-
μενος οὕτω.

ΕΡΜΙΠΠΟΣ

Μηδαμῶς, ὦ ἑταῖρε, μὴ πρὶν τῶν ἐγκωμίων ἄρξῃ
πρὶν ἄν μοι καὶ τὴν αἰτίαν ἀποδῷς ὑφ' ἧς εἰς τούτους προήχθητε τοὺς λόγους.

ΧΑΡΙΔΗΜΟΣ

Εἰκῆ διατρίβεις ἡμᾶς, ὦγαθέ, πάλαι δυναμένους
τὸν ἄπαντα λόγον διελθόντας ἀπαλλαγῆναι. πλὴν
ἀλλὰ τί τις ἂν χρήσαιτο, ὁπότε φίλος τις ὢν βιάζοιτο;
ἀνάγκη γὰρ ὑφίστασθαι πᾶν ὁτιοῦν. 5. ἦν δὲ
ζητεῖς αἰτίαν τῶν λόγων, αὐτὸς ἦν Κλεώνυμος ὁ
καλός· καθημένου γὰρ αὐτοῦ μεταξὺ ἐμοῦ τε καὶ
Ἀνδροκλέους τοῦ θείου, πολὺς ἐγίνετο λόγος τοῖς

---

[1] For the Dioscuri (Castor and Pollux) as protectors of
mariners and appearing as St. Elmo's fire see *The Ship,* 9.

dangers [1] and so had paid his thanks to them in this way, particularly as they had told him to do so, when they appeared at the top of the sails while the danger was at its height.   4.   Then there were many others at the party.   Some of them were related to Diotimus, others were acquaintances of his, but noteworthy for having graced the whole party by delivering encomia of beauty were Philo, son of Dinias, Aristippus, son of Agasthenes, and I myself.   Another of our companions at table was Cleonymus, the handsome nephew of Androcles, a delicate effeminate lad.   He seemed, however, not to be lacking in intellect, as he listened very eagerly to the speeches.   First to begin speaking about beauty was Philo, whose introductory remarks were as follows :

HERMIPPUS

No, my friend !   Please don't start on the encomia before telling me the reason which led you to discuss this topic.

CHARIDEMUS

You're wasting my time, my good fellow.   I could have reported the whole discussion long ago and been on my way.   But what is one to do when a friend [2] constrains ?   For then one must submit to anything.   5. You ask what caused the discussion ; it was handsome Cleonymus himself.   For he was sitting between Androcles, his uncle, and me, when much discussion of him arose amongst the less

---

[2] Apparently a quotation of a lost original; cf. *Charon* 2, *Menippus* 3.

ἰδιώταις περὶ αὐτοῦ ἀποβλέπουσί τε εἰς αὐτὸν καὶ
ὑπερεκπεπληγμένοις τὸ κάλλος. σχεδὸν οὖν πάντων
ὀλιγωρήσαντες κάθηντο διεξιόντες ἐγκώμια τοῦ
μειρακίου. ἀγασθέντες δὲ ἡμεῖς τῶν ἀνδρῶν τὴν
φιλοκαλίαν καὶ ἅμα ἐπαινέσαντες αὐτοὺς ἀργίας τε
πολλῆς εἶναι ὑπολαβόντες λόγοις ἀπολείπεσθαι τῶν
ἰδιωτῶν περὶ τῶν καλλίστων, ᾧ μόνῳ τούτων οἰόμεθα
προέχειν, καὶ δὴ ἡπτόμεθα τῶν περὶ κάλλους
λόγων. ἔδοξεν οὖν ἡμῖν οὐκ ὀνομαστὶ λέγειν τὸν
ἔπαινον τοῦ παιδός—οὐ γὰρ ἂν ἔχειν καλῶς,
ἐμβαλεῖν γὰρ ἂν αὐτὸν εἰς πλείω τρυφήν—ἀλλ'
οὐδὲ μὴν ὥσπερ ἐκείνους οὕτως ἀτάκτως, ὅπερ
ἕκαστος τύχοι, λέγειν, ἀλλ' ἕκαστον εἰπεῖν ἰδίᾳ ὅσ'
ἂν ἀπομνημονεύοι περὶ τοῦ προκειμένου.

6. καὶ δὴ ἀρξάμενος ὁ Φίλων πρῶτος οὑτωσὶ τὸν
λόγον ἐποιεῖτο· 'Ὡς ἔστι δεινόν, εἰ πάνθ' ὅσα
πράττομεν ἑκάστης ἡμέρας, ὡς περὶ καλῶν, ποιού-
μεθα τὴν σπουδήν, αὐτοῦ δὲ [1] κάλλους οὐδένα
ποιησόμεθα λόγον, ἀλλ' οὕτω καθεδούμεθα σιγῇ
ὥσπερ δεδοικότες μὴ λάθωμεν ἡμᾶς αὐτοὺς
ὑπὲρ οὗ σπουδάζομεν τὸν ἅπαντα χρόνον εἰπόντες.
καίτοι ποῦ τις ἂν χρήσαιτο πρεπόντως τοῖς λόγοις,
εἰ περὶ τῶν μηδενὸς ἀξίων σπουδάζων περὶ τοῦ
καλλίστου σιγῴη τῶν ὄντων; ἢ πῶς ἂν τὸ ἐν
λόγοις καλὸν σῴζοιτο κάλλιον μᾶλλον ἢ [2] πάντα
τἆλλα παρέντας περὶ αὐτοῦ λέγειν τοῦ τέλους ἡμᾶς
τῶν ἑκάστοτε πραττομένων; ἀλλ' ἵνα μὴ δόξω
λέγειν μὲν ὡς χρὴ περὶ τοῦτο διακεῖσθαι εἰδέναι,
εἰπεῖν δὲ μηδὲν ἐπίστασθαι περὶ αὐτοῦ, ὡς οἷόν τε
βραχέα περὶ τούτου πειράσομαι διελθεῖν.

educated people present, who were staring at him utterly amazed at his beauty. Scarcely heeding anything else they sat delivering encomia of the boy. We felt and expressed admiration for the men's appreciation of beauty, and thought that it would show the greatest idleness on our part to be outdone by the uneducated in discussing the highest forms of beauty ; for in this respect alone do we consider ourselves superior to them. Thus it was that we also started discussing beauty. We decided to pronounce our praises of the boy without mentioning his name, as that would be wrong and merely give him further airs. We agreed to avoid their disorderly, haphazard manner of discussion and that each of us in turn should make his personal contribution on the topic under discussion.

6. Thus it was that Philo began first and spoke as follows : "How scandalous it is that in all our everyday activities we are full of zeal, as though for something beautiful, while beauty itself we hold of no account, but remain seated thus in silence, as though afraid that a word might escape us unawares concerning the thing we pursue zealously all our days ! But what would be the right occasion for a man to speak, if he showed zeal for what's worthless and had nothing to say about the most beautiful of all things ? And what more beautiful way of preserving the beauty of speech than for us to leave aside all else and talk about the actual end of all our actions ? But, so as not to seem to you to claim knowledge of the correct attitude towards this without being able to say anything about it, I shall try as briefly as I can to discourse on this subject.

---

¹ δὲ τοῦ edd.. ² ἢ τῷ Gesner.

κάλλους γὰρ δὴ πάντες μὲν ἐπεθύμησαν τυχεῖν,
πάνυ δ' ἠξιώθησαν ὀλίγοι τινές· οἳ δὲ ταύτης ἔτυχον
τῆς δωρεᾶς, εὐδαιμονέστατοι πάντων ἔδοξαν γεγενῆσθαι καὶ πρὸς θεῶν καὶ πρὸς ἀνθρώπων τὰ εἰκότα
τετιμημένοι. τεκμήριον δέ· τῶν γοῦν θεῶν ἐξ ἡρώων
γενομένων Ἡρακλῆς τέ ἐστιν ὁ Διὸς καὶ Διόσκουροι
καὶ Ἑλένη, ὧν ὁ μὲν ἀνδρείας ἕνεκα ταύτης λέγεται
τυχεῖν τῆς τιμῆς, Ἑλένη δὲ τοῦ κάλλους χάριν
αὐτή [1] τε μεταβαλεῖν εἰς θεὸν καὶ τοῖς Διοσκούροις
αἰτία γενέσθαι πρὶν αὐτὴν εἰς οὐρανὸν ἀνελθεῖν τοῖς
ὑπὸ γὴν συνεξητασμένοις. 7. ἀλλὰ μὴν ὅστις
ἀνθρώπων ἠξιώθη τοῖς θεοῖς ὁμιλεῖν, οὐκ ἔστιν εὑρεῖν, πλὴν ὅσοι μετεσχήκασι κάλλους· Πέλοψ τε γὰρ
τούτου χάριν τοῖς θεοῖς ἀμβροσίας μετέσχε, καὶ
Γανυμήδης ὁ τοῦ Δαρδάνου οὕτω κεκρατηκέναι
λέγεται τοῦ πάντων ὑπάτου θεῶν, ὥστ' αὐτὸν
οὐκ ἀνασχέσθαι συμμετασχεῖν αὐτῷ τινα τῶν
ἄλλων θεῶν τῆς θήρας τῶν παιδικῶν, ἀλλ' αὐτῷ μόνῳ
πρέπουσαν ἡγούμενον εἶναι εἰς Γάργαρον κατα-
πτάντα τῆς Ἴδης ἀναγαγεῖν ἐκεῖσε τὰ παιδικά, ὅπου
συνέσεσθαι τὸν ἄπαντα ἔμελλε χρόνον. τοσαύτην δ'
ἐπιμέλειαν ἀεὶ πεποίηται τῶν καλῶν, ὥστ' οὐ
μόνον αὐτοὺς ἠξίωσε τῶν οὐρανίων ἀναγαγὼν
ἐκεῖσε, ἀλλὰ καὶ αὐτὸς ἐπὶ γῆς ὅ τι τύχοι γινόμενος
συνῆν ἑκάστοτε τοῖς ἐρωμένοις, καὶ τοῦτο μὲν
γενόμενος κύκνος συνεγένετο Λήδᾳ, τοῦτο δ' ἐν εἴδει

<hr />

[1] αὐτήν edd..

[1] Cf. Isocrates, *Helen* 61.
[2] Cf. Philostratus, *Imagines*, 394, 405.
[3] Ganymede, the Trojan boy who was carried off by Zeus
to be his cup-bearer (see Vol. 7, p. 269, etc.) is here loosely

Beauty is what all men have ever yearned to have, though very few have been considered worthy of it. But those who have had this gift have ever been thought the most fortunate of all and have been fittingly honoured by both gods and men. This can be proved. Among heroes who became gods are Heracles, the son of Zeus, the Dioscuri and Helen. One of these is said to have gained this honour for his bravery, Helen to have changed into a goddess herself on account of her beauty and to have won godhead for the Dioscuri, who had been numbered with those in the underworld [1] before she ascended to heaven. 7. Moreover one cannot find any humans who've been thought worthy to associate with the gods except for those who've had beauty. For that was why Pelops [2] is said to have shared immortality with the gods, and Ganymede, son of Dardanus,[3] is said to have mastered the highest of all gods so completely that he could not bear to let any of the other gods share his expedition in pursuit of his darling boy, but thought it an expedition befitting himself alone that he should fly down to Gargaron on Ida [4] and take up his darling boy to the place where he would enjoy his company for all time. He has always paid such attention to beauties that not only has he given them a title to life in heaven by taking them up there but he himself, each time he joined his loved ones on earth, would become anything at all, now becoming a swan to court Leda, now in

described as " child of Dardanus," because Dardanus was the founder of Troy.

[4] Ida was a mountain near Troy, and Gargaron one of its peaks. Cf. *Iliad* VIII. 48, *Dialogues of the Gods* 10, *Judgement of the Goddesses*, 1 and 5.

ταύρου τὴν Εὐρώπην ἁρπάζει, εἰκασθεὶς δ' Ἀμφι-
τρύωνι γεννᾷ τὸν Ἡρακλέα. καὶ πολλά τις ἂν ἔχοι
λέγειν τεχνάσματα τοῦ Διὸς ὅπως ἂν οἷς ἐπεθύμει
συγγένοιτο μηχανώμενος. 8. τὸ δὲ δὴ μέγιστον καὶ
οἷον ἄν τις θαυμάσαι, ὁμιλῶν γὰρ τοῖς θεοῖς—οὐ
γὰρ ἀνθρώπων γε οὐδέσι πλὴν εἰ μὴ τοῖς καλοῖς—
ἐν δ' οὖν τούτοις δημηγορῶν οὕτω πεποίηται
σοβαρὸς τῷ κοινῷ τῶν Ἑλλήνων ποιητῇ καὶ θρασὺς
καὶ καταπληκτικός, ὥστ' ἐν μὲν τῇ προτέρᾳ δημη-
γορίᾳ τὴν Ἥραν, καίτοι πρότερον πάντ' εἰωθυῖαν
ἐπιτιμᾶν αὐτῷ, ὅμως δ' αὐτὴν οὕτως ἐφόβησεν,
ὥστ' ἤρκεσεν αὐτῇ τὸ μηδὲν παθεῖν, ἀλλὰ μέχρι
λόγων στῆναι τὴν ὀργὴν τῷ Διί· τοὺς δ' ἅπαντας
θεοὺς ἐν τῇ ὑστέρᾳ πάλιν οὐχ ἧττον κατέστησε
φοβηθῆναι γῆν ἀνασπάσειν αὐτοῖς ἀνδράσι καὶ
θάλατταν ἀπειλήσας. μέλλων δὲ συνέσεσθαι καλοῖς
οὕτω γίγνεται πρᾷος καὶ ἥμερος καὶ τοῖς πᾶσιν
ἐπιεικής, ὥστε πρὸς ἅπασι τοῖς ἄλλοις καὶ αὐτὸ τὸ
Ζεὺς εἶναι καταλιπών, ὅπως μὴ φαίνοιτο τοῖς
παιδικοῖς ἀηδής, ἑτέρου τινὸς ὑποκρίνεται σχῆμα,
καὶ τούτου καλλίστου καὶ οἵου τὸν ὁρῶντα προσαγα-
γέσθαι. τοσοῦτον αἰδοῦς καὶ τιμῆς παρέχεται τῷ
κάλλει.

9. καὶ οὐχ ὁ μὲν Ζεὺς οὕτω μόνος ἑάλω τοῦ
κάλλους, τῶν δ' ἄλλων οὐδεὶς θεῶν, ἵνα μᾶλλον
ἔχειν δοκῇ ταῦτα κατηγορίαν Διός, οὐχ ὑπὲρ
τοῦ κάλλους εἰρῆσθαι· ἀλλ' εἴ τις ἀκριβῶς ἐθελήσει
σκοπεῖν, πάντας ἂν εὕροι θεοὺς ταὐτὰ πεπονθότας
Διί, οἷον τὸν μὲν Ποσειδῶ τοῦ Πέλοπος ἡττημένον,

---

[1] Homer.   [2] *Iliad* IV. 30 ff.   [3] *Iliad*, VIII. 19.

the shape of a bull carrying off Europa, or adopting the likeness of Amphitryon to produce Heracles. One can enumerate many devices adopted by Zeus in his schemes for enjoying the company of those who excited his desire.

8. But what is the most important thing and a surprising one is that in his conversations with the gods—he had none with any human beings unless they were beautiful—in his harangues amongst the gods, I say, he has been depicted as being so dashing, bold and terrifying by the poet of all Greeks alike,[1] that in his earlier speech [2] he so frightened Hera that, though she had been used before that to censure everything he did, she was then content to escape unharmed and allow the anger to Zeus to be confined to words. Again, in his later speech,[3] he struck no less fear into all the gods by his threats to pull up land and sea and all men with them. Yet, when he's about to keep company with beauties, he becomes so kind and gentle and so completely reasonable that, in addition to all else, he even leaves off being Zeus, and, so as not to appear unpleasing to his darlings, he adopts some other appearance, and, what's more, one that's very beautiful and likely to attract the beholder. Such is the respect and honour shown by him to beauty.

9. And, so that these words may not be thought to be spoken in criticism of Zeus rather than in defence of beauty, let me tell you that Zeus isn't the only god so to have become the captive of beauty. No, anyone willing to consider the matter carefully would find that all the gods have been affected in the same way as Zeus. For example, Posidon fell victim to

Ὑακίνθου δὲ τὸν Ἀπόλλω, τὸν Ἑρμῆν δὲ τοῦ
Κάδμου. 10. καὶ θεαὶ δ' ἐλάττους οὐκ αἰσχύνονται
φαινόμεναι τούτου, ἀλλ' ὥσπερ φιλοτιμίαν αὐταῖς
ἔχειν δοκεῖ τὸ τῷ δεῖνι συγγενομένην καλῷ διηγεῖσ-
θαι παρεσχῆσθαι τοῖς ἀνθρώποις. ἔτι δὲ—τῶν μὲν
γὰρ [1] ἄλλων ἁπάντων ἐπιτηδευμάτων [2] ἑκάστη θεῶν,
ἑκάστου προστάτις οὖσα, οὐχ ἑτέραις [3] ἀμφισβητεῖ
περὶ ὧν ἄρχει, ἀλλ' Ἀθηνᾶ μὲν τοῖς ἀνθρώποις
ἡγουμένη τὰ ἐς πολέμους πρὸς Ἄρτεμιν οὐ διαμά-
χεται περὶ θήρας, ὡς δ' αὕτως Ἀθηνᾷ κἀκείνη
παραχωρεῖ τῶν πολεμικῶν, τῶν δὲ γάμων Ἥρα
Ἀφροδίτῃ, οὐδ' αὐτὴ πρὸς αὐτῆς ἐνοχλουμένη περὶ
ὧν ἐφορεύει. ἑκάστη δ' ἐπὶ κάλλει τοσοῦτον φρονεῖ
καὶ πάσας ὑπερβάλλεσθαι δοκεῖ, ὥστε καὶ ἡ Ἔρις
αὐτὰς ἀλλήλαις ἐκπολεμῶσαι βουλομένη οὐδὲν
ἄλλο προύβαλεν αὐταῖς ἢ κάλλος, οὕτως οἰομένη
ῥᾳδίως ὅπερ ἤθελε καταστήσειν, ὀρθῶς καὶ φρονί-
μως τοῦτο λογιζομένη. σκέψαιτο δ' ἄν τις ἐντεῦθεν
τὴν τοῦ κάλλους περιουσίαν· ὡς γὰρ ἐλάβοντο τοῦ
μήλου καὶ τὴν ἐπιγραφὴν ἀνελέξαντο, ἑκάστης
αὐτῆς ὑπολαβούσης εἶναι τὸ μῆλον, μηδεμιᾶς δὲ
τολμώσης τὴν ψῆφον καθ' αὑτῆς ἐνεγκεῖν, ὡς ἄρ'
αἰσχροτέρα τῆς ἑτέρας εἴη τὴν ὄψιν, ἀνέρχονται
παρὰ τὸν τῶν μὲν πατέρα, τῆς δ' ἀδελφόν τε καὶ,
σύνοικον Δία ἐπιτρέψουσαι τὴν δίκην αὐτῷ. ἔχων
δὲ καὶ αὐτὸς ἥτις ἐστὶν ἀποφήνασθαι καλλίστη καὶ,
πολλῶν ἀνδρείων ὄντων καὶ σοφῶν καὶ φρονίμων

[1] γὰρ om. edd..
[2] sic L. A. Post.: ἐπιτηδεύματα ω, suppl. in mg. 1859: om.
edd..
[3] ἑτέραις ω: ἑτέρ' 1859, edd.: ἑτέρᾳ tentavi.

Pelops,[1] Apollo to Hyacinthus,[2] and Hermes to
Cadmus.[3] 10. Goddesses too are not ashamed to
reveal their subjection to beauty, but seem to take a
sort of pride in intercourse with this or that beautiful
man, and giving accounts of the favours they've
bestowed on men. Furthermore, in the wide range
of all other customary pursuits, each goddess is a
patroness of one particular thing and never quarrels
with another over her sphere of power, for Athena is
leader of men in matters of war but does not compete
against Artemis in the chase, while she in the same
way yields to Athena in military matters, and, where
marriage is concerned, Hera yields to Aphrodite,
while in her own department she meets with no
interference from her. But each so prides herself on
her beauty and thinks herself so superior to all
others that, when Discord wished to make them
fight against each other, she merely made beauty the
issue amongst them, for she thought that thus she
would easily achieve her wish, and her calculations
were shrewd and accurate. One can see the pre-
eminence of beauty from this : when they had taken
up the apple and read the inscription, since each
assumed the apple was hers, and none of them would
vote against herself and admit her inferiority in looks
to another, they went up to Zeus, who was the father
of two of them, and brother and husband to the third,
to entrust the decision to him. But though he
could himself have pronounced who was the most
beautiful and though there were many brave, wise

---

[1] For Poseidon and Pelops, cf. Philostratus *Imagines* 789.
[2] For Apollo and Hyacinthus see Vol. 7, p. 317.
[3] The love of Hermes for Cadmus is not mentioned
elsewhere.

ἔν τε Ἑλλάδι καὶ τῇ βαρβάρῳ, ὅδ᾽ [1] ἐπιτρέπει τὴν
κρίσιν Πάριδι τῷ Πριάμου ψῆφον ἐναργῆ καὶ
καθαρὰν ἐξενεγκών, ὅτι καὶ φρονήσεως καὶ σοφίας
καὶ ῥώμης ὑπερέχει τὸ κάλλος.

11. τοσαύτην δ᾽ ἐπιμέλειαν ἀεὶ πεποίηνται καὶ
σπουδὴν ἀκούειν εἶναι καλαί, ὥστε καὶ τὸν ἡρώων
τε κοσμήτορα καὶ θεῶν ποιητὴν οὐκ ἄλλοθέν ποθεν
ἢ παρὰ τοῦ κάλλους πεπείκασιν ὀνομάζειν. ἥδιον
ἂν οὖν ἀκούσαι λευκώλενος ἢ Ἥρα ἢ " πρέσβα θεὰ
θυγάτηρ μεγάλου Κρόνου ", Ἀθηνᾶ δ᾽ οὐκ ἂν
βουληθείη Τριτογένεια πρὸ τοῦ Γλαυκῶπις καλεῖσθαι, Ἀφροδίτη τε τιμήσαιτ᾽ ἂν τοῦ παντὸς καλεῖσθαι Χρυσῆ. ἅπερ ἅπαντ᾽ εἰς κάλλος τείνει.

12. καίτοι ταῦτ᾽ οὐ μόνον ἀπόδειξιν ἔχει πῶς οἱ
κρείττους ἔχουσι περὶ τοῦτο, ἀλλὰ καὶ μαρτύριόν
ἐστιν ἀψευδὲς τοῦ κρεῖττον εἶναι πάντων τῶν ἄλλων.
οὐκοῦν Ἀθηνᾶ μὲν ἀνδρείας ἅμα καὶ φρονήσεως
προέχειν ἐπιψηφίζει· ἀμφοτέρων γὰρ προΐσταται
τούτων· Ἥρα δ᾽ ἁπάσης ἀρχῆς καὶ δυναστείας
αἱρετώτερον ἀποφαίνει συνηγοροῦντ᾽ αὐτῇ καὶ τὸν
Δία παραλαβοῦσα. εἰ τοίνυν οὕτω μὲν θεῖον καὶ
σεμνὸν τὸ κάλλος ἐστίν, οὕτω δὲ περισπούδαστον
τοῖς θεοῖς, πῶς ἂν ἡμῖν ἔχοι καλῶς μὴ καὶ αὐτοὺς
μιμουμένους τοὺς θεοὺς ἔργῳ τε καὶ λόγῳ πᾶν ὅ τι
ἔχομεν συναίρεσθαι τῷ κάλλει;

13. Ταῦτα μὲν ὁ Φίλων περὶ τοῦ κάλλους εἶπεν
ἐπιθεὶς τοῦτο τῇ τελευτῇ, ὡς καὶ πλείω ἂν τούτων
εἰρήκει, εἰ μὴ τὸ μακρολογεῖν ἠπίστατο τῶν ἀδοκί-
μων ἐν συμποσίῳ. μετ᾽ ἐκεῖνον δ᾽ εὐθὺς Ἀρίστιππος ἥπτετο τῶν λόγων πολλὰ πρότερον παρακληθεὶς

[1] ὁ δ᾽ edd..

and intelligent men in Greece and elsewhere, yet he entrusted the decision to Paris, son of Priam, and thereby gave a clear honest vote to show that beauty is superior to intellect, wisdom and strength.

11. These goddesses have always been so eager and zealous to hear their beauty praised that they have persuaded the glorifier of heroes and poet of the gods [1] to take the names he gives them only from their beauty. Thus Hera would prefer to be called " white-armed " than " reverend goddess, daughter of mighty Cronos," Athena would not choose to be called " Trito-born " rather than " grey-eyed," and Aphrodite will set the highest store on being called " golden." All these words refer to beauty.

12. Indeed this not only shows the attitude of the mighty to this question but is also an infallible proof of the superiority of beauty to everything else. Thus Athena's verdict is that it is superior both to courage and intellect, for she was patroness of both these, while Hera proclaims that beauty is preferable to all power and authority, and she also had Zeus to support her plea. If then beauty is so divine and august and taken so very seriously by the gods, how would it be right for us not to imitate the gods ourselves in word and deed and use all we have in the service of beauty ? "

13. Such was the speech on beauty made by Philo, who added at the end of it that he would have said more had he not known that long speeches are unpopular at dinners. Immediately after him Aristippus began to speak, though only after much persuasion by Androcles, since he was chary of following

[1] Homer.

PSEUDO-LUCIAN

ὑπ' Ἀνδροκλέους· οὐ γὰρ ἐβούλετο λέγειν τὸ μετὰ Φίλων'[1] εὐλαβούμενος λέγειν. ἤρξατο δὲ ἐντεῦθεν·

14. Πολλοὶ πολλάκις ἄνθρωποι τὸ περὶ τῶν βελτίστων καὶ ἡμῖν συμφερόντων ἀφέντες λέγειν ἐφ' ἑτέρας τινὰς ὥρμησαν ὑποθέσεις, ἀφ' ὧν αὐτοῖς μὲν δοκοῦσι δόξαν προσάγειν, τοῖς δ' ἀκροαταῖς τοὺς λόγους οὐδὲν λυσιτελοῦντας ποιοῦνται, καὶ διεληλύθασιν οἱ μὲν περὶ τῶν αὐτῶν ἐρίζοντες ἀλλήλοις, οἱ δὲ διηγούμενοι τὰ οὐκ ὄντα, ἕτεροι δὲ περὶ τῶν οὐδαμῶς ἀναγκαίων λογοποιοῦντες, οὓς ἐχρῆν ταῦτα πάντα καταλιπόντας ὅπως τι βέλτιον τύχωσιν εἰπόντες σκοπεῖν· οὓς νῦν ἐγὼ περὶ τῶν ὄντων οὐδὲν ὑγιὲς ἐγνωκέναι νομίζων ἄλλως τε καὶ τὸ τινῶν ἀγνοίας τῶν βελτίστων κατηγοροῦντα τοῖς αὐτοῖς περιπίπτειν τῶν εὐηθεστέρων οἰόμενος εἶναι πάντη, τὴν αὐτὴν λυσιτελεστάτην καὶ καλλίστην τοῖς ἀκούουσιν ὑπόθεσιν ποιήσομαι τῶν λόγων καὶ ἣν πᾶς ὁστισοῦν ἂν φαίη κάλλιστ' ἂν ἔχειν ἀκούειν [καλλίστην].[2]

15. εἰ μὲν οὖν περί τινος ἑτέρου τοὺς λόγους ἐποιούμεθα νῦν, ἀλλὰ μὴ περὶ κάλλους, ἤρκεσεν ἂν ἡμῖν ἀκούσασιν ἑνὸς εἰπόντος ἀπηλλάχθαι περὶ αὐτοῦ· τοῦτο δ' ἄρα τοσαύτην ἀφθονίαν παρέχεται τοῖς βουλομένοις ἅπτεσθαι τῶν περὶ τούτου λόγων, ὥστ' οὐκ, εἰ μὴ κατ' ἀξίαν τις ἐφίκοιτο τῷ λόγῳ, νομίζειν δυστυχεῖν, ἀλλ' ἢν πρὸς πολλοῖς ἄλλοις κἀκεῖνός τι δυνηθῇ συμβαλέσθαι πρὸς τοὺς ἐπαίνους, τῆς ἀμείνονος οἴεσθαι πειρᾶσθαι τύχης. τὸ γὰρ οὕτω μὲν περιφανῶς ὑπὸ τῶν κρειττόνων τετιμημένον,

Philo and didn't wish to speak. He began as follows.

14. " Many men have on many occasions forgone discussion of the topics best and most advantageous to us and have embarked upon other subjects from which they think they bring themselves renown, although to their audience their words are of no profit. In their expositions some of them vie with each other on the same topics, some impart information that is untrue, while others discourse on quite unessential topics, though they ought to have left all these aside and been at pains to say something of greater value. Since I think that they have formed no sound opinion of the truth and since moreover I consider it quite inane to accuse people of mistaking the highest ideal and then to be guilty of the same oneself, I shall make the subject of my speech at once most profitable and most beautiful to my hearers, and one which anyone at all would admit to be ideal to hear.

15. If, then, we were now discussing anything other than beauty, we should have been satisfied to have a single speech and be rid of the subject ; but this topic affords such boundless scope to those wishing to embark upon its discussion that a man does not consider himself unlucky if his speech should fail to do justice to the subject, but rather does he consider himself comparatively fortunate if he can add to the praises paid by many others some contribution of his own. For, when something has been so conspicuously honoured by the Higher Powers, when it has been held so divine and pursued so eagerly by

---

¹ μετὰ φίλων ω.　　² καλλίστην del. L. A. Post.

οὕτω δὲ τοῖς ἀνθρώποις θεῖον καὶ περισπούδαστον,
πᾶσι δὲ τοῖς οὖσιν οἰκειότατον κόσμον, καὶ οἷς μὲν ἂν
παρῇ παρὰ πάντων σπουδαζομένων, ὧν δ' ἀφίσταται
μισουμένων καὶ οὐδὲ προσβλέπειν ἀξιουμένων, τίς ἂν
εἴη τοσοῦτον λόγων μετεσχηκὼς ὥστ' ἐπαινέσαι
πρὸς ἀξίαν ἀρκέσαι; οὐ μὴν ἀλλ' ἐπειδήπερ οὕτω
πολλῶν αὐτῷ δεῖ τῶν ἐπαινεσόντων ὥστε μόλις ἂν
τῆς ἀξίας τυχεῖν, οὐδὲν ἀπεικὸς καὶ ἡμᾶς ἐγχειρεῖν
τι λέγειν περὶ αὐτοῦ, μέλλοντάς γε μετὰ Φίλωνα
ποιεῖσθαι τοὺς λόγους. οὕτω δὴ σεμνότατον καὶ
θειότατον τῶν ὄντων ἐστὶν ὥστε—ἵν' ὅσα ¹ θεοὶ
καλοὺς τετιμήκασι, παραλείπω.

16. ἀλλ' οὖν ἐν τοῖς ἄνω χρόνοις ἐκ Διὸς Ἑλένη
γενομένη οὕτως ἐθαυμάσθη παρὰ πᾶσιν ἀνθρώποις,
ὥστ' ἔτι τῆς ἡλικίας οὖσαν ἐντὸς κατά τινα χρείαν ἐν
Πελοποννήσῳ γενόμενος ὁ Θησεὺς οὕτω τῆς ὥρας
ἰδὼν ἠγάσθη, ὥστ' οὔσης αὐτῷ καὶ βασιλείας ἀσφα-
λεστάτης καὶ δόξης οὐ τῆς τυχούσης ὅμως οὐκ ᾤετο
βιωτὸν αὑτῷ ταύτης ἐστερημένῳ, παρελθεῖν δὲ
πάντας εὐδαιμονίᾳ, εἰ ταύτην αὑτῷ γένοιτο συνοικεῖν. οὕτω δὲ διανοηθεὶς τὸ μὲν παρὰ τοῦ πατρὸς
λαβεῖν ἀπειπών, μὴ γὰρ ἂν αὐτὴν αὐτὸν ἐκδοῦναι
μήπω ἡλικίας ἐμμένην, τὴν δ' ἀρχὴν ὑπερφρονήσας
ἐκείνου καὶ παριδών, ὀλιγωρήσας δὲ καὶ τῶν ἐν
Πελοποννήσῳ πάντων δεινῶν, κοινωνοῦντ' αὐτῷ τῆς
ἁρπαγῆς καὶ Πειρίθουν παραλαβών, βίᾳ λαβὼν αὐτὴν
τοῦ πατρὸς εἰς Ἄφιδναν ἐκόμισε τῆς Ἀττικῆς, καὶ
τοσαύτην ἔσχε χάριν αὐτῷ τῆς συμμαχίας ταυτησί,
ὥσθ' οὕτως ἐφίλησε τὸν ἅπαντα χρόνον ὥστε καὶ τοῖς
ἐπιγενομένοις παράδειγμα γενέσθαι τὴν Θησέως καὶ

men, when something is the most proper ornament
of all living things, making its possessors to be
courted by all, while its absence makes men hated
and unfit to be seen, who, I ask, could be eloquent
enough to praise that thing as it deserves? However, since it needs so many to praise it that it can
scarcely receive its due, it is in no way unfitting for
me too to say something about it, even though I
shall be speaking after Philo. Indeed, it is so much
the most august and divine of all things that—but
I won't go into all the ways in which gods have
honoured beauties.

16. Be that as it may, in olden times Helen,
daughter of Zeus, excited such admiration amongst
all men that, even before she had reached marriageable age, Theseus, who had gone to the Peloponnese
on some business, upon seeing her, was struck with
such admiration for her beauty that, though he had
the most assured of thrones and no ordinary glory, he
considered that life would be intolerable without her,
whereas he would surpass all men in good fortune,
should it fall to him to have her for wife. With these
thoughts in his mind, rejecting the idea of receiving
her in marriage from her father, since he knew that he
wouldn't give her before she had reached marriageable age, and, because he held her father's power in contempt and scorn and despised everything formidable
in the Peloponnese, Theseus took Peirithoüs with
him to help carry her off, and, after seizing her against
her father's will, brought her to Aphidna in Attica.
He conceived such gratitude to Peirithoüs for aiding
him in this that he loved him so dearly for the rest of
his days that the friendship of Theseus and Peirithoüs

---

[1] ὥστ' ἐνεῖναι ὅσα . . . παραλείπειν L. A. Post.

Πειρίθου φιλίαν. ἐπειδὴ δὲ ἔδει κἀκεῖνον ἐν Ἅιδου γενέσθαι τὴν Δήμητρος μνηστευσόμενον κόρην, ἐπειδὴ πολλὰ παραινῶν οὐκ ἠδυνήθη ταύτης αὐτὸν τῆς πείρας ἀποσχέσθαι καταπεῖσαι, συνηκολούθησεν αὐτῷ ταύτην πρέπουσαν οἰόμενος αὐτῷ καταθήσειν τὴν χάριν περὶ τῆς ψυχῆς ὑπὲρ αὐτοῦ κινδυνεῦσαι. 17. ἐπανελθοῦσαν δ᾽ εἰς Ἄργος, αὖθις ἀποδημοῦντος αὐτοῦ, ἐπειδὴ καθ᾽ ὥραν ἦν γάμων, καίτοι γε ἔχοντες καλάς τε καὶ εὖ γεγονυίας ἐκ τῆς Ἑλλάδος σφίσιν αὐτοῖς ἄγεσθαι γυναῖκας οἱ τῆς Ἑλλάδος βασιλεῖς, οἱ δὲ συνελθόντες ἐμνηστεύοντο ταύτην τὰς ἄλλας ἁπάσας ὑπεριδόντες ὡς φαυλοτέρας. γνόντες δ᾽ ὅτι περιμάχητος ἔσται, καὶ δείσαντες μὴ πόλεμος γένηται τῇ Ἑλλάδι, μαχομένων πρὸς ἀλλήλους, ὀμωμόκασιν ὅρκον τουτονὶ ψήφῳ κοινῇ, ἦ μὴν ἐπικουρήσειν τῷ ταύτης ἀξιωθέντι μηδ᾽ ἐπιτρέψειν ἤν τις ἀδικεῖν ἐγχειρῇ, ἕκαστος οἰόμενος ταύτην αὐτῷ τὴν συμμαχίαν παρασκευάζειν. τῆς μὲν οὖν ἰδίας γνώμης ἀπέτυχον πάντες πλὴν Μενελάου, τῆς κοινῆς δ᾽ ἐπειράθησαν αὐτίκα· οὐ πολλῷ γὰρ ὕστερον ἔριδος γενομένης ταῖς θεαῖς περὶ κάλλους, ἐπιτρέπουσι τὴν κρίσιν Πάριδι τῷ Πριάμου, ὁ δὲ τῶν μὲν σωμάτων τῶν θεῶν ἡττηθείς, τῶν δωρεῶν δ᾽ ἀναγκασθεὶς γενέσθαι κριτής, καὶ διδούσης Ἥρας μὲν τὴν τῆς Ἀσίας ἀρχήν, τὸ δ᾽ ἐν πολέμοις Ἀθηνᾶς κράτος, Ἀφροδίτης δὲ τὸν τῆς Ἑλένης γάμον, καὶ φαύλοις μὲν ἀνθρώποις γενέσθαι ἄν ποτε νομίσας οὐκ ἐλάττω βασιλείαν, Ἑλένης δ᾽ οὐδένα τῶν ἐπιγιγνομένων ἀξιωθῆναι, προείλετο τὸν ταύτης γάμον.

became an example even for later generations. When Peirithoüs for his part had to go to Hades to court the daughter of Demeter, and Theseus despite his many pleas could not dissuade him from this enterprise, Theseus went with him, thinking that he would thus fittingly pay his debt of gratitude by risking his life for him. 17. Helen returned to Argos during another absence of Theseus, when she was now of marriageable age, and, though the kings of Greece had no lack of beautiful well-born women to marry, they ignored all other women as inferior and assembled to court her. Since they realised that she would be fought for and they feared that Greece would be cast into war if they fought against each other, by common agreement they took a solemn oath to support the man thought worthy of Helen, and not to allow anyone to attempt anything unjust, since each thought that thus he was securing allies for himself. All accordingly failed in their private aim except Menelaüs, but they very soon put their common aim to the test. For shortly afterwards a quarrel about beauty started among the goddesses, and they left the decision to Paris, son of Priam. Though overpowered by the physical attractions of the goddesses, he was compelled to decide between the gifts they offered. When Hera offered him the kingdom of Asia, Athena prowess in war and Aphrodite marriage with Helen, he reflected that, while mean fellows might on occasion obtain a kingdom as great, the privilege of Helen's favours would fall to nobody of a future generation, and so preferred marriage with her.

18. γενομένης δὲ τῆς ὑμνουμένης ἐκείνης στρατείας κατὰ τῶν Τρώων καὶ τῆς Εὐρώπης τότε πρῶτον κατὰ τῆς Ἀσίας ἐλθούσης, ἔχοντες οἵ τε Τρῶες ἀποδόντες τὴν Ἑλένην ἀδεῶς οἰκεῖν τὴν αὑτῶν, οἵ θ᾽ Ἕλληνες ταύτην αὐτοὺς ἐάσαντες ἔχειν ἀπαλλάττεσθαι τῶν ἐκ πολέμου καὶ στρατείας δυσχερῶν, οἱ δ᾽ οὐκ ἠβουλήθησαν ἀμφότεροι, οὐκ ἄν ποτε νομίσαντες εὑρεῖν ἀφορμὴν καλλίω πολέμου περὶ ἧς ἀποθανοῦνται. καὶ θεοὶ δὲ τοὺς αὑτῶν παῖδας σαφῶς εἰδότες ἀπολουμένους ἐν τῷ πολέμῳ οὐκ ἀπέτρεψαν μᾶλλον, ἀλλ᾽ ἐνήγαγον εἰς τοῦτο οὐκ ἐλάττω δόξαν αὐτοῖς οἰόμενοι φέρειν τοῦ θεῶν παῖδας γενέσθαι τὸ μαχομένους ὑπὲρ Ἑλένης ἀποθανεῖν. καὶ τί λέγω τοὺς αὑτῶν παῖδας; αὐτοὶ πρὸς αὑτοὺς μείζω καὶ δεινότερον ἐνεστήσαντο τοῦ πρὸς Γίγαντας αὐτοῖς γενομένου πολέμου· ἐν ἐκείνῳ μὲν γὰρ μετ᾽ ἀλλήλων, ἐνταῦθα δὲ ἐμάχοντο πρὸς ἀλλήλους. οὗ τί γένοιτ᾽ ἂν ἐναργέστερον δεῖγμα, ὅσῳ τῶν ἀνθρωπίνων ἁπάντων ὑπερέχει τὸ κάλλος παρ᾽ ἀθανάτοις κριταῖς; ὅταν γὰρ ὑπὲρ μὲν τῶν ἄλλων οὐδενὸς ἁπάντων οὐδαμοῦ τὸ παράπαν φαίνωνται διενεχθέντες, ὑπὲρ δὲ κάλλους οὐ μόνον τοὺς υἱοὺς ἐπιδεδωκότες, ἀλλ᾽ ἤδη καὶ ἀλλήλοις ἐναντία πεπολεμηκότες, ἔνιοι δὲ καὶ τρωθέντες, πῶς οὐχ ἁπάσαις ψήφοις προτιμῶσιν ἁπάντων τὸ κάλλος;

19. ἀλλ᾽ ἵνα μὴ δόξωμεν ἀπορίᾳ τῶν περὶ κάλλους λόγων περὶ ταὐτὰ [1] διατρίβειν ἀεί, ἐφ᾽ ἕτερον βούλομαι μεταβῆναι οὐδαμῶς ἔλαττον ὄν, ὥστε δεῖξαι τὴν τοῦ κάλλους ἀξίαν, τῶν πρότερον εἰρημένων,

---

[1] ταὐτὰ Guyet: ταῦτα codd..

18. When that celebrated expedition had been
made against the Trojans and Europe then for the
first time had invaded Asia, though the Trojans could
have given Helen back and lived without fear in their
own country, and the Greeks could have allowed them
to keep Helen and be rid of the hardships of war and
campaigning, nevertheless neither side proved willing
to do so, since they thought they'd never find a war
with a better cause for which to die. The gods too,
though well aware that their own sons would die in
the war, did nothing to stop them but encouraged
them, thinking it brought them no less glory to die
fighting for Helen than to have been born sons of
gods. But why talk of the *children* of the gods ?
The gods themselves then engaged with each other
in a mightier and more terrible war than the one they
had fought against the Giants. For in that they
fought alongside each other, but on this occasion
they fought against each other. What clearer
proof than this could there be to show how much
beauty excels everything else connected with men
in the judgment of the immortals ? For, when they
can be clearly seen never to have quarrelled over
anything else at all, and yet for beauty not only to
have sacrificed their sons but once even to have
fought against each other and some of them even to
have suffered wounds, are they not showing by a
unanimous vote that they value beauty above all
else ?

19. But, lest I be thought for want of things to say
about beauty to be lingering on the same theme for
ever, I wish to pass to another proof of the merit of
beauty no less weighty than what I've just been

τὴν Ἀρκάδος Ἱπποδάμειαν Οἰνομάου, ὅσους τοῦ
ταύτης κάλλους ἁλόντας μᾶλλον αἱρουμένους ἀπέφη-
νεν ἀποθνήσκειν ἢ ταύτης διῳκισμένους τὸν ἥλιον
προσορᾶν. ὡς γὰρ ἐλάβετο τῆς ἡλικίας ἡ παῖς καὶ
τὰς ἄλλας ὁ πατὴρ οὐκ ὀλίγῳ [1] τῷ μέσῳ παρενεγ-
κοῦσαν ἑώρα, τῆς μὲν ὥρας αὐτῆς ἁλοὺς—τοσοῦτον
γὰρ αὐτῇ περιῆν, ὥστε καὶ τὸν γεγεννηκόθ' [2]
ὑπηγάγετο παρὰ φύσιν—καὶ διὰ τοῦτ' ἀξιῶν αὐτὴν
ἔχειν παρ' ἑαυτῷ, βούλεσθαι δ' ἐκδιδόναι πλαττό-
μενος αὐτὴν τῷ ταύτης ἀξίῳ, τὰς παρ' ἀνθρώπων
φεύγων αἰτίας, μηχανήν τινα μηχανᾶται τῆς ἐπιθυμίας ἀδικωτέραν καὶ ἣν ᾤετο ῥᾳδίως ὅπερ ἐβούλετο
καταστήσειν· ὑπὸ γὰρ ἄρματι, ὡς οἷόν τε μάλιστα
ἦν, εἰς τάχος ὑπὸ τῆς τέχνης ἐξειργασμένῳ τοὺς ἐν
Ἀρκαδίᾳ ζεύξας ἐν τῷ τότε ταχίστους ἵππους
ἡμιλλᾶτο πρὸς τοὺς μνηστῆρας τῆς κόρης ἆθλον
τῆς νίκης παρελθοῦσιν [3] αὐτοῖς αὐτὴν προτιθεὶς ἢ
στέρεσθαι τῆς κεφαλῆς ἡττηθέντας. καὶ ἠξίου δ'
αὐτὴν αὐτοῖς συναναβαίνειν τὸ ἅρμα, ὅπως ἀπο-
σχολούμενοι περὶ ταύτην ἀμελοῖεν τῆς ἱππικῆς.
οἱ δ', ἀποτυχόντος τοῦ πρώτως ἁψαμένου τοῦ
δρόμου καὶ τῆς κόρης ἐκπεσόντος μετὰ τοῦ ζῆν,
τὸ μὲν ἀποκνῆσαι πρὸς τὸν ἀγῶνα ἢ μεταθεῖναί τι
τῶν βεβουλευμένων μειρακιῶδες εἶναι ὑπολαβόντες, τὴν δ' ὠμότητα μισήσαντες Οἰνομάου ἄλλος
ἄλλον ἔφθανεν ἀποθνῄσκων ὥσπερ δεδοικὼς μὴ τοῦ
τεθνάναι περὶ τῆς κόρης ἁμάρτῃ. καὶ προῆλθέ γε
μέχρι τρισκαίδεκα νέων ὁ φόνος· θεοὶ δ' ἐκεῖνον τῆς

---

[1] οὐκ ὀλίγῳ Fritzsche: οὐ πολλῷ codd..
[2] γεγενηκόθ' codd.: corr. edd..
[3] παρελθοῦσιν Guyet: παρελθόντας codd..

saying and to tell of Hippodamia, the daughter of Oenomaüs of Arcadia, and all those victims of her beauty whom she induced to choose death in preference to the light of day, if parted from her. For, once she was of age, and her father saw that she far surpassed all other women, he was overpowered by her beauty, for she had such a superabundance of it that her own father was unnaturally attracted to her. He therefore wished to keep her for himself, but in order to escape the censure of men, he pretended to be willing to give her in marriage to the man worthy of her, and devised a plan even more wicked than his lust and one which he thought would easily secure him what he wished. For he would yoke the swiftest horses then in Arcadia to a chariot skilfully constructed to ensure the greatest possible speed and compete against his daughter's suitors, offering her to them as the prize of victory, if they passed him, or death if they were defeated. He also insisted that she should mount the chariot with them so that they might be distracted by her and their attention wander from their horsemanship. But, after the first competitor in the race had proved unsuccessful and lost the maiden as well as his life, the others, considering it puerile to show fear for the contest or to change any of their plans and detesting Oenomaüs' cruelty, vied one with another in being first to die, as though afraid they might lose the chance of dying for the maiden. And so the butchery went on till thirteen young men had died. But the gods were filled with

πονηρίας μισήσαντες ταυτησὶ τούς τε τεθνεῶτας
ἅμα καὶ τὴν κόρην ἐλεοῦντες, τοὺς μὲν ὅτι κτήματος
ἀπεστέρηνται τοιούτου, τὴν κόρην δ' ὅτι τῆς
ὥρας οὐ κατὰ καιρὸν ἀπολαύοι, κηδόμενοί τε τοῦ
νέου, ὅστις ἔμελλε—Πέλοψ δ' ἦν οὗτος—ἀγωνιεῖ-
σθαι, ἅρμα τε χαρίζονται τούτῳ κάλλιον τέχνης
πεποιημένον ἵππους τε ἀθανάτους, δι' ὧν ἔμελλε
τῆς κόρης κύριος εἶναι, καὶ γέγονέ γε, τὸν κηδεστὴν
ἐπὶ τέρμασι τῆς νίκης ἀπεκτονώς.

20. Οὕτω τὸ τοῦ κάλλους χρῆμα ἀνθρώποις τε
θεῖον εἶναι δοκεῖ καὶ τιμώμενον ὑπὸ πάντων καὶ
θεοῖς ἐσπούδασται πολλαχόσε. διὸ δὴ καὶ ἡμῖν οὐκ
ἂν ἔχοι τις μέμφεσθαι δικαίως προὔργου λογισαμέ-
νοις τὸ ταῦτα περὶ κάλλους διεξελθεῖν. οὕτω μὲν
δὴ καὶ Ἀρίστιππος διῆλθε τὸν λόγον.

ΕΡΜΙΠΠΟΣ

21. Σὺ δὴ λοιπός, Χαρίδημε. ὅπως δ' ὥσπερ
κορωνίδα τῶν τοῦ κάλλους καλῶν ἐπιθήσῃ τὸν λόγον.

ΧΑΡΙΔΗΜΟΣ

Μηδαμῶς, ὦ πρὸς θεῶν, περαιτέρω προελθεῖν με
βίασ9· ἱκανὰ γὰρ δηλῶσαι τὴν συνουσίαν καὶ τὰ
νῦν εἰρημένα, ἄλλως τ' οὐδ' ὅσαπερ εἶπον ἀπομνη-
μονεύοντα. ῥᾷον γὰρ ἄν τις μνημονεύοι τῶν
ἑτέροις εἰρημένων ἢ τῶν αὑτῷ.

ΕΡΜΙΠΠΟΣ

Ταῦτα μὲν δή ἐστιν ὧν ἐξ ἀρχῆς ἐπεθυμοῦμεν
ἐπιτυχεῖν· οὐ γὰρ δὴ τοσοῦτον ἡμῖν τῶν λόγων

hatred for Oenomaüs for being so wicked, while they pitied the victims and also the maiden, them because of the prize they'd lost and her because she wasn't having the proper enjoyment of her beauty, and were also concerned for the young man, Pelops by name, who was about the enter the contest. They therefore presented him with a chariot even more skilfully constructed than that of Oenomaüs and with immortal steeds. These were to enable him to gain possession of the maiden, which he did after he had killed his father-in-law at the end of his victorious race.

20. Thus beauty is regarded by men as something divine, and valued as all-important, and many are the places to which its eager pursuit has taken the gods. Therefore no one could justly blame me for considering that this discourse of mine on beauty serves a useful purpose."

Such was the discourse of Aristippus.

HERMIPPUS

21. That leaves *you*, Charidemus. You must add *your* speech to set the final seal on the beauties of beauty.

CHARIDEMUS

In heaven's name, please don't force me to continue any further ; for what I've already told you is sufficient to show you how our conversation went. Besides, I forget what I said. It's easier to remember other people's words than one's own.

HERMIPPUS

But that's what we wanted to get from you right from the start ; for we were not so much concerned

ἐκείνων ὅσον ἐμέλησε τῶν σῶν ἀκοῦσαι. ὥστ', ἢν
τούτων ἀποστερήσῃς, κἀκεῖνα μάτην ἔσῃ πεπονη-
κώς. ἀλλὰ πρὸς Ἑρμοῦ τὸν ἅπαντα λόγον, ὥσπερ
ὑπέστης ἐξ ἀρχῆς, ἀπόδος.

ΧΑΡΙΔΗΜΟΣ

Βέλτιον μὲν ἦν τούτοις ἀπαλλάττειν με τῶν
δυσχερῶν ἀγαπῶντα· ἐπεὶ δ' οὕτω προθυμῇ καὶ
τῶν ἡμετέρων ἀκοῦσαι λόγων, καὶ τοῦθ' ὑπηρετεῖν
ἀνάγκη. ὧδε τοίνυν καὶ αὐτὸς ἐποιησάμην τὸν
λόγον·

22. Εἰ μὲν πρῶτος αὐτὸς ἦρχον περὶ τοῦ κάλλους
λέγειν, προοιμίων ἂν ἐδεόμην συχνῶν, ἐπεὶ δ'
ἐπὶ πολλοῖς ἔρχομαι τοῖς πρότερον εἰρηκόσιν
ἐρῶν, οὐδὲν ἀπεικὸς τοῖς ἐκείνων κεχρημένον ὡς
προοιμίοις ἐπιφέρειν ἑξῆς τὸν λόγον, ἄλλως τ' οὐδ'
ἑτέρωσε τῶν λόγων γινομένων, ἀλλ' ἐνταῦθα καὶ
τῆς αὐτῆς ἡμέρας, ὥστ' ἐνεῖναι καὶ τοὺς παρόντας
λαθεῖν ὡς ἄρ' οὐχ ἕκαστος ἰδίᾳ λογοποιοῦσιν, ἀλλὰ
τὸν αὐτὸν ἕκαστος ἐπὶ μέρους διεξέρχονται λόγον.
ἑτέρῳ μὲν οὖν ἦρκει γ' ἂν εἰς εὐφημίαν ἅπερ ὑμῶν
ἕκαστος ἔτυχεν εἰπὼν περὶ τοῦ κάλλους ἰδίᾳ, τούτῳ
δὲ τοσοῦτον περίεστιν ὥστε καὶ τοῖς ἐπιγιγνομέ-
νοις ἔξω τῶν νῦν εἰρημένων οὐ δεῖν ἐπαίνων τῶν
εἰς αὐτό· πλεῖστα γὰρ πολλαχόθεν, αὐτὰ πρῶτα
δεῖν λέγειν ἕκαστα, δόξαν παρίστησιν, ὥσπερ
ἀνθέων εὐτυχοῦντι λειμῶνι, ἀεὶ τῶν φαινομένων
ἄρτι προσαγομένων τοὺς δρεπομένους. ἐγὼ δ' ἐκ
πάντων ἐκλέξας ὅσα μοι δοκῶ μὴ βέλτιον εἶναι
παραλιπεῖν, λέξω διὰ βραχέων, ὅπως τῷ τε κάλλει

to hear their words as yours. If therefore you
deprive us of *that*, all your efforts so far will have
been in vain. By Hermes, I beg you, give me the
full discussion, as you promised at the outset.

It would have been better for you to be content
with this much and relieve me of an unpleasant task.
But since you are so set on hearing my speech also,
I must oblige you with this further favour. This
then was how *my* speech went :

22. " If I were beginning the first speech on beauty,
I should need many introductory remarks, but since
I am following many previous speakers, it seems
reasonable for me to treat their speeches as introductory remarks and continue the argument where
they left off, since the discussions are not being held
in two different places, but here, and at one and the
same time, so that it's possible even for those present
to forget that each of us is not making a speech of his
own, but each is proceeding in turn with the same
discussion. Therefore what each of you has said
individually about beauty would be sufficient to
bring honour to any other man, but I have the very
much greater task of ensuring that later generations
too shall be well supplied with praises of beauty over
and above those just delivered. For beauty brings
to one's mind from many quarters a great many ideas,
each of which one feels one should mention first, as
though one were in a meadow rich with flowers, where
each successive bloom that appears invites one to
pick it. I shall choose out of everything those points
which I feel should not be omitted, and speak briefly,

τὰ γιγνόμενα ἀποδώσω ὑμῖν τε τὸ μακρολογεῖν
παραλιπὼν δράσω κεχαρισμένα. 23. τοῖς μὲν οὖν
ἢ δι' ἀνδρείαν ἢ καθ' ἑτέραν τινὰ τῶν ἀρετῶν ἡμῶν
προέχειν δοκοῦσιν, ἢν μὴ τῷ καθ' ἡμέραν ποιεῖν εὖ
ἀναγκάζωσιν ἡμᾶς εὖ αὐτοῖς διακεῖσθαι, βασκαί-
νομεν μᾶλλον, ἐξ ὧν τἂν [1] οὐ καλῶς αὐτοῖς τὰ
πράγματα πραττόμενα [2] σχοίη· καλοὺς δ' οὐ μόνον
οὐ φθονοῦμεν τῆς ὥρας, ἀλλ' εὐθύς τε ἰδόντες
ἁλισκόμεθα ὑπεραγαπῶμέν τε οὐδ' ἀποκνοῦμεν
ὥσπερ κρείττοσιν, ὅσον ἂν ἡμῖν ἐξῇ, δουλεύοντες
αὐτοῖς. ἥδιον ἂν οὖν ὑπακοῦσαί τις ὥρας εὐτυχηκότι
ἢ προστάξειε τῷ μὴ τοιούτῳ, καὶ πλείω χάριν ἂν
εἰδείη τῷ πολλὰ προστάττοντι μᾶλλον ἢ τῷ μηδ'
ὁτιοῦν ἐπαγγέλλοντι.

24. καὶ τῶν μὲν ἄλλων ἀγαθῶν, ὧν ἂν ἐνδεεῖς
ὦμεν, οὐ περαιτέρω σπουδάζομεν τοῦ τυχεῖν,
κάλλους δ' ἡμῖν οὐδεὶς οὐδεπώποτε γέγονε κόρος,
ἀλλ' ἐάν τε τὸν Ἀγλαΐης, τὸν εἰς Ἴλιόν ποτε
συναναβάντα τοῖς Ἀχαιοῖς, ἐάν θ' Ὑάκινθον τὸν
καλὸν ἢ τὸν Λακεδαιμόνιον Νάρκισσον κάλλει νικῶ-
μεν, οὐκ ἀρκεῖν ἡμῖν δοκοῦμεν, ἀλλὰ δεδοίκαμεν μὴ
λάθωμεν τοῖς ἐπιγινομένοις ἂν καταλιπόντες ὑπερ-
βολήν. 25. σχεδὸν δ' ὡς εἰπεῖν πάντων τῶν ἐν
ἀνθρώποις πραγμάτων ὥσπερ κοινὸν παράδειγμα τὸ
κάλλος ἐστί, καὶ οὔτε στρατηγοῖς εἰς κάλλος ἡμέ-
ληται τὰ στρατεύματα συντάττειν οὔτε ῥήτορσι τοὺς
λόγους συντιθέναι οὔτε μὴν γραφεῦσι τὰς εἰκόνας
γεγραφέναι. ἀλλὰ τί ταῦτα λέγω, ὧν τὸ κάλλος τέλος

---

[1] τἂν Fritzch τ' ἂν codd..

[2] πράττομεν codd.: corr. Guyet.

so that I may pay due tribute to beauty and also act in a way acceptable to you by refraining from a long speech.

23. Those whom we think superior to ourselves for courage or in any other virtue tend to incur our envy, unless by their daily benefactions they force us to be well disposed to them ; as a result of this the things they undertake may not go well for them. But so far are we from envying the beautiful for their loveliness that, immediately we see them, we become their captives, show them inordinate affection and unhesitatingly act as their slaves in every way we can, as though they were our superiors. Thus one would more gladly obey someone blessed with beauty than issue orders to a person without beauty, and one would feel more gratitude to the beauty who gives many orders than the one who gives none at all.

24. Our enthusiasm for all other good things which we lack ends when we obtain them, but of beauty we have never ever had too much; no, even if we surpass the son of Aglaia,[1] who once set sail with the Achaeans for Troy, or beautiful Hyacinthus, or Narcissus of Lacedaemon, we are not satisfied, but are afraid that we may unwittingly be surpassed in beauty by later generations. 25. Beauty is, as it were, the universal ideal in very nearly every human activity ; beauty is considered by generals in arraying their armies, by orators in composing their speeches, and moreover by artists in painting their portraits. But why should I only mention those things which have beauty for their end ? For, in constructing the

---

[1] Nireus, the most handsome of the Greeks at Troy. Cf. *Dialogues of the Dead* 30, Homer *Iliad* II. 672.

ἐστίν; ὧν γὰρ εἰς χρείαν ἥκομεν ἀναγκαίως, οὐκ
ἐλλείπομεν οὐδὲν σπουδῆς εἰς ὅσον ἔξεστι κάλλιστα
κατασκευάζειν· τῷ τε γὰρ Μενέλεῳ οὐ τοσοῦτον
ἐμέλησε τῆς χρείας τῶν οἴκων, ἢ ὅσον[1] τοὺς εἰσερχο-
μένους ἐκπλήττειν, καὶ διὰ τοῦθ' οὕτω πολυτελεστά-
τους ἅμα κατεσκεύασε καὶ καλλίστους, καὶ τῆς
γνώμης οὐχ ἥμαρτεν· ὁ γὰρ Ὀδυσσέως οὕτως
ἀγασθῆναι λέγεται τούτους, κατὰ πύστιν τοῦ πατρὸς
εἰς αὐτὸν ἀφιγμένος, ὥστ' εἰπεῖν Πεισιστράτῳ τῷ

Ζηνός που τοιήδε γ' Ὀλυμπίου ἔνδοθεν αὐλή.

Νεστορίδῃ, αὐτός θ' ὁ τοῦ μειρακίου πατὴρ οὐκ ἄλλου
του χάριν μιλτοπαρῄους ἦγε τὰς ναῦς συστρατευό-
μενος τοῖς Ἕλλησιν ἐπὶ Τροίαν ἢ ὅπως τοὺς ὁρῶντας
ἐκπλήττειν ἔχῃ. καὶ σχεδὸν εἴ τις ἑκάστην ἐξετάζειν βούλεται τῶν τεχνῶν, εὑρήσει πάσας ἐς τὸ
κάλλος ὁρώσας καὶ τούτου τυγχάνειν τοῦ παντὸς
τιθεμένας.

26. τοσοῦτον δὲ τὸ κάλλος τῶν ἄλλων ἁπάντων
ὑπερέχειν δοκεῖ ὥστε τῶν μὲν ἢ δικαιοσύνης
ἢ σοφίας ἢ ἀνδρείας μετεχόντων πολλά τις ἂν
εὕροι τιμώμενα μᾶλλον, τῶν δὲ ταύτης τῆς ἰδέας
κεκοινωνηκότων βέλτιόν ἐστιν εὑρεῖν οὐδέν, ὥσπερ
δὴ καὶ τῶν μὴ μετεσχηκότων ἀτιμότερον οὐδέν·
μόνους γοῦν τοὺς μὴ καλοὺς ὀνομάζομεν αἰσχρούς,
ὡς οὐδὲν ὄν, εἴ τί τις ἔχων τύχοι πλεονέκτημα τῶν
ἄλλων κάλλους ἐστερημένος. 27. τοὺς μὲν οὖν ἢ
δημοκρατουμένοις τὰ κοινὰ διοικοῦντας ἢ τυράννοις
ὑποτεταγμένους τοὺς μὲν δημαγωγούς, τοὺς δὲ κόλα-
κας καλοῦμεν, μόνους δὲ τοὺς ὑπὸ ταύτῃ τῇ δυνάμει

[1] ἢ ὅσον codd.: ὅσον τοῦ Schaefer.

things which we have come to find indispensable, we show the greatest zeal for making them as beautiful as possible. For Menelaus was not so much concerned with using his palace as with astonishing his visitors ; that is why he lavished such wealth on its construction and made it so very beautiful. Moreover he succeeded in his purpose, for the son of Odysseus [1] is said, when visiting Menelaus in search of news about his father, to have admired it so much that he said to Peisistratus, son of Nestor

‘‘ ’Twas like being in the palace of Olympian Zeus.’’[2] Furthermore Odysseus himself, the boy's father, had ships ‘ with cheeks of red ’ [3] simply because he wished to be able to astonish those that saw them. And, if one cares to examine each of the arts and crafts, one will find that they all more or less aim at beauty and regard the achieving of beauty as all-important.

26. Beauty is thought so superior to everything else that, though one could find many things more honoured than those that partake of justice or wisdom or courage, nothing can be found better than the things informed with beauty, just as indeed nothing is held in less honour than the things without beauty. At any rate it's only those lacking beauty that we call ugly, since we regard any other advantage possessed by a man as immaterial if he be without beauty. 27. Therefore those who transact state affairs for citizens of a democracy and those subject to tyrants are called by us demagogues and toadies

---

[1] Telemachus.
[2] *Odyssey* IV. 74, also quoted *Essays in Portraiture Defended* 20.   [3] Cf. *Iliad* II. 637.

PSEUDO-LUCIAN

γενομένους θαυμάζομέν τε φιλοπόνους τε καὶ
φιλοκάλους ὀνομάζομεν καὶ κοινοὺς νομίζομεν
εὐεργέτας τοὺς τῶν καλῶν ἐπιμελητάς. ὅτε τοίνυν
οὕτω μὲν σεμνὸν τὸ κάλλος ἐστίν, οὕτω δὲ τοῖς
πᾶσιν ἐν εὐχῆς μέρει τυχεῖν κέρδος τε νομίζουσι τὸ
τούτῳ τι διακονῆσαι δυνηθῆναι, πῶς ἡμᾶς εἰκότως
οὐκ ἄν τις ἐμέμψατο, εἰ τοσοῦτον ἔχοντες κέρδος
κερδαίνειν ἔπειθ᾽ ἑκοντὶ προϊέμεθα, μηδ᾽ αὐτὸ τοῦτο
αἰσθέσθαι δυνηθέντες, ὅτι ζημιούμεθα;

28. Τοσοῦτον μὲν δὴ κἀγὼ τὸν λόγον ἐποιησάμην,
πολλὰ τῶν ἐνόντων μοι περὶ κάλλους εἰπεῖν ἀφελών,
ἐπειδὴ τὴν συνουσίαν ἐπὶ πολὺ παρατεινομένην
ἑώρων.

ΕΡΜΙΠΠΟΣ

Εὐδαίμονές γε, οἱ τοιαύτης ἀπολελαύκατε τῆς
συνουσίας· σχεδὸν δ᾽ ἤδη κἀγὼ οὐδὲν ἔλαττον ὑμῶν
ἔσχηκα διὰ σέ.

respectively, but we reserve our admiration for those subject to the power of beauty, calling those who show concern for the beautiful diligent and aesthetic and regarding them as common benefactors. When, therefore, beauty is so revered and so much a part of all men's prayers, and, when people count it gain to be able to serve it in any way, could we not have been blamed with good cause if, when able to gain so great a benefit, we have been wilfully relinquishing it without even being able to see that we're punishing ourselves?"

28. Such was the extent of *my* speech, for I excluded from it many of the things which I could have said about beauty, because I could see that the discussion was becoming protracted.

HERMIPPUS

How lucky you are to have enjoyed such a discussion! Still, thanks to you, I have now become almost as lucky as you.

NERO

NERO is attributed to Lucian in N and two other
Lucianic manuscripts, but there can be little doubt
that it is the work of one of the three Philostrati, and
probably of the first Philostratus, whose other works
have been lost though their titles are listed in the
Suda, rather than his son, Philostratus the " Athenian," who wrote *The Life of Apollonius of Tyana* for
the empress Julia Domna, though her death in 217
A.D. seems to have preceded its publication. The
reasons for ascribing Nero to a Philostratus are as
follows :

(1) The style is quite unlike that of Lucian, but in the
view of C. L. Kayser, the Teubner editor, it is very
like that of the Philostrati.

(2) C. 4 of Nero is very like *The Life of Apollonius*
4.24, while the only other mention of Musonius digging at Corinth rather than being in exile at Gyara is
ibid. 5.19. Note that elsewhere the " Athenian "
mentions Musonius as imprisoned, presumably at
Rome (ibid. 4.35 and 4.46), and as under detention
in Gyara (ibid. 7.16).

(3) The title *Nero* is included in the Suda's list of the
works of the first Philostratus. (It must however be
borne in mind that the Suda's evidence is often unreli-
able, and in this instance it arouses misgivings by
describing the first Philostratus as a contemporary of
Nero, while in an adjacent article describing his son
as alive almost 200 years later. Furthermore it is
not quite certain that Θεατής which follows *Nero*

in the Suda's list of titles is to be separated from it.)
(4) K. Mras, *Die Ueberlieferung Lucians*, p. 236 notes
that a few Lucianic manuscripts also contain the
works of Philostratus and other sophists, so that
Nero might have been mistaken for the last work of
Lucian rather than the first of Philostratus in such a
codex.
(5) Lemnos, the home of the Philostrati, is mentioned
in c. 6.

Kayser and F. Solmsen, *Transactions of the
American Philological Association*, 1940, pp. 556 ff.,
think that *Nero* is by the author of *The Life of
Apollonius*, but this theory is perhaps to be rejected
in view of the evidence of the Suda and *The Life of
Apollonius* 5.19 *fin.*, which looks like a polite reference
to another writer.

A more probable view is that of K. Münscher, who
following the Suda, ascribes *Nero* to the first Philostratus. This view is developed by J. Korver,
Mnemosyne, 1950, p. 319 ff., who suggests that the
dialogue was inspired by Caracalla's murder of his
brother Geta in 212 A.D. and that Nero's fate is
meant to serve as a warning to Caracalla to curb his
vicious behaviour before it is too late.

The dramatic date of the dialogue is 68 A.D. and
the scene is probably Gyara, a small island of the
Cyclades, which Menecrates is visiting from Lemnos.
(Alternatively the scene could be Lemnos, though
Musonius' presence there would then be unaccounted
for.) One of the speakers is Musonius Rufus, the
famous Stoic philosopher, who was banished by
Nero to Gyara, but later returned to Rome and
received favourable treatment from Vespasian. The

other speaker, Menecrates, is usually taken to be an imaginary character. Nero, however, had a favourite lyre-player of that name (cf. Suetonius, *Nero*, 30, Dio Cassius 63.1 and Petronius 73.19), so that it is a strange coincidence that the Menecrates of this dialogue should ask about Nero's musical accomplishments. The Menecrates of *Nero* could therefore be the historical Menecrates ; if so, it is most unrealistic for him to ask questions to which he knows the answers ; more probably the writer has forgotten Menecrates' connection with Nero, just as he blunders in other ways (cf. notes on cc. 2 and 5).

ΝΕΡΩΝ[1]

ΜΕΝΕΚΡΑΤΗΣ

1. Ἡ ὀρυχὴ τοῦ Ἰσθμοῦ, καὶ σοί, Μουσώνιε, διὰ χειρός, ὥς φασι, γεγονυῖα, τῷ τυράννῳ νοῦν εἶχεν Ἕλληνα;

ΜΟΥΣΩΝΙΟΣ

Ἴσθι, ὦ Μενέκρατες, καὶ βελτίω ἐντεθυμῆσθαι Νέρωνα· τὰς γὰρ περιβολὰς τῆς Πελοποννήσου τὰς ὑπὲρ Μαλέαν ξυνῄρει τοῖς θαλαττουμένοις εἴκοσι σταδίων τοῦ Ἰσθμοῦ ῥήγματι.[2] τοῦτο δ᾽ ἂν καὶ τὰς ἐμπορίας ὤνησε καὶ τὰς ἐπὶ θαλάττῃ πόλεις καὶ τὰς ἐν τῇ μεσογείᾳ· καὶ γὰρ δὴ κἀκείναις ἀποχρῶν ὁ οἴκοι καρπός, ἢν τὰ ἐπιθαλάττια εὖ πράττῃ.

ΜΕΝΕΚΡΑΤΗΣ

Ταῦτα δὴ διέξελθε, Μουσώνιε, βουλομένοις ἡμῖν ἀκροάσασθαι πᾶσιν, εἰ μή τι σπουδάσαι διανοῇ ἕτερον.

ΜΟΥΣΩΝΙΟΣ

Δίειμι βουλομένοις· οὐ[3] γὰρ οἶδ ὅ τι χαριζοίμην ἂν μᾶλλον τοῖς γε ἀφιγμένοις ἐς ἀηδὲς οὕτω

Codices rettuli N et Pal. Gr. 174 (14/15 saecl.).
[1] titulo Η ΠΕΡΙ ΤΗΣ ΟΡΥΧΗΣ ΤΟΥ ΙΣΘΜΟΥ add. edd..
[2] MEN. τοῦτο ... ἕτερον. codd.: corr. Gesner.
[3] οὐ Gesner: εὖ codd..

NERO or THE DIGGING OF THE ISTHMUS

1. Tell me, Musonius, about the digging of the Isthmus, for people say that you took part in it with your own hands. Did that enterprise reveal a Greek spirit on the part of the emperor?

MUSONIUS

I can assure you, Menecrates, that Nero's intentions were even better than Greek; for by breaking through two and a half miles of the Isthmus he proposed to save seafarers the voyage round the Peloponnese past Cape Malea. This would have benefited not only commerce but also the coastal and inland cities; for the inland cities find their home produce sufficient for their needs when the seaboard prospers.

MENECRATES

Tell us about this, Musonius, for we are all of us eager to hear, if you've no other serious business in mind.

MUSONIUS

I'll tell you, since it is your wish; for I don't know any better way of obliging those who have come for

509

φροντιστήριον ἐπὶ τῷ σπουδάζειν. 2. Νέρωνα
τοίνυν ἐς Ἀχαΐαν ᾠδαὶ ἦγον καὶ τὸ σφόδρα αὐτὸν
πεπεικέναι μηδ᾽ ἂν τὰς Μούσας ἀναβάλλεσθαι ἥδιον.
ἐβούλετο δὲ καὶ τὰ Ὀλύμπια, τὸν γυμνικώτατον
τῶν ἀγώνων, στεφανοῦσθαι ᾄδων· τὰ γὰρ Πύθια,
τούτων μὲν ἑαυτῷ μετεῖναι μᾶλλον ἢ τῷ Ἀπόλλωνι·
μηδὲ [1] γὰρ ἂν μηδ᾽ ἐκεῖνον ἐναντίαν αὐτῷ κιθάραν τε
καὶ ᾠδὴν θέσθαι. ὁ δὲ Ἰσθμὸς οὐ τῶν ἄποθεν
αὐτῷ βεβουλευμένων, ἀλλ᾽ ἐντυχὼν τῇ φύσει τοῦ
τόπου μεγαλουργίας ἠράσθη, τόν τε βασιλέα τῶν
ἐπὶ τὴν Τροίαν ποτὲ Ἀχαιῶν ἐνθυμηθείς, ὡς τὴν
Εὔβοιαν τῆς Βοιωτίας ἀπέτεμεν Εὐρίπῳ τῷ περὶ
τὴν Χαλκίδα, ἔτι γε μὴν καὶ τὸν Δαρεῖον, ὡς ὁ
Βόσπορος ἐγεφυρώθη αὐτῷ ἐπὶ τοὺς Σκύθας· τὰ δὲ
Ξέρξου καὶ πρὸ τούτων ἴσως ἐνενόησε, μέγιστα τῶν
μεγαλουργιῶν ὄντα, καὶ πρὸς τούτοις ⟨ὡς⟩ τῷ [2] δι᾽
ὀλίγου ἀλλήλοις ἐπιμίξαι πάντας ἔσοιτο [3] τὴν
Ἑλλάδα λαμπρῶς ἑστιᾶσθαι τοῖς ἔξωθεν· αἱ γὰρ
τύραννοι φύσεις μεθύουσι μέν, διψῶσι [4] δέ πη καὶ
ἀκοῦσαι τοῦτο [5] φθέγμα. 3. προελθὼν δὲ τῆς
σκηνῆς ὕμνον μὲν Ἀμφιτρίτης τε καὶ Ποσειδῶνος
ᾖσε καὶ ᾆσμα οὐ μέγα Μελικέρτῃ τε καὶ Λευκοθέᾳ.
ὀρέξαντος δ᾽ αὐτῷ χρυσῆν δίκελλαν τοῦ [6] τὴν

---

[1] μηδὲ Pal.: μὴ N.
[2] ὡς τῷ Kayser: τῷ Gesner: τὸ codd..
[3] ἔσοιτο L. A. Post: εἴσαιτο codd.: εἴσοιτο Kayser.
[4] διψῶσι Kayser: ψαύουσι codd..
[5] τοιοῦτο Kayser.　　　　　　　　　　[6] τοῦ Bourdelot: καὶ codd..

---

[1] Suetonius, *Nero* 23 describes Nero's introduction of
musical contests to Olympia as " praeter consuetudinem."
[2] This seems to be an erroneous reference to Agamemnon.
[3] Cf. Herodotus 4.83 ff.

serious study to such an austere schoolroom. 2.
Nero, then, had been brought to Greece by the call of
music and his own exaggerated conviction that even
the Muses could not surpass the sweetness of his
song. He even wished to win a victor's crown for
song at the Olympic games, where if anywhere the
contests are for athletes [1]; for the Pythian games he
regarded as belonging to himself more than they did
to Apollo ; for he believed that not even Apollo
would dare play the lyre or sing in competition with
him. But the Isthmus had no part in the plans
which he had formed from far away ; it was only
when he had seen what the place was like that he fell
in love with a grandiose scheme, when he thought
of the king [2] who once led the Achaeans against
Troy and how he severed Euboea from Boeotia by
digging the Euripus at Chalcis, and when moreover
he thought how Darius [3] had bridged the Bosporus
to attack the Scythians. Perhaps even before either
of these he had thought of the feat [4] of Xerxes, the
mightiest of all mighty works, and how moreover by
giving men a short route of access to each other he
would make it possible for foreigners to enjoy the
glorious hospitality of Greece. For tyrannical
natures, though intoxicated, yet somehow thirst to
hear praises [5] of this sort. 3. He advanced from
his tent and sang a hymn in honour of Amphitrite
and Poseidon and a ditty addressed to Melicerte and
Leucothea.[6] After the governor of Greece [7] had

[4] The canal across Athos; cf. Herodotus 7.22.
[5] A meaning suggested by the context, though hardly by
the Greek.   [6] All four are deities of the sea.
[7] Strictly speaking of Achaia, the southern province of
Greece; cf. Suetonius, *Nero* 19.

PHILOSTRATUS

Ἑλλάδα ἐπιτροπεύσαντος ἐπὶ τὴν ὀρυχὴν ᾖξε κροτούμενός τε καὶ ᾀδόμενος, καὶ καθικόμενος τῆς γῆς τρίς, οἶμαι, τοῖς τε τὴν ἀρχὴν [1] πεπιστευμένοις παρακελευσάμενος ξυντόνως [2] ἅπτεσθαι τοῦ ἔργου ἀνῄει εἰς τὴν Κόρινθον τὰ Ἡρακλέους δοκῶν ὑπερβεβλῆσθαι πάντα. οἱ μὲν δὴ ἐκ τοῦ δεσμωτηρίου τὰ πετρώδη τε καὶ δύσεργα ἐξεπόνουν, ἡ στρατιὰ δὲ τὰ γεώδη τε καὶ ἐπίπεδα. 4. ἑβδομηκοστὴν [3] δέ που καὶ πέμπτην ἡμέραν προσεζευγμένων ἡμῶν τῷ Ἰσθμῷ κατέβη τις ἐκ Κορίνθου λόγος οὔπω σαφὴς ὡς δὴ τοῦ Νέρωνος μετεγνωκότος τὴν τομήν. ἔφασαν δὲ τοὺς Αἰγυπτίους γεωμετροῦντας τῆς ἑκατέρας θαλάττης τὰς φύσεις οὐκ ἰσοπέδοις αὐταῖς συντυχεῖν, ἀλλ' ὑψηλοτέραν ἡγουμένους τὴν ἐκ τοῦ Λεχαίου περὶ τῇ Αἰγίνῃ δεδοικέναι· πελάγους γὰρ τοσούτου νήσῳ ἐπιχυθέντος κἂν ὑποβρύχιον ἀπενεχθῆναι τὴν Αἴγιναν. Νέρωνα δὲ τῆς μὲν τοῦ Ἰσθμοῦ τομῆς οὐδ' ἂν Θαλῆς μετέστησεν ὁ σοφώτατός τε καὶ φυσικώτατος· τοῦ γὰρ τεμεῖν αὐτὸν ἦρα μᾶλλον ἢ τοῦ δημοσίᾳ ᾄδειν. 5. ἡ δὲ τῶν Ἑσπερίων ἐθνῶν κίνησις καὶ ὀξύτατος [4] ὡς τῶν ἐκείνης νῦν ἁπτόμενος, ὄνομα δὲ αὐτῷ Βίνδαξ, ἀπήγαγεν Ἑλλάδος τε καὶ Ἰσθμοῦ Νέρωνα ψυχρῶς γεωμετρήσαντα· τὰς γὰρ θαλάσσας ἰσογαίους τε καὶ ἰσοπέδους οἶδα. φασὶ δ' αὐτῷ καὶ τὰ ἐπὶ [5] τῆς

---

[1] ὀρυχὴν Peletier.
[2] ξυμπόνως codd.: corr. Kayser.
[3] ἑβδομηκοστὴν coniectura Oleario nota: ἑβδόμην codd..
[4] ὀξύτατος ... Βίνδαξ del. ex Pal..   [5] ὑπὸ N.

---

[1] C. 4 is very similar to the *Life of Apollonius* 4.24 which

handed him a golden fork he fell to digging amid clapping and chants of applause. When he had directed blows at the ground to the number of three, I believe, and exhorted those delegated to start the work to tackle their task with energy, he went to Corinth believing he had surpassed all the feats of Heracles. The men from the prison started toiling away at the rocky and difficult ground, while the army worked where there was soil and flat ground.

4. When we had now been chained to the Isthmus for seventy-five days,[1] an unconfirmed report came from Corinth that Nero had changed his mind about cutting the Isthmus. They say that the Egyptians when calculating the features of both seas had found they were not both at the same level but thought the sea on the Lechaeum [2] side was higher and were afraid for Aegina ; for they thought it would be swamped and carried away if so mighty a sea poured over the island. But Nero would not have been dissuaded from cutting the Isthmus even by Thales, the wisest of men and greatest natural philosopher ; for he had a greater passion for cutting it than for singing in public. 5. But the revolt of the Western nations and the fact that the energetic Vindex has now joined it have forced Nero to leave Greece and the Isthmus [3] after his inane calculations ; for I know that the seas keep the same level as the land and as each other. They say that affairs at Rome

---

says that four stades (half-a-mile) of the digging had been completed.   [2] I.e. on the side of the Corinthian Gulf.

[3] The whole historical and chronological background to the dialogue is muddled; in particular (cf. Suetonius, *Nero* 40) Nero was at Naples when he heard the news from Gaul. Cf. also *Life of Apollonius* 4.24, which describes Nero's plans about the canal as dating from the seventh year of his reign (i.e. *c.* 61 A.D.).

Ῥώμης ὀλισθαίνειν ἤδη καὶ ὑποδιδόναι. τουτὶ κα
αὐτοὶ χθὲς ἠκούσατε τοῦ προσπταίσαντος[1] χιλιάρχου.

ΜΕΝΕΚΡΑΤΗΣ

6. Ἡ φωνὴ δέ, Μουσώνιε, δι᾿ ἣν μουσομανεῖ καὶ
τῶν Ὀλυμπιάδων τε καὶ Πυθιάδων ἐρᾷ, πῶς ἔχει
τῷ τυράννῳ; τῶν γὰρ Λήμνῳ προσπλεόντων οἱ
μὲν ἐθαύμαζον, οἱ δὲ κατεγέλων.

ΜΟΥΣΩΝΙΟΣ

Ἀλλ᾿ ἐκεῖνός γε, ὦ Μενέκρατες, οὔτε θαυμασίως
ἔχει τοῦ φθέγματος οὔτ᾿ αὖ γελοίως· ἡ γὰρ φύσις
αὐτὸν ἀμέμπτως τε καὶ μέσως ἥρμοκε. φθέγγε-
ται δὲ κοῖλον μὲν[2] φύσει καὶ βαρύ, ἐγκειμένης
αὐτῷ τῆς φάρυγγος· μέλη[3] δ᾿ οὕτω κατεσκευα-
σμένης[4] βομβεῖ[5] πως. οἱ δέ γε τόνοι τῶν
φθόγγων ἐπιλεαίνουσι τοῦτον, ἐπεὶ μὴ θαρρεῖ αὐτῷ,
χρωμάτων δὲ φιλανθρωπίᾳ καὶ μελοποιίᾳ εὐαγώγῳ
μὲν δὴ καὶ κιθαρῳδίᾳ εὐσταλεῖ καὶ ⟨τῷ⟩[6] οὗ καιρὸς
βαδίσαι καὶ στῆναι καὶ μεταστῆναι καὶ τὸ νεῦμα
ἐξομοιῶσαι τοῖς μέλεσιν, αἰσχύνην ἔχοντος μόνου
τοῦ βασιλέα δοκεῖν ἀκριβοῦν ταῦτα.

7. εἰ δὲ μιμοῖτο τοὺς κρείττονας, φεῦ γέλωτος, ὡς
πολὺς τῶν θεωμένων ἐκπίπτει, καίτοι μυρίων φόβων
ἐπηρτημένων, εἴ τις ἐπ᾿ αὐτῷ γελῶν εἴη· νεύει μὲν
γὰρ τοῦ μετρίου πλέον ξυνάγων τὸ πνεῦμα, ἐπ᾿

---

[1] προσπταίσαντος L.S.J.: προπταίσαντος codd..
[2] μὲν Pal.: μὴ N. [3] μέλει Pal.: μελῳδεῖ Kayser.
[4] κατεσκευασμένα N. [5] βομβῶδές Pal..
[6] τῷ deest in codd.: suppl. Kayser.

too are now slipping and receding from his grasp. This you heard for yourselves yesterday from the military tribune whose ship ran aground.

MENECRATES

6. But tell me, Musonius, about that voice of his which makes him mad about music and enamoured of Olympian and Pythian victories. What is the tyrant's voice like ? For some of those who have sailed to Lemnos expressed admiration for it, while others laughed at it.

MUSONIUS

But in fact, my dear Menecrates, his voice deserves neither admiration nor yet ridicule, for nature has made him tolerably and moderately tuneful. His voice is naturally hollow and low,[1] as his throat is deep set, and his singing has a sort of buzzing sound because his throat is thus constituted. However, the pitch of his voice makes him seem less rough when he puts his trust not in his natural powers but in gentle modifications, attractive melody and adroit harp-playing, in choosing the right time to walk, stop and move, and in swaying his head in time to the music ; then the only disgraceful feature is that a king should seem to strive for perfection in these accomplishments.

7. Should he ape his superiors, then, good heavens, what laughter emanates from the audience despite the countless threats hanging over the head of anyone laughing at him ! For he holds his breath and sways

[1] Suetonius, *Nero* 20, describes Nero as " exiguae vocis et fuscae."

ἄκρων δὲ διίσταται [1] τῶν ποδῶν ἀνακλώμενος
ὥσπερ οἱ ἐπὶ τοῦ τροχοῦ. φύσει δ' ἐρυθρὸς ὢν
ἐρευθεῖ μᾶλλον, ἐμπιπραμένου [2] αὐτῷ τοῦ προσώ-
που· τὸ δὲ πνεῦμα ὀλίγον, καὶ οὐκ ἀποχρῶν που δή.

ΜΕΝΕΚΡΑΤΗΣ

8. Οἱ δ' ἐν ἀγῶνι πρὸς αὐτὸν πῶς ὑφίενται, ὦ
Μουσώνιε; τέχνῃ γὰρ που χαρίζονται.

ΜΟΥΣΩΝΙΟΣ

Τέχνῃ μέν, ὥσπερ οἱ ὑποπαλαίοντες· ἀλλ' ἐνθυ-
μήθητι, ὦ Μενέκρατες, τὸν τῆς τραγῳδίας ὑποκρι-
τήν, ὡς Ἰσθμοῖ ἀπέθανεν· ἴσοι [3] γὰρ κίνδυνοι καὶ
περὶ τὰς τέχνας, ἢν ἐπιτείνωσιν οἱ τεχνάζοντες.

ΜΕΝΕΚΡΑΤΗΣ

Καὶ τί τοῦτο, Μουσώνιε; σφόδρα γὰρ ἀνήκοος
τοῦ λόγου.

ΜΟΥΣΩΝΙΟΣ

Ἄκουε δὴ λόγου ἀτόπου μέν, ἐν ὀφθαλμοῖς δὲ
Ἑλλήνων πεπραγμένου. 9. Ἰσθμοῖ γὰρ νόμου
κειμένου μήτε κωμῳδίαν ἀγωνίζεσθαι μήτε τραγῳδίαν, ἐδόκει Νέρωνι [4] τραγῳδοὺς νικᾶν. καὶ
παρῆλθον εἰς τὴν ἀγωνίαν ταύτην πλείους μέν, ὁ δ'
Ἠπειρώτης ἄριστα φωνῆς ἔχων, εὐδοκιμῶν δ' ἐπ'

---

[1] δὲ om. N: δ' ἵσταται Fritzsche.   [2] πιμπραμένου Pal..
[3] ἴσοι codd.: εἰσὶ Jacobs.   [4] Νέρωνι Schaefer: Νέρων codd..

---

[1] The Greek is difficult, but there may be a pun on two
meanings of τέχνη, " technical skill " and " guile."

his head immoderately, and stands on tiptoe with feet apart and with his body bent back like men bound to a wheel. Though his complexion is naturally ruddy, he grows redder still and his face burns, but his supply of breath is short and insufficient.

MENECRATES

8. But how do the competitors yield to him ? For I imagine they have craft enough to humour him.

MUSONIUS

They show the craft [1] of wrestlers who fall down on purpose. But bear in mind, my dear Menecrates, how the tragic actor was killed at the Isthmus. For craft too carries no less danger if its practitioners carry it too far.

MENECRATES

What's all this, my dear Musonius ? I've heard nothing at all about it.

MUSONIUS

Listen then to a tale that may be extraordinary but yet took place before the eyes of Greeks.

9. Although custom [2] ordains that there should be no comic or tragic contests at the Isthmus, Nero resolved to win a tragic victory. This contest was entered by several including the man from Epirus,[3] who, having an excellent voice which had won him

---

[2] Or the Greek could mean " a law "; no such law is known ; cf. p. 510, note 1. This chapter contradicts Philostratus, *Life of Apollonius* 4.24. where Nero's Isthmian victories are said to be in the contests for lyre-players and heralds, and only an Olympic tragic victory is mentioned.

[3] Alternatively Epirotes may be the man's name.

αὐτῇ [1] καὶ θαυμαζόμενος λαμπρότερα [2] τοῦ εἰωθότος ἐπλάττετο καὶ τοῦ στεφάνου ἐρᾶν καὶ μηδ᾿ ἀνήσειν πρότερον ἢ δέκα τάλαντα δοῦναί οἱ Νέρωνα ὑπὲρ τῆς νίκης. ὁ δ᾿ ἠγρίαινέ τε καὶ μανικῶς εἶχε· καὶ γὰρ δὴ καὶ ἠκροᾶτο ὑπὸ τῇ σκηνῇ ἐπ᾿ αὐτῷ δὴ τἀγῶνι. βοώντων δὲ τῶν Ἑλλήνων ἐπὶ τῷ Ἠπειρώτῃ, πέμπει τὸν γραμματέα κελεύων ὑφεῖναι αὐτῷ τοῦτον. αὐτοῦ δὲ ὑπεραίροντος τὸ φθέγμα καὶ [3] δημοτικῶς ἐρίζοντος εἰσπέμπει Νέρων ἐπ᾿ ὀκριβάντων τοὺς ἑαυτοῦ ὑποκριτὰς οἷον προσήκοντάς τι [4] τῷ πράγματι· καὶ γὰρ δὴ καὶ δέλτους ἐλεφαντίνους καὶ διθύρους προβεβλημένοι αὐτὰς ὥσπερ ἐγχειρίδια καὶ τὸν Ἠπειρώτην ἀναστήσαντες πρὸς τὸν ἀγχοῦ κίονα κατέαξαν αὐτοῦ τὴν φάρυγγα παίοντες ὀρθαῖς ταῖς δέλτοις.

ΜΕΝΕΚΡΑΤΗΣ

10. Τραγῳδίαν δὲ ἐνίκα, Μουσώνιε, μιαρὸν οὕτω πάθος ἐν ὀφθαλμοῖς τῶν Ἑλλήνων ἐργασάμενος;

ΜΟΥΣΩΝΙΟΣ

Παιδιὰ ταῦτα νεανίᾳ τῷ μητροκτονήσαντι. εἰ [5] δὲ τραγῳδίας [6] ὑποκριτὴν ἀπέκτεινεν ἐκτεμὼν αὐτοῦ τὸ φθέγμα, τί χρὴ θαυμάζειν; καὶ γὰρ δὴ καὶ τὸ

---

[1] αὐτῇ Peletier: αὐτὴν codd..
[2] λαμπροτέρᾳ Kayser.
[3] καὶ om. N: suppl. N².
[4] τι Fritzsche: τε codd..
[5] εἰ δὲ ... ἐτιμώρησαν Menecrati tribuunt codd.: corr. Solanus.
[6] τραγῳδίας Guyet: τραγῳδίαις codd..

fame and admiration, was unusually ostentatious in pretending that he had set his heart on the crown of victory and wouldn't give it up before Nero gave him ten talents as the price of victory. Nero was mad with rage ; for he had been listening under the stage during the actual contest. When the Greeks shouted in applause of the Epirote, Nero sent his secretary to bid him yield to him. But he raised his voice and went on competing as if they were all free and equal, till Nero sent his own actors on to the platform as though they belonged to the act. For they held writing tablets of ivory and double ones indeed poised before them like daggers and, forcing the Epirote against the pillar near-by, they smashed his throat in with the edge of their tablets.

MENECRATES

10. Did he win the tragic prize, Musonius, after perpetrating so monstrous a deed before the eyes of the Greeks ?

MUSONIUS

That was child's play to the youth who had murdered his mother. Why need one be surprised that he killed a tragic actor by cutting out his vocal chords ? Why he even set out to seal the Pythian

Πυθικὸν στόμιον, παρ' οὗ αἱ ὀμφαὶ ἀνέπνεον,[1]
ἀποφράττειν ὥρμησεν, ὡς μηδὲ τῷ Ἀπόλλωνι
φωνὴ εἴη, καίτοι τοῦ Πυθίου καταλέξαντος αὐτὸν
εἰς τοὺς Ὀρέστας τε καὶ Ἀλκμαίωνας, οἷς τὸ
μητροκτονῆσαι καὶ λόγον τινὰ εὐκλείας ἔδωκεν,
ἐπειδὴ πατράσιν ἐτιμώρησαν. ὁ δὲ μηδαμῶς
εἰπεῖν ἔχων ὅτῳ ἐτιμώρησεν, ὑβρίσθαι ὑπὸ τοῦ θεοῦ
ᾤετο πραότερα τῶν ἀληθῶν ἀκούων.

11. ἀλλὰ μεταξὺ λόγων, τίς ἡ προσιοῦσα ναῦς; ὡς
ἐπάγειν τι ἀγαθὸν ἔοικεν· ἐστεφάνωνται γὰρ τὰς
κεφαλὰς ὥσπερ χορὸς εὔφημος, καί τις ἐκ τῆς[2]
πρῴρας προτείνει τὴν χεῖρα παρακελευόμενος ἡμῖν
θαρρεῖν τε καὶ χαίρειν, βοᾷ τε, εἰ μὴ παρακούω,
Νέρωνα οἴχεσθαι.

ΜΕΝΕΚΡΑΤΗΣ

Βοᾷ γάρ, Μουσώνιε, καὶ σαφέστερόν γε, ὅσῳ τῆς
γῆς ἅπτεται. εὖ[3] γε, ὦ θεοί.

ΜΟΥΣΩΝΙΟΣ

Ἀλλὰ μὴ ἐπευχώμεθα· ἐπὶ γὰρ τοῖς κειμένοις
οὔ φασι δεῖν.

---

[1] ἀνέπνεον Coraes: ἐνέπνεον codd.
[2] τῆς om. N.
[3] ΜΟΥΣ. εὖ γε, ὦ θεοί. ΜΕΝ. ἀλλὰ ... δεῖν codd.: corr.
Fritzsche.

cavity [1] from which the oracular utterances came wafting up, so that not even Apollo should have a voice. And yet the Pythian god had merely classed him with men like Orestes and Alcmaeon, to whom matricide even gave some claim to renown, since they had avenged their fathers. But he, though quite unable to say whom he had avenged, considered himself insulted by the god, though he had been described in kinder terms than the truth warranted.

11. But what is this ship which has been approaching while we have been talking ? It seems to bring good news, for they have garlands on their head like a chorus that has good tidings to tell. Someone is stretching out his hand from the prow, bidding us be of good courage and rejoice. He is shouting, unless my ears deceive me, that Nero is dead.

MENECRATES

Yes, he is shouting that, and all the more clearly the nearer he draws to the land. The gods be praised.

MUSONIUS

No, let us not thank the gods, for they say we should not do so where the dead are concerned.

[1] Suetonius, *Nero* 39, 40 gives a different account, saying that Nero accepted without rancour a Delphic response given him. Suetonius also quotes an iambic trimeter linking Nero with Orestes and Alcmeon, but doesn't ascribe it to Apollo. More probably Nero resented Apollo as a rival musician; cf. c. 2.

EPIGRAMS

FIFTY-THREE epigrams in all have been attributed to Lucian. Some of these are without doubt the work of others; but those who reject all fifty-three as non-Lucianic are perhaps going too far, as at least a few are not un-Lucianic in style and thought. Here it is only necessary to print the spurious epigram *On his Own Book* which is quoted in Photius, *Bibliotheca*, 128 fin., and also occurs in a few inferior MSS. of Lucian; the other fifty-two have already been included by Paton in the five L.C.L. volumes of the Greek Anthology, having reached us from that source rather than through manuscripts of Lucian. Epigrams ascribed to Lucian in Paton's edition of the Anthology are:

(Teubner) no.	(L.C.L.) vol.	page	
2	3	200	(IX. 367)
3	4	18	(X. 26)
4	4	20	(X. 31)
5	4	18	(X. 28)
6	4	18	(X. 29)
8	3	62	(IX. 120)
9	4	18	(X. 27)
10	4	20	(X. 36)
11	4	42	(X. 42)
12	4	22	(X. 41)
14	4	20	(X. 35)
16	4	22	(X. 37)
18	4	276	(XI. 431)

LUCIAN

Paton's edition gives the authorship of the other epigrams printed in the Teubner Lucian as follows :

EPIGRAMS

20	4	110	(XI. 80)	:	Lucilius
21	4	112	(XI. 81)	:	Lucilius
24	4	184	(XI. 239)	:	Lucilius
25	4	132	(XI. 129)	:	Cerealis
27	4	72	(XI. 10)	:	Lucilius
33	1	308	(VI. 20)	:	Julian
40	4	264	(XI. 405)	:	probably Nicarchus
51	4	272	(XI. 420)	:	Anon.
53	4	172	(XI. 212)	:	Lucilius

34.1. 382 (VI. 164) is perhaps by Lucilius, though Paton assigns it to Lucian. (XI. 411 is anon., though attributed to Lucian in the index to vol. IV.)

ΕΠΙΓΡΑΜΜΑ

Εἰς τὴν ἑαυτοῦ βίβλον.

Λουκιανὸς τάδ᾽ ἔγραψα[1] παλαιά τε μωρά τε εἰδώς,
μωρὰ γὰρ ἀνθρώποις καὶ τὰ δοκοῦντα σοφά.
οὐδὲν ἐν ἀνθρώποισι διακριδόν[2] ἐστι νόημα,
ἀλλ᾽ ὃ σὺ θαυμάζεις, τοῦθ᾽ ἑτέροισι γέλως.

[1] ἔγραψε deteriores.
[2] διάκριτον Guyet.

EPIGRAM

" ON HIS OWN BOOK "

This is the work of Lucian's pen,
Who follies knew of bygone men.
For e'en the things considered wise
Are nought but folly in mine eyes.
No single thought that men embrace
Can merit have or pride of place.
For what seems wonderful to thee
Others deride with mockery.

INDEX

529

INDEX

INDEX

INDEX

INDEX

INDEX

534

INDEX

Printed in Great Britain at the Aberdeen University Press

THE LOEB CLASSICAL LIBRARY

VOLUMES ALREADY PUBLISHED

LATIN AUTHORS

AMMIANUS MARCELLINUS. Translated by J. C. Rolfe. 3 Vols.

APULEIUS: THE GOLDEN ASS (METAMORPHOSES). W. Adlington (1566). Revised by S. Gaselee.

ST. AUGUSTINE: CITY OF GOD. 7 Vols. Vol. I. G. E. McCracken. Vol. II. W. M. Green. Vol. IV. P. Levine. Vol. V. E. M. Sanford and W. M. Green. Vol. VI. W. C. Greene.

ST. AUGUSTINE, CONFESSIONS OF. W. Watts (1631). 2 Vols.

ST. AUGUSTINE, SELECT LETTERS. J. H. Baxter.

AUSONIUS. H. G. Evelyn White. 2 Vols.

BEDE. J. E. King. 2 Vols.

BOETHIUS: TRACTS AND DE CONSOLATIONE PHILOSOPHIAE. Rev. H. F. Stewart and E. K. Rand.

CAESAR: ALEXANDRINE, AFRICAN AND SPANISH WARS. A. G. Way.

CAESAR: CIVIL WARS. A. G. Peskett.

CAESAR: GALLIC WAR. H. J. Edwards.

CATO: DE RE RUSTICA; VARRO: DE RE RUSTICA. H. B. Ash and W. D. Hooper.

CATULLUS. F. W. Cornish; TIBULLUS. J. B. Postgate; PERVIGILIUM VERERIS. J. W. Mackail.

CELSUS: DE MEDICINA. W. G. Spencer. 3 Vols.

CICERO: BRUTUS AND ORATOR. G. L. Hendrickson and H. M. Hubbell.

[CICERO]: AD HERENNIUM. H. Caplan.

CICERO: DE ORATORE, etc. 2 Vols. Vol. I. DE ORATORE, Books I. and II. E. W. Sutton and H. Rackham. Vol. II. DE ORATORE, Book III. De Fato; Paradoxa Stoicorum; De Partitione Oratoria. H. Rackham.

CICERO: DE FINIBUS. H. Rackham.

CICERO: DE INVENTIONE, etc. H. M. Hubbell.

CICERO: DE NATURA DEORUM AND ACADEMICA. H. Rackham.

THE LOEB CLASSICAL LIBRARY

CICERO: DE OFFICIIS. Walter Miller.

CICERO: DE REPUBLICA and DE LEGIBUS; SOMNIUM SCIPIONIS. Clinton W. Keyes.

CICERO: DE SENECTUTE, DE AMICITIA, DE DIVINATIONE. W. A. Falconer.

CICERO: IN CATILINAM, PRO FLACCO, PRO MURENA, PRO SULLA. Louis E. Lord.

CICERO: LETTERS TO ATTICUS. E. O. Winstedt. 3 Vols.

CICERO: LETTERS TO HIS FRIENDS. W. Glynn Williams. 3 Vols.

CICERO: PHILIPPICS. W. C. A. Ker.

CICERO: PRO ARCHIA, POST REDITUM, DE DOMO, DE HARUSPICUM RESPONSIS, PRO PLANCIO. N. H. Watts.

CICERO: PRO CAECINA, PRO LEGE MANILIA, PRO CLUENTIO, PRO RABIRIO. H. Grose Hodge.

CICERO: PRO CAELIO, DE PROVINCIIS CONSULARIBUS, PRO BALBO. R. Gardner.

CICERO: PRO MILONE, IN PRISONEM, PRO SCAURO, PRO FONTEIO, PRO RABIRIO POSTUMO, PRO MARCELLO, PRO LIGARIO, PRO REGE DEIOTARO. N. H. Watts.

CICERO: PRO QUINCTIO, PRO ROSCIO AMERINO, PRO ROSCIO COMOEDO, CONTRA RULLUM. J. H. Freese.

CICERO: PRO SESTIO, IN VATINIUM. R. Gardner.

CICERO: TUSCULAN DISPUTATIONS. J. E. King.

CICERO: VERRINE ORATIONS. L. H. G. Greenwood. 2 Vols.

CLAUDIAN. M. Platnauer. 2 Vols.

COLUMELLA: DE RE RUSTICA, DE ARBORIBUS. H. B. Ash, E. S. Forster and E. Heffner. 3 Vols.

CURTIUS, Q.: HISTORY OF ALEXANDER. J. C. Rolfe. 2 Vols.

FLORUS. E. S. Forster; and CORNELIUS NEPOS. J. C. Rolfe.

FRONTINUS: STRATAGEMS AND AQUEDUCTS. C. E. Bennett and M. B. McElwain.

FRONTO: CORRESPONDENCE. C. R. Haines. 2 Vols.

GELLIUS. J. C. Rolfe. 3 Vols.

HORACE: ODES AND EPODES. C. E. Bennett.

HORACE: SATIRES, EPISTLES, ARS POETICA. H. R. Fairclough.

JEROME: SELECT LETTERS. F. A. Wright.

JUVENAL and PERSIUS. G. G. Ramsay.

LIVY. B. O. Foster, F. G. Moore, Evan T. Sage, and A. C. Schlesinger and R. M. Geer (General Index). 14 Vols.

LUCAN. J. D. Duff.

2

THE LOEB CLASSICAL LIBRARY

LUCRETIUS. W. H. D. Rouse.

MARTIAL. W. C. A. Ker. 2 Vols.

MINOR LATIN POETS: from PUBLILIUS SYRUS TO RUTILIUS NAMATIANUS, including GRATTIUS, CALPURNIUS SICULUS, NEMESIANUS, AVIANUS, and others with "Aetna" and the "Phoenix." J. Wight Duff and Arnold M. Duff.

OVID: THE ART OF LOVE AND OTHER POEMS. J. H. Mozley.

OVID: FASTI. Sir James G. Frazer.

OVID: HEROIDES and AMORES. Grant Showerman.

OVID: METAMORPHOSES. F. J. Miller. 2 Vols.

OVID: TRISTIA and EX PONTO. A. L. Wheeler.

PERSIUS. Cf. JUVENAL.

PETRONIUS. M. Heseltine; SENECA; APOCOLOCYNTOSIS. W. H. D. Rouse.

PHAEDRUS AND BABRIUS (Greek). B. E. Perry.

PLAUTUS. Paul Nixon. 5 Vols.

PLINY: LETTERS. Melmoth's translation revised by W. M. L. Hutchinson. 2 Vols.

PLINY: NATURAL HISTORY.
10 Vols. Vols. I.–V. and IX. H. Rackham. Vols. VI.–VIII. W. H. S. Jones. Vol. X. D. E. Eichholz.

PROPERTIUS. H. E. Butler.

PRUDENTIUS. H. J. Thomson. 2 Vols.

QUINTILIAN. H. E. Butler. 4 Vols.

REMAINS OF OLD LATIN. E. H. Warmington. 4 Vols. Vol. I. (Ennius and Caecilius.) Vol. II. (Livius, Naevius, Pacuvius, Accius.) Vol. III. (Lucilius, Laws of XII Tables.) Vol. IV. (Archaic Inscriptions.)

SALLUST. J. C. Rolfe.

SCRIPTORES HISTORIAE AUGUSTAE. D. Magie. 3 Vols.

SENECA: APOCOLOCYNTOSIS. Cf. PETRONIUS.

SENECA: EPISTULAE MORALES. R. M. Gummere. 3 Vols.

SENECA: MORAL ESSAYS. J. W. Basore. 3 Vols.

SENECA: TRAGEDIES. F. J. Miller. 2 Vols.

SIDONIUS: POEMS AND LETTERS. W. B. Anderson. 2 Vols.

SILIUS ITALICUS. J. D. Duff. 2 Vols.

STATIUS. J. H. Mozley. 2 Vols.

SUETONIUS. J. C. Rolfe. 2 Vols.

TACITUS: DIALOGUS. Sir Wm. Peterson; and AGRICOLA AND GERMANIA. Maurice Hutton.

TACITUS: HISTORIES AND ANNALS. C. H. Moore and J. Jackson. 4 Vols.

THE LOEB CLASSICAL LIBRARY

TERENCE. John Sargeaunt. 2 Vols.
TERTULLIAN: APOLOGIA AND DE SPECTACULIS. T. R. Glover; MINUCIUS FELIX. G. H. Rendall.
VALERIUS FLACCUS. J. H. Mozley.
VARRO: DE LINGUA LATINA. R. G. Kent. 2 Vols.
VELLEIUS PATERCULUS and RES GESTAE DIVI AUGUSTI. F. W. Shipley.
VIRGIL. H. R. Fairclough. 2 Vols.
VITRUVIUS: DE ARCHITECTURA. F. Granger. 2 Vols.

GREEK AUTHORS

ACHILLES TATIUS. S. Gaselee.
AELIAN: ON THE NATURE OF ANIMALS. A. F. Scholfield. 3 Vols.
AENEAS TACTICUS, ASCLEPIODOTUS AND ONASANDER. The Illinois Greek Club.
AESCHINES. C. D. Adams.
AESCHYLUS. H. Weir Smyth. 2 Vols.
ALCIPHRON, AELIAN, PHILOSTRATUS: LETTERS. A. R. Benner and F. H. Fobes.
ANDOCIDES, ANTIPHON, Cf. MINOR ATTIC ORATORS.
APOLLODORUS. Sir James G. Frazer. 2 Vols.
APOLLONIUS RHODIUS. R. C. Seaton.
THE APOSTOLIC FATHERS. Kirsopp Lake. 2 Vols.
APPIAN: ROMAN HISTORY. Horace White. 4 Vols.
ARATUS Cf. CALLIMACHUS.
ARISTOPHANES. Benjamin Bickley Rogers. 3 Vols. Verse trans.
ARISTOTLE: ART OF RHETORIC. J. H. Freese.
ARISTOTLE: ATHENIAN CONSTITUTION, EUDEMIAN ETHICS, VIRTUES AND VICES. H. Rackham.
ARISTOTLE: GENERATION OF ANIMALS. A. L. Peck.
ARISTOTLE: HISTORIA ANIMALIUM. A. L. Peck. Vol. I.
ARISTOTLE: METAPHYSICS. H. Tredennick. 2 Vols.
ARISTOTLE: METEOROLOGICA. H. D. P. Lee.
ARISTOTLE: MINOR WORKS. W. S. Hett. On Colours, On Things Heard, On Physiognomies, On Plants, On Marvellous Things Heard, Mechanical Problems, On Indivisible Lines, On Situations and Names of Winds, On Melissus, Xenophanes, and Gorgias.

4

THE LOEB CLASSICAL LIBRARY

THE LOEB CLASSICAL LIBRARY

DEMOSTHENES IV-VI : PRIVATE ORATIONS AND IN NEAERAM.
A. T. Murray.

DEMOSTHENES VII : FUNERAL SPEECH, EROTIC ESSAY,
EXORDIA AND LETTERS. N. W. and N. J. DeWitt.

DIO CASSIUS : ROMAN HISTORY. E. Cary. 9 Vols.

DIO CHRYSOSTOM. 5 Vols. J. W. Cohoon and H. Lamar
Crosby.

DIODORUS SICULUS. 12 Vols. Vols. I.–VI. C. H.
Oldfather. Vol. VII. C. L. Sherman. Vol. VIII.
C. B. Welles. Vols. IX. and X. R. M. Geer. Vol. XI.
F. Walton.

DIOGENES LAERTIUS. R. D. Hicks. 2 Vols.

DIONYSIUS OF HALICARNASSUS : ROMAN ANTIQUITIES. Spel-
man's translation revised by E. Cary. 7 Vols.

EPICTETUS. W. A. Oldfather. 2 Vols.

EURIPIDES. A. S. Way. 4 Vols. Verse trans.

EUSEBIUS : ECCLESIASTICAL HISTORY. Kirsopp Lake and
J. E. L. Oulton. 2 Vols.

GALEN : ON THE NATURAL FACULTIES. A. J. Brock.

THE GREEK ANTHOLOGY. W. R. Paton. 5 Vols.

GREEK ELEGY AND IAMBUS WITH THE ANACREONTEA. J. M.
Edmonds. 2 Vols.

THE GREEK BUCOLIC POETS (THEOCRITUS, BION, MOS-
CHUS). J. M. Edmonds.

GREEK MATHEMATICAL WORKS. Ivor Thomas. 2 Vols.

HERODES. Cf. THEOPHRASTUS : CHARACTERS.

HERODOTUS. A. D. Godley. 4 Vols.

HESIOD AND THE HOMERIC HYMNS. H. G. Evelyn White.

HIPPOCRATES and the FRAGMENTS OF HERACLEITUS. W. H.
S. Jones and E. T. Withington. 4 Vols.

HOMER : ILIAD. A. T. MURRAY. 2 Vols.

HOMER : ODYSSEY. A. T. Murray. 2 Vols.

ISAEUS. E. S. Forster.

ISOCRATES. George Norlin and LaRue Van Hook. 3 Vols.

ST. JOHN DAMASCENE : BARLAAM AND IOASAPH. Rev. G. R.
Woodward and Harold Mattingly.

JOSEPHUS. 9 Vols. Vols. I.–IV.; H. Thackeray. Vol. V.;
H. Thackeray and R. Marcus. Vols. VI.–VII.; R.
Marcus. Vol. VIII.; R. Marcus and Allen Wikgren.
Vol. IX. L. H. Feldman.

JULIAN. Wilmer Cave Wright. 3 Vols.

THE LOEB CLASSICAL LIBRARY

LUCIAN. 8 Vols. Vols. I.–V. A. M. Harmon. Vol. VI. K. Kilburn. Vols. VII.–VIII. M. D. Macleod.

LYCOPHRON. Cf. CALLIMACHUS.

LYRA GRAECA. J. M. Edmonds. 3 Vols.

LYSIAS. W. R. M. Lamb.

MANETHO. W. G. Waddell: PTOLEMY: TETRABIBLOS. F. E. Robbins.

MARCUS AURELIUS. C. R. Haines.

MENANDER. F. G. Allinson.

MINOR ATTIC ORATORS (ANTIPHON, ANDOCIDES, LYCURGUS, DEMADES, DINARCHUS, HYPERIDES). K. J. Maidment and J. O. Burtt. 2 Vols.

NONNOS: DIONYSIACA. W. H. D. Rouse. 3 Vols.

OPPIAN, COLLUTHUS, TRYPHIODORUS. A. W. Mair.

PAPYRI. NON-LITERARY SELECTIONS. A. S. Hunt and C. C. Edgar. 2 Vols. LITERARY SELECTIONS (Poetry). D. L. Page.

PARTHENIUS. Cf. DAPHNIS and CHLOE.

PAUSANIUS: DESCRIPTION OF GREECE. W. H. S. Jones. 4 Vols. and Companion Vol. arranged by R. E. Wycherley.

PHILO. 10 Vols. Vols. I.–V.; F. H. Colson and Rev. G. H. Whitaker. Vols. VI.–IX.; F. H. Colson. Vol. X. F. H. Colson and the Rev. J. W. Earp.

PHILO: 2 supplementary Vols. (*Translation only*). Ralph Marcus.

PHILOSTRATUS: THE LIFE OF APOLLONIUS OF TYANA. F. C. Coneybeare. 2 Vols.

PHILOSTRATUS: IMAGINES; CALLISTRATUS: DESCRIPTIONS. A. Fairbanks.

PHILOSTRATUS and EUNAPIUS: LIVES OF THE SOPHISTS. Wilmer Cave Wright.

PINDAR. Sir J. E. Sandys.

PLATO: CHARMIDES, ALCIBIADES, HIPPARCHUS, THE LOVERS, THEAGES, MINOS and EPINOMIS. W. R. M. Lamb.

PLATO: CRATYLUS, PARMENIDES, GREATER HIPPIAS, LESSER HIPPIAS. H. N. Fowler.

PLATO: EUTHYPHRO, APOLOGY, CRITO, PHAEDO, PHAEDRUS. H. N. Fowler.

PLATO: LACHES, PROTAGORAS, MENO, EUTHYDEMUS. W. R. M. Lamb.

PLATO: LAWS. Rev. R. G. Bury. 2 Vols.

PLATO: LYSIS, SYMPOSIUM, GORGIAS. W. R. M. Lamb.

THE LOEB CLASSICAL LIBRARY

PLATO : REPUBLIC. Paul Shorey. 2 Vols.
PLATO : STATESMAN, PHILEBUS. H. N. Fowler ; ION. W. R. M. Lamb.
PLATO : THEAETETUS AND SOPHIST. H. N. Fowler.
PLATO : TIMAEUS, CRITIAS, CLITOPHO, MENEXENUS, EPISTULAE. Rev. R. G. Bury.
PLOTINUS: A. H. Armstrong. Vols. I.–III.
PLUTARCH: MORALIA. 15 Vols. Vols. I.–V. F. C. Babbitt. Vol. VI. W. C. Helmbold. Vol. VII. P. H. De Lacy and B. Einarson. Vol. IX. E. L. Minar, Jr., F. H. Sandbach, W. C. Helmbold. Vol. X. H. N. Fowler, Vol. XI. L. Pearson and F. H. Sandbach. Vol. XII. H. Cherniss and W. C. Helmbold.
PLUTARCH : THE PARALLEL LIVES. B. Perrin. 11 Vols.
POLYBIUS. W. R. Paton. 6 Vols.
PROCOPIUS : HISTORY OF THE WARS. H. B. Dewing. 7 Vols.
PTOLEMY : TETRABIBLOS. Cf. MANETHO.
QUINTUS SMYRNAEUS. A. S. Way. Verse trans.
SEXTUS EMPIRICUS. Rev. R. G. Bury. 4 Vols.
SOPHOCLES. F. Storr. 2 Vols. Verse trans.
STRABO: GEOGRAPHY. Horace L. Jones. 8 Vols.
THEOPHRASTUS : CHARACTERS. J. M. Edmonds. HERODES, etc. A. D. Knox.
THEOPHRASTUS : ENQUIRY INTO PLANTS. Sir Arthur Hort. 2 Vols.
THUCYDIDES. C. F. Smith. 4 Vols.
TRYPHIODORUS. Cf. OPPIAN.
XENOPHON : CYROPAEDIA. Walter Millar. 2 Vols.
XENOPHON : HELLENICA, ANABASIS, APOLOGY, and SYMPOSIUM. C. L. Brownson and O. J. Todd. 3 Vols.
XENOPHON : MEMORABILIA and OECONOMICUS. E. C. Marchant.
XENOPHON : SCRIPTA MINORA. E. C. Marchant.

DESCRIPTIVE PROSPECTUS ON APPLICATION

London
Cambridge, Mass.

WILLIAM HEINEMANN LTD
HARVARD UNIVERSITY PRESS